D0345415

An Invincible Memory

Also by the author

Sergeant Getulio

A n
Invincible
Memory

JOÃO UBALDO RIBEIRO

Translated by the Author

HARPER & ROW, PUBLISHERS, New York
Cambridge, Philadelphia, San Francisco
1817 *London, Mexico City, São Paulo, Singapore, Sydney*

AN INVINCIBLE MEMORY. Copyright © 1989 by João Ubaldo Ribeiro. All rights reserved. Printed in the United States of America. No part of this book may be used or reproduced in any manner whatsoever without written permission except in the case of brief quotations embodied in critical articles and reviews. For information address Harper & Row, Publishers, Inc., 10 East 53rd Street, New York, N.Y. 10022. Published simultaneously in Canada by Fitzhenry & Whiteside Ltd., Toronto.

FIRST EDITION

Copyeditor: Marjorie Horvitz

Designer: Cassandra J. Pappas

Library of Congress Cataloging-in-Publication Data

Ribeiro, João Ubaldo, 1940–
 An invincible memory.

 Translation of: Viva o povo brasileiro.
 1. Brazil—History—Fiction. I. Title.
PQ9698.28.I165V5813 1989   869.3   88-45052
ISBN 0-06-015622-8

89 90 91 92 93 AC/RRD 10 9 8 7 6 5 4 3 2 1

For Manoel Ribeiro, with admiration

The secret of Truth is as follows:
there are no facts, there are only stories.

NOBODY EVER ESTABLISHED FOR SURE THE FIRST INCARNATION OF WARrant Officer José Francisco Brandão Galvão, now standing in the breeze at Whale Point, just a moment before his head and chest are struck by the little iron balls and round pebbles fired by the Portuguese matchlocks which will soon arrive from the sea. He is to die in the prime of his youth, without even knowing woman and without having done anything memorable. In all likelihood, his imagination is empty as he enjoys this waft that ushers in his death, for he has not lived sufficiently to really imagine, as do the very aged in his land, too old to want to experience anything, who hunker down with their two-foot-long pipes and maunder on, surrounded by the fascination of the young and lying stupendously. Maybe there is only one minute left, maybe less, before the Portuguese appear in the strong winter sun in All Saints Bay and make those little stone and iron spheres swarm all over him and kill him with great pain, piercing one of his eyes, splintering his head bones, and forcing him to bend over, hugging himself, unable even to think about his death. In the painting *Warrant Officer Brandão Galvão Harangues the Sea Gulls,* one can see it is the tenth of June, 1822, in the writing on a calendar page that soars aloft, borne on one side by the beak of a sea gull and on the other by a spearhead festooned with the colors and insignias of Liberty. Already mortally wounded, half rising, with an eye slithering down his beard, he harangued the sea gulls that moments before had been hovering absentmindedly over the brigs and whaleboats of the Portuguese commander known as Thirty Devils. He spoke not just one but many famous sentences, in the quavering though stentorian voice ever since imitated in classrooms or, if not in classrooms, during official visits that necessitate listening to speeches. For if after the Portuguese broadside there was little there but the sea birds, the ocean, and the indifference of natural events, enough remained to imprint forever on the minds of men the words he now pronounces, although they are not heard either here or closer by, nor do his lips seem to be moving, nor can anyone see on his face more than the bewildered expression of one who dies unknowingly. But they are noble words, against tyranny and oppression, whispered by death in the ears of the warrant officer, and therefore they are true.

Of those opposites, glory in life and glory in death, only the latter seems to pursue the ever-incarnating soul of the warrant officer. Otherwise he would not be there, at that time and place, for he could very well have gone to any other part of the bay area, where the people might be gathering together to drink and to acclaim the regent and immortal prince Dom Pedro, Perpetual Defender of the Austral Hemisphere. Already a corpse and a hero, his words to the gulls ever extending as they passed from mouth to mouth, the warrant officer would not hear the high proclamation that was made in the many celebrations in the city of Catu, just as he would not witness the sundry others that followed the ominous day on which the Senate of the Chamber of Bahia, boiling with resentment and hatred because the royal court had boarded ship to go back to Portugal with the same hauteur of its arrival, refused to acknowledge the royal writ appointing Brigadier Inácio Madeira de Melo commandant-in-arms. The Brazilian people was rising against the Portuguese, and torrential speeches rumbled within the walls of the churches, apothecaries, and salons where conspirators prophesied the glory of Austral America, fulcrum of splendor, fortune, and abundance. Everywhere new heroes were anointed, one each day in each village, sometimes two or three, news of brave feats flying about as swiftly as the swallows that spend the summer on the island. So it was when the famous corvette *Regeneração* put into the port of Bahia, bringing back important heroes, now amnestied after having been imprisoned in the Castle of Saint George, in the capital city of the oppressors. Enwrapped in the mists of legend, those men of destiny soon became renowned throughout the land for their incomparable valor, the beauty of their every gesture, the unerring force of each word they uttered, and for their character, never enfeebled by human weakness. And José Francisco's heart could not but beat faster, his chin trembling and his head spinning, when the great warrior Lieutenant João das Botas, one of the *Regeneração*'s passengers, looking as though battle drums were thundering around the edges of his scarlet-selvaged cape, came ashore on the island at sunset for a secret visit and spoke to a few men the apothecary had gathered at Whale Point. José Francisco heard his wrathful denunciation of the Brazilian deputies who had opposed amnesty in Lisbon. Barely able to breathe, he was made to realize how Brazil stood for freedom, opulence, justice, and beauty, heretofore denied by the iniquity of the Portuguese, who took away everything and gave nothing in return. He learned to say with contempt the name of one of the deputies, and later on, when he had already donned the green, galloon-cuffed doublet given to him by his aging, blind godmother, the widow of a first-class private, when he was already accustomed to feeling his breast tighten whenever he saw militiamen grouping here and there, the name of that deputy was the only thing he knew how to say during the meetings at the apothecary's. Most often the speeches were made by the apothecary and his frequent visitor, the exalted orator Sousa Lima, but the others could venture a word or two while the great revolutionaries caught their breath, and so, stroking the sparse beard granted him by his seventeen years, Warrant Officer Brandão Galvão grumbled coarsely: "Gonçalves Ledo, you cowardly traitor!" Then, running his defiant gaze over the room as if trying to follow the movements of a distressed fly, he would punch his knee, grunting an unintelligible curse, and return to his motionless silence. It pleased him that though he repeated those words and gestures nearly every night, because he was slow to learn new things and the only letters he knew were his initials, the other conspirators always listened as if he were saying something quite necessary and never heard before, and some of them even echoed his grumbles with somewhat solemn nods.

Before death brought him glory and conferred upon him the gift of fine words, maybe he even thought now and then that if it were not for his embellished garb and the vague but sublime tingling he felt at the mention of war, his former life as an apprentice fisherman, although he was a bastard and a poor man, was preferable after all. The work of a fisherman, albeit uncertain by its nature, was akin to the succession of days and nights, and if it demanded attention and discipline, it also brought about a rousing sentiment of freedom that the warrant officer did not understand well but could perceive, especially when the fish were transfigured into a throbbing silvery mass that cast a soft light over nets and canoes, and the men then calling it a day laughed for no reason. It embarrassed him that he had no idea of what was going on, and every time he gathered enough courage to ask, he lost it at the last moment, and just grumbled again. He did not know where Portugal was, he knew only that his father had returned to live there as soon as he was born. Sometimes he sneaked his way around to go see from afar the Portuguese warship *Dona Maria da Glória,* anchored like a haunted ark off Cross Point Harbor. Because he did not have a firearm, the only military object he owned being a doublet, he would squeeze his fingers around a three-hooked gaff while crouching in the dark and watch the boat, feeling his breath rush, thinking with his eyes closed of how he might board her to kill the Portuguese with his fishing weapon. He expected to see the fearsome face of the Portuguese commander Manoel Pereira da Silva, who was said to be one of the most ruthless colonists among the many evildoers sent over by the tyrannical court, but he never discerned anything but the shadow of a scrawny dog sliding along the edges of the jetty, and never heard anything other than the water sloshing the sides of the boat, and the murmurs that night magnifies, making the scampering of the little night crabs sound like a convention of chatterboxes. Of his duties as a warrant officer he knew not a thing, not even what the rank stood for, not even whether he really was a warrant officer. He actually suspected that in order to be a warrant officer, one needed something besides being called one, as happened for the first time in the apothecary's and ended up being adopted by everyone at Whale Point.

Perhaps if he had not been afraid to be alone with other warrant officers or commanders or pilots or captains or so many other stern-faced, monument-like, splendidly dressed figures, if he just could understand certain words whose sounds, in his secret and lonely anguish, only reminded him of outlandish imaginary objects, if his lack of knowledge about everything did not weigh on his head like a lead helmet, he would have made a trip to Cachoeira, where the conspirators were so exalted that they flew among the clouds and felt a different blood flowing inside their bodies, ready to irrigate the sea and to inseminate its foam with more and more heroes, more and more gods and goddesses of Liberty, as could be seen in picture books and sketched in the mind by the orators' words. The Paraguassu River, very murky, placidly deceitful, almost lethargic down at the bottom of the valley, made one feel, just by looking at the bend where it faded away, that the many entities living in it were gearing up for combat, and every day somebody, any time of the day, stood at one of its banks with his eyes clinging to the horizon and his thoughts painting visions of battle. But the warrant officer knew of those and other portents only from hearsay, because he feared meeting another soldier, who might ask him questions. What did he know about weapons and the arts of war? How many battles had he fought and what memories had he garnered to share with his companions and his family? What does he think about Brazil's struggles, what is his opinion about Independence, what great commander, barely regaining his wind after an arduous encounter, told him, "Give me ten others like you, my brave fellow, and the entire terrestrial orb will be ours"? Where exactly is Brazil, since all that is known is that this land here is Brazil, but it is not all of Brazil, and may the good soldier ignore where Brazil is? No, José Francisco would not leave Whale Point, not only because he did not want to, but also because fate was already weaving above his head the crown of laurels and thorns that signals the making of a hero. There at Whale Point, in the date inscribed in the winged calendar of the painting and with great rage and fury, the Portuguese launched their first attack against the revolutionaries of the island of Itaparica. Aware of the ongoing conspiracy through information turned over by the Portuguese João de Campos, who will be reviled and cursed for all eternity every time someone makes a speech about Warrant Officer Brandão Galvão and his audience of sea gulls, the hard-willed General Madeira, forced to draw in the reins of the Austral Hemisphere unwitnessed and unsupported, dispatched to the village of Whale Point Commander Thirty Devils' fleet of brigs. For very long after the attack, even centuries later, people would cross themselves as they recalled the *Dona Maria da Glória* transmuted into a sea monster of fire and smoke, and launches lowered from the brigs overwhelming the shore, with their oars, resembling deadly spikes, lances, and poleaxes, flashing their tips closer and closer. As it was written, the only one who succumbed was Warrant Officer Brandão Galvão, even before the Portuguese set foot on the sand, because he was very visible, one of those shapes that one who is carrying a virgin gun feels a compulsion to shoot at, the cuffs of his doublet shining and his slender silhouette against the dull-colored timbers of the jetty. Brought down as soon as the first launch began to spit out slugs in every direction, he could only notice that those bites from an air suddenly alive and hissing were killing him, and it was then that he harangued the sea gulls. He did not even see João de Campos jump off a boat at the head of the first group, to point out with his fat, greasy finger, blubber trembling under his loose breeches, the houses of the conspirators. Fortunately, as the brigs came into view, tacking into the bight, only the warrant officer remained at the station he had assigned himself, while the others, from the apothecary to the parish priest, from sailors to shellfish pickers, beat a retreat to the woods in the vicinity of Amoreiras, thus preventing, with their astute, prompt, and courageous action, the Revolution's suffering casualties of inestimable consequence. Running rabidly over the immense bank of hard sand like a host of demons, the Portuguese committed such awesome atrocities that books of verses were written about them, and the hatred of the many who were outraged has not yet been wholly appeased in the hearts of their descendants. The artillery arming the beach and the fortress was defiled, the gunpowder was watered, the iron pieces were plugged and made to roll on the grass and the dirt. The Church of Saint Lawrence was invaded, the mantle of Our Lord of Martyrdom was torn out, the Vera Cruz oratory was destroyed. And so many sacrileges were perpetrated that had God not already been on the Brazilian side out of justice and avocation, He would have joined it then and there, faced with the enemy's boundless brutality. The apothecary's shop was almost demolished and there were great losses, but José Francisco, having nothing in the world but a crippled mother, a sister not even maidenly, two hens, a three-hooked gaff, and a galloon-cuffed doublet, did not cause or represent any loss. On the contrary, he bequeathed the people his words to the sea gulls on the day he was smitten down by Portugal's impious, merciless talon while mounting guard at Whale Point.

The behavior of souls who disincarnate unexpectedly, especially the very young, is the object of great controversy and even of diametrical versions, with the result that in this whole field there is not a single point of agreement. In Amoreiras, for instance, it is said that a special conjunction of cardinal points, equinoxes, magnetic lines, mental meridians, highly potent stellar influences, esoteric poles, alchemical-philosophical currents, attractions of the moon and of the fixed and errant heavenly bodies, and hundreds of other arcane forces all causes the souls of the dead to refuse to leave, and to continue moving about freely among the living, interfering in everyday life and sometimes making countless demands. People used to say it was because of the Tupinambá Indians that lived there, who by means of a thousand Indian ruses and wiles tied up the souls of the dead until they paid back the favors they died owing or solved some disagreement of which they were part. But after the Tupinambás came the Portuguese, Spaniards, Dutchmen, even Frenchmen, and the deceased, though there were no more Indians to tie them up, still would not go away, defying the orders of the most respected priests and sorcerers. After that came the blacks from many nations in Africa, and no matter where they hailed from and what gods they brought with them, not one of them was ever able to get rid of his dead, so much so that they were the ones who learned best how to bear with this circumstance, there being for example no orphans or widows among them. The many of them who could not endure living in the company of an infinite memory and in the presence of everything that ever existed moved away to places very far from Amoreiras and never ate anything that came from there.

There are parts of the bay area where young souls disincarnated without warning yield to a first impulse and mistakenly enter the womb of a nanny goat or she-ass, or a hen's egg. Once inside, they cannot leave until the animal they entered is born and raised, and dies or is killed, which is the reason why there are individuals who from birth prefer starvation to having to eat the flesh of certain animals, because of the people incarnated in those animals. It is possible to extract a soul thus victimized by inexperience, but this requires powers more than human and a more than delicate conjugation of factors, and most families so afflicted choose to act with resignation and charity. In other areas, the souls take possession not of animals but of trees, and a discussion is warranted about whether they do it on purpose, some maintaining that the souls, much distressed by what happened while they were incarnated and quite fretful at their immortality, think that the condition of a plant is better than that of humans or animals. A soul learns nothing while a soul, for it needs incarnation in order to learn, and reasons abound to embrace the opinion that as a plant it learns better than as a man, particularly as a large fruit-bearing tree.

Neither is it possible to deny that in all of the bay lands one can find souls in torment, since one cannot doubt the testimony of the many, many people who come across them and help them with candles, novenas, prayers, and sacrifices. A good number of those souls in torment are in that predicament only temporarily and are not in torment at all but resting before they climb up to the Souls' Perch, where sooner or later they will have to overcome a great fear and incarnate once again. There is no need to compel them to do so, because it is unbearable not to be able to learn anything, so every minute multitudes of them can no longer keep a hold on themselves and come dashing down precipitously in darting flights from the Souls' Perch to incarnate. Those are very complicated occurrences, total comprehension of which escapes the wisest men and brotherhoods, and that is surely the reason why there is so much support for the opinion that holds Warrant Officer Brandão Galvão to have been the first incarnation of that dazed, startled little soul who abandoned the hero's sacred body and, since souls are lighter than air and many of them do not know how to fly too well, floated for a while in the wind that had moved the Portuguese fleet, oscillating at the whim of the breezes between the fortress and the Island of Fear, and gazed with great love, disenchantment, and helplessness at the body down below, reflecting the light on its military cuffs. But to think that the warrant officer was the first incarnation of that little soul adrift in the northeasterly now blowing lower is dictated by human vanity, which seeks to change the world in the manner that suits its needs. Yes, what greater glory could there be for the people than to have as their inspiring and eloquent hero the first incarnation of a new little soul, a soul especially begotten to cement more strongly everyone's pride and to display the mettle of the nation?

However, it did not happen that way. There are not many new souls, although every day a few of them are created in the great cosmic soup surrounding the planets and constellations. It is known by modern science that many, many millions of years ago there were no living beings, though the substances that presently constitute them drifted loosely in the primordial broth of the seas, and then one fine sunny day light struck some of those substances at the very instant the waves were stirring them together, with the result that something live appeared for the first time. The same thing scientists show to be so simple happens to new little souls when they are created in the great cosmic soup. Little souls are like certain particles of matter, also described by modern science, which have colors, flavors, and preferences but have neither bodies nor charges. Nevertheless, both little souls and particles exist, depending on the quantity of nothing that goes into their composition, and almost certainly on the presence of other scientific conditions, such as pressure, temperature, and the presence of catalysts good for reactions of nothing with nothing. In the sidereal amplitudes, immense and copious masses of nothing flow on, to gather at the proximity of some Souls' Perch. Whether the nothing seeks the Souls' Perches or the Souls' Perches seek the nothing, there is no way of knowing. The fact is that in the vicinity of a Souls' Perch what occurs is nothing, nothing on all sides, an infinitude of nothing unimaginable in all its amplifications. Nothing and more nothing and more nothing keeps on agglomerating there, to a point where so much nothing is accumulated that it becomes a critical nothing, and thus something comes forth from that nothing. This sudden nonform is nothing but a little new soul, inexperienced and innocent like all very young creatures and for this very reason subject to a great number of problems, since the only thing it knows is that it must go to the Souls' Perch to wait with the others for the hour when it will have to incarnate in order to learn.

Indeed, the little soul that remained disconsolate and aimless after having been obliged, still so callow and helpless, to leave Warrant Officer Brandão Galvão's body was not a Brazilian soul originally, because it is very unlikely that souls are destined to be born to only one nationality, whatever it may be, nor are they likely to become attached to one. In this case, it all began, like so many important events, by dint of chance. In any fortuitous occasion when the Souls' Perch is packed with newly created little souls, the feverish agitation of so many young ones anxious to learn and to fulfill their fates goes as far as to make the cosmos fibrillate and to slightly disturb the perfect functioning of astral clocks and other celestial mechanisms. What usually happens then is that, with the nervous and spasmodic flight of beach-grubbing birds scattered by a stone, the souls descend like arrows shot in the direction of the planet, and then scurry from one point to another as fast as lightning until they find an egg, a uterus, a seed, something living for them to animate. And of course they do not descend the way they would if they were bodies, or perhaps they do not really descend, inasmuch as their trajectories are simultaneously perpendicular to the planes of all three dimensions, and if it is not possible to understand this, it is because little is understood about fourth, fifth, or sixth dimensions, even by little souls, who before they arrive never know where they are. And it often happens that the first incarnation of little souls is not in people but in animals or plants, and it might well be supposed that quite some time before entering the dispirited womb of the warrant officer's mother that little soul was a monkey or a parrot, someplace in the vast woods of the bay area. Since at that time most monkeys and parrots did not have as many serious problems as they do now, one is led to believe that the little soul did try to return to the same species but could not resist, in spite of the intense fear it always causes in souls, the opportunity to incarnate in a human. So it came about that the little soul, roaming loose among plants and animals, was virtually sucked in by the strong attraction exercised upon it by the belly of a Tupinambá woman, inside which conception had taken place a few hours before.

Maybe the collaboration of singular circumstances that ended up making the warrant officer's a Brazilian soul began that way. It was born a female Indian around the time when the first whites were coming, having been raped and killed by eight of them before she was twelve. Without understanding anything, as soon as it left the girl's body and started its way back to the Souls' Perch, it was sucked in like a whirlpool by another human belly, and the little soul was born an Indian again and again and again—it is impossible to know how many times—until the day when, after having lived as a half-breed in the time of the Dutchmen, ensconced in the wilds and swamps with three or four women and many daughters and eating people now and then, it spent some time on the Souls' Perch, in much fear of incarnating in man or woman once more. And surely something must be written, because that soul, shivering with fright and apprehension in the dark space among the worlds, made the firm resolution to avoid the Austral Hemisphere on its next descent, but since it actually had not learned anything and was better at being a parrot than a person, it ended up flitting by in a fateful way, and eighteen years, two months, and twenty days before the tenth of June, 1822, it found itself inside the entrails of the frail woman who would soon bring it forth in the body of Warrant Officer Brandão Galvão, the hero of Independence.

And a hero whose name, almost as soon as his little soul had finished watching from above the simple funeral they gave him, was exalted wherever revolutionary patriots gathered, was evoked as an example of gallantry and eloquence, was the object of enraptured and poignant discourses. Maybe the little soul spent too much time in Amoreiras during its disembodied wanderings about the island, for souls do not have a very good sense of time. But it may not be true that the soul was entranced by the deceptions, snares, and necromancies that interweave in the Amoreiras air, because it took to frequent with assiduity and interest the places where the warrant officer was being honored, to thrill with delight and a happiness it had never experienced, as the details of his talk to the sea gulls were recalled for the people by declaimers, in symphonic alexandrines, breathtaking anastrophes, proparoxytones booming like hammered boilers, metaphors whose contours never dissolved, adorning the air with gelatinous, quivering sculptures. It wondered more and more at itself and heard so many accounts of prodigies worked by men such as the one it had been that it could not think of anything else. And so, an electric-blue invisible ball suspended by the many winds that inhabit the firmament, the little soul postponed and craved the moment it would be overtaken by a burning passion and would become a Brazilian soul forever and ever, a phenomenon that may be better understood if one remembers that, yes, souls do not learn anything, but they dream uncontrollably.

Pirajá, November 8, 1822

Sitting under a jack-fruit tree with his legs outspread, eating half-dry corn bread and biting enormous chunks off a piece of broiled sausage, Perilo Ambrósio Góes Farinha decided to rail at the two slaves who were keeping him company, even though they had not done anything wrong and were just watching him with hungry eyes. He was annoyed at the food. Ever since he was a boy he had been like that, very sensitive to disappointments related to food. It could be just a frustrated expectation, it could be anything, even someone's beating him to a portion of food he was after, in spite of his mouth being full and despite the vigilant attention he dedicated to all the food on the table while clamorously devouring all he had piled up in the two or three earthenware bowls he used as dishes. He remembered—his heart as usual offended and hurting with injustice's heavy loneliness—his father's threatening for the tenth or thirtieth time to expel him from the village and the farm on the day he attacked one of his sisters with a roasting spit because she had beaten him to a coveted hunk of meat. He had no way of reaching that piece of jerked beef, resplendent among gherkins and bittersweet eggplant at the other end of the table; he could not even reserve it for himself with shouts and threats, because he was glutted with slabs of pork fat mixed with manioc flour, which he thrust anxiously into every nook and cranny of his mouth, nor could he allow himself to stop agonizing in fear that someone might steal from his brimming bowls morsels already anticipated with sniffs and sighs, if he failed to heed them for a few moments. So he had no choice but to fly, his eyes like a wounded whale's, over the intolerable abyss between him and that piece of meat, and before his sister could bite what was his, to impale her hand with that grimy, greasy spit. "Why do you persecute me?" he still thought of crying out in revolt, but while they carried his sister inside, her hand run through by the spit from back to palm, his father wrenched the chunk of meat from his teeth amidst a rain of blows, and forced him to leave the table and to eat no more that day. Inside the room in which his father locked him, he burned with hatred and spite and wept most of the time, his sobs so deep and grinding that at times he thought they would never finish. Among other revenges, such as he dreamed of once in a while, then woke drenched in sweat, he swore aloud that one day he would force that sister to starve while he ate in front of her, because now that he had been deprived there would never be enough meat on earth to dispel the hunger for that usurped piece yanked violently from his desperate teeth. Yes, he ended up being expelled from home, a long time afterward. But that did not mean a thing now; it happened when all his other rancors were already poisoning him every moment of the day.

"So they give me water to drink!" His voice was more strident than usual, as always happened when he talked to blacks. "Water! Should it not suffice that I have to eat this pestiferous stodge—do I also have to wash my gullet with water? Come on, give me that gourd!"

Feliciano, the younger black, came out of the sun, where his master had made him stay together with the other one, and slowly picked up the gourd to hand it over.

"Be quick, you numbskull!" Perilo Ambrósio yelled.

Pulling the cork by the little cord that ran through its thicker end, he took a few noisy swigs, lowered the gourd, and kicked Feliciano's legs as strongly as his straddling position allowed.

"No doubt you look so shit-faced because I left you both in the sun—and I shall leave you two there for all eternity if I care to!—and because you want to put your manured mouths to this gourd from which I am drinking the filthy water you brought me! Why have you filled the gourd with such filthy water? Why? Answer me, you jackass, you turd of the devil! And if I leave you in the sun, the more you should hold me in high regard, for I am doing you a great favor, seeing as your brains are cooked by the sun of the Africas, so you'll be more comfortable. And don't look at me with that expression of a friar of the silent orders, you cynical monkey, don't look at me with any expression. Negroes have no souls and have as much right to express themselves as hogs and chickens! What you are supposed to express is your master's will, as when you give an account of my bravery and valor in this combat against the hosts of Madeira, suffering the saddest of conditions, eating this deadly pig swill, drinking this pestilential water, in the company of two dirty, stinking Negroes who fart like drunken Indians and dampen my resolve to fight—that is what you have to express, and more if I order you!"

Raising a little dust, a group of riders came into view on the dirt road that bordered the woods. Perilo Ambrósio was startled.

"Help me here!" he said to the slave, who stretched out his hand to him so he could get up, which he did with difficulty, his belly stubbornly clinging to the ground while, his knees bent, he panted in a great effort. "What is the matter with you—can you not bear a weight any longer? Then you do not take after your mother, whom I fucked often, laying all these pounds on top of her. I do not recall her being crushed, and had she not become a dewlapped mule, covered with the mange she caught from the dogs, I would still be of a mind to have a go at that pitchy arse. But no harm done," he added with an obscene laugh, rubbing his fat, hairy hand over Feliciano's backside, "because I have not yet had my full share of your family's arses, and the day will come when I will call you to my room so you can go down on all fours while I stick all of this rod of mine into your fundament; you should be good at it. But what—are those militiamen coming yonder? Are they Madeira's men running away? They're hauling an artillery piece—that is why they are moving so slowly—and they will take some time to get here. It suits me fine. Do you think they are really ours? You have better eyesight than I—look well. If you lie to me, if you tell me they are ours and they are not, it shall be your last treachery, because I will flay you alive before they get here. Hark, are they really ours? How goes the battle? I cannot take any chances—how goes the battle?"

Not even the sound of the battle reached them as before, though there had never been the tremendous thundering they had expected. Perilo Ambrósio —who had chosen to spend the day at that spot so distant from the fighting because he wanted to wait until the Brazilians won, then join them at once—was afraid that the combat had not finished yet, so he might be obliged to take part in it. He wanted the Brazilians to prevail, not because he was a Brazilian—in fact, he considered himself a Portuguese—but because, having been expelled from home, abominated by his parents and by all his relatives, and threatened with disinheritance, he had decided to acquire fame as a combatant on the side of the rebels. That way his loyalist father, already a fugitive accused of all conceivable crimes and perfidies, might lose everything after the Brazilian victory, his justly confiscated properties devolving upon his male child, for his intrepid actions on behalf of the national cause. Perilo Ambrósio's preference was for his family's banishment to a very faraway place, maybe Angola, among Negroes cooking humans to eat and horseflies transmitting fatal diseases, but since that seemed impossible, he resigned himself to the idea—which made him spend hours on end curling a strand of his hair with his fingertips and looking stupid—of becoming the absolute master of the estate, the blacks, the houses, and everything else. What happened to the family did not matter now; it was something to be taken care of later, after the present situation was turned to his best advantage.

They were ours, no doubt. Something, one could surmise from here, had happened to the wheels of a cart transporting a small cannon. Two sorrel mules were tugging hard at the cart, but it barely moved in spite of all their effort. Five or six riders paraded their mounts back and forth as if in a tournament, a few foot soldiers worked on something around the right wheel; the dust raised by the hoofs dimmed the air, otherwise very clear, and everything was seen as in an ancient painting, while the cracks of the cartman's whip, the curses and the shouts, were heard a bit after they happened.

"What are the two mules pulling?" Perilo Ambrósio asked, squinting to study the distant figures. "They are dragging a little field cannon, a falconet —is that how they call it? A most toilsome job it is; they ought to stop and mend the wheels; one of them is wobbling loose; it can be seen from here. I believe I should go meet them. Who among the regulars wears four galloons and gold or silver aiguillettes? There are some who always go about with epaulets flapping on their shoulders and other ornaments. Let's see: after squad leaders come staff sergeants, and then we have ensigns, and from there up they are all great captains, sergeants major, and field marshals. Listen, do you think they will welcome us and take us to be volunteers of Barros Falcão, gone afield? How goes the battle, that is what we must find out, that is for sure! For if we go over there and it is not finished yet, it is as certain as the good Lord is in heaven that they will summon us to march with them. In that case I will tell them a few stories, for it is of lies and cock-and-bull tales that the narrations of war are made. And after all, we were on the other side of the river, and the enemy could have caught us by surprise, could they not? But no, in matters of combat, the ones who appear to be tired of the fray are not dismissed if the fight has to go on. No, no, if I am to converse with that commanding officer, it will not be an empty conversation, with nothing to show for it. So I am not going to him without making a few arrangements. Come hither, you sooty blockhead, come on! Be quick, you wretch!"

A while later, with only Feliciano accompanying him, Perilo Ambrósio greeted a lieutenant, who, as he saw them approach, slackened his horse's reins and galloped in their direction, coming to a halt in the middle of a cloud of red dust.

"Bullet wound?" he asked. Perilo Ambrósio's left arm was wrapped in a sling as blood-soaked as his jacket and undershirt. "Are you still able to walk? I see you are losing a lot of blood."

"My Commandant, had I twenty almudes of blood, I would gladly give them all, and more, for liberty," Perilo Ambrósio answered, his voice feeble and broken by tearful wheezes.

"But you are Portuguese, are you not?"

"Yes, my Commandant. Portugal was where I first saw the light of day, and I was raised among the Portuguese because that is what my father and mother are, as undoubtedly your elders are too. But if I was born over there, it was over here that I came to life, and if my speech sounds as it does, it is because of the notions they always strove to cram into my head, even trying to send me to study in their country, which they did not accomplish because I resisted being brought up amid the enemies of freedom and Independence. Yes, my father, most unfortunately, allied himself to the cause of the oppressors, and this breaks my heart, inasmuch as I am a Brazilian for more reasons than simply living here, but rather because I feel as native to this land as the birds and the boscages. That was why I left my parents' house, relinquished my estate and my patrimony, and came here to battle until my dying breath, though it may be of little worth. We were coming through the dawn without a rest to join the men of the great field marshal Colonel Barros Falcão, when, as soon as we had forded the river, one of their details caught up with us. If it had not been for the valor of the Negro Inocêncio, who was coming with us and attacked two enemy backswordsmen as I was already succumbing from some blunderbussman's shots fired at us from behind, we would not be here now. That faithful and dauntless Negro Inocêncio is still there under that tree, badly hurt, maybe at death's door, unable to move or even to be carried. But I am still ready for combat, good my lord Commandant, and awaiting Your Excellency's orders."

"No, my brave comrade," the lieutenant said, his eyes filled with admiration, his body leaning forward, his hands on the pommel. "It is necessary for you to rest, to heal your wounds. Here across that flank, a little southward, Madeira's forces are choking us; there are those who say he has been reinforced by three or four thousand men, perhaps many more. But we, too, have been receiving reinforcements from everywhere and cannot allow our good comrades, the ones that fight and shed their blood for the insurrection, to remain helpless and unassisted. Those men over there, with the exception of one, are riding horses but are actually foot soldiers, stableboys who enlisted. One of them will show you how to get to a place where you can find some help for those wounds. You cannot afford to lose any more blood; you've already lost too much."

"No, my Commandant, my wounds have been bandaged by this Negro that follows me, whose bravery and dedication are worthy of a real person, so much so that if the Brazilian cause triumphs as God shall see fit to provide, my intent is to give him emancipation, although he is the only property I possess in this world. I fear it is too late, because he was bleeding heavily when we left him to seek help, but my greatest concern is that other Negro lying under that tree, who conducted himself with such valor in defense of his country and his master. As for myself, I can manage. If you could let me borrow one of those dobbins, it would be a royal courser to me, and even at a slow pace it will certainly take me to some resting place where I may be given shelter, for many are the friends I have everywhere, and generous hearts are still more countless."

With a short, forceful nod, the lieutenant, who did not seem to be more than twenty years old and spoke with a noticeable effort to make his voice sound deeper than it really was, said, "Very well, then," in a martial tone, and steadying the cocked hat that had been teetering on top of his head, galloped back to his party. He made one of the privates dismount after riding to where Perilo Ambrósio was, handed over the horse and a jug of water, and waved goodbye as if vaguely saluting. With Feliciano walking, head lowered but rapidly ahead of him, Perilo Ambrósio rode at a leisurely pace toward the place where the road approached the woods and disappeared. He stopped for a moment, watching in the distance the lieutenant alight near the tree where they had been, walk a few paces, bow briefly, doff and replace his hat, and maybe cross himself—it was too far for him to be sure of that. The lieutenant remounted and dog-trotted back to his dusty group. Perilo Ambrósio was pleased to note that everything had turned out very well to the last detail, although he had been certain the lieutenant would find Inocêncio dead. After all, when he decided to smear himself with his blood in order to report to the lieutenant as he had, he ended up stabbing him more than he had planned, because his arms and hands lost control and he attacked the slave as though having spasms. It is a good thing that he died quickly, and it cannot be denied that he shed his blood for Brazil, Perilo Ambrósio thought, turning his back and gently nudging the horse's sides with his heels, to finally ride onto the road.

Cachoeira, March 5, 1826

Yes, the emperor did not spend more than a couple of hours here, and the princess empress never did leave the flotilla's flagship, but this Sunday whose sun rejoices in all the houses, plants, and bodies of water, this morning in which the air you breathe almost makes you float, the colors of the Street of the Mother Church and of the village square, dresses and umbrellas of every hue, bells tolling as if gone mad, men in white satin breeches and pumps as in an ancient court, the visitation day's stalls and banderoles, smells of boiling food and coriander and fresh red pepper and fish and African fried foods, a dark blue sky bordering the mock fortresses built to please His Majesty, heaps of fruit by the river, black men and women glistening among garish fabrics and with voices like exotic flutes, boys running among the trees in their Sunday best, roofs reverberating light and heat, somebody singing, somebody looking at the river, somebody fishing, open doors and windows, flowers in tall, leafy vases—all this, experienced from the door of the Mother Church after the Mass is finished and the day begun, testifies that the emperor and perpetual defender of Brazil resides here and is soon to emerge from one of the three two-story houses that were turned over to him as palaces, giving his arm to the empress to go out for a stroll among his courtiers and his people, tall and handsome like a god, greeting the sun and rivaling with it in splendor. All this proves it is worthwhile to be alive, thought Perilo Ambrósio, baron of Pirapuama, standing at the Mother Church's front door and wiping the sweat off his face with an English brocade handkerchief. He raised his massive paunch, sniffed the air, made sure with one glance that his carriage, hitched to a pair of corpulent white geldings, was waiting at the place he had ordered, with the two black coachmen sitting stiff-backed in the driver's seat, their clothes also black and their rigid collars coming up almost to their ears. He considered vaguely the idea of rebuking them for having left the precise spot he had determined so they could avoid the sun under a mango tree. But he did not do so. He was feeling benevolent, and besides, the horses and the carriage, which involved so many expenses and annoyances, were protected from the heat too. He knew that when he climbed up to the carriage to return to the sugar plantation, he would want to look for stains made by resin dripping down from the tree on the blacks' clothes, the seats, and the roof, and if he found them he might lose his temper again, as happened more and more often when he dealt with blacks. But he would think about it later; he would not allow himself to be irritated now. He had just attended Mass, he had once more given so much in alms for the Church that the sexton's hand almost collapsed under the weight of the coins, he had felt his heart flustered and his eyes wet as the bells of the Eucharist sounded, and he had seen in the faces of those who greeted him so much affection, admiration, and pride at being recognized by him that though he disliked walking and had a certain repugnance toward some of the people who would probably speak to him and even try to touch him, he decided to saunter down the Street of the Mother Church, enjoying the blissfully charged atmosphere of the first Sunday after the emperor's visitation and the total happiness of knowing he was important to God and men.

He thrust his voluminous handkerchief into his pocket without folding it and undertook a pachydermal amble in the direction of the square. Damned lace cuffs, damned women who force him to uncover his head and to repeat his salutations. The second coachman, his lumpy Adam's apple bobbing between the collar flaps, rushed out of the carriage, expecting to have to help him up, as was his function.

"Cadge-cadge?" the black asked.

He did not know how to speak the language of the white yet; he was a new Negro. Perilo Ambrósio stopped and looked at his tall figure, grotesquely broad-shouldered inside his black coat.

"Cadge?" the black repeated, with an oafish smile. "Go-go? Suga mil, go?"

"Filthy Negro," Perilo Ambrósio said, not really knowing why.

"Fiffynigga," the black echoed. "Fiffynigga take to cadge, go-go?"

"No, I am not going to the sugar mill now," Perilo Ambrósio answered after a while, hearing the black repeat "cadge-cadge" and watching him make the gestures of someone who is carrying something gingerly. "Go back there and wait for me. Go back!"

"Gobah." The black spoke with the same frightening smile.

But he cut off his smile as suddenly as he had begun it, and seemed not to know which way to turn, until he finally made an about-face and ran back to the carriage.

"Addlebrained," Perilo Ambrósio decided.

That was not enough to calm him, though, because he had to admit that, faced with that silly-looking Negro and his unpleasant smile, he had felt a kind of fear once again. Maybe he even had chosen him to serve on the carriage not just on account of his size, his health, and his strength, which made him an envied slave, worthy of a baron. It might also have been because he wanted to put that fear to the proof, that inexplicable, almost bodily fear which always came over him when he spoke to that black. Maybe he would not call him a filthy Negro if he could understand it. No, no, of course he would; it was not that bad. Would it really be fear? How could he be afraid of something that belonged to him, just another one of his Negroes among so many dozens of them, something to which he could do anything he wished? Yes, but people are also afraid of a wild bullock, of many animals, even of the peck of a goose, whose neck can be twisted with one hand. No, it was not fear; it was the uncomfortable sensation everyone feels when talking to a lunatic, that was all. Nevertheless, that Negro would be better off serving at the city house, hauling to the beach the barrels of shit produced by the household, pumping and carrying water, and doing other heavy chores his size called for. Well, but those are just vexing trifles that come to mind to try to spoil a day like this, with the square already showing itself ahead with its Sunday crowd, everything in the world within reach of hand or desire—and nothing can be more intoxicating than to be in such a state of grace, knowing that everything evinces one's power. No matter what, it was no trivial event, the arrival, so natural and unpretentious, of a baron at this square where the emperor and his entourage still seemed to be milling about near the luxurious tent in which His Majesty had received the village's keys, and to which even freed mulattoes were permitted to come close to hear the voices of the court, accents and tones so unlike the ones found here and imitated, sometimes to perfection, by refined ladies and distinguished gentlemen. If the emperor, his admirals, his men-of-war, and his royal appurtenances were no longer there, all the imperial aura had passed on to the great noblemen of the land, such as Perilo Ambrósio, who, though not born in Cachoeira and hardly familiar with it, had aggrandized their fame and fortune throughout all the bay lands. Did not his austere, imposing person belong a little to all the people of Cachoeira? Was he not also, in a certain way, a nobleman of Cachoeira, someone its people could mention with pride, saying to strangers, "We, too, have our noble barons"?

Yes, he was, Perilo Ambrósio thought. I am a baron, he said mentally. He no longer had to repeat this obsessively as before, trying to convince himself of something absurd that was resisted by his own mind the first few days after the confirmation of his barony. I am the baron of Pirapuama: it is I. Pirapuama means "whale" in the language of the savages. This could not be verified with the certitude he had desired, because the Indians hardly existed anymore, and the few who remained were either hiding in the deepest wilderness or spent their time stealing and begging for money to get drunk, roll on the sidewalks, and flaunt the ugly diseases brought about by their own nature. But everyone in the bay area and beyond knew that a pirapuama was a whale, and if it was not, it would be from now on, for after all, there stood the baron of the whales, the one who, leaving a wake of suffering and tribulation behind him, struggling for the Motherland, facing hatred and incomprehension, forced to fight against his own family, was presently the highest among the grandees who fished for the great sea animals that every June came to parade their gigantic bodies in the midst of the green waves of All Saints Bay. Pirapuama—a name that affirmed a national singularity, that proclaimed proudly its austral origins, inseparable from those lands and its original inhabitants, the noble savages of yore.

So many struggles, so many sacrifices, Perilo Ambrósio thought, again wiping off his sweat with the vast brocade handkerchief whose nubbiness he cursed but whose studiedly casual exhibition for the eyes of the passersby gave him an irresistible compulsion to once more rub it slowly over the fat folds of his jowl and, that done, to pull out of his pocket a crystal flasket, and keeping his forefinger on the little bottle's mouth, sprinkle the handkerchief with drops of a perfume that aromatized all around, amazing the street boys with those essences that came out of a glittering stone and invaded the universe. Yes, the Revolution had rewarded its heroes. And in fact taking over all his family's properties had been much easier than he had imagined. It had been easy even when, after his father had been placed under arrest and charged with treason, he found the gold dust that was rumored to be buried illegally in the backyard of the sugar plantation's main house and secretly kept most of it, taking a fistful to the authorities as sad evidence that his family was really as bad as it was said to be, perhaps worse. He had wept as he turned over that gold, not out of regret but because he acknowledged that no matter how his filial heart ached, he could not, in the name of the Motherland and of the people who had made the Revolution, conceal the recreancy of his father, his mother, his sisters—of all who used to live in that house from which he was expelled for being the only Brazilian. Unselfish he was, since he might have kept everything for himself to spend the rest of his days in the peace, obscurity, and simple comforts befitting a man who, having done his duty to the nation, harbors no reason for celebration but the contentment of his conscience, such had been the adversity that had victimized him from all sides. Exhausted and bloodless in Pirajá, his wounds having barely stopped oozing vital fluids, there he was at the front line as he always would be, advising, ministering, orienting, serving in a thousand ways until the glorious moment when, driven away among the shadows of night and the thunderstorm sent by the gods of the New World, General Madeira fled back to Portugal on his ships.

Yes, the Revolution had rewarded its heroes, Perilo Ambrósio thought again, weighing his phrase and finding it elegant and expressive. Some had been rewarded in well-earned money, as had happened in Itaparica, on orders from Lord Cochrane himself. Even before Madeira ran away, a certain Captain Tristão Pio dos Santos traveled there as the bearer of what was said to be one thousand of something called hard pesos, to be divided among the commanders of the ships 25 de Junho, Dona Januária, and Vila do São Francisco, for their many heroic feats on the seas of Bahia. What in the world were one thousand hard pesos, an amount that evoked deluges of silver and gold coins? No one on the island or in the bay lands was sure, but they knew about that and many, many other great prizes, so many that if now there were sugar mills, cane crushers, farms, whale oil factories, barons, counts, viscounts, noblemen of the land, millionaires the people could be proud of, it was to a great extent because the Motherland had known how to recompense those who gave up everything for her, the great commanders, captains, and troop leaders who had borne on their tireless shoulders the burden of conducting and inspiring the people for victory, for liberty, for happiness. There on that very facade shines Dom Pedro's coat of arms, designed by himself. On that same spot, Perilo Ambrósio had once seen Dom Manuel's armillary sphere replaced by the escutcheon of Portugal, Brazil, and Algarve, which in its turn was chiseled out and covered with mortar, which would support throughout the centuries the symbol of the new era: a blessed and bountiful symbol, the herald of an explosion of prizes and rewards, Nature itself seeming to be summoning from heaven a cascade of patrimonies and rich farms, medals and pensions, titles and grants, decorations and lifelong positions, guerdons more plentiful and generous than the very hallowed land over which the mantle of freedom now unfolded. The same men who had led in war would now lead in peace—and Perilo Ambrósio remembered with a surge of pride his admired steam machine, his abundant production of sugar, molasses, and liquor, his widespread properties, the bonds he had so generously bought, which augmented the high regard in which he was held by the Provisory Council's Board of Finance, without whose support the barony would not perhaps have been granted. Progress is here, through the work of men like him. He himself made it possible for slaves, uncouth, practically irrational Negroes, to find in their humble service the way to Christian salvation, which otherwise would never open itself for them, and to do their chores, receiving in return food, clothes, shelter, and medicines, more than most of them deserved, considering the worries and vexations they inflicted upon their masters, and their brutish ingratitude, equally inborn in both blacks and natives. As for the people in general, they had many farms to work and many trades to practice, they could sell and eat whatever they fished in the now liberated sea, they could in short lead the same life they led before, with the sublime difference that they no longer were under the oppressive yoke of the Portuguese but were giving their service to Brazilians, to a wealth that stayed in their own country, in the hands of those who knew how to make it fructify.

I am going to have a refreshment, Perilo Ambrósio decided, but before he could get to the kiosk they had set up for the never-ending celebrations, he found himself surrounded by curtsies and bows, the street boys admiring him from a distance and turning away their eyes when he looked at them. A very good morning, Baron; how are you, sir. He had found the best way to treat the populace and the minor functionaries and merchants who encircled him, stretching their necks with solemn faces to hear his opinions about the world and its events. He had always spoken with facility, that was no problem, but a few pauses and expressive gestures were also necessary, to show how profound was the spirit out of which those observations were drawn. He pulled out his handkerchief and sniffed it with dignity. Was it true that His Imperial Majesty was very much inclined to accept Cachoeira's petition to be elevated from village to township, with the exalted name of Petrópolis? Yes, it was true; His Majesty had personally manifested such an intention when they had met in Itaparica, just before the visit to Cachoeira. At that time, by the way, he had had the opportunity to discourse to His Majesty about the painting made by Master Almerindo Conceição depicting Warrant Officer Brandão Galvão's harangue to the sea gulls, on that fateful, unforgettable tenth of June. And curiously, although His Majesty was touched by the warrant officer's story and showed interest in the details of the painting—which incidentally cannot be compared to true art as it is practiced in advanced countries and should be taken for a valuable document, nothing else—he preferred to make an extended comment on the baron of Pirapuama's explanation, which he deemed estimably erudite. His Majesty is very generous, the baron said, waving for someone to bring him a mombin juice. Had the baron had the chance to converse with the princess? Quite briefly, just a few words, for she was indisposed because of the heat and spent most of her time indoors being fanned and refreshed by her ladies-in-waiting. How does the juice taste? It tastes very good, it tastes fine; the princess is not the only one to be discommoded by the canicular sun.

Normally he would wait for the carriage to come, after its being called by a solicitous group of children as soon as he made clear his intention to leave, but this time he decided to meet it halfway, walking as though the crowd were tied to him by a rubber band. He took out of his pocket a chamois purse and distributed coins among the children, old people, and cripples who gathered around him. A stooped old woman wrapped in a black shawl kissed his hand and told him she had known his father and his dear mother very well, before they had been expelled to Portugal. The old woman was being shoved aside by the bailiff Desidério, who was embarrassed by her mentioning a subject so afflictive to the baron, when Perilo Ambrósio stopped him and, with the simple unaffectedness of a great man and hero, said, "Leave her alone, Desidério, for, alas, I too miss my parents and family, a fortune much greater than the one which presently weighs on my shoulders." The crowd froze; everyone stood in silence. And Perilo Ambrósio, biting his lower lip, spoke exactly as he had so often planned:

"Between Motherland and family, my good woman, may the good Lord always give me the strength to choose the former, since the fate of a people is worth more than a man's lot."

He noticed that an enraptured Desidério was quietly mouthing the words he pronounced, which would soon be discussed and repeated by all, in the poignancy of their painful candidness, their bitter courage. He stroked the old woman's shoulder, handed her a coin, and marched toward the carriage in unhurried steps, under the pregnant silence of those who now pondered how so much had been said in so minuscule a speech. Supporting himself on the second coachman, he climbed up on the carriage without looking at him, wiped off his sweat for the last time, crossed his hands over his stomach, and disposed himself to be gently rocked into a nap during the trip. In the Cachoeira sky, mixed with the luminosity and the warm vibration of the heavens, Warrant Officer Brandão Galvão's little soul, still dazed by the vision of the emperor, by the great events that followed one another irresistibly, and by the lovely painting in which it now believed unconditionally, followed the baron's actions and throbbed with admiration and reverence.

2

Settlement of the True Cross of Itaparica,
December 20, 1647

Caboco Capiroba enjoyed eating Dutchmen. In the beginning he did not differentiate between the Dutch and any other strangers he found under favorable circumstances, because he only started eating people after a certain age, maybe almost thirty. And also he had not always lived that way, in the midst of the thickest bushes and the most treacherous mangrove swamps, apt to leave a man stuck up to his groin in the mud long enough for the tide to come and drown him slowly, among serried midge clouds and razorlike mussel shells. It happened only after the many clicks, buzzes, and whistles he started hearing in his head, according to some because he was the son of an Indian woman and a runaway black to whom the Indian settlement gave refuge and who never left his house except at night, when he had to go out for some reason, so he developed a certain kinship with bats and goatsuckers and became unable to see in daylight. And the truth is that the *caboco* had suffered a little ever since he was a boy, being half black and half Indian and having a father who was changed into a night animal most of the time, seeing with his ears and hiding from the sun in the leafiest trees. But the clicks, buzzes, and whistles, as well as the great hotness that incinerated his mind and caused him to behave in the strangest ways anybody had ever seen, manifested themselves for the first time soon after the arrival of the priests, who came with the intention of never going away and began to call all that settlement and its lands a reduction. Nothing happened suddenly, but as each day passed in the reduction, the *caboco* saw himself more and more harassed by the clicks, buzzes, and whistles, which often erupted all at once like an orchestra of devils, during the morning Doctrine or during the afternoon Doctrine or anytime the priests were talking, that is to say most of the time. Then the day came when, in desperation for being unable to see a priest without having to bolt away, trying to hide his head between his legs and with that deafening din exploding his skull, he stole two women, ran into the bushes, and never returned. Some maintain that he continued to be able to speak perfectly, others that he gave up speaking and went on to become a bat just like his father, possibly even flying with the same type of black wing, something his father never accomplished, not even on the day everyone encouraged him to do it so he could soar away from the Portuguese to whom the priests turned him over, because a runaway black is not legal and nothing illegal is permitted in a reduction. And that the *caboco* ate people, sometimes keeping one or two in his pen for fattening, was known by one and all, although it started by chance.

When the priests arrived, a great rash of miracles, portents, and resurrections was set in motion. They built the chapel, consecrated it, and the next day the ground opened up to swallow one by one all who had considered the raising of that edifice an absurd endeavor and refused to work in it. They put up the images on the altars, and for a long time no one died for good anymore, including old people who were tired and interested in passing away once and for all, until everyone began to protest and nobody in the realm paid any attention to the letters and chronicles in which the priests related the prodigies they had effectuated or witnessed. They would lay down a dead old man at an image's feet, and after it sweated, bled, or demonstrated an equally strenuous effort, the deceased, to his and his family's great annoyance, became restless and finally went back home alive once again, in extreme disappointment. Thus it cannot be alleged that the priests were successful in every respect, but they accomplished much that was useful and advantageous, although it worsened the suffering of *caboco* Capiroba's head. In the morning, as soon as the sun rose, they lined up the women to take them to the Doctrine. After the Doctrine of the women, who were then herded to go learn how to weave and spin so they could make the fabrics in which they now wrapped their bodies, came the men's Doctrine, it being known that women and men need different doctrines. In the morning Doctrine, crazy stories were told, involving dead persons with exotic names. In the afternoon Doctrine, sometimes they taught how to imprison in interminable drawings the language spoken in the settlement, with the consequence that the priests were soon showing how to use the language properly, correcting mistakes and unacceptable usages and causing great consternation in many, some of whom, fraught with shame, decided not to say anything else for the rest of their lives, while others spoke only after apologizing for their ignorance of the rules of good language. And special attention was given to Good and Evil, whose differences the reduction's inhabitants did not understand if they were explained abstractly, so every day a new item was added to the lists everyone dedicatedly strove to memorize. To kill an animal: does that go into the Evil list? No. Yes. No. Yes, yes. No, that depends on other things on the Evil list and on other things on the Good list. Few, not to mention *caboco* Capiroba, could boast of knowing those lists entirely, and just two or three knew versions of them, which they memorized as if they were prayers and which, as they were repeated, changed a little to become even more mysterious. But the wisdom of those questions of Good and Evil was put into evidence and amply demonstrated when everything began to happen according to what had been foreseen in the Doctrine. Before the reduction, the settlement was composed of very ignorant people who did not even have small lists for Good and Evil, and in fact did not even have at their disposal good words to signify those most important things. After the reduction, it was seen that some people were bad and some were good, though this was not known before. Bad woman does not want to go to Doctrine, wants to go around naked, does not want the priest to daub her son's forehead with a greenish grease while saying magic words that can forever derange the child. Ugly, ugly bad woman. Good women do not speak to bad woman, bad woman remains alone, bad woman's husband also good man, bad woman alone more and more, gets very bad temper, looks crazy. Crazier all the time, punishment from heaven for being bad woman. Bad men are also unmasked, also end up getting their deserts. Bad man says he makes neither head nor tail out of priest's story, all claptrap, goes fishing. And he also remains alone more and more, drinks liquor, no one talks to him, bad man worse and worse, heavy punishment for badness, gets drunk and drowns, goes to a place where fire burns endlessly and pernicious lizards attack all day long. And finally people were apprised of Temptation, formerly so dissimulated that no one noticed it, but now caught redhanded in the most unsuspected places, so much so that as they leave the Doctrine many young people spend their whole time trying to find out whether everything that happens is not Temptation in one of its manifold guises, and are always in great apprehension, refusing even to sleep, so as not to allow Temptation to ensnare them.

In this long chain of episodes, among Temptation, Good, Evil, resurrections, sins, punishments, penances, hell and all the glad tidings brought by the priests along with Salvation and the Good News, the events inside *caboco* Capiroba's head had sooner or later to come to somebody's attention, and this declared itself most scandalously the day he, after having unnerved himself until his teeth gritted, and walked back and forth as if trying to sew up the ground, started the morning with a fever and nodes all over his body, chewing up words only heard at the time his father still spoke the language he was born with and always used before turning into an animal. Fortunately, in the midst of a growingly obscure world that sometimes seemed to be made of shadows, he had moments of luminosity, when he managed to talk and even to laugh. Otherwise he might have been given the same fate as other men and women who turned out to be absolutely demonized, permanently carrying within their entrails and minds some fiendish, inimical, Beelzebubian, diabolical, accursed, infernal devil, and resisting everything the priests did to rid them of their damnation. For the most part, they were always either trussed up or incarcerated, some of them in such a sorrowful natural condemnation through demonic possession that when the priests visited them to sprinkle holy water on them and to show them crosses, rigid cadavers, crowns of thorns, and the other symbols of the New Life, they were overtaken by convulsions, cataplexies, licentious smirks, and several other much-feared symptoms of bedevilment. *Caboco* Capiroba, however, in the intervals between his more and more frequent head torments, was an open, cordial, and peace-loving person, thoroughly justifying the priests' trust in him, so they let him go untied most of the time and observed with satisfaction that he normally would not enter into contortions at the sight of crosses, sacred corpses, crowns of thorns, hemorrhaging hearts, and similar signs of Divine Love.

It was thus untied that he, with all the reduction's community, listened to the famous story of the cruel suffering and great travails incurred by the good folk whose ship was wrecked along the coast of this very same land, a very long time ago. No one remembered such an event either from memory or from hearing it told, but the priests did not lie and consequently the story was true, which brought about inescapable suspicions among the inhabitants of the reduction, each one thinking that the others had been secret participants in the events of the story. Which was the depiction of said castaway good folk who came ashore when there existed in this land many savages in a state of wildness and no Christianity, so that said savages killed all those good folk to eat, slaughtering one of them every morning by clubbing him after most cruel rituals, not paying any heed to the supplications the sufferers addressed to them, nor caring for the weeping and clamor raised by the unfortunates who would be eaten in the following days. And those savages gorged themselves so much on human flesh, and became so used to it, that the idea of at least sparing the priest and holy man of that ill-fated expedition did not even cross their minds, not even when he spoke to them of the great sin they were about to commit and of the mortal offense that eating him would direct against God and all His flock. With a tear running down his pale cheek, the good priest closed his eyes in front of a huge, terrifying brute whose teeth were filed so as to better tear off the flesh of God's people, now executing a monstrous dance with satanic imprecations and pagan invocations, before he brought down his mace. And thus these savages were much demerited in the eyes of God, and fell deeply, very deeply, to a position whence they might never come back up to the light. And with these and more reasons and plots it was shown that one should never again eat people, one of the worst deeds among the most sinful ones, a perfidious custom which, though the reduction's residents had never heard about it before, now made them shudder for having been capable of such malefactions and made them willing to forever repent through penitence. And while most of them had only a little trouble understanding how they had done something they never knew they had, in *caboco* Capiroba's case there was an aggravation of his head illness, which attacked with such a bombardment of clicks, buzzes, and whistles that on the dawn of the day after the narration he stole the two women and disappeared. Six days later, downcast and famished, roasting a skinny little squirrel monkey to eat in the company of the women, he happened to see birds flying about in the bushes as if someone had startled them. He skulked over and recognized one of the priests, no doubt determined to drag him back because of his love for him, to tie him up and to sprinkle holy water on him until the foul spirit abandoned him. *Caboco* Capiroba then picked up a cudgel he had been polishing ever since his disappearance, approached the priest from behind, and flattened his head with precision, immediately slicing off some of the prime beef for a charcoal barbecue. As for the rest, he salted it very carefully in beautiful pink flitches, which he hung on a cord to get some sun. With the giblets they made a slumgullion, a brain stew in palm oil, well spiced with red peppers, tripe with squash, heart bits on a skewer with boiled cassava, broiled testicles, kidneys softened in coconut milk and papaya, liver tidbits fried in loin fat, deep-salted face parts and ears, chitlins left overnight in seasonings to enhance their taste, and a few sausages made by stuffing the guts after cleaning them with lemon, according to the recipe that very same priest had taught the reduction's women so they could make some for him. They also used some unwanted pieces for crab and fish bait, the lights and other soft parts being the best for that purpose, as the *caboco* found out in no time.

However, the priest did not sustain *caboco* Capiroba and his women very lone, for two or three reasons, the first of which was the smallness of the priest's carcass and his cartilaginous meat, of which even certain tenderloin pieces caused revulsion on account of their toughness and resistance to preparation and seasoning. The second was that provisions usually ended up spoiling in this atmosphere, extraordinarily rich in noxious vapors and putrefying principles, so that only the jerked beef and the sausages remained. The third, fourth, fifth, and all other reasons that could be enumerated would all be subordinate to their having become very fond of people meat, so that *caboco* Capiroba applied himself more and more to hunting a white here and there, among those who seemed to increase in quantity and quality all over the island. In the first year, he ate stockroom clerk Nuno Teles Figueiredo and his assistant, Baltazar Ribeiro, Father Serafim de Távora Azevedo, S.J., halberdier Bento Lopes da Quinta, stableboy Jerônimo Costa Peçanha, two deckhands, four young sons of the settlement's judges, a few sharecroppers, an occasional Spanish officer who happened to be passing by; nothing very notable. In the second year, he stole two more women and ate

Jacob Ferreiro do Monte, a converted Jew always remembered for his exemplary chicken savor, among the best ever tasted in these parts; Gabriel da Piedade, O.S.B., who yielded an irreproachable smoked ham; Luiz Ventura, Diogo Barros, Custódio Rangel da Veiga, Cosme Soares da Costa, Bartolomeu Cançado and Gregório Serrão Beleza, Portuguese from Minho with unrivaled white meat, which seldom failed in boiled dishes; Jorge Ceprón Nabarro, a Biscayan with a tangy, energetic flavor, a juicy bone marrow, and an ample gut; Diogo Serrano, his wife, Violante, his houseman, Valentim do Campo, and his graceful daughters, Teresa, Maria do Socorro, and Catarina, an uneven group but generally substantial, unassumingly tasty and very easy on the digestion; Fradique Padilha de Évora, a bit old and stringy, but the best bacon in memory, after proper salting; Carlos de Toledo e Braga, from whom two hefty gammons were made; six of Captain Ascenso da Silva Tissão's sailors, all of them with excessively hard briskets and just a tinge of musk, though of acknowledged excellence in casseroles and pot roasts; quartermaster Lourenço Rebelo Barreto, greatly missed for the unequaled texture of his rump beef; and many, many others. In the third year, the *caboco* stole two more women and saw the birth of a few daughters, so that with many mouths to feed he started utilizing a greater number of whites, to the point where a certain scarcity established itself at times. Then, a long time later, the summer fruits growing in clusters and dropping to the ground, the insects in great activity and mullet schools capering restlessly along the island's coast, he went out to try his luck without much hope, and came back hauling a very blond Dutchman, whom he had already quartered and skinned to get rid of useless weight on the trip back to his hovel. The Fleming had a taste a bit too bland and a meat a touch too pale and sweetish, but so tender and delicate, so light in one's stomach, so prized by the children, lending itself to every culinary use in such a versatile way, that soon everyone took to favor Flemish meat over any other food, even *caboco* Capiroba, whose formerly rude palate became so habituated to it that sometimes he went so far as to retch a little just from thinking about certain Portuguese and Spaniards he had eaten in times past and who now evoked only an oily, almost tallowy memory of great rancidness and invincible fetidity. Better game than this, so pale and translucent, solid but at the same time delicate to the touch and taste, firm yet soft, wholesome and savory, rare yet easy to hunt for—game such as this there has never been and there never will be, and so what a man must do is avail himself unquestionably of what Nature bestows upon him, because what is given now may be taken back later, that and no other being the structure of life.

This year, in the beginning of which the *caboco* and his ever-increasing family ate the first Dutchman, there was great plentitude, and sometimes it was easier to catch a couple of them in the bushes than to hit a land crab with a mud ball. Even so, when one of those heads like corn ears tossed its golden locks among the shrubs, or when one of them stopped his slow movements to breathe in the air around like an unsuspecting deer, the thrill of the hunt overwhelmed the *caboco*'s chest, his heart jumped, and his mouth went dry in anticipation of the stalking, capture, and slaughter of that animal which through its tenacity, cunning, and stamina emphasized the most transcendent and noble aspects of cynegetics. As he finally cornered and killed one of them, with as swift a blow as possible, sometimes still able to hear the meaningless sounds it uttered before being clubbed down, *caboco* Capiroba swelled with pride and respect for his prey, often remarking at dinner how gallant had been its demeanor and what an honor it was to be able to chew and swallow that chunk of what had been its leg, arm, or loin. As long as the *caboco* could remember, those yellow-haired newcomers, whose speech was different from that of the other whites, kept passing by in confusing waves, always fighting those who had settled there before, setting fire to plantations, and thundering toward the beach from massive boats. But there were never so many of them as now, sometimes in swarms like red ants, building palisades and fences, rummaging the whole island, and occupying the fortifications as though they had taken the others' place for good. All the better for the *caboco*'s family, who did not know whom to thank for such bounty, for it was clearly not the deities and holy figures the reduction's priests had told them about, since they abhorred the eating of people, in spite of having taught it to everyone through their narratives. If experience did not indicate that the keeping and fattening of people was an enterprise of doubtful outcome, he would already have started a little ranch on the sandbank surrounded by thick mangroves where he now dwelt most of the time. At any rate, on a night that began to diffuse a pitch-black darkness and the sticky air that precedes thunderstorms, *caboco* Capiroba, carrying some twenty yards of thin piassava rope rolled around his shoulders, a cane cutter taken from a bushwhacker he had eaten, a strong-meshed net, and the people-killing cudgel, was hoping to bag two or three Dutchmen alive, or more or less alive, to take back to be raised for beef. He figured he was getting old, all his women gave him only daughters, and life became more difficult all the time, so he wanted to be able to rest for a few days without having to work so hard at hunting. He sighed deeply and began to cross the shoal, seeing to it that neither the net nor the rope got wet.

Not long before *caboco* Capiroba's net slumped down on their heads like dozens of intertwined snakes, and Nikolaas Eijkman had his neck bludgeoned in such a way as to leave him gnarled for the rest of his existence, he and his companion, Heike Zernike, were talking about religion. They had spent the whole afternoon leaning over the banks of a little river and brandishing a shoemaker's blade, without managing to stab any of the four or five large fishes they spotted near the tall grass that bordered the river.

Afraid of the thunderclaps he felt were coming and hungrier than Eijkman, Zernike remarked that it was useless to trust Providence. Two good, God-fearing Christians, faithful servitors of valorous princes and captains as they were, had they not been abandoned and left on their own, suffering hunger, terrors, and all the punishments of hell itself, among insects the size of sparrows, animals never before witnessed, and plants with hostile leaves? Without any hope, any weapon, any friends, any food, any horizon?

"Damn the Company!" Zernike blurted out, sticking his blade in the soft earth with a vengeance. "Damn the Company, damn Schkopp, that accursed commandant, damn Banckert, that stinking admiral, damn all of them and all they stand for, and damn a thousand times their words and their forsworn beliefs and everything else they brought us, through misfortune upon misfortune! And night is already falling suddenly, as is usual in this pestilential, upside-down summer, and it is plain to see we will not have anything to eat yet again—as if, come to think of it, there was ever anything to eat in this land of poisonous pears and malevolent roots and meats that make you shit blood, damn, damn all of them a thousand times! And if they do not sink on their way to Paranambuco or whatever place they are heading to along this accursed coast, may they sink anywhere else, and may this storm that is coming to torment us reach them and not leave two boards together in the frames of that fleet of vipers, that squadron of scorpions, damn, damn them all for all eternity!"

"It would be better if you held back your blasphemies and did not say such things about our superiors," Eijkman answered. "After all, we are still in Schkopp's service, and we are still Flemish. Little has changed over this week we have been stranded here."

"Little has changed? Do you really think little has changed, if all we do is run away from the savages and from those Spaniards who want to kill us by chopping off our heads and casting the rest of us to the dogs, if we do not see a living soul and are starving to death?"

"They are not Spanish, they are Portuguese; it seems most of them are Portuguese now."

"They are all the same to me, the same bloodthirsty pigs. How can you say nothing has changed if we ourselves, hiding in the bushes and shaking like eels, watched the beheading of Zeeman, of Willem Stoffels, of poor Einthoven, who would live in peace anywhere, under any master or religion, Pieter Onnes, a fine comrade, poor devil . . . "

"Van der Waals . . . "

"Van der Waals! A feeble old man with almost no strength left in his arms, a man of good ancestry, a patriarch esteemed all over the Randstadt, and they . . . they made him go down on his knees and decapitated him with those horrendous cutlasses and those demonic battleaxes! Beernaert, they butchered Beernaert, they butchered him just as you saw, with his forehead cleaved in two and his body dropped near the water, so the crabs would claw him to shreds! And you say nothing changed? You are mad—that is what you are. You have lost your reason under this unacceptable sun and eating those deadly pears—that's it!"

"No, I am just saying that as far as we are concerned, little has changed. We are still Flemings in the Company's service and are engaged in this expedition—that is what I mean."

" 'Engaged,' if we were left here on our own, and Banckert sailed away with all his ships? Engaged in what—in garrisoning this strip of hell for the Company?"

"We are not the only ones they left behind, Many others are here too, and I am sure they will send over reinforcements to fight the Iberian armada that was dispatched against us."

"Sure, sure! Reinforcements? Bah! Reinforcements! Yes, they left behind a few others, like Beernaert, who is now fattening the crabs, like old van der Waals, like Einthoven and all the others whose necks the Spaniards chopped off or whom they strung up on the tops of those malignant, filthy trees."

"No, I am sure we will meet one of our detachments, I am sure."

"They will have to come to us, then, because we cannot hope to be able to leave this position, since on one side we will have at our heels those naked savages, now made worse by the sorceries the Jesuits taught them, and on the other side we will run into Spanish patrols—"

"Portuguese."

"Spanish or Portuguese, or any of those barbarians whose priests broil people as if they were roasting ducks and pour oil down their ears—this vile, greasy-skinned race with a language like that of dogs and pigs!"

"You are talking like this because you are hungry and did not manage to spear a fish with that awl of yours. Do as I tell you, eat one of those fruits you call pears. It will make you feel better; they are good."

"They burn my mouth, they sear my lips and gums, they shrivel up my tongue and teeth, they give me colic, they give me caustic urine—damned piece of hell, a thousand times damned! And I did not try to catch fish with an awl; this is a cobbler's blade—a cobbler's blade, you hear? A cobbler's blade! Who do you think you are to disparage a tool that does you good service, as it does to all who do not wear horseshoes instead of footwear? You had better not flaunt this rich man's arrogance of yours!"

"Come on, come on, did I not tell you that you are upset? All right, it is not an awl, it is a cobbler's blade, all right; I did not mean to offend you."

"Yes, a cobbler's son I am, and I inherited my father's trade. I did not have a palace in Leyden like your father, nor did I go around in four-hackney coaches like you, because millers like your father grow rich from the flour everyone has to buy, and shoemakers and cobblers are humble people. But you and I are here as equals, equally imbecilic for having believed that here we would find wealth, riches, immense harvests, mountains of gold and spicery, perpetual happiness and peace of mind—and what befalls us is this bile-green, fetid hole peopled by repulsive savages, mud, mosquitoes, rats, and astounding fevers, this place where everything is a menace and one never gets any respite from Nature or man. Your palace in Leyden is of no worth to you now. Your would rather be in your soft bed, with your hot onion-and-beet soup, your nightcap, and your oil lamp, but you are here, and if you want fish soup you have to pray for a cobbler's blade to be able to catch a fish."

"Yes, hot soup . . . Are you married?"

"No."

"I am not, either. There is a lady, however . . . or rather a girl, almost a girl. You know the houses by the river, the tall houses? Well, she lives in one of them, near one of the river's inlets and a footbridge that leads to her place. Her name is Geertge. I saw her at the harvest festival; I even talked to her father."

"And you enlisted to forget her?"

"No, no, of course not. I do not know why I enlisted; I did not need to. Maybe I wanted something not given by my father, maybe it was fate; I do not know. Now I remember Leyden, I remember Geertge, I remember beets. . . . You made me remember them. Did you use to eat mutton mince pie? Do you remember the tall stoves the pies came out of, smelling of noble herbs and of dough made with honest flour?"

"Don't talk about that—you torture me. What kinds of fish are there here? There can be no good fish in such warm waters. Nothing here is adequate, nothing can be enjoyed here. There are things that can be taken away from here and put to good Christian use elsewhere, but man cannot live here. It is a world for menial, brutish races."

"Eat one of the yellow pears," Eijkman said, somewhat regretful for having dwelt on so disagreeable and futile a subject at such a time, and he was getting ready to stand up and pluck a cashew when *caboco* Capiroba sprang up from behind the shrubbery and, swirling his club horizontally with the force of a windmill, dislocated his quarry's neck with one blow, after which he threw the net over both of them, tightened the cord that closed it with a knot, tied it to the cashew tree, and stood waiting for one of his victims to stop thrashing about and cease screeching, so he would not have to club him, too, and risk spoiling both of them, wasting food.

Caboco Capiroba's hovel, December 26, 1647

Dutchman Seeneeky agreed to eat a little piece of Dutchman Ackee-mun after resisting for a few days, ranting and raving inside the little cattle pen and shaking the fence posts in such a manner that *caboco* Capiroba, much to his displeasure—for he had smoked a head weed and wanted to sit still, looking at the trees—was compelled to break a finger in each of his hands. He thus also ensured that Seeneeky, whose restless ways and incessant jabbering were beginning to annoy him, would not again dig a hole to dislodge the posts. He could tie him up, but he knew it was not good for livestock to be kept tethered; it was sure to cause weight loss. He tried to persuade him in a friendly way, for he disliked mistreating animals unnecessarily. But this one behaved like a demented peccary, insisting on showing his teeth and yelping his incomprehensible sounds, and there was nothing the *caboco* could do but to run a ring through his snout so he could be moved about more easily and to give him a little drubbing, although not as hard as the only blow he had dealt Dutchman Ackee-mun. Ackee-mun had managed to wake up sufficiently to stagger back all the way from the creek to the hovel, but he no longer could stand erect, and one of his arms would not stop twitching. The women and the girls pinched him, appraised his flesh, and deemed it better to do the slaughtering as soon as possible, before his weight dwindled too much, for it was plain to see he was a sick animal. It was this way that they learned the Dutchmen's names, because the one that was left in the pen seemed to be more disconsolate at seeing the other being dragged to the butcher's block than a whale when its suckling is blooded, and cried out "Ackee-mun, Ackee-mun!" and pummeled the posts. The *caboco* found that repetitive chant interesting, became curious, stopped a short distance from the pen, and smiled at the cooped-up Dutchman.

"Ackee-mun?" he asked, pointing amusedly at the Dutchman that was being dragged away.

The prisoner's face brightened. Would that savage be one of the many Schkopp had turned into allies of the Flemish? He must be; he had recognized the other man's name.

"Eijkman, Ockee-mun," he said, almost smiling and trying to imitate the *caboco*'s pronunciation.

Delighted at the novelty, the *caboco* this time pointed at the man in the pen: Ackee-mun? The man said no by waving his hands palms out.

"Zernike, Zernike!" he said, poking his own chest with a forefinger. "Zernike!"

Ah, so they were different creatures; how could that be? The *caboco* compared the two with an experienced gaze. Same size, same hair, same clothers, same bestial sounds, probably the same taste. It could not be said that one was an ackee-mun and the other a seeneeky; there was no difference to justify two words. They were names, then; they had names. The *caboco* felt proud of his intelligence. He pointed at the one that was going to be slaughtered.

"Seeneeky?" he asked, laughing heartily.

The Dutchman waved his hands once again and poked his chest: "Zernike, Zernike!"

"Ackee-mun, Seeneeky." The *caboco* spoke triumphantly, after pausing to think.

The Dutchman approved, nodding several times as strongly as he could. The *caboco*'s laughter became merrier, and he started to point rhythmically at each one of them. Ackee-mun, Seeneeky, Ackee-mun, Seeneeky, Ackee-mun-ackee-mun, Seeneeky-seeneeky. The Dutchman laughed too, the women and the girls laughed, and they almost sang a ditty: Ackee-mun, Seeneeky, hoom-hoom, Seeneeky, Ackee-mun, hoom-hoom, ackeemunseeneeky! Ay, the *caboco* sighed, wiping a tear of laughter at the corner of his eye. Ay-ay. He almost started the song again, he had even imagined a few variations, and that festive mood pleased him, but it was getting late and the world was not made just for fun. He got serious and said, "Whoa! Off you go!" to the prisoner, although not expecting much because he knew that, like the others of his species, the animal was very stupid and did not understand the simplest commands. He turned his back on him, resigned to the blabbering that had started once more, took Ackee-mun to the block, put his foot on the Dutchman's face firmly but not brutally, and bled his neck over a bowl with a little lemon juice in it, preferring this method over bashing the head, which damaged the brain.

Vu, the *caboco*'s eldest daughter, was pleased when Seeneeky ate a little piece of Ackee-mun, not really just a little piece but almost a bowlful of very nice sun-dried meat with cassava mush. She had taken a liking to the Dutchman, and twice the *caboco* saw her trying to do with him the same thing the *caboco* did with his women. The *caboco* knew that was wrong, that it was the Dutchman that had to do as he did, making the woman go down on all fours, holding her by the fat on the sides of her thighs, using a little spittle, and getting it over with quickly, but he felt too lazy to teach her. And he figured that the way Vu had been behaving lately, rubbing herself against smooth-trunked trees and wandering out to go hide in the woods for hours on end, she was sure to think of something, and besides, it was not his problem; he had plenty to worry about as it was.

And she really did think of something, because after the *caboco* broke two of the Dutchman's fingers and put the ring in his nose, he no longer managed to push her back and fling himself about as soon as she held on to his breeches and pulled them down. When she finally got him naked from the waist down, he lay motionless, for as he had attempted the customary reaction, she squeezed his broken fingers and tied his nose ring to a short rope. And it was with great eagerness that, unable to overcome the engineering of his breeches, wrappers, drawers, garnitures, and all those voluminous fabrics that covered his loins, she cut open whatever she could with a knife and tore the rest apart with her teeth. As she at last saw him exposed, his russet pubes sparkling in the sun that passed in strips through the fence, Vu, still on her knees, raised her torso and, her lips quivering, her hands fluttering, her breath convulsed, her blood incandescent, her heart turbulent, almost flew away, not knowing in the beginning how to draw her body closer to his, what parts of her body to draw closer and press against the naked, supine Dutchman being watched by her with an almost unbearable pleasure, as though a ridge of goose flesh, muscles, and tingled skin had sprouted in the middle of her breasts down to just underneath her navel. But she knew, because a spasmodic, urgent undulation overtook her from every point in her body toward her crotch, and then, after caressing the Dutchman with her hands cupped, drawing them together gently and moving them up and down like somebody playing at letting water slip through her fingers, sat down on him in just one motion, let out a short cry, and burst out in the biggest laugh she ever thought possible. After that she took to going into the pen every now and then to turn the Dutchman over belly up and to sit on him, with many signs of happiness, sometimes staying for a long time with her eyes closed, swinging her trunk and hips slightly, sometimes almost jumping up and down as if galloping on horseback, sometimes simply penetrated and settled down, doing one chore or another and talking.

Because of those visits to the pen and everything she did with the Dutchman, *caboco* Capiroba thought, when he saw her beaming as she emerged from the pen, hopping from one leg to another and clicking her tongue as she liked to do when she was contented, that what had happened to her was the same thing that came over his women at times, making them, especially one of them, behave strangely while being fucked, having shudders and making noises of pleasure. If that might occasionally bother the *caboco,* forcing him to tell the woman to keep still and to whack her a couple of times so she would not display an improper and annoying behavior, it also gave him a mysterious satisfaction, so much so that there were times when he asked the woman afterward: You had thing? I had thing, she answered, and he laughed with relish—"Cah-hah, cah-hah, cah-hah!"—and gave her a little slap on her bottom.

"You had thing?" the *caboco* asked Vu. "You had thing today? I can see you had thing today; good, very good."

But she simply showed him the empty bowl whose contents Seeneeky had eaten. Oh, that. Yes, good, the animal had finally decided to eat what was given him, even if before that he insisted on not accepting anything, although Ackee-mun's meat, prepared in the form of so many delicacies, was at his disposal. The *caboco* complimented his daughter on her persistence, for he had seen her time and again trying to cajole the Dutchman into eating something, into nourishing himself so as not to remain so wasted, into stopping his refusal of everything, overturning the bowls on the ground and grunting ever so woefully. Now at least he would regain a little of the heft he had lost since his arrival, thus sparing the *caboco* the trouble of going out to kill another one in the near future; very good. Vu was cheerful all afternoon, and the next day taught the Dutchman a new art, which was to eat slices of Ackee-mun's fried spleen, sausage, and jerked beef that she put in his mouth in loving morsels while, with meticulous attention so as not to hurt him, making sure she had sat in the right position and housing inside her everything of his she could take, she bobbed up and down, watching tenderly that thing going in and out, in and almost out, in and almost out, until the moment that, her groin wet and splashy all around, everything inducing moans and undefinable sentiments, everything reeking of head-turning sea smells, she rolled her eyes, held her breath, and bit her lip, pulling harder into her the Dutchman's parts, which then vibrated faintly inside her, a dying, panting bird that left in there, mixed with hers, a lukewarm juice which afterward trickled down her thighs in milky rivulets and which, not knowing why and not even noticing, she gathered with her hands and rubbed over her skin.

She told her father everything she could about all those matters, and the *caboco* was glad, though not excessively, to hear he had a domesticated Dutchman as livestock. He thought vaguely about owning many domesti-cated Dutchmen, serving him faithfully on his piece of land until the day when their age and diminished production made slaughtering them advis-able. But those were just dreams, things to talk about in sleepy afternoons, futureless plans. And indeed before nightfall the Portuguese—now unques-tioned masters of the island again after the Flemish fled at the news of the coming of João IV's armada—negotiated the swamps with ease, taking advantage of the high tide and passing in flat-bottomed shallops over the shallow water that covered the mud. The *caboco* had grown used to the safety of his sandbank, had forgotten about tides and boats, and could not guess the meaning of the hunting dogs that accompanied the Portuguese, noisy beasts with odd-colored fur and teeth like a jaguar's. He did not know about other modernizations, either, such as the little harquebus a Portuguese drew from his belt to strike down with a shot in the back the girl Rõ, who had been running away into the bushes. He did not want to be shot too, so he did not fight back; he just stood there looking at his hands and wrists as he often did, and he did not say a thing while the Portuguese buckled him into a collar fastened to a chain, lined him up together with the women and the girls, and dumped them all hastily on the shallops, to be in time for the high tide. When they arrived in True Cross, all the people had gathered to see the great man-eating *caboco,* a throat-cutting, blood-drinking, Satan-serving giant, and the general opinion was that they should all die at the stake, not only the *caboco* but his women and daughters. However, the labor scarcity engendered by so many combats and conflicts, the helpless widows, the good men who lacked resources to till their land, all this caused the *caboco*'s women and children to be pardoned and charitably welcomed as slaves, including Vu, pregnant with the Dutchman's child. The *caboco* was hanged at dawn, looking at his tied-up hands and wrists with the same expression as that of Warrant Officer Brandão Galvão beholding his gallooned cuffs and his hands that would kill the enemy with gaff blows. A priest was sent to him, and he did not object, listening impassively to the words pronounced in magical language by the priest, with his right arm raised, and echoed by some in the large audience come to see the *caboco* writhe. His last thought was that he might be able to eat that priest, if there was no other choice and necessity commanded, but he knew that his meat, the meat of all those present, could not be compared to a Dutchman's. And while they slipped the noose over his neck, he even imagined how good it might have been if, instead of all that low-grade beef congregated in front of him, there had come and stayed, since the beginning, superior Dutchmen. So superior that Seeneeky, as soon as he arrived, was taken to the ironsmith, who filed off his nose ring; to the barber, who treated him and dressed the small injuries natural in pent-up wild animals; to a family's home, where he was given hot water, Christian food, and a clean bed and linen; to a war council, which sentenced him to be decently shot; to a pole, where he was hog-tied, said a few words no one understood, received many badly placed slugs, and took a little while to die. When his little soul dashed over Our Lady Point, bound for the Perch, *caboco* Capiroba's was already there, wishing never to go back to that mad place where he had lived, but very disquieted for only knowing there were other places and never having learned where they might be.

3

City of Salvador, Bahia, June 9, 1827

It looked as if the gig had gone under, and for a brief moment only the women's parasols remained visible above the waves. Perilo Ambrósio speculated that with all those frocks, petticoats, mantles, corsets, and so many other cloth and whalebone constructions, the two sailors would probably not be able to save the women if the boat sank, especially Antônia Vitória, as usual the one most bedecked with absurd trinkets and fripperies. But of course the gig had not sunk, nor would it sink, and he did not like that, he did not like having to face another execrable crossing over to the whale fishery on a choppy sea such as today's, he did not like all that retinue that Antônia Vitória, also as usual, had mustered, he did not like the muggy weather that kept him in a *bain-marie* inside his gabardine overcoat, he did not like sailing on the steam ferry with its nauseous-smelling boiler and noisy Negroes, he did not like having to chat with the distinguished guests who were waiting along with him for the gig to return to the beach, he detested the idea of pretending to be interested in the feast of Saint Anthony at the blubber-melting plant, he detested having to repeat tedious explanations about the whale fishery, the plantations, and the slaves, he detested being forced to bear with the norms, rules, and restrictions enjoined by Antônia Vitória on such occasions, he detested everything that would happen in the next few days, he hated Antônia Vitória, Sundays on the island with his family, unpleasant stepchildren, and abominable relatives, refined meals and manners, loathsome animals, discussions about agriculture and prices, questions on whether the tide was coming in or going out—he felt an urge to kill something. He had considered waking up afflicted by gout once again, writhing in pain and roaring if somebody touched his feet, but even if Antônia Vitória went to the island alone with her cortege to fulfill the

37

addlebrained promises she made to her most hallowed saint every year, he would not be rid of her. On the contrary, he could expect a visitation by some apothecary to force syrups and tisanes on him, and by the surgeon Justino José with his sinister lancets, his repulsive leeches, his sniffing of urine and stirring of feces, his Charonian bearing, his lugubrious admonitions and vampiric laughter. And also the espionage carried out by the slaves in their house in the Bângala district, who dared not disobey his orders to serve him all the forbidden foods and beverages and to pour into the pisspots those evil-smelling concoctions he would never drink, but when Antônia Vitória returned they would tell her everything, in spite of his threats and the fits of fury against all blacks by which he was overcome. Antônia Vitória, with her infinite capacity to say the same thing for days, weeks, months, or years on end, would force him to hole himself up somewhere her voice could not reach him, so he would not go crazy once and for all. And she would also complain to her father. Perilo Ambrósio bitterly recalled marrying that chalk-white widow, almost as fat as he was, with her very direct eyes, aggressive nose, and metallic voice, with her pride in the carved ivory that reconstituted offensively her upper front teeth, because thus he would be able to enter another business line through the Soares de Almeida Emporium and Warehouse, owned by the Brazilian Portuguese Afonso Soares Matinho de Almeida, her father. But his father-in-law kept himself distant and suspicious, which initially had mortified Perilo Ambrósio but now just annoyed him, because the old man was sinking deeper and deeper into illness and debility, and if Antônia Vitória had any good qualities, the chief one had to be as an old father's only daughter. The gig bordered the submerged reef's dark shade, its bow went down once more, and it reappeared almost dazzlingly with its cargo of multicolored satins and tulles. As it hove to the ferry anchored offshore, the blacks stood up to man the ropes and moor alongside her. Disgustedly guessing at the words Antônia Vitória was saying to the deckhands while she drew her skirts together and stretched out her other hand to be helped aboard, Perilo Ambrósio turned away his eyes and smiled at the visiting canon Dom Francisco Manoel de Araújo Marques. The canon answered in a curious way, pursing his lips into a kind of beak and nodding abruptly. Perilo Ambrósio could not find anything to talk about, and indeed he had no wish to speak.

"We shall soon be there," he said finally. "The ladies are already accommodating themselves on the ferry, and the gig will be back on the beach promptly."

"Yes, yes, I can see that," the canon replied. He nodded briskly again, resembling a cockerel examining from a distance something grubbed up unexpectedly. His glossy black enormous-brimmed hat, ornamented with fuzzy tassels, fluttered as if about to fly away, but it was fastened to his chin by black leather braid tipped with gold aglets. He adjusted the hat with the grave expression of someone who considered it a complex task. He pressed it down, tightened the braid under his chin, checked the knot with a thumb, slapped the brim back to its mushroomlike contours, and after an extended period of blank concentration as if to ascertain that everything was in order, stared at Perilo Ambrósio as though expecting approval or admiration. A cool breeze was starting up, the early-morning bustle was intensifying, sloops and canoes loaded with fish and fruit were putting in to shore; a small crowd huddled near the other dignitaries, under the mango trees at some distance from the beach. They wanted to see the steam ferry, for she was different from the first one that had crossed the bay, many years before. She was smaller and not as apparitional, but none of them could hold back their admiration, now that her side wheels reflected the sun coming up from behind the clouds, her long smokestack, topped by an iron crown, let out puffs of gray smoke, and her flanks huffed forth in hissing sprays billows of steam and water droplets that framed her in iridescence. And the baron, now standing there unassumingly in the right reverend's company to supervise the proceedings, had chartered the ferry at great expense and effort in order to take his wife, the baroness Dona Antônia Vitória, his entourage, and his guests to the feast of Saint Anthony: It was no trivial matter, nothing within a common person's reach. And people also wanted to see the councillors, the professors of Latin grammar, the superintendent of orphans, and the others who were grouped under the escutcheoned canopy the baron had made his blacks fetch from his house to unfold over the guests' heads while they waited to go aboard.

The canon turned toward the mango trees and extended his hand at the group. "Would it not be a good idea to tell them to get ready?" He spoke with some impatience, repeating the head gesture that was beginning to irritate Perilo Ambrósio. "There will have to be another trip on the gig besides the one that will take us aboard, because there are so many chests and trunks for those Negroes to carry, and I fear that the storm now looming over us will reach us before we manage to clear the bar. If I am not imposing on Your Lordship, of course—I do not wish to be importunate."

"Your Reverence is not importunate, Your Reverence cannot be importunate. I am going to summon them, of course, but I beg Your Reverence's leave to inform him that there is no reason to fear a storm is coming, and as you see, the zephyrs common this time of the year are beginning, the sun is almost out; this type of sea warrants no apprehension, nor have we to clear the bar, Your Reverence. We shall be skirting the island on our way, right inside this gulf, of which Your Reverence is seeing the outline, on very protected waters. And we will not even have to yield to the whims of the wind, which sometimes compel us to sail sideways, to wear ship, as they say here, because the ferry negotiates the distance on the power of machines and boilers."

The canon pursed his lips again, and gave the impression he was not going to stop nodding until his neck cracked.

"Yes, I know it perfectly well," he said. "But if you pardon my frankness, perhaps even my rudeness, in saying this to Your Lordship, that is precisely the reason why I seem to be impatient. It is just that those steam machines . . . You know they explode, do you not, their boilers blow up and reduce everything round about to splinters and shreds—does not Your Lordship know that? I imagine that if we encounter opposing currents that might force her mechanisms and engines of propulsion, we should be in a pinch."

"Oh, but Your Reverence does not know about the improvements that this most modern machine boasts; maybe she is not like the ones Your Reverence has seen."

"I have seen them in all manifestations and conceptions," the canon said, with ill-concealed disdain. He assumed a professorial posture, articulating his words almost syllable by syllable, and punctuating his speech with his right thumb and forefinger, forming a circle. "There are such engines in England and in France, or rather in all of Europe. I am therefore familiar with them, inasmuch as even before His Holiness bestowed upon this humble servant of his the canonry I humbly seek to honor, Divine Providence granted me the boon of getting acquainted not only with those but with many other states and kingdoms. And forsooth I say to Your Lordship that even in those advanced civilizations, where man's spirit is not perverted by a lustful and corrupting nature, where mongrelization does not wither away one's blood and temperament—in sum, where it is possible for there to exist what here will never be, that is to say, a culture and a life befitting superior men—even in such nations those machines cannot be said not to offer danger. I am sure that your vessel's mariners are really of the first order, and we shall be transported with every care, but you must admit it is better for us to sail out with the good weather we have now than to run the risk of facing a tempest, what with so many Negroes manning the boat."

Perilo Ambrósio pondered some reply, and even started to open his mouth, but decided it was not worth it and beckoned to a young black who was standing not too far from them. He was to go to the illustrious councillors and other high-ranking gentlemen and, after requesting permission without shouting or talking loudly, inform them that they ought to come over to the beach, for it was necessary to embark without delay. The canon pivoted as if caricaturing a military about-face, and followed the black with his eyes.

"The servile element is indispensable for the country and the society to be maintained," he commented, crossing his hands behind his back. "There can be no disagreement on this, since without it, costs would become prohibitive, and it would be impossible for this nation to aspire to become the granary of the civilized world and the provider of some of the chiefest materials that are essential to civilization. But there are limits to what one can suffer from a constant contact with those simiesque, obtuse creatures that have come to this world so that we may praise God for having made us normal men and put our charitableness to the proof."

"Yes, I, too, find Negroes repulsive. I own them in great numbers because the work at the sugar mill, the plantation, and the fishery requires many arms. But so countless are the troubles they give me, so many the expenses and irritations, that sometimes I ask myself whether I should not be better off without them."

"No, you would not. But that does not mean it is not difficult to bear with them; that is a price we pay over and beyond everything else we endure in this vale of tears, and consequently we have to make such a heavy burden as tolerable as possible. *Dives placet ubique, pauper ubique jacet,* as the ancients used to say; is it not so? There they come at last. But what an awesome parade! Is there not a guard to hold back that mob that surrounds them like hounds at a fox?"

After a crazy dance by the water's edge, the gig creaking, the blacks like dizzy ants, packages, oars, trunks, bundles, exclamations, laughs, and confusion everywhere, Dom Araújo Marques refused to embark like all the others in the arms of a slave so as not to get his feet wet, and they had to have him sit in a chair borrowed from the parish house and carry him over to the gig like an effigy on its litter. Aboard the ferry, Perilo Ambrósio noticed with satisfaction that the women had made themselves comfortable on the quarterdeck, sitting in their wicker armchairs and making the black girls rush to and fro, occupying themselves with useless tasks. Very well, that is the way it should be; let them stay there, where they will not be disturbed, and let them not come here to disturb. Right after he got to the upper deck, panting in spite of all the hands that helped him up the ladder, he saw the ferry's captain, whose oddly pitched voice and nasal tones he would recognize from any distance, welcoming ceremoniously the canon and the other guests, assisted by Amleto Ferreira, the bookkeeper. As always happened in the presence of important visitors, Perilo Ambrósio was not too pleased, though it was unavoidable, by the evidence of his dependence upon that light-haired, lanky mulatto, a somewhat better speaker than he should have been, who was bowing deeply to the canon before taking his leave, walking almost backward. I hope the captain will not come by to declaim his speeches and explanations, Perilo Ambrósio thought. Astern in the ferry, his three step-children, Vasco Miguel, Florbela Maria, and Felicidade Maria, were playing games with the black girls; Antônia Vitória was exhorting all to moral and exemplary conduct; and Teolina, Amleto the bookkeeper's wife, was watching over the children and the blacks. Shambling heavily to a chair beside the canon and the superintendent of orphans, he held on to everything out of fear he might slip as the result of the boat's slight teetering, and sat down with a sigh.

And, finally, the happy navigation, the wheels at first turning so slowly that it was hardly noticeable, only the noise from the engine room, the skipper's bells, and the shouts of the black machinists and stokers being heard. Moments later, the wheels moved a little less slowly, and before long they turned as fast as teals' feet paddling the water, a hoarse toot startled the sea gulls away from a fish school leeward, the bow, rising and falling gently, pointed toward the island's coastline. Dom Araújo Marques nodded two or three times and seemed to smile.

"It sails smoothly," he said. "I think the boilers are adjusted with precision. Despite the permanent humidity of this region's atmosphere, one is forced to admit that their heat facilitates the introduction of the phlogistic element in the wood to be burned."

With two enthusiastic handclaps and a laugh perhaps too loud, Amleto Ferreira applauded the canon.

"Amleto Ferreira, my bookkeeper," Perilo Ambrósio hastened to explain. "A person very dear to my household, my right-hand man."

The canon appeared not to have heard him. Now his head, instead of going up and down, raised itself by stages, in short jerks, so that finally his line of sight slanted sharply in relation to his very erect neck, giving the impression that even though short, he dealt with everyone from on high.

"Did you find what I said facetious?" he asked, pointing his nose sideways and directing his pupils at the bookkeeper.

"Why, yes! Your Reverence shows great wit, yes. Yes, has not everybody realized it?"

The canon's head, made smaller by the absence of his hat, immobilized itself.

"Realized what, if you would be so kind as to tell me?"

"That Your Reverence was speaking in jest, being ironical about the machinists' skill."

"I was not being ironical at all."

"Oh, I beg Your Reverence's pardon, but was it not an irony when you referred to phlogiston?"

"Certainly not. I said a very sensible thing known to any half-wit, and that thing is that phlogiston impregnates combustible materials with more ease when the atmosphere is warm, as it is here."

"Oh, Your Reverence must forgive me, then. I thought that by mentioning phlogiston . . . Pardon me, Your Excellency, it was an error of judgment."

"But what was it that you thought?"

"No, I did not think anything; it was a misunderstanding."

"What was it that you thought? Come now, have you lost your tongue?"

The canon started to syllabicate his words as he had done at the beach, and looked around with his hands raised shoulder-high, like in a painting of the Sacred Heart.

"Phlogiston, yes, explain phlogiston to me," he intoned. "No doubt you thought I was inventing words, I was making a little quip. But no, my dear fellow, I did not invent the word. His Lordship the baron for one knows it; it is known by all who went to good schools and lyceums."

"I, too, know it, Your Excellency."

"Call me Monsignor; I prefer that. It is a reasonable adaptation of the French term *monseigneur,* and after all, it is a little preferable to 'Excellency,' for it is not granted by His Holiness the Supreme Pontiff to just anybody. His Holiness said that to me personally in one of our many audiences in Rome. An excellency is everyone, even Your Excellency. . . . "

He continued to look around as he spoke, making pauses, sometimes fixing his gaze on a spectator's face, sometimes closing his eyes and delighting in his own words. Now he joined and separated his fingertips, and cackled a laugh, whose echo he immediately commanded from the audience with his eyes, and was obeyed. Pale like an ex-voto image, Amleto sat stiffly on a bench's edge. "Oh yes," the canon said. "I was changing the subject. Your Excellency was saying that you know about the phlogistic element, and yet you considered jocular a perfectly trivial remark upon it. Therefore, *cetera desiderantur.* There remains something to be clarified forthwith about this most singular phenomenon. *Pericula in mora,* hah-hah! Go on then, enlighten us on this mystery."

"I thought that when Your Reverence the monsignor mentioned the phlogistic element, Your Reverence wished to allude in a jesting way to a concept that, according to what I was able to learn from the few sources within my reach, is now thought to be part of an outdated natural philosophy, for it is known that the modern science of inanimate bodies maintains that fire is the result of a combustion of gases, and so—"

"What did you say your name was?"

"Amleto Ferreira, at the monsignor's service."

"Is it a Christian name? Amleto . . . I never heard it before."

"As far as I know, it originated from an English legend, an English poem or tragedy."

"An English tragedy, a poem? We have something here, then, we do have something! England is excessively benevolent toward poets and frivolous arts. If she had musicians too, she would be lost. So your parents read English profane books, is that it? What books are those?"

"I do not really know, Monsignor, but my father is English."

"Your father is English? Now we really have something, we really do have something! But you are brown, are you not? The ordinances that used to bar browns from public service are not in force any longer, you may speak freely, for it will still be possible for His Lordship the baron, after you have served him well, to place you in a good position, as a bailiff or, who knows, as the parish mule tender, so you can spend your old age in clover and with nothing to do, hah-hah! And where is this English father of yours; what is his trade?"

"He lives in England; we have had no news from him in a long time."

"In the company of your dear mother, of course. Tell me."

"No, Monsignor, my mother lives here in Bahia by the grace of God; she is an elementary-school teacher."

"No doubt. She is a freedwoman. I see. And your dear English father?"

"He used to be a seaman; he was a seaman when he came to Bahia."

"A corsair? And was he not hanged by the king's soldiers? Hah-hah!"

"No, Monsignor, he was in the crew of a merchant ship."

"And you were brought up by some religious order for browns? They must have done a good job; one can see you are literate, and when you speak you do not perpetrate abusive solecisms such as the ones one hears so much around here. You probably know how to count well too, or you would not be His Lordship's bookkeeper."

"I was brought up by my mother, with God's help. There are public lessons in the town where I was born, I was able to study—"

"Yes, I can see that. I do see you have something in your pate, and also the cleverness that is natural to mulattoes, which can be very useful to you, of great worth to you. That is, if you manage to overcome this foolish arrogance of yours, which is quite common among those who came up from the gutter, but nevertheless sufficiently prejudicial to make you stick your nose in matters of which you know naught."

"But, Monsignor, I was saying—"

"Shush! I have had too much patience with you, and I am no longer joking, as I was before; I am being serious now. I shall show you the truth in the Socratic way. I realize you are not versed in philosophy, and if you hear Socrates mentioned you may imagine that the talk is about some other Englishman who visited your mother's home. But no matter. I shall ask you a couple of questions, and in no time will demonstrate the falseness of your puerile arguments. Mr. Bookkeeper . . . What *is* that Anglican appellation of yours?"

"Amleto. Amleto Ferreira."

"A curious appellation for a Brazilian, a curious surname for an Englishman. I must remember this, to relate it at the French court; it will be enjoyed. Very well, then, Mr. Amulet. I ask you—and please reply using as few words as are possible for you—why this famous combustion of gases is not produced if no one sets fire to the wood or uses the sparks of a flintstone?"

"The initial impulse is missing, the reaction—"

"And what is that impulse?"

"The impulse provided by the flame already in combustion."

"And what does that flame contain?"

"Combustible material and gases in combustion."

"Very well; for that flame to burn it was necessary that another one was set to it, and another one for the latter, and another one for the latter, and so on, *ad infinitum*. And the first among all flames, how was it lighted?"

"By means of any of several methods, I imagine."

"Setting fire to it or using some other form of ignition? How could that be, if there was no fire, if I am asking about the first one, the first among the first?"

He stood up, opened his arms, and turned around slowly, facing at intervals each sector of his silent audience, some of whom nodded their agreement and whispered at the mulatto's arrogance, trying to rise to the heights of the immense sapience that now seemed to hover over them with its black frock and cloak.

"How could that be if there was no fire, if I am asking about the first one, the first among the first?" the canon repeated.

Sitting in the same position, Amleto Ferreira gulped. He felt dizzy, he was sure no more words would come out of his mouth, and he did not know where to look, but just the same he tried to speak. He did not go beyond one syllable, however, because everyone started whispering ecstatically about Dom Araújo Marques's triumph, which was already being culminated with a final stroke.

"It is the desire of impious naturalists," he said very loudly, "to revoke the existence of the phlogistic element, in the same way that they wish to revoke God's existence itself—it is an inevitable analogy to them. But no, Mr. Bookkeeper, mere logic, with no need to resort to faith, demoralizes them. Mere logic!"

Now nearer the island's strand, they could see ahead a few huts, plantations, long, curvilinear whale-rib fences, one or two canoes aground in the low tide. It was not a beautiful day, but the muggy weather was almost gone, the sun was challenged by just a few transparent clouds, the ferry's stern left behind a continuous wave that went as far as the eye could see. A school of flying fish leapt out of the water like glittering gems, and the children cheered. Perilo Ambrósio stood up, held the canon by the arm, and walked with him over to the gunwale.

"Actually," he said, pointing a hand outward, "my lands start over here, although on this part I only use them to grow sugarcane, as you can descry from here, for those light green spots are sugarcane spikes. At the Good Jesus Fishery in Amoreiras, to which we are headed, I own more or less three thousand braças from coast to coast, with a shoreline of more than half a league, if I am not mistaken. Though modest, our establishment there is quite important. We try to surround ourselves with some comforts, albeit not excessively, as Your Reverence will see, because whaling has not produced good yields the past few years, in my judgment on account of unfavorable lunations. Last year we captured no more than forty or fifty large ones and a few small ones. The taxes and contributions we pay, however, are still exceedingly heavy, and sacrifices upon sacrifices are demanded of us."

"How many kegs of oil are extracted from one whale?" the canon asked, blinking repeatedly as all that opulence unfolded before him.

"Well," Perilo Ambrósio answered, "this varies in proportion to their size. But in a general way I should say thirty or forty barrels, plus cheap meat, which we cure and sell for a mite per pound, some tens of tons of meat, much of it unusable except by Negroes. And on top of that we have all the work and expense with the Negroes, the whaleboats, and the plant facilities, which are always in need of repairs, since those African creatures are so villainous that they deal with their working implements as though they belonged to some enemy and not to their own masters, who provide their sustenance. I do not know whether Your Reverence will endorse my opinion, but I believe that if the lax authority and absence of rigor with which the servile element is treated these days keeps on, if crossbreeding continues among blacks of the worst African stocks—and nowadays that is what most of them are, herded by unscrupulous merchants—I do not know what will happen to this country's wealth and mercantile production."

"I not only endorse your opinion, I carry it further! The institution of slavery, which merited from the sublime Stagirite a most wise, judicious, perspicacious, and indisputable defense, inasmuch as it is rooted in the natural differences of character and propensity among races and peoples, is not, has not been, cannot be, will never be foreign to the church. What is foreign to her is rather the perverted concept of servitude that one sees practiced today by cultivators of a false, dangerous, and mainly heretical humanism. There is not a single freethinker who does not place himself on the side of the Sadducceeism that clearly constitutes the web of such reasoning. All this cannot but cause great concern, Your Lordship. *O tempora! Spes et fortuna, valete!* The decadence of public authority, the flaccidity of the spirit of honor and decency, the compliance with the insolence of the servile classes, the abandonment of the most elemental principles of social hierarchy, the confusion of values and criteria, even the lack of a real war to educate the great mass of the people and to season their mettle, all this, my dear Baron, is for me a source of great fear and ruth for a land such as this, which in hands that were firm and conscious of the fundamental truths would have much to offer to the European civilization that the good strive to implant here and the bad to cast down. *Abyssus abyssum invocat,* Your Lordship. I do not really know where all this will lead us."

The southeaster whiffled more strongly, the brim of the canon's hat flapped like the wings of a large bat. And he, his eyes wide open and his elbows on the ship's rail, continued to hold forth with vehemence, while the ferry, moving her wheels at varying speeds, set course to Amoreiras.

Settlement of Holy Port, Itaparica
June 10, 1821

First Dadinha spoke in detail about how it was a cool day, no doubt the same as exactly one hundred years before, the day she had been born. She did not know whether it had been Sunday too, they did not tell her, or if they did she could not remember. She waved her hand near her right ear, as she always did when she became upset for having forgotten something. Finally she declared it had to have been Sunday, not only because she had heard that every one hundred years the weekdays coincide but also because her mother, whose name was never revealed to her, had told somebody that it had been very cool the day she was born. Seeing that Sundays are always cooler than the other days, she explained, it must really have been Sunday, at precisely the moment the vespers bells were ringing. Some people disagreed with her, pointing out that Sunday was just as warm or cool as any other day, it was just that most people did not work very much on Sundays, so one's body did not get as hot. So, she said, so is it not the same thing? Cool like this, a breeze flowing through the window and flapping the flounces of the white madras smock that descended from her neck like the flanks of a pyramid. She had been unable to walk for a long time now. When she had to stand up, she had to summon help from many people, and when she had to remain on her feet she had to be propped up. But she did not seem to be one hundred years old, she did not seem to be of any particular age, turning young or old repeatedly several times a day or in the course of a single conversation. And she was majestic, sitting amidst colorful patchwork cushions and fringed madapollam shawls, with beads and shells of every color on her neck, her round face framed by a greenish-blue kerchief, and around her the delicate smell of the pitanga leaves she had ordered them to crush on the floor. Unlike her legs, her arms and hands moved with agility, adorning her conversation among graceful shrugs and sinuous elbow movements.

"I am hot," she announced. "Isn't it cool? Well, I feel hot!"

She bent sideways, turned her head as if to hide her face, and, almost imperceptibly at first but afterward giving the impression of an earthquake, started to shake her immense body, swaying to the rhythm of a soundless guffaw. Pursed moments before, her lips exploded, and she bent forward, tugged at her smock's frills, rolled her eyes, and laughed her heart out, her head buried in the convoluted mass of her breasts, arms, and shoulders. Ooy-ooy, she went, wiping off her tears, and burst out in a new cascade of laughter, this time sonorous ahs and ehs and ohs modulated in every way, her head moving in counterpoint to the rest of her body. Soon there was no room for anything but that laughter, and all those present, blacks who were not under punishment and could take the day off on Sunday, visitors who had trodden all the way from the Good Jesus Fishery to see the ever-enchanted greatest old mother in the world, people who never missed an occasion to come and stand before her as in front of an ancient mountain, a witness to all that ever happened on earth—the whole audience, from the old people to the infants in arms, started to laugh, stomping their feet, slapping their thighs, and hiding their open mouths with their hands. No one expected Dadinha to shout as she then did.

"Wha' be this?" she cried out. "Wha' be this?"

Without even her blood relatives and those close to her noticing any transition or motion, she was no longer curved in laughter, she was towering like someone who swallowed a coconut tree, stiff-backed and scowling so hard that only her eyes and mouth could be seen. The laughter stopped like a drumroll cut off by a command, two lines wrinkled her chin down from the corners of her mouth, her face became thin.

"Now, now," she spoke. "It is *my* hundredth birthday, it is I that am going to die, and that means I am the only one who can find it funny. I know why; nobody else here does. Let each one do their own best to be able to have their hundred years and to be able to find it funny when the time to die comes; the only ones who can do it are the ones who have the right. After I die, there will have to be some crying—it is the right thing to do—but I may laugh. Just now it was cool and I felt like warming up the wind and I did it, that is why I complained about the heat and laughed. But that is not all that is funny, although a person of wisdom will find that enough to make him realize all the rest, but only a person who really has knowledge. I am the one who is going to die; only I may laugh."

She furrowed her mouth some more, put her hands on her thighs, with her elbows pointing outward, and closed her eyes. When she said she was going to die today with the same naturalness as someone who remarks it is going to rain, many had thought that once again she wanted to play an innocent prank, because they could never tell if she was being oracular or being playful like a young girl. Bur her face, tautened in an aquiline mask, let no one mistake that for a joke. As she began her speech it could be seen she was really being herself, serious and at the same time ironic, with an absent-minded gravity and assuming fleeting appearances like the things one sees in dreams. No entities were speaking through her, at least at the outset, when her voice, full of curves and peaks, broke the silence.

"What I am going to tell you I already told someone here, someone there, a piece here, a piece there," she said, breathing deeply and opening her eyes. "As I do not want everything to be mixed up and misremembered after I die, I am going to tell you the important parts, will answer questions, will teach precepts."

Finally accepting that Dadinha was really going to die, they made themselves comfortable in order to learn everything they could and not embarrass her at the time of her farewell, and she made the following speech, voice in C major, long arpeggios, dissonant chords, scrupulous harmonies, multiple ranges, surprising attacks, expressionistic tempo, unerring dialogue:

"I was born in the slave quarters of the Good Jesus Fishery, the granddaughter of Vu plus the German *caboco* Seeneeky, this Vu being the daughter of *caboco* Capiroba—proshantane, proshantane, proshontane, prrr-pprrrr, outa heah, poppin' and buzzin' in the brain! Ahoom, proshantane, proshontane, outa heah, damn clicks in the head, words of blood and sin in the brain! Outa heah, 'cause *caboco* brain cannot take it! Outa heah, buzzin' and whistlin', hah, I'll be!"

"You received him, great old-old mother?"

"Why, no! Capiroba great *caboco* has not come down in more than fifteen years; he must have entered a new body being born and had no choice but to stay in it. No, what I have is a general receivement, things of the past that come and go, so your answer is yes and no."

"*Caboco* Capiroba saves prisoners?"

"Said *caboco* stands by that door with his cane cutter hanging from his hip and his two *caboco* brothers, Seeneeky and Ackee-mun, who never run from a fight and will live on and on. In-God-believe, most-holy-virgin, val' o'tears. I was born in the year twenty-one in the beginning of the seventeen hundreds, my father I did not know, he died as I was being born, even before I was born, nor my mother did I know, she was sold before I was weaned, and taken to Serigi, never to return here. When I was just about to be born, there were eighteen crazed souls in Amoreiras, all of them come to incarnate in this here me, though the parish priest said later that I would not live. My soul was incarnated after a great disputation, a disputation so great that people still remember it, and in that disputation my body was like a brothel visited by more than a hundred souls, sometimes fighting much. My father was a Negro whaleman; his eyes were light-colored. My older-eldest brother died at night doing work with whale oil, the boiler overturned on him, he died burned by the oil, he died fast, but the Negroes of the whale oil work almost all of them had their skin sometimes all live flesh, sometimes all blisters and scabs, and many became blind from the oil that splattered from the caldrons that tipped over when their trivets came apart. About the same as today. My grandmother Vu did not speak words, she spoke shouts. So when they took her to this house to work in it doing all the housework, she shouted and attacked the kitchen, and the more they yoked her up in the stocks to flog her with all their cats-o'-nine-tails and their straps, quirts, rods, and horsewhips, standing stocks, squatting stocks, head-down stocks, the more she attacked with no fear. They dressed her in a hair shirt, they squeezed her breasts with a cow's barnacle, they cracked her fingers with a

49

pilliwinks, they made her sleep with an oxbow on her neck and lying on corn seeds, they branded her with hot iron on many parts of her body, they threatened everything and then some, and the more they did it, the more she attacked. Then on account of all that untamableness and everybody thinking she was inhabited by the spirit of the Foul Fiend, they waited for her to give birth so they could have her child, and after that they buried her alive head down, digging a very deep hole to make sure she was very well buried, and the priest came after the burying to bless everything very well blessed, spilling holy water on the place of the hole so she would not come out to attack once again. *Caboca* Vu very fierce, she does not come down, she incarnates in wild banana trees, if anything. Whale fishing has the *cacharréo* which is the male, the *madrijo* which is the female, the *baleote* which is the suckling, the *seguilote* which goes alongside its mother but already eats food besides milk, and the half-fish, which is the young fish that would grow big if it was not harpooned. The whaling songs were the same as today, aru-eh-pun-pun, aru-eh-poon, I am going to catch the whale with the barbs of my harpoon, only it used to be sung faster—aru-eh-poon-poon-poon-poon. This was during the flensing; during the fishing trip there were others. The priest came all vested up to bless the dories that were going out to catch the whales, always three dories, once in a while four, they were not whaleboats like today's, today's whaleboats are like warships. The priest blesses the dories, which sail out very, very well armed, for all the whales are here this month bringing forth their young. The *madrijo* does not leave her *baleote* alone, does not leave her *seguilote* alone, and then when the *baleote* goes capering and capering and capering over the water, everybody knowing that the *madrijo* must be swimming around nearby, the *baleote* goes on playing and leaping and bounding and hopping on top of the waves like a dolphin made foolish by youth, the dories then go to it, and it looks at them as if he wanted to talk to them, and then all they have to do is to stick the harpoon in it, which they do from close by because the *baleote* knows nothing and is not afraid of them. So they kill the *baleote* with this harpoon, which is the same they use for the bigger fish, only not as big and with more barbs and prickles with the intent of causing much pain for the *baleote* to cry a lot before dying and being tied to a boat's side, and then arrives the mother, having heard those cries and whines, and when she comes she is already crying too, and then they stick in her the big harpoon, which makes her run leagues and leagues chased by the three dories, but they put in the middle the boat that is bringing her calf roped up to its side, because even badly wounded and badly tired she always comes back to see it, and she runs and is chased again and harpooned again, and sometimes they use great sickles and whale scythes and many irons, then she cries much like a person and squirts blood in a red water dust, the sea also becoming all red, and then this whale dies together with her *baleote,* and then they tow them one behind the other to the fishery, with their mouths and jaws tied shut by good ropes so the water will not go in, as well as the fishes that like to go into the mouths of whales and the creatures that drink their blood."

"What animals should she who is in her courses not eat?"

"Poison, not to eat. Venom, not to eat nor drink. Forbidden food, not to eat. Toadfish, not to touch. Scorpion fish, not to step on. Sullied water, henbane either black or white, wild taro, datura, spurge flax, puffer fish, all of them, all of them, my child. Realgar . . . Be careful! Do not eat in bad company, attention! Do not eat food prepared by a friend who used to be an enemy, much attention! Ah! Ah! Ah! Twee-twee-twee! Saint Kalendeh is coming, my people, it is on the twenty-third, my boy, make your offerings to him, my boy, *lobara Eshoo Lonah,* come here, come here, *Aloree-ay!*"

"Did you receive him, old-old great mother?"

"Dang-bay, snake of the woods! Hew-hay, ssssssu! Saint Lawrence has the same name as the time, he is from here! Obessem in the heavens, all prettied up! Avreekeetee, ooy, ooy, ooy, ooy! Let us go with Dom Pedro under the loko tree, playing the drums amelay and batakoto, long live the king of Byssinia, good *caboco* Solomon Darissa, from the land of Abobbas!"

"Are you seeing everything there?"

"Nearly-nearly. But what is it zit-zit-zit-zit, man? Mmmmm! Believe me very much, it is how I tell you: *emo-zhubah, ebbo-coshay,* all mixed together here, a veritable painting! Look at the twelve knights of France, people, but what rebrilliance! In the garmenture of the queen of Sheba, Solomon's sign, David's battle, great wonderments here, first-rate thing, what a lively feast! Come hither, little princess of Guinea, celebrating a celebration! Not to mention food, all kinds! Hey! I cannot tell you!"

"Anything with the Curukera moth there?"

"Nothing like that. That moth arrived here over the heads of the priests and of the one who touched the head of the brave *caboco* Capiroba, ay! The one who touched his head before they hanged him, ay! Hoom-hoom, haaan!"

"Did you receive him, great mother, is he here?"

"In the sheven hundred, around the Sheventy or the eighty, when not a sign of anything that there is now existed, only the whales and the people, came Darissa from Byssinia, who was crazy, crazy, most deranged. The city of Byssinia is Dze-Abobbas, but he did not bring any abobra gourds with him, he brought an ancient religion he could not defend here. The name of his people is Chicken in our speech, but he did not bring any chickens with him, either, and he did not cackle. This was before they ran the regular zezuit priests out of here, I tell you, hoom-hoom. There was the great king Zoceph, who stayed in the realm, in the dovecote of a marquis, and the marquis came and said: I do not care to have, understand me here, I do not care to have any zezuits in my lands, if I see a Zezuit I kick him out, heh-heh-heh-heh! They rounded them all up and took them very far to

Jiquitaia, heh-heh-heh-heh! No-good zezuits were all put together in irons and taken by Colonel Gonçalo to be punished in the realm, well over one hundred priests loading that ship, he-he-he-he! Bishop Zoceph Boteio, much distressed by this, quite fearlessly quit his job as archbishop, and moved out to live with the Itapagipe nuns, heh-heh-heh-heh-heh! It has nothing to do with Father Roma, the one who was killed with his sons, this comes much later in the events, he was taken to the gallows for having made sedition. They nailed a protest paper to the church's door, but if it was sacrilegious to hang a priest in this case it was forgiven, for he was a baby-making priest and very much of a seditionist, so that is the history, tra-la-la-la, if you want a better one you can tell it yourself, heh-heh-heh-heh-heh, got a little pipe there, a little pipe?"

"Are lovegrass roots good?"

"Lovegrass is good. Attention to the holy saints. All saints are good, all very good, all very good, Saint Anthony, the Saint of the Conception, all very good, but when in need call a saint of your color, remembering that captive slave Negroes cannot wear either smocks made of fine linen or gold chains, attention to what happens, to see you just have to look. Saint Solomon the Fighter's prayer goes like this, clap your hands, clap your hands: Hoom, cover yourself O body, defend yourself O brother, in Saint Solomon's holy ark, did you learn it? Saint Elesban, Saint Benedict Urumillah, Saint Figenia, you can remember a few more, good. For the evil eye, sprinkle cool water, use a spurge nettle branch to make the prayer or else broomwort, go on making crosses, making crosses, making crosses: God made you, God created you, may God rid you of the eyes that looked at you evilly, with two eyes they gave it to you, with three powers I take it out of you, the powers of God, the Velgin Mary and Zezus of Nazareth, her son conceived without strain or sin. If it was to your head, Saint John the Baptist; if it was to your eyes, Saint Lucy; if it was to your teeth, Saint Polonia; if it was to your body, the three persons of the Holy Trinity, Father, Son, and Holy Ghost; if it was out of ambition or envy, hatred or revenge, all will disappear in the abyss of the sacred sea or over the boundaries of the world where neither the cock crows nor the ox moos, with the powers of God and the Holy Trinity. One our-father-who-art, one hail-mary. A bath in scented water, an *aree-ashay,* put rue leaves in it, put hollyhock, basil, broomwort, put rosemary, and after they are dry burn them, make like incense, fumigate very much, and it is done. Headache, the following: Saint Flavius asks Saint Laurius, 'Where goest thou, Laurius?' To which answers Flavius, 'I am going to the river Jordanius, where lived Saint Joannius, to fetch very cold water to cure headache, migraine, and splitting head, with the powers of God and the Velgin Mary.' Sprinkle cold water, three our-father-who-arts, three hail-marys. Stabbing pain, ask for Saint Joseph's help.

Snakebite, Saint Dominic, also business with dogs. Head blow, Saint Stephens. Knotted bowels, plugged bladder, Saint Tolentine, as well as woman or beast with a stuck delivery. Impossibles, Saint Rita; traveling, Saint Chrissofer; stone blows, Saint Polinary; flaying, Saint Bartolomew; running sores and blains, Saint Lazar; arrow and spear wounds, Saint Bastian; playing music, Saint Cecilla; lost on the sea, Saint Clemento; fishing with a net, Saint Peter; fishing with a rod, Saint Zenon; scythe cuts, Saint Simon; tanning leather, Saint Crispin and Saint Crispinian; festering wounds, Saint Catherine; hunting, Saint George; raising children, Saint Gonzaga; stolen things, Saint Anthony; empty-headedness, Saint Ignassus; blood spilling, Saint Pintaleon; lunatic madness, Saint Hermes; firing cannons and harque-buses, Saint Barbra, as well as in thunder and in every detonation; pain in the balls, Saint Nereus, as well as raising capons; making jests, Saint Philip; chest maladies, Saint Casimir! When no saint answers your call, call Saint Judas Tadeus! Saint Judas, you know, is not the Jewish Judas, he is a different one, but people think they are the same, so when somebody remembers him he gets very pleased and never fails to come, do not forget that. The orison for heartburn is with Saint Iria, to be repeated three times: Saint Iria has three daughters, one spins, the other sews, and the other cures heartburn. Maggots on cows' backs, you can pray them out through the power of the five wounds of Our Lord, starting, 'Evil eaters, the Lord is not praised by your work! And in this sore you will never eat again!' For asthma, grind hermit crab shells, or use well-toasted powdered sea horses, drink them with water, it relieves coughs and wheezing chests. Wild fern, clove, and honey, good, good, good, good! Infusion and cataplasm of savanna flower! Pepper trees! Coral beans! Milkwort! Take the amulet agheree under your arm when you go out for a fight, prepare it well! Pray eh-tootoo prayer! Stay on guard, do not accept gifts of bracelets nor necklaces nor anything that might tie you up, do not let anyone touch your head, I warn you, laralah-lerelay! Do not turn your back to the window ignoring the door, do not accept food from everybody, do not trust, do not tell your secrets, if you will see, heh-heh-heh, oh my God, there is no telling. . . . Careful with the cururu toad, hoom-hoom! Do not lend salt on Friday, do not baptize, do not clip nails nor hair on Friday. On the first Monday of the month of August, no fishing, no going to the water spring! Do not count the fish as you fish them, nor the crabs as you put them in the creel, nor the shellfish as you pick them! If the wedding is on Saint Ann's day, the woman will die when she gives birth! Keep away from iron and metal when thunder is about to roar! To kill a spider brings bad luck, to keep a spider makes you rich. To make a birth faster burn pepper leaves, fumigate well, pray as follows: 'Go, smoke, so that my child is born.' Do not sharpen knives on Good Friday! If a woman rings a church's bells, she will no longer bear children. Pay attention to

Mother Cattatee, the new moon, pay attention! Mother Cattatee in the month of October, what happens? Thunder! If after nine days the rain goes on, it means rain with every moon! North wind blowing till noon, rainstorm the next day! Show your child's ass to Mother Cattatee as soon as you can! Ask Mother Cattatee for money! New moon, heh-heh. But plant only when the moon is full."

"Are many people going to win their mancipation papers?"

"Only if it is like my mancipation. I was mancipated because of a promise to a saint, and my legs could hardly walk after raising on my breast almost the whole family of the baron from great-grandfather to great-grandson, at the fishery and at the sugar mill. Some mancipation it was, they gave me four silver coins and put me in a straw-covered shed with no walls and at first would not do me the favor of letting some of the boys come here Sundays to put up the walls. And if I did not know how to weave lacing and if I did not have some help, I might even have gone without food, since I do not eat just on Sundays when people come to see me. In the old days they used to add bittter poison and black dregs to the oil in the lamps, so the blacks would not lick it. But I really did not go without food, one can always pick something in the woods or in the swamp, and I got used to eating leftovers, I like leftovers better than anything, this is the sincere truth. The Byssinian, when he arrived, he arrived with great renown among the others, he being the tallest one. They could not break him, they had to tie him with a rope the first day, he gnawed the rope, escaped to the woods, maybe received *caboco* Capiroba—then, you know, he made a quilombo, a rebellious settlement, you know. Took people with him, took women, made big quilombo. The men-in-arms came, they hunted him. But he did not want to be hunted, and when he saw he was going to be surrounded, he invaded here and spent hours and hours fighting, he only died because the dogs ate him. I knew him, he was bought for twenty-five milreis, he thought he was better than the whites, he was mad in his brain, very, very crazy. He said that if they gave him mancipation he would not accept it, he was the one who was going to give mancipation to the master, he had completely demented ideas, raving crazy, really. Little master Perilo Ambrósio is going to give mancipation when he is full master? It is more likely that the flounder fish will talk again to Our Lady as it used to. I raised him myself, and I myself am afraid of him, for his is a bad spirit. Now, there is one thing: If today you have food, tomorrow you will not, everything is going to finish, heh-heh-heh! My father was no longer strong enough for whaling, they made him a shit-barrel carrier. Shit trickled down the sides of the barrels, sometimes they burst apart and covered him with shit. But he did not die on account of the weight of the barrels, though they were really heavy and he was old and his body was all cut up from fighting the whales; he died of shame. The Negroes are still carrying shit, but many of them do not die, heh-heh-heh! Mancipation or no

54

mancipation, he-he! Crazy Byssinian was called Darissa, I knew him. *Caboco* Capiroba used to eat Dutchmen a lot, one, two, three, green, ripe, or in between, heh-heh-heh-heh! Among you people who eats Dutchmen? Liars, there are many Dutchmen everywhere, their kind will never be finished. I want you people to be very pretty, dressed up and nice-smelling. When it is time to cry, cry. For the reason that tears are like piss, sweat, or shit, they are things the body has to get rid of, do you understand that? But do not forget anything, proshantah, proshantan, proshantah, ay, ooy—hold it, head!—hoom, proshantan, proshantan. Forget not nothing, understand what I mean, heh-heh! The Curukere moth arrived on the priest's forehead, it arrives on many people's foreheads, attention! The gypsy spoke!"

"Did the gypsy speak pretty, great mother?"

"He did, but it was not possible to understand everything; it is a speech worse than the talk of foreign *cabocos* or *cabocos* of very ancient times, but you can try to understand it if you like: preches, mongogreches, cacheches, and the Santa Quisición, el granofício de la mu-erte and the sanctidá de la desgracia. And he said beware of those who teach surety, that was what he said before they made the ordinance that anybody who spoke to a gypsy would be hanged, and this gypsy, because he talked much, was killed and burned. If they had known I had listened to him and listened to him good, they would have cut my tongue off, maybe poured hot oil in my ears, they sure would have, heh-heh-heh. So they did not cut off my tongue, which is very good, but I talked to the gypsy and did not become either less or more infidel; it was another one of those things of life that I learned without really learning. The gypsy said:

> " 'Hear me now, O mammy,
>   Die the king of Spain,
>   'Cause hell is certain
>   And heaven far.
>   To live is to steal;
>   If you ask instead of taking
>   You will never get to Rome.
>   There'll be little food,
>   There'll be little life,
>   Though there will be plenty
>   Of people to be robbed.'

"And preches, leches, mongogreches, for days and days on end, it is a word to the wise, although I do not understand much of what he said. Fate is as follows: there is nothing you can do. If there is something you can do, it is because fate wanted it, there are many here whose fate is to complain about their fate, go on laughing if you like. Hey! Whazzat? Bless my soul, look! I see you did fish a lot of round pompano, you are telling me! Yellow weakfish, very good. A heap of needlefish, bless me, Turíbio Cafubá must have done this, would you say? Listen, girl, I think I will be on my way."

"You going riding, old great mother?"

"Sitting nice and pretty. Let us see if you can come up with a few good dirges, we will see! Mos' blessed Velgin, what a sugarcane field! They brought loads of cane from Angola, loads and loads by ship, and the blacks planted them all, you should see it. And they planted cane, cut cane, crushed cane, got all nicked by the canes, all slashed, all covered with splinters, he-he! And every day they brought more black slaves, and also girls from the Azores to marry the whites here that the king sent over by his own command, so many beautiful kings there are, each one more beautiful than the other. First died Dom João, bedecked with silver and gems, eating gold-dust cheese and wallowing in riches and feeling much compassion for the people. After this king Dom João came King Zoceph, there being many alterations in all his nations, but here nothing happened, or to be fair there happened cane and Azoranian girls. And then what comes next but a queen by the name of Dona Maria, who brought us all great happiness by sending here great expeditions to fetch cane and bring Azoranian girls, and every queen and king who is born is a great hope for those who keep on suffering, heh-heh-heh-heh, *caboco* Capiroba. Do you also eat kings, dearest *caboco*, huh, do you eat queens? Ugh, good heavens, how disgusting, tee-tee-tee, tee-tee-tee!"

"Is he back, great mother, do you see him?"

"Why, what a question! King, kingling, kinglet, is every king a kingly knave? You want to see something? Attention then, wait here, attention. Last month that other Dom João who was in the realm here moved away to the kingdom there, did he not, was it last month? Something like that? He moved from one kingdom to another, and I am here dying with grief—heh-heh-heh-heh! Hah-hah-hah! Ho-ho-ho! Ay-ay! Leave me alone, son, I am seeing many kings here, such kings. . . . All of them covered with gold, all gold, all gold, heh-heh. Now, now, get . . . All right, all right . . . The king is the one who gives! The people their good life! It was he that gave to me! The straw that is now my roof! Hah-hah-hah-hah! Ouch!"

"Feel a little pain there, dearest great mother?"

"No-no. Do not bother me, you, now I lost the kings' party because of you. They are gone now, it is too much work to call them back. Have the vespers sounded? I only want to go at the ringing of the vespers, the way it was when I came. Very well, all set? Take care of my youngest granddaughter's child, mind our blood! I am going, but I will stay awhile in Amoreiras. Do not let them kill little master Perilo Ambrósio. You did not forget anything, did you, Nezinha, better check. Do not forget anything, you hear?

Did you fix the gutter, did you pay for Crispim the Thief's fish? All right, then, I will drop by once in a while. Have you not forgotten anything really, Nezinha, are you sure? Why those faces? Is there anything else you want to know? Why all the fuss?"

But the vespers bells started to sound in the chapel, and Dadinha interrupted herself like somebody whose interest is aroused by a new subject. She crossed her arms very composedly, closed her eyes, and looking as if she was going to watch something fascinating, died exactly as she had chosen.

Good Jesus Fishery, June 9, 1827

The fall of Saint Bona and Saint Lucius happened at the precise moment Antônia Vitória was opening her mouth to order the tale-teller Justina Bojuda to put a stop to the story the children and the black woman Honorata were listening to. The young house black Martina was going to climb on the footstool to dust the images in the oratory, but her slipper got stuck, the footstool overturned, and in the fall she knocked down the sacred couple, who somersaulted to the floor. The images were not broken, because when the girl saw the saints diving head first onto the flags, contritely bracketed together as they had always been at the forefront of the oratory, she softened their fall with her arms, outstretched in despair. Only the pedestal that united the images was cracked apart, in a sinuous, capricious line, separating them for the first time since time began. Very blue, his mouth round and crimson, Saint Lucius trolled over and stopped belly up, his gaze, which moments before was fixed with perennial enchantment on his holy wife and companion, now turned to the side opposite where she had rolled and was nesting, her face to the joint of wall and floor, right by the settee where Justina Bojuda was just about to finish the following story: In a place no one knows where, by the sea or by the woods, on an island or on the mainland, once upon a time there was a parish priest. And there was the priest's parish, there was his church, there were the people who lived in that place, who were most devout, churchgoing and pious. Before Mass the priest could not rest because devout women came for confession; after Mass he could not rest because devout women came for confession; so the priest did not do anything but attend to those churchly women. So the priest thought and thought and came to a conclusion which was to prepare a list to be read at Mass. Halfway through Mass, the priest picked up the list and read as follows: My dear worshipers, people of this parish, I am getting old and tired, and have no more time and stamina for so many confessions every day. That is why from now on we shall obey the following dispositions, which I thought out myself very well and wrote very well, everything very well considered: Sundays I confess the lazy and the ones who do not wash; Mondays, those who steal and tell lies; Tuesdays, the ones who drink; Wednesdays, the ones who deceive their husbands or sin by contubernium; Thursdays, the nags and the gossips; Fridays, the witches, the conjurers, and the troublemakers; Saturdays, the gluttonous and the envious. And when the priest finished, nobody said anything, but everybody looked at one another in a funny way, and from that day on there were no more devout women to confess in that parish, and the priest rested to his heart's delight with his good Mass wine, and that is the end of the story.

"Gammer Justina, hush, not one more word from you!" Antônia Vitória trumpeted from the door, but she had barely prepared herself to make another speech with her hands up in the air, as she had done all around the house since her arrival, when the house girl screamed, the images spun their way down, Justina opened her eyes very wide, and Bona and Lucius trundled on the floor. "O, Jesus, Our Lady, great Saint Rita of the Impossible, my divine godfather Saint Anthony, the most ill-boding of all misfortunes has descended unto us! Oh, my beloved saint Saint Lucius, my saintly Saint Bona, given to me at my nuptials by my parents, oh, what have you done, you wretch, there they are, my little saints in shards, woe is me, see how far apart they fell and how their pedestal was shattered in a hundred slivers, and another hundred I shall make out of you, evil and bunglesome little Negress, a more than worthless thing, piece of the devil, buzzard, benighted, stupid Negress doing everything by bumps and pushes, oh, forgive me, O Christ, for having allowed the reliquary to be dusted by an unthinking Negress that is not good anough to rinse a clay chamber pot, may He forgive me, yes, if I do not rip you apart—and take your hands off them! Keep your donkey hoofs off that which you have already ruined, and who knows what else your mindlessness may have destroyed! Oh, my God, I hope there will not pour a rain of adversities upon our house and our establishment, for if it was the Infernal Enemy that directed this unserviceable Negress's blundering hands, they were her hands, not ours! Very well, then, if you want to cry with more zest and reason, I will give you motive. Go in the kitchen and explain to your mother that the slave I promised Saint Anthony I would free, paying him as if I had bought him and not just made him free, and giving him a plot of land, wood, and thatching, was going to be her, but I changed my mind, it cannot be her anymore, not because of any fault of hers, as her only one is the stench she gives off by dint of her race—tell her then that it is no longer her that I am going to free after the celebrations, not because of anything she did but because the shameless little Negress she brought into the world saw fit to triturate the holy spouses who have always watched over the happiness of this home—tell her then, you unfortunate, that it is no longer her that I am going to free out of devotion, but another, man or woman. And do not forget to say also that it is your fault that I made this decision, for it is against my wish that I am punishing your mother—it is just that I cannot let go unnoticed an act as sacrilegious as yours, an omen as bad as the one you now bring to this home! And say also that I am not sending you right off to the whip and do not have you cut in slices as I should because you are her daughter, and it is with her in mind that I choose so. Go on, go on, go tell her everything, go on, move, and do not forget a single word, you cursed little Negress, because later on I am going to ask your mother if you said to her everything the way I ordered you—go! And do not pass near me on your way, because I do not want to begrime my hands on your loathsome face, oh, my God, Saint Catherine, Saint Margaret, Saint Agatha, my Saint Joseph Calasanz of eternal resignation, help me through this most painful ordeal which makes my head heavy and weakens my body with distress! Go away! You are killing me, you are killing me, that is what you are doing! Go! Go before I strangle you, go! And you, Negress Honorata, to stand by silently as this heinous woman, who comes here for good food and the coppers she procures from our household and from the baron's generous purse, tells us preposterous stories and makes the children listen to the filth and the offenses that come out of her mouth! I told you I do not want you to tell such stories! I told you not to take advantage of this home's indulgence to fill the children's ears with anecdotes of low morals and high debauchery! What is this contubernium thing that is mentioned in the narrative? Do not tell me; I will have a hot egg shoved into the mouth of the first of you who repeats such a word or this vile tale you were stuttering to the children! Chut! O Lord of the Forsaken, I know that as sinners we owe Thee penitences for Thy mercy, but so much suffering obtains for those who leave Europe and come to live here, in such a crude, unwholesome, and thankless place, among so many unacknowledged, uncelebrated efforts and travails, enduring so much deprivation and anguish, dealing with a people brutish in such a way a Christian could never have thought possible—yes, I know how suffered the saintly Catholics among the Moors, but alas, a life so fraught with misery I lack the strength of the saints to bear! Did you know it was to you, Honorata, that I was going to give the same freedom I was just about to grant Negress Constantina, the mother of that M . . . she whose name I cannot allow to come out of my mouth—did you know it was you? I know only too well you are a giddy-as-a-fly featherhead and want even a trace of character, but even so I should forgive you those bad traits; what I cannot forgive is disobedience! Disobedience! Disobedience! Shall I have to clamor to the heavens for all eternity that in exchange for the food we give you, the roof we provide you, the tribulations and vexations we have to stomach on account of your worthless kind, for all that I only demand obedience in return? Obedience! It is not too much to ask from dogs and beasts of burden, but it seems to require excessive comprehension for your race's absence of intelligence and feelings. Obedience! Obedience that did not cross your dregs-filled mind, when with the most intolerable insolence, the most unpleasant bestiality, you allowed this brown hag to tell that blasphemous story, causing heaven to punish us through the shattering of my dearest saints—oh, my dear little saints, oh, how weak I am feeling, how much more agony shall I still be able to suffer? Saint Lucy, do not let the light of my eyes be extinguished before I arrange for the reparation of so many sins, which were not of my making—for God knows of the pious life I lead—but are mine to remedy. O Saint Anthony of Lisbon, my holy godfather, thou didst not know how to forgive me for not having attended all thirteen services in thy honor as I do every year, but thou knowest that it is not up to me to make decisions on what I should do, it is up to my master and husband, the baron, who only now consented to our coming here, and at the cost of so much beseeching—thou knowest it for thou hast seen everything, my holy godfather! Well, then, ungrateful Negress Honorata—and few names would be more inept for you—dismiss from your thoughts being freed, because my forgetting your disobedience and the harm you did to the children will never stretch that far, and they like you so much, the poor little ones. My Most Holy Mother, *mater dolorosa,* give me succor at this sorrowful hour, O most suffering, loving mother! Do not budge, do not budge, Negress, stay where you are, because I do not know if we should touch the saints before a priest sees them, what will become of me now, where is Brother Hilário, I feel I am fainting, oh, God, I have lost all my strength, oh, so much grief. . . ."

When Brother Hilário finally arrived, having been found as he slumbered, dreaming of bountiful pantries, a line of slaver trickling down to where his belly met his drooping chin, a rich snore settling the tempo of his nap—and he arrived as fast as his short steps allowed as they rasped his sandals against the floor through all those trellised corridors haunted by niches, sideboards, tripods, silverware closets, and so many other things—Antônia Vitória was already reclining in the cushioned daybed, stretching her neck toward the fan with which Teolina was refreshing her. The friar ran his little eyes over the room, looked at the two fallen images, and saw the petrified black women standing by the porch's threshold and the children sitting stiff-backed on the settee.

"Ah, my good father, counselor, and director!" The baroness sighed, rising faintly and then falling back on the bed's bolster, her eyes closed and her bosom palpitating.

"Did you give her a little vinegar to smell?" the friar asked, and when they said yes, and they had also put a grain of salt under her tongue, and her hands, which had been trembling so with cold, were now warm, he gestured for them to go out, to leave him alone with the baroness until somebody called them. "All right, all right, all is well now, all is well, it is all over now."

Antônia Vitória opened her eyes laboriously. She turned to the friar, now sitting on the footstool that had tipped over and which he had placed near the daybed. Oh, did not the good friar know how much she suffered and suffered and suffered, with never a respite from the woeful lot that the Fates seemed to enjoy inflicting on her? Why, had she not been just moments ago almost at death's door, after having come into that room to go on with the incessant drudgery of a house so full of illustrious visitors who required refined luncheons and even more refined suppers, as was to be expected from nobility, and that disaster had had to happen to her? Was it not enough that luncheon had made her so anxious because not only was it served late, almost at noon, but also the canon had not touched the seafood stew and seemed not to have liked the wines? Was it not sufficient that the baron, her master and husband, had told her with asperity in everyone's presence that the roast beef was not too different from the food of the Negroes, although he had devoured almost all of it? A misalliance, that was what her marriage was, though she could make such a terrible confidence only to the friar, her counselor, friend, and director, a confidence that could hardly be made to come out of her parched mouth, and gave her vapors. If it were not for her sweet old parents, if it were not for her children, whom the baron treated with so much indifference, if it were not for the good friar, maybe she would not find in herself the spirit to go on living. And now he could see for himself right there, lying on the floor in such ungainly positions, the two saints on whose blessings depended peace in her home and her marriage. The two little saints broken to pieces!

"But they are not in pieces, it was just the pedestal, and it is perfectly possible to glue the two parts back together. We will have some flour-and-egg-white glue made, and the mended part will be even stronger than before."

"Does Your Reverence think so? And do you not believe that a punishment will fall upon the household?"

"I think the saints will be like new, and we will have no punishment whatsoever."

"Will Your Reverence bless the glue, will you?"

"I will, I will; give it not a thought."

"Oh, how grateful I am to Your Reverence! But do you not think that there will be a punishment because that—forgive me the word—that dirty tale-teller was telling the children a quite near-the-knuckle story, that blasphemed against a man of the cloth?"

"No, not a punishment; maybe a warning."

"A warning! An admonition! So that such things do not happen again! So that our piety is put to the proof! Therefore, I must punish her myself! In view of so many affronts, the only punishment I applied was to revoke the promise for my dearest father's health of freeing the Negress Constantina."

"Revoke the promise?"

"No, by Jesus Christ on the Cross, a thousand times no! I shall simply free another one in her place, for it is necessary to punish her daughter, the brash, no-good young Negress that did that to the saints."

"She has been properly punished, then."

"Has she? But suppose I punished the young Negress directly for causing me so much revolt, and Negress Honorata, and also that terrible-looking ogress who tells stories?"

"Bojuda?"

"Yes. What a formidable name—she well deserves it."

"But she is a freedwoman, is she not?"

"Well, let every militiaman in the Empire come here, all the men-at-arms, all the Crown's inspectors and judges, and they will not snatch away from the baroness of Pirapuama either an old brown woman or anything else!"

"Of course they will not."

"Well, then, may I then punish her as I please? Has she not offended me, has she not offended so monstrously a man of God, has she not abused the children's innocence and Honorata's stupidity, in return for the food she takes from the kitchen all the time and the coppers I never denied her?"

"To tell the truth, perhaps it will not find support in the Doctrine."

"No support in the Doctrine, Lord of mine? Who disapproves?"

"Uh . . . Saint Jerome, Saint Jerome. *Sum cuique tribuere* . . . Yes . . . *Sum cuique tribuere, ibis, redibis, qui . . . quod.*"

"Are those the holy doctor's words, in such precious Latin, which my few lights do not let me understand? And those precepts befit a case such as this?"

"If memory serves."

"Ah, memory has always served you well, blessed Father, your wisdom is not of this world, and by listening to it, all paths seem clear to me, everything in its right place. What does good Doctrine indicate in this case?"

"A penance. A penance to teach them the evil they have done, and to show repentance to the eyes of the Lord."

"That is what Saint Jerome advises?"

"And Saint Anselm. Saint Anselm . . . "

"Saint Anselm! I shall give them a penance, then! My good Father, the envoy of Divine Providence . . . Should I give the children a penance too?"

"Maybe not Felicidade Maria, who is too young and can barely repeat half a prayer."

"We shall see about the children. At least, for the girls, two or three rosaries said on their knees and a little abstinence would be good. It is for their own virtue's sake. And I shall never leave them again under Honorata's care. Honorata! I shall punish them all after all, except Constantina, whose freedom I have already taken away and who should not pay for her daughter's

62

sins. My good spirits are back. Why do I not find by myself those things that said by Your Reverence seem to be so easy? Will Your Reverence really bless my dear saints' glue? Will you help me set the penances? What mortifications do penitent monks practice on themselves?"

Urinating sonorously in a porcelain chamber pot, Perilo Ambrósio felt great pleasure. He did not close his eyes to hear himself being emptied, because he also wanted to enjoy himself by looking at the foam, which started to reflect the light of the oil lamp in white and gold scintillations. And down there, her neck twisted up in an unnatural position, Antônia Vitória could not manage, in spite of tossing and turning in every way, to avoid the implacable spurts of endless piss that hit her face. And it was not only Antônia Vitória he was pissing on, he was pissing on everything, he felt he could piss on anything he wished, could do anything he wished. The enormous chamber pot, its brim gracefully curved like the petals of a giant lily, with its filigreed edges and with riparian scenes covering its sides and bottom in subtle lines and evocative colors, vibrated like a sun rained upon, and Perilo Ambrósio wanted to go on pissing forever. But he finished and stood a long time, his arms hanging loose and his chin touching his chest, squeezing out one more drop, another drop, one last drop, a drop dangling like a stalactite and hesitating briefly before it fell. He walked over to the window as he was, exposed and still dripping. He could not see the toads, he could not even see the ocean and the trees; everything was covered by a dense blackness. He had often been afraid of darkness, but now he had no fear. Propping his belly against the windowsill, he lowered both his hands to touch himself, and felt that everything down under was growing larger. It did not get as hard as it used to, when just to think of some of the black men and women of his house made it seem to want to explode, taut and aching as though it were going to detach itself from his body. Sometimes it did not even get completely hard, but he felt proud of the thick, blunt mass on which he was gently rubbing his hand. He hefted his balls, looked as if he was going to smile, and with an expression he knew he would never assume in front of anybody, not even before a mirror, began to masturbate by the window, barely able to hold back his urge to yell and howl, because he was masturbating for all that was infinitely his—the Negroes, the Negresses, the others, the world, the steamboat, the trees, the darkness, the animals, the estate itself. Yes, he could go sauntering around naked as he was, his glans like the head of an irresistible battering ram, and could make everybody look at it and revere it and yearn for the mercy of touching and kissing it. He imagined himself acting with kindly prepotency, drawing to his lap and groin the heads of those surrounding him, thus distributing blessings and happiness. And finally grabbing the young Negress Vevé without a word, to throw her in a bed, open her legs, make it very clear he did not want her to move, and, rubbing spit on that

63

swollen, brutal head of flesh, deflower her with a single stroke, then, waiting for her to wince with pain, stop her motions with a paralyzing embrace, feel skin or cartilage snapping as he broke them, find out if she was shallow or narrow, and push her knees upward, sticking everything into her with a rude motion to almost hurl her against the head of the bed, following this motion with short stabs after penetrating her until her bones pressed his fat, as if he was transfixing her, impaling her, running her through all the way, for her to die with her entrails battered to pieces at the precise moment when he would come inside her, needing to make no other gesture, the complete master, the complete master, getting up and wiping off blood and slime with her frock. It had not happened yet, but it was going to happen; he had already given orders for them to make all the arrangements so he could have the young Negress. He would not allow them to tell her anything, because there was always the danger that Antônia Vitória might hear about it, and especially because he did not want to forgo the pleasure of showing up suddenly in front of the girl and starting to take off his clothes without speaking anything, enjoying the fear or astonishment on her face as she saw sprouting from the folds of his underclothes the instrument of her submission. She had almost run away from him, the day she first set eyes on him—strangely light-colored eyes for a Negress, so wide open and elusive. He had called the foreman, Almério, to ask who she was. Dadinha's granddaughter. Yes, very well, I want to fuck her—is she a virgin? Yes, she is; she is going to ask permission to marry the harpooner Custódio; they are waiting for Saint Anthony's Day to speak to the baroness. Good, it is better that way; I want to fuck her even more, now that I know this. You know what to do, do you not? Do not bungle the job. Did the baron want him to go fetch the Negress today? No, I will talk to you later.

I will talk to you later, I will talk to you later, Perilo Ambrósio repeated, rubbing himself against the wall as if using a paintbrush with his eyes closed. Only then did the clouds of the pitch-black night allow a few stars to come forth. On the north side of the heavens, behind the famous constellation called Swan by some and by others seen as a congregation of kings, the warrant officer's little soul remembered again the light of its land and again trembled with pride. And since disincarnated little souls do not live in time, and all things for them may be past, present, or future, it passed at the same instant over the wavelets then doing the tide's night work, rippling along the beach at the Good Jesus Fishery. Nocturnal masses with shapes different from those they would have in daylight, the houses and the trees had only one eye, glowing at the window where Perilo Ambrósio was starting to squirt sperm on the wall, in jerks that made him bend his knees at short intervals. The little soul beheld that and everything else in the night with its now customary love, and not knowing why it was sure that someday it would animate the creature of Perilo Ambrósio, baron of Pirapuama, hero of

64

Independence, builder of the most beautiful and the strongest nation in the world, the wellspring of goodwill, abundance, and peace. For this was its glorious destiny, which began when it had inhabited Warrant Officer Brandão Galvão's brave body, smitten down in the defense of his land and her freedom, in Whale Point's peerless breeze. And it celebrated as do little souls during these epiphanies, tracing the air with lines and sparks along the borders of the zodiac, disappearing far away between two stars and coming back to shine so briefly no one could see it, now at the head of the constellation of the winged horse, now looping among the many celestial crowns that here adorn the firmament, recomposing all year round their glittering configurations and giving reason to believe that everything changes but is permanent, everything is permanent but changes, as is necessary for life. The little soul rejoiced greatly, turned into a happy spark, oblivious of anything that was not part of that rejoicing, and so, fortunately for it, it did not see that, slouching and panting by the window, Perilo Ambrósio was sticking his head into the darkness outside, and with nothing occupying his mind, had on his face so much indifferent baseness, so much crudity and absence of good feelings, that if his slabber dropped on the ground it might kill the creeping plants, and his only wish was that everything existed for him, a wish that cannot be easily distinguished from death. No one saw that terrible face nor could anyone see it, no one thought of it nor could anyone think of it—and Perilo Ambrósio toweled his sweat off with his shirttails, remembering with satisfaction that he did not like anybody.

4

When Vevé was about to be born, Roxinha thought she was sweating too much between her legs. It was natural for her to be sweating, because the heat coming out of the stove where she was poking firewood and balancing clay pots converted everything into a furnace. And besides, not even a whiff of air blew through the tops of the carambola and cashew trees, nor did the young sugarcane spikelets stir, and in the woods all was quiet, just a grassquit sounding off now and then, a scaled dove, beetles buzzing their wings, twigs crackling, pods popping out seeds, the subdued sibilance silence assumes at a time such as this. And she, so fat and heavy, having to stop time and again to catch her breath under the sticky, warm blanket that covered the world, was expecting rivers of sweat to run down her body, but even so, she put her hand between her thighs to find out what was happening. She knew the child ought to be born any moment now, but she had to do kitchen work even if it was Sunday, and besides, she had already given birth six times and had three miscarriages, all six children sold right after they were weaned and the three fetuses dumped on the beach together with the garbage, so she was annoyed at having to bring forth another one, she became impatient to think that there would be a new child hanging from her breasts, a child who as usual would not be hers. She sniffed her hand, smelled the stench of the water coming out of its broken bag, put her hand down again and touched Vevé's head beginning to emerge as though someone were pushing it out from inside. She did not remember to drop the piece of firewood she was holding in her left hand, and tried to rush out palming the girl's head, but she only managed to take a few steps, her legs straddling wide, and plopped down just beyond the doorstep, as her daughter slid down from her lower parts. She leaned against the wall, bent one of her knees upward and almost did not have to pull the girl up, because she was already winding her way out and about to start crying.

Not much later Dadinha arrived, in time to help the others bind the navel cord and bury the secundines according to all precepts, and she said she was very, very happy about all that. In the first place, the girl had been born on a Sunday like herself; it was a wonderful thing. In the second place, she had a birthmark like her father's; she was the first among her son Turíbio's children to be born with that mark. And on a Sunday, good, very good, very good. The spot on the child's forehead could be seen clearly, a patch of lighter skin more or less over her right eye, almost the same as her father's. This mark, Dadinha told them once more, came from *caboca* Vu, and it often used to light up when she was fighting. But it never lit up on Turíbio Cafubá, he-he-he, she laughed. She spat out some of the powdered tobacco she was cleaning her teeth with, and scrutinized it intently. Oh yes, oh yes, she went on mysteriously, this granddaughter of mine will go a long way, hoom-hoom. This birthmark means everything is continuing, and it is through her that it is going to continue. When they asked her if they could hold that to be the written truth revealed by her entities or pictured in her shells and beads, she answered it was rather something she wanted, not really something she knew. But it turned out to be the same thing; she was not in the mood to explain that.

"The name they are going to give her I do not know; when it is a woman they are not too choosy, and they do not brand women or anything," she said, holding her arms akimbo, as she always did to announce her speeches. "By the way, there is something I should say, although it will be like other things I say, which will go in one ear and out the other, but I will say it anyway: When they tell you, 'Dear Massa Felisberto Góes Farinha is a very kind master,' you say, 'Yes, yes.' But do not let that make you forget, though you shall not say it, that they are kind because they do not brand the black women, only the men. Hah-hah! I find you all very funny, very funny, I find most anything very funny. All right, that is that. Well, I do not know her white name, but the one she will have here I already know. I will say it: Daê. Daê. It can also be Naê. And she will grow to be a strong woman, you can see that, you can see that well."

That was what was told to Turíbio Cafubá, who started dancing as soon as he heard the news, even before he jumped out of the canoe on which he was bringing a rush basket full of gray snapper, pompano, salema, and small fish, hooked or seined since three in the morning.

"Daê-ay!" he shouted, saluting his daughter as if she were the clouds that were floating by over the beach. "And she has the mark on her forehead, no?"

He alighted from the canoe with the basket balancing on his head and did a few dance steps in the knee-high water. So she was born out of doors, huh! It is all very well and good! He was a man of good fortune, was he not? He was supposed to have been castrated, but they let him stay whole after very narrow escapes. He was supposed to have been sold off, but he ended up staying on the plantation of the good family whose mark they had branded on his chest, kindly, charitable people who treated Negroes well and gave light punishments. He was supposed to be too old for women, sixty almost for sure, but he filled up Roxinha, who was twenty-two and no match for him, with one child a year, and maybe he had made fifteen more with other women, they must all be grown up somewhere, hoom-hoom, what you say, huh? A man of good fortune, yes sir, there he was with his first-rate fish, it was all his, did not Massa allow him to fish and never wanted the fish for himself? Hah-hah-hah! The name is Turíbio Cafubá, friend, known by this word that recalls white soot because he had almost changed from black to white with the powder and the burnings from lime, he had almost become blind, he had almost had his body all cut up inside, but nothing like that had happened, man of good fortune! And had not Daê been born on a Sunday, so he could dance all day, carrying the spirit who came from the land of Dahomay or maybe Mahomay? Daê-Naê-ay! As for the fish, he was going to take just a few of them with him to make a sick person's broth for Roxinha, to fry, to make a stew with manioc flour mush and okra, gherkin, squash, and plantain—yes sir!—to make food for all! Go on and pick up the fish, take the fish, carry the fish!

Turíbio entered the slave quarters after many wiggles, comings and goings, rascally laughs, curtsies to all present, and a few songs, which he no longer understood but repeated in the manner copied from the old people who had taught them. Cafubá-ay! What you say? How about that! So that is what happened, what does the good friend say? Did you see that, girl, now get ready and I will make one in you too, just as easy as that! Is there any other woman here who wants to have a baby? If so, leave it to me! With me it is like that, no stalling, no mistake, no misses. Zup! There you are with a baby!

Sitting on a stool with her legs wide apart and her body shaking with laughter, Dadinha said that someone must have given him the brain of a porpoise to eat when he was little, for him to have become crazy like that, already old and still acting like a child. But he did not mind, he just leapt up twice and fell with one knee on the ground in front of the girl, who was lying quietly on a straw mat.

"Naê-ay!" he shouted. "Little Queen of Aiokah! And the mark!"

"And you speaking nonsense," Dadinha complained.

But again he did not mind, and as if there was much more music there than the sound of his heels stomping the ground, his hands clapping in a thousand tempos, and the tongue and lip clicks and throaty melodies resembling bass flute solos that came out of his mouth, he stretched his muscles, now glistening with tension and sweat, and danced. Many among them could dance, and were admired when in the feasts in which they were permitted to make music they rolled their eyes and bounced madly over the ground's hard clay, they floated in the air, they made their bodies be many things at the same time, they brought fire to the others' hearts, and at those times they were deities. But such a dance as Turíbio Cafubá's celebrating his daughter had never before been seen, for he became transparent and then very black and then he was everywhere, at times halting and vibrating like the wings of a cicada, at times dissolving into so many forms that people did not know in which to believe, and soon all the rhythms that sprouted from his figure were rhythms of something happening inside each one of them, blood pulsating, fingers stretching, breaths rushing, all that can happen in the body, all to which the spirit surrenders. No one was aware of how long Turíbio's dance lasted, not even he, whose face now soared way ahead of his body like the figurehead of a war canoe, while he bent forward and brandished his *araçanga,* the club he used to kill big fish as they were pulled up to the boat, and came forth with one leg independent of the other, each one marking its own beat and walking its own way, in the great war dance of his nation. His eyes bulging out, his chin jutting forward, he stopped for a moment, but at the same time everyone heard the vertiginous drums of a battle band, and in a vision no one would ever forget, he danced in honor of his daughter like the proudest warriors they had known about, a proudness mirrored in each gesture, each foot stomping the ground, each look upward, each shoulder raised, each agitation of arms and hands, everything one can do to display pride.

"Aaaah!" he shouted again, stopping his invisible drums in front of the girl, his mouth open wide and his arm made longer by the *araçanga.* "Arah-oomboh! Arah-oomboh, look who has arrived! Hail! All right, my fishing girl, when are you going to fish with your father?"

Dadinha's smile almost vanished, and she said to him that it was all right to celebrate and to dance, but he should not let himself be overtaken by fantasies; fantasies led nowhere. Of all his children, more than twenty for all she knew, not one had ever in any way remained there. And even if they had, they would have been not his but his master's, so he had better stop speaking meaningless things and take those fish inside to be cleaned and let Roxinha and the girl rest. But he did not accept that, and as if it were night, and time did not exist, he told a bedtime story. One upon a time, he said, there was a lime-sooted captive black man who made over twenty children, more than twenty, although he did not get to know any of them, because they took them all away soon after they were born. One fine day this lime-sooted captive black man is spooling his lines, folding his seine, and heaping up his fishing tools, when they come to the beach and tell him that a daughter of his had been born with a star on her forehead, with a name that the great old mother Dadinha soon discovered to be Daê, or also Naê. This lime-sooted black man steps out, and when he looks up in the air, there flies the great spirit of dancing who came from the land of Dahomay, or also Mahomay, and this spirit grabs this lime-sooted black man, and between one dance and the next this spirit whispers to him the following other story: Ah, my lime-sooted old black man and fisher of fish, I will have you know you ought to pay attention to that girl, you know that? Very well, the girl is born, learns to walk and every day she goes with her father to work at the kiln house, and she learns all the works of the kiln house. And since the master is very kind, she also goes fishing with her father, and the father, with much fatherly patience, teaches her the fisherman's patience with all its secrets, which are many, and one opens onto another which opens onto another, so that the fisherman never learns all but learns more than those who do not fish. He who fishes knows many things, things you cannot tell, you have to fish to know. Very well, this lime-sooted black father gives his hand to his daughter and they talk in long chats, during which the father shows himself to be more wise and more anything that is good than any other father, this being necessary for all fathers and much more so for the father who is a slave and therefore needs every piece of pride he can gather. This father will not teach what to expect from life because he does not know, but will teach about all the vines to make nets and baskets with, all the special bites of the many fishes of the sea, all the markings over the water and the qualities of the winds, all the things he had learned alone, talking to the tide. On Saint Francis Xavier's Day, this old lime-sooted black father goes to ask permission to join the cavalla fishers. The sea foreman answers: That is all right with me, let the father and the daughter stay with the motucas, the blacks who help when the net is dragged out of the water with its leaping fish, motucas because from far away they look like motuca flies swarming over the fish. But the girl does not mind being a motuca, nor does the old father, and she learns so much about that kind of fishing that from motuca she moves up to net tier, from net tier she moves up to shore chief, or maybe boatwoman. And then this father and his daughter, because there is another time inside time, will live happily forever, that is what I am telling you. There they are, hand in hand by the sea, the father just talking and talking and talking, and she like all daughters loving her father just the same, not allowing anybody to say anything bad about him and being patient with him and making soft food for him when his teeth are gone, holding his hand when his legs no longer walk by themselves, listening to what he says when nobody else is listening, loving her father just the same, just the same, it will be like that, it will be like that, and if someone had not enjoyed the story it was because they did not have a daughter, starred or not.

Dadinha never cried, and for that reason she did not cry, but she felt a pang between her breasts. Maybe she was feeling happy in a small way because the father saw a future for the girl and she also saw one, although they were different, and because there could not be two futures, one of them was wrong. She looked at her son, who seemed to be covered with colored beads of his sweat, felt sorry for him and felt proud of him, found him beautiful in his lack of sense and his delirium of mixed tongues and deities, and was able only to sigh. Not to mention that she knew, though she had not spoken to anyone about it because she did not want to be an ill-boding old nag, that soon two or three white farmhands would come on Massa Felisberto's orders to fetch Turíbio, to take him to be flogged and to make him stay overnight in the standing stocks, because he had given away the fish without speaking first to the master or the mistress. No special reason; it was just not to let a bad example go unpunished; it always happened, as sure as day and night.

And it did happen moments later, and Turíbio moaned when the straps landed on his back, only to keep the men from beating him too much; he was a little tired. He wanted to go to sleep; he knew what to do not to get too uncomfortable with his wrists fastened above his head, and to be careful not to let his knees bend during his sleep so he would not wake up with his hands torn off. A light punishment, they did not even take away his fishing privileges, they are good Christians, good people who know things no one else knows or imagines, it was just because he should have asked for permission to give away the fish, since merely knowing that the permission was sure to be granted did not do away with the need to ask for it, one just cannot allow those things to go unnoticed, if that kind of thing went on where would it stop? That is the way it is indeed, Turíbio thought, feeling blood trickling down his lashed back, and shaking his wet head after they threw two bucketfuls of seawater on him. And he even was glad while he prepared himself to sleep the way he had learned with practice, because he figured he had done a good job of predicting all that was going to happen, and he fell asleep dreaming of those happenings. Dadinha, her eyes open in the dark, figured she would surely not be able to see what was going to happen to the girl, for she was going to die at the age of one hundred years, as she had always known. But that youngest daughter of her youngest, late-coming son had a strong fate, and this could be anticipated in the slave quarters' heavy gloom, near the shed where Turíbio Cafubá, fettered up and with his back burning, grinned and, even sleeping, agreed with himself that he was a man of good fortune.

Good Jesus Fishery, June 11, 1827

" 'Illerman!"

Amleto Ferreira was startled. He knew there should be people beginning to man the whaleboats at that hour, because it was soon going to be dawn, and there were those who even in the dusk, as he did now, could discern far away the puffs of fog made by the whales' warm spouts, not long before the sun began to spread itself over the waters of the great bay. It was time to get to work; the crews were making ready to sail off. But he was startled anyway, maybe because the wind had changed direction all of a sudden, or maybe he had been absentminded, dwarfed among the boats shored up on the beach, listing on their stocks, their exposed frameworks like the ribs of half-eaten animals, barnacles covering the hulls with a whitish mass sprinkled with eye pupils, stanchions like weapons driven into the sand, the wind slipping through the holes in the hulls like a harbinger of ghosts.

"Cuddy man!"

Through the fleshless frame of the dory *Nossa Senhora da Penha,* formerly glorious and emblazoned in the maritime processions but now a skeleton populated by water bugs and little crabs, he saw at the other end of the beach the silhouette of the shore chief, mustering the crew. The cuddy man, a very lanky black who ran as if he had trouble lifting his feet, walked out from the woods by way of the cashew tree footpath, carrying two iron boilers and a bunch of firewood. He set everything down on the ground as he got near the chief, thrust the firewood in one of the boilers, and stiffened up, standing almost at attention. Ten or twelve men could be seen: the six boathands with their blue burlap caps, the tillerman, the harpooner, the diver, the cuddy man, and the shore chief, standing still like a statue.

"Balay balay balay azhoh balay!" the chief seemed to say to the tillerman, raising his arm. " 'Arpooner! Harpoon-ay!"

The tillerman ran off to the fish shed, disappeared into the darkness inside, and came back followed by two other blacks, a man and a woman. By the man's low-brimmed hat and by his height, Amleto could tell it was the black harpooner Custódio, but he did not recognize the woman. The shore chief waved his arm once more and said other things in the language of the blacks. Amleto felt a sudden indignation.

"Why, confound it!" he grunted, taking the first step to cross *Nossa Senhora da Penha*'s gaping hull, instead of going around it, as he always did. "Did I not tell them already? Did I not tell them? Yes, I told them! That black scum never has enough, they never have enough!"

He enjoyed routing the water bugs, the little fiddler crabs, the white crabs, and the other small animals that as he passed turned the boat's defunct beams into something swarmingly alive, going in and out of holes and crannies and continually giving everything a new texture. He had come here at four in the morning just as a precaution, because he wanted to pay one last visit to all the places the guests would be shown, for it would be he who, at the baron's imperious, weary beckoning, would have to explain the functioning of the fishery, the mill, the plantations, and anything else of which the visiting canon or the other guests cared to be informed. He had rehearsed a few short phrases and remarks, and hoped to recall with his customary facility things learned in the recommended grammar and rhetoric manuals, in the musty tomes he had forced himself to read nights on end, with his forehead dewed by sweat and his mind delirious, in the conversations and speeches to which he had paid such determined attention, in the Latin apothegms printed after plump, leafy initials, and memorized in imitation of the Saint Anthony Beyond Carmo parish priest's pronunciation. He was going to make a few clever constructions, using fine words such as the ones he collected avidly, writing them down in a little notebook and spending the day repeating them aloud. This demesne was no more, Most Reverend Monsignor, than an agrestal, untilled fallow, before it was subdued by the resoluteness of His Lordship the baron of Pirapuama, *cum dilectione hominum et odio vitiorum,* in the inspired words of the one who must needs have been the most august among the Holy Latin Doctors. Well, then, downstream of this brook . . . And now that he was building his judicious, florid sentences, which would amply demonstrate his ability, sending into oblivion the disaster that had occurred during the trip and justifying his heretofore almost undisputed social condition, the speech of those black whalers, the sound of those words, which was more like the noises of trees and animals, the harpooner's lithesome gestures, the dancing motions of the other blacks, all those things, without his knowing why, made his face feel cold, his heart pound, and his throat choke with anger, while he opened a fan of scurrying little crabs ahead of him, plodding the soft sand in the direction of the group. So what is all this, what is going on here?

The chief, who like all the others had stopped speaking the moment Amleto's presence was felt, looked bewildered. They were getting ready to sail out, they were manning the whaleboat, she was the last one, all the others had already pulled out—what was going on?

"I will not stand for that!" Amleto yelled. "I will not stand for it!"

His neck veins were swollen as he spoke, going up and down on the tips of his toes at each shout, and shaking a pointing finger at the blacks. The cuddy man, his nostrils gaping, his eyes popping out, and his gapped teeth pointing forward, gobbled like a turkey, changed the position of his legs with an exaggerated wiggle, rolled his eyes, and sniffed loudly. Amleto ran toward him and halted almost doing a jig. Although he had to turn his head up because of the black's height, he nailed his eyes on him with authority. The black glanced back at him a couple of times, turning his face away and again looking at him, and seemed to be going to weep, but when tears appeared ready to start pouring out of every crease on his face, he gobbled once more, stuck out and drew back his tongue with a slurping noise, and stood at attention.

"What? What?" Amleto shouted at the chief. "What is this? Huh?"

"He is out of order in the mind," the chief explained, and the cuddy man smiled, shaking his head.

"Does he not know I can send him to the whip for behaving worse than an animal?"

"He whips himself; he likes it."

The cuddy man heard that as a cue, stood on one foot, bent down like a wading bird toward the pan where he had placed the firewood, picked up a long twig, and, intoning sucked-in ooy-ooys that ended in whistles, started to flog himself, at first chaotically and afterward in a syncopated rhythm that he completed with short jumps.

"Stop!" Amleto shouted, but the cuddy man, his irises like two little black dots in the protruding whites of his eyes, smiled ceremoniously, took a deep bow, sweeping the ground with his fingertips, and struck his own back so hard that when his arm returned, a drizzle of blood arched in the air, and a few drops splattered on the pince-nez Amleto was holding tremulously in front of his face. "Stop, stop!"

"He does not understand the language of the whites well," the chief explained, while the cuddy man, in a dance with long pauses, went on lashing himself all over that section of the beach, yelling ooys and ays and sharing the blows with an invisible companion.

"How many times do I have to tell you to use the Christian language, never this animal babblement that cannot be comprehended and cannot be permitted?"

"Yes, but he does not understand that."

"Was he not born here?"

"He was, he was. But he does not understand most of what is spoken, he does not understand anything; his mind is out of order."

The cuddy man stopped jumping and whipping himself almost as suddenly as he had begun, stood with his arms hanging loose, and, with not another sign from his body of what was happening, burst out in sobs and tears, interrupted by brief grins and by the licks with which he received the tears that reached his mouth. And though he remained motionless, he did not stop staring obstinately at Amleto's small figure wherever it moved.

"So! So he stopped!" Amleto said. "So what now?"

"It was not because you told him to. He is out of order, he—" the chief started again to explain, but the cuddy man gobbled once more, even more loudly than the first time.

"Does he think he is a turkey?"

"No one knows. He does not say. He—"

"I do not want to hear about it any longer. Tell him to cease that. How can you take a dunderhead like this along on a mission of such responsibility?"

"He is a good cuddy man, helps in every task, makes good food. And if he cannot be the cuddy man he will not be anything else, no one can make him; all he does is man the cuddy."

74

The cuddy man looked at Amleto as if he were seeing him for the first time, changing postures from time to time like someone who is evaluating something, closing an eye, leaning his head sideways, and clicking his tongue.

"Well, what are you waiting for? Have I not told you to get him to work? Go on with your job. It is almost daylight; it is getting very late!"

The chief hesitated. Had not the boss man arrived there fuming and shaking with anger because they were using black talk? What now? The cuddy man understood only black talk; there was no other way to talk to him. Amleto, his hands on his waist and his elbows pointing backward, did not know what appearance to assume, and ended up by turning around and making a head gesture.

"All right, speak to him in that language of animals. Go on, make haste. This job is going very badly, very badly; this is very, very bad!"

The chief sang out the stange syllables that made Amleto want to plug his ears and almost shout so he would not hear them. The cuddy man immediately picked up his boilers, his firewood, and his implements and ran out to the pier, where the moored whaleboat slackened and tautened her cables to the cadence of the tide. The others remained as they were, their eyes on Amleto.

"Now go, go! What a pack of wastrels, what stupid, lazy people. Come on!"

Measuring his steps so as not to make them either too hurried or too slow, he followed the blacks who were now crowding the pier before jumping down to the boat. He walked on the jetty's boards without looking over its edges, treading down the middle just enough not to expose his fear of falling in the water. Aboard the whaleboat, a svelte, forty-foot-long craft with two faces, because her job requires her bow and stern to have the same external shape, the crew were taking their stations, and from above it all looked like a precise, calm ballet. As though he were on firm land and not on that keelless hull that sometimes seemed not to capsize only because it was held in place by the cables, a black man tied a piece of tow over each oarlock, hanging out of the boat with only one foot on her. From the mast bench, the sea chief followed the movements of the others and stroked the cables, the lowered sail's footrope, and the stirrups around the biriba-wood lift that would soon be hoisted up, oversaw the counting and stowing of the harpoons in the arms chest, and approved with his eyes the cuddy man's routine of preparing the sand in the box that took the place of a stove, the cleaning of the gourd used for measuring manioc flour rations, the packing of the boiler and of the hooks brought along for fishing. The harpooner had sat down astern on the capstan bench, patting the charred wood around which the harpoon cable was spooled. And then, everybody ready, a boatman jumped back on the jetty to unmoor the boat. But he stopped in front of Amleto and glanced at him and at the chief, who looked up from below, not knowing what to do. Amleto, experiencing for the first time at close range the sailing off of a fully tackled whaleboat ready to go and kill the great animals that could demolish a house with a tail blow, was surprised at his envy of these blacks, who much to his discomfort seemed to him to be expeditionary warriors, slaves but with powers he did not have, and at the last moment he thought he should say something to them, give an order, issue an indispensable direction, show them what they really were.

"Attention!" he bellowed, and the whole crew obeyed. "Attention!"

Because Amleto was in front of the sun, which had started to rise over the bay, the chief cupped a hand over his forehead and waited. He waited a long time, the first blush of the day unfolding itself, the water becoming rufous and gold-colored, shredded clouds flying away, the birds starting all sorts of activity, the waves sloshing like clockwork. Amleto inhaled deeply. What could he say that they would understand; what did they know how to do besides what they were doing?

"All right," he said at last. "You may go."

He realized that he was not necessary there nor could he ever be, that nothing had happened which he could tell about without lying, that the air became musical when, her oars drawn in like the legs of a hermit crab, the whaleboat *Liberdade,* clearing the small bar of the harbor, happy as a young goat, hoisted her tawny, square sail, veered larboard, gathered wind, and stood for the heart of the bay, where one could now easily see the contours of the whales like small moving volcanoes bordering the coast.

I shall talk about this departure during the tour, Amleto decided, wondering if he had in his notebook a verse or two by Virgil about heroes sailing off. Could he possibly memorize them before seven o'clock, the time the tour would start? Indeed, he still remembered them vaguely, because he had asked the priest to make a note of them after a sermon at the Our Lord of Seafarers Mass. Yes, he remembered well: I found so much evocative power in those verses, Reverend Father, that I beg you leave to copy them for my elevation. *Stabant orantes primi transmittere cursum, tendeban . . .* Was that how it went? And French, nothing in French? No, he had never heard anyone speak French, he had only a nebulous idea of how the words were pronounced. No, Latin. Latin, after all . . . *Stabant orantes!* And he was so engrossed in this exercise that he had already walked halfway back on the pier when he raised his head and saw coming to the beach the black girl who had been in the fish shed with the harpooner. She was probably young; she had a thin waist, broad, well-made hips, long legs—how would her breasts be? Amleto was flustered, his mouth salty, his groin almost creaking; he wanted to see her breasts, he could see them if he wished, touch them, do with them whatever he wanted!

76

"Hey!" he called out, and started to hurry along the pier without being aware of it. "Hey! You there!"

The first thing he noticed when she turned around was her hair. It was different from the hair of most blacks, neither kinky nor smooth, running down around her neck like a downy shawl. The face, yes, the face was very comely, the eyes large and long-lashed, the nostrils sculptured, the mouth and the chin strong but not hostile, a strange mark on the forehead. And the breasts Amleto could not stop looking at: they held up her hopsacking shirtwaist, live animals under it.

"Who are you, what is your name?"

"Venância."

"Oh yes, I have seen you before around here, a long time ago, fishing with that scatterbrained black—what was his name?"

"Turíbio, Turíbio Cafubá, my father."

"Your father? Whatever became of him?"

"He has been dead for years."

"Your mother, do you have a mother?"

"She was given away as a cook."

Although her face was stern and she was looking straight ahead almost contentiously, Amleto became even more excited than before at her deep, feminine voice, his pants almost bursting with his desire to touch her, and he got very close to her, who neither moved nor changed her appearance.

"I want to see your breasts."

She did not say anything; she remained as she was. With unbearable anticipation, he lifted her shirtwaist, quivered as he saw first her belly and navel appear, and almost exploded when, first the left one and then the right, her breasts, bouncing a little because of his upward tug, settled in delicate curves, the nipples pointing buoyantly up, the cleavage between them covered by a secret down. Amleto gasped and wanted to shout for having them so close, so visible, so touchable—how can one voice such feelings?

"I am going to feel them," he said, and she did not answer.

Slowly at first, and then as though he wanted to turn them into bread dough or to fuse his fingers with them, he squeezed her breasts, with his eyes closed, bent down and sucked them as hard as he could, filling his mouth as much as possible.

"Don't you feel anything?" he asked, flurried and frenzied, pinching both her nipples between his thumbs and forefingers.

He pushed her back, holding her by her shoulders, the folds of her shirt multiplying themselves over her exposed breasts. Feeling he was pale and flushed at the same time, and sweating intensely on his face and legs, he stretched out an open hand and showed her his tumefied fly. She followed his gesture with her eyes, her expression unchanged.

"See? See? See what happens to me because of you?"

Once again she did not say anything, and grabbing her limp hand to rub over his fly, he was going to order, "Squeeze it, squeeze it!" when an overpowering spasm constricted his scrotum, and unable to stifle his moans, he slid his hands down her arms and finished coming sitting on the ground, almost lying down, his legs stopping their jittering only little by little.

"May I go now?" she asked, her voice as indifferent as her face.

He did not find an answer and, too embarrassed to look at her, waved his hand hastily before getting up and composing himself. She pulled down her shirt over her breasts, gave it a light tug to cover her belly, turned around, and walked out unhurriedly toward the cashew tree footpath. Feverishly jamming a handkerchief down into his trousers, Amleto inspected himself and figured he still had plenty of time to go back to the house and change his underwear.

Many things in this world cannot be described, as is known by those who live by the pen, drudging away among lexicons and other people's books in the pursuit of the right word or the most eloquent sentence, hoping they will be able to produce pages of prose afforded by some wonder or portent they deem of interest to their readers, thus increasing their output and what little money they are paid. They resort to comparisons, they make up metaphors, they fabricate adjectives, but everything ends up sounding pale and wan, that wonder or portent fading away, losing its life and greatness for lack of that which a good word no matter how good cannot do—that is to say, make one a witness to the undescribable. In the minutiae of plot and intrigue, foiled love affairs, cruelties against innocents, dilacerating dilemmas, decrees of fate, ingenious coincidences, cleverly conceived surprises, ecstasies of passion, and all else that constitutes the just matter of novels and romances, they fare more or less well, according to their competence in their trade, as those plots and intrigues have been the same since Creation. How, though, is one to describe a smell? Nay, not a smell but this fatal vapor, this miasma manufactured in hell, this gaminess of putrescent things, rancid things, grangrenescent things, festering, repulsive things, things unbearable to imagine, now that the wind is channeling itself through the place where the latest whale carcass congregates clouds of buzzards, and the oil-making boilers huff out dingy puffs of an impossibly stenchful smoke. The two-and-seventy stenches, all well defined, that grieved the poet in the city of Cologne? The smell of the famous egg of two hundred years? The smell of the Augean stables at high noon?

Certainly all this, plus the malodor of six hundred devils, now begins to envelop the austere, ponderous procession that yonder comes, turning at the end of the long path that winds down from the manor and taking the dirt strip parallel to the beach. Out in front, in identical litters, rustic as befits country utensils but no less comfortable than others for both passengers and litter-bearing Negroes, come the visiting canon and the baron of Pirapuama. Formerly those litters had only four shafts apiece, necessitating the use of only two blacks, or four if each held just one shaft, both instances being quite discommoding for all concerned, especially on longer, more demanding trips. For that reason the baron ordered his master carpenter to make out of good wood those litters whose front and rear shafts are bifurcated in such a disposition as to allow four blacks, without crowding or discomfort, to carry one of them, using their eight hands. And that is how the baron and the canon are coming, swaying softly in the rhythm of their teams' footsteps and surrounded by the retinue of the walking guests, with Amleto to one side, explaining the whole itinerary with an orator's gestures and style. Already the blacks at the boilers are able to see them coming from afar, when the canon raises his arm and the procession stops.

"Down, down!" the baron commanded as soon as the blacks stopped. "Does not the monsignor feel well?"

No, the monsignor felt well enough. But on second thought, maybe not. What tremendous smell was that, stronger and more overwhelming all the time, arriving interspersed with blasts of an ocherous, equally mephitic smoke? He had heard and read accounts of the sufferings of chaplains obliged by priestly duty to administer the last rites to the war dead, and many times he had had nightmares in which he was horrified by the unimaginable fetidity of battlefields, but nothing he might have dreamed, let alone felt, could match this diabolical emanation. He understood now why His Lordship the baron had extolled so much the manor's location, upwind and at a safe distance from the source of that prodigious smell. Was it always this way at this establishment?

"Well," the baron answered, "they are finishing the flensing of a *madrijo* that could not be completed yesterday because it was Sunday and time for Saint Anthony's festivities, and Your Reverence was arriving to visit us. No matter how careful we are, those animals are like mountains, and the flensing is never total. But we cannot afford to let the blubber go to waste; the catches have been small and the oil production has been much below what we were expecting. Does the most reverend canon wish to attend the flensing of a whale in our industry? You would witness how many cares, expenses, and labors costs us the production of the oil without which one could not live with some decency in these parts and many others. And you would also see, with Your Most Reverend's leave, something one does not see in Rome."

"One of these whales? *In acto moriendi?*"

"No, already dead, and quite dead at that. When they arrive here they are dead, roped to the sides of the boats."

"That is not so bad, then. But begging Your Lordship's pardon, what can one do to be able to bear with that smell which makes itself felt with such potency even from here?"

"After a while the nose grows accustomed to it; it is as if it became numb, insensitive to it."

"And the smoke?"

"As we draw closer, it will stop coming over us; the wind is taking it upward in that direction. Unfortunately, I cannot order them to stop now, because all the meat and the blubber they are melting would spoil. Sometimes it takes over a day and a night for a whole whale to be liquefied, if it is a big one. We have thirty-two boilers, with a capacity of about fifteen tuns, but in season sometimes we are not able to keep up with all the work needed, even with the Negroes stopping only at lunchtime and working at night."

"How many Negroes work there?"

Perilo Ambrósio looked at Amleto, who sprang up animatedly to talk. There was not a fixed number, he explained; it depended on the amount of work and the urgency of some production goal, such as dictated by the need to load a merchant ship docked at the port of Bahia with oil destined for Europe. At those times, the number of Negroes working at the flensing was doubled or tripled, which was not easy, for the task required aptitude and practice. At any rate, they had several masters and skilled workers to make the main cuts, while the others prepared the blubber, a not very difficult job, which required mainly the cutting of cubes weighing about two pounds, to be taken to the boilers. The melting was also simple work, though complicated by the smoke, the heat, and the carelessness with which the Negroes sometimes let themselves be burned by spurts of boiling grease, especially the boys and girls who composed the majority of the workers in charge of carrying the blubber to drop it in the boilers. His Lordship the baron, so immersed in the high thoughts and businesses through which the interests of the Motherland took all his hours, had been prey to a little slip, because on his own orders the boilers had been increased from thirty-two to forty for over two years now. There remained to be done some repairs in the pipes and tubes connected to the chimney, the capacity of which had to be augmented so it could give passage to the smoke from all boilers, which was why, begging His Most Reverend's forgiveness, the smoke now came over them occasionally instead of being dispersed upward by the chimney as it should be. There were nevertheless advantages to all that smoke, no matter how paradoxical it might seem at first. It had the effect of reducing the copious swarms of common flies and horseflies, here known vulgarly as motucas, insects of insufferable impertinence, frequently appearing in numbers so vast that in spite of the smoke they give the black cutters and boilers the aspect of lamps that are surrounded by multitudes of moths and winged ants in winter. Neither did the smoke favor the buzzards, although those repulsive vultures demonstrated invention, intelligence, and daring by flying low under it to approach the installations via their natural entrances, even walking on the mud, even attacking one Negro or another for the possession of hunks of meat or fat. But did not the monsignor wish to put a perfumed handkerchief to his nose, so that he and the baron could go closer to the factory without being offended?

"If that were possible . . . "

Amleto went over to the two blacks who were in front of the canon's litter, picked out the fat, short one, and told him to run back to the manor to fetch perfumed handkerchiefs. The black ran off much faster than his weight seemed to make possible, and the canon laughed.

"A rather peculiar choice, I should say. If you wanted a fast messenger, would not the thin one be the right choice?"

"Negro Sabino is fat, but he is one of the quickest we have. I imagine he comes from a part of Africa where the Negroes are runners and scouts. And this other one cannot speak."

"Oh, is he mute?"

Amleto started to answer but took too long to articulate something, and looked helplessly at the baron. But the baron, with his fist tightened around one of the litter's stanchions, was not unsettled. On the contrary, he spoke more loudly and with more vehemence than he had intended, as though he was making an indignant proclamation, getting rid of something that was obstructing his chest.

"He is not mute!" he said, looking fixedly at the black. "He is disloyal! He used to enjoy great trust at my father's home and my own; I even took him along to the combats of Pirajá and other fronts during the War of Independence. Contrary to the other Negro who was in my company and who died fighting bravely—I do not wish to repeat a story everyone already knows and that brings me no merit, as I was only doing my patriotic duty—contrary to the other one, this one proved himself to be a cowardly poltroon. But I would have attributed that behavior to his race's natural flaws if it were not for the fact that as soon as he returned to our house he took to telling such dishonorable lies that were I a less benevolent master, he should no longer be alive on account of his impudence, his vileness, his turpitude, even. But guided as usual by compassion, I punished him commensurately with his fault, the chief one among many, of which I forever ridded him. He will lie no more, he may be absolved of that sin, if only at the cost of having compelled me to overcome my natural abhorrence for punishments, for I apply them only when they leave me no other choice, no other choice!"

"What was the punishment he received?"

"I simply had his tongue cut off, enough for him to be able to go on eating the food he does not deserve my giving him, and for people not to understand the tall tales I am sure he would still be telling if he could."

The canon looked at Feliciano with interest. "You had his tongue cut off, huh?"

"*Audi, vidi, tace,*" Amleto said.

"Yes, no doubt. Is it a common usage here—are there many of them in that condition?"

"No," the baron explained. "I hear that in the backlands of this province, where life is harsher and the use of more severity is required, even in some of the mills along the shores of this gulf, there are masters who are very rigorous toward their blacks. That is not the case here; here we have only whatever discipline is indispensable. Since running away from these lands is very difficult, none of them ever tries, so that Your Reverence will not find here a Negro with his foot chopped off, which is the manner second-time runaways are punished. We do not have many geldings, either, only two or three among the oldest ones.

"My brother, who raises some cattle, castrates the blacks who do housework and other light chores on his farms. And he tells me he obtains good results; they become calmer and more docile, more apt for their duties."

"I do not doubt it; conveniences vary. Now, here we do not castrate them, because actually . . . "

"Now, now, Baron, you may speak freely, I know what you mean. Since the work of the pickaninnies is very useful here, one must see to it that the Negroes reproduce themselves. It is the same thing at the mines, for there are always galleries and excavations where the rocks do not allow the passage of a grown body."

"Absolutely. And not only that, we also think it is uncalled for. Some of them die if we castrate them with a knife, and with a mace we sometimes have even more of a headache. You can render a Negro useless for work that way, and the risks of losses are too great, although we do have good pig gelders with some experience in the castration of Negroes. Neither do I brand them anymore, as they used to do in my father's time, branding the males and the house Negresses in the service of my late grandmother, the latter with the monogram she herself designed for her belongings. Nowadays it is a useless practice because the Negroes have no place to go, and without our assistance they would die unattended everywhere, as is already happening to so many derelict, pernicious freed blacks."

"Yes, one can no longer walk the streets without seeing their mobs importuning passersby and fouling everything around."

"Precisely! But where is the authority of the government, where is the discernment of the general good, since one cannot even mention sending that idle rabble to do forced labor in public works and many others where they would do some service, without arousing those who deem it possible to make an empire prosper with kid gloves and charitable deeds? What we see today is that it is more worthwhile to be a loafer with no occupation than a serviceable individual, and people still speak badly, not knowing anything that is going on, of men such as I, who are ostracized while carrying the nation on their backs! What would they do without any production? Would they live by lunching on speeches and drinking the tears they shed for the workless and the useless? And the ones they defend will be the first to stab them in the back as soon as the limit is reached, as it is being reached already, by anarchy and by the neglect of austere standards of conduct! I am being sincere with Your Reverence when I say that as a patriotic, God-fearing Brazilian, I cannot help harboring some hope, although I do not justify it but for my faith. Otherwise, Monsignor, I fear, I fear, I fear for the future of Brazil."

The canon pursed his mouth into the habitual beak, nodded his approval, and sighed like someone who has despaired of trying to make people listen to reason. He commented absentmindedly on the solution devised by North America, a rather uncivilized country but with a resolute people of strong character, to clean herself of her blacks and emancipated mongrels—for they do not do there what we do here, they do not allow browns and darkies a life in common with white people as if white they were—and this solution was to establish for them their own state somewhere on the Pepper Coast, near the lands of Guinea, where they can proceed with their bestial living as they please without being a nuisance to anybody. By doing that, incidentally, the Americans followed the example of their English ancestors, who long before had done the same in Sierra Leone. He sighed once again and prophesied a brilliant future for North America as compared to Brazil, although one does not know whether the speakers of the English tongue are more advanced because they practice those ideas or they practice those ideas because they are advanced, and in the final analysis you cannot really distinguish one thing from the other. *Parvis componere magna?* he asked with a shrug, while the black Sabino was coming back with two large white handkerchiefs and a flask of vetiver oil from India, much recommended by Her Ladyship the baroness for purposes such as covering up foul odors. The baron dampened one of the handkerchiefs with the oil, waved it in the air so he would not be inebriated by an excessive fragrance, tied it over his face, covering his mouth and nose, and asked the canon to imitate him. Many in the company also accepted some of the essence to sprinkle on their handkerchiefs, the blacks picked up the litters, and the procession, now masked and aromatized, went on down the beach trail. They were soon in front of the wall-less shed that spewed smoke out of all its holes, where a few boys and two or three girls went in and out, doing boiler work. A little farther ahead, sprouting behind the other shed like crooked obelisks, the ribs of the whale lay among droves of buzzards. On the side facing the sea, undulating over the soft-lined hillocks that rose beyond the shores of the island, the sugarcane field was swept by the breeze, the stalks bending and unbending at intervals, and no one knew if the light hiss modulating the air came from the wind sieved by the thin canelets of from the ceaseless wingbeats of the buzzards and flies.

"This demesne was no more, Reverent Monsignor, than an agrestal, untilled fallow, harrowed only by the natural hand of the Creator and never ployed by the hand of civilized man . . . " Amleto began, lifting the handkerchief from his mouth so that the fine words could take wing unimpeded.

Fine words that now, under the great bower woven with rustling granadilla and coral vines displaying a lavender flower here and there, among the sounds of bird song and washing waves, were like the fruits, the sweets, and the pastries deployed immeasurably all over the table, overfilling the pieces of enameled faience and painting the white tablecloth with all kinds of colorful patterns. They were that solid, those words, maybe more so. They were even more palpable than the fruits and the food, punctuated by the general chewing and sometimes perduring a long time in the air, like those guavas in a crimson syrup, these napoleons whose sculpturing one admires before biting them, these sweet egg strings whose tendrils are threaded in one's memory, this tapioca couscous collapsing little by little in coconut milk, these pineapples, these pomegranates, these sapodillas, these cherimoyas, these red and yellow Malay apples, these mangoes, these sweetsops, these jaboticabas, these ambarellas, these star apples, these strawberry guavas, these golden bananas, these watermelon slices, these carambolas, these pitangas, these ingas, these jambolans, these papayas, these refreshments of changing colors that sparkle in the glasses. And the canon was the one who was enouncing the fine words, ornamenting and enriching the shade under the bower and making everyone renew contact, always so elusive and rare, with Culture, Civilization, and Truth.

"Luigi Capponi," the canon said. "No doubt you have heard of him."

But of course! The great Luigi Capponi! The Latinist Luigi Capponi or the physiologist and surgeon Luigi Capponi? The latter, if memory serves, was Caroni, Caloni . . . Luigi Capponi, yes, he sure comes to mind here, no doubt about that! Very well put, a very appropriate thought: Luigi Capponi!

"Luigi Capponi," the canon said again, touching his fingertips against one another and closing his eyes, "the great sculptor of saints' images who became notable in Rome for his pure, sublime art, which complied with the best canons."

The best canons! Luigi Capponi, yes! Saint Ambrose with his beehive of honey-rich bees? Saint Jerome with his lion at the entrance of the sacred cavern? Saint Theodore with his shield, his armor, and his battle gear? Saint Ann and Saint Joachim receiving the holy sacrament of matrimony?

"Luigi Capponi," the canon repeated after a long pause, during which he seemed to rejoice at everything, especially himself. "The magnificent master sculptor of the Church of Saint Gregory in Rome! The great Saint Gregory, Saint Gregory the Great, Saint Gregory of the thirty Masses, Saint Gregory who from the flame-vomiting innards of Purgatory extracted even the soul of Emperor Trajan, of so many and so obdurate sins, Saint Gregory of whom it was said—and he is represented accordingly—that he used to hear the contents and style of his impavid sermons from the Holy Ghost itself, that Saint Gregory, that Saint Gregory, that Capponi! That Capponi!"

He made another pause, closed his eyes again. The lector of grammar Emílio Viana, his hand on the high collar that propped his chin, nodded affirmatively. The superintendent of orphans Manoel Boaventura Bandeira became even more serious than usual, frowning hard and puckering his lips. Capponi, exactly, the Church of Saint Gregory in Rome, that Capponi!

The canon let out a sudden guffaw.

"But what am I saying?" he said, after he had finished laughing and slapping his knees alternately. "Here I am in the company of distinguished persons, men of the highest caliber, enjoying the unrivaled, unequaled hospitality of His Lordship the baron of Pirapuama, whom I admired before for his renown and now admire much more for his accomplishments—yes, here I am talking in such a way as to be taken for a madman. Indeed, it does not seem to make sense for me to be reminiscing about Capponi, Saint Gregory, Rome. . . . Believe me, it is not my purpose to make an exhibition of myself, it would not be here among lettered and learned men that I should dare to give lessons, and neither does vanity tempt me, as you well know. But . . . but . . . how can I put it? We made it to the top of this very pleasant hill after that most demanding trip through the industrial establishment and its . . . its extraordinary odor, and then . . . then the slaves' chapel, and now, with everyone sitting here, I mention Capponi. And do you gentlemen know who came to my mind just now? Tiepolo! Yes, Tiepolo!"

He could no longer hold back convulsive laughter, and stopped speaking so he could go on haw-hawing, sometimes giving the impression he was going to turn serious all of a sudden, only to bend over laughing once again. In the beginning, the others looked at each other hesitatingly, but after a while through mutual encouragement, they burst out laughing too, and soon the black men and women were also laughing, the bower in agitation with so much mirth. The canon wiped off a few tears, sighed, and resumed his talk with some difficulty.

"I hope you will forgive me, but perhaps I shall be better understood if we share a few reflections, the sort of reflections I am sure have occupied or even permanently occupy the thoughts of those present. They are bound to occur, perforce they occur, it is imperative that they occur, it is inevitable that they occur, it is ineluctable that they occur to the civilized spirit here perplexed by how so much is uncustomary for the European mind in the New World. I was talking about Tiepolo, Capponi—and you might ask: Why? I shall answer you. I shall answer that question with another question, even though, ha-ha, I am not a Jesuit. I shall answer in the manner of the rhetoric masters of antiquity, I shall employ the very justly celebrated maieutics, if you know what I mean."

"The Socratic way," Amleto interrupted.

"By all means," the canon said, with a perforating smile. "I see I labored under a misapprehension a few days ago, by not making a correct estimate of your knowledge. Of a mulatto one could say you have only the appearance, and even so very lightly, for your good fortune. *Gnothi te auton*—do you know what that means?"

"No, no."

"It is also Socratic, it is Platonic. It means 'Know thyself,' *nosce te ipsum*, most wise advice. In other words, see yourself in the mirror, look at yourself, etc. Do you understand that? I must admit, and congratulate you for it, that I was very agreeably surprised at the way you performed in the conduction of our excursion; you speak well, you are literate. Would you therefore like to speak in my place, to say what I was going to say, to discourse upon what was to be my discourse? Your father, as you tell us, comes from a people that prides itself on being the spiritual child of the libertine King Henry, so one can expect anything from you. Go ahead!"

"No, forgive me, Most Reverend, it was only a comment that escaped me our of enthusiasm, an impulse."

"Half-bloods are very enthusiastic; one cannot deny they have that and other qualities that sometimes superimpose themselves over the laziness that marks their reputation. Indeed, I sustain that crossbreeding is one of the real levers of this country's progress, because the European spirit can hardly stand the contortions necessary to understand circumstances so foreign to human experience and avocation. The truth is that Brazil cannot be a people in itself, so the civilizing forces must be exercised through a class, in the case at hand the half-bloods, combining the ruggedness of the Negroes with some of the intelligence of the whites. The social classes of the Greek cities offer precious lessons, to be utilized within modern demands. Only leisure, *otium cum dignitate*, permitted the flourishing of Greek thought, because the slaves took care of all the rest. But they were slaves from literate, intelligent races, whites from Asia Minor, sometimes even Greeks themselves. The circumstances were different, quite different. The challenges ahead of us are formidable, are immense, are incommensurate, are unheard of. And whom do we depend upon as our servile element? Upon Negroes, the most backward race on the face of the earth, the degenerate descendants of Hamitic lineages, whose savagery not even Christendom's invincible hand has yet been able to overcome or even mitigate. In a certain way one can see here Providence's hand, though at first it is not noticeable. It is just that the savageness of the land can only be countered by the equal savageness of the Negroes—and in this they are unsurpassable, for they come from a land even more antagonistic than this one, more fraught with perils, fevers, and harmful animals. If we do not have intelligent slaves to whom we can trust even the education of the young, as the Hellenes used to do, to compensate for it we have sturdy slaves, capable under good, tenacious, strict direction of being up to the tasks necessary for our farms and factories. There remains only the question of who is going to be occupied with the immediate foremanship of the slaves, who will take care of intermediate matters, of those subjects that while not requiring a superior intelligence—on the contrary, they have a wilting effect on that kind of intelligence through their sameness, their lack of invention, and the absence of the sublime and the transcendental, the hallmarks of true thought and superiority of spirit—cannot be assimilated by the stupidity of the Negroes, either. That is where our contingent of half-bloods fits like a glove in the perfect social organization, the only one that might impart to this country an *élite,* as the French say, a cream of the cream, an aristocracy able like the Greek one to beget and make thrive a culture of the first order. I do not even see—and here again I emphasize what might be our happy fortune, our only happy fortune—the need for laws to curb mongrelization, because as our aristocracy of European fundaments solidifies itself, grows roots, nourishes its traditions, and strengthens its bloodlines in purity of race, temperament, and adherence to the highest values, social forces will by themselves prevent excessive mongrelization from occurring. The civilized man's natural abhorrence of contact with Negroes or browns and the cultivation of good instincts with spontaneity and no greater concern than the establishment of governments conscious of their historic responsibilities will set things happening in their normal tendencies, dictated by the correct impulses of history. This is how I see the role of the half-bloods, an important, a very important role, and do not assume I do not like you, because I do, I just find you a trifle arrogant, a vice it is my constitutional disposition to repulse. Believe me, ha-ha, there is a place on earth and a place in heaven for you. *Your* place, of course, if you know what I mean, ha-ha. But now see how you have made me lose my trend of thought, the same way you did the other day by insisting on debating with me matters of natural philosophy; you have done the same thing now. I was going to say that . . . I was going to say something. . . . See, you make me sound like a chatterbox, and to think that one of the virtues I cherish best is to listen more than to speak, to hear more than to say! I wanted to listen to you people, not to speak so much. But under provocation . . . What was I saying?"

Yes, what was he saying? What a fluent speaker, what a fiery delivery, what well-aimed, sharp thinking, what a refined candidness, what knowledge of life and history! When are we going to have statesmen of such stature? How everything seems easy when he speaks, how his thoughts are articulated, how his reasoning follows a perfect chain! He was speaking of Catoni, Capponi, Saint Gregory. . . . His Reverence was laughing very heartily, everyone was laughing, remember? And how unpresuming he is, a man of such position, such standing, such importance! And his wit, his quips, his bantering, his jocularity . . . "I am not a Jesuit," he had said.

"Yes!" exclaimed the canon, who, his eyes lowered and his hands drawn together in his lap, had been enjoying with modesty the recognition of his gifts that was erupting all over his audience. "Yes! I was saying I was not a Jesuit, because the Societas Iesu has a reputation for acting thus: Ask them a question, they fire another one at you. This frequently unnerving practice characterizes the alumni of their lyceums and colleges. But I was going to do as they do, because after all I am not like Horace's fools, who in order to avoid a vice *vitia in contraria currunt,* indulge in the opposite vice. No. If an assiduous pursuit of this dialectical vice makes it tiresome, perhaps odious, an occasional resort to it has its charm and usefulness. Coming to think of it, the question I was about to put to you has to do with what I spoke just now. Because I was simply going to ask: What is the baron doing in this place? What is he doing? What is his mission? Well, I myself, *data venia,* will answer. What he is doing here is to fight his natural propensities as a superior man and to struggle, while weighed down by the deficiencies of this country, against the disheartening difficulties of the environment and the existing conditions. You all see how he treats us, his chivalry, his graciousness, his consideration. And here, in this short interlude, under this delectable shade, *sub tegmine fagi,* one might be tempted to say we are in an Austrian parkland. But we are not. His Lordship the baron, a hero of many merits and even more a hero when one thinks about the continuous war he wages here, knows we are not. You shall see that there are still more arguments than those I have already exposed for the national organization to be made in the configuration I described, for the reasons I described. I mentioned parklands. Are there parklands here? Or is such a sweet word for us no more than an ancestral memory persisting in our hearts, inasmuch as our race was not made to inhabit this land, and is here in an act of sacrifice to Christendom and civilization, as missionaries, veritable missionaries, for that is what we are? It is necessary that Christendom and civilization be brought here; we are their bulwarks, their front line, their most martyred soldiers. But that does not mean that we should let ourselves be corrupted by the enfeebling, debilitating, degenerative, isolating environment in which we are forced to live or that we should forget who we really are. On the contrary, for if that happened, being here would lose its meaning, we would no longer be the loyal representatives of what it is up to us to represent and is in our constitution itself. If we were to change, we would no longer be the emissaries—missionaries, I insist—of the Christendom and civilization I mentioned. It is our duty to preserve, to conserve, to maintain. And to preserve is not just to keep alive the memory of who we are but to provide ourselves with the conditions to which we are entitled and without which we will decline. I had asked: Is this here a park? It is not a park. Now it is showing itself in a pleasant guise, but we know there are no parklands here, nor can there be any bucolic peace among poisonous animals, snakes, plants that cause all kinds of afflictions, inordinate rains, insufferable heat, and perpetual insalubrity, in a climate the humidity of which so sustains the vapors and miasmas which transport plagues that it is a wonder there are not more of them. We have no seasons; either it rains or it does not. We have no fruits—and I know how His Lordship the baron, this most eminent man among men, strives to introduce new cultures here, but good fruit-bearing trees simply do not thrive here, they cannot endure the soil's excessive richness of humors, the inclement sun, and other conditions. We have those that are shown here, and most of them do no harm if eaten rarely and prudently. But if ingesting them becomes a habit, we know very well that our organic systems will not be able to tolerate their caustic juices and the principles, of which they are so endowed, that disrupt the balance of Galen's four classical categories, for no greater reason than their growing and having roots on this soil, which is good only for some applications. Where are autumn cherries, perfumed peaches, health-giving apples, delicate pears, exquisite plums? Where is the luminous joy of spring, the succession of seasons each year, always reminding man of the hand of the Creator and inspiring him to new conquests? Where are the grapevines and vineyards, the inspired spirits of wine which derive from them their ineffable principles? No, gentlemen, it is as I tell you and as you well know: Either we keep ourselves within aristocratic standards organized the way I have had the opportunity to broach, or we are doomed to become the rulers of a weak people, we ourselves being contaminated by everything we must abominate. I was laughing a few moments ago, while talking about works of art and their very illustrious elaborators. 'What does the baron do here?' I had asked. Well, he makes an effort to bring here culture and civilization, but I am afraid I can demonstrate that without resorting to a complete policy for the nation, in those general lines and many related details, his struggles and his meritorious labors may even come to results opposed to those intended. Think of me not as impertinent but rather as a good friend. For in every conversation in which the baron entertained and enriched me, we noticed, we verified, we felt, we understood, we recognized—in a word, we acknowledged—the perfect similarity, I might even say identity, between our ways of thinking; let him say otherwise if I am falsifying the truth. Therefore I speak not out of impertinence but out of great friendship and selfless interest, since meditating upon our condition is becoming more and more imperative. What did we see at the slaves' chapel, where the baron has generously permitted freedmen and half-bloods to work in arts they have no aptitude to grasp, for those arts are the province of superior civilization—the art that has grown white hair, as the great master of sacred oratory once said? We saw many things, all of which corroborate what I say. We saw paintings of visions and miracles executed against all good rules of artistic composition. Credences, chandeliers, angels, cymae, palms, candleholders, the delicate carving—in every work, each and every one of them, one could feel the churlish touch of an uncultured, unskilled hand. We saw mulatto saints! Offensive representations of holy doctors whose appearance was made to be that of people who express themselves by drumbeats and grunts, unable to assimilate an instrument as noble and perfect as the Portuguese language, which they debase astoundingly every day, to the point where it makes one's ears hurt and one's mind agonize to hear their nescient, primitive blabber. You all know very well that the Greeks called the barbarians barbarians in imitation of the prattle of those vandalic, delinquent peoples. For everything they uttered sounded like bah-bah-bah—forgive me if I cannot hold back my laughter. *Ubicumque lingua roman, ibi Roma!* See what happens right in front of us. The language, they defile it and degrade it. As for morals—we know that, and how we know it!—the Adversary himself would pale if he knew of the deeds and practices of those we call the people, and Brazilian people on top of that, as if it were possible for Athenians to call by their own name helots and slaves, as if the spirit of Attica were the result of breathing the same air and living in the same place, instead of birth, ancestry, and good racial and pedagogic background. I do not mean to make any allusion to Brother Hilário, here present, whose probity I know is above any suspicion, but he himself will confirm that that even monasteries and brotherhoods have through the corrupting influence of the environment become veritable wells of iniquity and crime, to the point that after having caught dozens and dozens of friars smuggling gold and precious stones, the Crown functionaries had to prohibit the establishment of those orders in the mining region. Would not the worthy patron of that chapel, one of the saintliest among all the great saints, tremble if he saw to what extremes a government not based on profound philosophical fundaments such as the ones I touched upon here may be leading this country over which we have a responsibility—we are the only ones to have that responsibility, the ones who have to bear the greatest burden on their shoulders, for history is watching and judging us—may be leading this country, as I was saying, to become such a hideous example of the degradation of civilization, culture, and the human spirit that perhaps not even infinite divine mercy may find reasons to acquit us of our incaution and, in some cases, base cowardice? Would he not tremble, that great saint? Work practices that should scandalize every serious man have for a long time now permitted leisure for the servile element, have long been slackened and vilified. If since the beginning we have never been able to maintain corporations formed according to the proper hierarchy of work—yes, because we are in a country where the companion is a master and the apprentice is an officer—now what we see each day is the violation of order and tradition, with consequences that, God help us, may be so horrifying that it is too painful to estimate them. Did a corporation sign the works of the chapel? No. The blacks and half-bloods who made them signed them. *Qui pinxit?* I have to laugh. *Pinxit* some Bonfim, some Conceição, some Amor Divino! Now, individual authorship is for great art, not for the grotesque apery now rampant all over the nation, whose leaders must see that we either pull in the reins now, at this instant, or we will never be able to pull them! But no, this kind of thing keeps on happening. They invite here a so-called French Mission to inculcate fine arts improperly, as if we had here a people like the French and not a riffraff of knaves, cadgers, and uncouth servants, an unsightly, ill-smelling, noisy, stolid, lazy, indolent, mendacious people, as we all know very well since we deal with them—*mea culpa, nostra culpa!*—all the time, to our great suffering and even greater penance. Shall we keep our arms crossed? Shall we continue to treat our servile element better than they treat it in civilized countries? Shall we allow education to be the same for all classes, thus perpetuating and aggravating the degradation already so visible everywhere? Pearls before swine? I ask you: Pearls before swine? True education takes into account the necessary distinctions among the several classes of men. The greatest evils are germinating now to shoot forth later. Where is the Great Foreman indispensable to organize the servile element and the intermediate element, leaving for the national aristocracy the task of erecting here a true culture, a true civilization? Where do we see the national destiny being plotted? Our burden is heavy, our path is cruel, more than ever *ad augusta per angusta!* That is the art and the essence of our politics, of the politics we can neglect only at the cost of our own survival, and of the survival of everything we cherish, love, and represent. The art of politics is no more than that: the art of conserving good and extirpating evil. Mark my words, gentlemen. We cannot avoid pricking the boil, no matter how painful it may be. In spite of everything, I have faith and confidence in the future, for, the Lord be praised, men like His Lordship still adorn our public life, our commerce, our industry, and our government, and they will not allow, will not acquiesce, will not consent, will not accept the sun of truth to be obumbrated by the atrous cloud of ignorance and inconscience!"

Under the whole length of the bower even the leaves stopped rustling for a moment, the light became vitreous, as though not capable of penetrating entirely the density of the silence, and everyone took a very long time to move again, like people rising slowly from a long sleep. Some of them, emerging from a distant world, looked around, seeming to want to say something and not to find anything. At the end of the green tunnel, over the canon's head, two black girls saw—and they secretly squeezed their amulets—the Curukere moth flutter by, as if going to set down on him, and then disappear. Perilo Ambrósio, standing up and talking to the canon about how regrettable it was for the most inspired and important speech he had ever heard to be lost in that wilderness, felt his mouth fill with water and an acrid taste as he thought once more of the black girl Vevé, as he had been doing all along.

Who can that be who yonder saunters, so saucy, so smart, so spirited? It has to be Black Leléu, all natty and dapper, with wide-brimmed slouch hat, stylish paletot, more than spruce pantaloons, plastron-type necktie, ruffled handkerchief, shirt of fine linen, undertrousers of the best calico, pair of shiny bluchers hanging from his fingers, knee-high socks with floss-silk garters thrown over his shoulder—and the worst intentions! Irreligious like the devil, why was he coming angel-faced to the saint's feast, traveling a league and a half all the way from the beach of Duro, the beach of Cachaprego, the beach of Berlinque, and so many, many others along the coast of the island? And so well dressed, so dashing, handsome, and debonair, carrying his shoes in his hand so they would not get wet or dirty during his walk; they were made to order in the city of Bahia, a great novelty, made individually for each foot, not a cheap cobbler's job! By his strutting march and his jaunty clothes one might have taken him for a very rich black slave merchant coming here to sell the cream of his stock, a sultan from Ceuta, a great ambassador king, a numen of wealth and elegance. But no, it was Black Leléu, rehearsing his innocent look and remembering the routines he was going to do, as they expected, because he was on a business trip, and a good businessman must always do what is expected of him. The routines could not vary, because the children always asked for the same ones and became impatient if he did not do all of them. The pumpkin-cheek routine: Crouching like a monkey, his hands almost dragging on the floor, he puffs up his cheeks to an impossible size, goggles his eyes, shakes his head, and then lets the air out slowly, his cheeks flapping like a streamer in the wind. The fit-of-laughter routine: He starts to tell a story in a complicated language and suddenly has an uncontrollable fit of laughter, roaring and coughing and beating on his chest and almost having convulsions, tries to get back to the story, says a few more unintelligible words, and laughs again until he rolls on the ground, covered with tears and sweat. The routine of the very old African man: He picks up a cudgel, dresses in rags, pulls in his lips over his teeth to pretend he is toothless, and comes in walking with great difficulty, speaking invented African words and dancing a hobbling dance, during which he seems about to fall all the time, but before he touches the ground he ricochets against something unseen and stands vertically, as if made of rubber. And many other routines, songs, and pranks all over the house, even taking liberties when he felt he could, calling the baron Uncle, the baroness Aunt, the children cousins, and Amleto a relative on the black side of the family, ho-ho-ho-ho! And what of letting the children ride on his back, clop-clop-clop, being spurred by the boy Vasco Miguel, carrying the little girl on his shoulders, blowing bamboo whistles, answering the same questions time and again?

But it's work! Everything you get in this world you get through work, and if you are black you get less with much more work, so you have to work additionally and work in all kinds of work and work without respite and always believe somebody wants to take away the result of your work. Does Black Leléu work? But how he works, that Leléu! Black Leléu was freed by the will of a Portuguese from Salinas da Margarida, but was not let go; they would look at the paper and read lies that were not written on it. Did Black Leléu act as if nothing had happened? You bet he did! He said he did not want to leave the farm, all he wanted from life was to be a friend and servant of his missy, and if they ever freed him he would stay right there—go where, for heaven's sake? He won his emancipation papers at Christmastime, won a patch of land too, manured it very thoroughly, planted good, big-sized vegetables that seemed to shine and puff out, built a stall in the market, set up a grocery, sold and resold, struck all kinds of deals in all those parts, in Salinas, in Cachoeira, in Maragogipe, in True Cross, in Whale Point, in Nazaré das Farinhas, bought a donkey, bought a cart, loaned money at interest, buried a box of silver coins in a marked place that only he knew how to find. His missy died, they decided his patch was too much for him, they took it back. Was Black Leléu discouraged? Never-never! He had saved money, had procured black and mulatto girls for many, had made favors, had heard secrets, had given presents. And he graduated as a tailor second rank, it's like I'm telling you! Tailor second rank, unerring scissors, master needle, faultless basting! And how many freed people with no place to go, destitute and homeless, real trash, men and women who had been thrown away, he had welcomed, given shelter and food, and now worked for him? If they did not want to work, it was their problem, everybody works, let them go back to where they came from, then. And it was like this that he became the owner of a shop that makes uniforms for the officials of the province, the black men cutting, the black women sewing, every one of them sound and hale and well fed, ask any of them if they want to leave it there to go live in the streets. If you want anything you have to work; that is how you make it in life. He learned how to read and count too, my friend, what do you say?

He learned the whole ABC in four or five days, slept with the schoolmistress, who was brown, old, and hard of hearing, moved in to live with her, won a home, food, and clean clothes, always respected the old woman, never acted dishonestly with her, used to give her good husbandly service three times a week or more, brought more black women to the household, brought lacemakers, had the women making confections, dresses, and embroideries to sell, bought a boat, opened a fish shop, hoarded whatever he could, buried more money secretly in the backyard. The old woman died, he wore full mourning, stayed in vexation of spirit longer than the usual precepts recommended, had Masses celebrated, built a niche in the cemetery, wept hard almost once every day for a whole year, closed the school, opened his tailor shop, put the blacks to work in it, all of them with good food, the right to discarded pieces of cloth, every other Sunday off, and permission to leave if they wanted. He became a friend of the colonel who bought the uniforms very cheap from him to sell them very dear to the administrators and split the money with him more or less in half, found women of the profession for the colonel, found places for fornication. He opened a whorehouse, appointed a madam, set everything up, treats his girls well, almost does not beat them. Does he buy slaves? Too expensive. And who ever heard of a black man owning slaves, particularly a poor black man, a humble black man always in need of the help of the whites, always eager for that help—why, these very clothes were made, with a little patience, from the leftover materials given by white protectors. Thank God there are people in this world like my uncle, my aunt, my godmother—your blessing, please. And slaves really are very expensive, everything is very expensive, and besides, there is no end to the down-at-the-heels blacks and browns one can find gratis anywhere, don't you know that?

And isn't that the reason why Black Leléu, always seeking some assistance and a helping hand here and there, is arriving at the Good Jesus Fishery with a pious face you have to see to believe? Isn't it because he knows that Her Ladyship the baroness is again going to emancipate a slave because of a promise, and who knows if that slave is not a good worker and will not come along with Leléu? Of course it is. He knows some of the ones who may be considered: Negress Esmeralda, still usable by the many who prefer fat women, also good as a cook of tidbits; Negress Constantina, old but spry, and unrivaled in the kitchen; Negro Lírio, a strong carpenter; tongueless Negro Feliciano, good for managing the whorehouse and other jobs requiring a sense of responsibility; Negress Martina, wasp-waisted, round-rumped, small-breasted—anyone will pay for that; Fried Negro, thus named because once a boilerful of hot whale oil happened to spill down his back, a good sailing and fishing master in spite of not being able to move one of his arms on account of the scar; Negress Inácia, all big, big feet, big mouth, big hips, for all household chores and also for those who appreciate large black women;

Negress Benta, seamstress, embroiderer, and spinner. And so forth, isn't that right? Even if Black Leléu does not manage to take anybody along with him, one has to cultivate one's good friends, one has to show up once in a while, offer one's services, make compliments, admire generously, say thanks for things done and not done, the given and the not given—it's all work! And had it not been work to memorize more prayers, chants, and canticles for good Saint Anthony to lead during novenas and other acts, and the orisons for catching a husband to teach to the young women, and all the forecasts with their verses? There is no doubt it was, no one can deny it was. And for no other reason, as Leléu is thinking now as he wipes the sand off his feet to put on his shoes and walk up to announce himself, than his not believing in saints or anything else, for he believes only in work; let him who believes lie down with his mouth open toward the sky, waiting for the saint. A buzzard will come and—bzzzt!—shit in his mouth from on high; life cannot be lived like that. Clearing his throat, composing his face, drying the sweat off his forehead, arranging his clothes, and breathing deeply, Black Leléu, now turned into another person, opened his mouth in a hoarse laugh and started to gambol up the pathway. My beloved San' Antony, I beseetcha from my heart, give me my first husband, and the next I'll find alone!, he sang, redoubling his prancing and looking to see if somebody was already watching from the manor.

5

Good Jesus Fishery,
June 12, 1827

Whales big and small, of any of the many families and races that every year
visit and are hunted here, do not marry like the other fish. The other fish,
from what little is seen of their love, at a still river mouth, in an underwater
grotto, in a pond, in a puddle among the reefs, thrash about in the water,
many dance, a few corner their females in a nook, but they do not touch,
they do not know one another, and their young are like grains of sand they
sometimes eat with indifference. But not the whale fish, which first sings and
whistles when it falls in love, riding the waves as if it wanted to convulse the
sea all by itself. And it also turns plaintive in the middle of its songs, its
soughs of passion being heard every hour, the night music of this time of the
year. From above and afar, a whale is seen streaking the surface of the water,
and then it is no longer one, but two. That is because they go so close
together and harmonized that they seem to be a single animal until the male,
out of nervousness and the need to show prowess, pulls away his head, which
was clinging to hers, swings his tail thunderously, erupts from the water,
and takes flight, forming a winged lakelet around his body, which then soars
in the air for a moment, sinuates to extend the jump, and, raising a
strepitous whitecap, falls down alongside her in the same position as before,
and they go on swimming, mirroring the sun on their bluish hides. Because
on cold days their spouts agglutinate in vaporous droplets, which become
rainbowlike circles against the light, people say this is the way whale brides
make their garlands and announce their weddings to the others. And suddenly he and she are singing together, and they prance on the surf, they
wallow with their bellies up, they roll, disappear, and emerge again, and
again they disappear, rolling and hugging and diving to the deep, and in the
deep they are so much in love they cannot contain themselves. Turning over

near him, she stares with admiration at the great colored pillar presenting itself like a maypole from the folds of his belly, her own folds blossoming in throbbing reds, purples, whites, and lilacs, and so, a tidal wave churning the water, a hump growing in the middle of the bay, a crest of water flickering swiftly, they burst out from the deepness, this time joined together and paired face to face, their songs transmuted into squeals and laughs, their garlands vibrating with the new droplets.

And this feast sometimes goes on for days on end, if the whalers do not come to chase them, while they navigate along all the island's great coast, as Vevé had so many times watched with joy and curiosity, dreaming afterward that Custódio and she were two giant fish courting in the ocean. And they might well have been like those fish, romping naked in the shallows of the sandbanks, loving one another freely in and out of the water, and weaving their own garlands on those nights when the water is especially luminescent and any of it that splatters is like liquid light. When she had seen the whales making love or when she had looked at Custódio, tall and muscular, his thick legs molded under his dripping-wet short pants, his round, well-shaped buttocks, all the curvy shapes she knew and did not know, she had felt her flesh quiver like the skin of a horse shooing flies away, and had thought for a long time, now and again rolling all night on her straw mat, of running out to see him, catch him in his sleep, and do things with him. She did not know precisely what things, but she knew she wanted to rub her hand over his skin, not his clothing, she wanted to discover him and reveal him, and when she was dreaming like that she did not want him to wake up the moment she got there; she did not want him to be a statue, she wanted him warm and alive, she wanted to see if his skin was aroused as she touched it with the tip of her fingers, but she did not want him to wake up at once. She preferred to enjoy him a little while he was helpless like that and beautiful like a child, to be able to look at him, celebrating all by herself that warm nearness which altered her pulse, and when he woke he would find her relaxed and serene, aware of being damp between her legs, opening them for him to enter her gently as she knew he would, with his tender, loving power, with the yearning to fly that would come over them, as fused together as the great fish that also take off as one to the sky.

Ah yes, she thought, her face stinging and her crotch not damp but burning and ravaged, a reason not for pride and contentment but for shame, nausea, and despair—and nothing, nothing, nothing, nothing in the world but nothing, nothing, nothing, and the retching that constricted her belly, pushing her cramped stomach up to her throat, and the hate that made her head crackle with a blinding pain, and the certainty that nothing, nothing, nothing would ever be able to clean her, not water, not blood, not sandpaper rubbed all over her body, nothing, nothing, nothing! What was she? That, only that thing, that heap, that bundle, that mop, that pile of trash and nothing, for she could not even bring herself to cry, though she wanted to very much. And neither could she move nor make any sound, as if the neck that the baron had squeezed with just one hand had become forever rigid and frozen, hardly allowing her to breathe, as she lay paralyzed and mute, a dead, stiff fish. What can be done now? To get up, to straighten her body, still twisted in the same position it had got into when he had pushed her and cleaned himself with the rags he had torn out of her white shirtwaist, one of the many positions he had forced her into, turning her around and about with brutality and exposing her like a chicken being plucked? To stroke her face, swollen by all the slaps and punches he had given her, to wipe off the blood trickling from her gums mixed with saliva, to straighten her lips, which she knew were flaccid and hanging limply—never again the same lips, never again anything, just nothing, nothing, nothing! Do something? Nothing to do, nothing to be, and she noticed she could not even hear any sound, not even leaves stirring in the wind, nor noises of animals, nor people's voices, nor anything. She could move her eyes, though, and then she saw the door he had not pulled shut when he left, the pictures of saints on the wall, foreman Almério's trunk, with a grimy piece of cloth sticking from under the half-closed lid, the china closet, with little colored glasses and knick-knacks on the shelves, the window, with half of it opening sideways and a transom of the bascule type, the lines made by sunlight squeezing through the slits in the wood, fine dust floating almost festively in those bright little beams that hit the flagstone floor, the smell of fresh coconut oil coming in through the door like a fallow vapor, the straw-matted bed all convoluted and rumpled, the stone vase bristling with dry daisy stems at the foot of the image of Our Lady of Support, the water pitcher inside a blue-rimmed white basin, the black wick of a candle rising in the middle of a mound of petrified tallow on the windowsill, a clay water jug decorated with painted bas-relief arabesques, a lamp about to fall down from its hook and a little green bug drowned in the oil around the wick, the glass shingle on the roof almost entirely covered with dust and dry leaves, the stained leather whip lying on the floor, the pot where the baron had urinated standing up and facing her before leaving, the polished wood clothes tree with two hats on it, everything too motionless, too heavy, too silent. Everything indifferent, like the world she now was not sure existed, at least the way it used to exist before, or maybe it never existed. For a time so short that as soon as it came she already remembered it as past, a thought occurred to her, the thought that it had all been a nightmare, similar to some of the many she had had before, one of those nightmares from which one wakes up sweating and anxious and thanking God because it was just a dream. To budge, to try again to move and walk? What for, how, what? Very slowly she noticed she was rubbing her fingers over her lips, the other hand going up and clutching her disheveled hair, together with her neck, her knees bending toward each other, and she heard the sounds her motions on the bed made. Other sounds crept back, and the straw of the mat almost rumbled when her legs twitched; nausea contracted her stomach again, the noisome smell of half-rotten, musty straw engulfed the room, all her body went taut, and with her arms stretched, her back rigid, and her head shaking without stop, she vomited and loosened her bowels and bladder, she sat in the middle of all that had come out of her, wishing that still more had come out, that she would become nothing, nothing, nothing, and finally she cried. She cried for a long time in the same position; she cried for many reasons, at times all of them together and at times one by one; she was angry for feeling sorry for herself; she was angry especially because she was feeling shame; why should she feel shame if she had not done anything? But she felt more and more shame, and hatred for that shame that she knew could not be hers, but it was, it was, it was, it was! Because he had passed on to her the shame that ought to have been his; for him it was a triumph, he had left the room strutting and high-headed; and even among the blacks there would be those who would laugh and make jokes when they heard about it, and so much more shame came over her that she wished she could no longer think. Dirty, very dirty, dirty in every way, hurting, hurting so much, she hugged herself, alone, so alone, so helplessly alone, and went numb. In the beginning her skin became prickly, she felt goose pimples and thought she was going to itch all over and pass out, but she just went numb. And without thinking or really being aware of what she was doing, she got up and started to tidy the room. She rolled the bedsheet and the blanket in a bundle, arranged the mat on the bed, tore off a piece of her skirt to clean herself, tied the bundle close, held it with one hand and with the other covered the hole in her shirtwaist through which one of her breasts was showing, looked around, and went out, pushing the door with her shoulder.

At the end of the corridor, in high boots, spurs, and leather doublet, the foreman Almério loomed into sight like a shadow against the light. He halted and then stepped in her direction, and she just followed the jingling and glittering of the spurs with her eyes lowered. He stopped in front of her.

"Is he done?" he asked, a slight grin slanting his mustache.

She did not answer and tried to make her way out, but the foreman gripped her by her collar.

"Don't be a brash little Negress. Is he done?"

"I'm taking out your bed linen to wash, *senhor*. I'm going to wash and iron them and bring them back later."

He did not release her, but held her collar even more tightly and started to talk to her as if he wanted to caricature a fatherly tone, his eyes fixed on hers.

"Look, I have always told all the Negroes, all the little Negresses such as you, that the only thing to learn is obedience. I like every one of you, I treat all of you fairly, but obedience is above all. You've heard me say that, haven't you?"

Because she remained silent and tried to lower her head, he grasped her chin and jerked it up.

"So? So you've heard me say that, haven't you?"

"Yes."

"Good. Good. So how about it, is he done? Huh? Is he? Is he done?"

"Yes."

"Very good, then. And how was it? Come on, answer me! Did it all come out well?"

"Yes."

He appraised her from head to toe, spent some time looking at the ragged spots on her clothes, and inspected the swollen bruises on her face.

"Oh well," he said finally. "That's the way it is; these things are like that; nothing to cry about. There's nothing here that a couple of compresses won't cure," he added, making way for her and giving a light pat on her backside.

What a washed day, this Tuesday, Saint Anthony's Day eve, on which Perilo Ambrósio raped the black girl Daê, more usually called Venância. Really washed, because it rained until early morning, a thick rain, a rain like a summer storm, not those icy little drizzles that never go away and keep on soaking the bones of all creatures during the months of June and July, often going all the way through August and more often than not going into September, remembering that the first waters fall in April, the month of a thousand rains. And this island, as the ancients used to say, is truly the sky's pisspot, so to speak, a spot clouds favor to flock together before proceeding with their travels. One squall after another since Monday night around eleven, and then another and another and another, real rain, the kind that makes land slide, that raises such an indecorous smell of wet earth that many people are disturbed, and clay-eaters are so incensed that they sink their teeth even in wet shingles and potsherds. After that the weather clears up abruptly, the sky appears, very light blue, the sun gets hotter and hotter, though not as hot as in February, and the day is born washed in a way everybody has seen once before, the land and the sand tamped down, the leaves glistening, the air very clean, many novelties right and left, a great bustling about of animals, and a certain unexplainable joy, a certain belief that washed this way, luminous this way, the universe is not indifferent but propitious. Heads up, noses in the air, confident chins—subtle things but just the same easily noticeable, as for instance on the baroness's face while she orders a somewhat nervous group of blacks to sit down on two long benches on the manor's veranda and listen to her speak about her promise to her holy godfather, Saint Anthony. They had brought over the velvet-quilted wing chair, the ash-wood throne, majestic in stature, with its two-rung ladder and its back topped by a finely carved lion, they even brought the French ottoman, but she chose to remain on her feet, because in addition to the flowery gestures with which she marked her words, she needed to pace the floor in order to make expressive pauses and about-faces. She had put on her jewels, not many of them, just a couple, because she knew how a baroness should present herself to her Negroes, although she had not been able to resist the diadem, after all a modest piece that well befitted a noblewoman's headdress—a princess for those Negroes, a queen, why not? She had poured a little flask of perfume under her neckline, had put on the damask shawl festooned with gold and silver, had ordered them to bring over the little secretary with its ivory inkstand and golden quill, had sent word to the children not to play the music box—the baron had bought only cylinders of frivolous music, and people are not supposed to listen to frivolous music on Saint Anthony's Day eve—had stood silently for a long time in front of her audience of black men and women with her hands joined together over her lips as if she was praying, had crossed the veranda in this posture several times. Black Esmeralda, all in white and smelling of fresh linen starch, followed the baroness's movements with fascination, opening her eyes very wide and making gestures of approval all the time. Fried Black, his trunk a bit bent because of his scar, could not stop chewing his gums, and looked around very nervously, afraid someone might reprehend him. Black Lírio had sat down with his arms around his cane, the white hairs of his three-day beard looking false on his smooth face. Black Inácia had brought along a rosary, and pretended to be praying by moving her lips silently and fiddling with the beads in hands as large as the face of Black Jeba, who was trembling a little and had leaned against her as if he wanted to hide. Black Leléu, his hat pressed carefully against his stomach, had not sat down with the others, and stood by one of the columns near the last step of the stairway with his hand on the stone jardiniere, careful not to lean on anything because the baroness berated most severely whoever propped himself against any object, a habit caused by natural-born indolence she could not permit, saying it gave her great shame. He did not have to sit with the others, he was not one of the house's blacks, he was a free and documented man, he was there as a friend of the family, to approve and nod when the baroness looked at him after one sentence or another, for he had attended two or three of those solemnities before and was sure of how to act properly, even of the expression he should adopt—a frown, eyes on the infinite, lips curved downward, a change of supporting foot now and then—which he had learned from watching the whites listening to important speeches. And while he was waiting for the baroness to begin speaking, he used the opportunity to evaluate the blacks present and was a little disappointed; there were few of them, and only two or three were worth anything—Black Jeba, for instance, he would not take if he were paid.

Sitting on the ottoman behind the secretary, ankles crossed under his vast scapular, Brother Hilário started to shake his legs and looked at Teolina, who was sitting very composedly and with her eyes lowered at the other end of the porch. The baroness uncoupled her hands, moved her head like someone who has just concluded some deep thinking, walked over to the secretary, rapped on it slowly, and inspected the group.

"Are the ones from the small quarters all here as I ordered?" she asked with a hollow grin.

The group fidgeted; Black Leléu changed his footing. The baroness looked at Teolina and sighed.

"Why, my dear friend, at each question we ask these people, each question that does not have to do with the duties of the kitchen and the economy, the simple tasks they can hardly perform, are we confronted with this . . . this fidgeting and this discomfort, as though their tongues were stuck? Are they perchance afraid of me? Hah, very few of them know what they should be truly afraid of in this world, very few! Have you ever seen anything like it? They all look like they do not have anything to say for themselves."

"The ones from the small quarters are all here; I counted them," Teolina said. "There is only one missing, Venância. They told me she is in a bad way."

"In a bad way? It must be really bad, for her to ignore a summons from her mistress!"

The blacks stirred again; Black Jeba almost cuddled up to Inácia. The baroness turned and stretched her arm in his direction.

"You!" she said with authority. "You tell me about this bad way in which Negress Venância is."

"Hoom!" Black Jeba answered, pouting so much he seemed to be about to cry. "Hoom!"

"Come on, tell me. Your tongue has not been cut off, has it?"

Black Jeba looked at Feliciano, and seemed to become even smaller than before.

"No, Missy, no, *senhora*."

"So . . ."

"I don't know very well; it was an evil that came over her. An evil, kind of."

The baroness sought a general opinion with her eyes.

"Come now, what is this evil?"

"It was a great evil that came over her," Esmeralda interjected. "A great evil. May I speak?"

The baroness sighed again.

"Then I will speak. I think it is . . . I think she has the disease."

The other blacks became very restless; the baroness thought she had blushed; Teolina started looking down again.

"But . . ." the baroness said, a little unsettled.

"My godmother, may I?" Black Leléu asked, holding his hat with both hands and taking a kind of half-step forward. "She does not have what Esmeralda said. I saw her, she is sick, she has the colics, the 'emorrhage, it was an illness that came but will go away. She took tea, she had a bath with *zunzo* herb, she put on a compress, the fever is nearly all gone, and she is just feeling dizzy now."

"I know that type of dizziness," the baroness scoffed. "These people are hopeless. Well, too bad for her. As long as she is not here, she not only misses an occasion to elevate herself a little but also, and most assuredly, the occasion to be contemplated, because I have not made up my mind yet, and were not a promise to a saint a sacred, inviolable act, I would have long desisted from all this that only gives me worries and headaches."

Very well, but it was time to settle the question her piety and love for good works had imposed on her, no matter how burdensome. What boorish faces, my God in heaven, what terribly ugly features, all there like monkeys on a limb. The baroness made it clear how resigned she had to be, mused silently for a while, and started to pace the floor back and forth in front of the group. Who among you knows the names of the three Persons of the Holy Trinity? Come now. I heard *Senhora* Teolina teach that to all of you time and again, reading from the lectionary loud and clear. The Persons are three; it is a very simple question. You, Inácia, praying with such fervor, do you know the answer? The Virgin Mary? The Virgin and Holy Mother of Christ, a Person of the Holy Trinity? But where are we, so much ignorance clamors to heaven, so much stupidity! And so much laziness! The great truth of the Holy Mother Church is not above the understanding even of Negroes and savages! For does not Black Leovigildo, here present, know the answer?

"Father, Son, and Holy Ghost," Leléu said, and crossed himself, with his eyes turned up.

Father, Son, and Holy Ghost! The baroness pressed her hands to her lap and quietly implored the saints for resignation and patience. All the Negroes had been bathed in the sacred water of baptism following the tradition of the house, but were they nothing but baptized animals? How could one celebrate the office of the vigil, receive the yearly invocative blessing, practice so many venerable, exalted liturgies, with the participation of such unlearned people? What a shameful experience for her; how ashamed they made her! Very well, what is baptism, what is the holy sacrament of baptism? Just the blessed water, just the holy oils? But of course it is the salt too, but of course that is not what I asked! What is baptism? Must we explain everything day in and day out, everything once again and again and again, until Judgment Day? What is the original sin? What is a confession? Confirmation? Eucharistic wafer? Excommunication? Nothing, nothing, nothing? Who knows at least the Hail Mary words? Brother Hilário, most kind and enlightened servant of God, how is it possible to illuminate the obscurity of these souls, almost lost through ignorance and lack of understanding? How can we practice charity without its recipient being able to extol God's infinite goodness? Would not the holy doctors of the Church disapprove of such conduct?

Brother Hilário rose and remained silent for some time, his head low and the light reflecting on his tonsure. Making a sign for the blacks to do as she was going to do, Teolina rose too, clasped her blue-ribboned prayer book, waited for the friar to start speaking, and crossed herself hesitantly. The friar said that Her Ladyship the baroness was right in wishing to enlighten the minds of those simple people, but there was a limit to everything in this world, even to the power and reach of good deeds. Therefore it was up to the good Christian to bear with resignation the burden imposed by the need to deal with people of such ignorance and such tenuous humanity. No, Your Ladyship, the holy doctors would not disagree, rather they would sympathize with your discouragement, your disillusion, your discontent, which but underline even further the merits your modesty strives to conceal but fame promulgates throughout all these lands. And let those blacks present raise their thoughts to the Lord. Let them try to verify, through an honest examination of their consciences, if their sins and faults would not make them unworthy of the grace that was about to be bestowed by His Ladyship's benevolent hands. He was going to tell them once more the fable of the black saint—and the good Lord, our good Jesus, could make saints out of slaves, nothing for Him was impossible—who was the slave of Levantine Christians and had often refused his masters' offer of the benefit of emancipation because he did not believe he deserved it. Let them ponder that example, let them appreciate the effort and dedication of their mistress, so willing to free one of them, although they did not deserve it, even if for no other reason than the little devotion they demonstrated.

The baroness's and Teolina's eyes were filled with so many tears by the images the friar evoked, which enthralled them so much and transported them to such dizzying heights, that they did not notice the little black Nicodemo tug at Black Leléu's sleeve and whisper a message from the baron in his ear. Leléu deferred a little—what if the baroness objected? But Nicodemo shrugged and hung his lip instead of insisting, and started going back the way he had come. Why, that no-good, double-faced, snaky black brat—if Leléu did not start out right away he was going to be in trouble, you could count on that! He ran down the stairway after Nicodemo and pulled him by the seat of his pants. What was the matter, why had the baron called him in such a hurry? Shoot, Nicodemo didn't know, he only knew the message. Leléu gave him a pair of light kicks and raised his hand to slap his face. Nicodemo tossed about to pull himself loose, Leléu gave him another kick in his bottom. Don't pull tricks on me, come on, let's have the story! Well, actually the baron was a little discomposed today, a little worked up, he would not sit still, he was sticking his hand on his hair all the time, he was drumming on the furniture and patting his legs, he was biting his fingers, it was really something. And then he had asked: Is Black Leléu here? And when they said yes, he said "Pst!" to Nicodemo, who was walking down the footpath carrying on his head two bunches of oil-palm nuts in a pannier, and really big ones too, heavy enough to make his feet sink into the rain-soaked ground. He called him with a "Pst!" and said: Drop that shit right away, put it down, come on! And he ordered: Go around the house, go to the back porch, find Black Leléu, and tell that double-dealing Negro I want to talk to him, tell that rascally Negro I want him here right now. Leléu frowned, clapped the boy's head just because he had repeated the baron's words with too much pleasure, and let him go with a shove. What could that mean? So the baron was worked up, was fretting and worrying, huh? Leléu almost stopped, and he took two or three very slow steps, his face brightening in a cautious grin. Why, that was it, but of course, it's more than clear, it's as clear as light! The black girl Daê, Black Venância, Dadinha's granddaughter, who was out of sorts in the big slave quarters, nearly dead, nearly bloodless, and shaking all over, had got that way because Good Massa Baron Perilo Ambrósio had visited her! That black girl who was not at the porch because she was putting on compresses and having several kinds of fits, crying fits, fever fits, shaking fits, but it will go away, it will go away! He started to walk faster, having to restrain his feet from jumping, flapped his arms like a rooster, and hurried toward the entrance of the baron's study.

"Did you see the Negress?" the baron asked as soon as Leléu entered, with barely time to doff his hat.

"The Negress Vevé, Massa, the one who was assigned to the small quarters and is now at the big quarters?"

"What other goddamned Negress would I be talking about if not that one? You know perfectly well what happened; don't start any of your clowning; I've got no patience for it. Tell me, has Her Ladyship chosen the black she is going to emancipate?"

"No, Massa. Friar Brother Hilário is still speaking; he hasn't even started his prayers yet."

"You're taking that Negress with you, then."

"But Missy Baroness said—"

"I didn't ask you what Missy Baroness said; I want to know if you are taking that Negress with you."

"Sure, sure, sure, right now!"

"Leave the rest to me. Go on, hop to it, call Almério; tell him to make short work of it."

And when Antônio Vitória, as expected, rushed into his study almost at lunchtime, her hands writhing in agony, her nose red, her eyes swollen, and her voice punctuated by sobs, with Teolina two steps behind, still clinging to her prayer book, Perilo Ambrósio remembered that everything had been taken care of, and this time he did not want to listen to the litany she repeated every year. He figured he would manage to hold back his urge to put her down loudly and would consent to explain his reasons to some extent but would have no patience for anything else. Antônia Vitória began her lamentation—"I know it might be said I am a victim of the weakness and indecision pertaining to the daughters of Eve, those—" but he raised his hand with as much calm as he could muster, for her to shut up and listen to what he had to say. He knew very well about the pains and worries inflicted on her by the practice of so much charity, the suffering she went through in having to choose whom to benefit among so many blacks unworthy of attention, whose freeing was likely to cause her more embarrassment than contentment for her good deed. Therefore he had made the choice in her place, a choice he admitted was dictated in part by practical exigencies. The finances of his establishments were not in good shape, those were difficult times. So he saw neither harm nor a contradiction of her promise to her holy godfather in giving the emancipation to a young but enfeebled Negress, who was suffering fevers, vomits, and faintings, and who could even, one never knew, pass her disease on to the other blacks, thus causing incalculable losses. She should take it easy now, go back to the affairs of the household, which were so demanding today, she should not cry anymore, she should not be sad, he had settled everything for her. The Negress Venância would be freed, and Negro Leovigildo would take her with him to arrange for her an occupation and a place to live. He himself would see to it that everything was taken care of by Leovigildo, he would give him some money, it was all settled, and he hoped today's roast beef would not be as bad as that served at the previous luncheons. Antônia Vitória did not answer, though she did open her mouth for a brief moment. She seemed to have started walking toward him but gave up before taking her first step, tried a tearful, halfhearted smile, made a kind of old-fashioned curtsy, her right hand drawing up her skirt to raise its hem a little, thrust up her head with irresolute pride, and left, perhaps a bit too slowly. Standing in front of the door to the corridor, Perilo Ambrósio followed the two women with his eyes. Everything had been rather easier than he had thought; a little firmness had been enough. He strode over to the other door, took two steps outside, and observed with satisfaction the clean, clear, washed day, the kind of day that gives a person great peace of mind.

Tuntum Clearing,
June 14, 1827

Someone who did not know, someone from another place, could think those people were the same. But they were not. And not because of the pallid light of the torches creating uncertain shadows on faces and bushes, not because of the apparition-laden night that surrounded them, not because of their clothes. On the contrary, their clothes were the very same ones they had been wearing at the feast of Saint Anthony to show the dances of the blacks to the visitors and to all the people who had turned up from neighboring places. From other places there also came blacks of renown in all of the bay lands and in many other parts of Bahia where they had visited or been heard about, in order to take part in the dances and mock combats: Black Nofre of the shawm, Black Júlio Samongo of the side drum and the two-headed rattle, Black Lálio of the hand akalimba and the battle wirebow, Black Miruca of the square tambourine, round tambourine, little guitar, big guitar, sackbut, and castanets, young dancing girls from Guinea, with their skirts crimped up on one side so the ribbons and sweet-smelling grass braids around their ankles could be seen, even many who had been cowhided for secretly playing drums in their ceremonies, even Black Leléu, dappled with red and yellow clay mud, and wearing a powdered wig and a coarse jelab with sleeves covered by colored strips fastened at the ends. But the canon refused to see any of that, because the din of the drums, tin bells, and rattles gave him a headache, and he asked how they could endure such a cacophony, a maddening exhibition of hell after the heights to which they had been elevated by the chapel's harmonium. He took his leave from the retinue with a backhand wave, almost a shove, and climbed up on the litter to be carried back to the manor. Perilo Ambrósio, who also felt uncomfortable with all that, was glad they could return to the coolness of his porches, far from the racket and the smell of the blacks, far from the uneasiness caused by those sounds, those colors, those motions. Many in the company decided nevertheless to stay, among trenchers of grits and cornmeal, wooden trays of salted hominy, corn and tapioca rolls, corn pudding, corn on the cob, sweets of milk and eggs, biscuits, confections and gruels of cassava paste and corn, bowls of cooked peanuts, peanut brittle, taffy, molasses, corn flour cakes, butter cakes and thick-crusted drop biscuits and so many other things the baroness had ordered for the people to eat in the day of her celebration. And because she felt an intense secret pleasure watching that multitude—men, women, children, old people, mulattoes, blacks, functionaries, workers, all those people whose baroness she was—gorging themselves on caldrons of porridge and mountains of sweet couscous, stuffing themselves into a stupor, carrying food in their cheeks, hands, hats, and pockets, so much pleasure that she sometimes laughed without a stop, unable to control herself, and because she had anticipated that pleasure, she was reluctant to follow her husband. But she could not refuse to accompany him, and so she did not get to see the blacks starting to form a circle at the far end of the yard, partially screened from view by the crowd around them and by the donkeys tied to the posts of the shed where they had gathered, from which now and then a disembodied shout or laugh came out, and partially concealed by the sunlight itself, which blinded those who tried to descry them from afar.

As if they had not gotten there on their own feet but had sprouted suddenly at the yard's corner, the blacks started out, aye-yay whoops piercing the crowns of the mango trees, an intermittent clangor of metals, incomprehensible announcements—and there comes that versicolor wave of bright-hued fabrics and black skins, clacking wooden soles on the cobblestones in the rhythm rapped by the drumsticks on the sideboards of the drums. They formed a circle, they closed it, they opened it, the voices of the women rose above all the singing and drumming, the circle stretched out like string off a spool, the sticks stepped up their tempo and stepped it up again on top of it, the circle turned into a shoulder-to-shoulder line, and over they come, marching side by side, their trunks swaying, their feet doing half-steps to the beat of the big drum, the sticks halting abruptly every few bars and bursting back out after only the feet, some dragging, some tapping, had held up the beat. A few of the white children escaped from the hands of the grownups to go dance too, as the square was overtaken by the clatter of the sticks, the clanging of the tin bells, the jingling of the rattles, the harmonies of the horns and guitars above the beat, and the black line drawing near like a dancing snake. But soon the grownups recaptured the children and would not let them do anything but shake their legs sitting on the churchyard's balustrade or on the window ledges of the storehouse, while, fascinated, they recognized the faces of the blacks leaping about in that manner never imagined before. Black Leléu stopped, jumped up, and recited by heart the words with which he explained he was the lord of the Great Horn of Africa, arrived there after travels of more than one thousand and six hundred days each on ships with spreads of more than four hundred braças, with his forty thousand lily-white horses, his eighty Dutch captains, his eight hundred brides, his many, many more than twelve thousand soldiers, and now he was going to present his blacks to that great population. Brandishing the cudgel he used for turning into the African old man, he pointed at a black here and a black there, and they executed magical gambols, they acted out a machete fight, the young black girls, one by one, broke loose from the line and glided flutteringly over the yard like water birds skittering on a lake, their heads turned up high, their feet hammering the ground tumultuously and at the same time seeming not to touch it. Black Leléu showed the trick of the cheeks, played the act of the Portuguese nobleman who sends his slaves for punishment at the whipping post, staged a butting match—I'll take on anyone for a good head blow!—danced the dance of Old Father João filling his head with yellow flour to puff on the other blacks, and oversaw all the proceedings until the baron sent the errand boy Nicodemo with the order to stop. They should go eat and then sleep;

they had work to do the next morning. Black Leléu, who had not been paying attention to what he was doing from the moment he saw Nicodemo coming around the corner of the yard, listened to the message with a hand on his ear without stopping his swaying but very intently, whistled with two fingers in his mouth to make the orchestra stop, pulled off his caftan over his head, to remain in short pants and undershirt like the others, rubbed the rumpled cloth on his face to wipe off sweat mixed with dyes, raised his arms, and commanded the end of the presentation.

No, they were not the same, those blacks previously frolicking at the yard and later dispersed in little groups here and there on the clearing. They were sorcerers, that's what they were, witches of the night, wizardly as can be, people versed in the secrets of the Crystal Stone, of the power of souls and of the deities brought over from Africa under the worst conditions, people adept at using wild plants to infuse the most terrible poisonous philters and the most irresistible love potions, at sewing and binding spirits through all kinds of sortileges, at seeing the future in all kinds of presages, at seeing the magical side of all things. Not all of them were alike, because some of them believed more strongly in one thing and others in other things. There were those, for instance, who held as sacred the great fig tree that dominated the clearing, and treated their drums as gods to whom they offered food and drink the same way they did to the air, wood, and water gods. They were the majority, but a few of them sometimes joined the ones who believed in different things. This was because it was common for them to try to believe in everything they could, for they needed to conjure all their manes and secret forces to win some battles, since winning the war seemed to be beyond the reach of their deities, constrained to live in hiding, disguised, and under false names, negated all the time, without receiving the homage due them, without anything that might help them to break out of that clearing once and for all, leaving behind their imprisonment and humiliation to roam freely among their people.

Yes, they were really not the same, those blacks, they did not have the same frisky demeanor they had sported at the celebration; here they did not belong to anybody, as they would anywhere else. And at least tonight they could beat their drums, because the baron, the baroness, and their guests had left. The foreman Almério, a mulatto with many slave relatives, was afraid of the sorceries, and he knew that because he was half black, the gods of his relatives would be able to reach him anywhere, as could the specters of his ancestors if summoned right. So much so that he never went near the clearing at night, and even by day he would expose carefully the cross he carried on his chest and bless himself before entering that ringlike territory where whichever way you turned your face you were always giving your back to something you should not give your back to. The day after a feast on the clearing, he invariably pretended not to have heard the drums and the chanting, even if he was provoked by some black's sarcastic look or by a ritual song murmured softly by some black woman, as though on a windy night such as this the wind did not cover the whole fishery with that sound which persevered through the night like a live being. When he once woke up to find by his door a heap of yellow food and sacrificed animals connected to his doorstep by a trail of manioc flour punctuated by blood drops, he trembled all the way to work, and although he beat the slaves very hard that day he could not hide his fear, and on his way back home he tripped on a root, fell down, broke a tooth, sprained his jaw, and was unable to speak and eat for days. He did not sleep in his house the seven days that followed, he forced both the women who knew invocations and the ones who did not to bless and exorcise the doorstep and the bedroom, and until this day he sometimes sprinkles holy water on the ground before taking his first step outside. Amleto, who had stayed at the guest house with Teolina, had sent for Almério and told him to see to it that the Negroes behaved, to be rigorous and not to forgive any faults, because his responsibility as a trusted aide was even more serious than that of the master of those properties. But he knew, too, that the drums were going to sound as they always did in the absence of the baron, and although his blood boiled and his anger was so intense that he felt like knocking down everything around him, he did not have the courage to open the door and face that darkness infested with threats and unknown events. Lying in the high-headed bed in Teolina's company, a tulle cap tightly fastened on his head to smooth his hair, his eyes wide open, his nightshirt buttoned up to his neck, his teeth gritted, and his palms pushing his thighs, he thought once more of how someday everything would be different, very different. One day I shall be master, he thought, knowing he would have great difficulty in falling asleep, and not just because of the distant rumble of the drums that would loom from behind the trees at any moment.

The orchestra of the blacks was also a different one now. There were no longer any tabors, there were *ilus* poised with their wooden pegs like an armed guard; there were no longer any rattles, there were *amelês,* adorned with beads and ribbons; the gourd was now called *aguê,* the metal rattle *adjá,* and the sound of a horn now came from the flute *afofié;* and there were also the drum *rum* and the great drum *batacotô,* of war fame, and all the other instruments they remembered from their lands or from the teaching of their elders to build here, because they had come from a great many separate nations and were now forced to join together their bodies, languages, and beliefs. Black Lírio, here called Alibbah or Abah-Shoroh and also several other names, according to the day, the place, and the person, made a sign, raised his voice, and with an expressionless face, looking down with half-closed eyes, sang out a few short verses and repeated them in gradually higher tones. From the dark side of the clearing a woman's voice echoed the refrain, and soon other women followed suit, the orchestra started the first beat, the bushes changed color and substance, and the women emerged from them to dance under the light of the torches. And right away, all over the clearing, whether the blacks were dancing, singing, talking, or just walking to and fro, everything became alive and everything was possible.

Because it was the hour when nothing could be doubted, Black Leléu, who did not believe in anything but perceived that the air in that place was different, had made a point of coming. He was supposed to leave the next day first thing in the morning, taking with him Vevé, who by the way was here, who by the way he needed to keep an eye on. He stood near a coconut tree outside the clearing, waiting patiently for his eyes to grow used to the deeper darkness inside, in spite of the torches. Right on the other side, where the music was coming from, he knew Black Lírio was sitting in his wood-and-leather chair, leading the singing, presiding over the feast, and receiving the visit of his deities. Over by some corner, maybe on the spot where the pathways leading to the clearing crossed, Black Inácia should be calling *cabocos*, and Dadinha's relatives talking with their ancestors. At another corner would be Justina, divining and answering any question about the past, present, or future, seeing in water, seeing in crystal, seeing in the moon and the stars. And in many other spots there would be people around somebody or some presentation of novelties. But Vevé is a relative of Dadinha's, knows all the *cabocos*, she has to be with her people, Black Leléu thinks, stroking the rugosities of the coconut tree's trunk and squinting, his eyes growing more accustomed to switch from the blackness of the woods to the flames of the torches. Yes, there they are like a bunch of opossums, bending down as if they had to go under a very low arch, there they go slipping into the woods, Black Inácia, her skirt tucked up, walking as if she was going to fall over on her face any moment while pushing ahead among the bushes. Black Jeba, wearing a white skullcap, Black Martina, Black Honorata, Feliciano of the tongue stump, Black Budião of the carriage, with all his size—all of them, including some Leléu could not recognize precisely from where he stood but more or less knew, and knew that at times like this they would be together. And how about Vevé, here known as Naê, where was she? Leléu was about to start worrying and thinking out a plan for the next day, when he saw arriving at the same place as the others two people he knew were the harpooner Custódio and Vevé, she bending over a little but walking steadily, and he holding her by her waist. Good, it's right there, Leléu thought, remembering that he knew the spot, a crossing of trails that when the moon was up high the light descended on like an upside-down brand, because the big trees packed thickly around opened a hole in their crowns above the crossing. And there the grass, crushed by the trampling of countless feet, displayed black scars, charred patches where candles had always been lit and hands had always been rubbed. He would not go after them, he would go around the other side, he would show up just after they arrived and started to settle themselves; maybe it was better for him to do it that way. He patted down the brim of his slouch hat, looked right and left, and darted back by the pathway to shorten his route to the crossing. As he had figured, he arrived the moment Inácia, sticking the hem of her skirt behind her knees, was squatting down right where the two trails formed a cross and instructing the others by gestures. Inácia had been drinking, something Dadinha never did, but no one minded, just as they did not mind the cigar wrapped in green tobacco leaves that she munched almost without ever lighting it, nor the way she pushed people in the middle of long conversations and arguments with *cabocos*. Black Leléu had almost stumbled over the crossing, but recovered from the surprise in time to be able to crouch down among some low bushes, while Inácia in a slurred voice asked them to be quick and alert, explaining it was going to be a very busy night, and all her *cabocos* were being expected, maybe even *caboco* Capiroba, she was smelling something in the air, she didn't know what, something different.

"Smelling me, Little Nácia?" Leléu yelled from the bushes, jumping out with his legs apart, to fall suddenly right in front of her.

But if the others were startled and frightened by that apparition, Inácia did not flinch and even took some time to raise her eyes, because she had been speaking while poking the dirt with a twig.

"Little you again, huh?" she said. "I'll be switched, I'll be damned, at your age have you turned into a toad, to come jumping at people this way, thinking nobody is expecting this silly prank—haven't you got anything else to do, my boy? What's the matter, you scared, sonny?"

She made some hospitable gestures, moving her neck like a lizard.

"Sit down," she invited. "You're taking Daê with you, aren't you? Sit there, make your butt comfortable. So, are you taking Daê with you? Go ahead, do it. But check things first, better check, won't cost you anything. Huh? Sit down."

A little out of countenance, Leléu chose not to look around to see if the others were laughing.

"You saw me coming," he said.

"I saw you coming, I saw you leaving!" Inácia laughed, enormously amused, and fell sideways as though somebody had bumped her. "But how conceited can you get, how very conceited, of course I saw you leaving, I saw you coming, I saw you scheming. I've knowed you for a long, long time, don't try to fool me, hooeh-hooeh-hooeh!"

"Inácia . . ." Leléu said, not knowing well what he could do to be treated respectfully, not even knowing if Inácia was presently supposed to be Inácia.

"Look at yourself, see yourself, put yourself in your place, know yourself, try to understand, try to learn, don't think you're too smart, taran-tarah!" Inácia shouted, rising and speaking *caboco* language very close to his face, and he moved his head back. "Tarah-tarah, toroh-toroh, tirih-tirih! Put some sense into your head! Sit down!"

He was reluctant to sit down and even started bending his legs once, only to give up halfway, but she was pointing her arm downward so insistently that he ended up hunkering down beside her. He was disturbed by the lengthy drunken stare she directed at him, but decided not to turn away and confronted her firmly. Little by little she went so far as almost to smile, running her eyes over him with a look of amused affection, and began to treat him with great friendliness.

"Yes, yes, yes," she said, nodding like someone who is listening to a secret. She then explained to Leléu that she was positive it was going to be a very busy night and maybe events never seen here before could be expected. And she had barely arranged her circle of beads, lit the candles, cupped her hand over her brow, and started her prayers, when she burst into a vigorous laugh that shook her body in short jerks, got up so fast no one saw how she did it, made a short run to the edge of the thicker woods, laughed again, and stretched her arms upward.

"*Reis!*" she roared. "*Rrrrreis! Ha-ha! Reish! Ha-ha!*"

Maybe he was happy, but he was also very agitated, this *caboco* who arrived in such a hurry. And he did not want to speak through seashells, he did not want to answer questions, and as a matter of fact no one knew what he wanted; he even gave the impression he had come just to dance to the sound of the music of Black Lírio's people, because he appeared to want to go there but stopped midway.

"Well, what you know!" Honorata said. "Who can that be, arriving like that?"

Black Jeba went over to him, took off his cap with a flourish, made a few dance steps in front of him, bowed deeply, and tried to palaver, but the *caboco* pushed him away and swaggered back to the crossing, throwing out his chest to stand in front of Leléu, who was now on his feet again.

"Zitzen down!" he barked at Leléu, pointing to the grass on the crossing.

"Seeneeky!" Honorata recognized him. "Hoa! O tramper of the woods, warrior of the sea, king of the skewer and the spit, *reis! Rrrreish!*"

Seeneeky enjoyed her greeting, and forgetting Black Leléu for a while, bowed in a graceful curtsy to her, as if pausing in a minuet. But he was soon scowling again, aiming his finger at Leléu.

"Hoond!" he bellowed out, brandishing a tremulous forefinger. "Hoond!"

"Dog," Honorata translated. "Yes, dog."

Seeneeky was not interested in Honorata's intervention and did not take his eyes off Leléu.

"Hoond!" he repeated, drawing close and almost putting his face against Leléu's. "Hoond! Zitzen down, minher! Zitzen, minher!"

Leléu took two steps backward and thought about tripping Inácia to knock her down. He was not afraid, but she was getting bigger and bigger and more and more threatening, and maybe she was going to hit him, on top of the strange words she was shouting at him. And she really did not seem to be Inácia; her eyes, voice, and demeanor were different. He leaned over, slightly sideways, just to be in position to trip her, and raised his right heel from the ground.

"Sit down, sit down," Honorata interfered. "Minher is 'Mister' in his talk. He wants you to sit down, he wants to talk to you."

"He wants to talk to me? What does he want to talk to me about?"

"He came because of his great-great-granddaughter," Honorata explained, pointing at Vevé with her chin.

Seeneeky remained with his arms crossed, eyes fixed on Leléu as if waiting for the effect of the explanations. Leléu thought maybe he was having a chill in his stomach, but he breathed deeply and put his closed fists on his hips.

"So he's calling me a dog?"

"Hoond," Honorata confirmed. "The late Dadinha—"

"Hoond! Hoond!" Seeneeky exploded again.

Leléu almost cringed, feeling his temples throbbing and the muscles of his legs tightening.

"Don't call me hoond!" He defended himself in an oblique, insolent way to demonstrate his willingness to fight. "I'm not a hoond, no sir, don't call me a hoond! I'm not a hoond! Better not call me hoond!"

"Who is it, then?" Honorata asked.

"It's not for me to say!" Leléu shouted with vehemence. "It's not for me to say; I'm not the one who came here to call other people hoond; I didn't do anything; leave me out of this!"

Seeneeky hesitated, seemed to be somewhat appeased, paced back and forth in long strides, put his hand on his chin, said "ahn-ahn" repeatedly, and returned to Leléu.

"Jess," he said. "Jess, Ich know. Ich know, Ich know, Ich know! Zitzen down, zitzen down, minher, von't you zitzen?"

Black Leléu crouched down next to Seeneeky, who told him in Dutch *caboco* language the long story of his family, his grandchildren, his great-grandchildren, and his great-great-granddaughter, Turíbio Cafubá's daughter—vanderdicken, vanderley, vanderhagen, shvarze people zuffer! Woman Vu, the *caboca*, she zuffer, zuffer, zuffer, eaten by ants, buried alife head down, you vouldn't beliefe it! *Caboco* Seeneeky wiped off a tear, pulled Leléu's shoulder for him to come closer, and decided to whisper in his ear what he had to say, instead of speaking aloud for everyone to hear. Dear minher, great Shvarze Leléu, Zeeneeky is trusting you, is trusting you fery much! And Leléu should not leave behind the girl's *araçanga* inherited from her father, he also said. And he said that many, many, many things were going to happen, and that Leléu should never presume to be able to imagine what was going to happen, because he was not; he might be very smart, but life was smarter. And that—commen here, commen here, Zeeneeky is putting much, much trust in dear Shvarze Leléu, mine boy, lizzen here, attention, minher, mine boy, lizzen here, attention—Daê was bearing a child in her belly, she had been impregnated by the baron, it was the honest truth!

Leléu tried to pull back to look at her, but she went on grabbing him by his shoulder, her mouth covered by her cupped hand over his ear.

"Inácia . . ." he started to say.

"Huh?" she said, and stopped whispering. "Mine horse, mine horse!"

"He means Inácia is his medium, his horse," Honorata said. "That's not Inácia, that's him. It's Seeneeky, can't you see?"

Leléu almost sighed.

"All right, all right," he said, and turned back to Inácia. "You mean Naê—"

"Zut!" Inácia opened her eyes wide, put her forefinger over her lips, and stood up brusquely. "Shh! Shht! Inzolent, big mouth, tattletale Shvarze! Zut!" and before he could make one move, pushed him hard, and he fell sitting on the ground.

"If he was whispering, it was because it was a secret," Honorata said.

"Get lost, Honorata," Leléu answered, patting his sleeve to shake off the dirt that had got stuck to it, and springing up to pounce at Inácia.

But he did not go on, because something, no one found out precisely what, happened at that moment which made time seem to come to a halt, perhaps a little, perhaps a lot, and some thought there had been lightning, although it was a starry night. Seeneeky, at first making hoarse sounds in his throat and then spinning precipitately toward the woods, disappeared in the dark, although one could hear a cock-a-doodle or a baa now and then, it being known that this *caboco* Seeneeky, usually for no apparent reason, likes to do voices of livestock. Leléu did not go after him, and in fact no one but Seeneeky moved during that unmeasurable time. Maybe it was because after having been attracted there hours before, the little soul got too close, and then, in such an instantaneous way that even souls cannot describe it, it went into a swirl and saw itself now with its memories erased and its conscience dormant, within the little egg that had not yet started to roll inside Vevé toward its nest. And if the little soul did not feel anything besides the impotent fear incarnation causes, and right now does not remember it will no longer hover dreamily in the island's breeze, even less was felt by Naê, who in that instant only breathed a little more deeply, as does every fecundated female the moment a spirit occupies her little egg.

For that reason no one was really able to answer Inácia's questions when she came back in disarray from the woods, her knuckles bruised, her clothes torn in two or three places, her huge bosom heaving, and asked how long she had been stranded out there. She complained bitterly of that *caboco* Seeneeky, who once again had driven her to the bushes, dashing over dry shrubs and thickets with no thought to nettles, razor sedges, scratchbushes, nor anything else, charging against every fence post and stake he happened to run across, to tear them down barehanded in such a hurry it looked like the world was coming to an end, leaving her once more in this condition—oh, how she wished never again to be a horse for any *caboco* whatsoever! But that, as everyone knew, was a wish in vain, because as soon as she had settled down, after having a drink of water, washing her eyes, and wrapping a head scarf around her head, her shoulders jerked once again, her neck threw itself back, and—*rrreish!*—there they went till almost daybreak among arrivals and departures of *cabocos,* friends and relatives, confabulations, conversations, consultations, embraces and advices, the whole night illustrated by apparitions and magical facts.

Farmhouse of the Good Jesus Fishery, June 15, 1827

It is possible that so much theurgy thus cast out in the atmosphere, so many singular events, the very busy night Inácia had anticipated, were what made the second coachman of the big carriage, Black Budião, go out that night to seek advice from the spirits of the forest. He always went to the clearing with the others, but had never participated except to help, particularly Feliciano, whose sign language he understood as if it were spoken. It was actually through him that they heard in detail about how Inocêncio had died in the field of Pirajá, with his blood stolen by the baron to fake war glory, and learned how Feliciano's tongue had been cut off, in spite of his crying and his swearing by all the white saints that if they spared him he would never say a word about it. It was no use—Feliciano told Budião, his arms shaking and his eyes wet—because they squeezed my cheeks on both sides until I opened my mouth, they pulled my tongue out with a nippers, they cut it off very deep with a butcher's knife, and they burned the stump with a red-hot iron. It is not just talking that is made impossible by the lack of a tongue—Feliciano said amid guttural snorts—but you can't swallow your spit, you can't feel your teeth, you can't feel any taste, you can't hold back your drooling, and sometimes in the middle of the night it's as if the tongue had returned to its place, itching and trying to move, but you can't scratch it or move it, because it's not there, it's a ghost.

Since the first time Budião translated Feliciano's gestures for those who were at the clearing, and he made everyone shudder with his story, he always repeated his curse against the baron, which was to the effect that the baron would die a painful, cramped death, unable to confess his sins and taking them bottled up to his hell. He would pat Budião's shoulder and pretend to be taking something out of his mouth to hurl it to the ground, and Budião knew: he wanted to cast his curse once more. And although Budião knew it by heart, he always waited for each word to be gestured by Feliciano, who listened to them with a glowering face, his forehead ablaze with hatred.

But Budião never went beyond lending a hand and repeating the curse every time Feliciano asked him, so they were surprised when they noticed his absence long before the end of the night. In the beginning they thought he had crossed over to the side of Black Lírio's people for a while or had decided to listen to Justina Bojuda's divinations, but when they left by dawn he had not come back. Inácia, dizzy from so much work, said, "He'll be back, he'll be back," but this was no more than an assumption. After all, where could he go and not come back? Only if a snake bit him or a beast ate him or the ground swallowed him.

But no snake, no beast, no ground, for who else but him is coming from behind the cornfield, passing among the manioc ditches, startling the chickens, and noisily opening his way through the bushes, carrying in his hand a pack of leaves and a bundle of herbs, his short pants and his shirt covered with cockleburs. Already daylight, Feliciano tying together a cockerel's feet to capon it, two young girls throwing crushed leftover crabs for the chickens to eat, the dew evaporating from the vegetable patch and the broad-leafed plants, and there comes Black Budião with his crazy eyes goggling more than usual and his Adam's apple bobbing up and down. He did not want to be seen, so he stopped by the flour house's corner and made a sign to Feliciano. He wanted to talk in secret; he was impatient. Feliciano untied the cock's feet, tossed it back to the yard, and rushed over to the flour house, near the plantain trees. Why all the excitement, what happened? Almost out of breath, Budião did not know how to begin, and pointed backward with his hand full of leaves. Had he seen a ghost? Yes, I have, he answered, yes! And letting the story come out the way it wanted, he said that the curse was in those plants. Not exactly the curse, for the curse was in Feliciano's head, but the power of the curse. Why, hadn't he, without knowing how, found himself in the middle of the woods last night all of a sudden, and as if a voice was instructing him and a hand was guiding him, hadn't he plucked those leaves he was now showing, and didn't those leaves have all the power of the curse, really, really? And also without knowing how, hadn't he arrived here unerringly through the wilds, and now if someone asked him where he had been he wouldn't be able to say because he didn't remember anything about the place? With these leaves you make a powder, with these you make an infusion! Feliciano opened his hands, made a puzzled grimace. Black Budião got nervous, flapped the leaves, almost jumped up and down. Could it be that Feliciano did not remember the curse, his own curse, the curse Budião had repeated for him over and over again? Feliciano answered yes, a half-yes, and Budião, with his lunatic smile, said: So? So? So isn't it with these leaves and everything else I've been carefully taught that the baron is going to die a painful and cramped death, unable to confess his sins?

6

City of Salvador, Bahia,
August 23, 1827

It had been over a month since the baron fell ill, and almost a month since Amleto Ferreira, by force of circumstances and the growing confidence assured by his competence and dedication, took personal command of the downtown office on Jesus' Yard. That meant he was in charge of all the baron's businesses, even the most personal ones, because after his illness set in, Perilo Ambrósio alternated his disposition between choleric, apoplectic fits, during which he would blaspheme and hurl chinaware at the walls, and states of abysmal melancholia, when he hardly spoke and spent most of his time sitting by the large window with his chin deposited on his stomach, and sucking his tongue interminably. In the beginning he still paid an impatient attention to the meticulous figures Amleto rattled off around 3 P.M. every day, rifling through ledgers, yellowing paper rolls, bills, and stamps, but he soon became weary of that and sometimes even refused to see his bookkeeper, who would then round off his evenings having tea and biscuits, and hearing about the many woes and grievances that never ceased to harrow the baroness, culminated in these black days of August, the month of anguishes, by the nefarious disease that threatened to deprive her of the loving company of her Perilo Ambrósio, who might have his faults but was a good man. Would perfidious fate always send her one ordeal after another, always a new thorn on her brow, a new wound in her bosom? Was it not enough that her dear, sweet father could not walk anymore and could not recognize even the people closest to him? Would she never again see health reflected on the baron's rubicund face? Alas, not even political and financial subjects interested him any longer; she felt life was escaping him day by day; what sins, what sins are those we are paying for with so much suffering; does not God thus put to an excessive test His best children?

No one knew what was causing the baron's infirmity, described by the surgeon Justino José as a visceral congestion aggravated by a pertinacious nervous weakness. The surgeon had the habit of agitating his lower lip as if scooping up air every time he was compelled to admit the seriousness of some situation, and therefore he devoted the greater part of his calls to flapping his lips while pacing back and forth, repeating his diagnosis and cracking his knuckles. He was not a good patient, His Lordship, for although the elected treatment prescribed his being lanceted twenty-six times and having suction cups and leeches applied as many times as was dictated by the need for decongestants, he would get into a raging fury by the third stab and chase everyone out of his room, among profanities and scuffles, to the extent that the presence of women came to be forbidden during medical visits. All this led to the aggravation of his malady, and presently he was afflicted by very painfully clogged bowels and bladder, which made him howl pitifully all night, leaning trouserless on the shoulders of two blacks, with his nightshirt tucked up, in front of a chamber pot held up by another black and squeezing in vain, his belly transformed into a bubble of fire, dripping globules of a reddish, burning urine at intervals that seemed eternal to everyone. Nothing in the pharmacognosial arts and sciences was left untried, from decoctions and electuaries recommended by the wisdom of the ancients to simmering cataplasms, enemas, footbaths, emetics, sitz baths, fumigations, physics, warm waters, fomentations, special prayers—even the leeches and lancets every time the baron, listless and unable to resist the surgeon's assault, let himself be slit like a rubber tree. But perhaps because the correct succor of good Medicine had been delayed so much, not even those measures were able to bring him relief, and besides, some of the wounds opened by the jabs of the lancet started to apostemate, there having been found no medication capable of overcoming the virulence of the abscesses that each moment blossomed out in new fistules on the patient's depleted body. Now the suffering caused by his choked-up evacuating channels was augmented by the infernal itch from so many boils smeared with vulneraries, salves, ointments, and powders, which turned his bed into a kind of unctuous slough and filled the room with unbelievable smells. Worse than that, when one of the nostrums he was getting used to drinking without even asking what they were happened to have an effect, he would not wait for the blacks to come to him after his call. Afraid that if he left the precise moment pass as he waited for bedpans and pisspots, his bowels and bladder would become jammed again, he let himself go wherever and however he was. And because a copious, irresistible cascade would often pour forth, he was nearly always found still halfway through his relief, surrounded by a waterish, indefinitely colored puddle, by detonations of farts, and by an almost tangible aura of fetidness, at the center of which his expression of beatitude for his voidance brought to mind the visage of a demented statue.

In spite of that, such occasions were invariably celebrated, the concoction that had caused the deluge was glorified, votive candles were lit, the beginning of the cure was announced. But if in the following few hours a shaken, enfeebled Perilo Ambrósio, afraid of again having all his body's outlets obstructed, subsisted on euphorbium tea and little else, he would soon succumb to hunger and to his resentment that the others went on eating as they pleased, and though even the kitchen blacks tried to dissuade him, he would stuff himself with everything he could lay his hands on, in brutish expeditions to the stove and the food cabinets. At first he would stick his fingers down his throat to vomit each time he felt surfeited, but later on he would ingurgitate in earnest and fall asleep afterward, to have nightmares, to moan, to cry, and to wake up feeling sick again. Brought back to work the previous miracle once more, the medicine no longer had any effect, no matter how they backed it up with prayers and promises, and no matter how tenderly, how devotedly even, the house black Emerenciana, better known as Merinha, made him drink sip by sip with endless patience from the cup that might bring about his recovery. Everything soon returned to the way it was before, and the halls of the city manor palpitated once more in the middle of the night, illuminated by the flickering light of oil lamplets and haunted by nervous whispers, while the baron yowled with the pain from all that was tumefying him and could not be discharged. And once more there was fear for his life, because off and on he would sink into a prolonged asthenia, sometimes crumpled like an overripe fruit for days on end, not even attempting to protest when the surgeon, now skeptical about the cure, opted for a heroic treatment and lanceted him an additional fourteen times, showing the family the dark blood to demonstrate the seriousness of the patient's condition. He also prescribed a well-reputed carminative formula based on cassia pulp; he recommended that when the baron felt thirsty they should give him a tea made with ash flowers and senna leaves, as they would give water to a Bedouin; he explained that when the baron vomited and seemed to go into convulsions as he had enemas injected hurriedly up his bowels, it was a reaction that denounced his organism's persistent vitality; he forbade his patient to eat anything that might increase the volume of an intestinal tract already so infarcted by fecal matter; he stooped over a sheet of ruled paper on which he wrote a description of the abdominal organs and their divers humors, sympathetic and antipathetic, listing what in Nature combated such sympathies and antipathies on the balancing of which depended the baron's recovery; he sternly warned everyone about the observance of the determinations he had so meticulously written out, and rising with sweat and science mingling on his dripping forehead, he asserted that the illness had been besieged, as besieged as any disease could be, there having been no chapter of natural philosophy, of anatomy, and of iatrochemistry itself that had not been judiciously applied, and now they could only hope for a good response from the baron's viscera, which were presently mobilized against death in all possible ways. And if, the baron having long not been able to give the slightest attention to his affairs, there was no need for him to remain in Salvador, he should try a change of air, maybe a water cure on the island of Itaparica; maybe he would be healed by the alteration of the surrounding atmosphere's ethereal principles. Carried in his bed to the dock, and from there transported in complete comfort to a boat, he would arrive at the Good Jesus Fishery after a pleasant journey and would certainly be better off there. And so it was decided that on Friday the twenty-fourth, Saint Bartholomew's Day, the baron would sail out for an indefinite sojourn in Itaparica.

Amleto looked at the clock, fixing his eyes on the scape wheel, its teeth visible behind the glass and the miniature-adorned enameled pendulum. It was past seven, because the long hand had started to slide over the second *I* of the exotically serifed *XII* at the head of the dial. He knew the hours sounded just a little after the time shown by the pointers, and waited impatiently for the moment when the wheel would stumble upon a stronger than usual obstacle, would turn with a little bump, and would set in motion the gong mechanism. Office hours started at seven, but he took pride in always arriving by six-thirty, even six, if one considered the time he spent strutting pompously around the yard and Maciel, putting on and taking off his pince-nez, and inspecting the surroundings and the passersby as if permanently evaluating them. Now and again he would interpellate one black man or another, asking if he had papers, whom he belonged to, and whether he had been granted permission to wander around at that hour. He would make comments to bystanders, criticizing the plight the nation was getting into with such a growing number of vagrants and the consequent dissolution of customs, and finally manage to bring into the conversation the very important transactions that were awaiting his decisions. Transactions of His Lordship the baron of Pirapuama, he would add, trying to sound casual about it. Lately, however, he no longer talked so much; he even got to thinking it had been foolish of him to make such an effort to let his position and activities be known. Yes, foolish, uncalled for, even damaging, any way you looked at it. He kept on arriving in the square at six, and he still made a tour of the adjacent streets with the appearance of being on the brink of indignation about something, but he gradually became more distant and reticent, stinting even his formerly effusive greetings to the people of station he came across with regularity. As for the blacks, they got to know him and feared his inquisition, so they would hide while he took his stiff-necked walk, with his tall hat, metal-tipped cane, and impeccably pressed black coat. At six-thirty sharp, promptly as the bells of the Church of the Third Order started to ring, he would pull out of his pocket rather solemnly the large key to the downstairs door and push the door wide open, until both sides touched the walls of the entrance hall. Then, dexterously, he manipulated the complicated system of bolts and latches on the door to the corridor, went in, latched the door back, and turned right, to climb up the wood-and-iron stairway to the upper floor. There the black João Benigno, who lived in a shed in the backyard, ought to have finished cleaning up and been waiting for him by the small office's door. Sometimes he would try to take liberties, like starting a conversation about the rats that had scurried back and forth all night long as if the place belonged to them. But Amleto seldom listened to him at all, usually making an annoyed gesture for him to keep his mouth shut, and complained about the dust he had found on his desk the day before and the garbage he had seen on the sidewalk near the entrance, refusing to listen to explanations, and after telling João Benigno twice not to move away from the downstairs door nor to open it for a stranger without consulting somebody, he locked himself in the small workroom. First he circulated close to the walls and the closets, in a kind of ritual inspection during which he really did not see anything, although he stopped here and there, rubbing his hand over a package of string-tied papers or sniffing a large inkstand like someone who lifts the lid of a pan to smell the food. He then went to the window, tidied the drapes, lost whatever time was necessary to unravel its fringes as if he were combing a horse's mane, paused to gaze at the people around the fountain down below. Here was his desk, under the light from the window, a cool breeze slipping through the blinds, his papers arranged in orderly stacks, the embossed, clover-shaped silver glass-holder in front of the pale blue English porcelain water jug, the accounting books all carefully aligned and pressed together on the shelf by two marble lions on straight-lined pedestals. In this first, lone half hour of his morning, behind closed doors and free to be whoever he wanted, for he was his only witness, all those things gave him a feeling of security and calmness, an ineffable but genuine contentment, a sort of joyful comfort full of vaguely happy prospects. At this moment when he stood leaning on the back of his chair, enjoying this feeling that engulfed him as thoroughly as a bath, he never failed to get up to walk a few steps and open the door to the baron's study. He concentrated especially on the towering carved ironwood desk, the velvet, gold-cushioned high chair, and the ponderously framed portraits on the walls, inside an almost absolute darkness, broken only by the dim light that passed through the opening of the little office's door. Only then he would sit at his desk, lick his right thumb and forefinger, and very carefully, so as not to crumple it, pick up a sheet of paper from the little pile at his side, fold it in two, and, flourishing his pen before touching the paper with it, write at the top: "Schedule." Usually there were no more than ten or twelve items, some of which were transferred from the previous day and copied from the list he had pulled out of his pocket before sitting down and which he would tear up in narrow strips, making sure nothing could be read by anybody who might want to know what they were all about. Most of the items required him to check over papers and documents, something he did unhurriedly, even thumbing through a stack of them time after time to make sure everything was as he wished. He was through around ten minutes to seven, beaming with contentment, even wishing he had a potbelly over which he could cross his fingers and wheel his thumbs around one another. Sometimes he would walk to and fro, sometimes he talked to himself, sometimes he took to arranging the objects on his desk with such precision that he closed one eye to ascertain the exactness of their alignment, sometimes he stared at the mechanism of the clock.

The scape wheel got briefly stuck, took more time in the same position than he had expected, tumbled forward suddenly, the gong spring whined, and seven o'clock started to sound. Amleto counted the chimes with pleasure, and at the sound of the sixth one he rose to unfasten the lock of his office's front door. He opened it, and before him, holding his hat and cane, stood Horácio Bonfim, a middle-aged mulatto clerk, bucktoothed and stooping, subservient and servile, though always with something insolent about his manner, something one could not put a finger on but that made everyone feel uneasy in his presence. He interrupted what he was doing when he heard the door open, and looked at Amleto a bit sideways, his cane pointing forward. He bowed in an odd way, still not turning to Amleto, and smiled.

"I heard the clock chiming as I was coming down the corridor," he said. "I knew Your Excellency would be opening the door precisely at this hour; Your Excellency never fails! A very good morning in the first place, a very good morning! Yes, sir, never fails; would that the friar who rings the bells had such a good timepiece in his head!"

He knew Amleto liked to be complimented on his methodical habits, and spoke as though he really expected to please him, although, maybe on purpose, his lack of sincerity showed through. Amleto smiled. He could not help noticing Horácio's ill-concealed scorn, but even so he took an assiduous pleasure in confirming that that disagreeable man, who could not be trusted and who obviously despised him, could only inveigh against him in this veiled, crafty way, cushioned by kowtows and disguised as admiration. He returned his "good morning" and interrupted a new compliment, this time on his coat, to hand him a piece of paper.

"These people are coming to see me today," he explained. "I have to speak to all of them. We have a very busy day ahead of us today, and on top of it, His Lordship is traveling to the fishery tomorrow; we have to see to it that everything is arranged in due time. And tell Benigno that when Captain Martinez arrives he should lead him upstairs and let him in immediately. And if my brother-in-law Emídio Reis shows up, tell him to let him in too, except if I am with Captain Martinez, but in any case don't let my brother-in-law leave without seeing me. Some Negroes are coming too; they want favors as usual; they can wait until I call them."

Horácio picked up the paper, put his glasses on, read the names with a kind of hurried mumble, praised Amleto's handwriting—yes, sir; yes, sir!—and assured him he would take expeditious care of everything.

"Yes," Amleto said. "And if you want to come in, knock only once, and wait for me to open the door. It is not necessary to knock insistently; I hear the first knock perfectly well. If I take some time occasionally, that is because there are subjects and transactions which cannot be interrupted at will; business and secrecy are synonyms."

"Absolutely!"

Horácio spoke with an intolerable irony in his voice and Amleto considered saying something to him, but decided there was sufficient ambiguity in Horácio's tone to make it wiser not to acknowledge his insolence.

"Very well," he said, with his hand on the doorknob. "Very well."

"Very well," Horácio echoed.

He *would* have the last word, Amleto thought as he got back in his office and latched the door. But the anxiety that would come over him now, as it did every day, was alone enough to spoil a little his almost perfect happiness. He looked at his schedule and had trouble rereading it calmly, so he admonished himself and undertook a second rereading, this time meticulous and slow, although it cost him a great effort. He fretted over the difficulties he might encounter in accomplishing some of the items, he envisioned in intricate detail how bad, scandalizing, shameful even, it all might be if something turned out wrong, he fantasized about betrayals, mischances, devastating coincidences. And it also bothered him to have to do things not in the same order as in his schedule. To cross out number 8 before number 2, for instance, seemed unacceptable to him, so much so that when those transpositions repeated themselves, he could not hold back the compulsion to write down a new list, with the order corrected, and there were days when he had to do it many times, ruminating a muffled hatred against everyone who had altered the appropriate sequence of events. Consequently it was with a certain irritation that as he got up to answer Horácio's always stronger than necessary knocks on the door, he found himself in front of his diminutive, agitable brother-in-law Emídio Reis. True, he was glad Emídio had not missed their appointment, but he was item 5, and somehow it was not right to confer with him before talking to the captain. He did not like it, and decided he was going to rewrite the schedule.

"Isn't it too early?" he said through the half-open door, without moving out of the way.

"I told him that myself," Horácio intervened. "And I also told him that Your Excellency was first expecting Captain Martinez's call. But as long as Captain Martinez isn't here yet, and since Your Excellency also said that—"

"All right, all right!" Amleto interrupted, and pushed the door aside rudely to let his brother-in-law in.

He latched the door, tested it, and turned around to speak to Emídio, who had sat down in front of the desk. He stopped a few steps from him, and looked at him disapprovingly. He had noticed only now that he had come in shirtsleeves, with one shirttail sticking out of his high-waisted pants, loose suspenders, a messed-up necktie, and a leather thong knotted untidily beneath his navel. And instead of shoes, he was wearing clogs. And he still had the same ridiculous little hat Amleto had censured so often as fit only for varlets, and he had not even removed it after stepping in.

"Why do you have go around town dressed like a tramp? Mind you, if João Benigno did not know you he would not have let you in; his orders are to allow in only decently attired people. This is not a market square; you ought to be ashamed of yourself—how do you expect to rise in the world going around in wooden shoes, with your shirttails hanging out? And wearing this indescribable little hat you don't even have the civility to remove as you enter someone's room!"

Emídio feigned an exaggerated resignation, took off his hat, stroked his hair, and tucked in his shirt disinterestedly.

"Oh, you have to excuse me; it's because of all the work I have to do. Do you think it doesn't take work to run that store? Do you think it's just doing what you do, sitting behind this little table to write and to do sums and to give out orders in the name of His Lordship the baron of Pirapuama? Do you know how long I have been up and about, stacking up merchandise, worrying about debtors and thieving employees, without a moment off, not even to wash or shave? I have no time for niceties; it's either one thing or the other."

"You should rather say one thing has nothing to do with the other. Work is no excuse for slovenliness. And in addition to that, it is plain to see that you muddle up the time available to you: I was expecting you at nine, and not this early. You think I do not work, but do you know that this kind of thing disorganizes my whole day? Each minute here is valuable, even the time I spend teaching you notions of commerce, which no matter how hard I try you never learn, although you say you work and I don't. Why did you have to come now, if you could have stayed among your hog heads and bacon flitches as you like and come to see me at the appointed time?"

"That's what I'd rather be doing, believe me. But I do not make the schedules of the Treasury Board nor of the customs officials nor of all the others who swarm over the store like flies. And today we're going to be visited by an auditor from the Board of Commerce, who was there yesterday asking for the stamps and the bills of lading of almost all the merchandise we stole from the fishery. I told him we had settled it all with His Excellency the customs inspector general and with His Excellency the registrar—"

"But for God's sake, you didn't let him know we supply free provisions to the inspector nor that we pay the registrar a stipend, for God's sake, did you?

Because if anyone ever finds out about that, the word "disgrace" will be inadequate to describe what will happen to us. And especially to you, let me remind you, so you won't think you're not into this up to your neck."

"I know that; you don't have to remind me. And I'm neither a fool nor a lunatic to tell a thing like that to the man from the Board of Commerce."

"But you do talk too much. For instance, I have told you before not to refer to the merchandise we withdrew from the fishery as—"

"The merchandise we *stole* from the fishery! Bah! No one is listening to us. You have a fixation on fine words that do not fit my lips well."

"You shouldn't say that even as a joke; you shouldn't even think about it! I forbid you to talk like that, for your own good! Let this be the last time you talk like that! You have to get some sense into your head, or it will no longer be possible to work with you, and I'll be forced to tell this to your sister, who by the way is not too happy about you as it is."

"Why isn't Teolina happy about me—what have I done?"

"It's not anything you have done; it is the way you are, the way you act, the way you behave."

"But I work like a dog, I—"

"But what about your recklessness, your lack of a sense of measure with words? Let this be the last time: When you mention the merchandise proceeding from the fishery, call it simply 'special merchandise'; it's enough. Get that into your nob! Special merchandise!"

"All right. So all right, so we don't have the bills for the special merchandise, as neither His Excellency the inspector nor His Excellency the registrar gave us any."

"Yes, they did; I have them with me. But those are different ones, they are different! We don't have the ones he's asking for."

"What do you say, then—should I offer him money too? Don't forget we always have a good profit with the special merchandise, because it doesn't cost us anything, and we sell it for whatever price we wish."

"No, no, not so fast, not so fast, let sleeping dogs lie. Wait till he says something; if he wants money you can be sure he'll take the initiative, he'll say something like 'Perhaps we can do something about this,' 'Maybe we'll find a way out of this,' and so forth. But even so, don't make any offer, ask him to come see me, your brother-in-law, older than you and your protector, the person who oversees your accounts, and so forth. This is no job for you; I'll talk to him myself."

"And what do I say to him—how am I going to explain our not having any documents?"

"Very simple. Tell him all of the merchandise actually belongs to His Lordship, and it's not there for sale, only stored temporarily to be shipped later to one of his many properties."

"But—"

"Leave the rest to me. If he wants to confirm that information, he'll have to come to me, because I am the baron's voice now. I'll know what to do, there are many possible solutions, many ways out; these things are to be expected in business, there are precedents to be followed. Sooner or later they would have to audit us, and the sooner the better; it will be one problem less. So we don't have to keep on going over this matter. I have something more important to settle. Tell me, how is your stock of pharmacy articles?"

"We're full. We even have white linen bandages, about eight hundred varas. Why, didn't it all come as special merchandise with the latest consignment?"

"Yes, sure. When I had those articles transferred to the store, I could never have imagined I would need them again, now that the baron is sick and going to stay on the island. If it was only for the blacks they would get along, for there's no need to take so much trouble with them; maybe if we didn't they wouldn't get burned so often at the frying plant; maybe some of them let themselves get burned because they know they will be given treatment, a bed, medicines, and time off. Many good and honest men wish they could have so many privileges."

"Then we'll have to return the pharmacy articles?"

"When I tell you you are a nitwit and seem to have manure in your head instead of brains, you refuse to believe me. So you really think we make such a huge effort for the store—an endeavor made even worse by your being in charge of it and asking me for assistance for the most trivial reasons—in order to give away our merchandsie? How much do you charge for a vara of white linen?"

"Four hundred reis."

"Is that what they charge around here?"

"They charge much less, depending on volume."

"Very well, then, the fishery buys all your linen for bandages, but charge four hundred and five or six a vara. And since we're buying all the other articles too, make more or less the same kind of adjustment in the prices, from the flagons to the barley, do you understand? At two or three reis per hundred, these little additions seem small but add up powerfully in the end. But let's do better than that. I have here the list of articles; I bought them for the baron previously, of course."

He slid his thumb along the edge of one of his stacks of paper and picked out two sheets, taking care not to displace the remaining ones.

"Here it is. Drugs: I bought three hundred and twenty milreis worth of them, I turned over two hundred and twenty to the store, I'm buying back the same two hundred and twenty for two hundred and thirty. Vinegar: I bought two hundred quartas, I passed on to you one hundred and fifty to be sold at two hundred and thirty a quarta, I'm buying everything back at two hundred and forty. Barley . . ."

He concentrated for a long time, now and then letting his hand rest on the pen he was dipping in the inkpot. Emídio, perhaps dizzied by the speed of it all, tried to speak, and raised his finger. Without lifting his eyes from the paper on which he was listing merchandise and writing figures, Amleto anticipated his gesture and kept him silent with a *pst*.

"Now here we are!" he exclaimed after he had finished. "See, here is the list of all the merchandise, with prices and quantities. This is what you're going to sell the fishery through me. I'm going to make out a receipt right now for you to sign, representing the store, for the total value. And as soon as you can, by noon at the latest, have the merchandise shipped to the fishery on the small lighter *Lidador,* which is docked at the Conceição pier."

Minutes later, signing the receipt over a row of stamps, Emídio interrupted his labors and turned to Amleto, who was behind him, looking over his shoulder.

"Are you going to pay right now?" he asked. "With this money I can make quite a few improvements in the shed and take care of a lot of little things I've been putting off."

"The shed doesn't need any improvement; our life is what is in need of improvement. No, I'm not going to give you any money now, and as a matter of fact I have no intention of turning this money over to the store."

"But didn't you buy the merchandise in the baron's name, and isn't it his money and our store? I don't see how—"

"You don't see anything, you never see anything. Our situation at the store is very good, we don't need any money for it now, this merchandise didn't cost us anything, it involved no expenses. Therefore this money must be used in other ways, for our benefit."

"What other ways?"

"If you do not understand the simplest, most trifling commercial transactions, how do you expect to understand high dealings? Leave it to me. When I yanked you away from your farm plot and your hoe to put you in charge of a few businesses, I didn't really expect you to have a talent for questions of high finance. All right, you may go now; it's all set. I don't know why you're standing there like a mooncalf—close your mouth, man! Come on, get going! Don't you have anything to do? What are you waiting for?"

"Do I tell the auditor to come see you, then?"

"Yes, sure, tell him to come here. All right, go, God bless you, go."

And as soon as he had closed the door, almost slamming it on Horácio's face, he rushed to the desk with trembling hands. He pulled the third drawer from the top halfway out, the fourth all the way, then the first all the way, the second halfway. The carved wood box that had previously seemed to be part of the desk's facade wobbled loose. Amleto turned it around with a slight jolt and picked up the little bronze coffer within its open side. He took a key out of a drawer and another from his inside coat pocket. He seemed on the verge of despair when in spite of his grimacing and sweating he could not make the second key turn. He stopped for a moment, fanned himself with his hands, wiped his forehead, made a new attempt—and this time the key rotated softly, the lock clicked, and the coffer opened, liberating some of the new ten- and fifty-milreis bills that had been compressed inside. Amleto raised the lid completely; a gentle draft stirred the bills. He examined the receipt Emídio had left, put it under the coffer, and counted the larger bills. Deciding that even the fifties might bulge out too much in his pocket, he rummaged through the coffer, pulled from its bottom a batch of five-hundred- and thousand-milreis bills, untied the ribbon that bound them together, smelled them with three deep whiffs, and, counting them in a low voice, separated the amount indicated in the receipt. He hesitated about which pocket to use and ended up dividing everything into four parts, two for his pants pockets, two for his coat's inside pockets. Now he had to close the coffer and put it back in its compartment, but held off for a while, gazing at the remaining cash. Finally, reluctantly, he closed it and reversed the steps of the combination. The facade returned to its solid, unbroken appearance, the round black drawer knobs beamed like living eyes. He sat at his desk, felt the soft lumps made by the bills under his clothes, and spent a very long time leaning back motionless in his chair, his thoughts wandering far and his eyes lost ahead.

Good Jesus Fishery,
August 24, 1827

Sitting on the back doorstep of the farmhouse, Budião and Feliciano were doubting Merinha would arrive with the baron's party. The fishery house blacks were not the same as in the city house, and although a few of them, such as Merinha herself, would sometimes be attached to his retinue, more often than not they would stay behind, depending on the baroness's whims, which shifted like the wind. So near to victory—for they imagined that by now the poisons were reaching the culmination of their persistent action—they feared it might elude them at the last moment, because there was no one at the fishery who could go on with the job Merinha had been doing with such efficiency that reports about the baron's illness reached them several times a week, many describing him as hopeless and some even announcing he was dead, only to be denied afterward. And besides, Budião said, slapping his legs in exasperation, master Júlio Dandão had had nothing to answer when he asked him about Merinha. But, Feliciano observed, crying with the anguish of his speechlessness, since this great Júlio Dandão had shown himself to be so unusual, couldn't he suggest something? How could they accept defeat after such a good start, such an auspicious advancement of a plan so forlornly entertained for so many years, trusting only in a vague justice from the Fates, of whose existence one could never be sure? Oh, I don't know, Budião answered, and got up to pace a little. Who could say anything with certainty about this Júlio Dandão, who could trust anyone in this booby trap of a life? I don't know, I don't know, he said, pummeling the stalks of the banana trees.

And there really could not be a more mysterious black than this Júlio Dandão, master of the lighter *Lidador,* about whom everything seemed to be concealed or disguised. Fond of sheepskin, he went around with one on his back and wrapped himself in another when he slept in his boat's cabin. He hardly spoke at all, but not because he did not know the language; he knew it, he might even have not been born in Africa, who knows—he would not say and no one would ask him. He was black, very black, pitch black really, one of those blacks whose blackness confuses the eye, melding facial features in the dark, his nose a fat, curved tree branch burgeoning in the middle of a mustache that stretched thickly around his chin, under a bowl-shaped, soot-colored hat that he tied with a chin strap made of black braided goatskin. If it rained or the midyear cold arrived, he donned a napped jacket like all sea people and covered his head with a thick hood, all on top of the loose clothes he was wearing before, so he became even more massive and at night he could only be seen as an enormous shade, the brief glare of a lamp sometimes showing the whites of his eyes and the white twig he always had in the corner of his mouth. His name, Dandão, was the same given to the most powerful nightmares, and it was well known that he had never crossed himself in his whole life, nor ever had any respect for crosses, even if just for show. Taciturn, with wrinkled eyes, a tight-lipped mouth, big, bold teeth, high cheekbones, he did not smile easily; maybe he was a Djeje black, maybe a fierce Mina black, the kind that does not trust anybody, blunt like a horse, thick-necked, long-armed, with a disposition to wallop anybody anytime. He might be an Ashanti, who knows, he might even be a rice-eating Hausa black, a Fon, a Bariba, a Somba from the Benin, the Dahomey, or the Sudan, any of those lands of the great King Abomey, who used to make war using troops of killer women. He did not eat pork, he did not like dogs, he neither spoke to the women he saw when he went out nor looked at their faces, maybe he was a Muslim black with an enigmatic mind, as ciphered as his plates and papers with writings like worms, leaves, and sickles, which were said to be as potent as the poison of the dogbane plant. It was also said that his name sometimes changed to Vodoonoh, and snakes had some affinity to him—maybe by way of the celebrated snake Dang, the snake Dang-Bay, the snake Danghee, the snake Obessem, the snake Oshoon-Maray of the rainbow. That could very well be, and other things could also be, and it could also be nothing of that sort.

Those were the reasons why Budião was greatly surprised when Júlio

Dandão had suddenly signaled him as his boat was about to dock at the fishery's pier only yesterday. The block had not even finished sliding down the mast, and the boat was still too far off for the boatmen to cast the docking hawsers to the blacks waiting ashore, when, one hand resting on the starboard belaying pin and the other helping to pull loose a rope that had coiled around the mizzenmast, Júlio Dandão raised his eyes, saw Budião, let go of the rope, and held up his hand palm out, like someone asking to be attended. What could he possibly want? Budião did not know anyone who had ever talked to this boatmaster Júlio Dandão, who never left his lighter when he was here, and spent most of the time in his cabin, fanning a brazier to grill and smoke fish or poking around ceaselessly inside his cavernous boat. What could it be? Budião had thought again, while the hulking boat bordered the jetty with her sails furled, glided to the docking station, and let herself be tied still like a big, tame fish.

In spite of Dandão's gesture, Budião could not wait, because Almério had discovered there was a great deal of merchandise on the boat, and had started to holler at the blacks to move and tote all that to the warehouse. Dandão took some papers out of his leather bag, and as he handed them to Almério over the lighter's side, he saw Budião standing next to the foreman and did not say anything. But Budião thought, from the way he nodded almost imperceptibly, that he had confirmed the signal made from afar, as if telling him to go on with his chores until they had a chance to meet.

The day did not remain as clear as it had been when Budião was at the pier, not only because they had a lot to unload but also because a few dark clouds were gathering around the northwest, hiding the setting sun. It sure is hot, he thought, noticing how quiet the birds were, the bats flying low, cockroaches and flies seeking shelter in the houses, little bugs sticking to people's skins. But of course a cool northeasterly would soon blow the clouds over to some distant place, and besides, his discomfort was probably due to all the work he had done, because Almério, perhaps for lack of something else to do or someone to shout at, had taken the opportunity to have a few extra jobs done at the warehouse.

From high up on the wharf, Budião could see Júlio Dandão's sheepskin moving within the cabin's darkness like a ghost in a cave. He went nearer, the skin moved heavily, and Dandão emerged from the cabin, his body giving the impression it would never finish coming out. The smoke from the brazier, filtered through rows of spits on which small fish were arranged like little mats, curled around his legs, rose up in front of him, and enveloped his head. Budião halted for a moment, thinking he really was a phantom, justifiably named for a bad dream. But he would not be afraid of him, for after all, whatever he was, he was just a man, and the fact that he was a freedman did not mean he was not a black like Budião. He resumed his march down the wharf, and when he got to the lighter, which was almost high and dry in the low tide, and he was ready to jump in, Dandão sprouted all of a sudden in front of him, his hand outstretched to help him aboard.

They spent a long time crouching silently in front of the master's cubicle, the smell of the smoked anchovies greasing the still air, now even hotter than before. Dandão reached out for a small clay bowl full of manioc flour and grayish morsels of corned mutton. He extended it to Budião, his arm stretched out until the other man's refusal seemed apparent. He crawled over to the grid where the fish were being smoked, picked up a spit, showed it to Budião.

"Huh?" he offered. "Huh?"

Budião, who had not touched the meat because he did not notice the offer, absorbed as he was by other thoughts and by that magical boat he had never boarded before, came around almost startled, took the spit, snapped off five anchovies, and returned it. Dandão bit off a couple of fish too, and they sat still once more, chewing in silence. But Budião, a little less entranced now, felt like asking what that unexpected conversation was going to be about. He rehearsed the question in his head, and thought a couple of times he was going to speak, but gave up every time—wouldn't it be a discourtesy to speak before the host did? But he did not have to worry about that, because scooping up some flour to eat and cleaning his mustache with the back of his hand, Budião drew closer to him in order to talk.

"The baron, your master, is coming tomorrow," he said very clearly, not in the raspy grunt Budião had anticipated.

"He's coming tomorrow? So he's coming tomorrow? So he's cured, and is coming tomorrow?"

"It's not because he is cured, it's because he is worse. He is coming for a change of air. He is very sick; he will likely die."

Unsettled, Budião felt his face burn. Why had Dandão spoken like that, with that look of complicity? What kind of trap was being set; what was this mystery? He clenched his teeth and remained very serious; he was not going to admit anything.

"Oh, the poor baron—is dear Massa going to die?"

Dandão stared at him for a long time with a curiously amused look, on the verge of smiling. He put his hands on Budião's shoulder and squeezed it.

"You don't have to say anything," he said. "I know."

"Know what? I don't know anything. You are the one who called me here, you are the one who wanted to speak to me."

Without standing up fully, Dandão, walking like a hobbling monkey, went into the cabin, opened a dingy little bag, took out two bundles of herbs, and tried to hand them over to Budião, who just looked at them.

"What is that?" he asked, crossing his arms.

"Take them. Come on, take them; they are the same ones you picked before and don't know how to pick anymore. Take them; maybe you'll need them."

"I don't know what you're talking about. What do I need that for?"

"If Emerenciana doesn't come, if she doesn't bring over the leaves, what are you going to do?"

Budião became confused and could not make up his mind what to do or say.

"By the way, today is the eve of Saint Bartholomew's Day," Dandão went on, placing the two bundles near Budião. "Tomorrow is Saint Bartholomew's Day, and the baron is coming—that's a good sign."

Budião started switching his gaze back and forth between the herbs and Dandão's stony face.

"I don't deal with those things myself, not really." Dandão continued. "But this saint is the god Oshoon-Maray, and this god only accepts sacrifices of animals if their tongues are cut off first, did you know that? He only accepts them if their tongues are cut off."

Budião opened his eyes wide.

"Only if their tongues are cut off," Dandão repeated.

But how could that be? What did he know, who had told him those things, how did he know about Feliciano, to make that reference to tongues being cut off? Who had told him that, what nonsense had Merinha made up, that empty-headed fool?

"She's neither empty-headed nor a fool. She knew she could tell me, she knew she should tell me."

"Why? And why didn't she say anything to me? I might even have—"

"Never mind why. I, too, want him to die."

"Did the baron do something bad to you too?"

"No, not to myself, no. Here, take the herbs, do your job."

"But how? How will I be able to do it?"

"I know it's difficult, especially if Merinha does not come with the baron's party."

"Isn't she coming? Do you know if she's coming?"

"No, I don't know. I don't know. But maybe she is; it's always possible."

"And what if she doesn't come?"

"Are you going to give up, now that you are so close?"

"No, but it's not a question of giving up, it's a question of having no way to do it."

"No, there will be a way, there will be. There will be a way."

"How's that going to be? I don't know about that. There will be a way is easy to say, but how?"

"There will be a way," Dandão answered with great conviction, and stood up, indicating it was time for Budião to go. "Take your leaves with you, put both bundles under your shirt, stick them under your waistband."

Without another word, he walked over to his hole and curled up inside, wrapping himself in the huge sheepskin that was waiting for him, and gradually disappeared in the darkness. Budião stood as he was, squinting at the cabin.

"Go now." A disembodied voice sounded from the back of the cabin. "There's going to be a thunderstorm."

As soon as he had set foot on the beach on his way back to the shed, Budião felt the first drops of the heavy rain that had started to fall. In the northwest, right where the clouds had begun to gather, there was only an impenetrable, leaden mass. At first with a distant rumble, and then closer and closer, the thunderstorm burst forth, sprinkling the sky with sparks and making the ground tremble. Like a jagged knife, lightning flashed in the center of the conglomeration of clouds, hesitated before freeing itself, and suddenly tore asunder the whole expanse between the clouds and the beach with an unprecedented blast, the firmament itself seeming to be toppling down, a sky of heavy metal and colossal stones. Budião bundled up in the shed, and was dazed when the lightning dived into the sea and did not return after such a dazzling manifestation, leaving there just that solid darkness and the patter of the rain, which, even if unseen and held back by the shingles, still spattered on him as though it wanted to show him it knew where he was.

He related all those things to Feliciano, convinced that something unusual was really happening, something they could not put their fingers on, something they could not understand. The baron had not arrived yet anyway; they would only know if he was really coming after the sun was more or less high in the sky, not this early in the morning, the ground still muddy and pocked by the rain that had poured down all night and had flattened the watermelon and squash stems, and even uprooted a few small trees. The herb bundles, wrapped in taro and banana leaves so they would not get wet, had been hidden inside the hollow of a trumpet tree, where no one would find them or even look for them, challenging the almost deadly black ants that lived there. And Merinha, Merinha would certainly come, of course she would. But Budião repeated that with little confidence, and Feliciano refused to go with him to the port to wait for the boat that would bring the baron. He said he had the work of the farmhouse to do, the hoeing out of the goose grass that shot forth every day among the patches, the sowing of the seedbeds for kale, cabbage, and bell pepper, the care of the sweet-potato scions, the fruit trees, the donkeys and the mules, the manioc patch, so he could not leave the place, it was his fate, better forget about it, and after all, the baron had already suffered a lot, they had had that satisfaction, that was how things were.

Budião, however, knew Feliciano was lying, disguising his fear that Merinha would not come and nothing else could possibly be done, so he promptly started resigning himself, according to his habit and practice.

Offshore because of the low tide, the smack *Flor dos Mares* had anchored, and the first trip of the gig had been completed, but Budião, unable to stop pacing up and down, rubbing the nape of his neck, could not discern any woman on the boat but the baroness. On the first landing, only the pilot and two oarsmen came ashore, bringing instructions for the baron's reception. They gave orders to air the house, change the bed linen, put fresh water in the pots, tell the black women not to make any noise, and call up some four strong blacks to carry a good bed over to the beach, so the baron could be transported in it from the gig to the manor.

"Black Budião!" Almério called out. "Come over here quick, I've got a job for you!"

"I'm carrying firewood for the cooper," Budião said, knowing he should not have talked like that.

And in fact Almério did not like his answer, and darted over to him, shaking a whip in front of his face.

"Did I ask you anything? Did I ask you anything, you black ass? Did I ask you anything, you black bastard?"

"No, *senhor*. But master cooper Zé Pinto told me not to forget to carry all the firewood today, or he wouldn't be able to finish the hoops for the new barrels, he wouldn't be able to do any caulking, he wouldn't even finish the two new tubs."

"Since when do you get your orders from Zé Pinto? Who gives the orders around here? Come on, tell me, who gives the orders?"

"You, *senhor* master foreman Almério."

"So now, you no-good trash, you barefaced, insolent Negro, you piece of black dirt, so now?"

"Yes, *senhor*."

"Go call Sabino, go call Jacinto Curió and Roque Quebra-Ferro, call Silvestre and Dionísio, call Astério, get going, call about five strong boys and then go to the manor to fetch a bed to wait here for His Lordship's landing so he can be carried over to his bedroom. Come on, go! Go and report to me afterward so I can tell you what I'm going to do to make you pay for your insolence; I'll show you my methods for treating slaves."

The baron was carried ashore right after the baroness, who was so disturbed she got the hem of her skirt wet while she fired off nervous instructions: Now what are you people doing, can't you see you are going to sprain his back this way, do you want to kill him once and for all? What are you doing now, oh Lord of mine, and on top of everything you have brought this unserviceable cot to transport the master of you all? If there is no gratitude, let there be at least some sense and diligence! Slowly, he's about to roll out of the bed, oh what are you doing, slowly, slowly, slowly! No, I can't look, I can't look. O God Who beholds everything from above with Thy merciful eyes, please have pity on this daughter of Thine who is already feeling her soul being drained away by so much suffering, oh the poor, dear baron, careful, careful!

But the baron only moved his bulging eyes and drooled a little, his mouth half open, his lips hanging limply. After an affectionate question from the baroness—Tell me, dear, tell me if you want anything, are you feeling better, dear?—whispered so the help would not witness so much intimacy, and pronounced with one of her hands on his chest and the other on his forehead, he kept the same expressionless face and did not make a sound, his lower lip twitching languidly for a moment, only to hang down again.

"To the house, to the house!" the baroness commanded, remembering the example of fortitude and forbearance given by her father when her mother had died, and determined to duplicate it.

She raised her head, straightened the hair that was slipping out from under her hat, tightened her lips, inflated her chest, and with just an interval, like someone who is mustering her last reserves, gestured energetically. Carry on, carry on! The blacks lifted the huge cedar bed and trudged up the beach and the pathway toward the manor, the bed waddling like an egg-laying turtle. Budião thought he should not have tried to avoid that job; it might mean he was going to be thrashed. And even here, near the anchored smack, he had not managed to see Merinha.

He was now sure she had not come, because defying Almério's orders to report to him right after finishing the baron's transportation, he had returned to the beach and waited for everyone to come ashore, from the surgeon Justino José, all in black and clinging obstinately to a little black bag, to the black women and the boatmen. He almost asked one of them if by any chance they had seen a happy-looking black girl, with shiny teeth, a round face, and smiling eyes, with well-shaped arms and graceful gestures, who found something funny in everything, who always smelled of sweet-smelling grass, who always walked as if she was dancing, one who no matter how much time she spent in the kitchen among greasy pans always came out as fresh as daisies. Without meaning to, because he had no time for it and it was not the right moment, he remembered how he had first approached her, how he had just whiffed the air in her direction and done a couple of simple things—wrinkling his nose, sniffing briefly, boldly raising his nostrils, his shoulders, and his chin—and then she received him at night as if it had always been and always would have to be that way, her lap seeming always to have been there, a lovely nest, the place where he fitted perfectly, a shelter, you know? What does one like in a woman? It's hard to say; there are those who like the ones with longer hair like Indian women, or the ones with broad hips, or the ones who affect a certain gait, or the ones who have proud features, or the ones who are quiet and withdrawn, and by those surly moods in which they wake up promise to be such tremendous women as to kill a man in bed, or the ones who only obey, and on and on it goes, that's the way it is, there is a woman for each man, even if she never appears. So he did not know what it was, but he knew what was special about this girl Merinha, maybe her special laugh, maybe her special way of becoming pensive all of a sudden, maybe the special little hairs that could be seen on her arms and guessed in the most secret parts of her thighs, maybe the cheerful face with which she faced the worst situations, anything, anything, anything, an irresistible pull, an unstoppable desire, something you don't understand—where was Merinha, the baron's sweet poisoner, his Merinha? Merinha who had not said anything when he had asked her to administer the herbs and leaves, who had just taken them and confirmed: this one as a powder, this one as an infusion. Dammit, goddammit, shit, Budião thought, finding he was suffering more for not seeing Merinha than for the failed mission, and feeling a little ashamed.

Maybe because of that shame he also felt weak when he went to see Zé Pinto, a soft-spoken brown master cooper submerged under his clusters of mallets, his chisels, his grindstones of several grades, his adzes, his hoop-fastening clamps, his planes, his vises, his pitches, tars, and malthas, his seas of flax tow, his reamers and driftpins, his augers, his anvil, and his thousand coopering hickeys, and asked him to confirm the story of the firewood. He did not want to get whipped, particularly on an unnerving day like this, and he was sure Almério wanted to whip him. He had tried to avoid carrying the baron, not because of the weight but because of the baron himself, so he had made up that story, and Almério had become very angry, he really seemed to be having one of those days when before washing and eating he trounced one black after another. Dah-dah-dah-dah, Zé Pinto crooned, as he always did to calm people down even when there was no reason to calm down. Dah-dah-dah-dah, don't you worry, Zé Pinto said, getting ready to suggest that Almério was too busy with the baroness's instructions to remember such an insignificance, when his eyes shifted to a point behind Budião, and he chuckled.

"We have company," he said, pointing his chin to the shop's entrance.

Budião turned around, and saw a silhouette against the light of the door, and could not believe in what he saw.

"I came on the *Lidador,*" the silhouette said, and Budião was assured by that voice he missed so much that it was really Merinha standing there, come to see him.

City of Nazaré das Farinhas,
July 29, 1827

Talk about aggravation. An individual hits the trail from Whale Point to Salinas, Encarnação, and Cairu, each of them with more entangled, deranged business problems than the next, a really complete bag of troubles, he gets on a wretched little boat rented for a higher price than a white ass in the Congo, and navigate he does, to Mutá, Matarandiba, Jiribatuba, the Jaguaripe River mouth, Maragogipinho, everything an endless annoyance. Then comes the part on land on the goddamned back of a jackass, dragging along a dray full of junk among bushes and shrubs so belligerent they have to have been invented by the Devil, everything teeming with mosquitoes, a life worse than a slave's, nothing but suffering from beginning to end. Then he gets here and he finds more complications and impossible demands, more people trying to make money without doing anything, more people trying to default on their debts, more tribulations. And now that! Now that, just to make things complete! But . . . but whoever heard of such a run of bad luck; it looks like something made to order, something especially aimed at making his life slide backward; its unbelievable!

"Goddammit!" Black Leléu snorted. "It can't go on like this!"

He stood up in order to work out his impatience, but he could not walk inside the tiny space at the back of his vegetable stall. He kicked a stool, it tumbled over, he turned it up and drove its legs into the ground and sat on it. All right, first comes that girl Vevé, always putting on airs as if she amounted to something, as if she was a veritable marquise—now, now, see here, what is she but Cafubá's worthless daughter, nothing but a cotton-picking slave; now I've seen everything! Yes, first comes this girl Vevé and says that His Excellency the honorable notary and registrar of the City Treasury had decided to return her. What you mean, return—did you refuse to serve the man? I don't know, I stayed there the past two days, and then he showed up and sent me back, and said he'd come here later to talk to you.

"And you tell me that as if nothing had happened? Don't you know what that means?" Black Leléu had shouted. "You mean he sent you back just like that? Aren't you a shameless little Negress? What did you do, what did you do there? Now what am I going to say, how is it going to be?"

She had not answered, she kept silent all day. And her saying something would have been of no use, because she did not know anything. But Black Leléu knew. He knew that His Excellency the honorable notary Pedro Manoel Augusto Dantas was expecting a young black girl, round-fleshed but not fat, to take care of his house in Aratuípe, to water the vegetable patch, to mind the chickens, and to receive His Excellency without the privileges of a mistress but with regularity and few requirements. An easy life such as that there are many who implore God for and never find it. Then Leléu thought: I'll pick this girl Vevé and take her to His Excellency so he'll stop picking on me, and peeking at my figures, and threatening to put me in jail for lending money at interest, and all that persecution. All set, all arranged, and now this! Could he possibly not have liked her? But of course he had liked her; she was just what he had asked for, even better: She had all her teeth, which he did not demand, she was clean, which he did not demand, either, had well-rounded legs and a shapely behind, just the way he had asked. That was not the question, then; the question was—no doubt about it, no doubt at all, I'll cut off an arm if it isn't!—that when she got there she wouldn't let him get near her. That is a cheap, good-for-nothing, worthless little black bitch, and it had been for no other reason that the baron had decided to give her away for nothing.

"Yes, but I won't take that lying down," Leléu growled, and stood up again. "She's going to serve him if I have to tan her hide; she doesn't know me!"

He stepped out of the stall and called the young black boy Salustiano, who was slicing pumpkins outside.

"Listen to this well," Leléu said. "Go to the fishhouse and tell Mané Mina to untie that black girl I brought with me and send her over here without saying anything to her—come on, go!"

But before Salustiano could wipe his hands on a rag to go do his errand, the Honorable Pedro Manoel Augusto came into view alongside the warehouse by the river.

"Forget it, forget it," Leléu ordered Salustiano. "You can do that later, I'll tell you when."

He thought maybe the best thing would be to pretend he did not know anything. Meanwhile Pedro Manoel Augusto, squinting behind his spectacles and walking in tight little steps, a bit hindered by a potbelly on top of a pair of skinny legs, stopped for a moment, cupped his hand over his forehead, and finally located him near the stall. He made a happy gesture as if he was saying, "Oh, good!" and resumed his march. Leléu started going in his direction, but he signaled: No, no, we'll talk inside the stall.

"Oof!" he said after he was inside and had sat on a stool. "What a terrible heat! It ought to be much cooler this time of the year, but now it seems summer is already here. Yes, sir, how terribly hot it is!"

He loosened his collar, puffed some air down his chest, and pulled out a handkerchief to wipe himself dry.

"Your Excellency wants me to tell the little black Salu to fan Your Excellency a little?"

Pedro Manoel Augusto hesitated, but finally agreed.

"All right, but only a little bit."

He closed his eyes for some time, while Salustiano worked in front of him with a straw fan.

"Ah! What a relief! Here, here, fan this side. Ah!"

Leléu waited for him to start the conversation, because he knew he would not want to talk in front of the boy.

"You may go," Pedro Manoel Augusto said to the boy. "All right, you may go."

The boy left. He looked at Leléu as if he was organizing in his mind what he was going to say.

"Well," he began. "That girl you sent me . . ."

"I know, Massa, I got very upset," Leléu interrupted, deciding not to do as he had planned because he thought he had better defend himself right off, settle everything once and for all. "Don't worry, I'm going to grab her and—"

"No, no, no," Pedro Manoel Augusto said, waving his hands. "No, no, you don't know."

"Didn't you return her, *senhor?*"

"Yes, I did, but she didn't do anything. It wasn't because of her."

"She wouldn't serve you, is that it?"

"No, she didn't do anything, and neither did I. See if you can keep your mouth shut for a minute; try to stop that crazy grimacing of yours and listen to me, I haven't got much time."

"Oh, come on, Your Excellency Notary Pedro Augusto, I know you are a fiery man, a man who doesn't miss any chance! So when the girl got back, I said to myself: The minute His Excellency set his eyes on her he wanted her, but she must have acted improperly. I started worrying as soon as I heard about it."

Pedro Manoel Augusto appreciated the reference to his impetuous temperament, and smiled, feeling his balls absentmindedly.

"Yes," he said, an evocative look in his eyes. "Yes, but a man must think of other things in life, life is not just those things."

"Your Excellency couldn't be more right, life is not just those things; very well put."

"Exactly. Do you know what day it is today?"

"What day it is today? Yes, Sunday. But I'm not working, my stall is closed, I know the law. Your Excellency is not thinking . . ."

"No, no, that's not it. Do you know who the saint of the day is?"

"The saint of the day? The saint of the day? Today is a feast day? The saint of the day . . ."

"You don't know. Today's saint is a woman saint, Saint Martha."

"Saint Martha . . . A great saint, I know her well, I've heard a lot about her, Saint Martha, everyone's heard about her, a very famous saint, the great Saint Martha. That's right, July twenty-ninth, Saint Martha, a saint of high caliber, a beautiful saint. So my good Massa is a devotee of Saint Martha's, congratulations, it's a fine devotion, Saint Martha is—"

"No, I'm not the one who is her devotee, it's my wife, Dona Marta de Betânia."

"Dear Missy Her Excellency Notaress, you don't say! A beautiful devotion, a really lovely devotion! Saint Martha . . ."

"Stop putting me on, you conniving black, you didn't even know she was the day's saint; don't start lying again."

"What you mean, I don't know? What you mean, I don't know? Saint Martha, O great Saint Martha," Leléu recited, "the great Saint Martha,

"who overcame the dragon of Provence
to take it tamed with Magdalene
for men to slay, also to prove
that God existed in their land.
Sister of Laz'rus, from the land of Bethany,
Christ was her guest for supper oftentimes,
but even He was one time heard to complain
of the attention to His service she devoted
for Martha thought of nothing but to serve him,
even railing with impatience at Mary,
who was her sister, but a different woman,
for she contemplated as the other worked,
but Jesus was aware that 'mid sisters
one contemplates, the other does chores,
and all is worthy if it comes from the heart.
Saint Martha who bears the ladle of the beans,
holds a broom, holds a duster and the keys
of the home where she toils ev'ry day
without a rest, for she is the patron saint
of housewives and of cleaning women,
the ones who work whose work is never finished,
the ones wiping the floor the others sully,
the ones remaining quietly contented
as they happily see they're not remembered,
by those who'd remember so sarcastic,
if all those things hadn't been done,
perfectly done, all in their place,
and this is the mission of Martha,
it's of sweeping and cooking and baking,
and sewing and cleaning and tidying,
and this great, great Saint Martha,
no one remembers; but not remembering

one remembers what one does not remember,
and thus remembers that which is unrememberable,
but for the memory of good Saint Martha,
only remembered by all the unremembered."

Pedro Manoel Augusto smiled; Leléu opened his arms like a circus performer who has just finished his act.

"Yes, you do know something about her, you really do," Pedro Augusto said. "In spite of those unmetered, bungled verses, one can see they have taught you something. You're . . . you're no fool, Leovigildo."

"Nobody taught me, Massa, I learn things by myself; I'm always learning from people better than I, and from the great ones such as you."

"Very well, if you know so much about Saint Martha, there's no need for too many explanations. *Senhora* Dona Marta, my wife, was given this name because she was born on this day; it's her birthday today."

"Oh, really, Massa? Is it too much impertinence if I send her a basket of fresh fruit? I haven't got much to pay homage to her, but if it's the thought that counts . . ."

"No, she'll like it; you may send it later on."

"Thank you, Massa."

"Yes, but as I was telling you, this morning before Mass, *Senhora* Dona Marta spoke to me at length about the life of her patron saint, and asked me to give her that which for her is the highest gift of all—that is to say, a life without sin."

"But that's easy! What is Massa's sin, Massa has no sins!"

"You're wrong, I do have them, and not a few. But I have made the solemn promise to try to acquiesce to my wife's wish; she is right to ask. She knows that every now and then I . . . You know what I mean; you yourself mentioned my reputation as an amorist."

"Bless my soul, Massa, you don't have to tell me! Here in Nazaré, people say . . . Hee-hee!"

"Stop that; they exaggerate a lot. But indeed sometimes I do think I have a disproportionate virile impulse, such a potency . . . Nah, let's forget about that; this is none of your business or anybody else's. The truth is, I have made the promise, I have made it of my own free will, and I intend to keep it."

"Oh, but I would like so much to do Your Excellency this little favor. I did my very best; I had so much trouble to handpick a special one like that . . . Didn't Your Excellency like her, didn't you find her first-rate?"

Pedro Augusto bit his lips, and hefted his balls again.

"You can't imagine. But a promise is a promise, and I shall do my best from now on to live a life without sin, a clean life."

"Yes, a promise is a promise; Your Excellency is quite right."

"And therefore, since I have not accepted the Negress and cannot accept her anymore, our agreement is no longer in effect; I have not received anything from you in exchange for ignoring your transgressions, and running that risk is no longer worth anything to me."

Leléu put his hands on his forehead.

"But Your Excellency can't do this to me; you mean I'm going straight to the poorhouse?"

"It's the law; there's nothing I can do," Pedro Augusto said in a definitive tone.

But he did not get up to leave; he stayed as though their conversation had not finished. Leléu understood.

"But, Massa, all the fines, will I have to pay all the fines, pay for the new permits, the special assessment . . . ?"

"What can I do? It's the law, the regulations, the edicts, the ordinances. . . ."

But he did not get up, did not leave, did not move. Leléu almost prayed he would play a good game.

"Massa could try to help Leléu find a way out of this, couldn't he? The promise was just not to sin; it wasn't to deny helping a poor man in need who's going to starve if he has to face so many expenses."

"Now, now, Leovigildo, that's not quite true. If you take into account all the money you have loaned out at interest around here, only the cases we know about . . ."

"But, Massa, dear Massa, what is this blessed money, just a few coins, a few coppers, and no one pays me back, those people don't pay anybody, oh, if Your Excellency just knew how I suffer!"

"All right, but at any rate there's nothing I can do. If you want to trade, you must trade within the law."

But he did not leave, did not get up, did not move. Black Leléu decided it was the right time; he couldn't let the chance pass.

"But, Your Excellency, is it impossible to obtain even a little reduction in all that money?"

"Well, maybe. I'll tell you what to do: You shall go to see me in my office tomorrow, where all your debts are noted down. You'll do this: You shall pay me half of what you owe, and I'll forget about the fines and the other things. But you will pay cash, understood? No notes or vouchers."

"But, dear Massa, half of it? All that? Couldn't it be a little less?"

Pedro Augusto became upset and assumed a stern countenance.

"Negro Leovigildo, I am a serious man, I have got responsibilities, I am not playing games! I manage to cut your debt in half, and you talk to me like a sewer rat? If that's not good enough for you, all right with me, go bargain with the Tax Bureau!"

"No, Your Excellency, for God's sake, it was just a manner of speaking. I kiss your hands, Your Excellency, Our Lady of Support will help Your

Excellency for this act of charity, Saint Martha is sure to see how kindhearted you are! First thing in the morning tomorrow I'll take the money to your office without fail, first thing in the morning!"

Pedro Augusto got up to leave. Already halfway out, he reminded Leléu of *Senhora* Dona Marta's fruit basket, and remarked that it should not be too much to expect the courtesy of at least one every week, maybe a little fish too, huh? Leléu agreed and tried to kiss his hand, but he did not let him, and saying farewell with an affable wave, he strolled down the street, with the self-assured step of one who lives without sin. Leléu kept his eyes on him until he disappeared behind the warehouse. One hell of a loss, a plague on everybody, curse everything, goddammit! And what if that no-good black trash was really pregnant, as Inácia had said? When he had asked her if she knew how to do anything, she had answered: to fish. Now listen to that, screw it, a pox on it, shit, shit! To fish! He looked at the stack of bills he had piled up on a wood tray, fished up the one on top, and read it slowly. Overdue many days ago. Ah-hah, but if this misbegotten wretch doesn't pay me, Leléu thought, I'm going to tell the priest he fornicates behind the church with the black girls of his parish, and I'm going to warn him. He punched the tray and wished he knew more cusswords. And that no-good pest who is no help at all knows how to fish! Goddammit!

7

It looked as if Júlio Dandão wanted to kill Budião. And as a matter of fact he did; he went so far as to drag out a big hook from the hollows of his cabin and shake it angrily in front of him, as if barely able to contain himself.

"You are the one who should have his tongue cut off!"

Budião did not say anything; what could he say? He did not even look at Merinha, who did not look at him, either. Making a great variety of throat noises, Feliciano asked the same question he had been asking for days now:

"But why did you have to do that, what was it that got into your head?"

"Oh," Budião answered, not knowing where to look. "I already told you, I don't know; it was something that came over me."

It was something that came over him around midnight, maybe a little before, maybe a little later, when he was standing watch at the door of the baron's room. The baron had been getting worse ever since he landed; the word was that Brother Hilário had already given him the holy oils, and no one expected him to speak again or to be conscious of anything. But Budião thought he had heard a moan coming from the room and went in. When he stepped in, although he had been forbidden to use candles or lamps there, he saw clearly, in the moonlight slipping through the openings between the drapes, that the baron's eyes were open. Open and alive, and not rolling wildly as before. Budião was sure he could see and hear, maybe he could even speak. He went near his bed, and whispered:

"Did you call, Massa?"

Perilo Ambrósio managed to move his neck to look at him.

"Did you call, Massa?"

Perilo Ambrósio's eyes opened wider, his lips moved weakly, and he babbled something incomprehensible.

"Yes, Massa?"

But the baron did not manage to utter another sound, and it was then that something came over Budião. He drew his face close to the baron's.

"Is Massa listening, is he? I have a secret to tell dear Massa."

He could not speak aloud, he had to whisper, but he was sure the baron was listening to everything and was scared! Budião contorted his lips, stuck out his tongue, flared his nostrils, made the ugliest grimace he could, and came nearer the terrified baron.

"Hound of hell!" Budião snorted. "You are going to die! You are going to die, son of the Devil!"

The baron shuddered, made a useless effort to pull back, and tried to close his eyes but was unable to.

"Now you are afraid, you bastard, goddamn you! This is for all the evil things you did, for the tongues you cut off, for the death of Inocêncio, for your wickedness, and for being who you are! And I'll tell you more—you hear, you sick bastard?—I was the one who killed you, this Negro here was the one who killed you! Aaarrrr, you are going to diiiiie, to diiiiie!"

He had difficulty stopping, he even thought he was going to finish assassinating the baron right then and there, but finally he returned to the door and immediately felt sorry for what he had done—he swore, he swore by everything, that he had felt sorry right away; it was something that came over him. And if the baron got better, as had actually happened on Saint Bartholomew's Day, when he spoke, gave orders, and did a lot of other things? What a life they had started having after that mindless act, that purposeless lunacy, that veritable treason—what a life! Now every time one of them was called he felt his heart go cold; he was sure it was the baron summoning him for his revenge—and what a revenge it would be! The same suffering every day, the same furtive questions to the black women of the house—did he speak, did the baron say anything? And those terribly long moments the surgeon spent alone with him in there, sometimes with the priest and the baroness—how could they know if the baron had spoken, if he had given any indication? Oh, what an unbearable torment, making them suspect each look, each gesture, everything around. And how much longer, how far into eternity would they have to endure that, waiting for the day the baron would die? And maybe he would not die, no one could guarantee he would die, because in spite of Merinha's arrival that day after the coming of the baron, on orders of the baroness herself, who liked her work, and her having continued to apply herself in the administration of the herbs, no one was sure of anything, and after all, the forces of Medicine were fighting against them, and nothing in this world is absolutely certain. They were guilty, they were conspirators, they would die a slow, painful death.

Budião insisted he had not mentioned anybody's name, he had only said he was responsible for the baron's agony, he had not been able to resist it, he had done it without thinking. And even if they caught him and submitted him to the worst tortures, he would not say anything, he would die in silence, he was not afraid of pain.

"Hogwash," Júlio Dandão said rancorously. "Everybody speaks; there is no such thing. Anywhere, in any war, you would be hanged for what you did, hanged without a doubt."

"But we are not at war," Budião countered. "And I—"

"We *are* at war," Dandão said. "This is a war, and let me tell you something: If the baron catches you and doesn't kill you, I am going to kill you. And by bleeding you, like he did to Inocêncio. Why don't you go out and kill yourself? Honor commands you to kill yourself."

It was late dawn, and it would soon be daylight. Dandão stood up, pulled the tips of his sheepskin over his chest, walked slowly to the cabin, and became invisible inside. Budião got up too, banging forlornly on the lighter's rail.

"All right," he said to Merinha, who was now by his side. "All right, but I don't know why he makes such a fuss about it, I don't know what he's got to do with it. If there is someone who has a right to be angry, it's Feliciano, because it was his curse, and we were the ones who got together to carry it out; this man Júlio Dandão's got nothing to do with it. And in that case I, too, have a right to be angry, because you spoke too, you were the one who told it to him; he wouldn't know anything if it wasn't for you."

So Merinha told him the whole story of the mystery, which in the first place was that the black Inocêncio was Júlio Dandão's son, a secret son no one knew about but who knew about his father. When Inocêncio was living under the power of the older Farinha, the baron's father, Dandão had always managed one way or another to help his son and pass on to him the knowledge of his people and his family, and this Júlio Dandão was a man who enjoyed great esteem among the people of his nation, and this Inocêncio was his only son. After the older Farinha had given Inocêncio to Perilo Ambrósio, Dandão was no longer able to see him but always got news from him through the two or three blacks who shared the secret. And this Júlio Dandão had been saving the money he earned, or sometimes accepted in donations, to buy Inocêncio's freedom, and then he was informed that his boy had been killed in Pirajá, serving in a war that did not serve him, for it was a war of his masters against his masters. He slumped into the deepest sorrow one can imagine; it seemed he would never again move, speak, or be interested in anything. And he soon found out, through one of the blacks who had heard Feliciano's story at the clearing, how his son had really died. A son, Merinha explained, cannot die before his father, the case is not known of a father who has not gone mad forever when his son died, because it is against the law of Nature, and it is the worst curse one can cast. And the author of the son's death is the father's worst enemy, because his presence will always be there, for he committed against the father the first among all offenses, since after that a man can never see ahead of him anything but death.

She then told him she was Dandão's niece, and many times had kept him company while he wept secretly, and therefore there was no more trustworthy man in the world and more deserving of knowing what was going on and with more of a right to be so upset by the possibility that the baron might triumph perhaps definitively, killing him after killing his son, and turning him into a person who never existed.

Budião lowered his head even more, and thought about dying. Dandão was right in saying that honor commanded him to kill himself. But he did not even have time to be comforted by Merinha, because sunlight was rising fast in the sky and the foreman Almério came into view at the top of the pathway to the manor. Budião jumped, although Almério was still too far away and was not looking at them.

"You're going to fetch some eggs at the farmhouse, I came to wash myself in the sea before getting to work, Feliciano came along with me," Budião said hastily, and they left the lighter without speaking to master Dandão.

But they did not go very far along the beach, because Almério saw them and ordered them to stop. He walked in their direction slowly, measuring his steps and striking his thigh with a whip at each stride. He got near them and stared at Budião.

"You, you stinking Negro, I'll fix you today, I'll fix you."

Budião swallowed, his Adam's apple going up and down. Almério turned to the others.

"Everyone to the manor, right now."

"Is Massa Baron calling?"

"Shut up!" Almério shouted, and stared once again at Budião for a long time. "Good, very good; today is the day I'll fix you; I'm going to deal with you my way. This time you went too far!"

He pointed at the lighter and asked if Júlio Dandão was still there.

"Then go over there and tell him he'd better come too."

An almost funereal procession in complete silence up the pathway, the five of them arrived at the manor. Not daring to look at Júlio Dandão, whose anger was piercing his back and heating the air around, Budião panicked at first, and even thought of dashing to the sea, as if he were able to swim over to Africa or some other land, but he changed from panic to a kind of frigid fear, cold spots all over his body, his limbs as if absent, his mouth dry, his stomach all shriveled up. And here is the veranda full of people, practically all the blacks of the fishery, many whites, murmured conversations in the corners, eyes attentive to their arrival. Thinking he was being scrutinized to his bones, Budião licked his lips and decided to keep his head high. Dandão took off his hat and stood still, looking firmly ahead. Feliciano disappeared in the midst of a group down below, Merinha joined the house blacks who were crowding together near the closed door of the baron's room. Almério vanished inside the house. Time became slower than Budião had ever experienced; his mouth got so dry he thought he was going to choke. Without paying attention to what he was doing, he crossed over the veranda to the big window, which was now open. He passed by it, looked inside, and only then did he realize that Almério's sour mood was because of the thrashing he had promised to give him some time ago and not because of the baron, who could be seen there, finally stretched out, stiff, dead.

A lovelier death than the baron's there never has been and there can never be. The memory of the bay lands abounds with beautiful deaths, so many have been the hallowed men who confronted in an edifying manner the scythe of the Grim Reaper, thus bequeathing to subsequent generations unforgettable examples of fine dying. Indeed, not one illustrious family can be found that does not take retrospective pleasure in the several superb deaths in its thanatological patrimony, on account of either the last words breathed out, or the mantle of sweetness and peace enveloping the precise moment of the demise, or the dying one's stoicism, or the splendorous surroundings and most special circumstances involving sudden deceases, or the despair of the people at the exequies—and that is the reason why in these mortal questions no other place in the world can be so proud.

Since the baron's arrival for the journey of no return, all details conjugated themselves harmoniously, in a configuration of unsurpassable beauty. It might have been said that the passing was very near, but it did not happen that way. Although after he was accommodated in the bed where he would hear the ringing of the fatal hour he never left it once, there were moments, even days, when the hopes of those tending to him were reconstituted, inspired by some sign of improvement. This happened on Saint Bartholomew's Day around nine in the evening, when the black Rafael Arcanjo, sleeping during his shift at the door of the baron's room, was awakened by a loud, sonorous call, produced by a chest that had to be healthy.

"Come here, you black sonofabitch!" Perilo Ambrósio hollered, and Rafael Arcanjo jumped up in astonishment, because the baron had been lethargic and speechless all afternoon, his eyes clouded and expressionless, his mouth flaccid, his arms limp, everything seeming to be announcing the end, the corridors still echoing the laments of the baroness and her Negresses, the whimpering of the children, and the strangled sighs common to those who are preparing to weep for a dear departed.

"Would you fry a fryer with a frying friar?" the baron continued to Rafael Arcanjo, repeating the question insistently, calling the slave "the honorable councilman," and finally asking him to bring his ear near his mouth, for he needed to make an important communication to the honorable councilman.

As soon as the black, impressed by the deferential tone, such as he had never heard from anyone, put his ear against the baron's mouth, the baron grabbed his neck and sank his teeth in his ear as hard as he could. No matter how the black tossed and turned, he could not free himself from the baron's embrace or from his teeth, so the house was soon startled awake by his terror-stricken cries, and the two of them were found still in that tumultuous entanglement, the baron answering only by snarls what was asked of him, and Rafael Arcanjo squalling like a hog being slaughtered. The baroness ordered the black to keep quiet; after all, one could easily see that he was not being bitten so hard, and they needed some silence in order to converse with His Lordship, although he refused to release the black's ear from his mouth, making it necessary for the surgeon to pull him by his arms and shoulders with the help of two blacks for him to let go of Rafael, who leapt up toward the door with his hand on his ear and a line of blood trickling down his cheek.

"It's the way I'm telling you, Honorable Councilman," Perilo Ambrósio exclaimed animatedly. "It's what I keep saying time and again!"

Spurred by the energy that invaded him, he did not go back to sleep that night. He ordered them to stack up pillows behind his back, sat up in his bed to examine the fishery's accounting books, with distracted exclamations, complained about Amleto's absence, declared he would dismiss him at the first opportunity, and told long stories of travels and wars. Soon after daybreak he asked to eat couscous, but when the surgeon discouraged it he agreed promptly.

"A little ham, then. Cooked ham with beans and broiled chicken," he suggested.

Justino José reasoned with him that his visceral situation still deserved a great deal of care, and nothing recommended that he eat such heavy meals; he should resign himself to the same tea and toast as before. He did not complain, and in spite of a fever that not even the most severe hot head bath was able to master, slept peacefully before noon. Antônia Vitória and Teolina lit candles in the oratorium, Brother Hilário received instructions to celebrate ten thanksgiving Masses as soon as the convalescence confirmed itself. Even the pustules seemed to recede, now that they had been submitted to the strong exsiccating action of the fresh coffee powder they tamped on them, admittedly a household remedy but respected by the surgeon, who was always emphasizing how right many popular medical practices were, to the point that he reduced the lancetings to at most eight or nine a week.

What they did not know was that through the insidious work of the Parcae, the disease had not relented in its pertinacity, it was just abeyant, treacherously dissimulated, ready brutally to renew its attack. The morning after what would later be acknowledged as health's last call, the baron woke up feeling great pain once more, and although the surgeon did his very best in the mobilization of his multiple resources, nothing could be done from then on to prevent the patient's remaining conscious but a few minutes a day, and some days not even that. Even when he was conscious, his speech was impeded by such a voluminous glossitis that his tongue no longer fitted in his mouth, and his gestures were thwarted by involuntary movements of his hands, perpetually engaged in shaking, his fingers twitching as if picking at invisible bedbugs on the sheets. He could no longer stand any light or noise, and he howled even in front of the slender flames of the candles with which they tried to bring some light into that drapery-muffled darkness. In the last days he could not move his jaw anymore, either to speak or to eat, remaining with his chin rigid, his mandible jutting, his lips curved upward in a stony smile. Such was the power of the visceral congestion that was crushing him with its talons of steel that his neck and shoulders hardened too, an unthinkable, undeserved cacothanasia for one who would later be celebrated in history as the Centaur of Pirajá, hero of Independence and martyr of the Economy. Nevertheless, Divine Providence, always fair when interfering in human fate, saw to it that all ended well through the singular coincidence that the departure occurred on the date on which, exactly five years before, the unforgettable call to arms that opened the pathway to freedom for the Brazilian people had risen to the sky. Because it was on the seventh of September, Independence Day, a windy, dusky Friday, that he gasped twice, with his chest heaving, and collapsed dead. It was not even necessary to bind his chin with a perfumed scarf, because his face remained rocklike, a sardonic smile permanently carved on it. Unfortunately, no one was sure about his last words, but Brother Hilário, who stood by his side until his expiration, wrote down the ones that, in a clear miracle for one who could no longer speak or even see, he murmured in the darkness of his room, a few minutes before the end: "Country, honor, struggle, abnegation. Have I served God and Brazil well?"

Lying in state in the principal church's nave, his ample cadaver surrounded by angelica flowers, whose redolence pervaded everything, he was visited by a contrite procession ranging from blacks to men of position, from the highest to the lowest, every one of them stopping for a short while by the side of his majestic silver-and-bronze-trimmed coffin, conscious that this was a day unlike any other. In a brief speech intercalated with spacious gestures, Major Lindolfo Pereira Neves, who as a lieutenant had given assistance to the blood-drenched baron in Pirajá, offered his testimony of the legendary gallantry of that pillar of the nation, now felled by physical death, but immutably perennialized in the hearts of Brazilians. He told them how the baron, recuperated from his wounds but with his health still weakened by his agonizing triumph against death, volunteered for the most arduous duties, advising, exhorting, deliberating, remonstrating when necessary, making it inconceivable that without men like him Brazil would have been able to affirm her liberty against Madeira's ruthlessness. The professor of grammar

Joviniano de Melo Fraga, in a not so brief speech terminated in an acrostic of rigorously metered ten-syllable verses, added an exaltation of the civic and personal virtues of the deceased, now with the steady, serene semblance of someone who sought the sublime sacrifice of selflessly serving our Sacred Motherland! And much more was spoken and written and will always be written about the baron, his deeds, his martyrdom, and his journey to glory, and thus all the obsequies were concluded, the bishop celebrated the funeral Mass, the baroness was prostrated by eight syncopes in succession, and the inhumation was made right there at the church, Perilo Ambrósio now just a shadow by the tenebrous banks of the Styx.

Big Slave Quarters of the Good Jesus Fishery
September 9, 1827

What a terrible situation, for heaven's sake, is the situation of Massa Baron Perilo Ambrósio of Pirapuama's blacks, every one of them feeling like laughing but having to display these long faces like someone who's lost his father, his mother, his brother, his younger, ripening sisters-in-law, and his last jug of liquor. It's like a reversed party, a happiness ensconced in despondent postures, a song playing only in their heads. And because this happiness could not be exposed at all, it became part of the celebration to exaggerate their expressions of pain, mourning, sorrow, and helplessness, and almost all of them were having fun as in a masked ball. There are always some who overdo things a bit, like that clown Esmeralda, who keeps going into the manor with her face melting in tears and comes back to the slave quarters barely holding back her urge to sing. She made a little doll out of a corncob and scraps of burlap and tow, put on its head a hat like the one the baron used to wear at the fishery, and talks to it.

"How are things over there, little Massa?"

"Oof, what a hot little hell this is, ouch, ouch, ouch!" the doll answers.

"Where is it burning, dear Massa?"

"It's burning my behind, it's burning my dear little butt, ouch, my dear little butt!"

But even if it was Sunday, and many of them were not supposed to be doing anything after Mass, and could loiter in the yard, talking or doing one thing or another on their own, without supervision, it was not wise for Esmeralda to take such a risk, particularly because the laughter caused by her talk with the doll might be heard outside by somebody who might be displeased at hearing laughter so few days after the baron's death.

"Better drop that doll somewhere, better get rid of it," Inácia advised. "Better stop that joking; this will come to no good."

"Come on, Inácia, are you going to do his death ceremonies, the poor, dear, dear, dear little Massa's *ah-shay-shay?* Of course not. So let me do it! *Laroh-yay!*"

"What you doing, girl, you shouldn't fool with those things, cut that out!"

"I think father Lírio is going to dedicate him to Eshoo, this fellow here," Esmeralda said, waving the doll. "So why not salute Eshoo—it's his time of the day, almost noon, isn't it? So *Laroh-yay!*"

Yes, it was the time of the day for Eshoo, the deity who eats anything, but he could not be seen there personally, in spite of Esmeralda's salutation. Instead of him, Júlio Dandão appeared through the beach gate, together with Budião and Feliciano. Dandão heard Esmeralda laughing, went over to her, and saw the doll.

"Better tell her to stop that," he said to Budião in a low voice.

"Why don't you tell her yourself?" Budião answered, finding the doll very funny.

"I can't speak to her; she may be somebody's woman, somebody's daughter, somebody's mother."

"So leave her alone; it's just that they are very happy and can't show it, but they have to show it once in a while."

Dandão did not like Budião's answer, and looked around as if asking silently for someone to interfere.

"Esmeralda, will you stop that?" Inácia shouted with severity.

Esmeralda hid the doll behind her skirt embarrassedly.

"Better burn that doll, go on and burn that ugly thing."

She left to go burn the doll, but first she crushed it to crumbs in a little mortar. Budião felt annoyed at Júlio Dandão. After all, they had accomplished what they had set out to do, they ought to be happy, why was his face so mournful—was he missing the baron?

"I am not happy," Dandão said very seriously. "That's why I want to have that conversation today. Is Lírio coming?"

"No, not Lírio. But Zé Pinto is coming."

"It's good to know Zé Pinto is coming. It's a good thing to have another freed black in this. But why isn't Lírio coming?"

"He says he wants nothing to do with this type of conversation."

"But how does he know what I'm going to talk about? I didn't tell anybody, not even you."

"I know, but he said he knows very well what type of conversation it's going to be, and he wants no part of it."

Dandão bit his mustache, stood silent for a while, grumbled "All right," and asked where they were going to talk.

"Right here," Budião said. "Why can't it be right here? We can go inside one of the houses and sit down."

"Only if I were brainsick. Do people hang around the fish shed?"

"All the time."

"Isn't there a place where people don't go?"

"There are people everywhere; here you find people in every place."

Feliciano tugged at Budião's arm and made a short pantomime.

"What did he say?" Dandão asked Budião.

"He said there shouldn't be anybody at the farmhouse, and the flour house is empty and closed today."

"The flour house? The flour house may be a good idea; he's right."

"It's all the same to me; we can go now."

"No, we shouldn't go together, the four of us. I'll go first, then Feliciano goes, then you and Zé Pinto go. Go call him; come on."

Budião started finding all that a needless complication, and Dandão's tone, as though he were a foreman giving orders, irritated him. Even if he was older and Merinha's uncle, it was not right. It was enough that he had Almério on his back, who had not beat him only because you don't beat anybody in the first seven days of mourning.

And he was still thinking about that, and figuring he would protest the next time, when he arrived with Zé Pinto at the flour house. He stopped by the door and did not hear anything inside. He looked about; there were only the vegetable patches, the sheds, the chickens grubbing around, the buzzing of dragonflies, the swash of the creek behind the thicket of banana trees. He pulled the wooden bolt, pushed the door slowly, and could not see well at first, in spite of the light coming in through the spaces between the walls and the roof. A smell of fresh cassava flour, of overripe manioc, of fermented mash. Budião breathed deeply. He had always liked the smells of the flour house, he even liked the warm vapor from the embers shrouded beneath the ash of the ovens. He peered hard and saw Feliciano standing like a jabiru stork, the sole of his right foot flat against the inside of his left thigh, his hand holding one of the props of the small press. In front of him, crouching near the grinder, was Júlio Dandão, his face only to be guessed between his hat and the sheepskin coming up to his neck. He gestured for them to make themselves comfortable, because first he was going to light his pipe and smoke for a few moments. He opened his haversack, took out a fist-sized pipe bowl and a bamboo stalk, which he fitted into the bowl. He filled it to the brim with tobacco, letting a few shreds slip through his fingertips, got up, walked over to one of the ovens, rummaged the cinders for a live coal, found a big one, blew on it to scatter away the ashes, and brought it back to his place, tossing it back and forth from hand to hand while he walked.

No one among the three others had ever seen a pipe like that; they did not even know what one had to do in order to drink the tobacco smoke, although they had heard many stories about people, whites and blacks alike, who enjoyed drinking smoke. It was not something they could witness every day, so they remained still during all the time Dandão took, after laying the ember on the tobacco and joining his hands over it like a lid, to suck repeatedly the tip of the stem and finally cover himself with a bluish, harsh-scented smoke, which flowed out of the corners of his mouth and out of his nostrils, maybe out of every hole in his head. He remained like a steam engine, solidly motionless, blowing out smoke in prolonged puffs, and every now and then spitting vigorously without moving his head. His face was now becoming gradually visible, and they could see his bloodshot, half-closed eyes and could feel his thoughts were far away.

He finally started to speak, although he did not leave his pipe entirely aside, going back to it once in a while and firing up the tobacco with short, energetic draws until he was again surrounded by blue clouds. He was not the same as usual, and not only on account of the smoke but also because of his less rude demeanor, his softened speech, his tone of comradeship. But just the same he was not an ordinary man, a man like the others, he was still mysterious, though now it was as if they would be able to share that mystery, maybe not now, maybe never, but maybe yes. First he mentioned Black Lírio, who had not come because he did not want to have anything to do with that type of conversation.

"Maybe he looked in his seashells and guessed what the subject of my talk was going to be," he said, with a kind of sneer twisting his mustache. "Then why doesn't he look in the seashells to see everything else we don't know, past, present, and future, and to tell his people what to do, a people that greets him by kneeling down and touching their shoulders to the dirt?"

No one answered, and Dandão, as if he was expecting that, explained that they could tell a people and a person by their greetings, and nothing could be hoped for people who are slaves and who pay homage to another slave by prostrating themselves in front of him as though offering their heads and backs to be stepping-stones or doormats. To greet, he said, is necessary, which is the reason there is no nation in which it's not done, for it means we're not crazy since we know we're not alone in this world, we live among others, and it's only due to the others that we can be who we are, otherwise we are not. It also serves to make the others know they exist, for if nobody greeted anybody, everyone would think he did not exist. It also shows that we're not ignorant, for there is a proper way to greet each category: children, younger people, older people, younger women, married women, older women, a friend's father, a close relative, a distant relative, a man of the same trade, a stranger, and so forth, and you show you're not ignorant through your correct knowledge of all those things. And also, to greet means much more because through it we can demonstrate what we think, what we don't think, what we accept, what we don't accept, what we respect, what we don't respect, it being sufficient that we greet in the precise way, or even deny or reject someone else's greeting.

Therefore, Júlio Dandão continued, this Lírio was proving himself to be truly a king of slaves, the slave king, with his greetings that serve no purpose but to confirm they are all slaves. And he who allows a man to prostrate himself before him will naturally prostrate himself before another. And this is the situation Lírio wants to last forever, because if you're afraid even of talking about it, it means you prefer to go on bowing to your white masters, as long as your black underlings go on bowing to you.

"Our greeting," he cried out suddenly, raising his closed fist and punching the air in front of his face, "is this: Long live the people!"

So you can see, he went on, as calmly as before, you can see this Black Lírio's real nature. How nice it would be if everything was the way it should be! But it's not; nothing is the way it should be. What should be is not the same for masters and slaves. Since we are we and not they, he explained, then the way it should be for us is not the way it should be for them, so it's up to us to be what we think we should be, because we are the only ones who think that we should be the way we want to be. And grinning almost happily, he commented that in the time of his ancestors they killed worthless people so they could carry messages to the otherworld. Had anyone remembered to ask His Lordship to take a message? They could have used his killing in a better way.

Zé Pinto seemed to be frightened by that, but Dandão turned to him, and like someone describing a trivial event, told him that, yes, they had killed the baron. They not only had killed the baron but would kill many more barons, and would do other things equally momentous. And it should be noted that it was not a matter of revenge, it was more than that, much more than that. As those landowners died, two things would happen. The first was that the land would be divided among several heirs, multiplying itself in smaller properties, not so capable as the former to support the same wealth, weakening all the landowners, and fomenting discord through the greed of the heirs. The second was that those landowners were always deep in debts and mortgages, even on account of their expenses with the purchase of black slaves, owing in notes and other obligations more than the worth of the production of their lands and farms, so that the creditors, most of them people who have nothing to do with those lands, will take over the properties. Some of them will take the machines, others will take the plantations, the houses, the blacks, and so on, disorganizing property and complicating production. Each dead rich man means ten living poor men, he added in a tone that suggested he had said it many times before, and out of every ten poor people, nine are black and the other has the blood, either in his veins or in the life he leads.

Budião felt so dizzy he thought it was because of the smoke from the pipe. He glanced at his two companions, and they seemed to be dizzy too, Zé Pinto shaking his head in disbelief, and a restless, exalted Feliciano practicing the salute taught by Dandão. Intrigued by the ease with which Dandão spoke those direful, difficult things, Budião turned to Dandão and ended up saying he had not understood his talk very well.

"Did you understand it, Zé Pinto?" Budião asked.

"Dah-dah-dah-dah," Zé Pinto answered, without looking up.

"You're going to understand," Júlio Dandão said. "I'm going to show you a secret. I'm going to show you many secrets, secrets I have been keeping alone but must now share. All those who used to know these secrets before me have died or disappeared, and I was the only one left for this mission. But a secret that only one person knows has no usefulness; it only makes your mind delirious and leads you to complete madness. So the time has come to share these secrets, which is the only way to keep them whole. But they are not just things to be seen; they are also things to be done."

He glanced at all three, the pipe in his mouth, and sucked in his cheeks until they touched each other, as increasingly larger billows of smoke veiled his head.

"Very well," he said, his face slowly regaining its shape under the smoke. "Let's see the secrets now. You three stay where you are."

He reached back, picked up a brown cloth sack that had been lying unnoticed in a corner by their side, drew it near, loosened the string that closed it, peeped inside for a moment, pulled out with both hands a wood-and-metal chest, held the sack with his feet so the chest could come out unimpeded, and held it up in front of the others. It seemed heavy, because even his arms, which were as thick as a paypaya tree giving its first fruit, wavered as he lifted it. He set it down in front of him, took off his hat, rummaged in it with his fingertips to find a piece of iron with jagged edges, and began to stick it with nervous movements into the eight side slots of the chest, murmuring a muffled chant and sounds like someone humming calculations between his teeth, until he hit the chest's corners four or five times and the lid rose like the head of a slow fish surfacing in the water, the slight creaking of the hinges sounding very loud in that silence. Dandão looked inside the chest and put his hand on the lid, almost shutting it back.

"These secrets," he said, without taking his hand off the lid, "are part of a great knowledge, a knowledge which is not complete yet. But on the other hand, no knowledge ever becomes complete, and it's part of this knowledge here to always want to become complete. And it's also part of it—for it's a secret trusted only to certain people—that every person who has it will continue to work for it to become complete. If everyone works, generation after generation, this is the knowledge that will prevail."

Budião, Feliciano, and Zé Pinto still could not understand fully what he was saying, but they did not feel like asking anything, as if they were sure they would understand it all in the end. And anyway, while speaking amidst his waves of smoke, Dandão became much, much bigger, taller than the house where he was, he acquired all colors and expressions, he even became transparent, he became moist like a woman's crotch and wise like the root of a tree, he turned into a kind of landscape. Then he released the lid altogether, it gaped back, seesawing until it found its position, and he started to draw out secrets, one secret after another, each of them as wonderful as the one before, and there are those who contend that freedom was given then to countless spirits of things, ways of being, diligent inspirations, papers one could not see with both eyes not to go blind, ethereal influences, the truths behind what you hear, inescapable suggestions, realities as clear as the imperative of living and raising children. It also was very sonorous, so melodic that nothing else could be heard in the flour house, and some say that at that hour a clandestine brotherhood was founded which took the name Brotherhood of the Brazilian People, and others say that nothing happened, nothing ever happened, there was never such a house of such flour of such plantation of such baron of such fishery, and it all appears more labyrinthian with each investigation. While Júlio Dandão is little by little picking things to show from the chest, and displays one, and explains another, this Brotherhood is perhaps being founded, perhaps not, perhaps it was founded forever and will persist forever, perhaps it is all a lie, perhaps it is the most patent truth and for that reason unperceivable, but no one knows, because this Brotherhood kills and dies, but does not speak.

City of Salvador, Bahia
September 13, 1827

Smile of Contempt was pale, his voice quavering, his hands clenched, his eyes popping out. And Zé Libório was not much better, only he had no patience to remain seated, and while the other spoke he kept shuttling from one end of the shed to the other, sometimes facing Leléu like a man who is expecting explanations for something indefensible. But Leléu, who at the beginning had just kept thrumming on the table with his fingernails, was now listening with an impassive face to their accusations, crossing his arms and giving them what might be called polite attention. The only thing he would not accept would be for Smile of Contempt to call him bad names, in which case maybe he would use the club that was resting between his knees, but Smile of Contempt had prepared his speech, and seemed to be more interested in demonstrating he was right than in calling anybody names, at least for the time being. He recalled that Leléu had been the first to assemble the fish retailers to fix the prices for purchases and sales, and to settle the unity that was the basis of good commercial practice, particularly in this shitty business where even the rain and the moon made a difference, a poor man's business about which everybody was always giving unasked-for opinions and in which every public official thought he could order anyone about as he pleased. Then Leléu's behavior the past few days, strutting like some kind of grandee among the fish baskets and setting prices as he damn well pleased, could not be called anything but sheer treasonableness. When he found a basket already traded, he would ridicule the price, call the fisherman the prince of fools, offer whatever more was necessary, and take away the basket. When he arrived early, he behaved in a way never seen in the Conception Market since the beginning of the world, even going out to meet the canoes as they dropped their killicks, back from fishing, in order to announce, as though he were the undisputed king of the sea with all its fish, that he would cover any bid past or future, and therefore it was no use taking the fish to the trading yard, better haul everything straight to one of his four stalls. If by any chance some fisherman hesitated or pointed to a previous agreement with another retailer, he would first deride him, then threaten him, then betray his colleagues' confidence by denouncing the buyers who used hollowed-out weighing stones to buy more for less, then predict bankruptcies and dirty deals, bragging and boasting, flaunting financial powers, and in short surprising everyone with so much brazenness, insolence, and cynicism. If he arrived at the market around four or five o'clock, like the others, he ruined all that had been so laboriously organized in the course of years and years of worries and tribulations. Because the fish, as everybody knows, is sold according to ratings, and the ratings are set unostentatiously, with courtesy and discretion, everything deliberated within the decency that should preside over every serious business, so much so that if you are not an old hand at it you can stay there and watch as much as you like, and you will not see what is going on. It has nothing to do with the way Black Leléu decided to act, interfering in other people's conversations, laughing loudly at the deals they made, taunting those who sold fish to anybody but himself, and scheming to sabotage his competitors' sales, either by saying their fish were unwholesome, old, and second-rate or by lowering his price so much that no one could match it without going bankrupt. What about the Our Lady of Perpetual Help Fish Merchants' Guild, invented and christened by Leléu himself? The guild had no address, no billboard, no license, no nothing, but it existed, and that was proved by the fact that after they had gathered together to decide about each one's quota, to set the price for each kind of fish and seafood, and to establish payment conditions, no more than a single buyer was necessary to represent them all, an uncontroversial, uncontested buyer who had only one offer, and if the fisherman did not like it he could pick up his fish and go sell it on his own, but because producing is different from selling, there was nothing the fisherman could do but accept. But not now; now Leléu's fish-salting operation was getting bigger and bigger, row upon row of fish and shrimp drying in the sun, and there was talk of loads of clams and other shellfish kept in troughs filled with muddy sand and seawater, waiting for buyers.

So, Smile of Contempt said, trembling like turtle meat, this kind of thing's got to stop, it just can't go on like this, this is an abuse, it's more than an abuse, who did Leléu think he was, did he think the others would keep their arms crossed while this affront went on happening? More and more incensed, Smile of Contempt looked to Zé Libório for support, and Zé Libório strode over to Leléu with his hands on his hips and planted himself silently in front of him. Leléu even considered telling them how really, really worked up he was, and het up, and hopping mad, how he felt he was fighting the world alone, and how he had begun to think it was every man for himself even more than he used to think before. His Excellency Pedro Manoel Augusto over in Nazaré, for instance, had come back to see him after all that rigmarole about Saint Martha and Dona Marta de Betânia and whatnot, to ask him again if he could not procure a black girl to mind the Aratuípe house, young, with well-rounded legs, a good behind, an industrious, amenable disposition, and not too much Negro smell.

"But Your Excellency Notary Pedro Manoel Augusto, didn't you say yourself you didn't want to have anything to do with those things anymore? Didn't you send back the girl I found for you, a first-rate choice from the best stock of the baron of Pirapuama's farms, so famous for the quality of the blacks raised on them?"

"Yes, I know," Pedro Manoel Augusto had answered. "Yes, I did send her back. But I've been thinking it over. A man cannot let himself be bound by a woman's promises, a man must be faithful to himself, and so I changed my mind."

"A man must be faithful to what, dear Massa?"

"Faithful to himself. You do not understand those matters, they are matters of moral philosophy, which are as unreachable to you as intelligence is to worms. Whatever happened to the girl—you haven't sent her away, have you?"

"And what about the promise, my good Massa Your Excellency Pedro Manoel Augusto, the promise to Saint Martha?"

"That doesn't concern you, it's none of your business, don't be disrespectful, what happens to the promise is between the saint and me, keep out of it. So where is the girl?"

"But, Massa Pedro Manoel Augusto, hasn't Your Excellency received all the money, haven't I done everything like Your Excellency told me? Isn't it all settled now?"

"So I do you a favor, a very big favor, I forgive your fines and keep you out of jail, I make all kinds of exceptions for you, and when it is my turn to need a favor, you refuse it?"

"But, Your Excellency Honorable Notary and Registrar Pedro Manoel Augusto, didn't I make that payment in place of the girl you refused? Wasn't it one thing or the other?"

"My father is right when he says that one should not bestow favors and benefits on people like you, because they do not understand them, and the virtue of gratitude is unknown to them! So then, you bastardly Negro, so that's the way you answer me, quibbling and shilly-shallying? Do you think that piddling sum, that insignificancy you paid me instead of your felonious debts, means anything to me? Who do you think you are, who do you think I am? I thought that after doing you the favor I have done, you'd see that in me you had a friend and protector. But obviously it's not so, you do not value what should be valued, I see I was casting pearls before swine, as they say. It serves me right for expecting to be able to deal with Negroes the same way I deal with whites. You're no good, you're a perfect example of ingratitude and stupidity. Very well, then, you have lost your friend and protector, and from now on we shall see how well you're going to do in your illegal trades and crooked practices. One would think you were the one who did me the favor of forgiving my debts and fines, and not the other way around—it's very funny, very, very funny; I wouldn't believe it if someone else told me. Serves me right, serves me right!"

Leléu frowned hard. The sonofabitch had planned to take the money first and then the girl, maybe there had never been any promise to any Saint Martha, the bastard! All right, Leléu thought, he's being smart and Leléu is being a dupe for not having expected this, and for having let Vevé stay in Nazaré instead of sending her away someplace to see if he could find something for her to do. The more you live, the more you learn, that's the way the ball rolls, and besides, a black has to be very smart, smart as can be; being a black in a world full of sharpers is no joke, right? Leléu remembered his own tenets and rebuked himself for having forgotten them to the point of lowering his guard to Pedro Manoel Augusto. All right, if that's the way it is, let's play the game. Leléu fell down on his knees at the notary's feet.

"Oh, dear, dear Massa, for the sake of Your Excellency's sweet mother's love, for the wounds of Christ, please don't ever say a thing like that, please don't do such a terrible thing to me. I may be black, but I can be trusted, dear Massa! I didn't mean to question anything; it was just that I thought the promise . . . But you are so right, Your Excellency Honorable dear Massa, a man must be faithful to himself—God bless Your Excellency for having so much intelligence. Oh, dear Massa, don't think I wouldn't do anything for your friendship and protection; Saint Lawrence keep me from losing the dear, dear Massa's friendship: why should I care about just another black girl that doesn't have any value to me! I wish I had more of them to place at your service—for God's sake, Your Excellency Pedro Manoel Augusto, don't ever think it could be any different!"

The notary resisted a little and continued to sulk, but this time Leléu managed to kiss his hand and was about to squeeze out two heavy tears from the corners of his eyes, when he finally yielded. Very well, all was forgiven this time, but Leléu should not forget the lesson and should try not to cause any more problems. When would he be able to see the Negress? What a pity! If Leléu had known, she'd be ready and waiting right there, but she was not, she had gone out with two other women to help them pick shellfish—by the way, did His Excellency like red crabs? He had received a very good load. But His Excellency would not hear about red crabs. Now that he had secured the delivery of the girl, he became flustered, he got up, he could not stand still, he rubbed his hands and scratched his balls incessantly, a nervous little grin flashing in his mouth intermittently like a firefly. Then he would do as follows. What he would do was the following. All right, he was going to do the following, the following. Tomorrow without fail he would be at the old riverside warehouse, behind the piassava bales that served as a wall. Leléu was to send the Negress there first thing in the morning, and he would meet her there; he was going to see—and he rubbed his hands again, in the middle of a short jump—how things would turn out, and then he would speak to Leléu.

"That's very well thought out, very well thought out indeed!" Leléu kept saying, with great admiration. "Very intelligent, very intelligent!"

"I'm going to tell *Senhora* Dona Marta that I have to go on a trip early tomorrow, before daybreak. This way I can spend the whole day undisturbed at the warehouse."

"That's very clever! I'll say! That's why I admire high learning; I would never be able to think out those things, so well thought out; a learned man is a great thing, God bless you. Does dear Massa want me to send along some food too? Dear Massa may get hungry; these things are . . ."

Pedro Manoel Augusto laughed, covering his mouth. Sure, let the Negress bring a few comestibles with her, nothing too heavy, maybe a light snack, and a few sweets wouldn't be a bad idea, either.

"Leave it to me, dear Massa; I'll send all kinds of things, Your Excellency will see. And forgive me, but what a clever man you are, how intelligent, what a quick thinker!"

However, as soon as Pedro Manoel Augusto finished talking about all the arrangements for the tenth time, from the appointed hour to the sign he would use for them to know he was waiting—an unobtrusive little red handkerchief with its tip showing at the corner of the warehouse's big window—and left rubbing his hands as though he wanted to fuse them together, Leléu's face turned grim, and he darted out to the cabin behind the fish shed. He called Vevé, and addressing her as he never had, begged her fervently to stay in the cabin for her own good, no matter what. He then opened a rusty old trunk, and after tossing up colored cloths, pieces of painted wood, rattles, whistles, horns, dolls, wheels, clay bulls, and all kinds of toys, beamed as he found an air-filled cow bladder. He picked up a string puppet and a spinning top painted with blue and red polka dots, and wrapped them in a rag, together with the bladder.

"I'll talk to you later; just stay there," he said to Vevé, and left after bolting the door carefully.

He found the boy Salustiano at the vegetable stall as expected, and had a talk with him. Salu knew the boy José Vicente, His Excellency Pedro Manoel Augusto's son, didn't he? Didn't they play together once in a while? Yes, they did. And where was Quelé, Salu's younger brother? He had a job for them both, a very important job, no questions, it was something of great responsibility. Could Quelé be here this afternoon? Yes, he could, and Leléu talked to them in whispers around sundown. Are you two listening carefully? All right, so tomorrow morning very early . . .

And very early the next morning, Salustiano and Quelé could be seen with the top and the puppet stuck in the pockets of their pants, the bladder going up and down in their hands like a magical ball, in front of the porch where José Vicente was not doing anything and had asked a young house black to tell him the same story once again. And she was going to answer as usual that telling stories in daytime makes one grow a tail, when José Vicente saw the bladder and dashed out to the street. The girl shrugged, figuring it was better for him to play in the street than to stick around asking for one thing after another. Before long, Quelé started complaining about how narrow and full of ditches that street was; it wasn't good for them to play in. Why didn't they go to the grass plot near the old warehouse? José Vicente looked to see if the black girl was keeping an eye on him, and she was not. Dona Marta did not like him to go play near the old warehouse; she thought there could be snakes there. But just a short time would be all right, wouldn't it? He hesitated a little, and Quelé insisted. If they didn't go with him, he'd go alone, taking his bladder and his puppet with him, and would not show them the other toys he had in his place. Salu objected and said he was not going, his boss, Leovigildo, did not like him to wander too far, either. Well, I am going, Quelé said, grabbing the bladder. José Vicente ran after him, and Salu went back to the vegetable stall.

Quelé could see from afar the piece of red cloth squeezing out of the window corner. Then everything was as expected; now he had to take the first opportunity to throw the bladder over the warehouse's wood fence, as Leléu had told him. And over it went, helped by the strong wind that was bending the sedges on the nearby marsh.

"Darn it!" Quelé said. "Now I lost my best bladder, the one my god-mother overlaid with string for me!"

"Jump over the fence and get it," José Vicente said.

Quelé appraised the height of the fence and grimaced. Who could possibly climb that high? Only if they had a ladder.

"Maybe the door is open," José Vicente said. "Go see if the big door is open, so we can go to the backyard through the warehouse."

"Not me; if I go in there they'll say I'm a little black thief; not me!"

José Vicente ran to the door and pushed it. It was a bit stuck, but it seemed easy to open. He pushed it again and was about to make a passage large enough for him to slip in, when it was thrown fully open by somebody inside.

"Dad!" José Vicente cried. "My father!"

A startled Pedro Manoel Augusto stood at the door. He had come to open it with a smile on his face, and now could not find what to say, while José Vicente, without even looking at Quelé, bolted back home, afraid of being spanked for playing in a disapproved place.

"José Vicente, come back here!" Pedro Manoel Augusto called out, but it was too late, and the small figure of the boy disappeared behind the pottery trees.

That does it, the notary thought; now the blasted kid is rushing home to tell his mother that his father is not on a trip, he is hiding in the warehouse like a barn rat. And he had barely started to concoct a hasty excuse when Vevé came into view by the church, holding by its tugs a wicker hamper full of fruit, pastries, and refreshments. He made an alarmed sign with both hands, and she thought it was for her to hurry up, so she began to rush down the trail, without understanding why the more she ran, the more he gestured.

"Confound it!" he said when she stopped in front of the door, still panting from having run so hard. "Didn't you see my signs? What are you doing here? Don't you see you can't stay here?"

"But wasn't the red handkerchief in the window? Wasn't I supposed to come when the red handkerchief could be seen in the window?"

"No! Yes. Yes, you were! Were! But not anymore!"

And he scampered off to his house without speaking another word to Vevé, who remained in the same place, looking amused, while he shuffled away as fast as he could, his ponderous belly balancing on top of his skinny legs—what a disaster, what a disaster, my God, what a disaster! And later on, when Senhora Dona Marta de Betânia, in spite of her husband's protests, decided to check on things at the warehouse, she found Vevé with her eyes down, answering all the Senhora's questions with just a cringing silence, exactly as she had been instructed by Leléu. Dona Marta opened the hamper, turned it upside down on the ground, and in an effort to do or say something else, without knowing what, sniffed loudly, bit her lips, and marched stiffly back to her house, ignoring Pedro Manoel Augusto's dejected gaze, as looking on the verge of tears, he chewed his hands.

Though Leléu was still listening vaguely to what Smile of Contempt had gone on saying, he remembered with satisfaction how everything had worked out fine, and how that accursed notary had not managed to get something from him for nothing. He had even gone so far as to feel a certain affection for Vevé, but everything soon became gloomy again: would you believe that wretch was really heavy with child, and her belly was already swelling up, even under the huge skirt he had given her so there wouldn't be any gossiping while he decided what to do? Then Black Inácia had been right, then she was really pregnant since that Saint Anthony's Day more or less, almost three months ago. She wasn't good for anything; what the hell was he going to do with a goddamned pregnant black wench, even if it was the baron's child, a dead and buried baron—aggravation, aggravation! Now that he thought about it, he should have let the notary screw the girl, because by then something still could have been worked out to make him believe it was his child, since he was almost as white as the baron. Everything happening out of control, everything turning backward, welshers everywhere, bilkers, profiteers, envious people, everything going downhill, a more than wearisome struggle—aggravation, aggravation! A man must be faithful to himself, Leléu sneered, but as for me, they owe me and don't pay, they abuse me, they try to make me lose money, they pester me, they are eaten up by jealousy for everything I own, all I get from everyone is trouble—shit and goddammit!

"You're both mistaken," he said to Smile of Contempt, much more calmly than he had rehearsed. "I don't know what you two are talking about. I don't understand."

Smile of Contempt concentrated, so his outstretched finger would not jitter.

"Leléu," he said in a strangled voice, "you're not the only one who's smart, you're not the only one who isn't afraid, you're not the only one who's willing to fight."

Leléu felt for his club and gripped it hard.

"My club is in my hand," he said. "You have spoken lies, you have threatened me, you have abused my patience. And you too, Zé Libório, and remember that when both of you were in need, I was the one who loaned you money."

"At interest."

"Sure! Sure! At interest, because I can't go on working from sunup to sundown, from full moon to crescent moon, to go around giving my money away. What's wrong with you is that you think you can get something for nothing. Nothing is for nothing, and if I own things I earned them and have to earn them back again every day. Instead of being envious, work the way I do."

"Everybody here works; stop beating around the bush."

"My hand is on my club, and I feel like using it, and I'm not making jokes!"

"Better think again, Leléu."

"Out! Out, both of you! You know the way out!"

All right, why not, he thought after they had left, deciding he was going to have a moment of weakness.

"Yes, I'm going to have a moment of weakness," he said aloud, and fished a dusty bottle of *cachaça* out of a basket packed with dry banana leaves. He held the bottle up against the light, shook it, wiped off the dust with a rag, pulled out the cork with his teeth, filled two tin mugs, drank one on top of the other, got drunk immediately, and was very high when he sauntered out. Someone who did not know him perhaps would not notice he was so drunk, but others could tell by his hanging jaw even with his mouth closed and by his aggressive way of looking askance at everyone. He also spoke very loud when he drank, so loud that even if he tried to whisper, his voice would reverberate all over the market, waking up those already asleep after having worked all night and having had their luncheon at six in the morning.

He burst out of the door, the sun struck his face, he pulled his big hat over his forehead. He licked his lips, spat to one side, and rubbed his hands on the sides of his pants, something he would not do if he were sober, not to soil them. He remembered the club, went back to get it, and emerged again, looking like a new man.

"Let's get to work, Leléu," he said, evaluating the surroundings with a confident look and starting to walk to where the fishermen were already lining up the baskets of the day. He knew he was drunk; he had got drunk on purpose; he liked that sensation of madness, though he disapproved of drinking and knew he would regret it the next day. But he never talked about it, never admitted he had been drunk and crazy, he changed the subject when someone asked him about it, and when he was alone he only had goose pimples and shuddered if he remembered something stupid he had done, and those goose pimples and the shuddering were enough to exorcise everything, and not let him think again about what had happened. He proceeded to the baskets, and the first one he saw belonged to Rat and Possum, two scrawny mulattoes, brothers on both sides, who used to go out to fish drunk and who lived with two women each, two mothers-in-law, four brothers-in-law, six sisters-in-law, and three nephews in the holes of the Conception Hill stone wall, together with the bats, which according to some were their relatives and according to others their food in family parties. Neither of them knew how to fish, or if they knew they were always too sodden to be able to haul in their catch, so Leléu knew what they had in their basket, and knew they would sell it for any price. He went near the basket and confirmed what he knew: a disorderly heap of small squid, third-rate crabs, bony little red snappers, puny gray snappers, tiny cavallas, worthless scads and sardines, two or three small mojarras, four or five bumpers, a really scrubby leather jack displayed as if it amounted to something, six garfish more properly thought of as needle pads—absolutely nothing of value.

"How much do you ask for that fine miscellany of fish, my dear Possum, how much, my dear Blond Rat?" Leléu asked, stopping with a minuet-like step and florid gestures.

Surprised, Possum grinned.

"One crusado takes all," he said, and raised his arm in case Leléu wanted to hit him with the club.

"My good man, my great Brazilian fisherman, Your Honor presents a combination of fish of this caliber, something for kings and queens on this market's ramp, and Your Honor asks one crusado? For this banquet?" Leléu declaimed. "Here, take six crusados for this precious basket, take it for my blacks to keep."

He thought he was being tremendously funny, and was still bending down with laughter when his eyes fell on Black Lodé's horse-eye jacks, the gloss of the sea still persisting on their scales, their bluish backs sparkling. He halted, and turned around on his heels. Hey, hey, hey! Well, bless my soul!

"Master Lodegário," he intoned, dragging his hat on the cobblestones in a salute to the fish. "With Your Excellency's leave, may I compliment Your Excellency with all my best greetings and reverences for the fine conduction of this great catch, yes sir, bless you, the Most High be praised, what beautiful horse-eyes!"

Lodé smiled, changed his footing, and looked contentedly at his fish.

"Very well, very well-well-well," Leléu said. "I'll take them, I must have those horse-eyes, I'm even going to have one of them gilded."

"It's pledged already," Lodé said with some reluctance. "I kept just the little smelt here."

He showed the smelt basket.

"Good," Leléu declared. "I'll take those shitty minnows, too."

"The horse-eyes are pledged."

"Who did you pledge them to?"

"To Smile of Contempt."

"You pledged them to a poor man!"

"He was here earlier than you."

"You pledged them to a poor man! Poor people are a disgrace, they don't do anybody any good! That's why I don't talk to poor people, I keep a distance from them, I give them at most a hand wave and a few alms. Poverty is catching, believe me! Give me those horse-eyes, man, don't be a fool; I'll double any price that pauper, what's-his-name, Spoiled 'n' Contented, offered you. Take that over to my stall—don't be a fool."

His hands akimbo, his head tilted, and one of his eyes closed because of the sun, he kept on looking as Lodé carried the two baskets to the stalls. He did not even notice when three blacks appeared behind him and one of them tried to snatch the club from his hand. But he always had a firm grip on it, and he turned around without letting it go. The one who had tried to take the club from him smiled and stood awkwardly in front of him, while the others stayed a few steps behind.

"What is this?" Leléu asked, looking at them sideways and spreading his legs apart a little to plant himself more solidly on the ground. "What's the matter, can't you see anything round and hard without reaching for it?"

"Smile of Contempt sent us."

"Oh, sure, I have seen you gentlemen before, yes, I know you gentlemen, you're all Negroes for hire who belong to this what's-his-name, this boy Smock of Bad Hemp. Can you imagine this—that barefaced mulatto, instead of picking up a hoe to work at least once in his life, keeps three Negroes for hire as shameless as he, hauling turds for two coppers, weeding farms for a coin an acre. You're nothing but a bunch of poor sons of bitches, all sons of bitches!"

He stepped back a little; he knew he had offended them, and wanted to insult them some more.

"I know the coffee in his house, in this what's-his-name's house, this Smack of Dungpile, the coffee in his house is never hot. His wife doesn't clean herself. He never brings home anything, he sleeps on the floor, he's so beggarly he doesn't even have a bed. He drinks, he gambles, and he likes men, he's false to his body. He lies even in his sleep!"

No one saw who struck the first blow, but Leléu knew he was getting into a fight, and as soon as one of them moved, he switched the club to his other hand so fast no one noticed, and knocked down the one out in front with two thumps on his back. But they were very strong, and Leléu, though he changed into a windmill of leg, foot, and head blows with so much speed that people around could feel the air being minced by his movements, could not help getting hurt too, covered with sore lumps all over. It cannot be said that he lost the fight, it can even be said that he won, because all three of them ended up running away, two of them hobbling and the third with his hair soaked in blood. But back in his stall, rubbing arnica on his bruises and putting compresses on his lumps, Leléu thought he was getting old. He did not know how old he was, but he was getting old for sure. He did not have any white hair on his head, but the sparse beard that grew on his chin was getting grayer every day. Also he no longer liked to bend down even when he had to, he felt his joints were not as nimble as they used to be, the flesh under his arm near his armpit was a little flabby, he had to push back the paper in order to read small print—yes, he was getting old, he almost had not stood up to those three, and in bygone days they would have caused no concern to a man like him, who knew all kinds of fights. Now he would have to carry a weapon, it was a necessity, something besides the club. He searched a drawer and picked up a hollow duck-cloth cylinder, closed at one end and open and hemmed at the other, a little over a handspan and a half long and half an inch wide. He rolled up the tube to inspect the stingray spine inside it. Cautiously, because everybody knows that a wound made by a stingray spine never heals, he tested the tip and the barbs, and they were hard as stone and sharp as if they had been forged of fine steel by a needlemaker. He pulled back the hem, and the spine was sheathed, its deadly point hidden just below the opening, just a little cloth tube that could be carried around like a handkerchief. And that empty, limp little tube would be the only thing he would have in his hand after having stuck it in someone's belly. It would plant itself there with little or no bleeding outside, impossible to remove because of the barbs. As for Leléu, no sign of a weapon in his hands, just that innocent cloth tube, as harmless as a peeled banana. He put the loaded cylinder in his pocket, considered drinking again and even picked up one of the mugs, but changed his mind. A heavy sleepiness came over him, together with the thought that the baron's seventy-day funeral Mass at the cathedral would be the following day, and he was going to be present, at a distance but present. A headache tearing his temples apart, a sour nausea, so many things to worry about. And how many times had he made an ass of himself? And what the hell was he going to do with the little mulatto Vevé was going to give birth to in about six months. That was all he needed, a kid living with him. Well, he would give the kid away for someone to raise, that should not prove to be too difficult, particularly if it took after its father and turned out to be a light-skinned mulatto, more or less a brunet, with its hair almost smooth. What a life; what else is going to happen? Well, that's the way it is, Leléu sighed, starting to fall asleep, and deciding to put on his black suit tomorrow and to shed sobbing tears when the baroness saw him by the church's door.

8

City of Salvador, Bahia, March 17, 1839

It had rained all week, and the day dawned as ugly as the preceding ones. At five in the morning, before spending the customary half hour locked in his study in front of an enameled basin and a ewer full of lavender-scented water, cleaning his teeth and washing his head, which had gone through the night under a thick layer of agave juice and a close-fitting skullcap to straighten his hair, Amleto Ferreira set his window ajar and inspected his garden with displeasure. Nearly always dark beneath tangled treetops, which canopied a thick conglomeration of leaves and boughs of the smaller plants, the garden was even more darksome than usual, a dripping forest, heavy raindrops splattering the water of the little ponds, where the water platters, the pillpods, the water lilies, the pickerelweeds, the water vines snarled together like skeins of anacondas, and the rest of the water plants were excessively wet, drowned in a sogginess that made everything damp, slippery and muddy. The continuous hammering of fat raindrops dribbling down on resonant croton, malanga, and elephant's-ear leaves reiterated a kind of monotonous discouragement to a day that should be festive, and only tape grasses, mosses, rockweeds, richweeds, and such beings, which thrive in sodden obscurity, did not seem soaked and sorrowful like the other plants. A humid, faded world in which the color of the foliage brought to mind funeral ornaments, a world that made Amleto doubly resentful. He decided to go outside to see what the weather was promising, though he did not believe it was going to improve. He wrapped himself in a bathrobe, protected his neck with a knitted scarf, put a nightcap on his head not to catch cold, opened the study's back door, walked down the two steps carefully not to slip, and treaded delightedly on the carpet of grass and creeping plants, feeling his feet sinking in the soppy earth. It was not raining any longer, and just droplets from the trees kept falling, sometimes like a light rain, when a sudden gust stirred the treetops. Amleto shivered and was afraid he might catch cold, but even so he decided to walk over to the iron gate that opened onto the Rosary neighborhood, to get a better view of the horizon and appraise the weather. He liked his garden, he derived an inexplicable contentment from spending hours on end sitting in front of the plants, his eyes fixed on them as if he expected to accompany their growing and blossoming. And he also liked it to be shady, because sunlight was a personal aggression against him, with the special purpose of mercilessly darkening his skin as it had before, turning him into a mulatto again. He was fond of his plants, and he walked down the row of chestnut trees, paying attention to every trunk, raising his eyes to the delicately hued orchids poised lightly on the limbs of the larger trees, fragile like paper birds, noting the ferns and polypodies, the masonry jardinieres embraced by vines, the statues of the seasons—summer so strange, its Greek form so soft, a gently curved bosom, rounded hips, a noble, tender visage among the uprising roots of a great acacia tree; would Summer be a woman and Spring a girlish ephebe, as could be seen now, very marmorean against the red-splattered green of the bromelias?—the Roman-style columns with their tops cut off obliquely like in the ancient temples of old engravings, the debris on the ponds, dead leaves, insects, and wilted flowers arranging themselves gently along the edges like an ornament, a cicada chirring out suddenly. He stopped to look at the climbing plants clinging to the furrowed parget of the garden walls, stroked a few of their leaves, tried the bounce of their tendrils with his fingertips, until he finally got to the gate. The clouds remained dense and low on both sides, the wind had stopped, the air had become oppressive. Amleto shivered again and made an about-face, to go back and lock himself in his study once more.

He had therefore a surprise when he walked into the living room later on and saw through the windows opening onto the main porch that the sun had appeared and a glaring light was sparkling on the wet plants. He rushed out to the porch, put his hands on the balustrade; only an evanescent crown of clouds still endured in a sky whose faded blue also seemed to have been washed by the rains. He smiled and banged happily on the balustrade. He had been brooding inside, saddened by the injustices life always had in store for him. The christening of Patrício Macário Nobre dos Reis Ferreira-Dutton, his seventh child, though three of them had died, would at least have a lovely day as background. And also a fine celebration. He could feel the smell of biscuits being baked, he knew they were kneading sour and sweet doughs, and all kinds of foods were being cooked. Like his beautiful house with all its comforts, that celebration was something no one could take away from him; no one could say it was not his right. When he now thought about how he had made so much money, he admitted only vaguely and more and more infrequently having used the baron's assets and embezzled everything he was able to lay his hands on, in every possible type of cozenage. No, no, it really had not been like that, it was high time he quit being excessively rigorous with himself; it even seemed to be a propensity to martyrdom. What about the business acumen he had put at the baron's service, the endless difficulties, the heroic solutions found for unsurmountable problems? And the blood, that's right, the blood and sweat poured out for the baron? And how about the comfortable position he had assured for the baroness, who admittedly was now rather impoverished but lived with all dignity in the same house in Bângala, with all of her needs and her children's taken care of? True, she no longer had many Negroes, because the difficulties of the present time and the mischances that troubled the baron's businesses from all sides made it indispensable to cut the number of slaves to a minimum. What could he do? Whale fishing was becoming worse every year, it was more and more a thing of the past, soon to be entombed by progress, so the sale of the Good Jesus Fishery had been an excellent deal, in spite of an apparently low price. He had not told the baroness that he himself, hidden behind an association with two French merchants, had bought the fishery, and now would in fact sell it at a good profit. After all, it had been a sale like any other, and how else would they face their mounting expenses, if the farm and trade crisis was scourging all the baron's businesses? Some of the baroness's friends had agreed it had been a good deal, among them the bachelor of law Noêmio Pontes de Oliveira, who was now Amleto's lawyer, since their very close collaboration in the inventory of the baron's estate. And by the way, what a disappointing inventory it had been, with so many debits, liabilities, and arrears that if it were not for the dedication shown by Amleto, who took responsibility for everything and even worked with no remuneration for months, the baroness and her children might have had a very sad fate. She had also inherited something from her father, of course, but her father's assets had been sustaining a great many losses, not only on account of his long illness but also as a result of raids by radicals, who sometimes attacked the Portuguese physically and vandalized their properties. Using a legal artifice which he engendered laboriously with the lawyer's help to safeguard the baroness's interests against the greed of her father's Portuguese heirs, he managed to sell most of the estate before they could lay any claim to it, at prices not so advantageous, to be sure, but the circumstances of the transactions had demanded expediency, and it is easy to make criticisms after the fact. Not to mention the expensive and very delicate negotiations they had had to face in order to obtain the understanding and support of the auditors and inspectors from the Treasury, the Board of Commerce, and the judiciary, all of them people of high rank and responsibility whom one could not trifle with. Now the emporium and warehouse, as well as other firms, were registered in the names of third parties, because after buying them with Noêmio through his brother-in-law Emídio Reis, Amleto deemed it wiser to sell them than to try to keep ownership, even if by means of a front man. The houses left by the old man were still bringing in some rent money, though nothing but a few coins that he used for paying the baroness's expenses, and heaven knows how often he had had to add to that money from his own pocket, so she would have enough for her living. The sugar mills, on the other hand, were not doing well, the sugar problems were getting more serious every day, and all they could count on was the small production of sugarcane rum, hardly enough to keep the work going while they waited for better days.

"That's right," Amleto thought, leaving the porch to go have his breakfast. "The truth is I am at peace with my conscience; I never did anyone any harm; I am a worthy man."

And that was the very reason why he felt a certain bitterness, because he could not risk spending in accordance with his social position lest he attract the attention of slanderous, envious people, capable even of filling the baroness's ears with false insinuations, maybe downright calumnies. It did not make a difference that everyone knew—and everyone did know, because he had told them himself, though it was not true; but that they did not know—Teolina had inherited a fortune from her Portuguese great-uncles in Trás-Os-Montes. There were gossips and comments just the same. What a rock-strewn path he had to tread, obstacles upon obstacles, so many unsuspected hurdles! You took care of one thing and another would immediately loom ahead; you solved one problem and another would immediately pop up. To think of the time he had lost on Latin books, quotations, and memorized speeches, an arduous trail leading nowhere, except to poverty made more serious by the envy of the ignorant, rich and poor. Now that he had found the right course, had dug up his wealth with his fingernails, he still had to face the racial problem, rejection by people of high station and the restrictions imposed by the mean-minded, to the point that even Patrício Macário's christening party, which could be lavish as any in Bahia, had been planned cautiously as almost an intimate reception, for their closest friends and relatives. And ironically enough, he could not help being blessed by good fortune, as Providence always gave him a hand and fate always rewarded his hard work and talent for business. He had bought some real estate in the backlands for a very cheap price, almost nothing, because of the 1835 drought, and now the talk was that cattle raising would make millionaires overnight in that region. He had planted tobacco on the farm he had purchased through Emídio in São Félix, and profits from deals with German buyers were piling up. He sold hardwood lumbered in the baron's abandoned lands and could not fill all the orders he kept getting. He had foreseen that the continuous building of new houses in the city would greatly increase the demand for lime, and so he took title to the large calcareous beds under the shallow sea on Whale Point's inner shore, and now his blacks, with water just below their chins, shoveled up tons of seashells to load the lighters that would take them to his kilns in Holy Port. And even his slaked lime found all kinds of use, including the treatment of coconut plantations such as the one he owned in Conde, where he would soon be manufacturing oil, soap, and solid grease, besides selling the fiber to English importers.

"Come on now!" he exclaimed in disgust. "This will have to be solved someday, this will have to be solved; life cannot be made of sacrifices alone!"

He thought hungrily about breakfast. He had had some difficulty adapting the kitchen blacks and Teolina herself to the kind of meal he demanded for himself, although he did not force it on others. But he always complained about not being imitated by his wife and children, at least by the eldest one, Carlota Borroméia Martinha Nobre dos Reis Ferreira-Dutton, whom he was bringing up like an English girl but who would not accept his breakfast of grilled kidneys, smoked herring, a raisin pudding, crumpets, tea, toast, and jam. She had turned out so white, so niveous, with her diaphanous skin, her light-colored hair, her slender, fragile figure suitable to a young lady of the Court of Saint James's, and she was very amenable in general, but she rebelled against that food so much that she would feel sick and slip unnoticed into the kitchen to ask the blacks for corn bread, couscous, tapioca pudding, cassava dumplings, and coffee with milk. Nevertheless, she would learn someday; after all, it was not a fabrication, her origins were really British, she was a Dutton. He remembered with pleasure the day the adjutant priest to the vicar general came to see him in his office, nervously slipping his hands into the folds of his cassock to draw out his false birth certificate, so tortuously obtained.

"Here it is, Your Excellency!" had said the little priest, one of those old men who cannot get themselves to laugh even when they feel like it, and just make a faint, twitching grimace, their lips quivering as if afraid to keep away from each other for more than a second.

"Most Reverend!" Amleto answered, recalling that just a few minutes before he had read at the top of his list of things to do: "Dutton Certificate." He took the paper from the priest, even ripping it a little at the corner as he anxiously unrolled it, and read aloud: " 'Amleto Henrique Nobre Ferreira-Dutton'! Ferreira-Dutton. Doesn't the Most Reverend think it sounds well, sounds exceedingly well?"

The priest did not answer, tried to smile again, and softly tapped his right sleeve on the corners of his mouth to wipe off the drivel that trickled ceaselessly down his chin. But he soon perceived that the occasion required a less unenthusiastic comment.

"Yes, yes, it has a fine sound to it. Ferreira-Dupont!"

"No, no, Ferreira-Dutton. Dutton, Dutton, it's an English name, you know? The name of my father, John Dutton, John Malcolm Dutton."

"Oh, Your Excellency, please forgive me; I thought it was a French appellation."

"No, no; English. My father was an Englishman, maybe a distant relative of the Duttons who do business here. And my mother was Ferreira, of the Ferreiras from Viana do Castelo in Portugal."

"From Viana do Castelo?"

"Yes, yes. Does the most reverend also come from there?"

"No, no; I am from Ribatejo."

"Ribatejo, huh? That's far, that's very far."

"So. So if I am not mistaken, before this correction Your Excellency's name was simply Amleto Ferreira."

"Yes, sure, vicissitudes, problems caused by the religious disputes in King João's time, maybe negligence on the part of a godparent, the Napoleonic Wars . . . Those were troubled times, things were not so perfectly organized as today."

"Yes, of course."

"So the correction is necessary, it has been necessary for a long time, and thanks to the most reverend's and His Excellency the vicar's understanding . . . Your Reverence realizes that in the first place we had to reestablish factual truth and our family's historical heritage, which is fittingly mirrored in our name, and after all, our lineage goes back to time immemorial, both in Portugal and in England. And second, I attach a great significance to names, a great relevancy. A name should not be chosen whimsically, at random. My name, for example, is Amleto, chosen by my mother in honor of my father. Henrique is because of the tradition of England's royal houses—Henrique, Jorge, Carlos, Guilherme, Eduardo, and so forth. Nobre because it has always been our Portuguese family's third name, and Ferreira-Dutton, which is our correct family name, the result of an Anglo-Portuguese union."

"Yes, of course."

"In the case of my children, whom also by dint of the understanding I have always merited from the Church I have been able to baptize with their real names . . ." He reread the certificate and kissed it. "Yes, my children's names are not chosen haphazardly. *Nomen est omen,* wouldn't the most reverend agree?"

"Yes, of course, in a way . . ."

"My children's first names are those of two saints: the one of the day of their birth and the one of the day of their baptism. That's why my daughter's name is Carlota Borroméia Martinha Nobre dos Reis Ferreira-Dutton, for she was born on November fourth, therefore on Saint Charles Borromeo's Day, and baptized on the eleventh, Saint Martin's Day. And all the others have been named according to this criterion, namely Clemente André, born November twenty-third, Bonifácio Odulfo, and the three now asleep in Jesus, with also the name Reis, which comes from my wife's Trás-Os-Montes family, thus called ancestrally because they have always been on royal service."

"Of course. Very well put, of course."

Amleto noticed the priest seemed in a hurry, and had even stopped displaying that quick little grin at each name's announcement. Yes, certainly. Amleto had the envelope ready; all he had to do was take it out of the drawer where he had been keeping it since the day before. He felt its edges and handed it over to the priest.

"Begging Your Excellency's permission," the priest said, opening the envelope and beginning to count the bills in it without waiting for an answer.

"Yes, by all means. It's a modest contribution for the parish works, a donation made from the bottom of my heart . . ."

"Of course," the priest said, finishing his counting of the bills. "Well, now, if Your Excellency will excuse me . . ."

Yes, that certificate was carefully locked in the safe; everything was coming along fine after all. Yes, there was no reason for being upset. True, life dispenses hardships at every turn, but hardships must be forgotten on a day such as this. Hadn't the sun come out, wasn't everything practically ready: the burnished baptismal font, flowers all over the house, white linen tablecloths gleaming, jubilation floating in the air? By now the kidneys were sizzling on the grill, the iron teakettle was hissing splendidly over live coals, the pudding, cold as he liked it, was awaiting him in a little bowl of fine porcelain, full of raisins unseeded one by one by the kitchen blacks. He entered the spacious pantry, where a table was set, and the black girl Luzia checked everything with her eyes when she saw him come in.

"Today I want the kidneys medium rare," he said, sitting down after sniffing the roses in the vase at the center of the table.

"Yes, Massa," Luzia said, and rushed inside, shuffling her feet.

Nibbling on a muffin, Amleto thought the tray with the kidneys was arriving when he heard footsteps behind his back near the kitchen door. He turned around in joyful anticipation, but frowned almost immediately.

"What are you doing here today? Today of all days! Haven't I told you not to come here unless I called you? What do you want now—haven't you got everything you want?"

A small, dark mulatto woman with her hair held on top of her head by two bone combs stopped and appeared to be going back into the kitchen, but ended up standing in front of him, her hands clutched over her bosom.

"I'm not going to be in the way," she said. "You don't have to worry."

Amleto got up, seeming unable to contain his impatience, and stood for a long time with his hands covering his eyes.

"Dona Jesuína," he said, like someone who is being forced to repeat something very unpleasant. "Dona Jesuína, what else do you want, Dona Jesuína? What else do you want me to say, what else do you want me to do, what else do you want me to give?"

"You're calling me Dona Jesuína, and we're alone."

"Of course I'm calling you Dona Jesuína, but of course I've had to get used to it, you know that!"

"But you said you'd address me like that only when there were people around."

"All right, all right, I said that. But what's wrong with my respectfully calling you Dona Jesuína, because you *are* Dona Jesuína, are you not?"

"Yes, I am, but I am also your mother."

Amleto halted, turned up his eyes, raised his open hands, stomped on the floor. Had anybody ever forgotten that? How many sons of humble birth like him, and even those of noble birth, very noble birth, how many sons did for their mother what he did? Did she have a house? Yes, she did. Did she have servants? Yes, she did. Was her pantry stocked with the best and most expensive food? Yes, it was. Did she have a gardener to weed the grass from her flower patches, now that she could not bend down anymore? Yes, she did. Did she have everything she yearned for, everything she dreamed of, everything she craved? Wasn't a note or a message from her enough for him to send her everything she wanted—twenty skeins of thread, a basket of fruit, a hundred pounds of vegetables, ten pounds of meat, ten pounds of fish, four fat chickens, anything whatsoever? What complaints did she have, what grudges was she bearing, could it be possible that she would never be satisfied? If she still worked at her school, it was because she wanted it, and by the way it was no mean expense to buy writing slates for all those derelict, irredeemable children, and to buy more food than for a battalion—only for *Senhora* Dona Jesuína to act as if she was a good mother to a bad son? Now, now, come on, let's see things clearly!

She seemed to be feeling sorry about something, maybe about everything. Appearing to be on the verge of crying, she stretched out her arms toward her son and asked him through her sobs to forgive her, because she had come to see him out of the love she had for him, the pride and admiration she felt for him. If she had known that her baby boy, poor from the cradle, a mulatto and an illegitimate son, would have come such a long way to become a very important man, she would have died of happiness before she could finish bringing him up. He shouldn't be angry with her, a mother's heart has many weaknesses, how could she ever forget the dedication and care her son lavished on her, his concern about providing her with everything she needed? No, she was not ungrateful; it was just that though she understood his reasons perfectly well, it hurt so much not to be able to tell everyone as she would like that the great businessman and distinguished citizen Amleto Ferreira was her son, brought forth, suckled, cleaned, nursed, suffered for, and raised by her. It hurt so much that when she heard about her new grandson's baptism—what name had they chosen for him?—she could not resist the urge to see him, even if he, like all the others, was going to grow up without knowing he was her grandson; it did not matter, all she wanted was to see him. But now she understood how she had behaved in an inopportune, meddlesome way; would he please forgive her, would he please not be angry with her; it had been a thoughtless action, something that would never happen again, he could be sure of that.

Amleto was moved; his chin quivered; he walked over to his mother and almost embraced her. Oh, my dear, dear mother, if I could only embrace you and hold you in my arms, that's what I'd be doing now! Oh, sweet mother, you know how this situation hurts me too; you think I have no feelings, you think I don't cry at night as I remember my dear, sweet mother alone in her place, and I can't even go out in the street with her! If it weren't for those confounded tattletale Negresses that can come in here at any moment, and for the children, because today is Sunday and they're at home, if it weren't for that I'd cover you with kisses and caresses; you know very well that's what I would do, my dear, beloved mother! But don't you know—tell me, tell me, for heaven's sake tell me—don't you know that all this, this terrible situation, is for our own good? No, you don't know, you always act as if you didn't know! But you do understand, don't you, my adored mother? It's for our own good, don't you know?

Yes, she knew, and she also knew about his suffering because she was aware of his good sentiments, and she could not think of a fault she could say he had. But couldn't she perhaps watch the baptism unobtrusively, from a distance, without getting into any conversation, without moving from her place, perhaps introduced as Amleto's old wet nurse, a trusted old servant, a nursemaid or a governess?

"A governess?" Amleto became exasperated and turned his eyes to the ceiling. "*Senhora* Dona Jesuína, my children have an English governess and a German tutor. My God in heaven, what sort of stuffing fills Dona Jesuína's head? A governess! Of all the preposterous . . . My children with a black governess! Are you blind, can't you see reality? The world is not the way we want but the way it is!"

"I'm sorry; that's not what I meant. But a servant, a nursemaid . . ."

"No, no, too risky. They might detect some resemblance between us, maybe someone in the company has already heard a comment somewhere, and that might confirm it. No, no; why don't you drop those crazy notions and go to your Mass as usual, and then go tend your flowers? I'll tell you what: I'll send you some carnation seedlings I just got from Portugal, I'll send you some books, the romances you like, and we'll forget about all this—all right?"

"But I see no harm in being there as a servant, as an old housemaid. . . . And besides, who could see any resemblance between us? You are so white, so milk white, your hair is so smooth. . . ."

Amleto stroked his hair.

"You're right," he agreed. "My hair is smooth and my features are not coarse, yes. . . . But no, no, I still think it would be a temerity. Forget that idea, come on now."

"You have run out of arguments; you know very well that the presence of an old nursemaid at a baptism is customary among wealthy people and families of tradition, who reward their good servants and blacks."

Amleto paused in his pacing back and forth alongside the table.

"Oh well, what wouldn't I do for you? But be careful, watch your behavior; you are the nursemaid who brought me up and will behave as such. I'll never forgive you if you betray my trust!"

The kidneys were arriving; Luzia set the dish on the table and stood waiting near the chair where Amleto had sat down.

"Very well then, Dona Jesuína, it's all settled," he said, tucking a napkin in the folds of his collar. "Now if you'll excuse me, I have to have my first meal of the day; that is all for now. Luzia, where is the herbs-and-spices sauce?"

It was nine in the morning, and the day had become extraordinarily transparent, so clear and cool that one might have said the guests were chitchatting at a country estate in Sintra, on one of those fresh April mornings when even the roughest heaths seem to blossom out and perfume the meadows. Amleto ordered the doors and windows of the study to be opened wide. Actually it was not a study, but a vast, somber library, two roomy compartments separated by a carved rosewood arch, which was covered by a curtain of camletlike grosgrain, tied at the sides midway between the floor and the ceiling. It did not get too clear inside those cavernous chambers so jagged with nooks, recesses, and protuberances, colossal bookcases bristling with convoluted ornaments, here and there a hidden concavity, a kind of lair, an unexpected niche, two redoubtable-looking canephori over to one side supporting a little black wood table, so minuscule for such a formidable base, leather-bound tomes in drab colors, the initials AHNF-D embossed like a shield on their covers and backs, papers of all sizes, blotters and pens arranged punctiliously, a crystal vase full of yellow roses shining solitary on a corner shelf. But near the doors that led to the terrace, light was reflected so strongly that as he accommodated the small masculine company that followed him, and sat down in his *fauteuil,* Amleto was a master of solar lands, illuminated by the chiaroscuro lacework made by the sun filtered through the tree crowns. The port wine, letting out an occasional spark under that light, was perhaps getting to their heads by different routes than just their stomachs, and Amleto excused himself with bonhomie for lying back and crossing his legs, and laughed at the comparison with Sintra, which had been made by the officiating priest, Monsignor Bibiano Lucas Pimentel. Interestingly enough and in contrast with his reputation for inflexible severity, the monsignor was proving himself to be almost a wag, making one witty observation after another. Very unassuming for a man of the church who enjoyed so much prestige, he was a widely reputed sermonist, the force behind educational works never dreamed of before around here, an aristocrat who evinced his origins with his perfect silk cassocks, the delicate perfume that wafted around him, his manner of one who had become used to the best from birth. He took a few hurried little steps to the veranda, came back just as quickly as he had left, and inspected the part of the library where they were gathered.

"Yes sir! Here we are inside the lion's den where *Senhor* Amleto Henrique Ferreira-Dutton builds under the roses his ever-augmenting fortune!"

He laughed at his own words to make it very clear he meant them as a joke. Amleto understood and laughed too, but without showing his teeth, in a way he had been practicing lately because he considered it most proper at social events.

"I see Your Reverence has decided to turn your satirical bent against this humble servant of yours, who has done nothing to deserve the irony. First you compare this house to an estate in Sintra, a retreat for noblemen and potentates. And then you compare me to a—how should I put it?—to a wily, treacherous wild animal and mention a fortune which I do not know how to find, let alone possess."

The monsignor sat down and made himself comfortable in the chair.

"But I'm not being ironical, *Senhor* Amleto; what I'm saying is the truth. In contrast to useful animals, such as the dog, the cow, and the chicken, the names of wild animals are complimentary to those who are called by them. So it is with the lion, the tiger. . . . Therefore when I called you a lion I did not call you a wild beast but an invincible, irresistible fighter, capable of being at the helm of—and here is the second truth—what is undeniably a great fortune, which thanks to the help of God and to your competence is being increased day by day."

Amleto felt his ears burn, and thought maybe he had blushed.

"A most undeserved laudation," he mumbled, trying to think of something more interesting to say but unable to, due to his sincere emotion at the compliments.

"Of course they are deserved!" bellowed a deep, rather churlishly accented voice from the other side of the arch, and its owner, Major Francisco Gomes Magalhães, chief of police and Patrício Macário's godfather, appeared with a small wineglass in his hand. His nose was red, and although it could not be said he was drunk, it could not be said he was sober, either, which was apparent in his excessively firm steps and his louder than usual voice. "Yes, they are quite deserved! I heard what His Reverence said with that eloquence one can never praise enough, and he's absolutely right! Only one person can be greater than *Senhor* Amleto Henrique, and that's his son and my godson

Patrício Macário! Hah-hah! That one is going to be more than his father and godfather put together!"

"I don't know," Amleto said. "I don't know. Not on account of his good qualities, for if he inherited half of his mother's he inherited more virtues than most of mankind—I say this with no false modesty. But I fear for our future, I feel we're living in turbulent times, with no peace and no confidence in the future, with no respect for that which we were taught to cherish above all, such as the virtues of probity, temperance, and public spirit."

"And mind you, we're being governed by Brazilians for the first time in our history!" Monsignor Bibiano interrupted.

"Yes, but that doesn't mean anything. It might even mean the opposite of what Your Reverence might have wished to imply, begging Your Reverence's pardon," the major said. "The truth is, if the regents are Brazilian, all the rest, from army officers to merchants, all the rest is Portuguese."

"It's not really like that, my dear Chief of Police; you know very well that it is a little like that but not as much as you say. And please do not take me for an advocate of recolonization. I'm not one of those radicals who go so far as to be separationists, even republicanists, but I do sympathize with the movement for the declaration of His Imperial Majesty's majority. I'm of course aligned with the enlightened liberals, and Your Excellency must admit we have not had much luck with our regental governments. Disturbances of public order, sedition and anarchy everywhere, are they not disquieting to you, *Senhor* Chief of Police? Right here in Bahia, if memory serves, Your Excellency has been arduously engaged in combating sedition, and established your renown at the celebrated Battle of the Three Days not very long ago, not very long at all. I may be Portuguese by birth, but I'm Brazilian at heart, and if I speak like a Portuguese, this should be credited to the scruples of one who loves his language and does not wish to degrade it through improper and unadvisable usage. Your Excellency, I pray, should not jump to conclusions."

"By all means forgive me, Your Reverence; that was not what I meant. It's just that concerning the subject of the future of Brazil I have differences of opinion even with my illustrious friend and *compadre* and perhaps get a bit carried away. Please forgive me; nothing is farther from me than having any doubts about Your Reverence's most commendable and irreproachable conduct. But I do see a grandiose future for Brazil, a future comparable only to the apogee of the great civilizations of yore. For we are endowed with everything necessary for progress and enrichment. Right here in our part of the country—"

"We are subject to terrible, prolonged dry spells, which inflict punishment upon agriculture, cattle raising—"

"Excuse me, Monsignor," Amleto intervened. "Droughts, as those dry spells are called, are not entirely bad. Rather they may perhaps be seen as a guarantee of social order and of the established economy. For example, only through the penury occasioned by the droughts will the small landowner surrender to the evidence that his activity will always yield a paltry, insignificant production, thus making it possible for the big landowners, the only ones who can take progress to those backlands—I shall soon tell you why—to buy the small properties at conveniently low prices, because otherwise, incommensurate, maybe impossible investments would be required. And I'll tell you why only big landowners can take progress to all those vast regions. It's because only they have the power to seek from the government, by dint of their political weight and influence, the necessary improvements, the dams, weirs, and related works, to be done, after which the droughts will cease to be a hindrance to production. And only the big landowner can provide the capital, knowledge, and investments necessary for production to be up to commercial demands, which are becoming more complex each day. Therefore the droughts play a most important role, since they actualize something which I'm sure would call for more than the force of arms to be brought about by artificial means. And besides, what labor force would the big landowner rely upon, since slavery is fated to be abolished?"

The major had started gaping halfway through Amleto's speech, and remained stunned with admiration. The monsignor took some time to say anything, but finally complimented their host effusively for his brilliant, innovative reasoning.

"However, I don't think the end of slavery is near. Does *Senhor* Amleto really think we can survive without it, that it will be abolished?"

"I don't think its end is near, either; I don't know when it will be. But I do know it will come, and if there were no other reasons for it, it will come on account of the most powerful reason of all, namely that it will become very unrewarding and excessively expensive to keep slaves. I deal with them in my work, and I can assure you the expenses are incalculable; they would make the coldest financier shudder. There'll come a day when these costs will rise to such onerous heights that it will be better to work on a piecework basis than to think ingenuously that we enjoy free labor by having slaves, which is not true at all. Gentlemen, try to imagine a farmer who needs labor only for planting and harvesting, once or twice a year. The rest of the time he will have nothing with which to occupy his Negroes, but he will have to feed them, give them clothing, a roof, and medicines, not to mention unforeseeable problems that arise every day. This makes production more expensive because its costs are increased, and the landowner loses money, for it's becoming more and more difficult to cover those costs. Now compare that to contracts made with free workers to be paid on a piecework basis, without obliging the farmer to give them what he gives to his slaves. I don't think it's necessary to do a great deal of thinking to agree that slavery must be abolished sooner or later, for otherwise we shall be doomed to perpetual backwardness. Men in our region who could in time become small landowners will not accomplish that, for geographical and historical reasons. Together with the destitute inhabitants of the backlands, they will thus be the labor force of the nation, in the terms the nation requires to avoid waste and excessive costs. I know very well that this situation may lead to the existence of great masses of idlers, paupers, and tramps, such as has begun to happen already. But in the first place this is unavoidable, there's no stopping it, and the temperament of our lower classes is lighthearted, easygoing, accommodating, and not too demanding, which makes it not much of a problem. But even so—and I have devoted a great deal of thinking to this matter, gentlemen—it is comforting to be able to rely for the maintenance of public order upon an organization such as the national guard, so wisely and so opportunely created, as no doubt our major will agree. Again, as in the case of the droughts, it's necessary to invert our perspective, to see the good disguised by appearances as the bad. The rabble has a rude, primitive, fetishistic, barbarian, insensitive, unenlightened nature, and no ambitions but the ones dictated by its cramped horizons. The natural tendency of those people is therefore to turn against one another, and not against us, unless we relax the preservation of social discipline. There will be so to speak a naturally conducted selection, with the disappearance of those who do not embody the conditions to face life with their own means, not even in the service of the army, for which they are amply indicated in that which does not collide with the universality of the national guard, so opportunely conceived, I must repeat. And those contingents will furthermore enjoy freedom, considered by many the most precious of commodities and which we shall grant them for nothing, under the sole condition that they do not turn it into licentiousness nor use it for the commission of abuses."

"But doesn't *Senhor* Amleto believe that our people . . ."

"My dear Major and *compadre,* observe how we often use certain words without paying attention to their suitability. That's what has just happened, *data venia,* for the long conversance and fruitful friendship which unite us make me anticipate what you were going to say. Let us see now, what is that which we call our people? Surely it cannot be a mass of boorish, illiterate, diseased, stunted, malarious mongrels and Negroes. That cannot be called a people, that would not be what we would show a foreigner as our people. Our people is like us, that is to say, like the Europeans themselves. The working classes cannot transcend their condition, they will never be a people. A people is a race, a culture, a civilization, an affirmation, a nationality, not the scum of this nationality. Even if purged, as I foresee, the working classes will never be the Brazilian people, since the people is represented by the ruling class, the only one with a true claim to standards of civilization and culture in the European mold, for what are we but transplanted Europeans? We cannot lose sight of that, allowing ourselves to make the abysmal mistake of exploring our riches and virtual greatness, only to turn them over to this so-called people, which in the first place would not know how to manage such a prodigious legacy and would soon degrade it, as is known by anyone who has tried to provide comforts and rights to slaves and servants, because they do not know what to do with those comforts and rights."

"I'll have to agree with that. If you are generous with the lower orders . . ."

"That's the point, my dear gentlemen. Reality must be seen clearly, logically, unsentimentally. Ahead of us lies perhaps the most herculean task ever faced by civilized man. And I hope to God I'm wrong, but I fear for the future. I fear we may let the Creator do His part and fail to do ours, that is what I fear. What are we today? A few civilized men and a fearsome horde of blacks, browns, and natives. As the foundation for a civilization we are very few, hence the magnitude of our labors. If it depends on me, and I'm sure on you gentlemen too, Brazil will never become a country of blacks, browns, and natives, will not become a haven for inferior, despicable people held in contempt by all true civilizations, because by the grace of God, one of those civilizations will thrive here too."

"Has the *compadre* ever thought of going into politics? With such fluency and such a clear reasoning . . ."

"No, no, I detest politics; I'm a completely apolitical man. My line of work is entirely unrelated to politics. Politicians must forgive me, I have nothing against them, but the muck politics involves, if you pardon me the rudeness of the expression, is sickening to me. No, no, I'd rather remain obscure as the most humble member of the productive classes, accomplishing everything in my power to augment the wealth of my country; that's all I want. I hold no ambition for power, and may God keep me from having that ambition."

He spoke these last words in a contemplative, almost brooding tone. And so the civic vibration that was beginning to flicker in the library cooled down a bit. It was too beautiful a day to persist in such efforts. The monsignor, closing his eyes and shaking his head slowly as if singing an ancient song, mentioned downy flakes of albescent clouds slipping through the bristling skeletons of centenarian trees, and was heard with evocative sighs and doleful expressions. The major helped himself to more port, the monsignor asked for a glass and was soon having another, Amleto did likewise, and bachelor of law Noêmio came from inside, in old Commander Almeida's company, to declaim a few verses about swallows in the Mediterranean summers of All Saints Bay.

Near eleven, when they were called for lunch, they were very happy. Arm in arm with the monsignor on the way to the dining room, Amleto remarked that they were going to serve boiled rice in deference to the guests' tastes. He himself had once been a "rice gobbler," he had even tried manioc flour, which now tasted like sawdust to him. But Miss Bennington, the English governess, had educated him in no time at all. Was the monsignor familiar with the delights of British cooking, an art in which as in everything else that admirable people was the image of excellence? Rice can only be had as pudding; it's the only acceptable way of eating it. If he was not mistaken, it was called *rice pudding* in English, and there was a peculiarity about the second of those words, since it was not pronounced "puh-dinghy," as might be expected but "pooh-dinghy"; it was one of the many exceptions to the rule of the extraordinarily rich English language, with almost twice as many words as Portuguese. Did they like mutton in mint sauce? Oh, there was much to learn from the English! Brazilian manufacturers, all in all a piteous herd of ill-prepared, behindhand artisans, complained that English products were given artificial advantages over products made here, or rather botched here. Why? Because of low customs tarriffs. Even so, there still were tariffs; yet products made here were not only more expensive but also inferior. Put two and two together, my dear Monsignor, and you will have four every time; do they want things to be as they are not? That's no way to overcome competition, is it not so? I'm in favor of free trade; it's the only way for us to make any headway with our industries, if we can say we have industries. It's like that matter of the people we touched upon a while ago. Who made the glory and fame of Rome—the Caesars, or the slaves and the plebs? We have to inspire ourselves in the example of England, whose flag—"

But he did not finish speaking about the English flag, because as he got to the dining room he spotted the baroness at the doorway, walking with difficulty and leaning on her son Vasco Miguel's arm.

"*Senhora* Dona Baroness of Pirapuama!" he exclaimed, rushing toward her with his arms open. "My *Senhora* Dona Baroness!"

The baroness was suffering from rheumatism again, afflicted by lancinating twinges in her back, which bent her into outlandish postures and made her speak in a permanently weeping tone: Oh, *Senhor* Amleto, God has laid a cross on my back through this unappeasable neuralgia, oh, God of mine! But why had she come, she should have excused herself, they had had such cold days, my dear *Senhora* Baroness, we do not deserve such a sacrifice from Your Ladyship, has Your Ladyship, if I'm permitted to ask, had some willow bark tea?

Yes, she had, but she had had so much of it that it no longer had any effect. Amleto listened to her with a distressed look on his face, held her hands, walked slowly with her over to her chair, and gently helped her to sit down. He looked sideways at Vasco Miguel, who had graduated at the School of Medicine in Bahia but had no occupation—drained of color and emaciated, chinless, with jumbled teeth, his excessively high waist emphasized by a protruding pelvis. Yes, but if it had to be done it would be done, he thought, figuring his daughter did not yet have enough maturity and common sense to understand the reasons for her marriage to Vasco Miguel.

185

True, Amleto had had other plans for her; he had fantasized about Scottish castles while leafing through travel books. But one does not live by fantasies, one must live by a system of implacable decisions, as he had been learning the hard way all his life. The young man was not rich but he was white; he was not intelligent but was of noble birth; and he might eventually succeed in life because in his profession, like in all the others, good connections are more important than ability; and to add an irresistible touch to it all, it meant no future litigation about the baron's or the baroness's estate, since it would be all in the family anyway. Yes, yes, the marriage was something to be considered very, very seriously. Carlota Borroméia Martinha was probably sick in bed, as she always was when Vasco Miguel showed up at their home. She could do as she liked; those were feminine ruses, which should not be taken into account.

The way to deal with women is to tame them! If the baroness herself was the first to wish it and suggest it, why not? Teolina neither agreed nor disagreed; she disliked interfering in masculine subjects; so much the better. He glanced at Vasco Miguel once again and did not find him so bad; there were plenty of worse prospects around. Sitting down with an attentive look to make sure everything was running satisfactorily, he decided to communicate his decision to his daughter and had another sip of wine. He pulled a notebook and a golden pencil from his pocket mechanically, and scribbled fast: "Schedule: Marriage Carlota B." She is a Dutton, he thought with an elated determination, and a Dutton will do what must be done. The Lord be praised, *Dieu et mon droit. Le roy le veult,* one might even say by now. And how is the mutton? What lovely boiled potatoes!

Puffer Fish Village, Itaparica, February 28, 1836

Most people do not know anything about the armadillo. Ask them what they know about the armadillo, and they will likely answer that the armadillo digs holes, and will say little else. That is not fair to the armadillo. Indeed, the armadillo digs holes, and is as competent in their engineering as in their actual construction. The armadillo has no teeth. That is to say, if you look close enough it does, not in the front part of its mouth but in the back, a few puny things that cannot properly be spoken of as teeth. It doesn't bite, but it chews, and with that gives a lesson in the realities of life for those who want to see it, because the armadillo is like many two-legged beings who do not bite but chew and swallow, literally and figuratively. It possesses excellent nails, strong, sharp, and disposed like rakes, so that those who deal with it exercise an attentive caution to keep it from using them, which it will whenever it can. There are many armadillo races on the island, the most hunted being the so-called chicken armadillo, which people say is the true armadillo, known by its color, its size, and, after it is savored, by a taste superior to that of any chicken or duck. It can also be distinguished by the nine bands it sports. As for the six-banded armadillo, there are those who will not eat it, because the general opinion is that it fattens itself on the flesh of corpses, for it has no difficulty at all in entering any grave, deep or shallow, rich or poor. And in fact the six-bander, which is also known for usually being yellowish, not white like the others, and hairier, is fond of rotten flesh, animals killed by plagues and other foods enjoyed by buzzards, so that before eating it one must cook it very thoroughly to boil away the poisons, it being equally advisable to use much hot pepper in the recipe, to purge away any pestilence. The soft-assed armadillo, designated by many as the false armadillo, though not in reference to its morality, as with other animals, departed from here a long time ago, nor can we find here the famous three-banded armadillo, which rolls itself into a ball, the best designed of them all, and let us remember that Nature did not build many animals of better design and mechanisms than the armadillo. It is also more perfected in certain aspects than man, whose family is born capriciously and without order, while the armadillo's family is born in a most felicitous tidiness and most assuredly does not register among its members the same tribulations observed among men. The reason for this is that the female of the armadillo may have three, may have four, may have five or six young, and all of them are either shes or hes, there not occurring brothers and sisters in the same litter, which greatly facilitates their upbringing. Neither do we have on the island the armadillo called tatou and several other names, all of them most likely untruthful, which as we are told by narratives and accounts has a body longer than four feet and a tail of equal length, and from its carapace good-sized tubs are made, but this is sure as fate held to be nothing but tall tales by the whole island and by all decent men. Nowadays the armadillo is hunted with armadillo terriers, which find the armadillo, ferret it out, kill it, and bring it to the hunter. In the old days, the hunt was done with bludgeons around the time the armadillos left their burrows to eat, as they still do. But it used to be much more difficult for many reasons, among them that it is not always possible to make the armadillo release its nails from the bottom of its burrow, and it is strong-willed enough to die without letting go. For an animal with no teeth, the armadillo is not short on bravery, and for one that does not speak, it is not short on pride, and it may be taken for the plain truth that what we think of the armadillo is not what it thinks of itself, for there is nobility among armadillos and there are some of them that are better armadillos than others and there are many armadillo stories, some of which only we know and others only they know, and they prefer theirs while we prefer ours. Either fresh or corned or cured in the sun, stewed, in palm oil, braised in fat, even broiled or fried, the armadillo is a highly special food that no one who has eaten it will ever forget, and when such people see an armadillo they see nothing but a volume of food. Likewise the six-bander, reputed a bad food for his fare of cadavers because man forgets that he also lives by eating cadavers, even embalmed as dry meat or sausages. Man accepts only that he eats animals, not that animals eat him, although animals do not care about that and go on eating man, either by little snacks like the mosquito, or by regular custom like the roundworm, or by hunting like the cougar, or in the form of decaying food, for fishes and crabs if the dead man is in the sea, for buzzards and wild dogs if he is on land, and for worms and armadillos if he is buried.

Black Leléu was forced to listen with great patience to all this science and art of the armadillo, plus many other observations about the philosophy of hunting and food made by Luiz Armadillo around nightfall, while they cooked cassava to eat with dried anchovies and sugarcane syrup just before leaving for the hunt. Why on earth Black Leléu was engaged in this crazy expedition was something not even he knew for sure; maybe it had something to do with all the talk about his becoming two different people. To him it was all nonsense, but now and then he would be puzzled by something strange happening, and everybody kept saying he really had become two, two completely different Leléus, in their speech, their ways, their gait, their faces, their behavior, so much so that at a distance one could tell which one of the two was coming, there was really so great a difference between them.

"That's just something they made up," he mused aloud, and Luiz Armadillo, who was stirring the fire and was hard of hearing, thought he had asked about the cassava.

"It'll take some more time," he said in a professorial tone that unnerved Leléu. "If you're not patient, you can't hunt anything, you can't have anything in life. And besides, it's still too early; not one critter's come out yet. See there"—and he pointed at the dogs with his lower lip—"see how they're all quiet. They know they're going out hunting, they're ready, but they also know there's nothing to hunt right now, armadillos don't come out this early. Does the moon change today? Or was it yesterday? You have to change the water in the cassava pan as soon as it boils for the first time, so the cassava won't get hard, and after you change it you have to hold the second boiling a lot for it to get soft, and soft is the only way I can have it—I haven't got any more teeth. The armadillo comes out late. The armadillo comes out only—"

"I know; you told me," Leléu answered, deciding he would not lose his patience with Luiz, who was turning into an armadillo himself from eating so many of them, talking about them, and even speaking to them. One of these days he would become a full-blooded armadillo and run around eating dead people. Of course Leléu didn't believe those stories, but it might very well be part of the natural order of the world for something to turn into something else. Didn't the food people ate turn into hair, into nails, into strength, into speech, into everything a person has? But to turn into two people, as they said about him . . . They wanted to drive him crazy; envy works in a thousand ways, and even in Puffer Fish, a place as poor and out of the way as can be, with a people more dispossessed than the livestock of many good farms, envy was after him, although he did not flaunt either money or privileges. Well, no use thinking about that; the hunt was practically on, the dogs were getting restless, Luiz Armadillo had prepared himself, there was no way back now.

Luiz Armadillo returned to his brazier and started to fan the embers, his eyes fixed on the little sparks streaking out from underneath the pan. But the wind began blowing low and it was no longer necessary to fan, so he just remained squatting, his arms resting on his knees and his backside propped on his heels. Maybe the smoke, the sparks, the smell of burning coals, or the wind itself was shooing away the gnats, because not even the tiny blood-drinkers were there at their customary hour to break the peace with their itching bites, and the silence with the slapping one was forced to do as they bit. A very ample silence, with the low tide uncovering an almost endless marsh that went as far as the Island of Pigs, the remnants of a crimson strip about to fade in the sky, a damp coolness, big fruit bats fluttering low and now and then, flying together in large groups in the direction of the clouds or the dense forest, fiddlers and other small crabs standing at attention by the entrances to their holes, the oncoming sea beginning to lick the borders of the swamp, a faint light glimmering at the door of the little house under a coconut tree, an easygoing, rather silly, rather senseless wish that all that would stop, that it were no longer necessary to do anything, almost as if one's soul could leave the body, and the body become a statue, and the soul no more than a wind embracing everything and clinging to nothing. Wishing that in a way he could really be two people, Black Leléu could remember having felt this way only in his childhood, very, very young as perhaps he had been, when they left him alone for a while and he sat looking at clouds changing shape, the ground seeming to roll over, capsizing the world, the daytime moon white as a tapioca ball, his thoughts drifting to some unknown place, his head a soaring balloon. He could remember he had been a little boy, he even remembered that there existed places that did not exist except inside little boys, but he could not bring himself to feel that way again, he could only remember. Oh, boys and girls, what force they have that we do not have, what power they have when we love them, what an anguish they give us when they suffer, for they start suffering unjustly the moment they arrive, their distressed little faces hurting us, their crying torturing us, their discoveries making us cry for no reason! Although he was happy or maybe because of that, Leléu wiped the tears that ran down his face when he remembered Dafé's little face, which was no longer chubby as it had been for so long, and even flashed a few signs of womanhood now and then.

But she was still a little girl, with her pearly little teeth, her cocky little chin, her smell a bit like a flower's, a bit like honey, a bit like people, a bit like newly washed clothes and lavender leaves, her gestures like a little goddess's, the little devil! And while he thought, Leléu knew he had a silly smile on, and was proud of it.

She had been born before the expected time, on the twenty-ninth of February, a crazy day for anybody to be born, since you have a birthday only every four years. Then she was not going to be eight the next day, she was going to be two. And wasn't it because of her birthday that he was sitting here like a saphead, waiting to go hunting with Luiz Armadillo and listening to all that jabbering hunter's talk? Could it be that he was really turning into two people? Who'd ever have believed he would go on any stupid hunt, especially at night, especially if he wasn't exactly a woodsman? When he asked Maria da Fé what she wanted for her birthday, she said she wanted to eat an armadillo stew. Why, who ever heard of that? Why don't you ask for something else, a rich gift—a boat ride, a colorful dress, a wooden doll? No, I want to have a dinner of armadillo stew. And she also said, with that defiant look of hers no one could get mad at, that if Grandpa Leléu did not want to give her the armadillo, all right, but then he couldn't say he always kept his promises. Can you imagine that, a pint-sized brat barely out of her diapers, talking like that? Leléu smiled again. The little whippersnapper was bright, she was mettlesome, she was going to be one hell of a woman, a real go-getter. And here goes Grandpa Leléu out on a hunting trip like an idiot because of that little jackanapes. He could have bought the armadillos, but then he decided—was he really becoming two?—that the appropriate gift would be for him to go get the critter himself; the adventure rather than the armadillo would be his gift. If the people you used to know could see you now, Grandpa Leléu . . . If someone had told him before that all this was going to happen, he'd have said it was a lie; he might even have got angry. He'd have said that even after she was born, because he was on a disastrous streak, troubles in his life piling up like hog plums plummeting down from the trees in March. Working in Nazaré das Farinhas was now out the question, he had trouble finding buyers for his businesses, spongers kept popping up everywhere, he had about four more fights with Smile of Contempt's blacks, that girl Vevé was just about to give birth, he was feeling a strong desire to prick a couple of bellies with his ray spine and flatten some twenty heads with his club, his tailor's shop was being harassed and so were his girls, everything was drifting backward. And there he was, having to drag that pregnant woman around and about—and to think the reason he didn't have a family was that he didn't want to be tied down! So he had no liking either for the mother or for the child who was going to be born; he didn't like even to see Vevé. If he believed in things like hexes and jinxes, he would say she had brought them on, that wretch of a human bane standing in the way of everything, with her jutting belly and her almost complete silence.

And to top it all, the girl was born not only before the right day but before the hour, so to speak. She was born practically on the pinnace that was taking them to Incarnation Village, and no one was expecting that because by all reckonings she was supposed to be born in March. Leléu himself had done the figuring, because it was very easy to remember the day the baron screwed Vevé by force, Saint Anthony's Day eve, during one of the baroness's feasts in the old days. So all right, so he would take that wet blanket to Incarnation about fifteen days before she was supposed to have her child, and Da Hora, the woman in whose house she was going to stay, would be in charge of the lying-in. But no, maybe because of the moon, maybe because of Vevé's or his own bad luck, maybe because of the boat's tossing, maybe because of an intentional irony of fate in view of Leléu's having chosen for a midwife a woman who had the word "hour" in her name, water burst out of Vevé's belly the minute they entered the harbor, and she gripped the bow cordage, sat down, bit her lips, and straddled her legs wide.

"Hold it, press those legs together!" shouted Leléu, who had never imagined he would become so disquieted seeing for the first time a woman giving birth. "We're getting there, we're getting there, we're just about to dock, we're docking!"

But they had not arrived yet, and as they hurriedly moored the boat, with people on land holding the boat's rail with their hands because there was no time to belay the ropes, Vevé was carried to Da Hora's place with the top of the baby's head pushing out between her legs, and as soon as she lay down, the delivery was finished. Da Hora could hardly believe it was a first child and from an eight-months-and-a-half pregnancy, such a strong baby girl with such strong lungs, a delivery that had been as easy as a fart; she got a little suspicious. And Leléu would be suspicious, too, if he had not been practically an eyewitness to all the events that had led to that birth, and if it could not be seen, even with her wrapped up in a piece of cloth and with her eyes closed, that the baby was a mulatto and might take after her father. And that was confirmed afterward, because in spite of her skin's dark tone, almost like her mother's, her hair was practically smooth and her eyes—what beautiful eyes the little devil had!—were green, green, green like two emeralds, so lovely that people came to see them: they had become famous.

Yes, but Leléu disliked everything about it; he didn't even want to talk about it. Now instead of one there were two, and he grumbled a lot the next Monday as he was about to sail off with the ebb tide because he had to give Da Hora some money for their support, plus the usual whining extortions he was already expecting, plus an order for Black Sofrê, the keeper of his canoes *Dawn* and *Hummingbird,* to give them fish when they asked for it, though he should be careful not to overdo it. The Lent flies swarming all over like thousands of little mad devils even in the hollows of the boat, a sweltering, stifling heat like a scalding blanket, nothing but headaches waiting for him in Bahia, and the outstretched hand of that fat, watermelon-breasted, niggardly, tightfisted Da Hora, whose wiliness was proportional to the size of her tits. And those two inside, one with her nose in the air like a princess who could only speak to dukes and cherubs of very high station, and the other pissing, shitting, sucking, crying, shitting, pissing, sucking, crying, pissing, shitting, suckling . . . Now really, what did he have to do with that, what a life, what a life—the more he wanted to do what he wanted, the more he did what he did not want!

Leléu smiled again and followed only vaguely Luiz Armadillo's preparations: rummaging through dusty trinkets, putting a knife under his belt, inspecting a couple of grimy leather thongs, sniffing the air, his nose groping out like a snout, rubbing his hands on his backside every two steps, talking to the dogs—ah-hoon, Friendship; lah-lah-hoom, Colonel; hoon-hoon-hoon-hoon, Philistine; sho-sho-sho-sho, Good Nuts; lie down, Wildfire; scat, Bad Brave; take it easy, Crab; now now, Cornmeal; come on, Nobleman; now what, Excellent, now what?—damping the fire under the cassava pan, and going to fetch the jug of molasses from inside the water basin, where he kept it because of ants.

I'll cook the armadillo myself, Leléu thought, again anticipating his return home and all the fun they would have. Though sometimes he missed the life of travels and hard work he had always led, he did not like to leave Puffer Fish; he would only leave it briefly when he had no other choice, to wrap up one of the few businesses he was still involved with. He had got rid of almost everything, and now he had just a few rented houses, some five canoes, the little Puffer Fish farm with its vegetable patches and orchard, Vevé's big boat, a little lighter, the Conception Market fish stall, and his good old buried money. What else did he need? That had freed him from so many worries that although old age was coming over him unforgivingly on every spot in his body, he felt strong, maybe stronger than when he used to walk league upon league all over the bay lands. Nothing was annoying him anymore, not even his anger at Vevé, which had become much worse the day he got the news at his fish stall in Bahia that Da Hora had died suddenly in Incarnation. He almost kicked the stall to pieces in an overwhelming rage, and went out to kill Smile of Contempt with his stingray spine and did not do it only because he could not find him. Though a self-seeking, snitching, brash, wily, meddlesome old hag, she took care of his interests in Incarnation, and in all fairness he had to admit that though shrewd, she was neither dishonest nor lazy. And now—and now that! What a goddamned, accursed, ill-boding black bitch—it could only be because of her; he was forced to acknowledge that he was jinxed, and she was the jinx! So there he goes hand over head to Incarnation once again, knowing that by now Black Sofrê might even have sold the canoes, because Leléu could bet he was neither fishing nor working, that was for sure. And when he gets to Incarnation, what does he find but despair, with Black Sofrê and everyone else in the vicinity refusing to go out to sea, it all looking as though Doomsday was here and the next morning would not come. No question, no question, no question about it, it had to be a bad influence, it was plain to see it was that wretch's and her misbegotten daughter's influence. A girl who had come into the world on a leap year Friday, the twenty-ninth of February at noon—it was almost stupid not to admit that she and her mother were bound to have something to do with all those misfortunes.

The cause of the fear and consternation was not just Da Hora's death, for there were many who might never miss her. It was the return of the fish, which according to most people came to those parts every four years, sprouting from the ocean depths inhabited by dragons, serpents, and all other sea monsters to punish people's sins, a messenger of fear, an executioner from hell, haunting those clear waters with its enormous mouth of one thousand teeth. The first ones to see it were the crew of the *Hummingbird,* who were clearing the bar to cast their mullet net and had started to heave to, when a gentle ridging of the still water claimed their attention and a boundless terror chilled their blood: silent like the death it represented and just as threatening, a grayish blue-backed shape slipped by the canoe almost on the surface, as big as she and no doubt capable of biting her in two with just one squeeze from its colossal mouth. Not daring to move even a finger after they lay down on the wet bottom of the canoe, with the sun freezing them into a shivering mass, they even tried to breathe without making a sound, while the light swaying of the canoe, the little ripples made by the passage of the fish, and the two indescribably long times it grated its back against the hull let them know it was persevering in its murderous patrol, waiting to see the shadow of a victim in order to attack. Many hours later, so scared that they felt as if they had no more blood, they went to the church to pray, they confessed their sins, they lit votive candles, one of them went into seclusion, and the two others took a very long time to agree to remember the story and tell it.

It was the great tiger shark, which had come back with its appetite for warm-blooded animals, but some remained skeptical about it, they thought that without a master to guide them, the three young men had just made up an excuse for the loss of a net they could not handle by themselves. And the whole adventure was about to be forgotten, when three days after Almiro's boat had sailed out to the middle of the bay with three aboard to fish for mackerel, some boys found on the beach gnawed, ripped pieces of bodies covered by crabs and seaweed, crushed bones with only two or three hunks of flesh hanging from them, to the extent that it was impossible to tell how many there were, and they were able to recognize them only because the gig's hull, practically a shapeless heap of shredded boards and beams, ran aground at the mouth of the river, with its ragged sail still hanging from the mast and flapping like death's flag. The shark was now expected everywhere; penances were made all day long, and many families prepared themselves for famine and plagues, now that the sea was sheltering the most fearsome of deaths and even the river waters might suddenly grow teeth and devastate its banks, together with all those who chanced to be around.

Leléu refused to go to Da Hora's house, so he would not see Vevé and the girl. He would decide what to do with them later; maybe he would let them stay right there—after all, he did not even know where they had come from. Well, maybe he knew where one of them had come from, but that did not mean anything, he did not have any obligation toward them, they could both drop dead for all he cared, with all the adversity they seemed to drag after them like a tail that coiled around everyone. He visited Da Hora's grave, doffed his hat, pretended he was praying silently, and then walked over to the beach to think about what he was going to do. He did not even hear the first calls from João Dadinho and João Loló, who ran after him as though the shark had swum over to the church and was there chewing up the priest and the altars. But no, the creature was lurking offshore, one could tell by the fish school leaping crazily ahead of the great, deadly shape whose bluish reflections sometimes glistened just beneath the surface.

"I see it, I see it," Leléu said. "What can I do? I'm not the king of the seas."

We eat fish every day, he was going to say, so the fish may want to eat one of us, too, sometime. But he didn't say anything, he just kept listening in disbelief to what the others were saying.

"You're both crazy, you're both raving mad."

All right, they might be crazy, but what did it cost Leléu to agree with their proposal?

"It costs my boat," he answered grouchily. "If that thing munched up the gig like he was munching a fried croaker, is it my boat he's going to use for a toothpick?"

But the two of them insisted. If no one did anything about it, that fish was going to stay there for as long as it cared to, maybe for the rest of its life, getting used to eating people and having it easy. It had a weak snout, everyone knew that, it was not invincible, it could be harpooned; could it be that Leléu was going to let them ruin themselves because of a tyrannical fish?

"It's your ruination—it's my boat."

But he ended up changing his mind, let them go after the shark; he knew that every time they tried to get at it, it would disappear—it was always like that. Besides, there was an interesting detail in what they told him. They told him they were counting on Vevé's supervision and command, because she boasted of knowing all about seafaring, fishing, and battling vicious fishes! He had heard that story; he knew about Turíbio Cafubá, who by the way had been a natural-born idiot, as was known by one and all, and he knew of her bragging about knowing how to fish. All right, take the goddamned, godforsaken, accursed, blighted, blasted, shitty boat. You know what I want from you? I want you to get lost—now leave me alone!

He did not even say anything to her, and she did not speak to him, either, when sometime later he joined the others at the ramp to see the launch *Prankster* set sail, taking João Dadinho, João Loló, about four burly blacks, and Vevé, giving the impression she really knew what she was doing as she manned the rudder to put about around the bar and go chase the fish. He thought perversely that if the shark did its job well, it would take care of a few of his problems. It would eat Vevé, who was always setting him back, and it would eat João Loló, who insisted on charging him for the hoeing of a couple of okra, bell pepper, and mint patches, a hell of a lousy job he was never going to pay for, but Loló never ceased to remind him. True, the boat might be damaged, but the *Prankster* was solid cedar and jack-fruit wood of the best quality, it was no shark biscuit like that little laurel gig, and he figured, with a chortle, it would be a suitable price for the peace it would bring him. But he did not want to go on thinking like that, so he shook his head to get rid of those thoughts and remained by the beach, whistling low, while, first pushed by João Loló's pole and then with her jib and mainsail hoisted, the launch started to pull away. Vevé, her skirt tied between her knees in a big knot like ancient pantaloons, looked at him, raising her *araçanga,* and he could swear she had smiled, as he knew now she had, while the *Prankster* yawed starboard and set course out to sea to stalk the big fish.

The *Prankster* soon disappeared, and took a long time to return, everyone thinking she ought to be empty of people by now, with most of those bluffers already filling the creature's paunch, and the others more or less in pieces. With second thoughts about having let them use the boat and surprised about it, Leléu could not bring himself to do anything but wait for Zezé, Sofrê's daughter, who was supposed to come to take care of the baby—what the hell was her name, anyway? But it seemed Zezé would never come, and then, just because he could no longer stand her cries piercing his ears like an auger, he picked the girl up, closing the door so no one could see him doing the job of a house girl, almost a wet nurse. She had grown a lot, the little bastard; she weighed more than a suckling pig. Why don't I throw this little tramp out in the woods, or dump her in the sea and forget all about her? He gazed at her little face. She was not crying any longer, she was now slipping her fingers among Leléu's three or four chest hairs, tugging at them as if she wanted to hang from them.

"Ouch, you little bitch!" Leléu shouted, feeling like slapping her hands. "I'm going to rap you on that soft noggin of yours, you little pest!"

His face was very close to hers when he spoke, and she laughed as if on purpose, as if someone had told her to. At first it was just a grin, showing her lower tooth and her two upper teeth, but she was soon shaking with laughter, then guffawing, then pulling his stubble, then pressing her little body against his chest, and when he scowled in order to reestablish order, even if he had to cover her mouth with his hand or let her have it in the mug so she would learn some respect, she became serious, her shiny green eyes wide open toward him, her little head resting on his shoulder, her laugh reappearing as a chuckle, so much attention to him it seemed he was the center of the world—could it have been then that Leléu started to turn into two?

Leléu smiled exactly as he had smiled then. Luiz Armadillo assumed it was out of contentment because the food was finally ready, and waved at him to come and get it. Doing distractedly what Luiz was asking, Leléu remembered he had fallen asleep that day, and had waked up feeling one of his arms numb because of the position he had had to keep so as not to hurt the girl, and hearing people shouting outside, "There is the shark, there comes the evildoer, yes, good Jesus has killed the devil, oh my, it must be more than thirty feet long, oh, God bless the *Prankster!*" He rushed outside, forgetting he still had the girl in his arms, and there she was, the *Prankster,* listing from the weight of the creature roped to its side, with the huge hook baited with a pig's flank still planted in its monstrous mouth, João Loló's flensing billhook rammed into it to the hilt like a picket, machete cuts near its gills and snout, five banderilla-like harpoons planted on its back—there it was, vanquished like Saint George's dragon. Among the cries of the crowd, Leléu ran to the pier and saw a flushed Vevé still holding her *araçanga,* her hand bandaged because it had got scratched on the beast's back, in the posture of a general who's won a war. Yes sir, they killed the beast, Leléu thought, and soon figured that the shark's liver ought to weigh hundreds of pounds, and the oil was his; they could take the meat, but the oil was his. He straddled the girl's legs over his haunch and dashed to the beach to see them drag the fish to the sand, hollering to Sofrê to go get blades and machetes to remove the liver, and not to let anyone lay a finger on that liver—a little flask of the oil was worth a fortune, it was good for all kinds of things. Vevé was the first to come ashore, and she smiled when she saw Leléu, who smiled too, but turned serious right after.

"Here, you can take back your whatever-this-is," he said, handing the girl over to her.

But from that day on it seemed he did not want to go back to Bahia ever again, he kept putting off his trips, kept making up excuses to be with the girl, liked the name Maria da Fé, took to spending an enormous amount of time carrying her back and forth, took to becoming jealous of her mother, took to complaining about her being neglected, took to turning to old women for advice about mushes and paps, almost went crazy when he thought she had caught cold, and nursed her for two nights without sleeping for a minute—yes, yes, yes, he had become a different man, no one could believe what they saw. And when he did go to Bahia, he would come back loaded with presents, complaining once more that they had not taken good care of the girl, calling Vevé a bad mother, demanding that the girl's clothes be impeccably pressed, nice-smelling, and properly starched, going out for strolls with her to show her plants and animals, and the day she peed in his lap he laughed so much he almost had a stroke; he thought it was the funniest thing anyone could think of. And it was because of her that he bought the little Puffer Fish farm, a decision he had made while, as he did very often, he stood lost in contemplating her sleeping in her little bed, thinking it was time to go but staying. The day she called him "Gwanpa" and did it once again, though nobody who heard it thought it was anything but meaningless baby prattle—what stupid people, can't you see she says "Gwanpa" when she sees me?—he decided he was going to live in Puffer Fish, to bring up the girl in peace and quiet, far from bad people and from all the talk about sedition and war that was now being heard everywhere, to everyone's disquiet. He did not understand that talk, he did not want to understand it, and he suspected that Vevé, who now and then disappeared to go speak with people he did not know, had something to do with those rumors, so he was forceful when she hesitated about going to Puffer Fish.

"I'm not going to let the girl stay here, to have a bad upbringing and run all kinds of risks!"

"All kinds of risks?"

"Yes, yes, risks, risks! You don't know about that because you're always involved in those crazy conversations, you're all high-and-mighty after I gave you the command of the *Prankster* and you became known as the fearless woman who killed the fish that catches man by his shadow. So very well, so be fearless, be a tiger-shark killer, amaze people as the only woman launch-master in the world, do whatever you like, but you will not cause the girl to be unhappy. If you don't know how to be a mother, I know how to be a grandfather!"

He said "grandfather" in a proud tone, as if it was an irrefutable truth. And Vevé, who wanted to lose neither her daughter nor the boat and knew she could sail wherever she wanted from Puffer Fish, decided to agree. Peace, peace at last, in this place where there is nothing, and therefore there is everything. But here, too, Leléu sniffed something strange in the air, something that was developing in a way he could not see; the air was not the same as usual, there was something, there had to be something. Maybe something having to do with Júlio Dandão, who no doubt was involved in the Muslim Negroes' rebellions, maybe something having to do with those stray blacks from the decaying farms of the baron of Pirapuama, things having to do with people who instead of working wanted to change a world that could not be changed, which is why people always say "since the beginning of time, since the beginning of man," thus demonstrating that nothing really changes, and the laws of life will always prevail, and they will never change. Besides, Leléu thought, who but grandfathers know anything?

"You wave the firebrand like this," Luiz Armadillo said, whisking about a piece of firewood with a burning end that cut into the darkness, and Leléu was startled. He was already out in the bushes, he had eaten the cassava and still had a few specks of manioc flour and molasses in the creases of his cheeks, the dogs were working, and he hadn't seen anything. And he also noticed that he was carrying a firebrand himself, though just hanging from his right hand and not brandished like Luiz's.

"What the hell is that, Luiz, what do we want these firebrands for? They don't light anything."

"They're not supposed to; they're just to ward off devils."

"Devils? What are you talking about? What devils—where are they?"

Luiz Armadillo used his teacher's tone again, and explained that Leléu was not familiar with forests, so he didn't know about the devils of the woods, but Luiz knew. There are many devils here, he said slowly; it's not like in Africa, where there are no devils; here there are many of them, so Leléu had better carry his firebrand the proper way, to avoid possible trouble. And he was about to continue teaching the wisdom of the woods, when he halted by the edge of a bamboo thicket and squinted.

"Say, say, say!"

The dog Excellent tried to squeeze in through the clumped bamboos but did not make it and started going around it without stopping, changing direction every so many turns.

"Excellent's not a ferreter," Luiz explained. "Neither he, nor Friendship, nor Crab—look there."

He pointed at Crab and Friendship, which were also making nervous circles around the stalks.

"But it's difficult to slip in there; that's a tight clump."

"Nah, it depends on the dog. Wildfire is the one that goes in bamboo and reed thickets like that; you can't believe how easily she goes in."

Yelping all the time, Wildfire nuzzled the roots of the thicket, and all of a sudden, as though the ground had opened itself just for her, she disappeared into a kind of tunnel. Good Nuts, the little balls that gave him his name looking like two tiny brown moons, drove half his body into the hole, wagging his tail at high speed. And to Leléu's surprise, an eruption of sand burst forth on the other side of the bush, followed by a frantic armadillo, scampering out toward the roots of a giant cow tree, going much faster than its short legs seemed to allow. But soon the dogs were on top of him, including Wildfire, which had squeezed out of the hole like a chick coming out of an egg. Turned on his back, the armadillo snorted, gave battle, and

198

ran its nails over Excellent's nose, but Excellent was not disturbed, and clenched his teeth around its neck and held it until Luiz came over with a bludgeon in his hand.

"A six-bander," he said. "Nice little armadillo, come here," he added almost tenderly, and killed it with a quick blow to its head.

Two hours later, with four armadillos in their straw bag, they made their way home silently, even the dogs trotting quietly and in order, knowing the hunt had ended. Luiz Armadillo was walking out in front, and Leléu tried to step precisely where he had set his feet, so they almost collided when Luiz stopped unexpectedly.

"Listen!" he whispered, pointing his forefinger at an indefinite place, half upward, half toward the forest.

Leléu strained his ear and heard the fleeting chirrup of a bird.

"A lark, isn't it?" he asked.

"Yes, but at this hour?" Luiz said, making a solemn pause to ask a question whose answer he already knew. "Why at this hour?"

"I don't know; it is a little strange. But—"

"Sh!" Luiz said conspiratorially. "Listen!"

"Tell me something, Luiz—how come you're so hard of hearing and can hear a teeny sound like that?"

"I'm only deaf for deep sounds. I'm not deaf for sharp sounds. And I'm not even deaf for all deep sounds."

Leléu considered getting into an argument, although he was beginning to find all that very silly and wanted to get back home right away, but the sound returned, accompanied by a kind of murmur, a very distant, wordless chant.

"Hah!" Luiz said. "Hear that? Souls!"

Leléu tossed his head and gave him a light push to get him on his way again. The chant did not go away, though, seeming to fluctuate with the wind, which was blowing to the inner coast of the island, and Leléu got goose pimples and shuddered lightly. Could those be really the voices of souls coming from Tuntum and Amoreiras? And what about those muffled calls that could also be heard, at times very close by, as if there were people around exchanging greetings? The bird song was repeated, this time much nearer. Leléu shuddered again; the voices and chants stopped entirely. Nonsense, Leléu thought, I must be getting dotty. But he did not want to look back, and sighed with relief when they went around a little knoll and descried, illuminated by the moon and its reflection on the shallow waters covering the marsh, Luiz Armadillo's little shanty, the Island of Pigs, and the outskirts of the village. I want to go home right now, Leléu thought, anticipating the fun he would have with Maria da Fé the next morning, and hefting the straw bag with satisfaction. But he was not completely at peace, and it bothered him not to know the reason.

Village of Saint John of the Little Swamp,
Itaparica, October 29, 1846

Hey, what ever happened to all those folks of the Good Jesus Fishery—could it be that the whales ate them all up? Oh, how fleeting are the affairs of the world, nothing one builds is perennial, nothing one does is well remembered beyond its day, nothing remains as it is, no one ever returns, no one ever returns. If the traveler treads down the pathway that links the manor to the blubber-melting plant, he will notice that the daisies bordering it are being smothered by cockleburs; they do not even blossom as in the old days. Closed and silent, the manor appears to be well preserved, and even the blue friezes of the cornice seem freshly painted; the veranda has been swept recently, the windows are clean and shiny. But it resembles a corpse bedizened for its funeral, a great dead female creature that will soon begin to decompose. There are people around, one or two blacks, moving slowly, carrying baskets, hoeing the ground around the trees, and walking indifferently by the blubber-melting plant—this one, yes, a wasted ruin, corroded walls, contorted, gashed iron plates, the skeleton of the roof exhibiting itself through gaping holes bristling with broken rafters, weeds growing out of the crevices of the mortar, the gate toppling over its wood support poles, chickens grubbing in the dirt outside and inside, a rancid smell permeating the walls, four whale vertebrae, like royal thrones, disposed around a sad cinnamon tree. The blacks who used to work there were for the most part sold to sundry buyers, others are still paying for their emancipation in installments, some were dispersed according to the wishes of their owners, a few ran away, and many died, including almost all of those who had got to know the old Great Mother Dadinha, who lived to be one hundred and fifty and had even the powers of making rain or sunshine, as well as carrying in her head everything known to mankind to this day. There are no people like her now. The whites no longer command the hunting, flensing, and melting of the whales, and the coast swarms with ships from other lands, hunting more and better, and selling their oil here. The whales still show up in the bay, sometimes in good numbers, but they are a chancy, risky business; commerce is different these days; the world is different these days. To hunt a whale here and there, maybe, but not like in the old days; nothing is like in the old days.

Even the Saint Gonsalo holidays nowadays are something a man has to see to believe, and people say it is because of the debauchery of the owner of the new sugar mill in Little Swamp, who in addition to being a feaster is fond of seeing his Negroes frolic and is a big spender, even though there is some talk that under the guise of kindness what he does is to instigate, promote, and take part in orgies. May God forgive him who thinks evil, may God absolve him who indulges in slander, but it is known through the ancients —not the ancients from Portugal, nor the ancients from the coast of Africa, nor these third-rate ancients who are the only ones to be found today, but real ancients, Prester John's ancients, ancients from the kingdom of Cathay, of Marco Polo in Turkey, of King Herod's time in Hebrewland, of the Twelve Knights of France, of the Lord's Donkey, of the time when animals still spoke, of the Seven Wonders, ancients old as the hills—ever since the time of those ancients people have known about the nature of the good saint Gonsalo, here nicknamed Gonsalino, which goes to show how overfamiliar people get with him. Why is it that if Saint Anthony's garments are of stone or clay like the rest of him, if Saint Joseph's garments, Saint Onofre's, Saint Simon's garments, the garments of all saints, men and women, are, Saint Gonsalo's garments are by custom made of cloth? Let shame kill us, but truthfulness is the first commandment of the storyteller, and the truth is that the saint's skirt is made of cloth so they can pull up said cloth and see underneath it the flaw in the sanctity of this famous saint, namely his colossal lower tools: larger balls than Saint Nereus, a bigger rod than Saint Moses, a greater cockhead than Saint Priapus, harder than Solomon of the Thousands of Women—that is the simple truth. The verses for the saint? More than lecherous. The chants for the saint? More than libidinous. The praising of the saint? More than lascivious, certainly lewd. The entreaties to the saint? More than licentious. The feasts of the saint? More than Lupercalian, in which they sing:

> Good my saint from Portugal,
> Gonsalo, find me a husband,
> So I'll get rid of the cobwebs
> That are growing you-know-where—

and this in the novenas, very bland affairs, though one can very well imagine what is this you-know-where: it can be anywhere there is an opening, bottomless or not, in front, in the back, in the head, any spot in the body, and the women show those spots, rub those spots on the saint, stroke the saint's private parts, and clap their hands outside when the men sing:

> Saint Gonsalo comes from Douro,
> Bringing some hide on a stick—
> The kind of hide you like most,
> Which is the hide of a prick.

In the words of Master Aurelino Fialho, every year for more than a score the organizer of the festivities and the rehearser of the most eye-filling groups of dancing girls, the celebrations today reach their fulminating point, no more, no less, in the great fish feast of the Holy Guitar Player, as Gonsalino is also known. But before that there were the holidays and other festivities, which have been going on throughout yesterday and the day before yesterday, and to judge from them, you would think no one stopped even to sleep, with libertinism more or less ruling the day, let's face it. Yesterday there was what was seen under the light of the bamboo-mounted cressets of the square and what was not seen behind bushes, in clearings, around walls, on boats, anywhere he and she could appease their lowly instincts without sinning, for there is no sinning when one goes wenching during Gonsalino's feast—as established by the most authoritative books of precepts. And there are huzzahs and double huzzahs for Saint Gonsalino, always with the utmost fervor, making old people wish for the return of the days when the government of Bahia used to send militiamen and other men-at-arms, in order to put fornicationists, perturbationists, hullabalooists, gambolists, and dissolutionists in irons. Though not the speculationists of the gambling stalls, all of them crooked and enormous sources of high sinfulness, to which, however, old people devote themselves with voluptuousness, throwing away their coins in games with little rings and in bets on egg-in-spoon races, quoits, wheels of fortune, paper-strip lotteries, cockfights, marbles, and other carnival inventions. And if ordinarily Father Bernabé is hard pressed to assist his parish, what with all the expenses incurred on account of his live-in woman, two concubines, and nine children, three by each woman, it can be imagined how much worse it gets during the feast, when greatly adding to his worries are the many stalls he makes his families set up on the fairground, which his families manage or supervise, so badly that he must be the first owner of a gambling stall ever to have lost money, notwithstanding his being a man of God. If at court one saw dances, tom-toms, tambourines, castanets, and mandolins inside churches, then there is nothing one could say. But since such things are not seen at court, nor black women peddling indecencies in churchyards, nor auctions of confections—"For such a nice piece I ought to get more, but since I find no takers I'll sell it this cheap, here's one, here's two, here's three, I'm going to sell it, I'm selling it, I've sold it!"—nor unbridled food sprees, nor friars capering about and pinching behinds, nor guitars and zithers pit-a-patting among bumps and grinds, nor noblemen openly rubbing themselves against brown and black women, nor folk dances at the door of the house of God, not to mention the worst black bands following a saint of the Holy Apostolic Roman Mother carried by libertine snare-drum and castanet players on a most profane litter adorned with mosses and other plants of low extraction—since such things are not seen at court, one cannot help but being scandalized.

There goes Gonsalino to the beach in his fully decked out beechwood box, leaving behind his guitar but taking his little golden cudgel, to await the roundup of the fish, which today are caught in every way—by net, seine, harpoon, gaff, hook, trap, even by hand—since the saint never fails during his celebration. That can be verified at dinnertime, around midafternoon, for in the whole square teeming with people you will not be able to find a single bowl, dish, or gourd that is not filled with fish, either broiled, stewed, boiled, in palm oil, or even raw, the way the black Zé Pinima likes to have it. And seafood, more than any other, does not limit itself to sustenance, but its marine humors irrigate viscera with erotic principles, which in their turn are goaded by the rich man's port, the commoner's muscatel, and the poor man's firewater. This happens to both men and women, altering the curbs that the former impose on themselves out of fear and the latter pretend out of convenience are part of their nature, and leading to general incontinence and widespread wantonness. That is probably the reason why after dinner, just as night began to fall, few were the people who were not capering in the square or playing the game of the two-backed beast in the dark. And besides, tomorrow is another day, Friday, not Sunday, not a holiday, nor Saint Gonsalino's feast, but time to toil and suffer, as is the fate of men.

Merinha was now serving in a rich house in Little Swamp, and the house black Martina, very pretty and with her hair straightened, stopped by the gate to talk to her. Martina, who had also been sold to people of those lands, was on her day off, because her masters were very devoted to Saint Gonsalo; and her young master, her master's youngest son, sixteen years old and very, very hot-blooded, had come along to the feast with her. If Merinha's owners did not mind her going to the feast too, why couldn't she join them? Why did she have to keep that long face, hardly even peeping through a narrow opening in the gate at the passage of a band, as though she were in mourning? Life is short, and a black's life is made shorter by hard work and humiliation, so no chance to have fun should be missed. Come on, girl, lots of people we know are there, even Inácia's come all the way from Holy Port, a little up in years but spry as can be, and the mute Feliciano, on a day off from his work at the kiln, is also there, and so is Nicodemo, who's a big man now, it's almost like a reunion, sadness leads nowhere, let's go to the feast!

Merinha looked at the young man who had come along with Martina, at his upper lip, shaded by a silky fuzz, and his curly, lustrous hair, combed sideways, and his appearance of having drunk a bit too much, as he stood waiting under a mango tree at the corner.

"I don't know how you can do a thing like that," she said, pointing her chin at him. "A young goat like that, who can't do you any good, a white and a master like any other, out to take advantage of you like all the others . . ."

That did not disturb Martina, who smiled with a shrug.

"Now, really, do you think I would miss the chance to enjoy a nice, clean, sweet-smelling, fired-up white boy—you think I would miss the chance to enjoy a little nobleman? Not on your life; I'm one of God's children too! I've been teaching him, coaching him; there can't be anything better—you wouldn't believe what I make him do!"

She put her hands on her hips, laughed loudly, raised her chin, shaking with laughter, and nudged Merinha with her forearm.

"I have him while he's having me, sweetheart. . . . Ha-ha!"

Merinha laughed too. Who could get angry with Martina? Who knew if there wasn't something right about her way of life; who knew what was right? She glanced at the boy once more, and he did not seem impatient. He put his hat on, found a coconut tree stump next to the mango tree and sat down on it, leaning on the tree with his legs stretched out and giving the impression he was going to doze off.

"Isn't he pretty?" Martina asked. "His name is Manuel Bento, but I call him Bem-Bem; it makes him melt all over. Do you know I was the one who grabbed him? He used to give me the eye all the time, and I used to pretend I didn't understand it. I can't sell myself cheap; he's got to know he's not putting his hands on fool's gold—this here is fine gold, my dear!" She wiggled, with her fingertips pressed together below her navel, and laughed aloud again. "But I could tell he would not force things, he acted like that out of innocence, and, friend, when they are innocent I can't resist. Ask me why I don't grab baby boys, and I can't give you an answer. . . . Then the day I set my eyes on those thick young legs squeezed inside his older brother's old breeches, that bulging little ass, that face like a suckling piglet's hankering to be cuddled, those ways of a little chick yearning for a wing over it, I didn't waste any time, I went over to him and spoke to him. I spoke to him as I was passing carrying a tray and he was as usual at the end of the corridor with his hand on his hip so his elbow would rub on my breast as I passed, thinking I did not notice it, but I did notice it, and I'd take longer and longer passing by him, and every time I went back in I'd adjust my breasts inside my slip so they would point upward like this, nipples up like this, so when I rubbed one of them on his arm he'd feel it slipping down, and sometimes I'd stop for just a little while without looking at him and rub my breast on him back and forth like this. So all right; so one of those times

I turned to him and said, 'Why don't you go call me at night to ask for some tea?' To ask for some tea? He didn't get it, and then I laughed and stared right at the place where he was swelling up, which was pretty tight under those breeches, and when a man is a virgin it looks like it's going to burst, and I took a long time to answer, enough to make him almost climb up the wall on his back, and then I said, without looking in his eyes for even a moment: Tea. I said it like this, very slowly: Teeeaaa. There was no way he wouldn't make it out, but even so, when he arrived at the bedroom door and said he'd come to ask me to make some tea for him, I'd been so anxious it hurt. I got up and went over to him and said: Teeeaaa? Poor thing, he looked like he couldn't stand on his legs, so I started taking him inside the bedroom, I took him inside, I made him sit down, I took off his clothes, and it was really a feast, I enjoyed it very much. You know what I say to them? I say, My little baby, my sweet little white baby, naughty-naughty, give your honeybunch Martina a kiss right here. . . . Hee-hee-hee-hee!"

"Now really, Martina, a woman your age, when are you going to get some sense into your head? Now really . . ."

"With God's help, never, sweetheart. How about it, are you coming or not? You don't have to take your things there out of the jar, though as a preserve it's never been any good; it's like breadfruit: it doesn't keep well. It's just to forget our troubles for a while, to see people, to have some fun! If I didn't know, I'd say you were a widow, not just jilted by Budião."

She regretted it as soon as she spoke. She saw her friend's face almost come apart with grief and put her hand on the back of the other's neck with a weeping look, about to speak again, when Merinha interrupted her.

"Budião never jilted me," Merinha said. "And his name is not Budião. His right name is—"

"His name isn't Budião? Does he have an African name?"

"No, no, of course not; forget it. By baptism he is Faustino da Costa, and they call him Budião because that's what they call parrot fish, and his mouth looks like a parrot fish's with those pouting lips, and the color of his skin also—"

"How do you know he hasn't left you? A good ten years have passed, my good friend, and no one knows his whereabouts!"

"I know he hasn't left me."

"You do? But you told me yourself no one knows if he ran away, if he set up a settlement for runaway slaves, if he went back to his land—no one knows! Do you know, Merinha? Something in your eyes tells me you know—do you know?"

"No, I don't; how would I know?"

"Then how do you know he hasn't left you?"

"Oh, I just know, I know, a woman knows those things; it's something that comes over your chest, a feeling you have at night, something that comes in the early morning, an aching in the middle of the day, a shortness of breath that arrives at bedtime. I know! I know he isn't dead, and I know he didn't leave me."

"How do you know?"

"There are ways, there are ways! There are ways to know those things!"

Pity her, who was talking too much about things that should be kept secret, who was not even sure of what was true or false, who received messages that did not sound like messages, advice disguised in recipes, inexplicable greetings, help from unknown sources, news so vague she could not understand it. Was there any truth in what she kept hearing from Zé Pinto, now so old he could hardly walk, making a living of planting coriander and wormseed in rotting halves of the old whale oil barrels he had also used to make a roof for his tiny hut, and considered a lunatic because he liked to go out at night without a purpose, when everyone was asleep and no one in his right mind would risk catching cold like that? Whenever she asked him, his answer was always, Dah-dah-dah, my girl, that black brute of yours is more than sound and hale; nothing can happen to that no-good sort! But if she went on asking, Dah-dah-dah-dah-dah, my girl, he is looking for trouble who wants to know too much. And then he would shuffle away like an old duck, looking up and around as if talking to mosquitoes.

She felt lonesome, very lonesome, more lonesome now than in all these years, these months, these weeks, these dragging days, these snail-like hours, these minutes elongated like taffy threads, this perpetual opening and closing of her eyes like long nights intercalated by endless days, these gestures that were never completed because he was not there. A warrior woman by blood, she did not know it until her uncle Júlio Dandão, gone since the same day as Budião, made her remember. However, it was not just a memory of the mind, it was a memory that belonged to her whole body—her nose, her ears, the palms of her hands, her pores, her crotch, her mouth, burning with the fire of many peppers—a memory of things that would not let her sleep. A memory, pity her, shared by so many women like her, women from any nation, women fractured by so many demands, by the lives of their men, like hers so weak in their strength, so needed at their side, but having to go, to disappear into their lives of enterprises and expeditions with no assurance of ever coming back, liable to forget their women, to find them ugly and ancient, but the women, even crying and grieving and dying of passion, did not want their men to be any other way, for they would not love them any other way.

Nine years had gone by, maybe ten, certainly one thousand and a hundred, and Merinha knew that her Penelope-like face was not just hers, it was part of the world and of the life of women, of slave women, always in exile no matter where they happened to be—why did it have to be that way? Her elders had taught her, as they had been taught and as their teachers had been taught: Beauty is not a good provider; a beautiful man will let his wife go hungry; let saints in their litters be beautiful and let us have good bread-winners. But it wasn't true, was it? It wasn't, because a beautiful man seizes a woman's eyes, he brings forth all that is mischievous in her. A beautiful man? Oh, a beautiful man! A beautiful man is like a new toy, and his beauty brings pride to the woman who won him, for she knows he is coveted by the others but he belongs to her—that smile is hers, that intimacy is hers, those ways of a rich-plumaged cock are hers, that lovely man is hers. Yes, that's the way it is. But what makes a man beautiful? This is not known, because the elders would not explain it well. Elder woman number one, who comes from an orchard- and vegetable-planting people, finds beautiful the man whose arms since his grandfather have been growing longer to pick the fruits and to scrape the land, achieving excellence in his production and the esteem of his peers. Elder woman number two, who comes from a fishing people, finds beautiful the one who distinguishes himself the most on a boat, who has the body and gestures of a seafarer, who recognizes the presence of fish at a glance, who brings in the fish and is respected by the earnestness of his calling, and so he is beautiful like all the others who look like him. Elder woman number three, who comes from a warrior people, finds beautiful the demeanor of the good fighter, admires him who will die before he will lose, falls in love with a great victor. So Merinha does not know, but feels a woman will find beautiful the man who will give her the best children, and this way, if she cannot be like him, her children can—and her children, after all, are herself. And thus she preserves herself, preferring to be the fifth woman of a man who is like what she wants her children to be than the first woman of a man whose seed would mean nothing to the memory she bears in her body, which Nature does not allow her to forget, one whose children she would not want to carry. That is why faithful women shall always exist, women faithful to the point of madness, of insanity, of senselessness, and the reason is that they are loyal to their wombs, valorous trustees of their heritage, and so there is admiration for the woman who awaits for her man, there being stories about it in every repertoire, and every woman, no matter how she may deny it, feels envy if she cannot be like that, because even if she does not know why, she knows there is superiority in being that way.

Budião had shown up at night suddenly, as he always did, though he could have sent a message, for they were both living in Little Swamp now, he at the sugar mill, she at the same house as now. But he always chose to turn up at night and chirrup like a nocturnal bird near the little back gate until she came to see him. That time he seemed impatient, and when she took some time to come because she had been asleep and dressed only in a slip, he started peeping so loud that he might have awakened the masters of the house, for though their bedrooms were distant from the backyard, such sounds travel very far at night. She was startled as she came out, wrapping herself in a piece of cloth and unlatching the gate, her eyes wide open. For many days now Budião had appeared to be more and more tangled up in secrets, spending a long time with his eyes set on a vague spot ahead, barely speaking, and disappearing in the night after staying with her no more than a few short moments. Though he would tell her much of what was going on, it was usually in an imprecise, reticent way. Was there really a secret brotherhood, was there a number of secret brotherhoods? Why was Júlio Dandão always around with his lighter, and how did Budião manage to slip off and stay out in the sea all day with him and a few others, without bringing back either fish or merchandise, arriving sometimes excited, sometimes gloomy? Why were things so easy for him at this particular sugar mill? If his master was considered a good man, who did not lock up his slaves and treated them almost like people and sometimes let it be known he had ideas that had led many to the gallows or to exile, would that alone explain the great freedom Budião seemed to enjoy, an impossible thing among slaves?

Budião had been waiting for her, pacing back and forth almost in leaps, and he hugged her as soon as he saw her, putting his hand over her mouth when she tried to speak. But he took so long in his hug, even seeming to tremble as he squeezed her, his arms vibrating as if shivering with fever, that she struggled to pull herself loose, because she wanted to see his face, to see what was going on.

"What happened?" she said, holding his face with both hands. "What happened, is anything wrong? Tell me, something has to have happened!"

"Yes," he answered after a long silence. "Yes. I'm leaving today; I've come to say goodbye."

"To say goodbye? Where are you leaving to? Leaving? But how come, all of a sudden, just like that? You're going to run away? Are you going to run away, Budião?"

"More or less. It's a mission. Captain Teófilo knows that tonight I'm going out on Dandão's boat to pick up a few men who are waiting along the coast, and then we'll come back here and sail out again, this time at dawn on a big canoe with eight oarsmen, including me."

"Captain Teófilo knows? Budião, I can't believe that; who ever heard of a slaveowner knowing one of his blacks is running away and not doing anything?"

"He doesn't know I'm running away. He only knows the first part of the mission, which he thought up with your uncle and others, many others; it's a complicated thing, very complicated, very difficult."

"I still don't understand. I don't understand anything!"

"Look, you're the only one who can be told about that, not because you're my woman but because you're the woman you are and have a great deal of service to your credit. Listen well, because I'm not going to repeat it; I haven't got any time; I'm leaving with the high tide; your uncle is waiting for me. There's a man who's under arrest at the sea fort, an important man who commands a sedition force very, very, very far from here, in Rio Grande, which is so far it's impossible to imagine how far, but it's in Brazil. Ever since this man's arrival there are people making arrangements for him to escape from the fort and go back to his land. Dandão always knew about those things, he knows all about them, and he's been talking to Captain Teófilo for some time. People don't know about those things, because those talks are secret, sometimes even on a boat out on the sea."

"The captain has talks with my uncle? I don't—"

"Sh! You want to listen or don't you? I've never told you a lie; if you don't want to listen it suits me fine—it'll save me time."

"No, no, tell me."

"So Júlio Dandão knows all about it and is helping Captain Teófilo, who is part of a group that wants to set this man free; it's all too complicated and secret for me to explain it now. And tomorrow morning, after we have mustered all the men, we're sailing out on a big canoe to ride at anchor just offshore from the fort and wait for the man. I am going and so are your uncle and Zé Pinto and others, like I said. Tomorrow is Sunday; he gets permission to go swimming on the fort's beach, and that's when he's going to find a way to fool the soldier who'll be watching him and swim to the canoe. Then we're going to bring him over here, and while he's on the canoe he'll shave off the beard he grew in prison so he could have a different appearance after escaping, and change his clothes, and spend the day hiding right here, to embark later on a merchantman bound to Rio Grande."

"Oh, you're coming back, then. So that's it. Then you're not going away; you're going to be a runaway for one day only. At first I thought—"

"No, I'm going away with him. Júlio Dandão and I are going."

"You're going away? To this faraway place, to the war of sedition, with this man you don't know?"

"We know who he is. Yes, we're going with him. You'll hear from me. Keep in touch with Zé Pinto; he's going to stay; he'll always know something."

"And does the captain agree with all that?"

"He doesn't know about the second part of the mission. He only knows I'm going to be one of the rowers on the canoe. He doesn't know you're Dandão's niece and my woman, nor that Zé Pinto is together in this with me and Dandão; he doesn't know anything else, he only knows about what concerns him."

"But why? Why are you going away?"

"You think I want to be a slave for the rest of my life? You think I was born a slave? You think there's nothing to do, not only for me but also for others?"

"But what are you going to do in that place? You're going to serve this new master, to be one of his blacks?"

"No. Only I have to pretend in the beginning. I think we're going to fight in this war; they haven't told me everything yet; maybe Dandão knows it all and will tell me about it during the trip."

"They haven't told you yet? Who tells you those things?"

Budião looked up and raised his hand to check the wind.

"The tide's soon going to be as low as it can get; I have to go. I'm going, but I'll be back; in my heart I'll stay."

He thumped on the left side of his chest, his Adam's apple bobbed up and down, he looked at Merinha's face and covered his watery eyes. Oh, what a strange thing, what a senseless thing to have to go away now that he was seeing his woman so enticing, so naked underneath those loose clothes, so good to hold with the plumpness the years had brought her. Sometimes he felt like ceasing to exist, like going inside those little fat folds, those recesses, the middle of those ever more abundant breasts, the lanes traced by those strong thighs, to mingle with her, to mingle together and then stop together to become part of the ground, united once and for all, without speaking, without moving, without needing anything but life, being a plant, a tree, a being made out of both of them in the same measure. What a very strange thing, he thought again, looking at Merinha's armpit, which was showing now that the cloth that covered her had slipped down a bit, and he wondered whether that cloth did not bear the stains of her sweat from the kitchen, giving off the smell that made him more of a man than the others. He thrust his face in her armpit, breathed in as if he would die if he did not do it, and, feeling that the cloth had imprisoned that smell, tore it away from her with an unexpected tug. The hem of her slip coming up to her thighs, she became a breast showing, another one about to, a groin being uncovered, and bare, glistening shoulders under that charmed light. Budião could not choose where to look, and for a minuscule, everlasting moment, as she stood in front of him like the statue of Beauty, he thought he was going to come apart. He knelt down, nuzzled her thighs, put his hand under her slip, felt the middle of her thighs as hot as a brazier, lifted the slip and saw, irradiating heat and pulsating with giddying calls, her pubis nesting among her many frizzy hairs, over which he had so often let his fingers glide to feel the petals of that dark flower unfold themselves and become moist at his touch, the dainty perfume of the scented water with which she washed herself blended with her own musk, the inebriating smell that never stopped coming from there, a smell that always made him act like a wild animal, putting his hand over her crotch and then in his nose and mouth, his humid fingers shining and smelling of all that is good.

"Give me strength," he said, leaning his head and face against the place of love, opening her delicate cleft with two fingers, pressing his neck against it and hugging her by her knees. He felt her legs opening a bit, he raised his back as though he wanted her to ride his neck, pulled her by her powerful buttocks while she straddled her legs a little more and he felt an urge to slip inside her and stay there, sheltered under the Great Navel. Realizing that from her insides something larger than herself was coming out, a power she was almost afraid of, she came convulsively, squeezing her thighs against his ears, almost killing him in this embrace, almost draining herself dead. Budião stood up, lowered his breeches, and said he needed to come inside her. He did not have to move after he penetrated her, they only held each other a very long time, before he groaned and felt his legs wobble, as he poured himself into her.

He turned back one last time on his way to the beach. Waved by his black arm in the dark, her cloth seemed to float in the air like a spirit. Then he dashed out to the jetty, where Dandão was waiting for him impatiently and declaring he thought Budião was not coming anymore, and he had been considering sailing out without him. They unmoored the boat silently, Dandão took the tiller, Budião and Zé Pinto manned the sails, and they cast off along the bar, running before the wind, making for Whale Point like a hurrying mackerel slicing the water. Before midnight they had picked up all the rowers, and the ebbing tide formed a current to Bahia. They cast anchor at Hard Point and went ashore to fetch the canoe and bring her to sea, her hull shining from the wax with which they had polished her that very day, her sails spanking new and her oarlocks reinforced, in the precise likeness of an attack boat. Though under sail only because it was still too early and they did not have to hurry, they did not take long to arrive in Bahia. As if they were fishermen stalking mullet, they saw the day rise just off Saint Marcellus Fort, they had broiled fish with coffee and manioc flour around five o'clock, they hoisted the red banderole that was supposed to identify the canoe though there was no other one around, and they lay back to wait. Around ten o'clock, Dandão, who was astern, pretending he was sleeping with his hat over his eyes, poked Budião with his big toe, pointed his lip starboard ahead, and grumbled softly, "Oarsmen to their stations." Leaving a foamy wake behind him, a man was swimming fast to the canoe, and Dandão put about toward him. On the fort's beach, a soldier seemed about to fire his carbine, but gave up and ran back inside, waving his arms. They pulled the man aboard.

"Welcome aboard, Commander Bento Gonçalves," Dandão said. "In this bag you will find a clean new suit, a shirt, and underwear. And in the box, a mirror and a razor. Will Your Excellency please take your place there, because we're scooting out of here under sail and oars."

"By all means," the man answered. "Just give me a piece of cloth for me to wipe myself dry, and don't worry about me; let's get going."

They hid the man in Little Swamp all day long, after having axed the canoe to pieces upon arrival and set fire to it. The next morning, on a small gig, Júlio Dandão and Budião took the man to a hoy moored innocently at the port of Bahia, and went from there, one as a volunteer and the other as a runaway, to the war that was being made by that man in that distant land.

Zé Pinto knew little else, or if he did he would not tell it. The gig ran ashore empty near Saint Lawrence Fortress, and their disappearance was attributed to an accident, maybe a big fish, maybe a sudden rogue wave. Could Martina possibly be right, had Budião disappeared forever? He might very well have; the heart cannot be used to deny reason. Maybe she was now having second thoughts about not having joined Martina to go to the feast, not to do anything really, just to while away the time. Who knew if she would not run across someone who would tell her something about Budião? She considered changing her clothes but finally decided to go as she was; after all, she was not the reveling type, she was just going to watch, and if someone disapproved, let him give her new clothes. She stretched her arm to bolt the gate shut, patted down her unironed skirt, remade the knot on her kerchief, and headed to the square, dragging her wood-soled slippers. But when she got near the stalls and the merrymakers, she no longer wanted to talk to anybody; she decided to go around the trees and sit down on the small pier, with her feet dangling over the water.

"Dah-dah-dah." A voice sounded behind her. "Dah-dah-dah-dah, is that your idea of a feast?"

Zé Pinto stepped onto the pier by her side. He seemed to have drunk a little; his eyes were different.

"I'm really in no mood for the feast, Zé Pinto; I'd rather stay here enjoying the breeze."

He smiled and put his hand on her shoulder.

"Don't say a thing like that, girl. I'm an old man, and you should see how much fun I've been having. Dah-dah-dah, cut the nonsense, go have a good time."

She lowered her head, kept gazing at her feet and shaking her slippers with her toes, and did not answer. And she even thought Zé Pinto had left, but when she looked up he was pointing his chin at something behind her. How strange; hadn't something very much like that happened to her once, a long time ago? She turned to see what he was pointing at and saw a figure set against the light of the cressets, a huge man in high boots, a large hat pressed deeply onto his head, a heavy, wavy cloth covering his trunk down to his waist, metal flashing on his boots and pants.

"*Buenas,*" the figure said. "I've just arrived."

Merinha stood up without knowing how and peered hard, but she could not make out the man's shadowed features. And she had never heard that type of speech before, words pronounced as if they had more sounds than the ones used here. But even so she was not fooled for a minute, because she knew at once that that wrapped-up man who had sprouted from the dark and stood there like the trunk of a big tree was Budião, returning from the war, and here to be with her.

City of Salvador, Bahia, December 19, 1840

After being stared at a long time, the warrant officer seems to be moving, the hole that once was his eye is squirting blood, the cawing of the seagulls is the stridulation of lost souls piercing the wind, the Portuguese are again going to open fire and destroy everything. Maria da Fé, wearing a white lace dress, her straightened hair drawn tightly into a round bun, has been leaning on her elbows over the sideboard, her eyes fixed on the reproduction of Warrant Officer Brandão Galvão's picture, which the schoolmistress Jesuína would dust every day, while saying the Hail Holy Queen prayer. It was not identical to the original, because at the upper-right-hand corner, on an inscription drawn with capriciously convoluted tips, one could read the first few words of his harangue, written in a very stilted cursive script: *About the voice you hear, O seagulls from these invincible shores, there is nothing you may know, but the clear, resounding Voice of the Brazilian People, O columboid gifts from Mother Nature, you shall always recognize, as it astounds the World!*

But Dafé did not pay attention to those words, which she knew by heart. In fact, she knew almost the whole speech from listening to it so often as recited by her teacher, who had a special preference for that great countryman of hers among all the many, many heroes boasted by Brazilian history. What Dafé liked was to gaze at that scene and immediately lose herself in distant thoughts, without feeling or hearing anything else. In her usual position, her elbows on the sideboard, her ankles crossed, she would plant herself before the picture, which in spite of being a black-and-white print would acquire colors—first the warrant officer's blood, then his gallant uniform with its gallooned cuffs, then the whole scene—and finally sounds. Weren't those gaping seagulls really chittering so loud they could be heard in the room? And though she had never felt pain in her life, didn't she now see the world spin the way the warrant officer must have seen it, didn't she feel her head tighten, didn't she feel a little dizzy and sick?

Dona Jesuína thought all that interest was an exaggeration. After all, there were many more important heroes to pay homage to; Brazil owed its Independence not only to that valiant but to so many others that their enumeration was well nigh impossible. Let Dafé remember we were a great empire—did she have any idea of what an empire was, could she possibly appraise the greatness of such a concept? Let her imagine the tall, noble, stately, even portentous figure of His Imperial Majesty Dom Pedro de Alcântara João Carlos Leopoldo Salvador Bibiano Francisco Xavier de Paula Leocádio Miguel Gabriel Rafael Gonzaga, of the great house of Bragança, in his green fifteen years of age already as wise as the child Jesus in the midst of the doctors, and even looking like Him, with his milky-white, innocent visage. Let Dafé think about the many great men who had existed, still existed, and would always exist, men who knew about lofty things that the people would never be able to know, men who made grave decisions in the company of saints and muses, with love for Motherland and God. Let her not imagine that those men were people like them. Those men were not ordinary men; they were men who could raise multitudes with one word or look, men who went sleepless for months on end, carrying in their fearless chests the pains of the nation, their virtues comparable to the great martyrs', their words always of bravery, selflessness, courage, abnegation, devotion, and above all love for Brazil. Let her recall the examples of dauntless bravery that were abundant in every episode of our history, giving ample reason to the poet who thanked Heaven for bestowing upon us so many admirable men.

She could not help but find that very intriguing, Dona Jesuína reminded Dafé affectionately, turning over the print to interrupt the girl's daydreaming. Dafé was happy to be going back to Puffer Fish, back to Grandpa Leovigildo, wasn't she? If so, she wasn't acting like it. She was now a young woman, for many girls of twelve are already married, and she had been taught everything Dona Jesuína knew, so was it proper for her to behave like a senseless child, staring at a print for hours, however inspiring it was? Sometimes she had doubts about Dafé's future. It ought to be the best possible, because with her gifts and her beauty, it would not be difficult to find a young man of her race, or even of a clearer complexion, to rise in the world, to have a good marriage, to raise a family, and to settle down for good. But her odd behavior caused doubts.

She had always treated Dafé like a daughter. If she had occasionally punished her, it had been for her own good; she would punish a child of her own the same way. She sighed, thinking silently about Amleto and proud of him once again. She had given her the same education as Amleto's, with the exception of that which a woman did not need and was indispensable for a man. Nowadays he was a distinguished man, a man Bahia should be very proud of, a man capable of even the terrible sacrifice—yes, because she knew how painful it was for him—of denying his own mother so as not to imperil the heavy responsibilities he had on his shoulders. She became a little irritated at Dafé, as she compared her to Amleto. True, she was a woman and a mulatto, but why did she have to do those crazy things? Even when she was being rebuked and stood silent, it was plain to see she was not bowing, and her gaze, even in moments of tenderness, was always rebellious. Even when she was being punished, struck with a ferule or made to kneel down on corn seeds, which terrified the other children, she appeared indifferent and would not cry even when her schoolmates suggested she pretend to, so as to abbreviate the punishment.

Becoming more irritated, Dona Jesuína drove Dafé out of the room somewhat rudely, reminding her that she hadn't packed her trunk yet; she was still acting as though she had no sense. If Grandpa Leovigildo arrived and was in a hurry because of the tide, she would be embarrassed by that; he would think she was a negligent teacher. She told Dafé to get everything ready and went to the kitchen to see if they were finishing the coconut candy she was going to give the girl as a present. After all, in spite of everything, she liked her; she had grown fond of her throughout all those years she had stayed at her house to receive the education Leovigildo demanded for her. She had also got a little memento for Dafé, a gold chain and a medal of Our Lady of Support to help the girl along, now that she could no longer rely upon her teacher's guidance. She was against the girl's going to Baiacu, she would have no future there; it was impossible to understand why someone would rather live in the middle of nowhere than in a big city like Bahia, especially a girl old enough to think about marriage. The more she thought about a marriage for the girl, the easier she thought it might be. It could even be to a man of responsibility, a well-off man, a widower; why not? Maybe it was not much, but the girl was sure to have a dowry. Everyone remarked that her grandfather was a smart, well-to-do Negro, which one could confirm by the things he was able to give her. Therefore there was nothing sillier than this return to Puffer Fish, even if her mother was living there too, as the girl sometimes reminded her. And what a mother she must be, probably an uncouth Negress who had become pregnant by some young master, an ill-natured, uneducated woman, certainly very coarse, to judge from her job as a fishing master, which had never been a job for a woman, much less a decent woman. Well, it was none of her business; she was not going to be upset because of someone else's child. She had done her duty and done it well; the girl even knew more than she should, for she had been often seen with books she should not touch, and it was no use punishing her, because she would do it again. But she was also polite, clean, modest, and proper; those were virtues Dona Jesuína had always insisted on inculcating in her female students, for without them a woman was nothing. Therefore, if it was not enough for her to spend just two or three months a year in Puffer Fish, as she had done all these years, she must suit herself. Dona Jesuína washed her hands of it, although she found it a pity, a real pity, but the truth is, if a person does not know what is good for her, there is nothing you can do about it.

Dafé ran her eyes over her room, which was quite dark in spite of its open window, and spent some time looking at the image of Our Lady of Support, whose head was slightly bowed, her hands offering help and consolation, the light of her little lamp casting on her mantle stains of reddish gold. Dafé had never learned to like that room in which she had slept for so many years and in which she had locked herself so often in spite of the rule against it, to read books, including some strange ones she did not understand. But she did not dislike the room, either; it was like a slightly unpleasant friend whose company one ends up getting used to. The wet corner, almost just a damp crevice, a space so narrow one could only go in sideways, was still there, scaring her with its restless little bugs making noises at night and flying onto her bed; when she was a little girl, she had asked to have a burning candle in it. She opened both doors of her closet and started gathering her things. There was not room enough in the blue trunk Grandpa Leléu had given her, so she was going to have to bundle up a few things, because she did not want to leave anything behind. She had even set aside a few articles she had thought she was not going to take along, but now she had decided to take it all; nothing that belonged to her was going to remain there. She might even give all those odds and ends away in Puffer Fish, but she was going to take everything.

When Dona Jesuína got back to the room, she was ready to travel. The old woman had been preparing herself to complain, and was caught a bit off guard when she saw everything in its place, the trunk locked, two very neat bundles, a bag, the bed with its sheet properly stretched, the dressing table spotless, Dafé sitting on the edge of the bed, her back upright. She realized she was going to miss the girl very much; she felt like crying and hugged her, stroking her head.

"Do you promise to be good? Huh? Do you? And are you going to come visiting once in a while? Remember I'm very old, I'm not going to last too long, you'll have to come visiting very often. Oh, my dear Maria da Fé, I'm going to miss you!"

"So am I, I will come, I will!"

And they were still embracing when the pantry black Rogaciana, still flustered because her behind had been fondled, came to tell them that Leovigildo was waiting in the drawing room, and happy as could be! Dona Jesuína was annoyed. Again she would not say anything, but she did not like Leovigildo's stepping into her drawing room just like that, as if he were a respectable person. He was not; he was a Negro who might have some money and be a good man, but his extraction was low, one could see it perfectly well in that face, so pitch black it looked purple. Well, from now on she would give the house blacks strict orders to let him in only through the kitchen, where he was to stay, waiting right there. She took out of her bodice a little box tied with a gold-colored string, handed it over to Dafé, asked her to open it, put the chain and the medal on the girl's neck, and kissed her on both cheeks. She started to cry openly and was startled when Leléu, always the smart aleck, popped up at the drawing-room door all smiles, felt Rogaciana's bottom again, and cried out:

"My little girl, today I woke up wishing the sun a good morning!"

"The ebony naiad evanesces.
Her dusky skin doth become eburnean
From the algid kiss of the lethal serpent.
In her turgid bosom there no longer throbs
    Her laden heart.
'Dandalay! Dandalay!' Harold howls,
And in an awesome plunge he descends
From th' eagle's claws to the ground in desperation.
    O Dandalay! Dandalay!
But lo! the copious, wrenching tears
Pouring forth from his innermost soul—
Oh, imperishable show of boundless woe!—
    Suddenly cease their flow,
As the thud of the fallen hero's body's heard,
And he lies dead, dead at the feet of his beloved,
Each of them but a victim of prejudice,
Both of them but martyrs of liberty!"

His face flooded by sweat, his hands still quivering in declamatory transport, the poet Bonifácio Odulfo Nobre dos Reis Ferreira-Dutton bowed briskly to the applause that thundered at the Mazombo Tavern, almost drowning out the last stanza of his tragic poem "Harold and Dandalay." Unable to smile as he had intended, he wiped himself with a garish, crumpled handkerchief, looked around nervously, waved to the group crowding the counter, filliped awkwardly Antônio Onofre's Velázquez hat, and stood for a while as if not knowing where to go, while the applause persisted, dying little by little among enthusiastic comments.

"That naiad verse, that one's here to stay! How does it go? The eburnean evanescence . . . No, yes! The ebony naiad evanesces . . . It's really capital, my friend; the truth is, I haven't heard such sonority in a redondilla—a verse that between us very few poets have managed to save from vulgarity—I haven't heard such sonority in quite a long time! The ebony naiad evanesces . . . It's really capital, my friend, and it proves that bankers *ne sont pas seulement des salauds,* but they can also beget poets of the highest caliber! It's here to stay, it's really here to stay!"

"To the glasses! Mazombo, my good publican, there's more dryness here than in all the deserts of Bessarabia! Don't you realize you just listened to a magnificently inspired masterpiece, and our envy cannot be borne without our resorting to the precious lymph you insist on hiding in your vats?"

"But *Senhor Doutor* Antônio Onofre, I agree it's a matchless poem, an extraordinary work, so powerful it grips me down to my lower parts, and *Doutor* Bonifácio Odulfo is more of a poet than all the poets in the realm, but it's been daylight for a long time now; I fear the police might—"

"The police? Let the *gendarmerie* come! Contrary to common opinion, poets are not the ones whose legs start jittering when they are confronted with tyranny; it's pusillanimous tavernkeepers such as you! Poets do not back away from a fight, poets are not afraid of anything, let alone the mayor's or the chief of police's myrmidons, no matter who they may be! Come on; as if it weren't enough for you to charge us a mandarin's ransom for the pigwash you serve us, do you still have to install in this house of freedom a sordid atmosphere of oppression? What makes the morning so unpleasant to you—are you perchance a bat?"

" '*Je dis a cette nuit: "sois plus lente"; et l'aurore
Vá dissiper la nuit!*' "

"Bravo! '*O temps, suspends ton vol! et vous, heures propices,
Suspendez votre cours!
Laissez-nous savourer les rapides délices
Des plus beaux de nos jours!*' "

"*Touché!* You hear that, Mazombo? They brought Lamartine in defense of Antônio Onofre's request! What else do you want?"

"He wants Garret; he's a hopeless Portuguese. Come on, bring the wine before we put you in irons and dispatch you back to Beira, you heel!"

"Anisette for me!"

"And for me a glass of hemlock!"

"I want to drink from a skull! Are there no skulls in this tavern? How can poets get drunk without good, capacious skulls?"

"To the ebony nymph!"

"Naiad!"

"To the bard Bonifácio's ebony naiad,
Who outshines today all of the *Iliad!*"

"Cheers! To our Lord Byron! To our Mérimée! To our Musset! To our Chateaubriand, truly a Chateaubriand! The exotic perspective, the Oriental tone, something from *Atala*, something from *Le Dernier Abencérage* . . . And I say this as a great compliment, as Chateaubriand himself was an ardent disciple of Bernardin de Saint-Pierre, who in his turn—"

"Now pardon me, my friend Prosérpino, you're not doing full justice to the greatness of Bonifácio's work. I for one see much that's new, very new, along with the puissance of its vocabulary, the richness of its images, its rhythm, which one might call symphonic. *Ça va sans dire.* But what transfigures this piece, what transmutes it into a true landmark, a true revolution, a revolution made with boldness, invention, and genius, is the subject itself, the subject itself! Does the revolution contained in the subject escape you gentlemen, though as visible as the facade of a theater? Harold and Dandalay . . . The story of a forbidden love between a white descendant of Portuguese Goths and a Brazilian Negress, a savage, primitive being, 'an inebriating, atramentous fruit of tropical fronds,' as the poet himself puts it. Can you grasp the magnitude of his boldness? Can you imagine the day this peerless work is published, the impetus of the reaction of the moralists, conservatives, and pharisees of whom unfortunately most of our society is composed? The abolitionists and—why mince words?—the republicans . . ."

"Gentlemen, by the blessing of the Most Holy Sacrament, not those subjects!"

"You have no greatness, Mazombo; you have the ideals of a snail. You could go down in history as the master of this salon, housing what could be an immortal coterie."

"Yes, but one does not take history books to forced labor camps or to the gallows. You gentlemen are all of high station; you would not be either hanged or jailed; they would give you a good dressing-down, then send you to vacation on some distant beach, and after that you'd all be pardoned. But as for me . . ."

"All right, *mon Tartuffe.* Help us to another bottle; do your stuff. But I was talking about Harold and Dandalay. By the way, what a splendid name you found for your heroine, my Odulfo—where did you dig it up? You're wilier than a wily cat; what sources did you use?"

"I didn't use any sources the way you think. Her name is a product of fantasy. I tried to invent a sonorous word, one that would evoke African sounds, the dances and the indolence characteristic of the Negro race."

"And it was a most fortunate choice! Dandalay . . . Now answer me, Prosérpino, which of your Portuguese and Frenchmen would be capable of such invention? And by the way, when are we going to do the burning of Portuguese books? We have to do it by a lake; somebody has to find a lake!"

"There's a lagoon near my uncle's farm in Rio Vermelho."

"Then that's where we're going to do it. We'll make a bonfire out of the books by those sinister jackasses who still have the gall to want to be our mentors. Are we, a generation immersed in the genius of Rousseau and Victor Hugo, between Death and Greatness, to read cow-eyed little pieces and whining lamentations?"

"But not Herculano. Herculano—"

"Herculano is a pompous ass, and you know it!"

"Take that back—better take that back!"

"I'd sooner let my mustache be shaved off, and you know I've killed two rotters who dared to try."

"You killed two men? Where?"

"That's none of your business. In Europe; you don't know European students; duels are very frequent."

"You're lying!"

"No, *you*'re lying! You're lying even about this Herculano, a dangerous bedlamite who grubs up archaeological jawbreakers to tell lies about Portugal, such fearsome lies that even the most stupid Portuguese—and they are not few, mind you, rather they—"

"Take that back, take that back!"

"I will not! And I am also going to throw the galimatias he had the nerve to print in the same fire with the gibberish authored by Their Excellencies Xavier de Novais, Soares dos Passo, Bulhão Pato, and all those other drooling mules who touch your sensitivity so much. To the fire! At midnight, by Eusébio's uncle's lagoon, the Abyssal Lake whence you can hear the fathomless voice of the Ages . . . And we shall drink from skulls too, Eusébio! Tomorrow we shall go to a graveyard, we shall violate crypts. . . . Maybe a church would be a better idea. We'll go in a church at night—"

"Gentlemen, I beseech you from the bottom of my heart—those subjects, those subjects!"

> "Oh, near the embalmed cadaver
> Of she who while living was so dear,
> Down I lie for love so eager,
> Caressing and kissing her gelid face . . ."

"Take back what you said about Herculano—take it back! All of you can see how he provokes me, and it's a good thing you do, before I whip his ass!"

"Take it easy, gentlemen; it's a night of poetry!"

"Take it back! Herculano is not an ass!"

"Let the poet of the night decide, then! The poet Bonifácio Odulfo will decide whether Herculano is an ass or not! Let's hear the verdict!"

But Bonifácio did not know what to say, and as soon as he had started his first syllables, he retched with a violent cough, which forced him to sit down, his hair unkempt, his face convulsed, his breathing fitful.

"Camphor!"

"Unfasten his collar!"

"Make him stand up!"

After the camphor had been whiffed and Herculano had been forgotten, Bonifácio recovered gradually, stroking his hair with a stoic laughter and a distant look.

"The lungs, this pair of rascals. But it'll go away. It—"

A new fit of coughing hit him. Supported by Antônio Onofre and Mazombo, he seemed about to faint but managed to get back on his feet. He insisted he was feeling fine and asked everyone to go on drinking and talking as before, but Antônio Onofre accepted Mazombo's anxious arguments and convinced him to go home. It was about eight o'clock, and it was a good idea for them to get some fresh air after spending the whole night in a damp, stuffy tavern.

They emerged arm in arm into the street. The sun was covered by heavy clouds, and instead of fresh air they encountered a suffocating mugginess, which brought an exclamation of horror from Antônio Onofre.

"Let's admit it's an uninhabitable city," he said. "The air is more pleasant inside the tavern."

Bonifácio did not answer, seeming not to have heard anything. Antônio Onofre stopped and tugged at his sleeve.

"What's wrong—don't you feel better?"

"Oh, I'm all right, I'm perfectly all right; I had even forgotten about the coughing. What a nuisance—we were having such great fun, and all of a sudden that fit came over me."

"Is that why you're so despondent? Are you thinking about your disease?"

"No, I'm neither despondent nor thinking about my disease. I consider it a malediction, an act of fate. I'm not the first one to have it, as you know, and in a way it's the lot of poets, as my mother says. No, I don't even think about it, and I'm not despondent at all."

"Yes, you are." Antônio Onofre stopped once more, took two steps backward, and spoke with his arms crossed. "An amatory problem again? Oh sure, that has to be it! *On ne badine pas avec l'amour.* What happened, did Dona X throw another one of her languid looks at you?"

"You know I don't want you to make any jokes about that. Do you want her husband's henchmen to club me to death?"

"But I didn't mention any names, I just said 'X.' I think it brings a touch of mystery and adventure to the whole thing."

"I hate to think about it; I haven't been able to see her lately. I'm afraid the old ogre locked her up in that dreadful estate in Barra again. Anyway, no plays are showing now, and the only place where I could see her would be a theater."

"But there'll be a reception someday; you shouldn't despair."

"I'm not despairing. I wasn't thinking about her, either."

"Then what the devil are you thinking about—because you say you're not upset, but you are; I know you very well; you're not the type to wear that long face. Is the old man giving you trouble?"

"The old man always gives me trouble. Poor man, he's learned, but his disappointments and his work have led him to become suspicious of men of letters and intellectuals. Now he's the head of the bank and involved with all sorts of other businesses, interminable transactions that make me dizzy just to hear them mentioned; I don't think he has enough time to hector me as before. He got used to the idea that I am the way I am and that I'll never be turned into a plutocrat like him. But I know that must make him suffer; he figures that after he dies our family will face immediate ruin, and he might very well be right. He can't count on his children. Clemente André is now practically a monsignor; his life is schools, seminars, and convents, and at times he seems unable to understand anything but his Gregorian chants and the confessions of his faithful. Little Carlota is a woman, and married to Vasco Miguel, that mooncalf, who just the same was awarded a few jobs in the old man's firms. You have to make do with what you can, as they say, and I suppose he has to get along with the chucklehead he's got for a son-in-law."

"But it's not his fault; after all, Carlota—"

"Carlota doesn't even speak, let alone think and make choices. She enjoys her books, she probably has silly fantasies, she's very contented with her music lessons and my two snotty nephews, who are always hanging on to her skirts. Although she did deserve a better husband, the poor girl. Better yet, any other husband. At least my father saved a few lives when he got him away from medicine. In the 1850 epidemic he lost his mother and his sister Felicidade Maria, who were both under his care. I'm sure that if they let him loose to practice medical arts, he would make more casualties than both the yellow fever and the plague put together."

"You're really venomous today, huh? I'm glad I'm your friend—what a tongue you have!"

"It's not that; it's just that in spite of that saturnine appearance of his, my father is very softhearted; he does all kinds of stupid things because of it. He took pity on the baroness after the baron died; he was always very devoted to them, and served the baron—who must have known about business as he knew ancient Sanskrit—with so much dedication that it almost cost him his health, maybe his life. They never gave him anything in return, as is the rule in those cases, but even so, he decided he must sacrifice himself for the baroness. He did everything he could for her: He straightened out the bankrupt companies that light-headed baron left her; he had to pay for the baron's funeral, because the baron must have gone out of his mind after fighting like a madman in the War of Independence and probably became incapable of any activity but being a hero. He even paid for the outfit of the other girl—what's her name?—for Florbela's outfit when she entered a convent. And if that were not enough, he guaranteed a lavish existence for that zebra Vasco Miguel, by giving him his daughter's—my sister's—hand in marriage. The baroness must have asked him. His mother died young, so he made the baroness his mother; he started doing everything she wanted. As a result, he bears an additional burden on his shoulders, for Vasco Miguel knows positively nothing about business, as indeed he knows nothing about anything. I think his vocabulary doesn't go beyond eighty words, if that."

"But you have another brother, don't you? A younger brother?"

"Tico Macário? It would be easier to make Father Clemente roll up his frock and go out dancing in the Feast of Kings than to get some sense into Tico's head. Incidentally, it's his fourteenth birthday today, but he looks like an eighteen-year-old monkey. He hardly knows the three R's and is always wallowing among the Negresses of the house and the farms, to the point that I don't doubt I have a couple of nephews in some slave quarters. Not long ago he punched his Latin teacher, old Queiroz; and on top of that, he poured ink on the old man's books and papers, a complete horror. My father punishes him, but it's of little use because my mother dotes on him; he'll always be her baby boy, and she always thinks people are being unfair to him or don't understand him. He's run away from home twice, and she invariably promises him the whole world for him not to do it again. He's been smoking and drinking and playing billiards—he's a real stormy petrel, that brother of mine. As you can see, my old man has his problems, but what is one to do? We all have problems."

"Yes, but it bothers you anyway."

"My dear friend Toninho, I see you insist on finding out what it is that seems to you to be making me sad. I'll be frank with you, because I consider you my brother and I wish that I could enjoy at home the fraternity, the understanding, the closeness, and the selflessness of our friendship."

"Thank you. I feel that way too."

"You don't have to thank me; you know it's the truth; one doesn't talk about those things."

"Le sort fait les parents, le choix fait les amis."

"That's right. So the truth is, nothing afflicts me but that which afflicts us all: the anguish of the world. What is a poet, an artist, a visionary, but one who feels more than other people? The thing that astounds me most is insensitivity. Sometimes I think I'm in a nightmare, as I realize how insensitive are my fellow human beings, how they do not cry out, they do not weep, they do not die, confronted with a world of iniquity and injustice. Take our people. What country could be richer, happier, more prosperous, more modern than ours? No other! Nevertheless, what we see is so much poverty, so much hunger, so much backwardness, so many human tragedies, and they look at all that as if it were part of the natural order. We could be the titans of the universe, the titans!"

"And we shall be! The power of the people, the power of the spirit, the power of courage!"

"But sometimes my faith wavers. One might say I alternate between a certain Weltschmerz, a disenchantment, a hopelessness—"

"Don't you think this kind of feeling is rather passé, something ancient, Wertherian? Times are different; the horizons of the New World—"

"That which you call Wertherian has nothing to do with time or place. As

Werther himself says, people here are like people everywhere. Why not acknowledge ennui, the dark bile of melancholy? Why not acknowledge that the poet's cup is of bitter gall, that his burden is heavy, that for him death is a dawning? It's the truth, my very dear friend Toninho: I alternate between this too deeply rooted and atrocious 'spleen' and an affinity for the heroism that leads nations, an affinity for rapture, for the affirmation of Race and Universal Vitality, for the Spirit of the People, and for Greatness—why not acknowledge all that? Who am I, then, where am I, what am I doing here? Do you know the weight this represents for a sensitive soul? Sometimes I envy the rude strength of the people, sometimes I clamor to heaven for not having been born poor or even a slave. Sometimes—this will astound you, my friend—I crave martyrdom; all of me turns to the idea of sanctity as an avocation!"

"That moves me deeply! It's true, I'm moved by what you say even more powerfully than by your verses, for are we not at this very moment living history? Won't they someday talk and write about how we used to walk unnoticed up the obscure slope of Saint Benedict Hill, suffering for all that will make us raise our voices louder than any power will ever be able to do? Imagine the future: 'Here the poets Bonifácio Odulfo and Antônio Onofre walked so many times, declaiming the magnificent dreams that brought fever to their hearts, and the indifferent passersby did not know that between the bard of "Harold and Dandalay" and the poet of "New World, New Future" there fermented the Universal Revolution!' "

"Oh yes! Sometimes I think precisely like that, I'm sure it's going to be like that. Why do I have this certainty? I don't know, but it's something inside me that allows no room for doubt—I just know, I know! Don't you feel at times a tourbillion in your soul, a maelstrom of unruly, sometimes contradictory ideas and sentiments, don't you feel anxious, thirsty, impatient, bewildered?"

"Twin souls, that's what we are! I, too, carry this certainty with me all the time, which comes to me in the midst of that same confusion of mind and emotions. I want to show you something I wrote, though it's still just a first draft, in which I tried to paint a verbal picture of those feelings. Are you going to Mazombo's tonight?"

"My dear fellow, if we don't go to Mazombo's, won't the world seem unbearable?"

"You're right; you're right about everything today. Well, I think I'm going to change course here; you're almost home, and from here I can get to Saint Raymond Street in a hop. I hope the old hag has gone out to do her grocery shopping and hasn't come back yet. Today the rent is due, and I haven't paid the rent for two months because I still don't have the necessary *cum quibus* to honor the debt. It's ironical that my father has just come into a fortune in diamonds, an immeasurable heap of money, but his remittances are tardy; everything comes on muleback from Lençóis, out in the middle of nowhere. Oh well, it could be worse. If she's not around, I can go in undisturbed and lock myself in my room; I'll think of something later. *Au revoir, mon p'tit.* 'Harold and Dandalay' has already been written with fire in the Pantheon of Immortality!"

"Wait a moment, Toninho—don't you want some cash to keep you going while you wait for your remittance?"

"No, I'll be all right. I can always eat at the back of the Church of Saint Peter with my uncle the priest. Lunch is well worth a Mass, *n'est-ce pas?*"

"Don't be silly. Come on; here you are."

"Well, if you promise you won't do what you did the other times . . . If you give me your word that it's a real loan, that you'll let me pay it back . . ."

"All right, all right. Won't you be swimming in an ocean of diamonds pretty soon? Pay me when you assume your station as a potentate."

"You save me from opprobrium once again, thank you very much. That old boardinghouse hag has no sense of propriety; she shouts out her complaints about me for all the neighborhood to hear. And you're preserving me from Mass too! Goodbye now; I'll see you tonight at Mazombo's!"

"Goodbye, Toninho; take care, huh?"

He stood still for some time, watching his friend cross the street and head into an alley toward Saint Raymond. He remembered he was a little drunk, maybe very drunk, but instead of worrying, he felt happy about it. He surveyed the street with a smile and thought about how he did not have to worry about a future that had already been written, how glory would come to him naturally, how that people he understood and interpreted so well would reach through his voice the plenitude of the conscience of its race. He saw himself at court, in the salons of Paris, returning in triumph to Bahia in the arms of the people as their poet, their highest poet. He felt a great tenderness for everything around, and greeted effusively a brown passing by carrying bundles of papers, who answered with an overeager kowtow to His Excellency. He ambled home slowly, full of love for the people and the land, and wrote mentally: "O telluric, indomitable power of the untamed land of Brazil, O you who toil in the fields, who brave the unknown in the forests . . ." He thought vaguely of writing down those words, but changed his mind because he was sure they would come back someday; he was not like the others: he was a genius for sure. And he was also sleepy, as he said to his mother when she greeted him with the usual tearful remonstration, before he locked himself in his room to sleep, closing the windows carefully to avoid catching some lung disease.

"What happens to a person who needs something desperately and when this something arrives it has nothing to do with what the person wanted? The person dies, that's what happens to the person! How can an establishment like Ambrósio Nunes and Brothers, which prides itself on its tradition and on serving the most distinguished prelates and statesmen, present this ill-fitting rag, this butchery, and dare call it a frock? Such cynicism would shame the lowest used-clothes dealer downtown! Look, look at this waistline, look at it—I feel like ripping it to pieces! I said very clearly that I wanted a high waistline; this makes me look like a fat old man, with his waist undifferentiated from his hips. And what is this? This here on the side, what is it? It's a placket! Who ever saw a frock with a placket, for the love of the Most Holy Virgin? For a minute I thought it was a pocket, but no, it's a horrendous hole; that's preposterous; you gentlemen must be crazy! That's why I have always had my frocks made in Rome, and when against my principles I decide to bring my business to a local firm, what I get is this . . . this abominable thing! I don't like anything about it: I don't like the trimmings, this is not the fabric I ordered, the skirt is not full enough, the cape was supposed to be held in place by a brooch and not by these funeral buttons—what an awful thing; I hate it, I hate it, I hate it! And what are these little threads, these little worms—are they braids? What ugly things; throw them away, throw them away, Domiciano—I can't even look at them! Listen to me, my dear sir: I don't live on sportulae, like the rest of your customers; I can afford to dress decently; the fact that I'm a priest doesn't mean I should walk around in tatters, wrapped in a bag of black tow! Please be so kind as to see to it that all the alterations are made at once! Indeed, I don't want any alterations; I demand the frock I ordered! And exactly the way I ordered it! You have three days, two days and a half, to finish the job, and woe to you if Sunday comes and my frock is not ready! That's all for now, I've had enough, there are limits even for the patience of a saint! You gentlemen may go now. Domiciano, get me a glass of water with a pinch of sugar. But be careful, huh? Don't bring me your customary syrup, or I'll pour it in your ears!"

Father Clemente André fell exhausted on the sofa, his hands on his aching forehead. He stretched out his leg and opened the door of his wardrobe with the tip of his boot. He gazed dejectedly at the long row of soutanes, capes, vestments, and hats, all worn and tired and lusterless, nothing befitting the Sunday he was anticipating so much. He got up, opened another door, thumbed through the hanging clothes, felt his throat tighten, and sat down again, this time to cry, with his hands covering his face.

"My son, what happened?" Teolina asked at the door.

"Oh, Mother, Mother!" Clemente André sobbed without uncovering his face. "My dearest Mother, am I going to meet the archbishop wearing an old frock?"

Teolina became upset and rushed to him to pull up his head and look him in the eyes.

"Now, son, don't keep that up; there's no reason for that. Didn't you order a new silk frock, which was supposed to be delivered today?"

"Didn't you see I had to run the two hackers from Ambrósio Nunes and Brothers out of here for having the insolence to bring me a sack—a sack, sweet, dear Mother!—and trying to force it on me as a frock! I told them to make another one, tailored the way I want, but I don't believe they'll bring it on time. I need it for Sunday!"

"Don't worry, dear, they are very experienced, and besides, they owe money to your father's bank; they'll do anything to please you."

"Oh, dearest Mother, do you really think so?"

"I can assure you. Come now, don't fret anymore. Today is your little brother's birthday, and instead of celebrating, your father is on the outs with him again; there's going to be trouble. Your other brother spent the whole night out in the taverns as usual and is now sleeping upstairs, which also makes your father very angry. Think of it, he's fast asleep at three o'clock in the afternoon—can anything be said for that? As for you, you spend so little time with us that you should try to make the best of these rare moments."

"You're right, my sweet, dear Mother. But I'm so worried about the frock . . . You know that ever since I was just a tyke I have admired His Eminence, a man above all others in his firmness, his courage, his proud demeanor, his conduct worthy of a true prince of the Church. I can still remember my confirmation, seeing him praying in his throne, magnificent like a king. I remember how I trembled with happiness as I received the *álapa* from his strong, stern hand—"

"*Álapa?* Speak more clearly, son; remember my letters are scant. Did you receive something special from him?"

"Yes, in a way. Don't you remember that a person being confirmed is slapped lightly on the face? Well, it's not called a slap, it's called an *álapa*. He struck my face and I felt a shiver, an unprecedented emotion, I felt my whole body fill with admiration for that man, a feeling so overpowering and sublime that I cannot describe it, I can't find the words. And how often I have found myself almost overwhelmed by a divine, angelic possession as I contemplated his imposing figure at the processions, the majesty of his noble face shaded by the baldachin, enhancing his august features. Oh, sweet, dearest Mother, the mere thought of being introduced to him personally gives me goose bumps: Will I be able to say something after kissing his hand, will I make a good impression?"

"But of course you will, son. You're no ignoramus, you're held in high regard by your superiors, you were among the first in your class at the seminary, you're a well-known teacher, you're making a name for yourself for your charitable work. . . . Don't you imagine the archbishop has heard a great deal about you and thinks well of you?"

"Do you really think so? Really?"

"I'm certain!"

"But, but even so, don't you think I ought to present myself well? Apart from being a priest, I'm a wellborn man; I can't be compared to one of those village priests, and I don't want anyone to be mistaken about that."

"No one will, dear. I've always told you you have a great destiny; I've always known it; there's no reason for you to worry. Forget about that. Go have something to eat; dinner will probably be late today. Your father is still receiving a few visitors in his study, business matters. Did you sleep well? I practically haven't seen you since yesterday. And your friend, did he sleep well?"

"One question at a time, dear, sweet Mother. If you could have been a priest, you would be an awesome confessor. No, no, I don't want a snack; I was just going to have the glass of water and sugar I asked Domiciano to fetch, which by the way is taking him an eternity. And Domiciano can't really be called a friend of mine. He's just a boy from the Charitable Works orphanage, whom I'm supervising personally. It's a difficult case; he's very rebellious, very bullheaded, very boorish."

"Sometimes I admire you even more than I always do, dear. You're not satisfied with being a father, teacher, counselor, and friend to those intractable creatures, but you still dedicate what little time you have for yourself to the assistance of those with an even greater need for support."

"Really, Mother, you can't imagine how much trouble he gives me. I can't even sleep alone, because if I leave him by himself I don't know what he wouldn't do; he needs constant vigilance. But I thank God for the opportunity to serve my fellowman; this is the essence of priesthood. By the way, where is he? He should have come back a long time ago."

"Don't worry. I'm going back downstairs; I'll find him and order him back. Maybe he had to do something else. But before I go, I want to ask you a favor."

"As many as you like, dearest Mother."

"Couldn't you have a talk with your brother?"

"Which one of them?"

"Patrício Macário. Bonifácio's already chosen his fate; he won't even talk about it; sometimes for days he says no more than two or three words to his family."

"That little savage, then? But what can I talk to him about? If not even Father can get anywhere with him . . . ?"

"But you're a man of the church, and a man of the church experienced in taming headstrong boys, like this Domiciano of yours."

"I doubt I could do with Tico Macário what I do with Domiciano."

"Of course not, he's your brother; he's not a street boy. But you might try to inculcate a few ideas in him, to show him how wrong he's been acting. I

228

fear your father might expel him from our house, such is his anger at him."

"Maybe it wouldn't be such a bad idea to put him out of the house. He might learn to value what he now takes for granted."

"God forbid; don't even mention that! How can you wish such a terrible thing for your little brother? Don't forget he's just a young boy, he has no sense; we must be patient with him."

"Very well, dear Mother, I'll see what I can do. But I'm not promising anything, you hear? Where is he?"

"Your father had him brought to the study, and that's why I'm worried; he was so incensed when he arrived home, he wouldn't even go see his plants, as he does every evening, no matter how upset he is."

"What did Tico do this time?"

"Nothing. It's just that today is his birthday, and since Monday your father has been talking about how grievous it was to have a good-for-nothing fourteen-year-old son who barely knows how to read and count. I think that because today is the tenth of March, he's really going to give the boy the rough side of his tongue. I fear for the worst, son, I fear for the worst. I think Patrício Macário took after your grandfather, my father, who they say used to be just as pigheaded, and the more they punished him, the worse he got."

"Oh Lord, oh Lord, oh Lord, all this makes me so very tired! Why can't we live in peace like other families? Why always a new complication? Isn't it tiresome, isn't it really tiresome?"

"But you are going to talk to him, aren't you? It's a promise, isn't it?"

"It is, it is. I'll talk to him, you can rest assured, although I don't believe it's going to be of any use. I'll do it as soon as Domiciano gets back, because I have to give him some chores."

"So that's settled; we'll talk later. You won't take long, will you? I have to go give the Negresses a few orders, so I'll find Domiciano for you. See! There he is! You were keeping us waiting, my boy!"

Domiciano, not saying anything, stopped at the entrance with a glass in his hand, his blond hair a bit tousled, his undershirt unbuttoned at the top, showing his chest. Teolina glanced at him quickly, waited for him to step aside so she could pass, and walked down the corridor. Clemente André took the glass, stroked the boy's hair, buttoned up his shirt, and rested his forearm on his shoulder.

"Where have you been? What took you so long?" he said tenderly.

"The Negresses were fooling with me; they took a long time to bring the glass."

"The Negresses were fooling with you? It's because you're so beautiful; it doesn't matter. Come on, don't be sad."

He embraced the boy, pulled his head close to his own, and stood a long time, stroking his head and the back of his neck.

10

Village of Saint John of the Little Swamp,
October 29, 1846

Because it was Saint Gonsalino's feast, Budião could stay with Merinha until the small hours. Around dawn, she sneaked back to the house by the back gate, not to sleep but to start grating the corn and the coconut for the couscous and to light the stove. He slipped into a boat that was moored almost on dry land, and slept until the sun began to warm his feet under the wide poncho he was using as a blanket. He did not know whose boat it was and felt embarrassed at the thought of reaching for the fish rack to pluck out a couple of dry fish, so he picked up his sack, stuck his poncho and his manta in it, and jumped out to the beach from the bow, which was high and dry in the low tide. But he was very hungry, so he decided to go back. He picked up a whole fish spit, filled his hand and mouth with manioc flour, slipped half a brick of brown sugar into his pocket, and, with his cheeks stuffed, jumped back on the sand. Since his hands were busy, making it difficult for him to hold on to anything on his way down, he staggered as he hit the ground and almost fell in front of a pair of tattered leggings, topped by gray pants in equally bad shape. He looked up and saw the face of a middle-aged mulatto man, wearing a straw hat, a seven-day beard, and a cape tied to his neck by a dingy piece of rope; he smelled of spoiled lemon punch and sugarcane rum. Budião chewed the fish and flour in his mouth as fast as he could so he would be able to speak; maybe that man was the boat's master, although he did not seem to be. But his face looked familiar, and Budião had some trouble paying attention to what he was going to say as he tried to remember who the man was.

"Last night was Saint Gonsalino's feast," Budião started to explain, "and, you know, people settle down for the night any way they can. But I didn't touch anything, and about this fish, I—"

"Whose Negro are you?" the man asked rudely, and when Budião heard that authoritarian, strident voice, he recognized Almério, the foreman of the Good Jesus Fishery. But he chose not to say anything about it and even hoped Almério had not recognized him, either, with his clothes from the province and the curved mustache he had let grow for the past eight years. It was strange for Almério to be here, especially covered by filthy rags like a beggar.

"I'm nobody's Negro, friend," Budião said. "Are you the master of this boat?"

"You barefaced Negro, who ever heard of a Negro asking questions? Where is your license—come on, show me your license!"

"Why should I show you my license? Who are you?"

"Every white man has the right to demand to see the license of any Negro he finds loitering around."

"I don't see any white man here."

"Listen here, you smutty piece of coal, don't get fresh with me or I'll slice you to bits right now."

Leaping back, Almério drew a sickle-shaped razor from his legging, opening it with the same motion, and cut the air in front of Budião. His legs straddled, he stuck out his jaw, spat through the corner of his mouth, and waited insolently for a reaction. Budião slipped his hand under his shirt, took out his papers, and handed them over to the other man, who reached for them with his left hand. So he would not lower the hand that was holding the razor, he was going to unfold the papers with the help of his mouth, but Budião took a step forward, unfolded them, and returned them.

"This is no license," Almério said. "I've never seen a license like this; this is nothing."

"They're upside down, *che*."

"I can see they're upside down; it doesn't matter which side is up; it's all the same either way; this here is nothing."

"This is proof that I was amnestied and emancipated as a former soldier of the Juliana Republic, the Republic of Piratini, a Farrapos War veteran."

"That's all a lie; there was never any such thing. These are ass-wiping papers. I'm going to tear them all up."

Before he could move, one of Budião's hands squeezed his wrist so strongly that he let the razor drop, and the other hand closed around his throat.

"Listen well, Almério, you're not going to tear up anything, you understand? You're not going to tear up anything, you're not going to do anything, you understand?"

"Don't I know you? It's no use speaking with a different accent, I know you: you're a runaway Negro from the sugar mill here; you used to be a Good Jesus Fishery black! You are the one who's not going to do anything; you're going to the stocks or to the gallows for being a footloose Negro!"

"You want to see me do something, you shameless mulatto trying to become white, you natural-born bootlicker? You want to see me do something?"

"No, don't hold me any tighter, no! Ouch!"

Almério crumpled to the ground; Budião put the papers back under his shirt, picked up the razor, snapped it shut, and tossed it out in the water.

"Give me that sack, and I won't tell anyone I saw you here," Almério said, still on the ground.

Budião almost laughed, and he thought about kicking him but decided it was not worth it. He felt in his pocket, found two verdigris-coated little coins, and threw them at him.

"Here, buy yourself some more liquor and go to sleep."

Almério scooped up the two coins, scraping the sand with his hands.

"I owe you a beating, you dirty Negro," he said. "No, not just one; now I owe you two beatings, and you're going to take them if it's the last thing I do."

"Listen," Budião said, starting to walk toward the village. "I'm not going to whack you into a pulp because I don't want to get my hands dirty, and I'm not going to dump you in the sea because I don't want to poison the fish. But if you go on speaking, if you say as much as one more word, I'm going to stick your head in the sand and make crab bait out of your guts."

He stood by a while longer, looking at Almério, who did not rise, and he left slowly, stepping off the beach and onto the tall grass beyond. There had been a time when he would not have been able to contain himself, he would have felt a salty taste in his mouth and wanted to kill Almério, and maybe he would have done it. But not today. Today it had made him very happy to throw the two coins at him. He could not care less about the man's insults and threats; he just wanted to saunter about, revisiting this island that was not his home but seemed to be, after his having lived so long in a place so far away that many people there did not believe this place existed. As he prepared his maté, passing the drinking gourd to his companions in those nights of the pampas so different from the ones here, holding in his teeth barbecued meat dipped in a boiling brine, to cut off a hunk of it with a knife held close to his mouth, learning new words and new tastes, he himself had doubted he had come from another place, he did not know too well who he was, except for the memory of Merinha and the conspirators of the flour house. Life was very difficult to understand, even after you had lived to the hilt, even after you had listened to very closely guarded secrets, even after you had thought you knew the truth, or at least some truth or part of it.

The truth was that nothing could be understood, he thought, though without worrying about it, as on other occasions. Everything was very beautiful here, very nice-smelling, clear and luminous. He stopped to admire a blossoming acacia tree and was surprised as he realized how vividly he

232

remembered the fishery's acacia trees; he'd had no idea before of how much they were a part of his mind. Among the roots of the great tree there were five or six white-crab holes, the blond little creatures startled by his presence, tense at the entrance of their homes, ready to plunge in as soon as he made one move. He figured that if he had told anyone in the province about the existence of a gold-colored tree surrounded by gold-colored crabs, he would have been called a liar. He pretended he was going to pounce, and the crabs scrambled, only the little round holes remaining to adorn the exposed roots.

Very beautiful, he thought, very beautiful. And he was finding himself beautiful too. He did not know what his face looked like, he had not even washed his eyes, but he felt good-looking, striding on with his field boots, his knapsack, his leather hat, his large mustache framing his face, his red kerchief around his neck. Well, he was still hungry; maybe the best thing for him to do before anything else would be to go see Zé Pinto, whose little house stood among the sedges not too far from the beach. Maybe there he would find some leftovers to eat, he would talk with the old man, he would make an appointment with him and Feliciano to straighten out a couple of things. Nothing in a hurry, nothing too anxiously, for things here happen slowly, and his life in the past few years had been lived altogether too fast. He hardly noticed that when he got to the pathway to Zé Pinto's place, a few boys were following him at a distance and everyone's eyes were fixed on him.

The old man had some okra, some gherkins, coriander, peppermint, onions, manioc flour, and two big jewfish heads. They made a stew and had it with mush steeped in a hot pepper sauce. Budião ate with such an unexpected pleasure that he kept laughing and moaning, while the old man, munching with his lips thrust out because he had no teeth, stared at him in amusement. A pitanga tree, some of whose branches were growing through the little window, displayed fruits to tightly bunched together that they seemed to come in clusters. Budião pulled down the biggest branch, filled both his hands with pitangas, and ate them one by one, his eyes closed. After that he did not feel like talking for a long time, and it was only with some effort that he got up to fix his maté. He dampened the leaves with a little cold water, got the kettle, poured boiling water in the gourd almost to the brim, and made himself comfortable on the floor again. Zé Pinto asked what it was, and he answered lazily that it was just another custom among the many he had picked up in the province of Rio Grande, where he had fought against the Brazilian Empire, though the province was also Brazil, but that was a hard thing to explain. As a matter of fact, everything was hard to explain, and even old Dandão had seemed not to be able to understand certain things; there was still a lot to learn. But how was one supposed to do that? Sure, he had learned much in his travels and in that great ten-year war, had won his freedom, had seen in a short time more than many people see in their whole lives, but would he always have to be in those combats in order to learn? And had he actually learned something: was it not necessary for him to learn how to learn? That war, he knew, had not been his war, although he had thought so at the beginning. But perhaps it had been his war. It was difficult to be sure of anything, very difficult, and not even partaking in some of the Brotherhood's secrets made him sure it really existed.

Unaware of what he was doing, as if the maté steaming up the metal tube with which he sipped it were making him drunk, he said in a rambling way that he had fought very hard, he had graduated from porter and odd-job man to fighter, but he had always fought as a black, always as a black, always different for more reasons than color, always at the bottom, even if at the top. That was what caused so much confusion in him, because he thought the war had been something that had to do with the Brotherhood of the Brazilian People—but how could it have been, if there still seemed to be no place for him? He had questioned Dandão on that subject, and Dandão told him that life and understanding are composed of many steps, and not all who take one step manage to take the next one, and not all steps reach the end of the way, and besides that, his own understanding did not go beyond a certain point, and he did not know either the future or the designs that he was sure were being set up for them. No one tells us what the design is, Dandão had said, but all you have to do is to follow the command of your conscience in order to do what is designed, for no one is denied the right to see what is necessary for him to accomplish his design, and you are the only one who can deny yourself seeing and accomplishing.

Dandão died in the seventh year of the war, as strong as he had always been and without having had time to say goodbye. However, he seemed to know he was going to die, because before he left for the patrol from which he would not come back, he had turned over to Budião his bag with the chest of the secrets. Budião still had it in his sack, and he could not say he knew those secrets well; they were visions that revealed themselves better only after you had lived through them. It was not a simple knowledge but something that was always changing according to the actions and the experience of those who sought to share it. Is there a Brotherhood; what is this Brotherhood? Yes, they were the Brotherhood, but they were not the only ones. There was something in certain people, the way they walked, the way they talked, their type of voice. There were mysterious helps, interferences, agreements without the need for conversation, things detested in common. Oh, he really could not explain those things, but he knew that someone's freedom was nothing without everyone's freedom and freedom was nothing without equality, and equality must be inside people's hearts and heads, it can be neither bought nor imposed. Oh, he did not know anything, he just wanted to talk with Feliciano and Zé Pinto together; he also wanted to know how life

234

had been going on around here, if there was any news, what had happened in all those years. After all, they were the conspirators of the flour house, were they not?

He asked Zé Pinto to keep the sack. He took out only his poncho, which might be useful at night, and cautioned him to be careful with Júlio Dandão's chest; it would be better if he hid it somewhere, forgot about it, did not try to open it. Budião was going out for a stroll in the neighborhood; maybe he would walk all the way to Amoreiras; he was not sure what he was going to do. Could Feliciano possibly come to see him here Saturday night? The slave quarters of the lime factory was far, and depending on the tide, Feliciano might have to work late on Saturday; no one could guarantee he would be able to come to Little Swamp. Well, we'll see. Budião put on the hat that had been hanging from his neck and raised his hand.

"Long live the people!" he said, smiling.

"Long live the people!" Zé Pinto answered, very serious.

Budião stepped from the house, stretched out his arms, breathed deeply, and marched slowly down the pathway. He came close to the square, pondered whether to walk along the beach to Amoreiras, and turned around absentmindedly when a hand touched his shoulder.

"Is this the one?" a man in uniform asked Almério, who was standing behind two other men in military garb.

"That's him, that's him."

"We're watchmen," the man said to Budião. "Your license."

Budião handed him his papers.

"This is not a license. These are worthless papers."

"These are my amnesty and emancipation papers."

"They have no validity; that's from the province of Rio Grande."

"No, that's from the Empire, the emperor. I'm an amnestied veteran of the Farrapos War."

"Maybe, but I don't believe it. To us you're a runaway slave from the Little Swamp sugar mill. Faustino da Costa, branded with the mark of the Good Jesus Fishery?"

He did not wait for an answer and yanked Budião's shirt open to check the brand on his chest. He beckoned his companions, who rushed over to him, one of them pointing his carbine. The other carried a staff, chains, and ropes, and he made Budião cross his arms behind his back, stuck the staff between them, and tied them together with three complicated knots. He fettered Budião's ankles with short gyves and put around his neck a collar fastened to a long chain.

"Move!" the first man said. "You're going to stay in irons in Whale Point until your master comes to decide what should be done about you. Move!"

He struck Budião's back with a kind of horsewhip he carried under his arm, crumpled the papers to thrust them in his pocket, and pointed to a cart hitched to two mules that was parked across the square. Almério followed them, until the man halted suddenly.

"What do you want?" he asked curtly. "You've done your part; you've got no more business with us; go away."

"He has money. It would be only fair that for finding him and informing the authorities, I—"

"That's not my concern; talk to Captain Teófilo about that. Go on, off with you before I let you have it too! And you there, hurry up with that Negro!"

"He had a sack! Ask him about the sack!" Almério still shouted as he stood under an almond tree, while they tied Budião to the cart, climbed on it, and made for Whale Point, dragging him behind.

Puffer Fish Village, Itaparica, May 12, 1841

One of the greatest pleasures in the world is to step outside after a heavy but short downpour and to feel among one's toes the tepid water of the puddles formed on the flagstones the sun had been warming. Dafé remembered that if Grandpa Leléu were in Baiacu instead of on a business trip to Bahia, he would chide her for being barefoot and with her skirt tucked up, dragging her feet in the puddles with wide-open toes to better enjoy the water's warmth. He complained so much, Grandpa Leléu! True, he was very good to her, he would do anything she wanted, but he complained a lot: don't do this, don't do that, that's not proper for a young lady, what do you think life is? Once she had tried to answer this question honestly. But she didn't know what she thought life was. Life . . . life . . . Life is when you're alive like her in Puffer Fish, among animals and plants. Was she satisfied with that? No, she wasn't; she could very well want to go see the world, see more things, talk to more people, go to balls, meet princes and princesses and heroes. . . . So that's what you think life is: life is to travel and to meet princes and princesses, huh? Well, it ain't that! It ain't that at all; that's a very big mistake; life isn't that!

Life is work, Grandpa Leléu had said. Life is work, tribulation, work, watchfulness, work, alertness, work, and so forth. She then answered that in that case, she wanted to work; why didn't he give her the command of a fishing boat, the way her mother had been given the command of the *Prankster?* And he laughed: Now, now, girl, what kind of an idea is that; better get some sense into your head! Did she think he had provided her with such a fine education and was bringing her up in abundance for her to become a fisherwoman? But wasn't Mother a fisherwoman? Well, he had said, your mother is crazy; it's not the same thing.

Then give me work to do, she had asked, because I want to know about life. He laughed once again and said there were many types of work she could do, such as embroidering, such as candy-making, such as weaving lace, such as making dresses and starching clothes. Well now, so he had provided her with such a fine education, which had taught her so much about princes and princesses and great heroes, for her to become a laundress? Was that what he thought life was: life was being a laundress?

No, that wasn't what he thought life was. But he himself had been a vegetable grower, a grocer, a tailor, a fishmonger, a clown, a downtrodden slave, he had been everything you can be in the world, and now look at him standing there: all he knows comes down to one thing, and that thing is that everything is work. Then find me work, she answered, but no embroidering, no candy-making, no lace weaving, no dressmaking, and most of all no laundering and starching.

Hah, that's not so simple, he had retorted. And besides, he added, what I have in mind for you, what's uppermost in my mind for you, is for you to get married and become a good housewife and give me many, many great-grandchildren: the first one Tadeu, the second one Jacinto, the third Belarmino, the fourth Vicentino, the fifth Lourival, the sixth Joaquim, and the youngest one Leovigildo, who I'm going to run away with and raise as my own son, hah-hah! All right, so find me a marriage, she answered, and it may be with a prince, it may be with a great captain, it may be with a viscount or a governor.

Grandpa Leléu got kind of nonplussed and tried to change the subject as hard as he could but did not find a way. If he said life was work or marriage, he had to prove it, otherwise life would be anything she wanted, and that was what she said to him, with her closed fists pinned to her waist. So after much rumination, Grandpa Leléu decided he would set up a school for her, a tiny but decent enough little school right there in Puffer Fish, so she could be the schoolmistress, which was nice work until marriage came along. And marriage will be guaranteed, for who wouldn't want to marry a pretty teacher? Therefore when he traveled to Bahia he was going to buy notebooks, a blackboard, several writing slates, reading primers, and all the materials necessary for the good teaching of letters and numbers. Dafé asked him to bring picture books too, and he said yes. And a pitanga-wood ferule for the Saturday question periods! And some inkstands and pens and ruled paper and blotters and a little bottle of glue!

Oh, Dafé thought, immersing her feet in a deeper puddle and enjoying the cold breeze that was blowing now, I hope he'll be back today. There was still so much to do before the school would be ready! Well, maybe not that much; all that had to be done was his ordering the rethatching of the roof of the little house he had got for the school. But everything seemed to take too long; she could hardly wait to start working and knowing life. She had

237

gathered together all the books and notebooks from her time with Dona Jesuína, she had even rehearsed a few sentences to say to her students. And by the way, who would her students be? Everyone, she decided, everyone was going to be her student, everyone.

Grandpa Leléu wouldn't be happy about what had been planned for today, either. They had decided she was going to sail out on the *Prankster*, along with her mother and the fishermen. Maybe it was just for fun, because it was already too late for serious fishing, but Vevé had promised they would go look for fish, yes. Fun or no fun, Grandpa Leléu would disapprove, but what the eye doesn't see the heart doesn't feel, and besides, it's silly of him to think so.

So they sailed out, Vevé in command, with Angelfish, Black Régis, Odorico, and Ugly Black, a more than lovely sight, the boat tacking like a porpoise, the ropes and the wood groaning, the bow striving to take flight and cutting the waves like a nimble scissors, a school of garfish dancing upright leeward, their tails whisking the surface of the sea. Dafé lay down at the rail and put her fingers in the water, leaving sometimes one, sometimes two or three little foamy wakes behind them. Ugly Black, the callus he had on his chest from pushing poles shaking like a deranged nipple, was going to practice the markings of the reefs, the shallow and deep parts, all the places fit for line fishing, which an apprentice must know. He stood up on the midship bench, shaded his eyes, cupping his hand over them, and pointed to two hillocks on the coastline.

"From there, pulling a line to here," he said, making invisible drawings in the air. "Better lie to, now!"

The *Prankster* creaked again, the crew started lowering the sails, Vevé made the boat yaw starboard, as if trying to arrive sideways at the spot indicated by Ugly Black, but got there almost straight.

"Ebb tide's flowing, so you've got to cast the killick about thirty *braças* ahead of the point and let the rope run," Ugly Black said.

"I'm on my way," Vevé said. "You call."

"Avast, avast, avast!" Ugly Black shouted.

"Cast the bow killick, Angelfish!"

"Just let it go, Dona Vevé?"

"Hold it awhile! How many fathoms straight down, Ugly Black?"

"No more than twenty at the deep spot, which is here. Drop it straight down, letting it run just a bit, because she's going to line up with the tide in that direction."

"Tell us when she's lined up."

"All right, we can cast the lines here," Ugly Black said, proud of his navigation, because the boat, swaying softly and echoing the breaking of the waves in her hull, her killick rope taut, came to rest in the position he had predicted, drawn by the ebb tide current. "That's it! Dog snapper, amber-fish, red snapper, cavalla, hake, all among the rocks down below!"

"Slice the squids, Dorico, get moving!"

"There's a lot of fresh water underneath, isn't there, Ugly Black?"

"It's from the river Paraguassu, Dona Vevé, but the fish are down there too; there's hard-tailed jack biting; once in a while one of them cuts the top of the water."

"Where are the squids, boy?"

Unable to decide where to look while all this was happening, Dafé was amazed at finding so much knowledge in these ordinary people and at never having read in books that people like this could possess that much learning and so many beautiful skills; she found even her mother to be an unknown, mysterious, and distant person, with a wisdom she had never witnessed before. How much studying they must have done, how all of them became beautiful doing their jobs; now she, too, was going to be a fisherwoman! Just a while before, she was a bit smug because she was going to be a teacher and therefore knew many more things than all of them put together, but now she saw it was not true. There were people who caught fish, people who planted vegetables, people who wove fabrics, people who worked with wood, all kinds of people, and all of that re-quires great knowledge and many things inside and behind this knowl-edge—maybe this was what life was, as Grandpa Leléu used to teach; oh, how many things there were in life! What a beauty life was, each object holding inside it a whole world with so many other things related to it, and even a piece of cloth had one day in which somebody paid attention to it alone, while weaving it, finishing it, and cutting it. Had anyone ever thought of a more beautiful thing in God's world than the great knowl-edge of those fishermen and sailors? Dafé even felt a little like dancing. She drummed on the boat's rail with fast, short pats, she giggled, she stomped her feet with excitement, she ran back and forth, watching the fish come up, over here a hook being baited, over there the plopping of sinkers being swallowed by the water—hey, hey, hey, isn't life beautiful and full of novelties? Now she wanted to work as a sailor and a fisher-woman too. But she also wanted to be a teacher. So what did she really want? She wanted everything, that was what she wanted! If every trade has its knowledge of life, how many sides does life have, Grandpa Leléu?

She was almost flying when she got near Angelfish, who was no longer frail, haggard, and sallow-faced as before, he was now the picture of beauty, with his white hake emerging shining at the tip of his line. All around, a coruscation of scales and droplets of every color, and the fish, their mouths transfixed by hooks that seemed too small to catch them, flapping their tails in the hollows of the boat—why, hadn't she herself, laughing nervously all the while, pulled up a mojarra? And what about the huge stingray, looking more like a frigate bird than a fish, that Vevé caught on her line?

As they returned just after noontime, Dafé found it impossible to leave the piles of fish heaped in the baskets. A few of them still tossed about now and then, others seemed to be panting, their gills going up and down more slowly each time, others had already stiffened up, twisted like sickles. On the beach, she followed the unloading of every basket, she observed the weighing and cleaning of the fish, she stood by the bowls and pans watching dinner being fixed, she oversaw her mojarra being fried so no one else would eat it in her place.

By late afternoon, this time of the year when it gets dark early, they decided they had better walk from Pig Island to Outeiro, because Leléu might land at another port, and he would not be pleased if he did not find Dafé home, especially if he had brought along the school's articles, as he very likely would. Since the little island turns into a peninsula in the low tide, they were able to use the sandbank trail and take a shortcut through the woods, near four abandoned big houses with plants growing over the walls and erupting out of the windows. So they had a surprise when they came across an oxcart of the type found in sugar mills standing at the gate of one of the houses and heard voices inside. Dafé, who after the fishing had begun to see every animal with new eyes, wanted to have a look at the two oxen, one white, the other spotted, both ruminating without raising their eyes. A young man's head popped out at one of the windows.

"Hey!" he yelled. "Here's what we were waiting for!"

"Let's get out of here," Vevé said, but the boy and three others came out of the gate quickly and surrounded them.

"Excuse us," Vevé said, trying to leave while holding Dafé's hand.

But they blocked her way, and the one who had spoken first held up an unstopped jug.

"A sip of wine, my flower?"

"No; much obliged."

"Eugênio, where you come from do they allow Negresses to refuse a white man's offer?"

"Not where I come from. I thought it was part of your liberal customs here."

"Not here! Here these cheap black sluts obey! Have a sip of wine! Are you going to drink it, or will I have to force you?"

"No; much obliged. It's getting late; I have to take my little daughter home; please don't do that; please let us pass."

"Your little daughter? You don't say! This great big wench here, this superb Negress, this rump, these tits—this is your little daughter?"

"Leave them alone, Leopoldo, let them go."

"Never! What kind of an impression would you get of Bahian hospitality?

Come here, Negress, stop shuffling around; we're not going to do you any harm, we just want to have a party—what do you say? We'll take you home afterward, we'll even pay you an honorarium—what do you say?"

"Let us go, Massa, please."

"You shameless Negress!" he shouted, and grabbed Dafé with a violent hug, fondling her bottom.

Dafé's skirt went up, the others came close, one of them started helping Leopoldo to hold her still.

"No, not this time!" Vevé cried out.

She dropped the bag of provisions she had been carrying on her back, pulled the *araçanga* out of it, and lunged against them, spinning the big club over her head. They let Dafé go, and Leopoldo walked back a few steps.

"You insolent black bitch! Don't get fresh, because I can make mincemeat out of you anytime I feel like it!"

"Keep away from me, keep away from me."

"I don't want anything to do with you, you filthy Negress; I want the other one."

"Keep away."

Dafé was never able to tell or even remember well what happened then. But she would remember clinging to her fallen mother, who was bleeding from the more than twenty stabs she had received, and the one called Leopoldo still tried to pull her up, but the one named Eugênio said they ought to leave.

"The other one is dead," he said. "This is not fun anymore; let's go."

Much later, past midnight, a cold northwesterly wind blowing strong and presaging a storm, Leléu and about eight other men, bearing torches and with hunting dogs, found Dafé sitting on her heels next to Vevé's body, so motionless not even her eyes were blinking. They wrapped a blanket around her, found a hammock to carry her dead mother, and took her to bed, but she did not sleep. And for the next twenty-one days she barely moved, she did not open her mouth to say one single word, she remained sitting with her head down, gazing at her hands, open in her lap.

City of Salvador, Bahia, March 12, 1835

"I told you, I've always told you: Spit from an empty stomach! What did I use to tell you, day after day?"

"Spit from an empty stomach."

"Say it again!"

"Spit from an empty stomach."

"Say it again!"

"Spit from an empty stomach."

"So? So? So? So why didn't you do it?"

"I never remembered."

"You never remembered? You never remembered? Is that all you have to say? You never remembered?"

"That's what I used to tell you then and what I can tell you now."

Amleto gave the account books lying on his desk a hard blow with his cane. That was what he should do to him, that perfect reprobate who was his son but one had to admit he was also a reprobate, a scapegrace, a ne'er-do-well. He hadn't applied the rod to his back often enough, that was it. And on the other hand, his mother protected him in every way, and Amleto was even sure that most of the illnesses he had had without ever developing a fever or losing his appetite, as if his soul itself suffered from bulimia, had been made up by her in order to shield him from discipline. And there was the result: that colossal boor, that oafish, uncouth person, with an unpleasant appearance, a low mentality, and even lower instincts, whom he had to call his son, for indeed he was. Yes, he was, but he did not seem to be, because all the others had turned out to look like people of good birth and character, and only he had been born with that indecently broad, flat nose and those lips so fleshy that they were rather like two thick sausages—a Negroid, undeniably a Negroid! Fortunately, his hair was not really bad, it was just a bit curly, but with a great deal of pomade and held down by skullcaps at night, it could be reasonably combed down, in a kind of brittle mass drawn onto the nape of his neck.

Amleto seemed to want to sit down but never touched the seat, and he stood erect to resume his striding back and forth. There had been a solution for that snout. His mother had done it with him, and Carlota Borroméia's nose had become very slender by means of the same technique. That is to say, spit from an empty stomach. You just moisten your forefinger and thumb with your tongue before you have eaten, then you massage the nose. Carlota Borroméia's nose had been much less simian then Patrício Macário's, so the treatment they gave it when she was a baby had been sufficient. But that was not his case, he should have gone on for a much longer time, but no efforts and no punishments had managed to make him remember such a common-place measure. As a matter of fact, the truth was that punishment could not force him to do anything.

Last Thursday, right after the argument in his study about spit from an empty stomach, Amleto had opened the door to let in Father Clemente André, this one, yes, a very proper young man, dedicated, studious, almost blond, with exemplary manners and culture. Maybe a little complacent, a bit of a fop perhaps, but a man of extremely high caliber. Poor Clemente André, he had come to give a word of advice to Patrício Macário, maybe even offer him a little solidarity as their father was about to lose his head. But all he accomplished was that Patrício Macário, after treating him with rudeness, threatened to let him have it in the face with hands and paws, as he himself put it.

"You're queer, that's what you are!" he had shouted at his brother, his neck veins bulging. "You're queer, and Father and Mother are the only ones who don't even see you wiggle your behind!"

"Have some respect for me, you scamp!"

"You have respect for me and don't put your hands on me, because I don't care if you're all silk and face powder—I'll split your chin in two!"

The tragedy feared for so long almost happened. Amleto picked from the rack his bronze-capped rosewood cane and started hitting Patrício Macário, but he stopped short of bashing his head because Clemente André raised his hand to his forehead, moaned limply, and collapsed on the carpet.

"My son!" Amleto shouted, dropping the cane and rushing to the priest, who was now rolling his eyes as though in fatal agony. "My son, what has this wild beast, this baptized animal, done to you?"

He got back on his feet in a rage and dove to the floor to get his cane to resume his attack on Patrício Macário, who had his arms crossed and was watching the scene as if he had nothing to do with it.

"You scoundrel! You pervert! You nitwit! You degenerate! I'll teach you to be insolent, you dog!"

But a pain in his chest, a lacerating, burning pain under his breastbone, arrested his raised arm. Breathless and dizzy, he leaned against the back of a chair, a sudden frigid sweat beading his face. Dashing to the study in the company of two house blacks, Teolina staggered at the door and also had to lean against something not to fall down.

"I'll kill him, I'll kill this freak of nature, I'll kill him," Almeto gasped. "Before he kills us all, I'll kill him. God could not have given me a worse punishment than having this quadruped for a son!"

"Don't talk like that, in Immaculate Mary's name! My Saint Anthony, my Saint Philip, my Saint Margaret, what happened? What happened, Patrício Macário, my child? O Holy Mother of God, Father Clemente!"

Of all the people in the house, Bonifácio Odulfo, who was asleep and did not wake up, and Patrício Macário, who moved only when his mother ordered him to help her, alone escaped at least a day of restrictions, rest, anxiety, and nervous weakness. Dr. Vasco Miguel, who fortunately arrived from the office a while later to bring Amleto some papers, examined them all. He worried most about Amleto, who was afflicted with an anguish-related dyspnea and pre-apoplexy, and prescribed a few bromides, confined him to bed, forbade him to eat heavily, and substituted green tea for his coffee. As for the others, chamomile tea, quiet, rest. As for Tico, patience; medicine knew very little about cases such as his. He had a colleague who was very interested in nervous illnesses; maybe he would know about something that might have an effect on Tico, although, as he had said before, little is known about the physiology of exalted temperaments. And finally, as for Bonifácio Odulfo, he was a poet, and like all parasites, as Vasco Miguel grumbled angrily to himself, he felt he was a creditor of the world while a debtor only to himself; no harm would come to him.

Amleto wanted to leave his bed on the first day, but the women of the family so implored him to rest, if only for the next three days, returning to work the following Monday, that he agreed to spend Friday lying down. He had to drink calmatives and one granadilla juice after another all day long to be able to hold back the fury that pumped blood to his head every time he remembered Patrício Macário. Even so, they had trouble containing him, but on Saturday morning he shoved aside all who tried to stop him and got to his office in the business district at a quarter past seven, as was his habit ever since he had left Jesus' Yard.

The first thing he did was to lock himself in and attack his books with his cane, mindless of the noise that could be heard outside. He was getting used to power and even enjoyed acting in ways people did not understand and seeing that no one dared to ask questions. Woe unto him who should have the audacity to want to know what all that noise was, and he even considered striking the door but changed his mind and hit the books so hard that he broke the cane.

He finally managed to sit down, staring ahead and rubbing his finger on the jagged end of the cane. That brat would get his comeuppance, that was for sure. A man like him, respected in all Bahia, he might say in all Brazil, allowing himself to be demoralized by a young rascal in his own home? Never, never! And it was high time to set in motion the plan he had conceived the night before, which now seemed increasingly well thought out. He looked at the list of things to do in front of him. He had to change it; something more important had come up. He started to make a new list, and wrote after the number 1: "Family Council." He was glad that the next thing to do, number 1 in the previous list, was a brief appointment right there in his office with the bachelor of law Noêmio Pontes, presently his associate in several enterprises, including the banking house, perhaps the most powerful in all the region, with assets of over four thousand contos.

Almeto interrupted the writing of the list and leaned back in his chair, scratching the side of his nostril with the penholder. As he thought about the assets of the banking house, he felt a sudden infusion of joy and serenity. Yes, he had nothing to fear. Why had he become so used to uncertainty, insecurity, and worrisomeness that even now, when there was no reason for it, he persisted in shaking with fear, in becoming almost terrified? Nonsense, nonsense; nothing was beyond his reach; he had to assume once and for all the total serenity and firmness he presented to people. But of course. Why all this disquiet now, all this anxiety? Away with it. He decided he would

244

return to the first list; there was no need to add "Family Council"; it was something that would take its course naturally; he would handle everything during his normal office hours, with no haste.

When Bachelor Noêmio came through the door that the secretary Octaviano Souza had respectfully opened for him, he found Amleto with his hands crossed over his stomach and exhibiting his usual slightly hurried affability. They talked about the recent yields of the Lençóis diamond mines, the tobacco plantations, the sugar mills, the lime factory, the warehouses, the shipping operations, and other matters. The bachelor was particularly impressed by the acuity with which Amleto touched upon the problem of the confederation of money-issuing banks, explaining its benefits to their interests. Unlike the bachelor, who had a few doubts about it because he thought it was a madman's idea, Amleto was sure it would be established.

"Mark my words," he said. "The exchange rates will go up like a sky-rocket. We shall buy pounds. More and more pounds sterling."

The bachelor agreed that buying pounds was always sound business, but he pondered that maybe it would involve too large a commitment of resources to an enterprise as uncertain as the confederation. Instead of becoming impatient, Amleto gave a cadenced, good-natured lecture about the logic of finances, which is, he said, a logic that establishes as its major premise the fact that those who are in command will unfailingly do anything to perpetuate that command and everything to justify such perpetuation. And the justification is needed because while they are in command, they do all right for themselves. And doing all right for oneself is a generous thing, it is actually open to everyone. Everyone, that is, who can see. In matters of public finances, he intoned, closing his eyes with a smile, more than in any other field, the old maxim is of the essence: *Cui prodest?* To whom is it profitable, to whom does it bring advantages? Any decision in the field of public finances represents profit for someone, no matter how diabolically this may be disguised, and it usually is not, because those in command hold it as their most refined art to make those who are not in command think that those who are have in mind the interests of those who are not.

He allowed himself a prolonged giggle, and apologized for talking like a sophist, though he could guarantee he was not. The confederation idea had ripened, it was a way to make money with paper that was too attractive to be ignored, if only for a necessarily limited time.

"In public finance," he added, laughing so much that he almost could not speak, "everything is for a necessarily limited time. We'll buy pounds."

He regretted that the country had not been colonized by the English. He asked leave to tell an anecdote, and said that his son Bonifácio Odulfo, an impenitent Francophile, a boot polisher of the little Corsican lieutenant—poets' whims he'll get over, just as he got over the measles—had rebuffed his father's request that he learn English.

"A language of barbarians!" he had said. "A language that has no sub-junctive must be viewed with suspicion!"

Amleto confessed it had made him laugh quite a bit. But afterward, following his custom of thrashing over everything that had made him laugh, he had arrived at the conclusion that the absence of verbal inflections in English was a sign of superiority.

"Overabundant verbal inflections tend to stall the mind in sterile paths," he said. "If a Frenchman thinks of doing something for which he doesn't find a precise mood, tense, and inflection, he won't think about it anymore."

He laughed again and even apologized once more for being in that irresistible vein; he didn't know what had come over him. But he soon regained his composure and looked among his notes for something he might still need to discuss with the bachelor. All the items had been crossed out with energetic pen strokes, but there was something else to be settled.

"There is still a matter I wish to talk to you about," he began. "The new lighter for the lime factory, the distribution of the fund's shares . . . But of course, how could I forget?" He made an exceedingly long pause, during which he opened his mouth a couple of times as if to speak, then he clapped his hands with his wrists touching, as though he wanted to mimic a butterfly. "As you know, throughout all these years we have been together, our personal friendship has prospered as much as our business, perhaps, to my honor, even more."

"My honor, Commander Amleto."

Amleto smiled. He enjoyed being addressed as "Commander"; it was incomparably better than *senhor*. He bowed his head slightly at the bachelor, and went on explaining that he considered himself a friend of the bachelor's, and therefore his confidant. He described how Patrício Macário caused all kinds of problems for him, creating an intolerable situation in his home. After much suffering, many doubts and hesitations, many moments in which he had been at the brink of precipitating himself into an act of madness dictated by rage, he had finally come to a definitive decision, the only one indicated for the case in point. He had thought of it after an incident between his son and himself that had almost put an end to his days and to this moment made him feel weak and prone to fainting. But he had formu-lated it in a prudent, balanced, and mature way, and was so sure of it that only very strong arguments, very, very strong, unanswerable arguments, would dissuade him.

He added that he was sorry he could not reveal the decision yet. But he would do it today, at the family council he was convening, which he expected the bachelor Noêmio Pontes to give him the honor of attending. Would two o'clock be all right? It was Saturday; they could close the office early. He himself would go home around eleven and would not come back in the afternoon.

246

"I'm deeply honored, my dear Commander and friend, deeply honored," the bachelor said, rising as if it had become impossible for him to remain seated.

"Believe me, my very cherished friend, the honor you do me is greater. I will also make arrangements for the presence of Monsignor Bibiano, who baptized the boy and is our spiritual adviser and confessor, and of Major Francisco Magalhães, who is the boy's godfather. In my opinion, we should also have the participation of Dr. Vasco Miguel, of my son Father Clemente André, and of Bonifácio Odulfo too, although I don't believe he's going to be interested. But he is my son too, and a grown man; I don't want him to say later that he was ignored in a family decision."

"Wise thinking, very wise. And I'm sure your decision is quite right; I'm sure I'm going to support it."

"I hope so. As I said, only extremely strong arguments would dissuade me."

He felt in very good spirits after the bachelor had left. He opened the window and looked out. It was a beautiful day; it was without doubt a beautiful day in every sense. There was nothing like determination, firmness, and the courage of making decisions to invigorate a man of responsibility. He got back to his desk, picked up a monogrammed writing pad, and scribbled four short messages: one for Monsignor Bibiano, one for Major Francisco Magalhães, one for Dr. Vasco Miguel, and one for Teolina, asking her to make sure that Father Clemente and Bonifácio Odulfo were home at 2 P.M. for a discussion of the highest importance. He addressed four envelopes and pulled the bell's cord; Octaviano came in at once.

"Have these messages taken right now to the people whose names are on the envelopes. Very well, *Senhor* Octaviano, that's all. What's wrong?"

Octaviano hesitated; his face turned red. Nothing was wrong; it was just that he was aware of the commander's directive not to be disturbed, but for weeks now, almost every day, a woman, a brown, humble woman, though one could see she was a decent person, had come to try to see the commander.

"Enroll her in the charity list," Amleto said. "That's all those people want; they think we can support all of mankind."

"I've already done that, Commander. But she says she does not want alms on feasts of saints; what she really wants is to speak to Your Excellency."

"But why speak to me? I have no time to see everyone who comes to me. Who is this woman?"

"She says she is the widow of an employee of His Lordship the baron of Pirapuama, later of Your Excellency—a certain Horácio Bonfim, if I am not mistaken."

Amleto was barely able to hold back an exclamation. What would that woman want here, so many years after her husband had been dismissed, to die soon afterward? Didn't she have a pension? She was sure to have one, and

247

maybe something else too; what could she possibly be after now? A good thing it couldn't be, but it was better to see right away what it was all about.

"All right, *Senhor* Octaviano, you may let her in."

"Yes sir. And here are today's documents, which you told me to classify and organize."

"Leave them over there."

He did not like the way Octaviano set down the folder containing the documents and moved it so that its upper edge was perfectly parallel to the edge of the table. Those little things were what made Octavianos different from Amletos, he thought. Or even Horácios from Octavianos, because that scum would never have tried to satisfy by himself his superiors' demands for tidiness; everything he did had to be ordered. He remembered the way Horácio was taken aback when he was dismissed after a workday like any other. He probably had felt secure, knowing that Amleto knew that he knew about Amleto's frauds against the baron's properties, because he was always eavesdropping, spying, and scrutinizing. What he did not know—and that could be seen in his ashen face when he was told—was that Amleto had had a locksmith open his drawers and his compartment in the big cabinet and had taken all his papers. All of them: not only the ones that compromised Amleto but also those that compromised Horácio, even the dice and card game IOUs he had not had the sense to destroy. Amleto chuckled, remembering the man's look of helplessness when he said to him very calmly:

"Take heart, *Senhor* Horácio Bonfim. I am obliged to you for having taught me a lesson. And that lesson is not to save too many papers, because our past is our business and nobody else's. You have just taught me a great history lesson, *Senhor* Horácio Bonfim. Get out of here."

He was almost repeating aloud the words he had said then, when the woman came in, introduced by Octaviano as Dona Maria d'Alva Bonfim. He stared at her sternly and did not ask her to sit down.

"Yes?" he said, crossing his hands over his desk.

The woman was nervous and had trouble starting to speak, especially after he got up and stood by the window, telling her he had no time to waste. Stammering heavily and apologizing at each sentence, she finally said Horácio had been a good man, had always been a good husband, had lived for his work and his home. If he had had his faults, that only made him equivalent to any man of his condition, very humble in origin and tempered by hard work since early childhood. The truth was, he had not left her unsupported, ever since that fateful day when he got home from work after having been dismissed and two hours later suffered the seizure that left him paralyzed in bed for over forty days, until a merciful death took him away. God had not given them children, and they had not managed to acquire any property worth naming, but she had inherited the house in which they lived in Tingüi, there was the small nest egg left at the savings bank, the little vegetable patch in her backyard, a few chickens, and two rented houses, which allowed her to survive modestly. But now the old house where they had lived ever since they had married, since the time of the baron of Pirapuama, whom God must have in His Holy Glory for having done so much for the common people, was about to collapse, after the rain had so damaged it as to make it almost impossible to go on living in. She had no money for the repairs, which were altogether too expensive, as he could see in the written estimate she was now showing him.

Amleto became impatient and refused to look at the paper. All that babbling was getting nowhere; he could not waste his time listening to stories in which he had absolutely no interest. She apologized again, took out of her purse a hardcover notebook, and explained that before he died Horácio had managed, with great difficulty, to speak to her about the notebook, and had even whispered it was worth money. Since she did not know how to read too well, was unfamiliar with those difficult words, and had no one in the world to resort to, it had occurred to her to seek His Excellency the commander and try to get something in return for the notebook. Who knows, maybe Horácio had been right, and it was really a valuable document.

Amleto took the notebook, pressed his glasses on his nose, and opened the first page. As if it were the title page of a carefully laid out book, it read: "DIARY OF EVENTS AT THE ESTABLISHMENTS OF HIS LORDSHIP THE BARON OF PIRAPUAMA UNDER THE MANAGEMENT OF THE BOOKKEEPER AMLETO FERREIRA—An account authored by HORÁCIO BONFIM, with the purpose of enlightening His Lordship and Posterity." He thumbed through a couple of pages, feigning just a slight interest. There were not many pages, maybe thirty, covered by a tight script with several corrections. But in a hard-to-believe profusion of details, they covered everything that had happened at the office since the day the baron had fallen ill.

"That blackguard!" Amleto said between his teeth.

"Did Your Excellency say something?"

"No, it was just a casual utterance. Do you have copies of this?"

"No sir; he told me to be careful because that was the only place where those notes were written."

"Good for you. This is absolutely worthless, but here there are secrets of the firm which your late husband saw fit to note down in this fashion, who knows with what purpose. Have you ever shown this to anyone?"

"No sir; I've never shown it to anyone; this notebook has been locked in a trunk and covered with dust ever since my husband's death."

"You've acted responsibly. And with luck, I might add, because your husband would have been in serious trouble, even after his death, if this here had been divulged."

"You mean it actually never had any value?"

"It's not impossible that it had some value for him. I don't know what people like him think. But just the same, I'm glad you have brought it to me, for I happen to be the only person to whom this irresponsible document can be trusted." He changed his expression and crossed his arms. "Unfortunately, I cannot give you the help you seek; it's quite beyond my available resources at the moment; we're living in a time of crisis. Nevertheless, I'm going to give you a letter to the Municipal Director of Public Works, requesting some assistance for you, within the bounds of possibility. That's what the government is for, anyway. And as a token of goodwill, I'm going to write another letter, this one to *Senhor* Emídio Reis, who owns a few stores, asking him to see if he can give you some leftover materials or something with imperfections but still usable."

He rang the bell and told Octaviano as soon as he came in to write the two letters. He made a sign for her to leave, but before she closed the door behind her, he called her back.

"Here," he said, handing her a five-milreis bill. "It's not for your husband's sake but for yours."

He locked the door, sat down, and opened the notebook at random. He came across a page topped by the title "The Plundering of the Provisions." A bit shaky, he began to read: "The provisions purchased for the establishments of His Lordship the baron are constantly turned over, sometimes in their entirety, to establishments owned by *Senhor* Amleto in collusion with his relative *Senhor* Emídio Reis. On Thursday, August 23, of the year of Our Lord 1827, *Senhor* Emídio Reis, who is Amleto's wife's brother, came to the office and upon that occasion . . ."

"That blackguard!" Amleto snarled, slamming the notebook shut.

Bonifácio Odulfo came down to his father's study over half an hour late. He found the door closed, with Teolina practically leaning on it, so anxious to know what was going on inside she did not even notice her son's arrival and was startled when he spoke to ask her what time it was.

"Son!" she said, raising her hands and running to the parlor and back to take a look at the clock. "It's almost a quarter to three, and you're still here? I thought by now you'd be inside; I've been ordering them to wake you up since noon! This time your father is really going to get his dander up; he's been in a stew since early this morning, and now you arrive so late for this discussion he considers so important! I only hope this won't make things worse for your poor little brother—oh my God, what do you think your father is going to do to him?"

"Take it easy, Dona Teolina; isn't Father Clemente in there to give his blessing to this famous scheme the commander has devised?"

"You mean you haven't heard? Don't you know Tico almost got into a fistfight with Father Clemente André and your father wanted to cane him to death and didn't do it only because he got a sudden spasm?"

"I heard some rumors from the Negresses, but I didn't give them a thought. Did Tico really maul Father Clemente's nose? That must have been a magnificent scrap, with the father tangled up in his silk skirts and Tico pommeling his mug with those two little elephant paws God gave him."

"Don't talk like that! I forbid you to talk like that! Not content with being late, which shows your contempt for our family affairs, you also deal with the problem as if it were a joke? Can't you be serious about anything?"

"Forgive me, Mother, but the fact is, that which you call family affairs are wearisome to me even before I know what they are all about. And after all, what can I do if Tico persists in his resolve to give the father a couple of wallops? If your intention is for me to intercede, *pardon, madame, moi je ne suis pas un suicide.* I have no esteem for pugilism; my muscles are in my head and not in any paws, as is our sweet Tiquinho's case."

"I told you you are forbidden to talk like that!"

"But I'm not saying anything against Tico; we've always gotten along fine. He is our dear youngest brother; I'm sure he's going to be the joy of my old age, as he is to you and Father. I'm just being truthful. It's a matter of vocation. Mine is letters, Tico's is—how can I put it?—corporal arts? There's a place in this world for both brain and brawn, for Bonifácios and Ticos. Well, do you think I should go in now?"

"But of course you should! Your father will be angry enough at your lateness, but he would never forgive you if you didn't attend; it would be a very, very serious offense."

"Far, far be it from me to commit a very, very serious offense against my magnanimous begetter. How does one enter this cavern?"

"Listen, try to say a word in your brother's favor. He's got no sense; he's still a child."

"A two-hundred-pound child, but a child."

"Listen to me, Bonifácio Odulfo, don't try to make a fool out of your mother! If you don't want—and you never do—to do me a favor, even if I seldom ask for one, at least don't make jests this . . . this stupid way."

"Is my hair too unkempt? Father always complains about my hair. How about it? I tried to comb it meticulously. What do you say?"

"You still look half asleep, but your hair is all right; it's just that you need a haircut. It doesn't become you when it's that long; it isn't the right look for a proper young man."

"That's what makes it untouchable, *amoreuse Maman.* My reputation would not withstand a proper young man's haircut; it would be fatal. Tell me, should I knock or call out?"

"I have to leave first. I don't want your father to think I'm eavesdropping.

But remember, defend your brother, who has no one on his side; he's been left to fend for himself."

"Worry not, Dona Teolina, *comptez sur moi.*"

She disappeared down the corridor. He started to knock on the door but changed his mind and tried the handle. The door was unlocked and opened more easily than he had expected, so he bumped it rather hard on Amleto's heel, interrupting his pacing around the room to better emphasize his oratory, as he was just shouting:

"To the barracks! To the barracks with him! The barracks! The barracks, the barracks, the barracks!"

"I'm sorry, Father," Bonifácio Odulfo said, holding Amleto's elbow so he wouldn't fall.

Amleto had been ready to let fly the next sentence, and he hesitated briefly between proceeding and acknowledging the entrance of the new participant. But he quickly put himself together, inspected his patent-leather boot heel, noticed the mark caused by the door, and filled his lungs to vent his anger. But contrary to his own expectation, he did not say anything; he just fixed his eyes on Bonifácio, his lips tightened, his brow furrowed, his chin going up and down, as he had learned to do through years of practice in dealing firmly with subordinates. Motionless except for his chin and for the thrusts that inflated his chest at short intervals, he did not take his eyes away from his son, who started to blush and felt his ears getting unbearably hot. Amleto was discovering a great pleasure in remaining speechless in the same posture, letting a throbbing silence engulf the room. More and more flushed, Bonifácio tried to focus on something, but he could not manage to make himself comfortable, and finally crossed his hands over his waist, with his head down. The silence was getting intolerably loaded, when a very perturbed Monsignor Bibiano decided to speak, having spent some time nervously stroking his stomach, which sprawled over his waistband.

"Yes, but the commander was saying . . ."

"I was saying something about sons, Monsignor. I was saying something about sons, about the inconsequence of this pithless, wayward generation, without a sense of true values and a notion of responsibility."

He returned his gaze to Bonifácio, who had not raised his head.

"Please do not give me explanations; I do not wish to hear your explanations, nor do I care for wisecracks in your popinjay French. The decision I am making in the case of your brother would not be unfitting for yourself, so try to act like a man of your age and origins, not like an ill-born wastrel. Take a seat and try to speak only if you have something, and I mean something, to say."

He followed Bonifácio's movements from the door to a chair and went on staring at him for some time. Finally, pressing together his fingertips, his forefingers touching his lips, he looked up as though trying to find on the ceiling the thread of the conversation.

"I was saying that after listening to the suggestions of those here present, which I consider sensible, constructive, and judicious, the decision remains definitely the barracks. I know the terrible consequences of that, even for the good name of the family. The army is not an honorable occupation, nor is it fit for a gentleman; it is something for the flotsam and jetsam of the nation, as is plain to see every moment, in front of our eyes. Not even its police duties are properly carried out, since the soldiers busy themselves with mutinies more than with anything else, that ragged band of ruffians recruited by force or sold for some five milreis by recruiting agents, that mob of derelict freed blacks, runaway slaves, and foreigners of bad provenance. Even among the officers you will not find one who belongs to a distinguished or renowned family, for no aristocrat will accept a uniform in his family. But there are extreme cases, and for extreme ills extreme remedies are required. The only way to avoid a tragic fate for that muddleheaded boy is to put him in uniform, so his unruliness will be corrected by dint of a few drubbings with the flat of a sword or by weights tied to his feet, which is how the army treats its vast contingent of rowdies and troublemakers."

"But, Commander, the army?" Major Magalhães asked. "Aren't you being excessively rigorous with the boy? Has my good friend thought of the navy, for instance? There are excellent English officers in the navy, and even among the common sailors there is a great number of Englishmen. And their discipline is also strong, but the navy, we all know, cannot be compared to the army; it is an ennobling profession. Even the Portuguese officers . . ."

"My illustrious friend and *compadre*, I know very well what is happening in your heart, for your affection for your godson is well known, and, as no one is unaware, I'm deeply grateful for it. But the navy . . ." He stopped, closed his eyes, looking for the right words, paled a little, and cleared his throat at length, with his closed fist over his mouth. "All right, let's be frank. I thought about the navy, yes, but two reasons kept me from choosing it. The first one is that I see that young man in uniform not only as discipline but, perhaps principally, as a punishment. And I deem his punishment to be much greater in the army than in the navy." He stopped again, cleared his throat so extensively that he had a slight coughing fit, and resumed his speech in a rather strangled voice. "In the second place, one might say that Patrício Macário, in his physical features and his temperament, probably took after—and I say this with no embarrassment, for I am proud of my Brazilian roots, even if they come by way of matrimony—the Brazilian side of Dona Teolina's family. I have never had the chance to tell you this, and I think not even my children know about it, but Dona Teolina's grandmother on her father's side was practically an Indian, the daughter of a

Portuguese—a very well-reputed bushwhacker, a man of noble origins who became a jungle ranger due to circumstances not worth mentioning here —and an Indian woman, the youngest daughter of a *cacique*, which is how the Indians call their kings and leaders. That Indian woman must have had very strong blood, because it crossed generations to get to Patrício Macário. The result is that Indian-like appearance, that swarthy complexion and maybe those rude, practically indomitable ways. Dona Teolina's dear grandmother, I'm told, was an admirable lady, who converted after being taken out of her tribe, and led a life dedicated to her family and to pious works. But her lineage must necessarily include many savage warriors, from whom I imagine Patrício Macário inherited those traits we referred to, in his character and appearance. I do not wish, therefore, to run any risks. In the army, if he is modified by work and discipline and if he is not court-martialed in the process, he can climb to positions less denigrating to his origins. In the navy he would not fulfill the physical requirements for officers, and I honestly do not believe he would rise above the rank of lieutenant, or whatever they call the highest of their low ranks. No, no, the young man is going to the military school."

"At Central School they also prepare young men for the army."

"He's going to the military school."

"Is he of the required age?"

"That's a matter of no concern; we have enough friends who can solve such trifles."

"And won't Dona Teolina be opposed?"

"It's possible, but a woman's opposition must be faced in precisely those terms: as a woman's opposition. Women, my friends, are all heart and no head, and we know very well there are more traps in the blandishments of the heart than in the cold reasoning of the head. Dona Teolina will have to understand because, as in relation to children, we have to do with women what is best for them, not what they want."

"Undeniably."

"That's the reason why I convened this council. I know that my decision, painful as it is for a father, is correct, but I did not wish to make it without the audience of my friends and my family. We must *e pluribus unum facere* —may the monsignor's erudition correct me if I used the expression improperly."

"Now, now, Commander, I wish I knew Latin so well."

"That's very kind of you; it's a friend's generosity. Well, speaking of friendship, I'm afraid I'll have to take further advantage of it. I'm sure the major's good offices will be useful for the entrance of the boy in the military school. I'm going to send him with no privileges of any kind. Do they give their students a soldier's pay?"

"I don't think so. The army doesn't pay even its mercenaries, and when it pays, it's such a miserly sum that it can hardly buy a three-hundred-reis meal a day."

"Then he may receive a small allowance, a few pounds parsimoniously allotted by our correspondent. And mentioning a correspondent reminds me to ask another favor, this time from my distinguished lawyer, friend, and partner, Dr. Noêmio Pontes."

"I am at your service."

"For which I am perennially grateful. It's to take care of the matter of a correspondent in Rio de Janeiro. I know that among the many friends you have in that city, there are enough men of responsibility and character to perform this function."

"Oh yes, of course. As a first thought, I might suggest Dr. Amarílio Veiga, or maybe Dr. Benjamin Furtado, or maybe . . ."

The decision having been made and ratified, the details went on being discussed, now as slowly as the approaching end of the afternoon, Amleto leaning back on his chair with a contented look, Vasco Miguel rising a little, impatient to leave, Major Magalhães immersed in grave thoughts and gazing out the window, the monsignor wondering if he was going to be invited to dinner, Noêmio Pontes noting down names and addresses, Clemente André worrying about the new frock that should arrive any minute now, Bonifácio Odulfo silent, resentful, humiliated, rancorous—how he hated the way all those people lived, how he abhorred his father's money and everything it stood for, how one day everyone would bow to his genius, how one day that house would exist only to honor his memory!

11

Leléu hid behind the oil palms to cry, and thought about how life is crazy, crazy, crazy. How can a man watch himself crying? He didn't know, but it was happening—there he was watching himself with his face furrowing, his chest heaving, his throat aching from choking his moans so hard, tears coming down like rain in spite of the effort he made to stifle them by squeezing the palms of his hands against his eyes. Maybe he had cried when he was a boy, but he didn't remember, because a little black slave boy with no mother, no father, no protector, learns very early he can't cry. And now this, just like that, right when the party was about to start, everybody arriving, the little streamers fluttering, the bonfires burning, the corn being roasted, the colored skyrockets ready to fly to the sky, the balloons with their tow wicks all set to go, the biggest Saint John's Day eve party ever seen in all those parts, the biggest Saint John's Day celebration in the world, as Leléu himself had said at the Puffer Fish square when he invited everyone to come to Little Pot Spring, where after the revelry they would all wash in honor of the great saint, Our Lord's cousin. If someone happened to see him crying like that, they would think it was because of the expenses he was having with the party, and he laughed in the midst of his crying, finding life even crazier than before. But after laughing, he resumed sobbing so hard that he couldn't remain sitting and walked a few steps toward the springhead. He had to stop that; after all, he was the host; he had even dressed like Saint John the Baptist to clown around, wrapped in a goatskin he was going to say was camel hide like the saint's, and had brought along his old guara-wood club to serve as a cudgel. And besides, wasn't the party being given to make the girl happy? And how can anyone be made happy, especially an innocent young girl, by all this boohooing and these yowls that reminded him of a pup abandoned by its mother?

He leaned his hand against a palm tree and asked himself what he could do. What could he do, even if he was a man who had seen everything in life? Nothing, it all seemed to indicate. His little girl, who as she closed her little arms around his neck to cajole something out of him brought a warmth to his heart he had never felt and a gratitude for life he had never found possible and a wonderment whose existence he had never suspected, his little girl, whom he wanted to protect from all the evils of the world and who used to be the very face of happiness and confidence, had been stolen. Not her little body, though it was now frail because she had been eating very little since the day her mother was murdered. Dafé's body was still there, even if it made him sad and sometimes sleepless out of fear she might get sick, even if it didn't have the vigor that had been the first thing people used to feel in her presence. But her spirit had been stolen, taken away, penned someplace where there was no way to reclaim it. The school materials, which he had brought in big, separate, ornate packages, so she could spend the night joyfully opening and arranging them, were still where he had left them, just the one with the slates open, because he had thought it might cheer her, but she wouldn't even look at it. He did everything that came to his mind: He took her sightseeing to Bahia and to any town or village where they were having an open-air feast, a carnival, or a celebration; he even paid mothers so that their children would keep her company; he did everything, really everything, but he never heard her laugh, never saw her run gleefully barefoot, never noticed a glimmer in her eyes, never listened to her tell stories of kings, princes and princesses, and heroes, never saw her even glance at the picture books he had taken so much trouble to find for her. And he himself had been losing interest in life and business, in anything but her, and was forced, during the many wakeful nights when he tiptoed to see if she was sleeping well and breathing, to make speeches to himself so he would not be defeated once and for all and would go on with the battle of life.

He couldn't do even that now, as he cried his heart out, propped on the thorny, vine-covered trunk of a palm tree. He wanted his little girl back; what use did he have for money, what use did he have for anything, if he no longer was Grandpa Leléu, if he had nothing more to learn in the world, if he had failed at the only thing in his life that he hadn't looked upon as work, but as life itself? For the first time, Black Leléu thought of dying, he figured that he, too, needed a rest, that death was a necessary, merciful thing, that turning into nothing was better than being what he had become, because his suffering was the usual one, it was work, but her suffering was impossible to bear, it killed more than death itself. He felt under his short breeches the stingray spine he had picked up absentmindedly on his way out of the house, he touched his heart with his other hand, he thought of how easy it would be to get that spine and thrust it in the place that was the residence of blood and go away for good; maybe after death he would find what he had lost, what he had never had, what had been granted him for so little time: the peace always denied to one whose body and mind were scarred. Clenching his hands until his fingernails buried themselves in his palms, he felt very sorry for himself, he wished he had someone to complain to, he wished for a father, a mother, bosom friends, he felt so alone that he saw madness close at hand, he saw how easy it would be to lose his reason, how it was something as simple as jumping off a cliff into the darkness of an abyss.

But is Black Leléu a quitter? Never on your life! You know the whale they nickname *toadeira*? It's the bravest of living beings, which, surrounded by the deadliest enemies any creature can have, its flanks harpooned, the sea a fatal thornbush, raises its back like a noble horse, shakes its head like a combatant who won't surrender, gives no one the satisfaction of its pants or groans, denies the sting of the many darts biting its back, asks its blood to be faithful to it in that hour, and with an impetus nothing on earth can resist, rends everything in front of it and drags the boats, the people, the ropes, everything, behind it in a sprint of spume and water over the seven seas, and thus triumphs over those who think they can beat one that will not be beaten, through the strength of pride and the will to fight. I'm nothing, Black Leléu thought, turning little by little into a *toadeira*, I'm a no-good Negro no one ever wanted, but I am I, and I want to work, there is no work I can't work at, and I'm pulling this rope, I'm destroying this enemy boat with my head, I'm diving into this sea—let's go, my Leléu!

And by the time he was out of the oil palm patch, he had a smile this big on his face, he was almost a deity of the woods after having wet his face under the cold gush of the spring to fight tears with tears, whirling to and fro, looking like a twenty-year-old he never knew he had been, a real devil, nimble like a monkey, wild like a bitch, with the power, with the spirit, with the fucking flags of the infinite, the force of the ostentation of the courage of the man who takes no shit from any sonofabitch, two Leléus, one good and the other bad like the plague, one hand caressing and the other striking, one side of his face smiling and the other scowling, one side of his heart pouring love and the other red hot with hatred, one ear listening and the other deaf, one leg fleeing and the other strutting forth, his chest high, his head separated from his neck and spitting fire, his teeth powerful enough to bite down all the trees on the island, his longing for Dafé's return saying like a drum that yes, she was there, that life takes precedence over death, that fighting takes precedence over bowing down, that a love that won't be defeated takes precedence over a love that hides, that a holy war takes precedence over a sick peace.

Who can that be who yonder saunters, so saucy, so smart, so spirited? It has to be Black Leléu, with his finely tanned goatskin, his finely cut guara-wood cudgel, his finely set smart sandals, his finely tuned puckish smile, breaking out of the woods in order to frolic! Come on, girls, or the saint will get mad—wake up, John! Wake up, John, bring down the bonfire of the firmament with your mother Elizabeth, your father Zachary, your cousin the master of heaven, your meal of locusts and honey, your hand that cleans water itself, your lamb of innocence—wake up John! Wake up, Saint John, come down here to see your party, to see how they're lighting the fire of the Holy Ghost, which spins above Jesus' head like moths around a light—come on, Saint John, come and vanquish Salome, who dances and kills, and dances and dies!

"What is this girl doing here all down in the dumps—you got no sense?" Black Leléu asked, prancing about by the wailing of Master Pautério's concertina. "Saint John doesn't want to see anyone sad! Are you that hungry? There's even armadillo stew, fetched by Saint John here, together with Luiz Tatu! There's corn cream, there's hominy, there's cornmeal, there's salted hominy, there's corn and tapioca rolls, there's corn on the cob, there's roasted corn, there's peanuts, there's sweet corn flour, there's corn gruel, there's everything!"

With his hands at his back, he touched the tip of a burning twig to a rocket he was hiding, pretended its hissing startled him, whirled around as if trying to find out what was happening behind him, and let go the rocket—hooray for Saint John! Sitting next to two other girls, who like her were not dancing with the rest of the frolickers, Dafé fixed her flower garland and smiled lightly, without showing her teeth. But it was a smile! Leléu thought. Wheee, hooray for Saint John!

He took her hand, started dancing around and greeting someone here and someone there, and went to the middle of a circle of people, jumping from one foot to the other.

"All right, folks, Saint John's arrived. Those who are not yet *compadres* better see to it right now!"

"Why, really, who ever saw a black Saint John like that?"

"Been out in the sun too much, son, han-han-han-han!"

"Work a miracle, my dear little saint!"

"Give me the tub. Is it virgin water? Let me take a look! Hoom! Hoom! Ah-hoom! I don't want to tell you, my dear, but I see a great many bad things inside this wet water—quite, quite bad!"

"Tell me, tell me, dear little saint!"

"Let me get rid of this camel hide, let me make myself comfortable. Hoom-hoom, a very bad thing, my friend!"

"Is this a camel hide, dear saint? In my dear saint's land, a goat is called a camel?"

"Goats are called camels,
And camels are called bucks.
Now go ask your dear mother
If it is true that she . . . Heh-heh-heh-heh—what's the rhyme for
bucks, sonny?"

"My dear saint, is all that the moon said written down on that water?"

"This water holds all the words
That the moon has ever said,
Including about your sisters
Living from bed to bed! Heh-heh-heh-heh—you ask it, I answer
it!"

"See my fate in the water, sweet little saint!"

"Looking here in the water,
I see your fate all too well.
It's to bear water in baskets
And gnaw the sides of a bell."

"You think I'll get married today, good my saint?"

"I'll tell you the whole truth:
Your marriage won't come to pass,
But with luck you'll find today
A good friend to screw your . . . Peep-peep-peep—look at the
little bird to air your mind a bit!"

"Should I stick a knife in a banana tree, so I'll know the first letter of my
love's name?"

"To stick is quite possible
And it is possible to stick,
So be careful all you can
Not to be stuck by a prick!"

"Should I light a candle at midnight, to know if what my heart tells me
is true?"

"Do light the candle, my boy,
If that is your belief,
To hear your heart tell you
That your father is a thief."

And there he goes, and here he comes, and away he jumps, how nice is
this tamped-down, hard clay ground, so there is no dust when you celebrate

and dance! Long live God, whose sainthood is old, and Saint John, who's an old saint, a new saint can be duped even by a cheating priest, this is good, all the way with that concertina, Pautério, let's have it, master! Chonk-chonk-chonk, ah-one, ah-two, ah-three, let's jump over the bonfire to become good *compadres*, whee-whee-whee, praise the Lord, good, good, good, good! I'll take offense at anyone who keeps still, you hear? All right, I want you to eat, I want you to dance, I want you to frolic, I want you to jump, I want you to speak well of the host after you leave, I want you to get home with your belly full of food, your head full of liquor, your private parts full of heat, because for that heat we have the water of Little Pot Spring, which was given to these people for them to wash themselves in the year's cold night, which is the Baptist's night, who was the one who stroked the Lord's head and made the water of the Jordan sacred, by bathing in it the holy body the world was going to sully.

Did Leléu work that night? How he worked, that Black Leléu! How he zipped and zigzagged about, how he seemed to be five, to be six or twenty, how he talked, how he said silly things, how he showed off to everyone, how he performed, how he popped up everywhere, how he got to be the very image of all the feasting saints, how he had a word for everything—what an artist Leléu was! What a love he had for his dear, dear, sweet little grand-daughter, as he decided that he would not allow her to stop to think, that he would wind up her body so much that her soul would not be able to resist, and would you believe, isn't that she dancing and prancing, jumping over the bonfires hand in hand with him, having a little of everything there was to eat, lighting firecrackers and helping with the balloons, all of them as pretty as can be, as they turn into little stars in the sky of the village? The only one who felt happier than she was Leléu, who almost prayed to the saint to thank him for having made his little granddaughter return just as she used to be—there is really happiness in this world!

And he was about to burst like popcorn out of so much happiness, when he got back from the spring carrying a pot of water to douse the ones who had not been brave enough to bathe in the spring, and he found her shaking, her chin trembling, her eyes popping, her arms pressed hard against her ribs, her legs folding as if she was trying to kneel down and couldn't do it. He dropped the pot and rushed over to her, but could not manage to make her speak right away. He almost had to lull her in his lap until finally, her hand rising so slowly that it seemed to be carrying a weight, she pointed at one of the bonfires, around which four young white men stood near some black women. They were having a very good time, one of them playing a kind of little guitar, the others dancing around the fire. Leléu felt a tight chill slide down his chest to the pit of his stomach.

"Are those the ones?"

"Yes."

He sprang up, holding the ray spine to draw it out together with the sheath that hid it. But Dafé almost fell down when he let go of her, and he figured at once that if he attacked them or killed them right there, or even if he waited for a chance soon after the party, he would be arrested, tortured, and hanged.

"No," he said to himself. "It's not going to be like that."

He laid the goatskin over her shoulders very tenderly to keep her warm and carried her slowly all the way back to the house, after telling Master Pautério to take over the party, because he had to help his granddaughter, who had felt suddenly ill. When he arrived, he woke the two old black women who slept in the backyard room and told them to make some tea for the girl and see to it that she was well covered and waited on. While the old women were fetching the leaves for the tea and lighting up the coals, he asked her if she was feeling better, and she answered yes, but she was sort of hearing clicks, buzzes, and whistles inside her head.

"That's nothing," he said. "It'll go away in no time. I'm going to tell *Sa* Benvinda to get two raw potato slices to put here on your temples under your hair, and your headache will go away in no time. Are you cold?"

"No."

"All right, then. Look, pay attention to what I'm saying, because it's very important that you help me in this—I'll tell you all about it later. I'm going to tell Benvinda and Nonoca that I'm going to bed in the other room and to call me if anything happens. But don't let them call me, you hear?"

"I'm sleepy."

"That's good, that's fine; go to sleep, then. But if you happen to wake up, don't let them call me—did you get that? Do you understand?"

"Yes."

Leléu pressed her head close to his for a short moment, arranged her sheets, and left to tell the old women that he had drunk too much at the party, he was very drowsy and was going to sleep in the small room.

"But if something happens, call me, huh? If she asks you to call me, you call me, huh?"

"There'll be no need for that, *Sô* Leléu; a little balm tea will take care of that; she'll be all right before you know it. That's just a stammacache."

"All right, then hurry up with that tea, because she's pretty much asleep already. And put two raw potato slices on her temples to suck out her headache."

"Leave it to us; you can go to bed without a worry; we'll do everything; leave it to us."

"All right; good night, then."

He went into the small room carrying a lamp, touched its flame to the four wicks of the spiderlike fixture hanging from the roof, and started rummaging through his belongings. He put on a pair of short pants, an undershirt, and a straw hat, wrapped around his waist a broad leather baldric, whose tip on the left side was good for sheathing his fish knife, tested the cutting edge of the knife with his thumb and put it back in its sheath, checked the ray spine, picked up his club, looked around to see if he had forgotten something, slapped down the top of his hat twice, muffled the wicks, covered himself with a black blanket, and jumped out of the window to hurry back to Little Pot.

It all had happened so fast that he had not really made up his mind about what he was going to do, and hiding once again in the oil palm patch, this time not to cry but to keep an eye on the four whites, he asked himself if he was sure he wanted to kill those men. Many times he had thought of killing a man, and once he had even stabbed one in the arm, but he had always found it better to settle things some other way; killing should be reserved only for a true need. Like now, like now! Would this be what they call mortal hatred? It must be, because he felt full of poison against those who had stolen his little girl's soul, had taken away her gaiety and her will to live, had ended the party that was saving her just by showing up, were so arrogant that they had returned to the place where they had murdered Vevé, because they knew nothing could happen to them, nothing happened to a white man who killed a black. And they were probably ready to do harm to other black girls, the ones who were not shameless or fearful enough to do all they wished.

Well, Leléu thought, they may be cattle, all that black bunch may be cattle, that can even be the way the world is disposed, but this time I'm doing the disposing.

It was almost dawn when they came out from behind some bushes in the company of a few young black girls, all four of the boys staggering and laughing loudly. Leléu stood ready, observing the direction they were going to take, because their boat might be moored either on Pig Island or in Puffer Fish. They took longer than anyone could bear in that situation, and bursting with impatience, he almost fell on them for better or worse, but finally they left the women, who had to stay to go to work the next morning, and walked away slowly, strolling down a trail that was sure to lead to Pig Island. Leléu went around the back of the palm patch and scurried into the dense woods to come out ahead of them, and when they arrived he was already hiding near the boat, waiting for something to happen so he would know how to act. A white man's boat for sure, all freshly painted, new rigging, burnished hull, smart design—was there a crew on it? Leléu felt uneasy, because if there was a crew, what would he be able to accomplish?

Almost forgetting to breathe, he stretched his neck over the little pinnace he was hiding behind, and saw with relief that no one was on the boat. Now all he had to do was wait until they settled the argument they had been having even before arriving, because two of them wanted to take advantage of the tide and sail out right away, and the two others thought it was better to wait and leave in the morning. He crossed his fingers, asking for luck for the first time in his life. It would be better if they slept right there, drunk as they were, because everything would be easier, there would be no problem in figuring out a way to dispatch them. But the bearded one, who appeared to be the oldest of them, imposed his will. They would go immediately; it was already Friday, they had promised to get back the same day, after some fishing, and whoever felt sleepy could sleep on the boat; he would hoist the sails and man the rudder.

Leléu spat to the side. Dammit! What now? Maybe he would never see them again, maybe it was the last chance to have his revenge; wouldn't it be better to pounce on them right now? He stroked his club, put his hand on the knife's handle, and stiffened his body. It's now or never! Careful not to make any noise as he walked on the water's edge, he started to go around the pinnace very slowly, still not knowing how he was going to do it. He did not care if he was wounded or killed too, but the idea that one of them might escape mortified him. Well, leave it to luck, leave it to fate.

But if one of them escaped, wouldn't people come to look for Dafé to hurt her or even kill her too? Sure they would. And could he leave the girl helpless? He could not. He stopped in the midst of a terrible anguish—what now, what now, what now? Was he going to have to give up, after having been so close? How come no idea popped up, how come he was going to be defeated this stupid way? He looked over the rail of the pinnace once more: They were climbing aboard. They were going to sail around the little bar, against the tide, which was still coming out, then coast the island close to the shore to get to the channel and probably catch a tail wind to Bahia. A curse on them! Leléu prepared himself once again to attack them blindly, took two steps and— No! No! But of course, it's clear, there can't be anything clearer! Aren't they going to pass near the beach and the sandbank? Leave it to me!

Making a great effort not to allow anxiety to rush him and cause him to make noise in a situation where even a loud sigh would be heard, he got down almost on all fours and, so slowly his leg and belly muscles hurt, managed to walk, with water up to his knees, to the bend in the beach that would keep him from being seen from the other side, and as soon as he got there he darted like a madman down the sandbank toward the Puffer Fish port, at the place they would have to pass.

A curse on them—may the liquor go to their heads more than it already has, may they take a long time, a very long time, to hoist the sails and maneuver around the little bar! Running with his lungs squeezing out of his throat and with only the thought of the need to work well fueling his will to run and giving strength to legs that wanted to crumple down and to a heart that could not beat faster, he described the Puffer Fish cove, the little fishing canoes, moored like a row of dark fishes, beginning to be floated up from the mud by the power of the rising tide. He passed by old Perelepe's vegetable garden, near the part that had been fenced to make a pigsty, leaned on some loose posts, and without really knowing why, with no time to think and feeling dizzy from breathlessness, pressed his shoulder to the fence, broke inside, jumped over a bunch of suckling pigs, stumbled on a sow, almost fell down as he pushed the shed's door open and picked up a rusty mattock that was always lying there. Finding it lighter than he had expected, he put it over his left shoulder, together with the club, and resumed his race to the canoes. He chose one of the smallest, dumped the mattock and the club aboard, and cut loose the ropes of more than ten neighboring canoes, imagining that many of them would be lost in the current. He got back on the one he had chosen, jumped aboard, and started rowing his way out.

He had been waiting for quite some time with his killick down just around the little bar, when the white men's mainsail came into view behind the tallest mangrove trees. He hid the black blanket in the hollow astern, picked up the mattock, and with two strong blows of its pointed arm made a hole in the bottom of the canoe, which started flooding slowly. He arranged his things near his feet, waited until he was within sight of the whites, and began to wave his arms and cry out like a desperate castaway, a tottering, feeble castaway, because he had decided to pretend to be very old.

The boat came near the canoe, two of the young men saw him, and one of them maneuvered close. They threw him a rope and lowered the jack ladder, and he climbed up it, taking even the mattock aboard, while the canoe heeled over.

"What does this old character want that pickax for?" one of them said, half amused, half annoyed.

"If I lose it I won't be able to afford a new one, Massa," Leléu answered in a quavering voice. "Now that I've lost my canoe, it's all I can count on to dig out a couple of clams."

He kissed their hands, bowed down elaborately, thanked heaven for answering the prayers of a poor old black and having him rescued by those four archangels, he didn't know what to do or say to show his gratitude. The man who had complained about the mattock told him to shut up and asked if he could steer a boat such as theirs, which was almost the same as the boats he was used to. Leléu said yes, of course, that was something he had been doing since his childhood, he had always been a seaman and a fisherman. They wanted to sleep, right? He could see—heh-heh-heh!—that the young masters had had more than a couple, and right they were, youth comes only once and all you get from life is the life you lead—ih-ih-ih! But there comes a time when all a man's body wants is rest, isn't that right? That's the way you get ready for another round, it's by resting and eating well. They could leave it to him—wasn't it to Bahia they were going? He would be their steersman, then, it was the least he could do as a token of gratitude; he'd find a way to get back after arriving in Bahia; these things could always be arranged.

The wind was blowing very gently, and Leléu maneuvered the boat toward the channel. The tide was still low, so they passed close to the shore on the starboard side and to the almost fully exposed sandbank portside, the markings left on the sand by the waves meandering as far as the eye could see under the moonlight. He looked at the four of them, and all of them were snoring, two on the bow, one midships, and the last one so near him that if he stretched his arm he could touch him. He knotted up the tiller, stood, saw that the boat was heading in the right direction, and drew out his fish knife. Much more easily than he had anticipated, for they were all sleeping with their faces up and their throats exposed, he went over to each one of them, and with a single stroke apiece sliced their necks noiselessly. He then went down to the bottom of the boat and dug a hole in the hull about five inches wide, through which the water started to gush. He dropped the mattock aside, picked up the club, rinsed the knife in the water, cut off the rope of the mainsail block to make it topple down, looked around, and dove in the sea at the very moment the boat was passing over the deepest spot in the channel. He swam the short distance to the beach and stood looking at the boat, now sinking faster and faster down to the bottom of the channel, where he was sure no one would ever find it, just as no one had ever found the others who had sunk in the thick mud of the bottom, forty fathoms below that surface slick as a blade. He inspected the sky, saw it was soon going to be dawn. It was time to rush back to Outeiro, before the old women found out he wasn't asleep there.

Whale Point, November 3, 1846

While washing himself with the help of a gourd at the jailhouse door leading to the backyard, the jailkeeper Manoel Joaquim, old and toothless, a mustache covering his mouth, was making a speech. One of his balls was swollen to the size of a squash by filariasis, and he would pat it to emphasize a point now and then. He was outraged by the lack of order that is the rule these days and against the low caliber of public men, who are a far cry from those of yore, those who made one proud to serve them, not these third-rate noblemen of today, these increasingly brash little merchants, and these new Negroes, who any day now will be demanding to be addressed as *senhor*.

With great difficulty because of the burden between his legs, and naked and wet as he was, he ambled over to the cell where Budião had been chained hand and foot to the wall, unable to sit down, since the day they put him

266

there. The old man looked at him contemptuously, cleared his throat, and spat to the side.

"A no-good Negro such as you, taking liberties, forging papers, abusing your master's confidence by running away—a no-good Negro such as you would not be here now, eating the very best food twice a day and enjoying the comfort of a warm, dry little cell, something many of the poor don't have in their houses. You would be in the stocks and under a whip to warm your back and make you learn!"

He returned to the backyard and started to wipe himself with a grimy piece of cloth. Still half wet, he put on the loose trousers he was forced to wear because of his disease, donned his shirt, and hung his coat on a wall hook.

"Very well," he said. "Your luck's run out. It's no longer Sunday or a holiday, and your rightful master, Captain Teófilo, is coming over to recognize you and decide about you. I don't think you're going to be spared a good thrashing or maybe something worse, something quite worse. Captain Teófilo is a very good man, too good, as a matter of fact, but he will not let what you did go unpunished; it's necessary to give an example."

He walked over to a water barrel, filled a bucket, and splashed the water on Budião.

"Only two or three days there and you already smell like a pack of mangy dogs. I believe Africa has to be the most smelly land on earth, with your race fouling it up." He doused Budião a couple of times more, complained that the church bells often did not ring at the right time, and griped about being given neither money nor assistants and having to watch over runaway blacks. "I'd sooner be minding pigs! Here we don't have even the most run-of-the-mill tools for a public jail; we don't have anything. This is the only exception—we've got this!"

He raised an enormous dark wood paddle, its five holes arranged in the shape of a cross as usual, one side smooth and the other dotted with small protuberances looking like blunt-tipped little nails.

"And we have this!" Showing a leather thong with braided strips at one end, he beamed. "But this you can get from any mule driver, such as myself. You see these dark spots here? They're blood, the blood of a no-good Negro like you. He left here to go straight to the cemetery; four men took turns punishing him. He was strong; he had a beefy body like you."

He seemed unable to stop speaking and moving about. Since there was nothing for him to do, he sat down but soon rose to adjust a birdcage, sat down again only to return to the cage, dusted off his coat with his fingertips, moved ceaselessly, while recalling in a very loud voice the better times he had known, times of respect and severity.

Dizzy and sometimes passing out, to wake with his arms and shoulders on fire, Budião had not felt his legs for a long time, no longer moved his eyes and head easily, no longer understood well what was spoken to him, no longer even experienced too much pain except in his head, which seemed to be pulled from all sides by sharp claws. He did not see Manoel Joaquim disappear down the corridor that the four cells faced, to open the front door and let in Captain Teófilo, the three watchmen who had made the arrest, and the garrison chief, Corporal Lourenço Frota.

"Is he dead?" Corporal Lourenço asked, after Manoel Joaquim opened Budião's cell.

"No way, Corporal. He's just pretending."

The corporal was not convinced. He pulled up one of Budião's closed eyelids, slapped his face twice, and kicked him lightly on his shin.

"He doesn't move. How long's he been here?"

"Ever since he was brought in. But he's being fed. I myself figured out the length of the arm chain for him to be able to hold his plate and eat. Yesterday he ate beans and pig hock, he ate everything. Today he hasn't eaten yet, but it's still early. Today I—"

"Set him free; unchain him."

"Hadn't you better call the militiamen? He's a strong Negro; he may try something."

"Unchain him, man; it's plain to see he's weak. You have coffee here, some strong drink?"

"Coffee? I wish I could afford coffee; I haven't seen coffee in a very, very long time! What does Your Excellency think I can do with the half a pataca a day they give me—do you expect me to live on cake and give the prisoners coffee, which costs such a fortune today?"

"Shut up, old man; unchain the black!"

They made Budião sit in a high-backed, upright chair. Because he would slide down the seat, they had to hold him up and hang him by his armpits on the back of the chair. The corporal ordered Manoel Joaquim to make a brine with water cooled by the night air and pour it on the black's head, dousing him all over. Then he had some firewater brought over to him, squeezed Budião's cheeks until he parted his lips, poured in half a glassful, and thwacked his mouth shut. Budião shook.

"He's alive," the corporal said. "Come on, Negro, what do you have to say?"

"*Pues entonces,*" Budião said. "*Nosotros* are goin' to keeck *todos* out."

"What did he say?"

"That's a kind of African talk. Doesn't he speak Portuguese?"

"*En marche-marche!*" Budião said, raising his neck, and the corporal slapped him.

"Listen here, you insolent Negro, I know you, you know how to talk like people, don't try to get fresh, don't try any tricks with me or I'll rip you apart!"

Budião opened his eyes, saw Captain Teófilo, and almost smiled.

"Captain Teófilo!" he said. "*Senhor Capitán* Teófilo, ees zat you? I hab come vack from the Farropilla War, *Capitán*! We took *el Comandante* Bento Gonçalbes, as *el Capitán* Teófilo *ordenó*! And the probince . . ."

Captain Teófilo turned pale.

"What war is that?" the corporal asked. "Didn't he say something about a war?"

"He must be delirious; I don't know about any war; I don't know who this commander is."

"I do. It's Commander Bento Gonçalves, who was once under arrest in Saint Marcellus Fort, a kind of Gallegan, a treacherous, seditious man. I was with the fort's garrison when he escaped, about eight years ago, maybe more."

"I don't know; I don't remember."

"This black knows a thing or two. Mané Joaquim, where are the papers he presented?"

"They're in the drawer, the drawer inside. I locked everything up because all those papers scare me. No one ever comes here, no scribes, no officials, and I'm supposed to keep those papers without knowing what to do with them. Wouldn't Your Excellency care to take them all with you once and for all?"

"No, Manoel Joaquim, I want the papers he was showing around. Go get the papers—stop all that talking!"

Captain Teófilo began pacing, his hands behind his back. Did the corporal believe that runaway black of his really knew about important things?

"You can bet on it. In my opinion, today we're going to find out how the Gallegan managed to escape."

"You think he'll talk?"

"That depends. But if I garrote him, either he speaks or he dies. That's up to Your Excellency, however; he's your black."

The captain did not answer right away; he needed to ponder carefully what he was going to say. If his slave had important information, he could not, without arousing suspicion or even ill will, deny permission for him to be interrogated by the usual means. On the other hand, if he spoke instead of dying, wouldn't the captain be irreparably incriminated? And he was still thinking about what he was going to do, when Manoel Joaquim returned with the papers.

"Let me see them," the captain hurried to say, to pick them up before the corporal. "Faustino, that's right. Faustino—"

But he did not finish, because a violent explosion, followed by two weaker ones, seemed to jolt the whole ground. A kitchen shelf tumbled down, Manoel Joaquim's water jug rolled along the table and shattered on the floor, the corridor door burst open with a bang, a gust of lukewarm air assaulted them. Outside, rolls of black smoke coming from the direction of Saint Lawrence Fortress started to envelop the trees and the housetops.

"Jesus and Our Lady! It's the fortress! They're having a mutiny!"

They forgot Manoel Joaquim and the prisoner as they dashed pell-mell out the door, and among all the turmoil and confusion already going on they saw that the fire indeed came from the fortress, not only from its walls but also from behind it, giving the impression the sea itself was aflame.

"The fortress is burning!"

"We're being attacked!"

"It's a mutiny—the soldiers are mutinying! They're going to put everyone to the sword! It's a mutiny!"

"Corporal Lourenço, you must hold back the mutineers!"

"Women to their houses, women to their houses, lock yourselves up in your houses and don't open the doors for anyone!"

"The garrison, where's the garrison? To arms! To arms!"

"Captain Teófilo! The national guard, the national guard!"

"In the name of His Imperial Majesty! Order, in the name of His Majesty!"

"They won't spare anyone who doesn't join their cause and doesn't pay tribute to them! It's the edge of the sword for everyone—oh my God!"

"The buckets! Everyone to the fort—everyone to the fort!"

Only many hours later, among recriminations, misunderstandings, insults, and a confusion that would last for months, it was learned that there had been no mutiny, no invasion, no fighting, and in fact nobody really knew what had happened. No one had been at the fortress except the cleaning man, Black Máximo, who was sweeping the leaves from the entrance. And Black Máximo did not have much to tell: he had become even deafer after those three thunderclaps that had burst over the north wall and that thick smoke that had almost killed him. It seemed to him that a powder keg had exploded, one keg, then two small kegs, then came that tar-and-dregs smoke. And all of a sudden the sea was burning, something that to his relief many others had seen, so people wouldn't think he was a liar, and indeed they found out later that someone had dumped a mixture of oil and tar over the water and set fire to it.

Some said, too, that behind the fire, standing out sharply against Friars Island, a little brig that had been holding fast in full sail put to sea quick as lightning, about three quarters of an hour after the explosions. And it is also known that when they returned to the jailhouse, the captain and the corporal no longer found Budião. They found abandoned the tools the raiders were going to use to free him from his chains but had not needed. And they also found Manoel Joaquim fettered where Budião had been, one of the ring bolts fastened around the base of his swollen scrotum. Blind with pain and in great lamentation, Manoel Joaquim, to the disbelief of some and the belief of

270

others, testified that at least five people had come to set the black free. Among them was a young, tall woman, very strong, whom the others called Maria da Fé.

City of Salvador, Bahia, April 5, 1863

What a shock! On the little balm-tea leaves gathered by the silver strainer was a tiny dark lump, identical to a dead fly. Amleto shivered. But before crying out in a rage, as he had intended, he decided to make a closer inspection of the object, in spite of the repugnance it caused him and the way it would make him retch if it was a fly. He raised the strainer in the direction of the window light, fastened his spectacles on his nose, and poked the leaf with the tip of a spoon handle. Confound it, even glasses didn't help his eyesight lately. But the texture was most certainly that of a fly; it was a fly, he was almost sure.

"Joviniana! Joviniana! Joviniana!"

Black Juvi, her head scarf sliding down, her eyes bulging, her apron askew, her stocky body making her look wider than she was tall, rushed nervously into the room. She knew the rule established by the commander, according to which one summons a black only once; one does not deign to do it a second time. Therefore something very serious must have happened, although after Missy Teolina's death Massa Amleto's nerves had been getting worse all the time; he almost wouldn't eat at all and had the oddest manias. She saw the strainer in the hand he was raising above his head, trembling with fury, and guessed it had something to do with the housefly mania, the most terrible of them all, agonizingly prolonging every meal, while he pored over each spoonful and made everyone jittery whenever he banged on the table, thinking he had discovered a fly. He had two blacks standing guard by the table to shoo away the flies with feather fans, he ordered them to burn camphor all over the house, he demanded a spray of spurge nettle and a nosegay of chrysanthemums in every vase, he made the rounds of the kitchen and the pantry to see if they hadn't left some food item uncovered, and even so, whether he was eating or drinking, he had to scrape his tongue in his teeth to prevent swallowing a fly by mistake. This made his meals arduous, not only because they were so protracted but also because they were full of anxiety and crises of postprandial melancholy, when in spite of his precautions he would be made miserable by the fear of digesting flies inadvertently swallowed. This was what caused the beaked appearance that more and more marked his features, because in order not to show his tongue while he rubbed it back and forth between his teeth, he had to hold back its advance by keeping his lips together, his tongue inflating his mouth as if there were a live animal imprisoned inside it.

"What happened, Massa?"

"This! It's this! This is a fly! A fly in my tea!"

Black Juvi bent down and stretched out her hand.

"Excuse me, Massa."

She took the strainer, squinted a little, poked the leaf with her finger, and smiled.

"No, it's not, Massa; it's a bundled-up leaf."

"Are you sure, Negress? Take a good look at it; it looks exactly like a fly to me! And if it's a fly, I know a lot of people who are going to live on fly tea, fly soup, and fly stew for the rest of their lives!"

"No, it's not a fly, Massa, it's a leaf. Look here."

She spread out the leaf and laid it down carefully in front of him. He pulled his spectacles closer to his eyes, took a long time staring at the leaf, and finally fell back relieved in his chair.

"It's not a fly," he said, smiling. "Indeed it's not, it's not. Well, take this tray away."

"But isn't Massa going to drink his tea?"

"No. No, I'm not."

"But the tea is just the way Massa likes it, Massa didn't eat anything in the morning, Massa's been on a empty stomach until now, the tea—"

"No, no. Take it away."

"Doesn't Massa want black tea instead of balm?"

"Take this tea away, Joviniana! If you say one more word I'll do to you what I did to the Negro Fidúcio: I'll have a hot egg stuffed in your mouth to cure your effrontery! Take it away!"

How could he drink tea, how could he drink anything, eat anything, with the thought of a fly making him gag? He actually had almost swallowed a fly once, a short time after Teolina's death. He became rigid with revulsion as he remembered what had happened, but he could not avoid recalling perversely every detail. He had been reading a newspaper absentmindedly, and had not even glanced at the goblet of port he had put to his mouth. As he took a sip, he felt a spongy little lump on his tongue, like a raisin or a piece of grapeskin. But the little lump fluttered on his tongue, and with an indescribable nausea he spat out the fly, still alive, and vomited on the carpet until he felt so weak that he fainted.

He pressed his stomach and shook his head energetically to get rid of unpleasant thoughts. He rubbed his tongue on his teeth and inspected it in the little mirror of the hatstand. Yes, ever since that day, the idea that there might be a fly in his food disquieted him so much that he practically did not eat anymore. He had grown much thinner, and now his hair, still submitted every night to the skullcap and the agave juice, dribbled down the sides of his fleshless head, accentuating his jutting cheekbones and his hollowed-out cheeks. In the beginning he had felt well, but little by little he was becoming weaker, his chest drooping, his thin legs losing all their stamina, his hands translucent and withered. But he did not find this asthenia entirely disagreeable, for sometimes it was very gentle and beguiling, as when a delightful drunkenness came over him, often accompanied by swift visions of colors, after his having for instance forced himself to drink some coffee with a lot of sugar in the early morning. And it was by all means preferable to the possibility of ingesting flies, a danger that not even the strictest vigilance could be sure of warding off completely.

But was it only because of the flies? He thought so, but after suggesting to people so often that his lack of appetite was due to his distress at Teolina's death, he could not entirely discard that conjecture. Poor Teolina! Always unassuming, always ready for work and cooperation, always conducting herself in an exemplary ladylike way. She had not died of the fever during the epidemic, although she did catch it, the terrifying yellow fever that had killed thousands on several occasions. Or maybe she had never caught the disease, because at the height of her fever she had not, like the other victims, expelled the roundworms that caused the illness. But her health had never been the same again; she always had a fever, an ache, a discomfort, all of it made more serious by Patrício Macário's absence, which hurt her much more deeply than he had expected. On her deathbed, she would pray through chaplet after chaplet, begging the saints to do as they did in the stories every family had to tell and grant her the grace of seeing her little boy before she expired. But that did not happen, because Patrício Macário did not manage to travel to Bahia in time, and his mother had already been buried when he arrived.

Yes, maybe it was also because of Teolina. He missed her, he missed her in a thousand ways that had not occurred to him before, so much so that the crying that for many months he had hidden in the corners of his study when he remembered her had been sincere. A widower, yes, a widower. He had never imagined the void a man falls into after becoming a widower, how life turns awkward, how habits are subverted, how people and things gain new appearances. But being a widower was mainly the void, the great void that made his afternoons endless and made him hole himself up in his business office until late in the evening.

A widower and a rich man. At first he had thought that with discretion and ingeniousness, it would not be difficult for him to have an amorous adventure or two, to arrange things so that he would finally be able to know women. And it had not been difficult, only he soon lost his taste for this activity, which for him was always costly rather than pleasurable. He saw a French actress a few times, but the woman he had seen shining onstage with such beauty and gracefulness was in actuality quite older than she had seemed, and her presence, so fraught with wiles, sulks, and pouts, unnerved him, so he sent her a billet-doux in which he professed eternal affection and gratitude but regretted that for reasons of conscience so private he would never reveal them, he could not go on seeing her.

Yes, maybe it was because of Teolina's death. For outside of that, after all, he was forced to admit he was a happy man. As he did very often, he leaned back, took off his spectacles, and prepared to give himself another mental lecture on how happy he was and therefore had to feel. His businesses now made him unquestionably one of the richest men in the province of Bahia, maybe in the whole country, particularly because he invested in diamond prospecting the public subsidies granted to his properties in drought-stricken areas. He made an effort to remember everything he owned, as he used to do, but could not manage to; it was too much for his tired memory. There was practically no one who did not owe him something or did not buy something from him, directly or indirectly. Even his Negroes, whom in order to show how consistent his positions were he had been freeing within the limits of possibility, were paying him for their emancipation titles in installments to which a small interest was added. And to be fair, it should be said that he almost did not touch that money, of which the larger portion was pledged to one of his many initiatives in the field of culture and social problems, the Fund for Abolitionist Studies.

Wasn't he happy, then? His eldest son had quickly gained the title of Monsignor, as everyone had foreseen, dedicating himself body and soul to the education of young men, both in the Charitable Works orphanage and in the private school he had managed, with great tenacity and persistence, to found, which now boasted over three hundred pupils, all full-time boarders. Bonifácio, approaching his thirtieth year, still worried him, but not as much as before, If it weren't for the expenses incurred by the publication of his books, each one flourishing on its cover the name of a different publishing house, as dictated by the poet's fancy, he wouldn't cause him the slightest dissatisfaction. Amleto had become used to his months spent without seeing the sun, as he himself put it; they did not have any more conflicts and even treated each other with some affection in their rare encounters. The poet had his circle of admirers, to judge from a few notices in newspapers and pamphlets, one of which pronounced the poem "Harold and Dandalay" a classic in the language, with characters worthy of resting in the universal bookstand alongside Dido and Aeneas, Helen and Paris, Ulysses and Penelope. He would never replace Amleto at the head of his firms, but Dr. Vasco Miguel, though pernickety and slow, like a scrupulous turtle, demonstrated, if not talent, at least a solid mediocrity, so precious in the world of business, so much more desirable in many cases than intelligence or originality. Come to think of it, he couldn't have hoped for a better son-in-law, and when he looked at Carlota Borroméia's pudgy, placid countenance, he knew the family would fare well under any circumstances.

And Patrício Macário, what a miracle! Military training, the stringent submission to Count de Lippe's twenty-nine extremely rigid articles of war, which Amleto had come to know and admire through his son, life in the barracks, and discipline—how good for the boy's character all that had been! He had no doubt found his calling. Though he was still quite young, his gallant conduct in the river Plate hostilities—where, he had said jokingly, every Brazilian considered it a question of honor to kill at least a Hispanic a day—had garnered him the respect of his commanding officers and a quick promotion to his present rank of lieutenant, serving in the military district of Bahia. The uniform fitted him well, it even disguised his mulatto looks, especially now that he had developed a taste for imposing accessories and dashing capes, to a point where, though he was just a lieutenant, he impressed the rank and file and the unmoneyed officers, who were in the majority, as a kind of marshal. His reputation as a valiant warrior and a soldier to the core had just earned him, by direct request of the captain in command, a commission to serve as second officer of the special company that would be assigned to eliminate the famous woman bandit Maria da Fé, who went on sowing terror and disorder in all the bay area and even in the backlands. Tomorrow, Monday, he would be off to lead his soldiers in this expedition, in which he would most likely cover himself with glory once again. Amleto even felt proud of him, although he had not freed himself entirely from the embarrassment of having a son in the military and felt compelled to give lengthy explanations every time he could not avoid the subject.

Therefore he was happy, wasn't he? He wondered if he had any worry, any real worry. No, he did not. Consequently he was very happy. He leaned back again to better assimilate this truth, and he even smiled contentedly, even laughed aloud, even thought about eating something before lunch, which would be late, well after eleven, because of the presence of the whole family. Yes, he was going to have something to eat, something light, maybe a rice pudding, maybe a few tea rolls. Very good, there was nothing he could not order, there was nothing beyond his reach, he was a happy man.

He did not know, of course, what was happening more or less at the same time, around nine, in his son-in-law Vasco Miguel's home. After returning from Mass, sending the children to their art and deportment lessons with Miss Clara, the English governess and tutor, Carlota Borroméia went up to the second-floor salon, opened the balcony doors, drew the curtains, put her hands on the rail, and seemed to be admiring the crystalline air that enfolded the house from all sides, the green fields stretching out to the horizon, the garden resplendent in every color. She went over to the writing desk, dipped a pen in the inkstand, bit the penholder for a long time, rolled her eyes, and very slowly, bending her neck sideways, like a sculptor who wants to contemplate his work from every angle, wrote a few lines, in an elaborate, round script:

> Well then, well then, well then!
> Well there!

Well then, well then? Well there?
Well, then may you forgive me, may you excuse me.
Well, then!
I discovered that seen from here the garden,
The garden and the madrigal, la-si-re-do!
Are not interested in existence!
Well, then! Wellthen, wellthen, wellthen,
To whom may read me. Signed, CBNFD.

She then sat down at the piano and played for more or less half an hour. She got up, opened one of the drawers of the big sideboard, and took out a solid-silver knife in a sheath also of silver, which according to Amleto had been inherited from an English great-grandfather. She went to all the many bisque figurines that populated the salon, and calmly picking them up one by one, she chopped off their heads, put the figurines back in their places, then threw all the heads out the window. When the house blacks noticed the rain of bisque heads falling on the garden, they gathered in front of the balcony not knowing what was going on, until Carlota Borroméia emerged up there, and at first smiling and then furiously, attacked herself with repeated stabs, tumbling down on the floor as she transfixed her neck. When they managed to bash the door in, they found her lifeless, grimacing enigmatically inside a sweet-smelling puddle of blood.

Amleto was informed just at the moment when he was going to dip his spoon in the rice pudding. He dropped the spoon, closed his mouth, and, without altering his voice, told Black Juvi to order the stable blacks to get his coach ready, because he was going to go see his dead daughter.

12

Puffer Fish Village, May 25, 1863

Only one question runs from mouth to mouth, only one speculation haunts eager hearts, only one doubt is whispered on the island, from Whale Point to Catu, from outer shore to inner shore, from boat to boat, from house to house, from apothecary to apothecary, from slave quarters to slave quarters, from plantation to plantation: Will she come? Will she once more prove her tremendous audacity, which the powerful consider insolent but the little people admire? Will she once more challenge, with the pride that never leaves her, the troops and arms of the authorities? Or, by not coming to pay homage to her grandfather, will she give the lie to the legends of her great feats told by all the people? Or could it be that she doesn't exist, in spite of the testimony of several people, who might nevertheless be simple rumor-mongers, of the many who abound among the rabble?

It is the dead of night on the island. Vast, leaden clouds, continuous as if dabbed on the sky with a brush, shroud a thick blackness, inside which nothing seems to move. At the foot of a hill, the windows of Black Leléu's house are open, little rectangular blades of light floating in the darkness and fluttered by the warm wind that blows now and then, oddly for this time of the year. And from those little windows, like waves flowing in a regular cadence, a whining, quavering wail wafts out, led by an old woman's nasal voice and echoed by other women. There is no mistake about what those songs are. They are dirges, threnodies for the dead, ululations that are always keened at funerals here, not so much for their words—for their meaning is no longer fully known—but for the melancholy in which they bathe all living beings and their surroundings, converting everything to the same tearful sadness.

Whose wake is that which yonder is seen, so sad, so sorrowful, so solemn? Why, if it isn't Black Leléu smiling in his coffin, more stately than a viscount, more dapper than a marquis, well-pressed black suit, boots sparklingly polished, an expertly shaven face, very-well-brushed kinky hair, very clean hands crossed over his chest, a very-nice-smelling starched shirt——nothing like death at all! Is Black Leléu dead? Of course he is, or they would not have washed him, dressed him, and left him lying there to be buried the next morning. He died halfway through his midday nap, and because he had more and more been turning into a boy, he thought he was dreaming. He was found by the other boys with whom he had been supposed to go play ball, fly kites, and spin tops. They saw he was dead at once, but none of them was scared, because his face looked amused, maybe even impish, and certainly happy.

For he used to be happy, no doubt, this Black Leléu, who had been so many things in life and ended up turning into a boy. It had not been too long ago, nor did it happen all of a sudden. It happened little by little, every day something new, and before they knew it he was jumping and running among the children and did not want to do anything but play. Come to think of it, he was already a bit like that even when his granddaughter used to live with him. But they did that to her mother, and her mind was affected, and after his having suffered a great deal for that, she decided, in a way no one remembers well, to disappear in the world, living in the wilds and making war for more than fifteen years now, condemned by all courts and all police.

What had come over such a well-raised, beautiful, and doted-on girl, who seemed almost white from so much care? No one knew, and there were even those who would cross themselves and mention the Devil, because only the Enemy would be able to drag a woman into a life so fraught with struggles and difficulties, too hard even for a man. Black Leléu, however, smiling over there in his coffin, knew all about it, and even as a child he never forgot he had his granddaughter and was always proud of her, only he couldn't go around saying that, for hadn't they threatened him because of her, and not just once or twice?

And poor girl, how she had suffered after her mother's death! The day he killed the four whites, she slept late, and so he was able to stay in his room, recouping his lost sleep. A little before eight o'clock he was ready to go out, he had put the fish knife, the club, and the spine back in their places and was thinking about how he would tell her what had happened, or even if he should tell her, when he heard her moaning. He hurried to her side to ask her what was wrong, and she complained of clicks, buzzes, and whistles inside her head again. But what do you mean, honey, what do you mean by whistles and buzzes? Oh, she didn't know; she only knew she had this crazy orchestra inside her head.

An orchestra that from then on could scarcely be contained. Sometimes it played softly or even stopped, though rarely, but at other times it knew no limits, making the girl run to the woods or the sandbank, where finally, after twisting her hands and moving as if trying to bury herself headfirst in the ground, she would get some relief. Not knowing what else to do, Leléu told her that the four men had died when their boat had sunk, and she listened to it unemotionally. He then narrated how he himself had been the author of those deaths, adorning his story and making very ugly grimaces to describe in fabricated details the execution of the four whites. He wheeled around and about, he swaggered in the manner of an ancient warrior, he showed with his club how he could wield a saber and a bayonet better than the best generals, he said he could defeat whole armies, become invisible, go through walls, and fly without wings, he put an arm around her to tell her, while punching and biting the air with ferocity, that nothing, nothing, nothing, nothing, nothing times nothing over nothing could happen to her, because Grandpa was as strong as 88 elephants, wild as 120 lions, and vicious like 360 regiments of hornets. So there, my purty-purty gurl, my coochie-coochie-coo of the emewald eyes, my pwecious gem, fuh-lower of my garden, dj-joy of my life, zolace of my zuffering, you cocky, brassy, lovely, no-good, sweet choo-choo-choo, coochie-coochie-coo, why dat weeping look on dat pretty-pretty face? Huh? Tah-tah-tah-tah-tah? Bah-bah-bah-bah-bah, boo-boo-boo-boo-boo? How 'bout it, how about a smile for the old man? Old man cwies, he cwies and cwies and cwies, you bad girl, old man cwies! You want old man to cwy? There he goes—ow-ahoom-ahoom-ahoom-ahoom, ow-oho-oho-oho-oho—old man cwies until he melts down, bad little girl not sowwy for old man cwying? Just a little shmile, little girl, a shmile, dat too difficult?

But she did not smile and commented earnestly that if the men had died not knowing why they had died, the revenge had been of little usefulness. It should have been an example, not only to them but to others. Leléu was startled, almost got mad at her, and asked her if she had lost her mind once and for all. That had been the only way, what did she think, did she think he could confront all of Bahia, all of Brazil, all by himself? She'd better shut her mouth and from now on think twice before saying stupid things.

She didn't seem to have heard him and, gazing at her hands crossed in her lap, said there should be justice, that if there was justice he wouldn't have needed to do that useless thing, running risks for nothing, for something that had neither brought her mother back nor erased her humiliation and terror, nor would it prevent the same sort of thing from happening again.

"Those four won't do it again!" Leléu shouted angrily. "What is this thing called justice? That's hogwash, that doesn't exist—it may exist in foreign lands, but it doesn't exist here!"

"But it will have to exist."

"But it will have to exist. . . . Who's talking, is it the empress? Is it the field marshal? Get some sense into your head, girl: You think heaven is near, but heaven is far! Maybe if you moved to one of those lands they say there are—but I don't believe even that, especially you being a mulatto, that is to say, black."

"No. It's going to have to be here: This is my land."

"This is my land. . . . What you talking about, girl? Your land are the little plots I have that you're going to inherit, and even so if you're not smart you'll end up with nothing, because there'll always be someone to try to take them from you."

"I don't mean land in that sense; I mean to say this is my country, we are the people of this country."

"You said it well, you said it very well. We are the people of this country, the little people. That's what we are: the little people. So remember that, get this into your head once and for all: we are the little people! And the little people are nothing, the people is nothing at all; who ever heard of the people having any importance? And black people, on top of that? Look at reality, see reality! This country belongs to the landowners, the masters, the rich, the powerful, and what we have to do is to try to get along with them as well as we can, it's to take advantage of what we can, it's to bend forward and back, it's to work and be smart—this is what the life of poor people is all about, my child, don't fool yourself. And with luck and plenty of work, a poor man rises in the world and improves his lot a bit, but the people are the people, and the masters are the masters! Are masters part of the people? Go ask one of them! If they were part of the people, they wouldn't be masters."

"And what about justice?"

"What justice? But, but really, what justice? Where did you hear about justice? Justice is a book word, that's what justice is! The only justice I get is from myself; you'd see what kind of justice I'd get if I hadn't worked like eight, like eight times eight people; if I hadn't made my moves and had sat there waiting for justice, we'd be eating grass today, if anything!"

"Yes, but there will be justice. Common people do all the work, don't they? Common people are the ones who produce, aren't they? So the people is going to rule."

Leléu couldn't stop gaping, his chin hanging loose as he thought he was hearing hallucinations. What were those ideas, what had come over the girl's mind?

"Don't you remember all those princes and kings and heroes in your books? And don't you remember that not even they could accomplish any of that, that nothing like that exists, that people must have their feet on the ground?"

"I don't know."

Yes, killing those men had been really useless, and not only because it had failed to bring back Vevé, as Dafé had commented. It also failed to bring back Dafé herself, who had not remained as despondent as before but was a different person now. She was still the same nice, loving girl, but she no longer played, she talked very little and went out to the woods a lot, spending hours lost there and walking back slowly, like someone burdened by heavy thoughts. When he had to travel—and sometimes he would just invent the need to travel—she always asked to join him, and he would take her along, but she never wanted to see what he suggested. She would remain still for hours on some street, sitting on a park bench or on a balustrade where blacks were allowed, looking at people passing by and seeming to be as far away as the moon and the stars. Later she asked her grandfather to take her to see people working. People working—what kind of a crazy idea is that? People working, people working, people working! Carpenters, cabinetmakers, ironsmiths, coopers, shoemakers, tailors, bricklayers, farmers, gardeners, alembic makers, bakers, barbers, painters, armorers, butchers, wagon drivers, cutlers, broom makers, grocers, cowherds, tripemongers, mule drivers, porters, salesclerks, bell ringers, goldsmiths, weavers, pan makers, miners, hunters, pharmacists, cooks, machinists, tooth pullers, witch doctors, coachmen, shellfish pickers, fishmongers, woodcutters, meatcutters, swineherds, vegetable peddlers, saddlers, saltwork hands, oil merchants, locksmiths, cleaning men, water bearers, taverners, scissors sharpeners, stokers, hawkers, used-book dealers, pottery workers, printers, scribes, streetlamp lighters, engravers, gravediggers, stableboys, houseworkers, harnessers, shearers, gelders, milkmen, innkeepers, millers—all those she went to meet and admired them in their work, convincing herself more and more that to make, to produce, and to serve are signs of the beauty of the world, and a man is only he who makes, produces, or serves. She also asked to see musicians, troupers, and clowns, market singers, guitar players, improvisers memorizing their improvisations, toymakers, town square performers, picture painters, music players, festival dancers, sculptors of clay bulls, dolls, and utensils, woodcarvers with their woods, gilders with their sheets of fine gold, magic makers, rocket makers with their perils, storytellers and yarn spinners, pretenders of Christmas plays, and birdmen. All that and many more things she went to study and admire in the company of her grandfather Leléu, who was also familiar with many of those arts and their good practitioners, often causing in her a wonderment similar to the one caused by Vevé, the day she saw her practicing her fishing profession.

But if the love and friendship between them spread out in many directions and created roots even deeper than before, that didn't stop her from keeping her strange, silent, elusive ways. There were even days when she seemed to have run away from home, making Leléu nervous and distraught until someone found her, sometimes in distant places where you could go only by boat. From that time on, he began to think she was going mad, mad enough to be in a madhouse, but since she wasn't a violent lunatic, and even if she were, he decided not to tell anyone about it and not to seek advice from anyone, so they wouldn't want to lock her up or think she was possessed by the Devil. Still, he didn't give up offering her advice. These thoughts are not appropriate either for a black or for a woman, he told her many times, they are thoughts of someone who doesn't know the world, doesn't know life. But though she usually listened to him without arguing, she would not change her behavior or give up explaining to him her strange ideas. In the beginning he wouldn't listen, but he ended up getting used to it. At least by talking only to him she didn't run the risk of needing to talk to someone else and being held as a seditious madwoman.

But didn't she talk to someone else? Why, for some time now, after she had met old Zé Pinto, an aged, half-retired cooper who showed her the practices of his profession, did she go on visiting him now and then, taking him food and spending hours in conversation? Why, after making this acquaintance, did she also start having talks with a black who formerly belonged to the baron of Pirapuama, lately digging up oyster shells for the commander's lime factory, a black who couldn't even speak properly because the baron had had his tongue chopped off? But she learned how to understand what he said, and would even catch a boat on Sundays to go listen to what he had to tell. She also became friends with a certain Merinha from Little Swamp, the house black of a rich family, whom she had never seen before, but now they seemed to be sisters.

Leléu went on worrying, got jealous, even staged a few bad fights. What the hell was that, what kind of life was that she was leading? If blacks were not supposed to have families, if black families were slave quarters and concubinage, how did she ever expect to be considered a family girl if she went on acting like that? Had she learned what a family girl was, studying with that old hag, or hadn't she? It sure seemed she hadn't, because he dared her to point out one single family girl who talked about those things, had those ideas and those attitudes, kept company with low-down Negroes, didn't use her chances to improve her race, and rather than leave blackness wanted to return to it! To be born black, all right, nothing you can do about it. But to want to be black? Is there anyone who wants to be black? Let her show him one that wouldn't become as white as a heron if he could! How can a person have the chance to try not to be a black anymore and let it go?

"I'm always going to be black, Grandpa."

"And are you black? You're not black but a mulatto, a green-eyed mulatto, and many, many others less good-looking than you, much, much less good-looking, are today nearly-nearly white, enjoy consideration, are well set up in life. I myself know about a lot of very mixed people, very, very mixed, that are now white, have important positions, are important persons. And you, what do you keep thinking about? You keep thinking about knowing who Dadinha was—why the hell should I know about Dadinha? You keep thinking about—"

"You know who Dadinha was, Grandfather."

"So I do! She was nothing, she wasn't anything, she was a fat, dumpy, lying, crooked old—"

"Wasn't she my great-grandmother? The mother of Turíbio Cafubá?"

"The mother of . . . Who's been telling you those things? It has to be Zé Pinto, that doting old fool—I'm going to get a club and wallop his head a bit, so he'll stop being nosy and meddlesome—who's been telling you those things."

"Why don't you tell me too? My mother's name, her real name—was it Naê?"

"I'm not telling you about any of those things! You fight and fight and fight, you fight so much that your body never stops aching even when you're resting, you fight and fight and fight to climb out of your condition, to improve, to rise, and then what comes up? Someone like you comes up, and I think I'm going to lock you up at home so you won't go around acting like a fool, trying to get back down, trying to know about those things, trying to get into trouble, to change what cannot be changed. . . . I know life, you understand? I know life!"

"Who was *caboco* Capiroba?"

"*Caboco* Capiroba? There never was any *caboco* Capiroba, there was never any such thing, it's all a legend! But can it be that I send you to a boarding school, I give you the best teacher, I buy you all the books you need to get knowledge, and now you decide to grow downward like a horse's tail, to unlearn, to prepare yourself to become an old black hag, instead of somebody? *Caroba* Capiboca, *caboco* Capiroba—there was never any such thing! Is that what you studied for? Is that it?"

"Wasn't there a daughter of the *caboco* called Vu? Did you ever meet a man called Júlio Dandão?

"Júlio Dandão? A bandit, a sorcerer, a warlock! He must have run away with more than forty thefts and more than twenty murders to his credit. Don't tell me you . . . No, not Júlio Dandão, you haven't seen this Júlio Dandão, have you seen him? That's no company for you, no company, you understand? He's no company for you!"

"But he's no longer around, he vanished; you said so yourself."

"So why do you want to know about him? He's not your relative, he's nothing to you—what do you want to know about him for?"

"I was just asking; it was just a question. And what about my father—did you know my father?"

Leléu rolled up his eyes. What else could he tell the girl, what else could he do? He became a little uncomfortable, got up to pretend he was going to see his plants, and ended up having his attention called by a boy who was trying to fly a kite and was about to run over the vegetable garden patches as he pulled the string. The boy thought Leléu was going to protest and run after him to give him a couple of raps on the head as he always threatened, but that did not happen. Very serious, Leléu picked up the kite, inspected it critically, and told the boy that with that tail it would never go up. In fact that was a disgrace of a kite, probably like the face of whoever had made it, so now he was going to show what a real kite was. He went to the room where he kept his things, picked up a heap of odds and ends, set out to make a new kite, and spent the afternoon flying it and giving lessons about winds to the boy and to the others who had gathered around.

It must have been then that he started turning into a child and little by little stopped reproaching his granddaughter. And he not only stopped reproaching her but one fine day called her for a conversation she could never have anticipated. He told her it might not look like it, but he had got to learn a great many things, among them that the wisdom of life has many sides, not just one side. Therefore it was quite possible that there were many wisdoms instead of just one, so he was no longer denying what his granddaughter thought. He found it wrong but did not deny it; that's how the world is, full of ways of seeing. So did she know what he was going to do? Well, he'd tell her. The money he had saved in a life of endless work was hers, it was buried in those places he had written down in the paper he was handing her. Everything was hers; he was now an old man, he just wanted to stay there with his little vegetable garden, his little orchard, his little house, his chickens, his pigs, his things, his toys, his children friends. He was an old man, really very, very old, he must be the oldest man she knew, so the best he could do was to stay there being a young boy, something he had never been and which now interested him very much, to make his life complete. As for her, she now had no excuse not to do what she thought she should do, and as a matter of fact she ought to go ahead and do precisely that: what she thought she should do. It was a gift he had thought about much before giving to her, and it was a gift of great love. Not the money, since he had no one in the world but her, and therefore it was his duty to take good care of her, for she didn't have anyone else in the world, either. The gift was her freedom, her freedom to be and to choose, something for which at least through him she would find help, though she would face difficulties on all sides, mortal difficulties really, tough, merciless difficulties. But he would give her this advice: Let her not be gullible, not trust, not confide, and not give up easily; let her not be a liar but not be foolhardy, either; let her not try to fight always the same way but see that for each fight there is a special way, depending always on circumstances; and let her love him, because he loved her so much that his heart ached, and if he hadn't been a better grandfather, it had been because he hadn't known how, but everything he knew and had tried to learn had been for her. Did she like him?

Dafé hugged her grandfather's head, pressed it against her bosom and cried noiselessly, so he would not raise his eyes and see her tears. She said there couldn't be anyone who loved anyone more than she did her grandfather, because for her he was not just a grandfather, he was a father, a teacher, a companion, a friend, everything in the world. A better grandfather than he, a better father, anyone better than he there could never be, and if she did go out in the world one day she would never forget him, nor cease to honor his name and memory and come to see him whenever she could, nor cease to love him so much that her heart ached also and her chin quivered with all the affection overflowing from inside her.

For a long time that day they just embraced without saying anything else, and in the early evening they dined together as though they were at a banquet, with Leléu drawing out of his chest a silver candleholder to decorate the table, she filling the vases in the room with gladioli, and the two of them laughing a lot because they decided to act like people of nobility, and there was never such a refined dinner party—isn't that right, Your Lordship the viscount? by all means, Your Ladyship the marquess!—in the whole history of Puffer Fish, the island, the bay lands, and the rest of Brazil. After dinner Leléu took a nap, to rest so that at night he could go on building the trap to catch nothing he had decided to make to show the other boys. And she, after laying a light blanket over him so he wouldn't catch cold and leaving a little cup of water by his side so he wouldn't have to get up if he woke thirsty, went inside for a few things, which she packed in a bundle. She then left, and no one knows precisely where she went, but it certainly was someplace where people from the conspirators of the flour house were gathering.

That was not the day she left for good, but it was the day she started leaving for good, and the boy Leléu already knew she would go away. When she did go, he neither spoke much nor made a scene, he behaved as he had promised, and dispirited out of loneliness and missing her so heavily he could not walk in his empty house and his garden, now deserted because of her absence, he refused to cry, although for that he had to swallow his sobs like someone who's fighting to keep a vile-tasting medicine in his stomach. He chose to feel pride, he didn't know too well in what, but pride anyway, a slow, full pride, which gave a flavor to the air he breathed while he remembered her.

And it was thus proud that he, according to some seeing his granddaughter once in a while and according to others getting only messages and notes, went on being a happy kid until he died many years later, very old, as old as can be, the oldest little boy anyone has ever seen or imagined. And in this tumescent night now smothering the island, where the news of his death has run around all the coast like a gunpowder circle, maybe he is still thinking he is dreaming, so nice-looking in his neat little coffin, so happy with his well-sung dirges. The night seeped into the woods, pressed its black velvet blanket over all beings, and became denser and stickier, as though it would not wish to go away when the morning came. And in the stretched-out notes that the old women of Puffer Fish moan through the air, the same question comes to everyone's thoughts, slipping through the grid of those pale labyrinths of funereal music, a question made by the aged ones repeating the sign of the Cross, and by the young ones anticipating feats of arms, the question about whether she will come, whether in an irresistible cavalcade tearing through the night, plowing the seas on an invincible fleet, Maria da Fé will be here to revere her grandfather's body, the great Black Leléu of irreprehensible memory. Night, waving her black gloves at her brother Dew, her sister Cold, her companion Unknown, her servant Mystery, her cousins Apprehensions, her friends Apparitions, her dinner guests Alarms, did not want and was not going to answer, thus decanting in the air of the island an insidious fear of everything, a fear of nothing, the feeling known to all, that something strong is about to happen.

Cemetery of the Blacks of the Settlement of the True Cross of Itaparica, May 26, 1863

Since early morning, under a fine drizzle that kept coming and going, Leléu's funeral procession had been slowly snaking its way up puddle-pocked trails covered by slippery clay. Almost at nine o'clock, with a feeble sun coming through here and there among the thinner clouds, they got to the foot of the hill where the little cemetery was placed. It was difficult to proceed over that mud, which covered the hill as with okra slime, but the soldiers decided to help. The tallest among them, most likely an officer, to judge from his engraved leather baldric, his golden garnitures, his many-tasseled sash, and his mother-of-pearl sword handle, summoned four strong black soldiers and ordered them to carry the coffin. He called two others and told them, in a hoarse, grating voice made almost unintelligible by the great mustache that covered his mouth and part of his chin, to go ahead of the procession with shovels to carve steps wherever possible, so that the hill could be negotiated with less difficulty.

The people in the procession balked at relinquishing the coffin to the soldiers. One of them tried to protest, but the officer pushed him and with a gesture of his baton ordered the soldier who had been restrained from the coffin to ignore the objections and take over his assignment. No one else complained, if for no other reason than because they had there a unit of about thirty men, all armed with two-barreled pistols and new carbines they had very seldom seen in the hands of soldiers. Besides, the truth was that many people had made a point of coming to the funeral precisely because of that unit. They wanted to see what would happen if Maria da Fé decided to show up, because this was the reason the soldiers were there. Since the day before, they had heard about the arrival of the troops, commanded by a dashing and very fierce captain, whose knowledge of military matters and of the arts of combat and battle was renowned all around those parts.

Could that stern officer of few words, a man one could see was not from here but from a part of Brazil where superior heroes were reared from birth, be the great captain? Maybe he was, he certainly was, because the boat that had brought the unit had suffered sudden damage upon its arrival at Whale Point, yet here was that detachment to show the power and the presence of the Empire. They must have treaded all the wilds and swamplands between Whale Point and Puffer Fish in forced march through the night, only to stop Maria da Fé from once again affronting one and all. Right now, unfailingly gallant, towering in his triple-soled, double-vamped boots, he was dividing himself like a she-jaguar minding simultaneously her young and her territory, pacing ceaselesly back and forth, instructing his men and sniffing around for the enemy, an enemy who, as could be easily surmised—for anyone recognizes professional competence when he sees it—could never surprise him. He had even stationed sentries at every spot from which people approaching could be seen at a distance, demonstrating how much military sagacity he had learned from his masters at war colleges. And also, ever since Leléu's coffin had left the house, he had been continually dispatching scouts ahead, stopping the procession whenever one of them took too long to return, so that those who hated men in uniform as functioning only to beat, trample, humiliate, coerce, plunder, kill, and intimidate them, started fearing for Maria da Fé's fate and praying for her foxlike cunning not to abandon her but to keep her away from such a fatal encounter.

What a captain, what curt manners, what perfect adherence to military mores! Invading the deathwatch, to the great fear of everyone present, he had not hesitated to defy the lamentation of the bereaved and had evacuated the house after ordering them to open the coffin, already shut for the procession. He doubtless wanted to find out if it was really Leléu in there, or if he had pretended to die in order to help his outlaw granddaughter in the setting of some trap. He spent a long time in the deceased's company, and a great nervousness was coming over those who had been expelled from the house, when finally he came out and by gestures only, as seemed to be his habit, ordered the coffin shut again and taken to the cemetery. Without doffing his wide-brimmed hat, himself almost a shadow under his cape, which was criss-crossed by coruscating braid loops, he clasped his hands behind his back to survey the procession on its way out; his smooth, swarthy face was impassive, his mustache tapering down like the horns of a mountain goat.

If by custom one does not speak at funerals, at this one the silence was almost visible, punctuated by the sloshing of feet on the soaked trail and broken now and then by the squeak of a heron as it hurled itself down from the hill, scraping the treetops, to hunt shellfish in the marshes. Finally the coffin reached the edge of the grave. The rain, which had stopped for some time now, started up again, brought by a gust of wind inching up the inner coast like a curtain being drawn with a slow, determined pull. The gravedigger Aristides looked up annoyed as the first drops began converting the puddles to rivulets on the clay, which would soon flood the rectangular hole he had dug so diligently at daybreak; jumping inside the grave, he stretched out his arms and waved his hands, asking them to hand over the coffin.

"Out!" the captain growled. "Get out! That's not the way!"

Aristides seemed not to understand, and he stopped with his arms outstretched, rainwater running down his face.

"Get out!" the captain said again, his voice strangely high-pitched for someone who a moment before had spoken as if he had sandpaper in his throat.

Aristides gripped the edges of the grave, pulled himself up, stood next to the captain and tried to say something, but gave up. The captain took a few steps toward the coffin, halted in front of it with his head down, and, so brusquely it alarmed those near him, took off his hat and threw it on the ground. And they had not even had time to think how odd it was for a captain to have his hair drawn into a bun on top of his head, when he closed his hand around his huge mustache, yanked it off, bringing a shiver of sympathetic pain to all, and flung it down near the hat, as if it were just a hairy spider.

"People of Puffer Fish Village and of all the land of True Cross!" the captain said, now in a clear, crystalline voice, a bellbird's peal above the fizzle of the rain and muffled cries of surprise. "We are here to pay the last homage to one who will always be an example to all who do not bow their heads to tyranny, all who dream of freedom, all who learn in their everyday struggle to have respect for their own worth, all who say: Down with the masters and long live the people! Long live the people and long live freedom!"

Lord in heaven, who was that statue of glory, beautiful in countenance and speech, if not the warrior Maria da Fé, bursting forth through incomprehensible arts, emerging from the clothes of a mean-looking captain like an obscure worm turning into a triumphant butterfly, shining like a sun amid all the rain, coming to unleash the pride that had been rotting away in their fearful hearts? Here she is in flesh and bone, not a legend but a truth you could touch, not distant but near, leading not soldiers but a squad of her militiamen—the Militia of the People, whom so many had heard of and so few had seen!

"People of Puffer Fish, people of True Cross, people of the island of Itaparica, people of my land, I want blown into your ears the revolt that saves!" she said, and there was no one on the slopes of that funereal hill who did not feel his hide twitch like a horse's and his head pulled forward by the vibrant voice that pierced the clouds.

Perched atop a purple-flowered tree, people's militiaman José da Rosa was absorbed in listening to Maria da Fé's speech, which came to him ricocheting off the rocks of the hillsides, and he almost forgot to keep an eye on the many trails to the cemetery, as he had been ordered. But he did not forget, and while the people down below were pressing closer and closer together to better see and hear Maria da Fé, he decided to draw aside the foliage covering him, and he saw a wide, squat sailboat coming around the bar. Squinting, he realized that the little dark spots dotting the boat's rail were heads, heads of people, many more people than was normal for a boat like that. Not a boat, a large lighter; not a lighter, a fat barge; not a fat barge, a really big barge; Aprígio Lopes's ferry! But what on earth was that old tub, with her scant canvas all up, doing right in the port of Puffer Fish, and with so many hands on board? They were surely not her hands, because four or five were more than enough to put an aged bathtub like that to sea, and besides, there would never be enough merchandise for her to ferry in these poor parts of the island, where nothing, or almost nothing, was merchandise. So those had to be the soldiers, getting ready to land on the beach—there they come! The bastards, they had given up too soon repairing the little corvette on which they had put into the port of Whale Point. Maybe the damage had been excessive, and they figured it would never be ready in time for them to be at the funeral. We did too good a job, José da Rosa thought, and without thinking any more, he burst down like a wind squall through the top of the tree to give the news to Maria da Fé.

On the barge, Patrício Macário cupped a hand over his brow to shade his eyes and inspect the almost deserted coast, just two or three women digging up mussels, two or three fishermen mending nets, empty canoes aground in the swamp. Would she be there, the so-called great bandit who was to be captured or killed by that expeditionary force? He looked around, disgusted at the ill-armed ragamuffins whose officer he was. He did not even know how many they were, but they were surely fewer than when they had finally left Bahia, after the captain, affecting generosity and understanding, assured them all that if they did not get their pay as soon as they returned, he would lend them the money from his own pocket, at no interest.

"This isn't an army," Patrício Macário said to himself, perhaps in too loud a voice for someone who did not want to be heard. "What the hell is it?"

"What?" asked the captain, who had come near him unnoticed. "What did you say, Lieutenant?"

"Oh, nothing, Captain. I was just thinking."

"You weren't just thinking, you were speaking."

"Yes, sir. I believe I was lost in thought and ended up speaking."

"I heard you. You were doubting we're really an army. That's not fitting for an officer, Lieutenant, not fitting at all."

"I'm sorry, Captain; I didn't realize I was speaking so loud. And I wasn't referring to the Brazilian Army, sir; I was just thinking about these men. I think the same way as a great part of our officers: I don't think we're being given even minimal conditions for doing our job."

"Yes, I know what you mean," the captain said, running his eyes over the men piled up all over the ferry. "But we'll not be the first to command a rabble and win."

"I'm sure of that, Captain. I know you're going to lead this expedition to success."

"I, too, know that. Are you familiar with the region?"

"No, I can't say I am. I have been here a couple of times; my father has a few properties on the island. But this was in my childhood, a long time ago. Anyway, we have with us a few men who come from here, so I don't think it will be too much of a problem to find our way around."

"We shouldn't be overconfident. I wish we had a few horses. I can't forget the splendid role played by our cavalry in Montecaseros."

"Yes, sir."

"Where was your baptism of fire, Lieutenant?"

"Against the Easterners, Captain. I served in the Seventeenth. I was—"

"Yes, yes. Just a moment."

The barge was starting to put about in the little cove, the coxswain maneuvering to bring her to rest. The captain went over to him.

"Do you think we'll have trouble landing?" he asked.

"Trouble? What do you mean by trouble, *Senhor* Captain?"

"I see the terrain is muddy; it's quicksand."

"Quicksand?"

"Yes, mud that yields too easily to a man's weight."

"Oh yes, that it does, it yields a lot. But it shouldn't go above the knee. The tide is pretty high, and we can cast anchor very near the beach; they won't have to walk too far."

"Isn't there a gig in this craft?"

"This is a ferry, *Senhor* Captain; there are no gigs on ferries. And even if we had them, we'd have had no time to haul them aboard, for you yourself threatened to have me shot if I didn't set sail immediately."

"You're doing service for His Imperial Majesty's Government. You should be proud of that, and besides, you're going to be reimbursed."

"Yes, *Senhor* Captain. I'm sure, *Senhor* Captain."

The captain walked over to the side of the barge and, his hands on the rail, inspected the beach. He spat in the water.

"Mud, mosquitoes, hunger," he grumbled. "It's the lot they reserve for the soldier."

He breathed deeply, banged on the wood, and filled himself with a sudden bravado.

"Lieutenant!" he shouted. "Take command of the landing; we have put into port! Let's crush that filthy rabble! The mud doesn't matter, obstacles don't matter, nothing matters—our duty will be carried out!"

"Yes, sir!"

"Men! The eyes of the Motherland are not upon us, for it is by obscure, forsaken combats such as the one awaiting us that the foundations of a nation are made. Rather than dishonorable, such a circumstance is ennobling, as it is not up to the soldier to ask questions, but to carry out orders! And it is not up to him to seek recognition beyond that of his conscience, which shall always display unconditional devotion to the Motherland! We are His Imperial Majesty's Army on a mission to police and pacify enemies of order and national unity, enemies of the Brazilian people! Lieutenant, take charge!"

"Company, attention! Bugler!"

Going up and down like a deranged bird, the company pennant oscillated among the other standards, whose bearers struggled to balance themselves in the mud. It tilted down, touching the water, but it unfurled again, kissed by the deserted beach's cold breeze. Patrício Macário, his sword in his hand, his neck veins bulging out, splotches of black, noisome mud covering his uniform, managed, in spite of getting mired at each step, to make the trip between the barge and the beach several times, directing the landing.

On land, while the men following orders to reconnoiter the surroundings picked fruits and chased chickens, whose necks they twisted as soon as they grabbed them, the captain had a few residents summoned to him for information. Did any of them know where that bandit could be found—had she really had the contumely to attend her grandfather's funeral? No one knew, even when the captain threatened to indict them all under the articles of war. And why were they so few; was the population really so sparse in a village with so many houses and a countryside with so many small farms? Yes, of course, everyone had gone to the funeral. Very well, where was the cemetery?

"With your permission, *Senhor* Captain," said one of the residents, an old man with a pimply nose and a straw hat with a frayed brim.

"All right, old fellow, but be quick about it; I've got no time to lose."

"It's the matter of who's going to pay for what Your Excellency's soldiery took from my farm, and though I haven't been able to add it all up yet, I know they bared all my trees of fruit, they didn't leave me a single chicken, and they took at least four suckling pigs and an old but still breeding sow."

"It's your fault for allowing them to enter your property. They couldn't go in without an authorization."

"That's what I told them, *Senhor* Captain, but they wouldn't listen to me, and they even gave my son a couple of whacks for trying to stop them."

"Your son probably behaved himself insolently. No one may offend the dignity of the armed forces, even in extreme situations."

"He just told them not to go in and that no one had invited them and that they couldn't destroy all our livestock and our fruits, for that was all we had."

"Enough of this! Don't be impertinent! You will be reimbursed, and that's sufficient, for you should be proud of assisting the army of your Motherland—not everyone is given such an honor! Poor illiterate lout, you have never heard of Napoleon, and therefore it means nothing to you that that great general of mankind said armies march on their stomachs. How did you expect us to proceed on such a perilous expedition, through unknown terrain and against a vicious, unscrupulous bandit, to protect people such as you from her violence, without feeding our men properly?"

"But, *Senhor* Captain, the truth is, this bandit never took anything from me, and without what your soldiers took from me and money to buy other things, my family is going to starve."

"Enough, I said! Do you want me to have you flogged for being insolent to an Imperial Army officer?"

"No sir."

"Then go explain yourself to the company quartermaster, make your complaints to him, present proof of ownership for the animals and the fruit, fill out the necessary requisitions and forms, pay for the seals, stamps, and emoluments required by law, and you will receive your miserable money in due time, at the paymaster's office of the military district. Don't make me regret my dedication to the people of which you are part and to which I shall always devote my life! Out with you!"

After the old man had left, Patrício Macário, who had been standing next to the captain all the while, asked him if he could not be allowed to pay for the expenses and damages out of his own pocket. After all, the soldiers' pay was eight months late, and everything led to the assumption that the poor old man's payment would take a year or two to be processed.

"Not at all. We can't give this riffraff bad habits. If we establish a precedent, they'll start considering it their right to be paid in cash whenever a war operation requires the commandeering of supplies. Besides, it's a legal procedure, and it's not up to a military man to question the law, but only to abide by it."

"Yes, sir."

Besides, the captain had other concerns. He ordered that two men be selected to act as scouts during the siege of the cemetery. The company was to march immediately, on the double; let them fall in at once. However, though the bugler played the assembly call almost frantically, a few soldiers tarried and others seemed to have disappeared in the woods. Purple with rage, the captain decided to pick out three of the latecomers to be punished with two hundred strokes of a sword side. He summoned two strong browns and called the medical officer, in fact a medical school senior, to observe the punishment. After the unit fell into formation in the village square, the three men were beaten, and when, after the prescribed number of blows, they were freed by the men who were holding them by their armpits and fell down, shapeless, bruised, and bloody, on the hard sand of the little square, the doctor pronounced all of them in critical condition. The captain shrugged, went near the crumpled men, examined them impassively, and gave orders for them to be kept in one of the nearby huts until they healed, if ever they did, and could be submitted to a court-martial.

Keeping the troops in readiness, he decided to have a tactical meeting with his two lieutenants and four warrant officers. He explained that there were two routes to the cemetery: the one recommended by a scout and the one he himself had chosen after some quick pondering. The scout had suggested they take the trail leading directly to the cemetery, but he thought they should go around it from the south, maybe by way of Thick Point, to prevent the enemy from using their time advantage to escape encirclement.

"Are we getting back on the barge?" Patrício Macário asked.

"Of course not. We're infantry, not sailors. We'll march. We'll ford the cove on the shallow part and from there we'll block the enemy's possible escape to the mainland by way of Funnel Channel."

"Sir, do you think we're prepared for this march? Most of the men are barefoot, and the terrain . . ."

"They're used to fighting barefoot or wearing sandals. Better that than the confounded regulation boots they supply them, which wreck their feet."

He closed the discussion about the march and explained further that from Thick Point they would carry out a rapid pincers movement around the enemy's probable position. It was von Blücher's lesson, Ney's lesson, Condé's lesson, it was the tactical pillar of the Auxonne School, it was the lesson of Valmy, the lesson of Jena, the lesson of Austerlitz. If they marched with the swiftness he was planning, he was sure he would pin down the enemy between two firing lines, and in a final bayonet charge he would liquidate them easily, for if nothing else, his men were far superior numerically, since the current information was that the bandit's practice was to make her excursions in the company of little more than twenty men. And he grinned triumphantly when it was reported to him that some people were already returning from the burial, and Maria da Fé had indeed been present with her men, dressed like soldiers, and by now should be on her way to Funnel Channel.

"Precisely as I told you, gentlemen," he said, opening his arms. "Lieutenant Patrício Macário, Lieutenant Alvim, we'll march immediately!"

The march, however, did not take place as foreseen. The tide had not yet begun to ebb when they arrived in Thick Point sometime past noon, and the troop had to make a stop, using the opportunity to barbecue the chickens, pigs, and goats they had taken from the farms of the village. Some of the men had also brought along bottles of firewater, and when the tide was sufficiently low for them to ford the wide cove, many had trouble walking. Instead of rain, there was now a suffocating mugginess, made unbearable by motuca flies and other blood-sucking bugs of all sizes. And the mud, covered by a shallow lamina of dark water, turned out to be much more treacherous and voracious than they had imagined, swallowing the men up to their waists and refusing to free them, which made the crossing several hours long. Besides that, black mussel shells hidden in underground clusters near the roots of the mangroves lacerated almost everyone's feet, dyeing the black mire scarlet and necessitating a long halt after they reached the other side of the cove, so that their blood could be stanched and their feet patched up.

The still-clouded sky brought darkness down sooner, and the captain very nervously rushed his officers into organizing the pincers movement. He himself would be in command of the west column, which would proceed along the inner coast. Lieutenant Macário, whose combat experience recommended him over Lieutenant Alvim's virgin sword, would command the east column, which would follow a curvilinear route, bordering the outer coast obliquely. That way there would be no chance for the enemy to escape, unless they retreated north, in which case they would fall into the hands of the garrisons of Big Sea Settlement or Whale Point.

Night came, and Patrício Macário, at the head of his column, considered whether it would not be wiser to halt the march. After all, nothing could be seen in those tenebrous wilds, his men were exhausted and fearful, and if both columns were correctly oriented, the enemy was bound to find itself surrounded as it headed south. He made up his mind; they would camp right there. Though there were few field lanterns and most of them did not work well, the column was close to a springhead and on a relatively dry grass patch; they would make a couple of bonfires, weave torches, and make do.

But more than the voices of crickets and owls punctuated the silence. There was something else, no one could say what, a kind of oppressive, invisible presence, signs of unknown living beings in trees and bushes, suggestions of terrifying visions, phantoms and demons. Patrício Macário, sleepless, his head resting on his haversack, lit up a cigarillo and offered one to Private Jonas, who, with very wide open eyes, was putting more wood on the fire and crossing himself again and again. He accepted the cigarillo avidly, excused himself, and lit it with a firebrand. Patrício Macário asked him if he was afraid of damned souls, and he said no, snakes were what he was afraid of; he would never fall asleep in the grass because he was sure a poisonous snake would come and bite him or eat his eyes. With due respect, he advised the *Senhor* Lieutenant to be cautious, for snakes were not picky about their prey, and as everybody knew, little children were the only ones they would not attack. Patrício Macário laughed and was going to say something, when a loud rustling caused all of them to raise their heads. And they still had had no time to wonder what had happened, when leaves rustled once again and a cavernous laugh seemed to run from one side of the bushes to the other. And soon came giggles, a taunting, almost indecent titter breaking out from several points in the darkness. But like the flame of a candle extinguished by a strong puff, all the noises came to a sudden halt and a stony quietness returned.

"What was that?"

"It's the Devil! Vadirretra! Satan!"

"What happened, what happened?"

"There's nothing there; I don't hear anything!"

"It's the *cabocos* of the woods who accompany her!"

"To arms, to arms!"

"Bugler!"

In spite of panic and general confusion, Patrício Macário managed to gather together most of the men, though some of them fled in terror or took the opportunity to desert. But there was no time to investigate that; it was necessary to form pickets and patrols, to light up torches, and to search the area in small groups, which would cover a circle with a radius of about three hundred yards from where they stood. Then they would meet there once again, in case they did not encounter the enemy. If they did, they were to open fire at once, and their companions would come to reinforce them.

Crossing over a small ravine, covered with razor sedge, the patrol led by Warrant Officer Azevedo sighted a few silhouettes formed by the light of torches or lanterns on top of a high incline, almost a cliff.

"Halt! Who's there?"

"Captain Vieira's men on patrol!"

The warrant officer smiled. They were comrades, all right; he could see even in that dim light that they were wearing uniforms.

"Warrant Officer Sacramento?" he asked the man who had spoken to him. "Sacramento?"

"Sacramento, yes," the man said, and it was the last thing Warrant Officer Azevedo heard in his life, because a furious firing commenced up there, and he fell with the first volley.

"It's them! They're Maria da Fé's men disguised as soldiers!"

"A curse on them—they fooled us!"

"Get back, get back! The warrant officer fell!"

"Fire! Fire at them!"

"Pull back! We have to report to the lieutenant! Pull back!"

Soon everyone knew, each one in his own way and all in conflicting versions, about the presence of an enemy with the appearance of the army, and the result was that despite the desperate efforts of the officers, there were many unfortunate encounters among the patrols. They killed each other in great numbers, and almost every one of them was wounded endeavoring to decimate the enemy or to escape to a safe place. For a long time afterward, people would remember this disaster known to history as the "Puffer Fish Debacle," a military catastrophe attributed to a blatant nonobservance of war ethics on the part of the outlaws, as well as their resort to tactics that would never occur to a decently trained officer. Not to mention the vast contingents mobilized by them, described by eyewitnesses as a frenzied horde of hundreds and hundreds of fanatical cutthroats, armed with colossal sickles and insensitive to pain.

That horde, however, must have beaten quite a hasty retreat after the fateful confrontation, because the only ones around were a small rear guard of twenty to thirty men. The very same men who after the routing of their troop lassoed Patrício Macário—who was lost in the forest and dizzy from a wound on his head—roped his arms tight to his body, and led him away with a few kicks on his behind.

Camp of Matange, May 28, 1863

No one is quite sure, but there are those who assert that Maria da Fé converses with birds and they understand each other perfectly. This goes for sea birds, for she has often been seen chatting with sea gulls or laughing with herons and kingfishers, and for land birds—tanagers, thrushes, cardinals, red crests, tyrant birds, seed eaters, fly eaters, canaries, parakeets, and many others that are found everywhere here. And to be sure, there she is now, sitting like a young girl on the fork of a mango tree, looking up and no doubt questioning a little black hummingbird that is working back and forth among the trees, doing those hummingbird stops in the air and flights backward. The hummingbird is voiceless, but that does not stop him from using other means to talk, and no one knows if all that dance is not an alphabet.

She, however, cannot stay too long, even if she is being informed of news by the hummingbird, because she has things to do. She must decide about the two officers captured Tuesday night, who are locked in two little rooms of the abandoned slave quarters of Matange that she and her men use for a camp whenever they are in the area. The ranking officer, the one called Vieira, had been very arrogant upon his arrival, threatening them with terrible punishments for the outrage to which he was being submitted, but he was now much calmer and even quite amenable, anxiously trying to find

296

out what they intended to do with him and even professing a certain sympathy for his captors. Pretty soon, she was sure, he would be holding out generous promises if they set him free, but it was obvious he could not be trusted. She had seen him only once and at a distance, but his scoundrelly face was the only thing in him that did not lie, an opinion shared by Budião, who had met with him a couple of times.

As for the other one, he seemed to be pride incarnate; he would not answer what was asked him and confronted them with a cocksure hatred that would be funny if it were not for the seriousness he displayed in his gaze and posture. On two occasions she had peeked at him through a crack in the wall while he talked to Budião. The first day he limited himself to demanding treatment compatible with the dignity of a military officer, to declaring that he did not acknowledge the legitimacy of his imprisonment, and to emphasizing he would be out of there and would come back to crush them as they deserved. Though all that sounded a little silly under the circumstances, it did contain a certain beauty, and he himself did not seem entirely ugly to her, with his tanned, ruddy skin, his tall, broad-shouldered countenance, his beautiful head topped by curly hair, his strong chin, his full lips, his appealing mustache. If his nose were not a little stumpy, he would indeed be a very beautiful man. No, no, even with that nose he was good-looking; maybe with another and better-proportioned one, he would become too good-looking. Yes, he was good-looking, a beautiful man—and Maria da Fé felt goose pimples and the wish to see him again.

But she was soon annoyed by that feeling. How could she allow that to happen, even if only in thought? No, it couldn't happen. Since the beginning she had learned that to be considered of equal value by men she had to be better, all the more so because she had to lead them. No, no weaknesses, no disturbing thoughts that might make her daydream or even slip, nothing of the kind. If she were a man she could even have several women, but being a woman she couldn't have any man, except one who wouldn't try to boss her or think he had subjugated her just because he had taken her to bed. But that didn't exist; it was useless to go on thinking nonsense.

She tossed away the twig she had had in her hand while sitting on the mango tree, ran her eyes around, saw the men busying themselves with one thing or another in the compound, waved at José da Rosa, who as usual had climbed on a tree to keep watch, and went into the shed, where Budião was probably already waiting for her. She found him dozing and joked with him, saying he was getting old.

"It's true," he said. "You are the only one that doesn't get old. You still have the same face; no one would say your more than thirty years are not just twenty."

"That's because my birthday is only every four years." She laughed. "You should have picked your birthday better."

"I don't even know when the hell it is; I think in my time they didn't have calendars. In my land in Africa, no one knows about dates."

"You're old as the devil, here or in Africa. And how about Merinha, is she any better?"

"Yes, there's nothing wrong with her. Serves her right, for being so stubborn about coming along with us no matter what. She can't take this kind of effort anymore."

"But you think you can take it, and you're older."

"Yes, but I don't have to drag along those fat legs and that big ass."

"That's no way to talk about your woman."

"But I like it! I like a big, fat black wench! I wouldn't be caught dead with a skinny one of your type; I think a man needs flesh in a woman. No, if she lost her big ass, she would lose Budião too, because I can still be of service and I have admirers."

"How shameless can you get, man; stop thinking foolish things. Follow my example—I never think foolish things."

"But you're different: you're Dona Maria da Fé."

"Yes, that may be so. And so?"

"And so what?"

"So let's decide once and for all what we're going to do with those two," she said, feeling suddenly a little tired of life and a little scared, because when she spoke of the officers she remembered the younger one again, and again she had a shiver, not from cold or fever but from something at the same time more tender and more overpowering, something that came up her legs, not on her skin, not in her flesh, not in her bones, not anywhere in her legs, but up her legs. "So?" she asked, more loudly than she had intended, rising to pace about the shed.

Budião remarked that those officers were of little or no usefulness. At first sight it looked like a good idea to ask a ransom for them, some money to help with expenses, since as she knew they were always or nearly always short, depending more and more on the help of friendly farmers and, increasingly, some looting here and there. But what ransom? The army didn't even pay its soldiers, who lived in rags, doing odd jobs, robbing blacks, and mutinying. Word was all over about commanding officers who had become rich advancing their subordinates back pay and charging interest three times higher than in any commercial transaction. And about others who stuffed their coffers with money just as much, by keeping for themselves the rare disbursements that were made, demanding commission for the purchase of arms and supplies, and so forth. Therefore nothing in the way of a ransom could be expected for those two, particularly because if they were in uniform it was because they used to be down and out and couldn't get a decent occupation, so it was unthinkable to demand a ransom from their families, if they had families.

298

"In my opinion," Budião said, "we club their backs a little and . . . They like this clubbing thing. In Puffer Fish they killed two of their own and crippled another with I don't know how many whacks with the side of a sword. So we give them a few good whacks, and after that we kill them. And the sooner the better, because we ought to get out of here fast; it won't be long before they send more troops after us, and not all of them will be like these. That's my opinion,"

Maria da Fé disagreed. What good would come to them from such silly vengeance, which had no other purpose than to nourish the low passions everyone carries but should not let thrive? She was surprised at Budião. It was true that violence and death were at times unavoidable. She herself had agreed that his vengeance against Almério had been more than fair, particularly because of the example it gave to all those who had witnessed the foreman's life of wickedness and treachery. And she also had not been against many other things they had done and were still doing. But to kill just for killing, for a vengeance that yields bad fruit? Those were not the terms of the conversations they and others had had so many times. It wasn't in those terms that they thought about the always uncertain but unforgettable existence of the Brotherhood. That was not what they were doing, that was not what they were fighting for.

Budião lowered his head for a moment, then raised it very high. He said he agreed there should not be violence, but there was, whether he agreed or not. There was so much of it that all through his life he had never ceased to have it as his companion, either inside himself or in brothers of his race or among the whites or anywhere else. So violence is part of existence, and it's better for it to be in our favor than against us. Indeed, violence ended up not solving things, but did anything else? If the two officers were set free and ran across them, wouldn't they beat them and kill them? So it was a matter of opportunity, of the law of life itself: Each side tries to beat and kill the other, and when one can kill one does, and when the other can kill the other does.

She had spoken about the Brotherhood, knowing she would find an echo in his heart. The Brotherhood was part of their lives, had always given them solace, cheer, and hope, had even seemed to confirm itself several times, but she had said herself that its existence was uncertain, and she was right. Then what were they doing, what were they really fighting for? Why had he fought in the province, obtaining an emancipation that did him no good? Why had they involved themselves in so many ventures, so many combats? Because it had to be; he accepted that. But what else, wasn't there anything besides that? Why hadn't they learned more from the secrets of Júlio Dandão's chest, what was everything's reason to be, what was all that, where would they get? Maybe he was getting even older than he thought, because lately he had felt more and more like that, doubting anything that wasn't very plain to see and not believing in too many things.

Maria da Fé said she didn't agree. He himself believed in freedom, so much so that he would rather die than live without it. And didn't he believe in justice too? She believed in justice, she believed justice would be achieved someday, that there was a people, not a soulless, worthless mass, she believed the people should believe in that too, and that both of them should do something for that to happen. But that didn't mean she knew the meaning of each action, because she didn't. She didn't know much more than what she had said. And he should remember that the chest's secrets were more secrets of the how than secrets of the why. In fact they were about how you can find out the why, since the why—and that was in the secrets—is discovered with practice, and they were practicing. If Júlio Dandão had said they should kill the rich, she replied that there are many ways to kill, and the least effective is the way that will kill one, for another one to rise in his place. That was probably because Júlio Dandão was still at the beginning of the discovery of the knowledge the doors to which the secrets only opened, and this knowledge was being completed by them, the way Júlio Dandão himself had said it should be completed. Not really completed, but continued by them, because as Dandão had also said while looking at the chest, knowledge could never be completed but should always be in the process of being completed, so that after them others would come to go on with this task—could it be the Brotherhood?

What did he think she had done the day she had been to the late Zé Pinto's place in Little Swamp, disguised with the help of Merinha and Martina, to get the chest that was hidden in a place only she knew? All those who could be trusted, even some who had later joined them, were there, because it was like a ceremony, and Maria da Fé had said yes, she was going to open the chest for a moment. Well, did he know what she had done? To everyone's amazement and even fear, she had left the group with the chest in her hands, opened it, looked inside it a moment, and instead of taking something out had slipped something in.

"I put something inside it," she said. "A paper with some more steps to the knowledge and the secrets I think I've found out."

"What steps?"

"I don't really know, I'm not sure. That's why I've kept them in the chest."

"All right, then do whatever you like with the men."

"Not what I like, but what should be done. Those men don't know it, but they ought to be on our side, because they belong to our side. If they thought a little, they would see they don't belong to the side of those who exploit them and send them out to be killed like sheep so that the masters have their good life guaranteed. They're dangerous because they believe the lies they tell each other, lies they have always imposed on the soldiers and in which they get to have more faith than in themselves. There's nothing we can do about their heads, but if we cut them off we could do harm to other heads. Of course we'll cut off the heads of all those who are about to cut ours off, but I think the way I said before: I don't want to cut one off so that another one will sprout in its place."

"Yes, all right. So what are we going to do?"

"I think I know. Tell the men we're raising camp tomorrow by sunup. And tonight I'm going to need a boat for a job. And ask Merinha to come see me too."

"What are you going to do?"

"Nothing; I'm not going to do anything. I'm going to make sure they have a strong sleeping herb mixed in their food, I'm going to wait for them to fall asleep and set them free at night in Whale Point."

"Whale Point? Why so far?"

"For two reasons. They don't know where they are and won't know how much time they traveled to get to Whale Point. And also because there are people there, and I need people for what I want to do with them."

"What do you want to do with them? I don't understand; it's too complicated."

"There's nothing complicated about it. It's just a joke I want to play."

She left the shed smiling, as if she remembered something amusing. She walked slowly, looking at the landscape, and without thinking stopped by the door of the room where the younger officer was locked.

"Open this door, Zé Popó. I'm going in," she said to one of the two men who were standing guard, herself surprised at what she was doing.

"You're going in, Dona Maria da Fé?" Zé Popó asked, startled. "You're going to let this man see your face?"

"Many people have seen my face. And now and then I like to show it. Come on, open up. Wait outside, I'll call you if I need you."

Patrício Macário was dazed by the light that poured in suddenly through the open door and thought he was having a vision when he became aware of the presence of that very tall, very handsome woman, dressed in clothes such as he had never seen in the women he was used to, with a proud demeanor they never displayed, either, but it was especially her luminous, warm, and calm beauty that made him rub his eyes involuntarily. She stopped, gazed at him for a long time; he tried to speak but did not find anything to say.

"So," she said finally, running her eyes over the room. "Are you being treated in accordance with the dignity of an officer?"

"Can you tell me who you are?"

"My name," she said, "is Maria da Fé."

He took a step backward, moving his head like someone who wants to shake something out of his ears.

"What?"

"Maria da Fé. I think you've heard of me. As far as I know, you've come here to see me. No, not to see me but to kill me, am I right?"

Patrício Macário stood at attention. "You're right, you're quite right. To make you a prisoner and maybe kill you, if you resisted."

"No. You came to kill me. You came to kill us all. That's what the army always does."

"This is not true. The Brazilian Army—"

". . . is nothing but a band of unloved ruffians whose main mission is to fight their own people."

"I protest! You cannot speak like that! This is a serious offense I cannot accept, and—"

"Of course it's a serious offense. Truth frequently offends. And please try not to shout; you're not in the barracks where you live with the other great heroes who compose the military. I didn't come here to argue, I came here to see the prisoner for the first and last time. I've always been curious about the type of man who makes it his ideal to kill or die and forever stand at attention. You may be at ease; I'm not a general."

"This is absolutely inadmissible! The arrogance with which you speak to me will not make me bow my head! I am an officer of the Imperial Army, I represent the highest power in the nation, and the fact that I'm being submitted to coercion here does not intimidate me. If you are here to try to frighten me with threats or announcements of execution, you are wasting your time. I will have you know I could not care less for what you have decided to do with me, and it does not make me budge an inch from my firm purpose, in case I manage to escape, to bring to justice and punishment those low-class rebels you represent and lead, in an activity inimical to the Motherland!"

"What is the Motherland?"

"I will not explain a sublime concept to a woman of the people, a well of arrogant ignorance, a vulgar bandit. I am the Motherland!"

"The Motherland is you," she said, laughing. "And the people is you."

"I was not talking about the people, I was talking about the Motherland!"

Maria da Fé changed her laugh into a smile and looked at him almost tenderly. She like his childishly defiant ways; what did she see in this man? But she soon changed her expression.

"Stop shouting, officer."

"Stop insulting!"

"Goodbye, officer. What is the officer's name?"

"Patrício Macário Nobre dos Reis Ferreira-Dutton. Lieutenant!"

"A horrible name. Goodbye, officer."

"Just a moment! I demand explanations! I demand—"

The door closed behind her, and Maria da Fé stood next to it for some time before she started to walk away. She ran across Merinha, who was looking for her and told her that if she mixed two plants that grew wild all over Matange, one part of the first for four parts of the second, and made an extract of them, two drops would be enough to make a big man sleep, two drops that had no taste and did not alter any food or drink. And they didn't make you numb, or sick, or incapacitated, they didn't actually make you sleep, but they blurred the consciousness of those who took them, perfectly for the case in question. Very well, Maria da Fé said, take care of it.

At night, when it was still early but very dark, Maria da Fé went out to see the boat and then got back to the camp to ask if the officers had eaten well. Yes, they had eaten very well, Merinha answered, and if those tricky tufted leaves had not failed her, they ought to be pretty groggy by now. Maria da Fé then ordered them to leave the two men naked in their rooms, saving their uniforms in case they might be needed later. But shouldn't they put other clothes on them? No, she said, naked. So it was done, and almost at sailing time, she came to see how everything was. Everything was fine, just as expected; they were waiting for the order to carry the men to the boat. She stopped once more in front of Patrício Macário's room and once more she ordered the door opened.

"There's still something I have to do."

"But he's sleeping naked in there!"

"Then cover him with a bedsheet."

She went in soon afterward and closed the door. There he was, only his head showing above the folds of the sheet, by the feeble light of a tin lamp. She stopped next to his cot, felt herself burn again, closed her eyes for a moment, her hands so tightly clenched her fingernails almost cut into the palms of her hands. Her heart running fast, her breath short, but feeling a great well-being in all her body, she bent down toward him, so beautiful and strong and sleeping like an innocent, and lifted the sheet, unveiling him as if afraid to wake him.

What did she do afterward? No one knows. What is known is that she came out some time later with an almost naughty look, which could have been on account of the prank she anticipated. She took both of the officers on a boat to Whale Point and left them silently in Glory Square, stark naked under the trees.

They were found the next day and caused great hilarity and agitation among the villagers, who gave them clothes and listened to the wondrous narration of their misfortune at the hands of the great bandit Maria da Fé. A misfortune, by the way, made still more vivid by the testimony of her friends, because all those who know about this episode attest that the tyrant birds woke up the people of the village to see the naked men, the tanagers with their innocent-sounding songs poesied the event, and the little black hummingbird went back to her to tell her how everything had happened.

13

Whale Point, January 7, 1865

Among the hundreds, maybe thousands, of exceedingly great heroes and patriots who populate the lands and the history of the island and the bay area, there looms no figure so formidable as to cast a shadow over João Popó. There may be some who are more famous, who have greater intellectual or martial merits, or who are more distinguished orators. But there is none among them whose heart shelters or has ever sheltered more love for the Motherland, more civic fervor, more inflamed passion for his country, than old João Popó. And on all the island there is no one who rejoices like him—his eyes submerging every moment under cascading tears, his heart almost bouncing out of his chest, his throat so narrowed that it hinders his speech—at the celebrations of the Seventh of January. That, as all true Brazilians know, is the date of the Itaparicans' final victory over the oppressor's hosts. They tried to take the island, the parasites, but as their men-of-war came into view by the lovely shore that faces Bahia, all the beaches turned into thundering gullies, such was the intensity of the Itaparican fire. They tried Amoreiras and were driven back, even with knives and stones; they tried Sand Point and were repulsed, even with punches and kicks; they tried Whale Point and were massacred by the island's sailors; they tried Mocambo and were decimated by an army of embattled women and children.

That is what old João Popó is thinking as he walks down Channel Street, in a big hurry because it is almost time for the civic parade. Folded inside his chest pocket, the notes for the ad-libbed speech he is going to make at the Municipal Chamber makes his breastbone, which naturally juts out like a rooster's, seem even more salient. He is better dressed than most of the well-dressed passersby, whom he greets discriminatingly, marking each one's degree of friendship or importance by the height to which he removes his hat. But he does not stop to talk, and apologizes whenever someone wants to exchange words: he has got to run, there are still many things to see to, today is the big day. And everyone understands, because everyone knows his uncompromising patriotism and the major contribution he makes to the celebrations, paying most of the expenses from his own pocket, because of the insufficiency and uncertainty of official disbursements.

So no one disturbs his march down Channel Street toward Fair Park, even if they know he chose this route out of prudence and does not want to be seen on busier Straight Street. He is a man of great responsibility, a responsibility whose execution is possible only for a man of means. And he does have means, not only the slaughterhouse and the meat shops on the island and in Bahia, but also the stores, the small farms, the rented houses, the six fishing boats. Thanks to all that, he is able not only to give money for the Seventh of January festivities but also to do what he is doing now. Whoever stops for a while to accompany his passage will see that a good hundred yards behind him come Militão and Boanerges, two of his black meatcutters, carrying packages of neck beef and chuck ribs in the pouches of their leather aprons, and two baskets with the carcasses of the weanling lambs he orders butchered every year to be eaten at victory luncheons. The idea came to him after a speech he himself had made in which he recalled the heroic feats of the islanders, declaring that they no longer were a flock of sheep herded by thieves and felons in the pay of the Lusitanian Crown. Consequently, nothing better for marking that day among Itaparicans than to ally the force of a metaphor to the force of food by having the lambs delivered to all homes.

Not, to be sure, all the homes of Whale Point, big and prosperous these days and upgraded to a municipality with the official name of Intrepid Village of Itaparica, but the homes of João Popó's families. Because one of his grave responsibilities is to provide support for descendants whose number is considered large even for a place of such feracious women as the island is. With Iaiá Candinha, his legal wife, he had eighteen children, all of them raised to adulthood except Olegário, who died at ten, felled by an inflamed tooth root. With Young Iaiá, Candinha's sister, he had eleven, but two of them were stillborn, so nine were left. With the black Laurinda, of Young Iaiá's pantry and kitchen, he had three, all male, burly mulattoes. With Maria Zezé, Candinha's niece who lives in Mutá but comes to stay at her aunt's festivities every year, he had four, still living with their mother with the exception of Perolina, who got married and moved with her husband to Santo Antônio de Jesus. With Rufina from the Hill, who is thought to be a witch, he had five, the same number he had with a woman for whom he set up a home in Rail Point and whose name is uncertain, though she is known in the neighborhood as Maria Silver Coin. With the young black girls of his father's property and his own he had more than twenty, maybe more than thirty, although Chico Popó, his older brother, who died in the Independence War, also enjoyed visiting the Negresses, so a few of the children may be his. And with other women—a goddaughter here, a goddaughter's mother there, a visiting cousin, a housemaid or two—he had a few more, sometimes more than a few, so that the exact number of his direct and indirect descendants is unknown, to which it should be added that their two main branches have different names: Candinha's is Azevedo, Young Iaiá's is Batista, with the result that one may lose track of their kinship, save for the fact that people call almost all of them by their given names followed by the surname Popó.

It is difficult to point out the most outstanding fruits of such an exuberant tree. What can be said is that anything can be found among the Popós, from Luiz Popó, who never washes, drinks rum all day, and lives among mules, to Lafayette Popó, who started out as a municipal construction foreman appointed through the old man's influence and quickly became the wealthy owner of several farms and manors. And there are Popós everywhere, since not all of them have stayed in Itaparica or even in the bay lands. Some of them moved to the backlands, others moved to the court, others went away and disappeared without sending news.

But among all of them, Rufina from the Hill's are the most famous. They are Zé Popó, Dionísio Popó, Vavá Popó, Geminiano Popó, and Rita Popó. Rufina's blood, Cape Verdean and Sudanese and Azorean, has always been held to be very strong, so it must have been after her that the boys took, although João Popó, who nowadays does not go out in the street carrying a club only because his position does not allow him, is also described by older people as having been a bit of a hell-raiser in his youth, a debaucher, a brawler, a street fighter, a troublemaker, and a master fistfighter. Anyway, they are all very tough customers, real devils, so to speak, with whom no one wants any complications. And to top it all, Zé Popó, who is old enough to have a little more sense, decided to join the bandits led by Maria da Fé, though that does not stop him from showing up in the village now and then disguised as this or that, to cause provocations, to visit and be disrespectful to family girls, and to defy the authorities.

João Popó's concern with his progeny at this time, however, does not go much beyond the need to dispatch the lambs, and he is signaling for Militão to proceed to Saint Anthony Hill, where he will make the deliveries at Rufina's and other women's, and telling Boanerges to use a side entrance to Young Iaiá's place to take care of his errands with the kitchen blacks. He arranged his new coat, straightened his high collar, stiffened up, and went in, looking straight ahead. Young Iaiá was as usual sitting in the rocking chair and sewing by the light coming through the window, and as usual she did not raise her eyes as he entered. Ever since the day he, then her fiancé, scandalized the family by having impregnated Candinha, thus being forced to marry her, Young Iaiá would not speak to him except to answer questions. The children they made together were made wordlessly, and when she needed to say something to him, she did it through Laurinda. In the beginning João Popó tried to convince her to abandon that muleheaded, haughty posture, but she would not change, so he ended up getting used to it.

He stopped at the door, waiting in vain for her to acknowledge his presence.

"Very well," he said, after clearing his throat. "I'm just passing by to let you know the black Boa has arrived with the two lambs for your luncheon. Where is Laurinda?"

She made a head gesture toward the pantry, and he walked inside, to find the black woman talking to Boanerges in the kitchen.

"I don't want any of this kitchen-door chatting!" he said sternly. "Have you unloaded the two lambs, Boanerges?"

"Yes, Massa."

"Have you delivered the beef?"

"Yes, Massa."

"So what are you doing here, like a babbling old wife? Go do your chores before I lose my patience!"

He turned to Laurinda, slapped her behind gently.

"All right, my pet, any messages?"

"Young Iaiá wants to know if Massa's going to come to luncheon here today. She says Massa's been promising to have luncheon here for eight years now, and it hasn't happened yet."

"How can I possibly come to her luncheon? Today I'll be entertaining authorities at home, people of high station; Dona Candinha's been working since four in the morning. This is a mindless idea; tell her I'll come next year, not this year."

"Yes, Massa."

"Tell her I'm coming tonight, after six. Tell her I'm going to need her tonight."

"She's been having rheumatism since Wednesday; I've already rubbed oil on her twice today."

"Then I'm going to need you. Leave the door to your room open as usual."

"I've got rheumatism too."

"Say that again and I'll show you your rheumatism. You want me to sleep alone?"

"There was a message to you from Rufina earlier on; she wants to speak to Massa."

"I know what it is. Militão ought to be arriving there now with the meat and the lambs."

"I don't think that's what she wanted, Massa."

"Shut up; don't take liberties with me. Come on, put your hand here, feel it here for a minute, come on."

"Not here, Massa—don't be crazy, Massa João Popó!"

"You juicy old bitch—"

"Massa João, people can come in here anytime!"

"If I didn't have to leave, I'd show you once again what I have been showing ever since you arrived here. See, see how it swells up? Many young men would like to have this potency!"

"Massa João . . ."

Young Iaiá came to the kitchen door, stopped, and made an about-face. João Popó turned away from Laurinda, who ran off to the stove with her hands on her head scarf, and went after Young Iaiá.

"What is it? You haven't seen anything, you don't have to look like that. Why that face?"

"My face is the same as always."

"It's not! I'm fed up with this; people act here as if I were a criminal! Answer me: Is this home ever short of anything, is it? Is it?"

"I never said it was."

"But you act as though it was! I never spared myself any sacrifice, never placed my interests above the interests of my dependents, I have always behaved correctly, and what do I get? Ungratefulness! If I didn't have to answer my Motherland's call now, you would listen to a good pair of truths! Where are my patent-leather shoes, the old ones? These are not broken in yet, I stopped over just to change them, I've got no time to go on putting up with your sniveling! You're an old nag, that's what you are, a rancorous old woman unable to forget a youthful mistake for which I have begged forgiveness so many times, and only a thick-skinned, thankless heart such as yours is able to deny it! My shoes!"

He was annoyed when he left, sweating a little, feeling discriminated against and exploited. Well, he could not let those things disturb him. How was it that the speech started? And the part about the war, wasn't it a bit lame? Were battles really taking place? Had Brazil really reacted against the criminal seizure of the ship *Marquês de Olinda*? Could it be that the nation was actually at war? So many rumors, so much gossip—what was the truth? He tried to remember the part of his speech that mentioned the war and was unable to; it had to be done from the beginning. He slowed down his steps, repeating his speech from scratch in a rather guttural voice, almost a yelp, in which the words were intelligible only to himself, and others would perceive only his dramatic intonation and his pauses of style.

"What is it, Father—are you starting your speech already?"

"Huh?" João Popó almost bumped absentmindedly into his eldest sons, Cochrane, Labatut, Lafayette, and Washington, as they were coming out of the market alley, bound for the Municipal Chamber.

"You were making a speech to yourself."

"Of course not; that's nonsense, Ostinho."

"Is the president of the province coming?"

"Maybe he's already here. I didn't have time to wait for his ship."

"It hasn't arrived yet."

"Oh, we have time, then. Has the ship come into view?"

"No, strangely. It ought to be here by now, but nothing is visible beyond the sandbank."

"Nonsense; it must be on its way. The president will be here; it's an important occasion, a very important occasion."

"Well, as I was saying to Labinha, maybe he won't come. This war talk is really true; we've been at war with Paraguay for some time now, maybe more than a month."

"Who told you? These rumors run around all the time; not one day goes by without somebody mentioning wars in the south, against the Easterners, the Argentines, and God knows who else."

"No, no, it's true. Everyone knows about it in Bahia. Things are serious—we're at war! Ask anybody who just came from there; everyone knows."

"My God! We're at war? War?"

João Popó staggered, feeling an uncontrollable burning in his chest. He raised his cane high, not knowing what to do. He felt like running in every direction, making a speech in everybody's ears, going for his arms, climbing up the church steeple to make it his tribune.

"The bells!" he growled. "Why aren't the bells tolling? We're at war! At war! Brazil is being threatened, do you understand that? Threatened, attacked, hated by the enemy! We're at war, we must have courage and determination, Brazil cannot succumb, it will never succumb!"

A while later, even in the absence of the president of the province or some high-ranking representative, João Popó, feeling even dizzier than when he heard the news for the first time, forgot about his memorized speech and, in spiritual exaltation, as if he were repeating something being whispered to him from the clouds, spoke for more than half an hour. He said how fitting it was that he and other Itaparicans had first heard about the war that very day. It was a divine presage, a coincidence worked out by Providence. He would like to say that once again Itaparica would save the Motherland and preserve her integrity. They had done that against the Dutch, against corsairs of all nations, and against the Portuguese oppressors, and now they would do it against the infamous Paraguayan enemy, who would never lay their filthy claws on the high-flying Brazilian banner. He personally knew how mettlesome Itaparicans were, mettlesome in the past, mettlesome in the present, mettlesome in the future. He had personally had the exalted privilege of knowing many of the heroes of yore, either Itaparicans or men with roots on the island, such as Barros Galvão, João das Botas, the baron of Pirapuama—a true and unjustly forgotten warrior and statesman of Independence—and so many others whom history would not let go unremembered but would forever honor on the highest peaks of the utmost glory, the glory of having served the Motherland for the Motherland's love. As for the future, he himself would be at the front line of combat if the years weighing on his back would allow him. But if he could not go personally, he would send out his sons. They were of age, all fully grown; he could not give them orders. But those orders would not be necessary, for he was sure that as soon as they heard the sonorous clarion call of the sublime invocation to carry out their duty as Brazilians, at least one of them would be ready to embark.

"And this I swear on my honor as a citizen, my honor as a Brazilian, and my honor as a patriot who will never cease fighting and resisting as long as one Paraguayan remains alive! Down with the Portuguese oppressor! Down with the Dutch invader! Down with Madeira! Long live João das Botas! Long live Maria Felipa! Long live Sister Joana Angélica! Long live Lord Cochrane! Long live the baron of Pirapuama! Long live the Intrepid Village of Itaparica! Long live His Imperial Majesty, Dom Pedro II! Long live Brazilian independence! Death to Paraguay! Long live the Motherland!"

Dissolving in sweat, an indignant drool trickling down the folds of his chin, he fell on the arms of the first of those who rushed to compliment him, was squeezed by a tearful, howling crowd. All over the square outside, people applauded with handclaps, huzzahs, and rockets. Even the group dressed up in loincloths and feather headgear to play the part of Indians in the parade, usually poor browns who do it for some rum and are always too drunk to care about anything, seemed to be aroused, and a few clubs swung in the air.

And of course João Popó did not know, but would hear later with unspeakable pride, that the fortunate coincidence to which he had alluded in his speech had been even more extraordinary than he had thought. Because on that same day, who knows if not at the same hour, while he vituperated the enemy on Quitanda Square and the specter of war unfolded its gelid shadow over Brazil, His Imperial Majesty's Government, from high up in the court of Rio de Janeiro, was issuing a decree creating the Volunteers of the Motherland, the flower of national youth who would go to war in the faraway fields of honor of the Paraguayan campaign.

City of Salvador, Bahia, May 23, 1866

Will they never be over, these maudlin compliments, these hanging lips, all this pantomime, this inane ritual? Bonifácio Odulfo received Professor Oscar Pedreira's warm, excessively long and vigorous embrace and had to hold back an urge to push him away. Yes, yes, all right, so he's deeply grieved by Commander Amleto's demise, he hasn't thought about anything but that each one of the 365 days that have gone by since the commander's death, and of course he believes all this toadying will prevent the bank's claim on his overdue promissory note. It will be sent to the notary today. How many people are there in this endless line? All in black, the women with their hands clenched mournfully together, the men affecting the most ridiculous types of somberness—what a grotesque procession! Everything a mere superficial act, destitute of true sentiment and, worse, of practical usefulness. In this respect Commander Amleto had always been right, as by the way he had been in many, many others: That which does not have a practical purpose makes no sense, is empty, is something mankind must learn how to get rid of. What does all this hypocrisy mean? What is all this for? People ought to evolve, they have to understand everything must evolve and each one of us too!

Just as he himself, incidentally, had evolved a great deal ever since the day when, as he returned home carrying under his arm a stack of press copies of his latest poem, "Cries at Sunrise," just launched at Mazombo's, he was surprised to find the door open at that hour, carriages parked out in front, indistinct human shapes and buzzing voices inside. He went up the stairway two steps at a time, and the first person he saw was the black Juvi, pressing her hands against her enormous bosom, her mouth wide open, her face wet.

"Oh, Little Massa, oh, Little Massa, Massa, Massa, Massa!"

Sure, the old man had died. They'd known he was going to die for some time now; he himself kept talking about it. He had continued working but had stopped going out, and since Carlota Borroméia's death he had begun to eat even less than before. He often had nothing but tea all day long, and at times would have just half a slice of fish for lunch and a bread roll with diluted milk for dinner. He would not even argue anymore if they urged him to eat. He would seem to be listening attentively to what was being said to him but would not answer anything back, as though he had a divine mission to starve. His hair became thinner and thinner, his skin very white and sallow, his nose longer, his voice raspy and weak, his movements slow like those of a man twenty or thirty years older than he. He was bound to die.

Bonifácio Odulfo set the stack of pamphlets on the living-room sideboard, went to his father's bedroom, sat down at his mother's dressing table, in front of the agave-juice jar, and stayed there without moving or speaking until it was time for the funeral.

In the following days he did not leave home, talked very little, and had them tell many of his friends who came to see him that he was not in. When they consulted him about something that had to be done, he asked that they please speak to Monsignor Clemente André, Dr. Noêmio, Dr. Vasco Miguel, or somebody. The house blacks, his relatives, and his retainers were even worried about him, as they had never imagined how deeply he would feel his father's death, spending day after day in silence, self-absorbed, absent, distracted, always locked in his room or sitting in the study at the same writing table at which the old man had worked until the end of his life.

Meeting in the study to discuss inheritance problems, Dr. Noêmio, Clemente André, Vasco Miguel, and the notary Pôncio Nogueira thought, when Bonifácio Odulfo entered the room, that their conversation would be interrupted for just a brief moment, because they of course believed he was there just to offer an excuse for not wishing to participate in the discussion. They were therefore quite surprised when they heard him speak.

"You gentlemen cannot have this meeting without my presence," he said. "I consider this a disrespectful action and an open door to the usurpation of my rights."

What? Usurpation? What did he mean? Why was he talking like that, when his behavior had made it reasonable to assume that he wouldn't be interested in attending, when all his life he had limited his interest in his father's businesses to receiving his allowance and having his publications paid for, when he professed a violent distaste for everything related to commerce, production, and money, when he had sworn eternal aversion to all that was not art and poetry?

"Those are excuses, an untenable succession of non sequiturs," he answered, pressing together his fingertips as his father used to do, bending his neck the same way, and speaking in the same slightly pretentious tone, so that for a minute it crossed everybody's mind that they were seeing a ghost. "The fact is that I am one of his heirs, interested in his inventory and co-responsible for the innumerable properties which constitute the estate left by my father, with the right and the duty to be informed of everything that's going on and to give my opinion about it. Moreover, considering the special circumstances surrounding the direct heirs—that is to say, considering that my elder brother, Monsignor Clemente André, has dedicated his life to the priesthood and to education, and my younger brother, Captain Patrício Macário, is following a military career and right now is at the Mato Grosso battlefront—the best candidate for Commander Amleto Henrique Nobre Ferreira-Dutton's succession is I, Bachelor Bonifácio Odulfo Nobre dos Reis Ferreira-Dutton. Not to mention that"—and he made a long pause, running his gaze in a circle over the others—"*fide, sed cui, vide*, a wise ancient precept, wouldn't you say?"

Yes, he had surprised them, and more surprises were to come. At the central office, discipline became more rigid, and the austerity enforced in Amleto's time doubled. At home, parallel with a rigorous control of household finances and severe punishments for blacks who broke any object or caused any waste, a ceremonious atmosphere was established in which excessive familiarity or spontaneity was unacceptable. His appearance changed so much that many of his friends from his bohemian times would not recognize him if they saw him, an unlikely event at best even if they wanted to see him, because he refused to receive the two or three who tried to visit, although he did send one of them an envelope with some cash and a note warning that that was the last help he could give him. He trimmed his hair, had his beard cut à la Prince Albert, started dressing exclusively in black, and abandoned the hacking breathing he had adopted among his friends to convince them of the debility of his lungs. Finally, he proved himself to be a still shrewder and more cold-blooded businessman than his father, mastering in less than three months all the subjects necessary to the efficacious management of his firms and accomplishing in less than a year results formerly considered chimerical. The only former activity in which Bonifácio Odulfo persisted was poetry, for in the rare moments of relaxation he allowed himself in the company of his associates, he admitted, feigning reluctance, that poetry was in his blood, it was a flame that would not be extinguished. But he no longer published pamphlets, nor did he show or recite his poems, but he preferred to keep them for later publication, perhaps under a pen name, in a serious volume which he would personally edit. He also cultivated in secret a genre he named erotic-Fescennine, nourishing a vague solitary fantasy of someday setting up a plan to print a selection of this poetry, even after his death. And in his spare time he would lock himself in his study to learn English and memorize Latin apothegms and quotations, having tea and eating raisin-filled muffins.

The parade of condolences seemed finally to have finished, and the squeezes, hugs, tearful faces, and standard remarks were mercifully over. Monsignor Clemente André, by now out of his solemn vestments but very elegant in a French cassock, emerged from the sacristy, kissed his nephews, was complimented on his sermon by Vasco Miguel, and grasped Bonifácio Odulfo's hands.

"Are you going to work today?" he asked.

"By all means. Today is a day like any other. Except of course for starting office hours late on account of this Mass. I'm on my way out now. What do you want?"

"It's about the new wing of the orphanage."

"My dear Monsignor, I know you aspire to sainthood and live for what they call good works, but have you ever thought you could lead your family to bankruptcy with your munificence?"

"Oh, you're exaggerating. And besides, the wing is practically finished; all we need now are the roof tiles."

"Isn't there any other company in Bahia interested in practicing charity? Even if not as much as we, because we practice it at an astronomical level."

"But it's only the tiles; it's not much."

"All right, but I mean it: we have to put a stop to this. If I were to debit to your account all you have withdrawn in the name of your forlorn children, you'd be a poor priest by now, and goodbye Roman cassocks."

"French. You like it?"

"Stop being so frivolous; behave according to your position, our position.

I'm serious; don't make the burden I bear even heavier, having to be at the head of all our businesses, without a minute of peace and quiet, while you do your charities, Patrício Macário covers himself with blood and medals, and Dr. Vasco Miguel spends his life scribbling letters and memorandums and poring over petty accounts."

"Don't get angry with me. I promise I'll talk to you before I incur any other expense."

"Even if you don't promise, that's what you'll have to do. I preside over commercial and financial establishments; I'm a responsible member of the productive class; I'm not running a picnic."

"Yes, I'm aware of that, you're right. But what do I do to get the money for the tiles? Should I go see you at the office later today?"

"No, you'd only be in the way; my schedule is full up. I'll do better than giving you the money; I'll give you the tiles."

"But wouldn't it be simpler to give me the money? This way, I myself would take the trouble to buy the tiles; it would make things easier for you."

"Believe me, my dear brother, no one makes anything easier for me. I make them easier myself. You don't want the tiles anymore? Are you hard up? What do you do with your monthly stipend, huh? Remember it's not small. Are your French cassocks too expensive?"

"You don't have to talk like that. Even though we're brothers, we have to preserve a mutual respect."

"That's precisely what I think. Do you see what I mean? Well, as for the tiles, so we won't waste any more time: Go see your uncle at the central emporium and tell him you've talked it over with me, and I've approved the donation of the tiles. No, not the donation, the sale."

"What do you mean? I don't understand."

"Of course you don't; you understand these things as much as I do your euchologies. What I'm saying is that he'll give you the tiles and also a receipt and a sales voucher, as if you had purchased them."

"But if you're giving them, why pretend they're being sold?"

"Sometimes this type of thing is necessary; it would be too complicated, and useless besides, to explain it to you."

He said goodbye impatiently, kissed his nephews as had his brother, and asked if Vasco Miguel would not like to come along with him to the office to save time. They would use his coach and send Vasco Miguel's back home with the children. Vasco Miguel agreed, and they went out together, climbed into the coach, and leaned back facing each other on the wide, padded seats. Bonifácio Odulfo drew the window curtains together, letting in only the light from the sun roof. He pinched the skin between his eyebrows for a long time, his eyes closed, his head down, his right arm nested on his chest. Maybe there would be no need to talk to his brother-in-law during the long trip, marked by the jostling of the wheels over the potholes in the pavement and by the syncopated percussion of the horses' shoes; maybe he could stay silent, as he preferred. If he did not speak, Vasco Miguel would not speak, either, because in his customary posture, his pudgy little hands crossed over his stomach, with his slightly open mouth, his moist lips, his expressionless eyes, and his pendulous cheeks, he seemed never to be thinking but to be always like an unwound clock, waiting indifferently for someone to set it in motion.

Nevertheless, having remained silent for so long, Bonifácio Odulfo could not hold back an association of ideas that renewed his irritation with his brother-in-law. He had been thinking at first about how odd and at the same time exasperating it was, though he did not know exactly why, that a learned man like his brother the priest did not even suspect the need to feign the receipt of a certain amount in order to cover up the expenditure or receipt of another. How stupid, he thought; most men really seem not to have too much imagination, reasoning power, discernment, vision. Yes, vision, something lacking, like so many other things, in this fellow almost dozing off in front of him.

"How are the contacts with foreign banks coming along?" he asked all of a sudden, in the harsh tone of someone who expects a disappointing answer.

"What contacts with foreign banks?"

"Dr. Vasco Miguel, I remember perfectly well that last Monday at a meeting of the bank's board I spoke exhaustively of the opportunities created by this conflict with Paraguay. Our troops don't even have uniforms, let alone the vast material resources needed to carry on the war. Even if they can count on the so-called allies, who don't mean too much, their inferiority in numbers is enormous, and so's their inferiority in equipment. You remember I spoke about what this meant, don't you?"

"Yes, yes, I do. You didn't have to remind me; I remember it perfectly."

"And what did I say?"

"You said that this means the government is going to need extremely heavy financing. I'm well aware of that."

"You don't seem to be. If you do, why haven't you expedited our contacts with foreign banks? With our correspondents?"

"I saw no reason for that. And I still don't."

"But for Most Holy Mary's sake, has Dr. Vasco Miguel heard everything I said at the meeting, everything I have just said, has he? Has he?"

"Yes, of course I have. But I don't see what one thing's got to do with the other."

"You don't see. This Paraguay campaign is going to last much longer than people think; I'm sure it's going to be exceptionally arduous, for the very reasons I mentioned. And how could we participate in the banking opportunities that will arise, if not through foreign financing? As agents for those funds, as middlemen! Or do you believe we have enough resources in our bank to finance the Paraguay campaign?"

"Yes, you're absolutely right. I'll see to that immediately, as soon as I arrive at the office."

"And don't forget to ask for information about purchases of matériel by the allies and by the Paraguayans."

"Are we going to finance the Paraguayans?"

"Obviously not. We may finance their suppliers, though. Some of them are also our clients abroad. This may result in a series of very interesting, even innovative transactions, an intricate, subtle network which only the talent of a great banker can conceive. And I think that by the grace of God I have that talent."

"I think so too. That's why banks have to have presidents, isn't it? My area of work precludes my anticipating . . ."

Bonifácio Odulfo was appeased; he waved his hand conciliatorily and went back into silence. Not because his irritation had gone away entirely, but because as he mentioned what he had called very interesting transactions, he remembered something he had been thinking about for two days now. Something he had given the secret name of "three-cornered game," in which he visualized a complex interrelationship among three participants in a financial operation. Not three but four, to be sure. He leaned back, delighted by the clarity with which he saw all the possibilities, in a consummate web he compared to the cat's cradles Amleto—now he knew why—had had as his only amusement in his last months. He could explain what he was thinking to Vasco Miguel, but that zebra would make neither head nor tail of it. He would take care of everything himself.

"Do you play chess?" he asked, looking askance at Vasco Miguel.

"No."

"That's what I thought."

He noticed the coachman pulling on the brakes, so they were probably going down Mountain Hill. He made a small opening between the curtains to look at the sea down below, brown, round Saint Marcellus Fort standing in the middle of the still water, the towers of the Seaside Church of Our Lady of Conception sparkling under the harsh sun. He was lost in the contemplation of the landscape for a while, maybe feeling the warm breath of poetic inspiration, certainly feeling some peace. Because it was not he, it was Patrício Macário who, very far from there, was kneeling down on the ground after a bugle call to pray to the Virgin of the Battles, Our Lady of the Immaculate Conception, next to other officers and soldiers, most of whom shall die tomorrow, right there in the swamplands of a place called Tuiuti.

Intrepid Village of Itaparica,
March 11, 1866

Grief is like that; grief kills. Old João Popó has taken to his bed for the fourth time since maybe November last year, and this time there are those who guarantee he will not escape. He is but a shadow of the man he used to be, practically unrecognizable, a sorry sight, especially to those who knew that even at his age he used to be full of vigor, had a brisk gait, a hearty voice, an authoritative manner. No such thing now, as he drags himself close to the walls when he goes out, does not raise his eyes, speaks as if he did not have enough strength to open his mouth, goes wherever they take him, does not react to anything. And now in bed, though his most alarming symptom is a slight fever that comes and goes, he will not eat or drink, he will not do anything but remain with his eyes nailed to the ceiling, praying with the old rosary he inherited from his mother.

Itaparica is of course entering the fray; it would not stay out of it at a time like this. Contrary to what could be expected in some other place, the problem was to contain the ardor of the volunteers, for the mustering costs of the island's expedition, the Second Infantry Company of the Volunteers of the Motherland, had been entirely defrayed by the citizens of the village, including João Popó himself, and such a circumstance was bound to limit the recruitment. But it cost a lot more to turn back the most fervent of them, who would not resign themselves to being excluded and threatened to commit the greatest follies if they were not shipped out to defend Brazil. The obstinate or lucky ones found themselves sponsors to pay for their uniforms and gear, besides using political influence to be signed up. Even so, many were left out and, embittered, were thinking of forming another company, of doing anything to go to the war, because everyone thought he should go to the war.

Everyone, that is, except the many sons of João Popó. If on the Seventh of January he had been the first to exhort the crowd to rise in arms for the nation, perhaps, to his honor, in the same sacrosanct instant the Volunteers of the Motherland were being created; if he had been the first to get into action, moving heaven and earth to organize the Itaparican participation in the conflict, indefatigable in his advocacy, unbending in his determination, unrelenting in his fervor; if, finally, he had been the one who, in the name of his own honor, had offered his sons to the holocaust, he had also turned out to be the one who after so much honor was seeing himself divested of it, downcast, crestfallen, defeated. In one word: disgraced. The new company had been in existence since the tenth of October. That day, the number of volunteers was higher than the enlistment goal. But João Popó's sons did not volunteer that day or any other day, not one of João Popó's sons with any of his past or present women, not a single, face-saving one.

In the beginning he tried to dissimulate, pretending it was just a matter of time, while the families chose the ones who were to go. He went so far as to suggest that there was jealousy among his sons because all of them wanted to go, which was not possible, hence the delay. But he was soon forced to stop lying, because the truth started being known by everybody in the village and even in other parts of the island. There was no way to hide it—and João Popó took to bed for the first time.

Back on his feet, he resumed with renewed zeal the campaign to convince one of his sons to enlist. Candinha's sons were the first he tried to persuade. Lafayette Popó declared he was too old to fight, and besides, his many responsibilities made it impossible for him to accept new obligations at the moment. If Lafayette, who was the fourth son, was too old, what would the first three say? They said the same thing, adding with cynicism that they were heroes and generals only by name. Then there were the girls, who were born in a series, and then the only one of the last group of males old enough to serve, Franklin Popó. But Candinha, among cries and lamentations, said that if Sister Joana Angélica had been transfixed by an ignoble Portuguese bayonet, she herself was willing to be impaled by her husband's cruel dagger if he insisted on sending her beloved little boy, the solace of her old age, to die or be maimed in the war. Later João Popó found out that Franklin himself, also in tears, had begged his mother to take that extreme position —and he fell sick in bed for the second time.

Recuperated after having, according to the opinion of many, pendulated between life and death, he tried to see Rufina's sons, but could not even discuss the matter properly with her because she would only engage in this type of conversation after settling the complex problems of the inheritance and the bequests João Popó ought to make to his natural descendants while still living. And what did Young Iaiá's sons say? They said the same, as did Laurinda's, Maria Zezé's, and Maria Silver Coin's. And besides, why should they be the ones who had to go, instead of the legitimate ones? Just because the others were legitimate? Were they not content with their many privileges; they still wanted more? The old man fumed, clamored, and threatened, but to no avail. He even suspended the furnishing of provisions to all of them, but his children and women would go to his stores when he was not in and take all they wanted, indifferent to the resistance of his employees and blacks. One of his mulatto sons, Ranulfo Popó, sprang up from no one knows where and offered to volunteer, but under certain conditions, including a substantial lifetime allowance, the Incarnation Village house, and the Rail Point farmlet. Outraged at what he saw as the worst of all crimes and sins, the prostitution of one's love for the Motherland, João Popó had a spell of sadness which almost prostrated him. One night during this period, Luiz Popó came to see him completely drunk, and after pronouncing an unintelligible speech among gestures that seemed to be attempts to catch invisible butterflies, said that he was going to Paraguay, he would go that very minute—which he did not do for several reasons, the most important of which was that he collapsed on the ground, to wake up only the next day without remembering anything, and João Popó became laid up for the third time.

They did not believe he would rally. He entered the new year almost unconscious, but recovered miraculously in time to take part in the Seventh of January festivities. Candinha was against it, his closest friends tried to dissuade him, but he insisted. They argued that besides the situation created by the absence of volunteers among the most numerous of progeny on the island, especially in view of that solemn promise, there was also the question raised by the disturbances in which Zé Popó had participated during the previous year's celebrations. And indeed, disguised as Indian participants in the civic parade, the brigands who call themselves the Militia of the People took advantage of the festive atmosphere to invade the tax collector's office and steal all the tax money. Not satisfied with that, they forced the collector to sign a document in which he admitted he kept for himself most of what he collected and that he had been cheating and extorting the taxpayers, taking the lion's share and welcoming all sorts of bribes. Still not satisfied, they distributed leaflets in which they asked if it was possible for a country to be independent if its people were enslaved and its masters were servants of foreigners. They also asked if people were going to Paraguay to fight in the defense of a country that belonged not to those who were going to fight but to those who were sending them away to fight while they stayed home, writing poems, making speeches, and getting richer every day. They asked if there were slaves and wretchedly poor people in Paraguay. If there were, little glory would come to them from their fighting, for a slavemaster was just like all other slavemasters, no matter what language he spoke or what color he was, and the slave who considers himself not a slave but a person cannot fight for this or that master but must fight against all masters. If there were not, why fight against a free people, for the sake of slavemasters and exploiters? If there were, also why fight there, since their fight was right here, not outside? And finally, not satisfied with all that, they painted house and garden walls with huge letters that said: LONG LIVE THE PEOPLE; LONG LIVE THE BRAZILIAN PEOPLE; LONG LIVE THE PEOPLE THAT ONE DAY WILL FIND ITSELF; LONG LIVE US WHO DON'T BELONG TO ANYONE; LONG LIVE US WHO WANT FREEDOM FOR US AND NOT FOR OUR OWNERS. And many more capers were probably brought off by Zé Popó turned into a devil, almost naked in his feather-duster skirt and raising hell all over the village.

Yes, João Popó remembered that very well, and even more, things he would not tell anybody. Zé Popó had had the nerve to jump over the backyard wall of Young Iaiá's house, where the old man was in bed with Laurinda and occupied, and had opened the window, looked inside, laughed, and said, "your blessin', Dad." João Popó had the biggest scare of his life, but managed to get up, with his underpants falling around his shins, and call down his outrageous son as he deserved, though by then he was probably skedaddling through the woods and did not hear anything. The disaster was rounded off by his subsequent inability to take up where he had left off with Laurinda, the second time this had ever happened in all his existence. The first time had been early in his marriage, when in the middle of an amorous act Candinha had let out a most obscene moan, which put him out of action for the whole night and left him traumatized for quite a while, for he had never imagined this type of conduct to be possible for such an apparently virtuous woman. But that time reason had been on his side; it was Candinha's shame, not his. What serious man would bear the suspicions begotten by that moan, which she fortunately had never dared to repeat? But not the second time; the second time, his duty as soon as the incident was over was to act like a man and slip back into Laurinda with the same energy. This, however, had not been possible, and João Popó changed into his nightshirt and spent the night wide awake, walking around the house, cursing his son, and mumbling a strong incantation to recover his virile disposition, with no result.

Yes, he had been through all those tribulations, but he would not give any satisfaction to his enemies and to those who envied him. He would rather die than not attend the celebrations that were part of his very soul, synonymous in a way with his life. He sent for Militão, ordered him to take the lambs to the usual people, took a complete bath, combed his hair carefully, put on his best clothes, and went to the Municipal Chamber, refusing the company of Labatut, Washington, and Cochrane. When he got there, he proudly ignored glances and whispers, and as soon as the floor was yielded to those who wished to speak, he raised his hand and marched to the rostrum, where he had so often received the most impassioned ovations. But he could not even start to speak, for he was submerged in the loudest booing ever heard on the island, in spite of all the not too heartfelt appeals to order made by the speaker of the chamber. He resisted, raised his voice as loud as he could, even threatened to step down to grapple with the nearest booers.

"You knaves! I'm not afraid of you! Scoundrels! I'll take you one by one. Come one by one, you knaves!"

Amid an uncontrollable tumult, he stepped down from the rostrum, supported by two or three friends, who after much confusion and shouting managed to take him home. But he ended up storming madly out the door to try to invade the little house where Cadet Mirabeau José conducted the enlisting. But it was Sunday, and the cadet was a-courting in the drawing room of his future father-in-law, the registrar João Bizarria. That did not stop João Popó, who burst like a whirlwind into João Bizarria's house and, falling on his knees, his hair mussed, his clothes in disarray, his eyes rolling out of their sockets, implored among clamorous sobs to be inducted, to be taken to combat. He would give them money, he would give them all his possessions, he would do anything; he was still in better shape than many young men, because the men of his time had more backbone. For the love of God, by the sacred galloons of the cadet's uniform, by everything in the world, allow him to enlist, under any condition, in any rank, for any task, provided it was at the front line; he couldn't bear the shame of seeing Brazil in jeopardy and not a single Popó standing up to offer his blood in her defense. He had to be dragged home, his crying turned to howls, his mind carbonized by the fire of passion, his body enervated by the force of so much adversity—and he took to his bed for the fourth time.

Now, on this other Sunday with so little in common with that one, João Popó may be about to expire, in the four-poster where he neither parts with his rosary nor gives any answer to what is spoken to him. They tried to hide all news from him, but he knows it all. There are always malicious people who make comments in an intentional loud tone near the window of his room. There are always visitors who come to enjoy the pleasure most people find in giving bad news and witnessing ominous events. He knows that the famous steamship *Union*, which will take the Second Infantry Company to the war, has docked. He knows there are parties for the future combatants, there are tearful but proud sweethearts, fiancées, wives, and mothers, there are bands rehearsing, people ornamenting the streets with streamers, women finishing embroidering standards and flags, young men anticipating the slaughtering of the enemy, men already presenting themselves as the fathers of the most lionhearted heroes. He also knows that along the breakwaters of Whale Point, enveloped by the same breeze that had kissed so many immortal faces, the mothers of the volunteers have planted tamarind seedlings, one for each son about to embark, so that those noble perennial trees, unhurried in growth and imposing in countenance, will always be there, even if those they will forever memorialize never return. He knows about all that, and that is why he is weeping a little and wishing to die in the company of his rosary, with whose beads he has just started his two hundred and ninth Hail Mary. The embarkation is set for Wednesday the fourteenth, everything has been taken care of, everything is ready, there will be no Popós in Paraguay, soon there will be no João Popó anymore.

The family's consternation cannot be said to have been equal to so great a loss as João Popó's. After all, he was getting old anyway, he had been frailer and frailer lately, and at his age death was often a rest, it was no use living without health, people have to resign themselves to their fate, that's the way life is, every life ends in death, isn't that right? To be fair to Candinha, it's true she was giving him the best sickbed care, was always offering him some tea or a light pap, which he would refuse, was at his side most of the time, but no one during all this ordeal ever heard a distressed sound from her or saw a tear of apprehension. Young Iaiá showed up every day to ask about him, but she would not go inside the room, and since she did not speak to her sister, either, limited herself to mumbling a few questions to the house blacks, crossing herself, and mincing stiffly back home. As for the other families he supported and their relatives and adherents, they did not seem to be affected by the situation. In the beginning, they would still comment on the subject and show some concern, maybe even sadness. But they soon got used to it and went back to living as usual, each one dedicated to his job or joblessness, adding through such indifference a cruel tone of melancholy to João Popó's inglorious decline.

A melancholy mixed with bitterness and scandal, if one believes the rumor according to which Coquinho, Ostinho, and Labinha—as Cochrane, Washington, and Labatut were known by their intimates—drinking in a tavern in Bahia, discussed openly the division of the old man's estate, because Coquinho had the conviction, strongly seconded by Labinha, who helped in the difficult task of opening Ostinho's eyes to the truths of life, that Lafayette had set up a plan to keep practically everything for himself, even the old man's personal gold jewelry. If they doubted it, let them remember the case of the gold and ruby crucifix on which no one had set eyes ever since Lafayette had borrowed it, alleging the need to add to the brilliance of a religious ceremony; let them remember the case of the Portuguese wrought-silver candleholders, of the gold-handled ivory cane, of the big gold chain, of so many others that the family's memory couldn't keep track of them. Coquinho became vehement. "If there's little flour, my bread comes first," he was said to have exclaimed rudely, just before expounding an elaborate course of action that involved the participation of a lawyer from Bahia, in order to appraise the validity of making the old man sign a few papers before kicking the bucket, and of course to indicate the nature and the terms of those papers. That implied a lot of work; there were inventories to be made, investigations, inquests, evaluations, and all of it covertly, so as not to arouse anyone's attention. Therefore they couldn't waste any time, for they were surely not the only ones to have brains and ambition among the countless known and unknown heirs of João Popó, whose precarious condition underlined the need for urgent measures.

Whether or not it is a falsehood cannot be stated without proof, but the fact is that Cochrane Popó started to visit sedulously the office of Dr. José Miranda, a lawyer reputed for his skill in organizing frauds, swindles, forgeries, humbugs, impostures, and even somewhat refined thefts. Such a persistent frequency had to mean interests in common, interests that perhaps were being manifested in certain papers that Cochrane, rarely Labatut, and never Washington, took to carrying back and forth between the island and Bahia, in ever more numerous trips. He transported them in the internal

322

pockets of a thick black overcoat, and they probably caused him to feel a bit cold, because whenever he arrived bringing papers, always at night, his overcoat was buttoned from top to bottom, his hands were in his pants pockets in a way that would be unmannerly if one could not see it was because he was feeling unwell, his shoulders drawn upward, his hat pulled down to his neck, his face in the dark, so cloaked that many people would only recognize him at night by the way all the Popós walked, just like their father, sort of hopping along. His new habit soon drew the attention of the villagers, and the most widespread suspicion was that he had taken to drinking in the company of a mistress he had found himself in Bahia, driven by the now practically fatal shame he had caused his father, and when he drank he got like that and ought to catch tuberculosis any day now. Now and then someone cannot resist, and as he looms all hooded at the end of the street, they shout that there comes the werewolf, the bugbear, a black devil, and so forth, but he does not care and goes on his way without answering.

As God writes straight with crooked lines, it was on account of this very practice that Zé Popó was able to do easily what he had to do on the island this Sunday. Zé Popó came to talk to his father, to tell him he was going to Paraguay to fight, his honor was saved. He had wanted to come before, but it was difficult for him to enter the village without being arrested, and in the second place, he had hesitated to talk to Maria da Fé about it; he thought she would be disappointed in him for wanting to go to a war that in fact was not theirs. But she was not disappointed; she told him she understood it very well. It was even a question of humanity, of duty toward the old man, who according to the news that always came from the island was bedridden precisely because none of his sons had enlisted.

"But that's not the only reason," he answered. "It's also because I want to go."

"Yes, I know; sometimes I feel like going too," she said, to his great surprise, as he had expected at least an ironic laugh. "I know all we think about this war and our country's situation is true, but this is also our country, all the more so because our people are the majority of those who were born and live in it. Therefore there's something in this war that is also ours; this is our country, or it will be someday. We have to do things in a way we believe is right; we can't forget our ideas, but we cannot forget other things, which are maybe secondary but exist anyway. I, too, feel goose pimples when we talk about Brazil, when I listen to anthems and see the people raise their eyes to the flag. Because it's not our flag, but it is our flag. But I can't go. I'm a woman, I'm a bandit, and I have a very great responsibility. If I let those ideas be forgotten, how is it going to be? But not you; you can go, you have to experience that too, to fight for what you love though it's denied to you, for what is ours but is turned against us, for what belongs to those who give the orders in wartime and dominate us in peace-time. That's the way it is; maybe life is like that; maybe you'll learn something you can teach us."

"I never thought . . ."

"I did; I've been thinking about it. I've been figuring you'd want to go since the Seventh of January, when some of our men were in Itaparica, disguised as parade Indians. And I also think the following: Could it be that after this war things might improve? The army has always been a ragged band of troublemakers, commanded by foreigners who despise everything here, and packed with equally foreign mercenaries, who also despise every-thing. The soldiers, who come from the people, have always been the worst weapon against the people, more than the police, more than the inquisitors. And even so the powerful snub the military, won't receive them in their mansions, won't allow their daughters to marry them, won't allow their sons to be in their company. Maybe now the army will understand, after sacri-ficing itself for those who stay home criticizing their actions and sending them orders that are impossible to follow; maybe now it will understand it belongs not to the masters but to the people; it's not the national guard but the people's guard; it's not a weapon against the people but one for the people. Maybe now it will realize that its side is our side, not the side of those it serves without getting even crumbs in exchange, let alone the honor of serving its own people. Many soldiers will come back as heroes, covered by glory and legends, and none of them will ever be the same after this war. And let's hope they become what they should be, the Army of the People. Yes, go, go fight in Paraguay, give back to your father his will to live, learn by doing and living. I didn't have a father, but I had my grandfather, who was more than a father to me, and once he did with me what I'm doing with you now. Go, do, learn, teach."

A brother is a brother, and no matter how different—one bucktoothed, the other toothless, one blond, the other dark-haired, one ugly, the other handsome, one bowlegged, the other knock-kneed—one fine day their brotherhood pops up, and *prrrrrr!* there they are, one the spitting image of the other, you see one, you see the other. That was the thought that came to Zé Popó as he skulked in the bushes, mulling over a way to get into the village and talk to his father that night. True, it was going to be a dark night, but people were used to recognizing anything in the dark; it was necessary to devise a way to get in his father's house unnoticed and to leave only after enlisting, for then he could not be arrested.

And he was thinking thus without hitting upon anything and almost deciding to have a go at it no matter what, when he saw himself walking along the beach by Friars Farm. He shook his head. What phantom was that, all in black, all huddled up, but resembling him so patently? He hid behind the shrubbery near the path the figure ought to take, so he could have the chance to see it close up, even if he probably would have trouble discerning its features. But he did not have to discern anything, because as soon as the figure got within ten yards of him, he saw it had to be his brother Cochrane Popó. He had never noticed how much they looked like each other, but they really did: he could see it in their postures, their bodies, and their gait, and he could remember it from the few times they had met face to face since becoming adults.

"Pst!" Zé Popó said, coming out from the shrubbery.

"Aaay!" Cochrane yelled, raising his arms and acting as if he was going to run, though he did not manage to move his legs. "Aaay!"

"Take it easy, Coquinho, it's me."

"Me who? Aaay! My time hasn't come yet, it hasn't come yet!"

"It's me, Coquinho, Zé Popó, your brother."

"Zé Popó? Are you really Zé Popó?"

"Yes, yes, it's me!"

"You scared the hell out of me, I thought it was death coming to get me, I thought it was the Devil. You shouldn't do a thing like that, I almost had a stroke! You shouldn't do a thing like that!"

"I'm sorry, I didn't mean it that way."

"What are you doing here? Are you trying to get arrested? One of these days they'll catch you, and I can assure you they won't be tickling you with feathers, you can be sure of that! If I were you, I'd be on my way out of here—what do you want here? You, too, start acting like a buzzard just because you heard the old man is not well?"

"Is it really bad?"

"Yes, yes. I mean, no one knows what's wrong with him, his fever is slight, he doesn't seem to have any disease. But he doesn't eat; he's lost a lot of weight and never leaves his bed now."

"Poor Father. Well, I want you to do me a favor."

"A favor from me?"

"Yes, a little favor that won't cost you anything."

"I don't know; my life is clean; I don't want to do you any favors so they can accuse me of helping bandits; I don't want my fate to be the gallows, as yours is bound to be."

"Now, don't be a crab louse!" Zé Popó said with impatience, and walked over to his brother.

A short while later, Cochrane Popó's shape could be seen, sinister in appearance, at Glory Square in front of Almiro's tavern, and someone shouted from inside:

"There goes the boogeyman!"

He didn't even look, and went on up the square. Contrary to what they expected, he didn't turn left to go home but took the little alley to go to

Channel Street. Walking almost noiselessly, he got to João Popó's door, found it ajar, marched into the entrance hall, and stopped in the drawing room, which was illuminated only by a glass-chimneyed lamp and by the little lamps of the oratory.

"Anybody home?" he shouted, clapping his hands, and a startled young black girl came to the drawing room, looked at him, and ran upstairs.

"*Seu* Coquinho is here, *Seu* Conquinho is here!" he heard her say upstairs.

Candinha came down the stairway soon afterward, carrying another lamp and squinting.

"What do you want here?" she asked. "You've stopped coming here, you never bother to visit the home you have abandoned, and now you drop in all of a sudden. What's come over you? I can't lend you any money; you still haven't paid back what you borrowed before, and I have to hoard coppers so all the needs of the house are taken care of."

"I want to see my father."

"That's not possible now; he finally had a little pap and looks like he's going to sleep."

"But I have to."

Without saying anything else, he grasped the table lamp and went up the stairway, with Candinha protesting behind him and holding him fully responsible for his father's death, if it was precipitated by that impromptu visit. He got in the room without doffing his hat and stopped by the old man's bedside. He was not sleeping, he was almost sitting up, his lips moving weakly in prayer. He was surprised when he saw his son, and spoke for the first time in a long time.

"You? What do you want here?"

"I came to tell you something important."

"Nothing you can tell me is important; you've got nothing to tell me. I don't want to see you."

"Who do you think I am?"

"Who you are. A poltroon, a coward, a milksop, a bum who's made me commit the unforgivable sin of giving him Lord Cochrane's sacred name! Get out of here—do you want to finish me off? Get out of here!"

"I'm neither Coquinho, nor Ostinho, nor Labinha," the man said, taking off his hat and unbuttoning his overcoat. "My name is José."

"You? Dressed in his clothes? What have you done? Have you killed your brother? O Lord of the Unfortunates, why dost Thou martyrize me at the end of my life? What terrible sins have I committed, for Thou to punish me so rigorously?"

"I didn't kill anybody, though it wouldn't have been much of a loss. I just gave him a couple of whacks because he wouldn't let me borrow his clothes, but I think I haven't even crippled him."

"I don't want to see you, either! On account of you—"

"I've come to tell you I'm going to embark for the Paraguay campaign."

At the end of her strength, almost too breathless to get to the door, Candinha could not believe her eyes after dashing down and back up the stairs, having fetched Militão and Boanerges, who slept in the backyard rooms. In front of the two blacks called to overpower the invader there unfolded a scene not of pain and cruelty but almost illuminated by a splendor coming from no one knew where, almost among antiphonies sung from both sides of heaven, father and son embracing each other, crying and laughing, João Popó sprightly like a young man, and Zé Popó, so strapping, looking like a little boy. Candinha passed out.

But João Popó did not even notice it, what with the embarkation set for two days ahead and his having to do the impossible to procure, even if he had to steal, a uniform and gear for his son and enlist him at all costs; fortunately, there was always a way to arrange those things. Because now he knew that on the fourteenth, his pigeon chest bulging out more than ever, the wind of the Motherland burning his lungs and bringing fire to his heart, his head floating in the air like a festive balloon, there he would be at dockside, mindless of the tears running down his face, raising his hat as high as he could to salute his heroic son, there waving his hand from the *Union*'s rail with a wide grin, sailing out to the fields of combat, a Popó in the first line of attack against the enemies of Brazil. As for Cochrane Popó, merciless fate saw to it that when Zé Popó put on his overcoat after giving him a couple of clouts, he took with him some of those incriminating papers, with the consequence that the old man found out everything and swore to disinherit the three conspirators, as sure as a son of his was fighting in Paraguay.

14

Tuiuti Camp, May 24, 1866

Not that he believed in those things, but the truth was that everybody who spoke for the goddess Yfah, the one who knows all, had always told Zé Popó that he belonged to Oshosse. A fine Oshosse accompanied him, a very fine, handsome, and valiant Oshosse, the *orishah* who hunts at dawn, eats roosters, and is an expert with the bow and arrow. Zé Popó would not say anything, but all *babbalaohs*, all *babbalorishahs* and *yalorishahs*, casters of seashells and beads, always said Oshosse was near him, without talking to others and without having ever seen him before. So he got used to his *orishah*, he learned to have a preference for his light blue color, and discovered to his great surprise that ever since his birth he had disliked everything Oshosse disliked. He disliked ants, he disliked okra, he disliked honey. They were all despised by Oshosse, but he did not know it before; he only found out after he had grown up.

Anyway, these are things that may or may not be, only Zé Popó, who was first put on KP duty, but after the inspection call was assigned to serve as one of the orderlies of his battalion's officer of the day and spent the first part of the morning without much to do, noticed a fleeting stir in the woods, something alive moving about—and he did not know why he felt sure it had something to do with Oshosse, he even felt there was a presage in the clouds, that the god wanted to warn him of something. Particularly because it was the weekday consecrated to him, the day, as Zé Popó was also forced to admit, when most of his own decisive moments happened. But could this *orishah* really be here? What was he doing so far from his cults and his people, here where there are no *orishahs* but other entities, monsters with ox heads and razor-tailed, serpentlike bodies, according to what is told by the men from these parts, as well as by the Argentines and the Easterners? But the truth was that according to the blacks more recently arrived from Africa,

328

Oshosse was a very Brazilian *orishah*, much more Brazilian than African, because in Africa he had got lost among hundreds of others, and many people did not even remember him. So it was not unlikely for him to have followed his Brazilian sons here, to fight by their side and to protect them.

Zé Popó decided that was all nonsense, he was giving his thoughts too much freedom. Instead of that, why didn't he try to see in order to learn, as Maria da Fé had advised? There was much to see and learn, even new ways of speaking, even that Bahians were not just those born in Bahia but all those not born in the Province of the South. Even new foods and drinks, which at first are repulsive but later become tasteful. Yes, much to learn, and Zé Popó gazed at the field surrounding the camp: the forest, the swamplands, the odd-looking shrubs. Tents multiplying down to the horizon—how many men could be there? Thousands and thousands, to be sure, and great generals, rarely seen, in their splendid uniforms and their legendary valor, whose names were whispered like those of gods by the soldiers talking around bonfires in the cold nights of the place.

A nice day, fortunately, a clear day, you could even say a nice-smelling day. But in the woods, what's happening in the woods? If it's Oshosse in the woods, what's he doing in those woods? What time can it be? Around ten, maybe eleven, Zé Popó sprang up to answer a call from his officer and on his way saw a group of soldiers scampering out of the forest.

"It's them!" one of the soldiers cried out.

If later they asked Zé Popó in what sequence everything happened right after, he would not have known how to answer, because all of a sudden a kind of rocket hissed and exploded, the call to arms sounded, soldiers scurried like ants from all sides, dismantling the musket stacks as if they were made of toothpicks, standards filled the air, the officers started to shout, and from the woods, the sand patches, and the swamps, among an infernal fusillade, erupted the Paraguayan cavalry and infantry, a copper-red wave made more fearsome by the cutting coruscation of their long, curved-bladed swords.

Pale but very firm, Captain Patrício Macário, his voice even stronger than usual, deployed his men in a triple line, firing upon one of the flanks of the enemy cavalry, which had penetrated the center of the Brazilian vanguard, forming a kind of wedge. Zé Popó, with a salty taste in his mouth and managing to see only what was ahead of him, obeyed the order to fix bayonets without paying attention to what he was doing, knowing just that he was to wait for a command to charge against the enemy riders, now hindered by the muddy terrain and cut off from their main body by a charge of Garibaldi Horsemen, who came down among great yells on their left wing, making a great many deaths. The bugle call for the bayonet charge sounded its murderous song, the whole band seemed to play in unison, and Zé Popó, running as if he would never want to stop, lunged ahead of the first wave, despite the fire from the Paraguayan

329

infantrymen on his left side, supporting their surrounded cavalry. He even had the sensation that he could see the deadly lines traced by the bullets and duck them, he did not believe he could ever be hit, and suddenly he was face to face with the first Paraguayan he had ever seen in his life, a strong, big, Indian-faced young man who did not know what to do on his restless horse, and without a lance or a sword. Zé Popó had never imagined that in a war like that people would look the enemy in the eye, but that was what he did, closing his own the minute that with a forward and upward thrust he gored the other's stomach, feeling his tunic tearing open, his entrails coming apart, and his blood spurting until it covered his fists. He waited until the Paraguayan, his mouth wide open, let go of his horse's trappings, which he had grabbed the moment he had been wounded, and would have stayed there looking only at that for a long time, until he remembered where he was and what he had to do not to get killed too. He spun his carbine around as if he suspected someone was trying to get at him from behind, and saw the enemy cavalry pulling back and being decimated by the Garibaldi Horsemen, while their infantrymen were scampering off, chased by a group of soldiers led by Captain Patrício Macário.

Some of Zé Popó's comrades near him applauded; he looked around in disbelief. There was not a single enemy in sight, there was nothing but comrades, and even the shooting had become a distant roar. They had won the battle, then; so this was a battle; he had been in worse scraps. He recognized, standing on his left and smiling with his hand on the visor of his cap, Joaquim Leso from Gameleira, son of the fisherman Né Leso, who had often helped Maria da Fé. He was going to embrace him, but as soon as he took the first step on the slippery terrain, he seemed to have been given a strong shove and slipped down to the ground on one knee. He looked around to see who might have pushed him, didn't find anyone close enough, and turned around in time to hear an awesome rumble come from the woods and see Joaquim Leso's head shattered by a projectile unknown to him. It had been a mistake, it had been a bad mistake, the battle was not over yet, it had just begun, and Death, seeking to touch every forehead, started again to soak with blood the fields and swamplands. During the whole day the carnage would proceed, wave after wave of men colliding among shouts, explosions, and groans, no one but Death seeing well what was happening, for no man sees a battle, he only lives his part to the end.

But Oshallah, the father of man, sees battles. Oshallah sees all, and he also saw when his son Joaquim Leso had his head destroyed by a cannon shell, so that he would never again captivate everyone in Gameleira with his placid manners, his friendly smile, and the confidence he inspired. He also saw when his son Oshosse darted out of the woods, visible only to him as a bluish streak, and shoved Zé Popó aside, preventing the shell from striking him. What did Oshosse want, what was he doing involved in that battle of men, in which many good ones were to die if it was so written?

He soon found out what Oshosse wanted, when the latter arrived in the home of Shango, the one who hurls stones. Shango was resplendent in his red and white colors, and greeted his brother with the proud joy that leaves him only when he is possessed by wrath. Oshosse addressed him with the following words:

"*Kah-wo-wo-kah-bee-eh-se*, hail, my great brother, king of Oyo, master of lightning, lord of the *ijeh-arah*, Jakoota, hurler of stones! Way over yonder, in a distant place called Tuiuti, a great battle is going on, the greatest battle ever seen in this side of the world, and in this battle many of our worthiest sons are dying, felled by a merciless and most strong enemy. There is no lack of courage in our sons, who are fighting for the honor they carry in their blood, but the fortune of the fray is uncertain, and I fear the time may come when not one of our brave sons will remain on his feet. Many times they bowed their heads to us, they fulfilled their obligations even with difficulty, and they gave us our food in offerings. Who will now remember me at daybreak, who will give me my rooster and my goat? Who will salute me by the edge of the forest? Who will honor your weapons, who will carry out your ceremonies, who will evoke you? It is not fitting that we stay out of this fight; rather we must enter it as if it were ours, for indeed it is. And that is the reason I am calling my brother Shango, master of fire and of the ax, of never equaled pride and courage, to accompany me to this great battle in which many of our worthiest sons are dying, so that we may change its face through the strength of our arms and our ingenuity."

The one who is named Jakoota, the hurler of stones, nodded his head, big as a church bell, and answered:

"*Oh-keh*, Oshosse, *Oh-keh-aroh*, imcomparable hunter of the dawn, king of the forests, lord of astuteness, unbeatable at the bow and arrow, to see you in my house brings joy to my heart! Yfah, the one who knows all, had already told me that this great battle was being fought and that many of my worthiest sons were dying in it. I know well that we are not supposed to join those combats, but I also know that we were compelled to join many of them, and all too often, to our great sorrow, we have not been able to help our people the way we would have liked. I admire your courage, I have witnessed how you are full of power and deserved importance, in this land in which you were not born, but reborn. I am proud to see you rising to help our sons, and even prouder that you came to call me to go with you to the battlefield. So I am going with you to the battlefield, taking my weapons and my strength, and together we will overcome those who want to kill our worthiest sons."

He spoke this and stood up, his stature comparable to a tower's and his gaze as hot as a hundred bonfires. And soon he was overwhelming the burning field of Tuiuti in the company of his brother Oshosse. What they first did was to enter the hearts and heads of their sons, bringing to their throats their ancestors' battle cries, each one a stunning Oshosse, each one an irresistible Shango, not one of them feeling any fear, not one feeling pain, all fighting like the wind bending back tall grass. Shango saw his son Capistrano from Tairu, surrounded by three Paraguayan horsemen in the swamplands, throw out his wet, jammed carbine, pick up a fallen lance, and make a grimace at one of the enemies, who spurred his horse in a maneuver that splattered bloody water all around and charged. Shango appeared to his son and said:

"Capistrano, it was not in vain that your head was consecrated to me, nor that you paid homage to me in my feast days, nor that your actions have always honored and aggrandized me. The food you served me, the animals you slaughtered for me, of all that I have a good memory. Hold your lance firmly, do not fear the enemy, for he fears nothing who is a good son of Shango. I am by your side and will fight by your side."

The brave son of the peaceful shores of Tairu, where fish are plentiful and women are pleasant, heard this and strengthened his resolve.

"*Kah-wo-wo-kah-bee-eh-see-leh*, my great father Shango! I had no fear when I often saw myself alone at sea, braving storms and big fish. I have never known fear and never trembled in the dark, and I will not tremble now, particularly having my father by my side. Before I die here in these foreign fields and my relatives make my *ah-shay-shay* in my absence and cast my sacred objects in the river water, I will take one of them with me, I will not die for nothing. And no one will see me turn my back or move my feet from here."

Shango, an incandescent red and white spark, found on the other side, on dry land, another son of his, Private Presciliano Braz, from Santo Amaro do Catu. Shango did not want to waste any time speaking to him, so he just entered his head and directed his eyes to the two other riders who were threatening Capistrano. Presciliano loaded his carbine and, guided by the god's hand, shot a bullet through the forehead of one of the riders, whose mount galloped off, dragging him over the puddles. Right away Shango brought another cartridge to Presciliano's hand, and once again he directed his aim unerringly. This done, he flew close to the rider who was charging against Capistrano, and when the rider lowered his lance toward his son, he puffed fire on him, such a strong puff that the man lost his balance on the saddle, missed his target, and was impaled on Capistrano's lance, almost a flag at the tip of pole.

Everywhere Shango and Oshosse could be seen fighting alongside their worthiest sons. But Oshosse saw that even with his efforts and his brother's extraordinary valor, their position in the battle was not good and the dangers were increasing. So the great hunter of dawn, expert at the bow and arrow, went to the abode of his brother Ogoon, master of iron and of tools, whose name is war itself. When he arrived, he spoke to him in the following manner:

"*Ogoon-eh*, peerless ironsmith, master of tools, singular in combat, whose name is war itself, bravest among all *orishahs*, I salute you, my most valiant brother! This very moment, in a place called Tuiuti, some of our worthiest sons are perishing in an uneven combat, attacked by a ruthless enemy. Our brother Shango and I are helping in this struggle, but our help is not sufficient, no matter how I dash through the woods supporting one here and another one there, and no matter how our brother Shango, the one who hurls stones, astounds the swamplands with his great prowess. That is why I am seeking the help of my insuperable brother, the great Ogoon, master of iron and tools, singular in combat, whose name is war itself, to join us in this fight, so that we will not come to regret the loss of many of our worthiest sons."

The *orishah* whose color is deep blue furrowed his brow, crossed his arms over his broad, naked chest, and answered:

"*Oh-keh*, Oshosse, my beloved brother, great hunter of the dawn, skillful at the bow and arrow! It brings me joy to see you in my house, but I must tell you, because I do not lie, that you would give me more joy if you had not come in the circumstances you came. Not that it bothers me to go to battle, for I dominate all weapons and tools, and my name is war itself, but because you have sought me only now, and I should have been the first to be called. I acknowledge the great valor and unequaled courage of my brother Shango, lord of lightning, hurler of stones, king of Oyo, but I cannot accept being shed of what is mine by right and vocation. With my arm the battle would be won and we would not lose many of our worthiest sons, now about to be in painful death throes in those fields called Tuiuti. But they forgot about me, and I should have been the first to be remembered. Where have they bowed their heads for me? Where is my place of offerings? What animals have they killed for me before the great battle? Who asked me to provide a good fate for the iron of the armaments? Who remembered me before the battle became untenable, even with the help given by you, unrivaled hunter, faultless archer, and by our brother Shango, who has never been surpassed in pride and courage? I am sad because this great battle is taking place where so many of our worthiest sons shall die, but honor does not permit me to take part in it. Do not mention this subject any longer, and I ask you that if you wish to remain in my house, with which you give me great joy, do not discuss something I do not care to discuss, because I know, and you know, that I am right."

He spoke this and pressed his arms even more strongly around his chest, scowling in such a way that the leaves trembled in the trees. Oshosse, courageous hunter, skillful at the bow and arrow, lord of the forest, also trembled before the just wrath of his irreprehensible brother. But he did not despair, and went to the house of Oshallah, the father of man. When he arrived, he said these words to him:

"*Heh-pah-babbah*, Babah-Oshah, Oshallah, father of man, son of Oloroon, lord of whiteness, highest among all, my father, the one who has the most names! For a long time now this son of yours has been suffering without ever seeking you to ask for anything, because I have always respected my fate and tried to understand there is a necessity in everything that happens. But now, in an unknown field called Tuiuti, many of our worthiest sons are dying in an uneven battle, facing a most strong and ruthless enemy. I myself and my brother Shango, called by me, are fighting in this battle, but our efforts are not enough to keep Death away from our sons' foreheads. I have just spoken to my brother Ogoon, master of iron and tools, whose name is war itself and whose valor is above any other, and out of hurt pride he will not agree to go to the battlefield to defend those he considers ungrateful, and nothing can dissuade him from that decision. I know this war is not ours and neither are we supposed to do anything in wars, nor Oshallah, father of man, wants to have anything to do with wars. But I would not be here if I did not know that your sons among men have also been dying in this great battle and this brings pain to your heart. I see my own life in this great battle and ask you to help me convince dauntless Ogoon, invincible in war, to fight alongside his sons."

That said, he embraced the knees of his father Oshallah, Oloroon's only son, lord of whiteness, highest among all. Oshallah took pity on his son, stroked his head, and answered with great friendship, saying the following words:

"I know well how you feel, for I have been observing your endeavor and your distress, as well as the death of our worthiest sons in the fields called Tuiuti. And you are right about what I can do, because indeed I can do very little. As you said yourself, this war is not ours, and neither is it up to us to interfere in it. There are many things that are written, there are many more that are up to men to write because their souls are free, and if they make war it is because they chose war. But do not be distressed, for it is also written that those who fight with faith for the good things they believe shall win in the end. As for Ogoon, master of iron and tools, insuperable in combat, whose name is war itself, you know very well his bravery can only be matched by his stubbornness. You said yourself that nothing would dissuade him, and he is like that."

The great Oshosse, fearless hunter, incomparable at the bow and arrow, persistent as the morning dew, became dispirited after his father spoke, all the more so because he knew it was all true. And he was already crying in the lap of Oshallah, lord of whiteness, highest among all, with pain for the loss of his worthiest sons, when Oshallah, his heart cramped by pity, spoke as follows:

"I do not want you to cry or be sad, my beloved son, unbeatable at the bow and arrow, hunter of dawn, prince of the woods. I promise you nothing, but I will give you an advice. Do not let vanish the hope that the valiant Ogoon, invincible in war, may change his mind and join his sons in this great battle. But do not be satisfied with just hope, for without diligence, hope leads but to fruitless dreams. Seek therefore your sister Yansan, queen of the winds and spirits, mistress of storms, plucky and bold as a typhoon, and ask for her help. She will not make up for the absence of Ogoon, whose name is war itself and whose arm knows no barriers, but she will give you new confidence, for even the most powerful trees fear the strength of your sister Yansan, tamer of winds and spirits. Go see her, salute her, and tell her that your worthiest sons and hers are dying in this great battle of the place called Tuiuti. Ask her to use her great gifts as a warrior to help out in the cruel combat of the great battle."

Oshosse pressed his head against his father's chest and without delay departed to the house of Yansan, mistress of winds and storms, guardian of spirits. When he arrived, he said:

"*Eppa-heh,* Yansan, mistress of winds and storms, queen of spirits, plucky and bold like a typhoon, of irresistible courage, I salute you! In the unknown fields of a place called Tuiuti, many of our worthiest sons are dying in the hands of a most strong and ruthless enemy. I have joined the combat in the company of our brother Shango, the one who hurls stones, redoubtable in the battlefield, but even so our sons are in danger and the fortune of the battle is very uncertain. So I have come to ask you to travel with me to fight in this place called Tuiuti, so that with your help the outcome will not be adverse to us, my great sister Yansan, queen of winds and storms, mistress of spirits, awe-inspiring in war!"

The goddess of scarlet adornments raised her lovely face of fulgent beauty and answered her brother Oshosse the following way:

"*Oh-keh,* Oshosse, my beloved brother, hunter of dawn, prince of the woods, expert at the bow and arrow, I welcome you for the joy your presence brings to my house! The beads of Yfah, the one who knows all, had told me that this great battle is being fought where many of our worthiest sons are dying, and that my brothers Oshosse, skillful at the bow and arrow, and Shango, the stone hurler, are engaged in it. I was beginning to find it odd that no one had summoned me to this fight, but the beads showed me that you would come to call me, and so I will follow you to the battle with all my arms. Today will not be the day the dead bodies of our worthiest sons will be strewn about the ground, for that will be thwarted by the strength of our arms and the power of my winds."

She spoke this and left with her brother for the fields of Tuiuti, where

Shango, the one who tames lightning, was riding the clouds in the fierce heat of the battle, toppling down enemies and shielding his sons, no more awesome vision being possible in heaven or earth. And soon Yansan, queen of the air, bolder than a typhoon, of whom even the most powerful trees are afraid, made her treacherous winds blow to instill bad spirits in the hearts of the enemies. Cowardly spirits, craven spirits, lying, dubious spirits, all those were blown by the goddess's winds, slipping into the nostrils of the Paraguayans and infusing great fear in them. Spirits of discord, spirits of envy, spirits of meanness, all these were also blown by the winds of Yansan, the one who does not run away from anything, and spread confusion among the enemies.

Oshallah, father of man, the highest among all, saw from his white throne what was happening, and smiled. But he still felt in his heart the sadness of his beloved son Oshosse, never surpassed in hunting, and so he called Eshoo, the one who eats anything, to his presence.

"*Laroh-yeh*, boy Eshoo, the one who eats anything, friend of dogs, messenger for the *orishahs*," said Oshallah, father of man. "I called you here for you to do me a service. Very far, in an unknown field called Tuiuti, a battle is happening in which many of my worthiest sons and the sons of other *orishahs* are dying, and this brings great grief to my heart. Ogoon, lord of tools and iron, whose name is war itself, by reason of pride and vanity does not wish to lend his arm to the defense of his sons. He complains they did not do their obligations to him, he was not the first to be called, he was forgotten, and now he refuses to fight. I do not want to expose myself to his tantrums and to the excesses of his ill temper, because I cannot step down from my greatness. So I order you to go see him, and without telling him anything I spoke to you, or that I spoke to you, convince him to go to battle, using one of your thousand ruses and stratagems, and do not ever come before me again if you do not accomplish your mission to my satisfaction."

Eshoo flew over to Ogoon's house and found him asleep. Then Eshoo, the one who eats anything, the perfect messenger, the one who laughs in the dark, slipped in the form of a dream into the sleep of Ogoon, king of iron, excellent in combat, whose name is war itself. But he did not go as Eshoo, he transmuted himself into the figure of Yansan, goddess of the air, of invincible resolve. Curving her rounded hips, Yansan appeared before Ogoon's sleeping eyes, and spoke to him:

"*Ogoon-eh*, great warrior! Yes, a great warrior who sleeps like an old sheep while his worthiest sons perish like trampled flowers in a foreign field called Tuiuti! Was it for you that I left the perfumed bed of our brother Shango, king of Oyo, lord of justice and thunder, the one who hurls stones? The one who is now fighting alongside his sons, not ceasing for a moment to attack and do battle according to his honor of an exalted combatant? *Ogoon-eh*, great

336

warrior, master of iron and tools, whose name is war itself, I hope your sleep of lead will bring you glory! I hope you will thus satisfy your small vanity, which sees nothing more important than the homages of those who are dying today without your protection, because you choose to lie here like a beautiless Oshoon, nourishing your spoiled little boy's pettiness. Do you think that this way you are punishing those you think have forgotten you? No, this way you punish yourself, belittling yourself in my eyes, making yourself insignificant and truly deserving of what you complain about with your arrogant sulking. My soft thighs you shall never touch again, my velvety breasts shall never again accept your head, I shall no more consent that you slip your hand under my dress, for if I formerly used to be stirred by the conquering hand of the lord of victory, now it brings me revulsion to be touched by the hand of one who sleeps while his people die. If formerly my womb wanted to receive your seed and be proud of it while bearing it and after it sprouted, now I do not want to have your children anymore; find yourself a woman with a low head and puny sentiments to serve as your seedbed, to bring into the world your children, who will soon see themselves fatherless, for you sleep out of vanity while your people die out of bravery. Farewell, great warrior, lord of iron and tools, whose name is war itself!"

Right after that Eshoo, the one who knows a thousand ruses and delights in stratagems, the one who laughs in the dark, left Ogoon's sleep and hid among the trees, because he knew that he whose name is war itself was going to wake up burned by the radiance of the great goddess Yansan's eyes, chilled by the glacial scorn that emanated from them, stunned by a beauty which let nothing else be seen when she was present, gone mad just to think he might never be with her again. Thus crazy with fury rose the great Ogoon, king of iron and tools, invincible in combat, boiling with hate because he could not answer her, for there is no way to give an answer to a dream. A dream he interpreted as a presage, as a whisper from Yfah, the one who knows all, trying to help him against a trap set up by treacherous Fate. So the brave son of Oshallah, lord of war, insuperable in combat, took his weapons and left for the great battle, the face of which he was going to change with the power of his irresistible arm.

Oshosse, the hunter of dawn, felt his great brother Ogoon had arrived to fight when a clangor of metal drowned the din of the battle, and the air became hot like the air blown by a bellows in a furnace. Ogoon, master of iron, lord of arms, whose name is war itself, halted his flight in the sky and said to his brother the following words:

"*Oh-keh*, Oshosse, my dearest brother, peerless hunter, expert at the bow and arrow! It is not fitting for me to sleep like an old sheep while our worthiest sons die in this terrible war. More important than the homages they did not pay me and the obligations they did not fulfill are their lives, and I cannot let pride go on blinding me. But if I have already wasted too much time by taking so long to answer your just summons, I will make up for everything with my fury and my most vigorous passion."

Oshosse's face was illuminated by an ample grin, and his chest filled itself with new ardor, in front of the towering figure of his great brother, tremendous like the thundering of bronze cannons. He saluted him with his arm raised, and said:

"*Ogoon-eh*, hail, king of iron, master of tools, invincible in combat, whose name is war itself. Your arrival is salvation to us. For all is turning into a nightmare in this awesome battle in which our sons are dying like flies and being mixed with mud, crushed by the enemy's merciless foot. Now with your arrival, I am sure we will turn the fortune of the battle in our favor and before the end of the day we will celebrate our victory."

Ogoon swooped down on the field like a squall, leaving nothing ahead of him, for he ignores all barriers and is known as the one who goes first. In front of him, on a green hillock, a group of soldiers was fighting around the standard of the Second Infantry Company of the Volunteers of the Motherland of the Island of Itaparica, held up in the air by Sergeant Matias de Melo Bonfim, consecrated to Ogoon ever since he was seven, one of his worthiest sons. He came from Amoreiras, where coral vines blossom and birds sing more often. He had left behind his two little children, Matilde and Baltazar, his wife, Maricota, his corn and bean field, his widowed mother, and his livestock, promising to come back as soon as he won the war. He had kissed his little girl, Matilde, and his little boy, Baltazar, at dockside, before embarking with his smart uniform to fight for Brazil, he had embraced his wife, Maricota, and his widowed mother and had sailed with the same proud smile he was showing now, as he held up the untouchable standard of the island's company, which floated in the breeze above the battle. Happy to see his son, Ogoon set out to encourage and comfort him, but the seething lead of an enemy bullet bit the lad from Amoreiras's tender neck, erased his smile, and clouded his eyes with the gray veil of Death, and Death drew out his soul through his mouth, a mouth which never again would kiss Matilde and Baltazar, and never again would speak to tell of the beauties of Amoreiras, where coral vines blossom and birds sing more often.

Ogoon let out a cry louder than the cannonade, and his warm tears of grief for his dead son sprinkled the ground, making the blood of the fallen even more steamy. The standard oscillated to one side and then to the other, until its flagstaff tilted over, and it got lost among the heads of the contenders. Like a tunny shoal ravaging a mullet shoal, like jaguars pouncing on their prey, like a swarm of berserk bees, like packs of wild dogs at each other's throats, Paraguayans and Itaparicans plunged into the fight for the possession of the standard. Corporals Benevides and Arimatéa, brandishing their carbines like clubs, made a wall around the standard, so their comrade Corporal

Líbio could raise it again. But as Corporal Líbio got up, his head was split by a saber blow, and he fell down dying, the memory of his lovely Gamboa, the land where seafood is plentiful and afternoons are cool, wafting out to the air from his torn brain. A Paraguayan hand seized the flagstaff, a lance blow to Corporal Benevides's chest felled him, and the enemy was about to rumple the untouchable banner, when Ogoon, lord of battles, master of arms, whose name is war itself, shot down from on high and yanked away the flagstaff with a tug that for a moment made it flutter among the clouds. Then the great Ogoon said to Corporal Arimatéa:

"José de Arimatéa, hold steady the untouchable standard of your land, which I am now handing over to you. This is your father Ogoon, lord of battles, invincible in combat, whose name is war itself, speaking to you! I have not forgotten my sons, and I am here to keep them from perishing in the hands of the cruel enemy. My pain is immense because I took too long to come and could not keep them from killing one of my worthiest sons, Matias de Melo Bonfim, pride and joy of Amoreiras, where coral vines blossom and birds sing more often. And for the same reason my fury is also unmeasurable, and I will now bring it down upon the enemy. I am at your side, you shall prevail! *Ogoon-eh!*"

And right away, like a whirlwind, like a steel windmill, like twenty thousand machetes pulverizing the air, the great Ogoon, invincible in combat, shielded his son Corporal Arimatéa, while he held the banner high up, immune to the bullets and lunges of the enemy. And then Ogoon, who knows no barriers and is called the one who goes out in front, ran over all sides of the battlefield, from one flank to another, from the vanguard to the rear guard, from foot soldiers to horsemen, from horsemen to artillerymen, bringing confidence and stamina to his sons, and death and terror to the enemy, still blind with hate for having witnessed the death of Matias, consecrated to him ever since he was seven. He was thus tirelessly over-whelming the field, when he came across Omoloo, who was waving at him from the shade of a tree, his poxy face covered by a veil of strings and beads. Then the *orishah* of plagues and diseases, master of leprosy and tetter, the one who kills without a knife, said to Ogoon:

"*Ogoon-eh*, most valiant warrior, lord of iron, master of arms and tools, hail my brother Ogoon, whose name is war itself! I saw in the beads of Yfah, the one who knows all, that this battle was being fought in those fields called Tuiuti, and that in it many of our worthiest sons were, and still are, being killed by a very powerful and pitiless enemy. The beads also told me that helping their sons in this great battle were our brother Oshosse, invincible at the bow and arrow, prince of the woods, our brother Shango, the one who hurls stones, lord of lightning, our sister Yansan, queen of winds and storms, who causes fear even in the tallest trees, and finally you, whom I mention last to emphasize I should do it first, Ogoon, owner of iron, master of arms, uncriticizable ironsmith, invincible in combat. Then I left my house and came here, because I, too, want to fight and help to keep many of our worthiest sons from dying. My heart also hurts when I see my sons fall, and I also cry from seeing them unassisted in this great battle, and decimated by a most strong and merciless enemy. So I ask you to take me to the battle, because I, too, want to fight to defend my sons."

But the great Ogoon was in a bitter mood, and spoke with bile in his throat and sulfur in his lungs, answering Omoloo with the following barbed words:

"*Ah-toh-toh*, Omoloo, owner of plagues, master of smallpox, lord of epidemics, the one who kills without a knife! It surprises me much that you have come to this great battle to try to take arms! Where is your old arrogance, which kept you from accepting the knife I gave as a present to the *orishahs* and to men, having rather killed your animals by exhaustion than saluted me for the use of my knife? Where is your sick pride, which makes your slaughters the only ones where I am not saluted? Now you want me to take you to combat, you want to handle the iron of my arms, you want to save your forlorn sons at the expense of my bravery and my war tools? Well, let me tell you, master of pustules, lord of deformities, owner of boils, king of leprosy and epidemics, unrivaled in rotting away alive and in slow death, I will not take you to any combat, here you shall not spread your pestilential breath and your contagious sweat. Carry your lame ugliness far away from here, find yourself another place and forget about your fantasies of being a warrior, for my arrival has changed the fortune of the battle, and by nightfall no enemy shall be standing on these fields called Tuiuti. You are of no usefulness here, and if my knife is not good enough for your sacrifices, neither is it good enough to help you seek glory, inasmuch as your glory is the glory of quarantines, of confinements, of hospitals, of leprosariums, and of cemeteries."

Thus spoke the lord of iron whose name is war itself, and set out to make more deaths among the enemy. Omoloo, lord of plagues, master of smallpox and furuncles, the one who does not eat crab, did not say anything back, and his poxy face could not be seen under his veil. But Oshallah, father of man, the one who has the most names, highest among all, saw Omoloo's face, and a shadow came over his joy. The great battle in which the *orishahs* had fought had been won, and the deadly peace imposed by Ogoon's never defeated arm with his brothers' help was arriving together with the night. But Ogoon's pride, dictating such harsh words at the god Omoloo, who does not forgive easily, would still cause a great many more deaths among his worthiest sons.

Oshallah, the one who sees everything, Oloroon's only son, highest among all, lord of whiteness, fountainhead of harmony, the one who is called by the most names, sighed. He had noticed that Paraguayan entities, strange beings of unbelievable appearance, were about to come out of waters, trees, and clouds to help their sons too. Oshallah, father of man, does not know either fear or uncertainty. He knows anguish, though, and again his heart felt pain, as he thought that that battle had been won, but the terrible days had just started when his worthiest sons would perish like flies, like flowers trampled by the cruel enemy, like tree trunks rotting from the fury of Omoloo, master of maladies, prince of plagues, owner of festers and pustules, the one who kills without a knife.

Corrientes, Argentina, June 30, 1866

With a little grimace of pain, Captain Patrício Macário stretched his left leg on one of the empty chairs of his table at the restaurant and cabaret *El Pericón*. He immediately remembered his father and his governesses because it was not a polite thing to do even at home, let alone in a public place. Well, he didn't give a damn. His leg felt much better, but it still hurt, especially when it was as cold as now, so he didn't give a damn, he had to stretch it out so that unnerving twinge would go away. Besides, considering there was no public except the waiter, the circumstances might even be considered private. He became annoyed once again for needing excuses, explanations, and defenses for his behavior, as though his father and governesses might come there to reprehend him, and as though he would pay any attention if they did. Recalling the air of permanent displeasure with which his father had treated him most of his life, he stroked his nose, smiled, then became serious again, in deep thought. He mused for some time about whether or not he missed his father, and could not make up his mind. Yes, maybe he did, maybe when he returned he might feel depressed. He found himself without references, was even a bit sorrowful. Although they had put him in uniform practically as a banishment, he had always thought of himself as someone who would always have relatives and a home. But now everything seemed empty in spite of his two brothers and his brother-in-law, suddenly turned into memories so distant that he felt very much alone. It was at the same time uncomfortable and exciting, a feeling so ambiguous that it bothered him and made him try to think of something else.

Yes, he was not really in public in that out-of-the-world place decorated in red and gold, full of tables with convoluted legs, stuffed furniture, portieres, rugs, bulky draperies, chandeliers suspended on heavy chains, windows opening onto carved black-wood balconies. Everything dilapidated and threadbare, the velvet of the backs of the chairs frayed, the candleholders dented, the windowpanes patched with paper and glue, and in a corner of the wall a large hole, barely covered by a wood partition. The waiter, attired in a kind of livery, also worn out but very clean, was waiting with dignity to be called, his hands crossed over his stomach. Patrício Macário took a liking to him, finding amusement in his turkeylike manner, puffed up and at the same time skittish. He looked around once more. No matter how decrepit, how bad, the place was princely compared to the hospital, the memory of whose stench almost made him gag. Fortunately, he had been discharged and given permission to convalesce in the city until he was fit enough to take a boat up the river, back to the camp of Tuiuti to resume his duties. His leg had stopped twinging and throbbing, the scar on his face was no longer hurting, he breathed deeply and felt almost happy. No, he felt completely happy, happy to be alive, to be healing, to have had his conduct in combat once again praised by superiors and subordinates, to have received part of his overdue pay and a remittance from Bonifácio Odulfo, to have found that half-ruined but pleasant place, to have nothing to do but whatever struck his fancy. He waved at the waiter, who rushed to the table and stopped two steps from it, bending forward, his head very erect.

"¿Para beber, que hay?"

With a gesture that almost startled Patrício Macário, he pulled out from under his vest a kind of folder on whose faded cover one could still read *Carta de Vinos*, in filigreed letters. He spread it out in front of his customer, whose eyes opened wide with surprise.

"¿Hay eses vinos todos acá?"

"Casi todos, mi Capitán, casi todos. ¿Puedo hacer, con su permiso, una recomendación?"

"Sí, claro, por supuesto."

"El Clicó, mi Capitán," he said, taking a step forward, halting with a click of his heels, and pointing to a name in the folder.

Patrício Macário read: *Clicquot, Finísimo Rojo de Francia.*

"El Clicó," he repeated, trying to imitate the waiter's pronunciation.

"Sí, Señor Capitán. Es el preferido de nuestros mejores clientes; todas las personas de más fino gusto que vienen acá lo prefieren."

Patrício Macário laughed and looked around. What persons? The waiter followed his look.

"Está así por causa de las guerras," he explained, with a look of wounded pride. "Hay muchísimo poco tiempo, tuvimos acá la ocupación del General Robles y del Comandante Resquin, siempre con grandes daños, Señor Capitán."

He pointed his chin to the hole in the wall. "¡Un cohete, Señor Capitán!"

"¿Un cohete?"

"Sí, un cohete. Ssssi . . . ¡Bám! ¿Lo comprende?"

"Sí. Ssssi . . . ¡Bam! ¿Cohete, se llama?"

"Sabe mejor que yo, Señor Capitán."

"Bien, hoy no me interesan cohetes o canones. Acepto la sugestión. El Clicó."

The waiter went into the pantry, and after a very short while came back carrying a colossal tray, practically a little silver tabletop, dwarfing the dark bottle and the sparkling crystal glass poised on it. Making a flourish, he started holding the tray just with his right hand, displaying on his face the effort it took to bear such a weight with only one arm, but insisting on maintaining his sylphic gestures until he managed to deposit his huge load on the table.

"*Traga una otra copa,*" Patrício Macário ordered.

"*¿Está mala esa, Señor Capitán? Es cristal veneciano, el mejor de la casa, yo mismo . . .*"

"*No, no, es para Usted. No me gusta beber solo.*"

The employee laughed, bowed effusively, and without much conviction refused the invitation. Patrício Macário insisted, affecting severity, and he finally agreed, but the captain would have to understand the need for a certain reserve. In spite of the apparent neglect in which he found it, that house had a great tradition, a very proud one. It had been founded by Frenchmen—real Frenchmen!—many years ago, and was now the property of a Castilian family, very kind people but a little strict. Besides, with the installation of the warehouses, the hospital, and other establishments of the allies, there were more people in town, more business. Other customers might arrive, and he might have to call more waiters, who at that time were busy with other chores. *Y por la noche, ah, el Señor Capitán no conoce las noches de sábado en El Pericón. ¡Son memorables—la música, los vinos, las lindas mujeres!* So if the captain did not mind, he would hide his glass after the customary toast, so that if someone came he would not be caught *en violación flagrante de los reglamientos.*

He ran off to fetch his glass, and poured some of the wine for the captain to taste. Patrício Macário had never imagined that a sip of wine, a simple little sip of wine, could be so inebriatingly delicious, so indescribable in the warmth it brought to his mouth and stomach, in the soft wave that engulfed his head, in the urge to breathe more deeply that overcame him, in the sudden clarity that established itself, making all the red velvets of the room appear to increase in brightness and size. He closed his eyes, leaned back in his chair, and moaned softly, while the very mild tartness of that little sip spread all over his mouth, biting and sweetening it at the same time and giving a delicious perfume to the air he was inhaling. He looked up; the employee bowed, filled his glass, and returned to his stiff posture.

"*Sirvase,*" Patrício Macário said.

"*¿El Señor Capitán hará un brindis?*" the waiter asked, raising his filled glass higher than his head.

"*No, hagalo Usted. Debe solamente disculparme porque no puedo ponerme de pie, como es la obligación de un caballero.*"

"*Es un honor para mi, Señor Capitán.*"

"*Adelante, adelante.*"

He listened to the toast attentively, though he could only understand a word here and there; the waiter seemed to be repeating fervently something very complicated, maybe a poem memorized in his youth. He finished with vivas to Brazil, Argentina, freedom, friendship between sister nations, and the many victories the captain was going to have in his glorious career in arms. Patrício Macário, very anxious for him to get it over with and barely able to hold back his urge to drink, thanked him with a *muy bien* and a brisk nod, then upturned the glass, drinking all its contents in one draft. He wanted to pause midway but was unable to; he had never drunk anything that did him so much good, anything he needed so much. Maybe he should not drink, having just left the hospital, but he did not feel weak nor had he taken any medicine, for the only thing they had done had been to wash his two wounds with a phenol solution and wrap them in new bandages every two days or so. And what the hell, a man has a right to a drinking spree after having been through so much suffering and seen so much misery.

Those were the very words he said to Pedro Vidal, the waiter, when a couple of hours later he had trouble balancing a bottle, one of the eight he was using to demonstrate the arraying of forces in the Battle of Tuiuti. Although he disappeared frequently behind the partition to fill and empty his glass, Pedro Vidal was one of those drunks who, the more they drink, assume a more collected, dignified poise, so he was able to help Patrício Macário with the bottle.

"Muchas gracias," Patrício Macário said, looking at the bottle with satisfaction. "This one no can fall, es el General Osório. Muy bien, entonces we have here Osório, en el hilltop, see? Here en este side está Mallet with la artilleria, here are las ditches with los abatises and las several defensas against el enemy cabalry, comprende? Muy bien, here we have Sampaio, Sampaio acá, la Thirda División. Here los hombres del General Flores, see? Entonces, Flores. Muy bien, here Flores and here Mitre! Mitre! Argentina! En Mallet's right sido, comprendes? Here los bushes, here la foresta, here la lagoona. Here, el general headquartelos, see? This way comes later el paraguayo Diaz, bien over el Thirda División, Sampaio. Sampaio here. El Diaz, when the battala starts, comes por acá, él ataca in this dirección, understando? Muy bien, the batalla breakas out here, see? Un Congreve rocketo—sssssssiz-bám!—many of them bursting, explodindo here, in the medio of el campamiento bivouacado here. Yo was here, and told el buglero to play el assemblea call, you know it? Ta-tara-ta-ta-ta-ta-ta-tara-ta-ta, tororeh, tororeh, tororeh . . . I had it played because mi posición es here, behindo this bottle, this botellita, see? Entonces I ordered assemblea, had todos fall in en this formación here. Tienes bread? Con pieces of bread I can demonstrado mi formación with exactitud. Mi bueno Vidal, fraterno comrada, when you go fetcho la botella you go fetcho now you could take la oportunidad to bring dos or three breads, I no care if they are old because they no to eat but solamente to complete this estudy. This time, I está make el toast, now I see how grandiosa this batalla was! Fifty thousand hombres, maybe sixty thousand, and el viejo Sampaio contra-attacking el Diaz like a horricane! Entonces what usted es waiting for, mi bravo Pedro Vidal? Uno dies of el thirsto in la grande city of the siete streams? El supplymiento of wines of la grande house El Pericón es exhaustido?"

He watched Pedro Vidal make his way to the pantry and noticed only then that other customers had arrived. On the other side of the vast salon, a bit ill-defined in the dim light, their long shadows distorted by the recesses and saliences on the walls, two groups were occupying two large tables. Standing next to a smaller table a little to the right, a third group was about to sit down. Patrício Macário resented it. Now El Pericón was not the same, there were intruders, soon there would be noises of plates, silverware, laughter, and conversation, there would even be more light, as in fact had started to happen, with new waiters appearing from nowhere and lighting the chandeliers, so that the room, to his displeasure, seemed to rejuvenate, like an oldish woman who is pretty only at night. But he soon resigned himself to it, and figured that with Vidal's help he would manage to keep his territory relatively protected, and besides, the new bottle had arrived. He filled the glasses, picked up his cane to get up; his bad leg seemed extraordinarily well, although he needed the cane because he became unsteadier as he stood up, and had to wait with his eyes closed for his dizziness to get better. He opened his eyes, stretched out his hand for the glass, and saw Captain Vieira in front of him in an impeccable uniform, glistening boots, gold galloons, a scintillating baldric, and immaculate white gloves, one of which was on his left hand while the other hung casually from one of the cuffs of his tunic sleeve, where he had tucked it in the manner of the most elegant officers.

"My noble Captain Macário!" he said, holding out his hand with a grin that twisted his mustache. "I'm very glad to see you! I see you have recovered fully," he added, pursing his lips as his eyes ran over the sea of bottles and glasses on the table, "and are ready to go back to the rigors of the camp, which I've only managed to leave today, and even so for a mission that will take very little time. We landed here just a few hours ago, and—"

"Vieira," Patrício Macário said without thinking, "you're the last person I wanted to see tonight. Go away."

"Hey, what's the matter? What's come over you? Has the news about your forthcoming promotion to major gone to your head?"

"Promotion to major? What promotion to major?"

"Don't tell me you don't know. Everyone in the camp's heard about it; the old man makes no secret of it."

"Is that really true? Who told you?"

"It's like I said, everyone knows, it's in the bag. Even old Polidoro, who's not the most laudatory of men, has spoken about you at a General Staff meeting. It's in the bag."

"Major?"

"Not yet, you're still a captain, and therefore guilty of a serious discourtesy to a fellow soldier and officer by not inviting him to your table to toast your coming promotion."

"No, no toasting. Toasting is contagious. Let's limit ourselves to drinking."

"You like Clicquot?" Vieira asked after sitting down, inspecting one of the bottles critically. "Well, I don't have to ask; it's obvious you do. It tastes good to me too. A bit sharp sometimes, but always serious, wouldn't you say?"

"Huh? Yes, sure. Major, huh? I wasn't expecting that, I really wasn't."

"What do you mean, you weren't expecting it? Of course you were! If your bravery in combat weren't enough, and you've really got plenty of it, you'd still have what's most important, an influential family with excellent connections."

"What? What do you mean by that? You mean to say I keep sending letters to beg for favors and getting close to superior officers to fawn upon them? Is that what you mean?"

"No, not at all. I spoke in a general way. You can't deny that good connections and an important family do count, can you?"

"If they do, it doesn't matter to me. I do my job, I carry out my duties, and the rest doesn't matter."

"Life is really very ironical. Ever since that episode in Itaparica, when I was already a captain and you were still a lieutenant, you have been getting promotions and I haven't. Mind you, I'm not making any insinuation, but modesty aside, my combat record is richer than yours, I've got more years of service than you, and you see how things are."

"You still have the gall to mention that Itaparica episode, with your so-called pincers movement and your night excursion?"

"I acted in accordance with elementary tactical rules, the norms applicable to a situation like that."

"And it turned out the way it did."

"You know perfectly well I can't be blamed for the failure of that mission. We were facing extremely hard, unusual conditions and a numerous, savage enemy familiar with the terrain, to the point that even with the tenacious resistance we offered them, they were able to inflict very heavy casualties on us, which, added to the paludal insalubrity of the region, forced us to retreat, enabling us to keep our casualties from being greatly increased."

"That is what you wrote in your report, with those very same words, if I'm not mistaken."

"More or less. I've always had an excellent memory and a certain literary propensity."

"It's one of the most cynical, dishonest pieces I've read in my whole life. Don't talk to me about that report; it makes me ashamed to think of it."

"Now, let's not be so sanctimonious; we're both seasoned men, we know reality. What did you want me to do, destroy our careers with a different report? At the time, you agreed with everything in it, I remember very well."

"Yes, that's true, but it was out of inexperience. I wouldn't have agreed if it had happened today."

"I believe it's easy to say that now."

"Vieira, why do you think everyone has your character; why do you judge everyone by yourself?"

"Because I think it's funny that like me you have accepted privileges for having served in a war zone and others derived from our heroic action in Itaparica, and now you decide to say you wouldn't accept them. Not only would you accept them, but anyone else would—that's the way life has to be led. What do you think the others are, a choir of vestals? If I could just tell everything I know . . ."

"Look here, Vieira, I just didn't contest the report, and I accepted the privileges so as not to contest it."

"But the truth is, you didn't contest it. And why should you? I've got more military competence than many who boast of theirs and have reached positions compatible with that boasting. Right now we're suffering the consequences of the incapacity of many of our commanding officers. You must know that life in the camp became hellish, under Paraguayan bombardment night and day. One of these days, weakened and unnerved by this impenitent bombardment, we'll have a new confrontation, and that time it'll be goodbye. I think not even your much-lauded manic bravery will be sufficient to save us from a debacle. And why is that? Because we didn't take advantage of our victory to pursue the enemy, to decimate them as much as possible and occupy new positions. It's the clear lesson of the great strategists, it's really basic in military theory."

"How could we possibly have pursued the enemy, Vieira? Pursue the enemy with officers like you, who disappear when combat starts, whom no one sees while the fire lasts, who limits himself to bullshit about the lessons of Zis-and-zat and Zat-and-zis and God knows what other Frenchmen, as if we were partaking in exercises about Napoleon at the academy? What do you know about real battles, about a real military operation, you virgin sword, rascal, poltroon, liar, and unprincipled scoundrel!"

"Measure your words, Macário! Measure your words before you come to regret them bitterly! I can make you swallow your words!"

"You can't do anything, you rat! You can't do anything! The same way you watch your soldiers dying without command or assistance, humble people, boys barely out of their diapers, people to whom you feel superior when actually you're very inferior to them, this same way you'll listen to whatever the hell I feel like saying to you. For your ludicrous sword I don't need more than my cane! The army that will come out of this war will have no more place for bums such as you, who disguise their knavery with affected manners and false knowledge, who only live to seek privileges, who use their position to obtain more and more benefits, who make their uniforms a polishing rag for the boots of the powerful, who turn military life into the garbage can of sponges who don't know how to do anything except to give themselves airs and to lay their hands on whatever they can, lying, cheating, bragging, extorting, and intimidating, even believing in their own tall tales, which they foist upon themselves and others in order to be able to look at themselves in the mirror. You lying, cowardly, venal, rascally conniver, brave against those who cannot resist you, you irresponsible parasite, you cynical profiteer and extortionist, you hypocrite, you thief! Son of a bitch! Did you hear that? Son of a bitch! Did you hear that well? I mean you, Captain Vieira. You turd in uniform, walking pustule, decorated sewer, I mean you! I mean you, you son of a bitch!"

"Watch out, I might shoot you!" Vieira said, very flushed, almost purple, and taking two steps back.

"Go ahead, you dog. I called you a son of a bitch. Did you hear that? Son of a bitch, son of a bitch, son of a bitch! Son of a bitch! Cuckold! Bastard! Pansy! Thief! What else do you want me to call you to prove you won't do anything? Son of a bitch!"

"Macário, the world makes many turns, and the day will come when everything you're saying to me now will be paid back with interest. Listen to what I'm telling you. I won't spoil my career by shooting down an ignoramus such as you, a mere troglodyte who considers himself a military man. You're drunk, and I neither argue nor fight with drunks."

"Come back here, you bastard! Come back here to make me swallow my words!"

But Vieira did not come back, and Patrício Macário did not feel like going after him. He considered talking to the waiter to explain to him everything that bothered him in people like Vieira, everything that caused him this uncontrolled anger, this feeling of impotence and frustration, but he decided he couldn't, he could never explain it to anybody, all he could do was hope there was someone, and there should be, who felt the way he did.

He sat down again, picked up a glass, and raised it, but did not bring it to his lips. What could he do now—eat? Was he hungry? He had to eat anyway, so although he was not hungry but only wanted to eat because he felt it was his obligation, he asked the waiter to bring him something substantial. He ate much more than he had expected to, and feeling less drunk but still very drunk, ended up sitting next to a woman called Corazón, professing a love for her he had never before experienced, and leaving to go sleep with her in a little room decorated with paper flowers, in *la plaza del Cabildo*.

15

One should not espouse a rigid determinism about such matters, because other factors, such as race, play crucial roles, but the truth is that the clear definition of the year in four distinct seasons is civilized and civilizing. Nations such as Brazil, where there is virtually only changelessness from January to December, seem destined to backwardness, and there is an abundance of historical and contemporary examples. Even culturally, seasonal variations assume enormous importance, since they force a diversification of interests and activities in keeping with climatic alterations, so that the peoples exposed to them have a wider range of aptitudes and a necessarily sharper sensitivity. Moreover, cold stimulates intellectual activity and obviates the inertia common to the inhabitants of torrid and tropical zones. One does not see laziness in Europe, and the inference seems fully justified that this happens on account of the goad of a cold climate, which, as has been demonstrated, while causing the constriction of blood vessels and the lowering of the temperature of lubricious viscera, not only creates organic conditions propitious to the pursuit of superior work and invention, be it technical or artistic, but also cohibits the somnolent sensualism of Negroes, Indians, half-breeds, and other inhabitants of hot climates, even whites who do not manage to overcome, through the pure force of the civilized European spirit, the overwhelming pressures of the physical environment. Thus, while one becomes stronger and greater, the other becomes weak and perverted.

The facts are clear, Bonifácio Odulfo thought. Not to see them is, as people say, to want to block the sun with a sieve. When was he going to write this essay, which came to his mind so finished, so whole, so polished and fluent, so founded on the evidence of facts and of dispassionate reason? Maybe never, he concluded with a certain sadness, for bankers don't write essays, nor is it convenient that certain things be said, though known by all.

It was a pity, as it had also been a pity that he had not been able to write down the poem that gushed over him as he huddled up to brave the wind that was sweeping downtown Lisbon and insisted on walking down Ouro Street, so he would have the thrill of stopping at the entrance of Comércio Square and come upon Ribeira das Naus, the pregnant, gray vastness of the Tagus River mouth, wavelets rippling over the ramp, as if that were the place where the sea began and the Infinite opened itself. O conquerors of oceans! O dauntless mariners, explorers of the Universe, dominators of worlds, travelers of the Unknown! Glory to you who opened the way . . .

Maybe the tears that flowed from his eyes then, like the ones now flowing while he looked down at São Bento Street from high up on a balcony, had not been caused only by the freezing wind striking his eyes. Maybe it was really emotion, the same emotion that was returning to him now, though serenely, as he gazed at the colorful houses of Bairro Alto and Estrela, which he could see from each side of the balcony. He squeezed the wrought-iron parapet, indifferent to the cold in his hands. What a beautiful small palace! No, not a small palace, a real palace, a residence worthy of a king. What a difference from the squalor of Brazilian homes, where the absence of comfort, refinement, and luxury was named "austerity," with undisguised embarrassment. And it was only one of the residences of his host, the marquis of Sassoeiros. No doubt the best of them, for he had insisted on treating his guests with nonpareil magnificence, putting at their disposal the palace with all its facilities, more than sufficient to house Bonifácio Odulfo, his wife, Dona Henriqueta, the servants brought from Brazil, and the Portuguese house help. But there were others: the villa in Lisbon, the villa in Sintra, the Estoril mansion, the what's-its-name in Restelo, and so forth, in a succession impossible to memorize, which brought Bonifácio Odulfo a twinge of envy. How could one be that refined in Brazil? Not even being rich is worth it in Brazil, he thought, taking his hands off the parapet and blowing into them to warm them up.

"How cold!" trilled Henriqueta, very coquettish in her wool-collared redingote, which she had gracefully put over her pink nightgown. "Close it, close it, Boduzinho; this cold kills me! What were you doing out there in the cold—do you want to get a chill and kill me with worry?"

"You're talking like a Portuguese already; it's wonderful how you have talent for those things!" a charmed Bonifácio Odulfo said. "And you're beautiful like a princess! My little Portuguese princess!"

"But I've never really spoken the Brazilian way."

"That's true, you've always had a very educated speech; it was one of the things that first attracted me in you. And your father, the old baron, speaks exactly like a Portuguese."

"He's always made a point of that. He always says that by his voice people will always know he's never lived among Negroes and is a Coimbra graduate."

350

"He's quite a wit, the old boy. I was thinking how lovely this house is, this palace, don't you think so? We've commented on that before, but I never get tired of comparing this wealth and refinement to the poverty of Brazil, where no matter how much money you have, you can't really have anything like that. It's not that you can't buy these things, import them, but there's something else, which you can't import—this atmosphere, this civilization in the air. . . ."

"Don't even talk about it; that's all I've been thinking about. How nice it is to be able to walk on decent streets without ever seeing a Negro or a tatterdemalion, as in Bahia, among people who speak correctly and obviously have a minimum of culture, even the poor people. Incidentally, you criticized me, but now you must agree that it was a good idea to bring the two white maids and Miss Gordon, and it was a very good idea to bring your lackey, what's-his-name? I always forget."

"My lackey, hah-hah! Octaviano. Yes, I didn't want to bring him; I thought I would be allowing him too much importance by offering him a trip to Europe after so few years of service. It's true; you're right. I thought that bringing only the Negroes was sufficient, but we would be greatly embarrassed . . ."

". . . if we gave everyone here the impression we live among Negroes and there are only Negroes in Brazil, which incidentally is what many of them think, and it makes me fume with rage. A man of your importance cannot take care of trivial matters personally, nor use a black to deal with them. Imagine the embarrassment! Now that the marquis has granted us the use of his house and his help, and so insists that we make full use of them, I don't think I'm taking any of the Negresses along on my shopping; I'm taking the Portuguese maids and Miss Gordon; I'm not even taking the Brazilian white maids."

"You're still going shopping today? Remember today is the reception at the royal palace, it's the eve of the celebrations for the restoration of independence; the streets are very busy. . . ."

"Oh, the reception in the palace! King Dom Luis—did you see his portrait? He has beautiful blue eyes: you can see he was born a king. What do you mean, am I going shopping today? If you knew how much there is to buy in Chiado, if you knew how they have everything here while we have nothing back there, if you knew how many things I still need to be perfect at the reception, a wife truly worthy of you, you wouldn't say that! Oh, what jewels, what gems, what perfect gold, what splendor! You can't imagine what it means for a feminine spirit imprisoned in the backwardness of Brazil to go to Lisbon shops and see how things that back there leave people agape are deliciously common here."

"I understand it perfectly, my worshiped one, and nothing delights me more than seeing you like a naughty child, with your eyes sparkling, eager to go shopping. But you haven't seen anything yet. We're still going to Paris, to London. . . . You can't imagine the opulence of Napoleon III's court, of the City of Light!"

"Yes, I can, I can indeed, and I'm also going to go shopping when I get there! I intend to take full advantage of this trip, and I'm going to use every minute to buy the things we need, besides other things, important things that will change our lives. We're not ordinary people."

"All right, all right, I'm getting used to your being right all the time. Have you had breakfast?"

"No, but it's been served, and I'm hungrier than I can remember in a long time!"

"Watch your manners, naughty girl! Who ever saw a lady talking that way about her appetite?"

"Yes, but have you seen all the foods they have here?"

"Of course I have; haven't we been here for three days now?"

"Then how come you're not excited? Everything is so much better, of such better quality. . . . The sweets, the meats, the preserves, the seafood . . . Ow!"

"Behave yourself, little girl!"

"Have you seen the apples? My favorite fruit is the apple—oh, what fresh, delicious apples! And the cherries? And the plums? Oh, why don't we have fruits in Brazil?"

"Better go have your breakfast now—go, go, before you eat me."

"Bow-wow! Wow! Wow!"

"Go, go. I'm just going in the bathroom for a minute to trim my beard and will join you in no time."

"Don't take long!"

"I won't. Now go."

He did not move before she got to the door of the room where breakfast had been set on the table, opened it, and turned around to wave her hand at him. What joy in living, what restless sensitivity, what wonderful intuition in a woman still so young! He had to confess he had learned a lot from her, that he was learning something new every day. He had got used to a certain self-sufficiency at the head of his businesses and his family, so he used to think he had little to learn. But he had been mistaken, because that girl with her impish ways in private and the public demeanor of a lady was truly the ideal companion for a man like him. She had opened his eyes to aspects of life whose importance he had not acknowledged before, she had educated his taste, she had called his attention to many things of great relevance; in short, she had made a new man out of him. Teresa Henriqueta Vianna Sá de Britto Ferreira-Dutton, practically a princess by origin and a queen by calling, the future mother of his children, who could not but turn out to be princes.

He went into the bathroom absentmindedly and looked at himself in the mirror. He raised his face and found himself even good-looking, with a visible nobility of features, a lithe young man at thirty-five. So many things behind this face, so many things inside this head! He had trouble opening the washbasin faucet and getting the right mixture of hot and cold water. Amazed once more by such an efficient mechanism, he almost could not take his hands from the spout to wash his face, so good was the feeling of the water running over his fingers. He was proud to remember that he had not needed to consult the Portuguese servants about how to use that and other modern apparatuses; he was sure his conduct would continue to be perfect and he would not be ashamed of it later. He knew all the right words, he knew what to like and what not to like, he did not appear nervous on social occasions; no one could say he was a provincial lout, typical of a backward, obscure country, with no character of its own and nothing to make it notable. And this was just Portugal—whose importance had been diminishing for everyone to see—and could not be compared to the great nations of Europe.

He raised his face again. If he had been born in France or England in conditions equivalent to the ones he had enjoyed in Brazil, what heights would he not have reached? It was true that with the suspension of remittances from Brazil due to the Paraguayan campaign, his importance in Portugal had grown considerably. It had not been for nothing that Minister Loulé himself, the prime minister, had insisted on honoring him with a personal invitation to the celebrations of December 1. The marquis of Sassoeiros, who treated him with so much attention and pomp, also had his reasons to be so pleasant to him, because the Brazilian sales of the products he imported from France had been practically suspended due to exchange problems, making it very important to be friends with an influential Brazilian banker, able to circumvent certain problems. There was also the matter of the marquis's connections with the duke of Saldanha. The marquis had mentioned those connections in a special way, as if he was trying to hint at something he could not be too clear about for a while. But Bonifácio Odulfo suspected that it was a plot of the greatest import, involving the possibility of Dom Luis's taking over the Spanish Crown, for which it was said he had the support of Napoleon III. Would an Iberian federation, widely held to be the duke of Saldanha's objective and supported by interests such as the marquis of Sassoeiros's, really be established? And in this historic changing of the face of Europe, could the participation of the one now prosaically looking at himself in the mirror be decisive, as far as the provision of capital and financial counseling were concerned?

Bonifácio Odulfo squinted to get a better view of himself; he saw better that way. Yes, he was an important man, a very important man, who surprisingly was viewing as his peers men who could decide the fate of the world. And very soon, together with men as important as he, he would be entering the imposing halls of Ajuda Palace. Brazil was backward, infinitely backward and unknown, but he was important, and personally he had nothing to be ashamed of. As a matter of fact, he would have nothing to be ashamed of if he were invited by the emperor of France himself, or by Queen Victoria. But of course he wouldn't be, because, as he thought with irritation, Brazilians are important only to the Portuguese.

Intrepid Village of Itaparica, May 14, 1870

Shame, shame, shame of shames! Supreme shame, indelible shame, a shame so heavy that it leaves João Popó unable to live with himself. If before that, in the hardest moments of a very hard life, they had never seen him with a glass in his hand, now they would; it was too much. And let them say whatever they pleased; he wouldn't give a hang, just as he didn't give a hang about the look from Lindaura of Jacinto, when he went into her husband's grocery stall and ordered a jug—not really a jug, almost a pot—of sugarcane rum, real sweat from the still, something to make the drinker's breath catch fire when he lit his cigar, something for a real man. A tremendous astonishment for everyone: a man of respect, instead of having a Negro do it, going personally to a grocery stall to ask in deafening tones for a big jug of cheap firewater? Now they had seen everything, even old João Popó making a scandal of himself and losing his decorum entirely, for after telling them not to wrap it and not to have it delivered to his place, because he would carry it himself under his arm, would you believe he ordered them to fill half a tin mug with said rotgut and guzzled it without batting an eye, as if it was water? He wiped his mouth with a handkerchief, clicked his tongue, and looked each one in the face before bursting out the door, carrying his jug.

True, there had been great changes in João Popó's life since his son Zé Popó's departure for the war, so the general astoundment was not as strong as it would have been in earlier times. To start with, after the embarkation the old man had spent some two or three sleepless nights in sheer trepidation, his eyes wide open as if he had drunk five coffeepots, a real spinning top whizzing back and forth at the most inconvenient hours. He had Coquinho Popó called to his house at early dawn and gave him a dressing down that lasted till daybreak, saying to him that if he had any dignity he must never again set foot in a home supported by João Popó, and that he'd better start looking for a place to live, because he was going to be evicted. He did more or less the same thing with Labinha and Ostinho and quit speaking to Lafayette, and when Candinha protested, he threatened to give her a whipping with a wild vine, going so far as to order the black Boanerges to go fetch a good quantity in the woods. Franklin Popó tried to defend his mother and lost a new shirt, torn by the vine lashes of the old man, who chased him from room to room, even jumping out a window after him, as though he were a twenty-year-old. Returning to the house, he announced that he had no interest in remaining there, he didn't consider them a decent family, and from that day on he was going to live with Young Iaiá. Candinha said she was going to cut her throat, and he went inside, picked up his razor, whetted it meticulously on a cork slab, tried its edge by cutting a hair held by only one of its ends, and handed it to her, recommending that she do the job outside, so as not to besmirch the whole house with that unserviceable blood, incapable of producing decent offspring. Candinha fainted, he complained she wasn't good enough even to kill herself, told the black women to pack up his bundles and trunks, rented two carts, and moved out ostentatiously, taking even the piano and the bisque statuettes that stood on top of it and had been a gift from the late Hermelindo, Candinha's father.

In Young Iaiá's house he made a speech for the blacks and the neighbors in which he declared that living with a kept woman was in many cases better than living with a legal wife who was only a dead weight, but they shouldn't get any ideas, because he was there exercising his right as master and breadwinner of that home, and he didn't owe any explanations to anybody. In the early evening, barely having finished his change of residence, he sent a message to Young Iaiá, saying he was going to need her later on, and when she sent word by Laurinda that her rheumatism had got worse, he kicked open the door to her room and told her he wanted to see her sufficiently sprightly even to dance the polka within a quarter of an hour as checked on his gold stem-winder, or he would cure that rheumatism the tough way.

And he was not satisfied thus to occupy Young Iaiá but seemed to have incorporated the most salacious of devils, for not a day went by without his engaging in carnal give-and-takes with at least one of his women, sometimes two, such was the lecherous fire that seared him all the time and the priapism that invaded his loins at the sight of any female, to the point that he would announce to his friends, in feigned confidential tones, that he wished the earth itself had a vagina, so he could possess it with his invincible rod, which brought to him epic sentiments as he stuck it ineluctably through the folds of a woman. He even started going now and then to Mutá, to see Maria Zezé. And Candinha, after her initial disappointment, still kept in the house everything he had left behind, including the china teacup, the English slippers, and the enameled chamber pot, so that when he showed up he could feel at home before taking her to bed, where she would cross herself and close her eyes.

Rufina Popó was the only one with whom he encountered difficulties, because even with his paying frequent calls, giving her more money than ever before, and praising everything he saw or heard, she would not give in; she would only give in if the proper arrangements were made, particularly now that it was her son Zé Popó who embodied the very honor of the family. João Popó could not bring himself to agree with the arrangements, and just held out the hope of a vague will he was going to make in the near future, but he promised that things would change after his son got back from the war. And as long as things were settled that way, why didn't they . . . Not so fast, she would answer, with a shove. First the papers in my hand.

This attitude caused him some nervousness at times, so much so that one day he stopped at her doorstep, right in the middle of Saint Anthony Hill and in everyone's presence, and staged one of the loudest hubbubs ever witnessed on the whole island, with cusswords and profanities of such diversity that many of them had never been heard before. He had to be held still by his sons Geminiano and Vavá, and Dionísio, the most hotheaded among them, threatened to get at him with a club if he went on calling his mother names.

So João Popó's conduct was not so unusual anymore; in a way, it had become part of the daily events in the village. But now that his son had returned a hero, promoted to corporal and with his chest covered with medals, it was expected that João Popó would change once again. And that was what everyone thought when they saw him in a resplendent black suit, new hat, new boots, new handkerchief, everything new, waiting for the ship to dock, bringing back the ones who had survived combat and disease, bringing back his son Zé Popó. Among sirens, whistles, serpentines, shouts, clarions, fanfares, and skyrockets, João Popó almost carried his son in his arms to take him, followed by a brass band, to Fair Park, where the party was waiting, the little square full of tables covered with food and drink. For four months he had toiled on an acrostic, and he could finally declaim it triumphantly at the height of the party, as the grand finale to his speech saluting Zé Popó. What joy, what rapture, what glory to see Zé Popó answering young boys' questions about the medals glittering on his chest, what an indescribable day! And it remained indescribable all through the evening. João Popó decreeing a holiday and celebrating all over the village, the very image of happiness and pride.

But now shame! Opprobrium! Shame! Rufina's contemptible, sorcerous blood, that no-good pest! Why can't happiness ever be complete? Isn't it incredible? Zé Popó, the cur, the wretch, the varlet, the rake, did he have to cut down the old man's happiness with that disappointment? No, not a disappointment, an offense, an aggression, an outrage, a veritable crime! That shame, shame, shame, not to mention the crime indubitably committed against the Motherland, for the vast satisfaction and amusement of his enemies and—why not say it?—the enemies of Brazil. João Popó, shivering as he remembered once again what had happened, filled a little tin cup with firewater and drank it all, finishing with a shudder.

The Seventh of January Society of the Sons of Independence, acknowledged as being of public service by the municipality and the province, had been created with literary and recreational purposes, having also in view the fomentation of the ideals of patriotism and public spirit, and the purest values of the nation. The election for the biennium 1869–1870 was won by the Liberty slate, in spite of the embattled opposition captained by João Popó at the head of the Authority slate, whose platform was a thornbush of barbs against the dissolution of customs, freethinking, republican, and abolitionist ideas, religious liberty, and whatever else might represent the undermining of the foundations upon which a real civilization must be built. Corinto Melo, the leader of the victorious slate, was an apparently unassailable figure, but João Popó saw in his complacency toward certain novelties an extreme danger, added to the obvious tarnishing of an organization created to conserve, not to change. His proposal to alter the statutes in order to admit browns as members had been within a hairbreadth of being approved, requiring from João Popó superhuman efforts of eloquence and regimentation to keep such a calamity from occurring. Where are we? he had asked at a general assembly meeting. In Sodom and Gomorrah? In the depraved kingdoms of the Orient? We will never allow the day to come when the destiny of a society which carries Independence in its name is ruled by slaves and sons of slaves!

On many other occasions, João Popó's vigilant, combative spirit confronted Corinto Melo's reformism, to the point that their relationship became rather shaken and the Saturday-afternoon meetings usually took place in an atmosphere of exacerbated tension. It was thus necessary for João Popó to gather support even among some of the members of the opposing faction for the tribute he wanted to pay his son at a special session. There were those who argued that the tribute should be paid to all former combatants, including the many dead ones, but João Popó counterargued that his son had by far been the most decorated, and therefore justice demanded that he symbolize the honor. After long, patient negotiations, during which João Popó often saw himself in the awkward position of asking for the payment of overdue debts and exercising other types of pressure, they arrived at a compromise. The tribute would be to all, but Zé Popó would receive the certificate of merit in the name of the others, and would address the audience about the campaign, perhaps even deliver a short lecture.

A short lecture that, covering compactly fifty-six pages of ruled paper, João Popó had already prepared during months of exhausting labors, during which he often felt feverish and was compelled to rise from his desk, such was his exaltation as he narrated Brazilian glories.

Lo, the Centaur of the Pampas gallops swiftly.

Under a merciless hail of bullets, he raises his majestic chest, and with his magnificent appearance our men recover their spirit, so beaten down by the bloodiness of the battle.

He is not a man. He is a god. His eyes glinting under the fluttering brim of his great black hat, he draws his glorious sword, and from his lips there bursts out, in a strong, stentorian voice like the clarions of Triumph, the order yearned for so long:

"Charge!"

From every throat there erupts a war cry, which resounds in unison over the fields.

It is the Brazilian soldiers, in their irresistible rush.

They no longer march; they run. They no longer run; they overwhelm, they overrun, they go like a giant billow, nothing can stop them.

A wounded body rolls on the ground.

It is a comrade, falling on the field of honor! A life still budding, now reaped down by the horror of war!

Meanwhile the battle proceeds, atrocious, horrendous, at each moment claiming more lives to immolate at the god Mars's flaming altar. The bugle sounds. . . .

But there was no way Zé Popó would read what the old man had written, no matter how pathetic the appeals he received. If he cared to, he could add something, give it a personal touch here and there, but how could he waste a work of that caliber, involving so much research, so many herculean feats of language? Useless. Zé Popó held firm, and so, on his festive Saturday afternoon, João Popó, in spite of his smiles and his puffed-out chest, could not deny to himself that he was a little apprehensive as he entered the large two-story building that housed the Society.

Shame installed itself right at the beginning of the ceremony, because Zé Popó refused to take his seat in the place of honor they had appointed for him, whose setting up had cost his father so much. He affirmed that he saw no reason for sitting in a different place from his comrades, who had as much merit as he did, and besides, merit in war is not always recognized where it really manifests itself. João Popó pretended he did not mind, and even applauded his son's words, but avoided looking at Corinto Melo, who was probably very happy about it.

Shame increased when after the conferring of the certificate and the complimentary speeches, one by the president and another by the official orator, Zé Popó was led to the rostrum, and instead of going straight into the subject of the day, said in a tone destitute of eloquence, almost flaccid, that he didn't know what to speak about. What did they want to hear? They shouldn't think war was made by people unlike those present. On the contrary, from privates to marshals, it was made by people like themselves; the same man who works in peacetime works in wartime. Nevertheless, if they wanted, he would gladly answer the questions they might have, although sometimes words didn't come easily to him and he didn't know how to use them properly.

A heavy silence came over the assembly hall, people moving their feet and looking at the floor, a few coughing, some changing their positions noisily, chairs being dragged, floorboards groaning. Feeling his ears burn, João Popó glanced around and did not see anyone who looked as if he was going to ask a question. It would all be a great fiasco, a dud, a shame. And if Políbio's son, who fancied himself a poet and a man of letters, decided to ad-lib and took away all of Zé Popó's preeminence? Humiliation! João Popó looked at Políbio's son and thought he was building the opening sentence of a speech; he had the dangerous expression of someone who's arranging intercalated clauses in his head. No, no, that couldn't happen, and João Popó started to raise his hand to ask for the floor. Since things had got to that point, he would assume control of the situation, he would read the lecture he had written; fortunately, he had brought it with him.

But he had to pretend his raised hand was to rub his eye, because Corinto Melo, after clearing his throat, his fist pedantically closed over his mouth, decided to ask a question. The room went completely still, and Zé Popó put his hands on the rostrum's railing, looking amenably at the presiding board.

Corinto Melo made a little preamble in which he repeated some of the best sentences of his previous speech, then he pressed his clasped hands on his lips, breathed deeply, and asked Zé Popó which among all his rich experiences as a hero of the Motherland had been the image that had been better preserved, the reminiscence that had remained more strongly, that had been more firmly planted in his mind, and Zé Popó answered: Maggots. Yes, maggots, he said unassumingly. In many parts of Paraguay and the border region of Brazil, blowflies were so abundant that at first the men spent all the time they could protecting their meat, which was often precious and hard to find. But they soon gave up that fight they always lost and got used to maggoty meat crawling with little white larvae, they got used to maggots in everything, and many even got used to eating the flies themselves or swallowing them along with any liquid they drank, because they swarmed over everything. As a consequence, even the lightly wounded turned little by little into larva hatcheries, walking maggot sores. They could wash their sores with potassium chlorate, but it was difficult to find, so some comrades were eaten alive, their bodies, their faces, their viscera fattening those little worms, causing at first itches, which made them tear off bits of their rotting flesh, and later unbearable pain, which they had to endure in solitude because not even the doctors would get near them. More than once Zé Popó had seen comrades with their faces half eaten, little worms wriggling in their cheeks, eyes, and ears, and maybe that was the reason why maggots were the war memory that haunted him the most.

João Popó had to be restrained not to interrupt his son, and he did not wait for any reaction to what had been spoken but immediately asked what was the feeling that dominated a soldier when the hour came to fight for the Motherland, to which Zé Popó answered: Fear. Even after many hours of combat, even after years of war, what one felt was fear every time. They fought on despite their fear because the enemy also had fear and because good officers, who similarly had fear, set an example, courageously pretending not to have fear. At certain times the fear was so great that the men would run away from the fight in terror, and this would happen to the best soldiers on both sides. Because of this fear the war became worse, since the men turned desperate for having to repress it so much and committed, whenever they could, the most horrifying atrocities even against defenseless people, which incidentally had happened a lot in this war.

Very flushed, João Popó contested his son and pointed to his medals, most of which had been bestowed for bravery in action. Talking incisively and with his eyes fixed on the presiding board, he asked if it was not true that one of the medals had been awarded for the rescue of an officer under circumstances of exceptional difficulty, and Zé Popó answered: More or less. They were in Curupaiti, where the allies suffered a great defeat and were chased away by the enemy, and his commanding officer, Major Patrício Macário, was pushing his terrified men forward, helped only by a few soldiers. Their situation was becoming more and more difficult, with the Paraguayans seeming to multiply by twenty each minute and the Brazilians in a panic, running back like flushed birds. He himself was thinking of running away too, now that the men who were fleeing announced in disconnected shouts terrible events right ahead. He asked the officer if he didn't think they ought to get the hell out of there, and the officer, seeing there was no way out of their predicament, said maybe they would be able to regroup a bit rearward. At this moment a bullet scraped the captain's forehead, and he was blinded by the blood that flowed uncontrollably down to his eyes, besides having become a little dizzy and unsteady. As a consequence, Zé Popó had to support him a little, and on their way back defended him against two or three attacks, and was lucky every time. But the major had walked on his own feet, had never stopped holding and using his sword, and if Zé Popó had defended him until they arrived at a safe place, that should not obscure the circumstances that he had been defending himself at the same time. He wasn't saying this out of modesty, which he didn't even consider a respectable virtue, but out of honesty and because he wanted them to see that special men don't exist and anyone can be a hero, depending on where he is, what he does, and how he does it, and on how what he does is interpreted by others.

João Popó got up, tried to offer an addendum to his son's comments, and got into a conflict with the president, who ruled him out of order if only because now there were other questions, many other questions. He considered leaving, hesitated, walked to the exit, and watched the rest of the session standing at the door, moving all the time as if about to leave, changing his mind, and gluing his eyes on the ceiling, unable to vent his anger.

Had Zé Popó been wounded? Yes, he had, and what he could say was that it brought about an enormous hotness and a tremendous thirst, thirst such as he had never felt in his life. But in this place where he had been wounded the water was fetid because it was taken from puddles where corpses were decomposing and was sure to cause cholera or any of the other plagues, such as smallpox, which killed more soldiers than the guns. So he refused to drink water until the next day, when they transported him to a hospital where there was some cleanliness but not much, and the men who could walk always asked not to stay in the field hospitals.

Hadn't he witnessed any of the great heroic feats of which so much had been said ever since the company had started? Yes, he had, he had seen many acts of bravery and courage on both sides. But he would like to say that they should not forget that they were also heroes who had endured fear, disease, hunger, fatigue, mud, lice, fleas, bedbugs, ticks, motucas, cold, despair, pain, indifference, dirt, injustice, mutilation. They were all heroes, and they hadn't been born heroes, they were men of the people, people like the people of the island and of Bahia, who also endured many of those things and even worse ones, without going to war and being called heroic. And the Paraguayans had been heroic too. He didn't have any hatred for the Paraguayans, nor did he think people should hate the Paraguayans, because they had fought for their country the way we fought for ours. The Paraguayans, too, were a people, they were people like our people, people like us. Now they had been decimated, and in the last months of the war there were practically only boys in their army, beardless, sharp-voiced boys with startled, courageous eyes, many of whom he himself had killed, and let no one ask him to be proud of that, nor to have heroic memories of it. He would be proud, yes, and he was sure that someday he would indeed be proud, if the fighting and the suffering had been not to maintain a Brazil where many worked and few made money, where the real Brazilian people, the people who produced, the people who built, the people who lived and created, had neither voice nor respect, where the powerful looked upon their country as just something to be pillaged and profited by without their giving anything in return, pirates of their own country. He would be proud, yes, if their fighting could be used, as it might well come to be, to arm the army in favor of the people and not against it, as it had always been, crushing the people to serve the powerful. He would be proud, yes, if their fighting had been, as it might have been, to defend a Brazil where the people ruled, a great country, a great Motherland, where there would be dignity, justice, and freedom!

João Popó leaned against the door not to fall down, but was almost knocked down by the tumult that ensued, among a disorderly chorus of "hear hear"s, bravos, "down with"s, whistles, applause, indignant shouts, and name calling.

"Long live the Brazilian people!" Zé Popó hollered out from the rostrum, his closed fist pointing upward. "Long live us!"

Tuntum Clearing, June 13, 1871

Souls and spirits sometimes buzz a little. It's not really buzzing, it's just that when the surroundings are charged with them, there appears to occur an atmospheric vibration, which to the ears of sensitive individuals sounds like a buzz. Rufina from the Hill, for instance, stated as soon as she got to the clearing that there seemed to be a beehive in every shrub.

"It's a real swarm," she said to her daughter Rita Popó, who was walking by her side carrying the little basket with her magical objects. "Tell these people to be patient; this is going to be a toilsome night. I have to catch my breath."

She grabbed the basket and strode over to the crossing, feeling the scent of the souls she knew were there, the *cabocos* and other entities. She was anticipating her exhaustion by the end of the night, and her mood soured a little. She got to the crossing, was annoyed at finding people around it, and shooed everyone away impatiently. A hell of a buzz; wasn't there any other place in the world where all those souls could go? She sighed and squatted down next to the crossing of the two trails, now so treaded on that it was rather lower than the ground around them, tucking her skirt between her knees and starting to take her things out of the basket slowly. The buzz was really bothering her, and before she kissed her beads and crossed herself with them, she ran her eyes with irritation over the darkness of the bushes and trees surrounding the clearing.

"Teeming with people out there," she grumbled, pouting her lower lip. "I hope there won't be a brawl."

She arranged all her objects, put one of her hands on her forehead and with the other lifted a jug of rum to her lips, pulled out the cork with her teeth, and took several long swigs. She spat aside and took out of her hair a black cigar, which she slipped into her mouth's right corner, between her cheek and her gums.

"Girl Rita, you can bring me these people!" she yelled out to the other side of the clearing. "No noise and not much conversation!"

When they got to her, they found her with her hair loose, her eyes bloodshot, and on her face an expression that made everyone a little restless, a little disquieted. Rufina was a great witch, one of the greatest witches among the many great witches of the island, and her nearly always blunt

362

disposition intimidated those who approached her when she was gathering together her magical powers.

"Light my cigar," she ordered, without meaning anyone in particular, and a skinny black boy dashed over to a little bonfire and came back with a firebrand.

She took a long time lighting her cigar and blowing great smoke puffs up in the air.

"All right," she said finally. " 'Centration. Prayer."

But she didn't have to spend too much time praying, in a soft voice, her fingers squeezing her brow, because her body began to tremble, her cigar almost fell out of her mouth, her head seemed to want to wrest itself loose from her neck, and she leapt up suddenly, making everyone take a step back.

"*Rrrreis! Rrrreis! Reish! Kereh-kesheh, kereh-kesheh, kereh-kesheh!* Where, where, where's all folks, this one here want to speak, all folks! Hoom! *Rrreish!*"

Rufina had been right, it was going to be a very busy night, because anyone could see that that *caboco* had arrived after having contended with others, in a very bad fight for the medium. And what a fine *caboco* he was, very proud, very snappy, very handsome, very communicative in his twisted speech. Rita Popó returned the gaze he was directing at her and felt a jolt on her spine. What a night!

Patrício Macário left Jefferson Pedreira's country villa without speaking to anyone. He was not going anywhere; he just wanted to step out for a while. The cigar smoke was making his eyes smart, and he was a bit tired of listening to the same arguments in favor of the republican form of government. He knew all that by heart, and the truth was they were not really having a debate inside. Instead of paying attention to what the others were saying, every one of them kept thinking about what he was going to say when his turn came, even if he was just going to repeat in other words everything that had been said before. Normally he had a lot of patience with that, he even enjoyed it when the speakers were good, but this time he was not in the mood.

The night was clear, and he walked over to a large tree whose name he did not know. He stroked its trunk, breathing the cool air washed by the light rain that had fallen a couple of hours before, and raised his face to look at the moon, very luminous in a cloudless sky. He had always liked Itaparica, not only the village but also spots like this little farm, sheltered by the woods, surrounded by pleasant trees and little plants of all colors, nights enlivened by fireflies and crickets, a cool, soft breeze stirring the leaves, windows brightened by soft lights. To stay inside conspiring, or playing conspirator, on a night like this was almost sinful.

He smiled, not knowing why, and noticed that for the first time in many days he was not facing life despondently, with a great, viscous tedium. True, he had become a major when still young, but now military life seemed to him a wearying desert, surrounded by mediocre colleagues and wheedling careerists like Vieira—who by the way was also a major now, with a new promotion anticipated, at a time when promotions were coming more and more seldom. What could he do, where could he go? Maybe it was still too soon, but the changes he had expected after the war did not appear as if they would ever materialize. On the contrary, the army went on being underpaid when paid at all, in rags, ill equipped, demoralized, corrupt, and despised. The blacks, who had carried most of the weight of the war on their backs and had returned as soldiers, could not be called soldiers because in fact they were slaves—and how can an army be composed of slaves instead of free soldiers? Nothing had actually changed, nothing of what he had so emphatically predicted to Vieira during that binge in Corrientes had happened. It was natural, then, for him to become discouraged, and the republican ebullience of a few idealists did not do him any good. He himself had come to share those ideals; he thought vaguely that a republic would lead the country into a better course; but what could he do to work for it, exiled in the military district of Bahia, in command of a bunch of illiterate peasants and irreclaimable drunks, keeping company with officers incapable of thinking about anything other than money and influence-peddling? He did not even have clear ideas on the subject, for lack of study and information, not to mention knowledge of what was going on in the country. And eloquent, well-intentioned conspirators like his friend Jefferson Pedreira were of little value, because they were practically in the same situation as he, all inexperienced provincials who had read two or three books in French. All right, it had been a good idea to come to this gathering on the island, it coincided with the vacation he had just started, maybe it was even a good chance to come out of the torpor that the sameness of life in the barracks had instilled in him. But Nature attracted him more than the comparative study of the degrees of advancement of the several nations that had adopted the republican form of government, a theme being expounded with exophthalmic fury by a bachelor of law he had met that night, who had not shut his mouth since he got to the villa.

Yes, but if nothing was more understandable than his discouragement, his euphoria was also understandable as he noticed it was dissolving, losing its reason to be on such a beautiful, friendly, calm night. Maybe he would be justified in having bad memories of Itaparica, for after all, it had been here, though on the opposite coast, that the great fiasco of the operation commanded by Vieira had occurred. But no, that did not bother him, it seemed to be something that took place in another existence and with another person. Only the memory of the extraordinarily beautiful woman with whom he had talked remained very vivid, as if that had not been the only time he

364

had seen her, as if she had something more to do with him than would be justified by a short, brusque conversation. Where could she be by now? People said she had gone on as the same bandit she had always been, had disappeared in the backlands, had become a saint, had freed slaves, had made war on the side of rebellious Indians, had made miracles, could become invisible, and was ageless. All a legend, of course, but even so he was curious about her.

And it was with a kind of nostalgia, a kind of indefinite longing, the feeling that he had once been there under the same circumstances, only happier and more innocent, that he began to saunter absentmindedly down an ancient trail in the middle of the thick grass patch that faced the villa on that side. Under the moonlight, the still wet leaves took on different appearances every moment, and he walked among them, shaking them to see the water droplets shattering in the rays that pierced the tops of the loftier trees. He did not notice that the trail curved excessively and he was no longer sure of where he was when he came to the edge of a spacious clearing and saw on the other side a large group of blacks and mulattoes surrounded by torches and little bonfires, gathering around someone who was crouched down. It seemed to be one of the blacks' forbidden fetishist practices, which, as everyone knew, persisted. It might be an interesting thing to watch, although if he let himself be seen, they would probably break up the ceremony. So he decided to hide among the tall bushes surrounding the clearings. He found an old tree stump, which he used as a stool, and, concealed by the shrubbery, started to watch the ritual of the blacks.

When Maria da Fé found out that Zé Popó, taking advantage of their passing by the Island of Tide, was going to pay his mother a quick visit, for he had not seen her since his return from the war, she said she was going with him, surprising herself. Why had she said that? There was no reason for her to take chances by making such a trip, although the risk was actually very slight, because if only the two of them and the boat's crew went, they would not be conspicuous and would know where to hide if necessary. But why go to Itaparica? She could not find a good reason. Saint Anthony's Day, novenas humming away into the night, the blacks probably using the day off for some religious ceremony: nothing to do there. Well, maybe she missed the island; after all, she had lived there for so long, and there Grandpa Leléu's memory was everywhere.

Her mind was made up anyway, and when Zé Popó left with the ebb tide and their little pinnace veered south, making for Itaparica, she felt her heart lighten as though it were floating in the soft breeze. Night would fall soon, the sky was becoming purplish on the starboard side, and suddenly, like a gray mountain emerging from the bottom of the sea, a great whale came into view ahead, enveloped in the brume created by the steam of its spout. Maria da Fé stood up in wonderment and ran over to the bow for a better view of the huge animal, now barely moving, with half its body out of the water, in a placid, imposing majesty. And as the pinnace got so close that Maria da Fé thought she would be able to touch the whale, it emitted a melodious, guttural sound, strangely delicate for an animal of that size, arched its back in a graceful curve, and dove down in the sea, leaving behind a crest of foam. Maria da Fé released her breath, which she seemed to have held all the time the wonderful vision lasted, and felt an exhilarating joy, a youthful transport of happiness and freedom that made her lips open in a wide grin, while the little boat jibed larboard and made straight to old Whale Point, now framed by a wholly crimson sky.

As soon as they moored in Whale Point, they were given a message by the boatman Bernardino, whom they had sent ashore before they landed, saying that Rufina, as expected, was going to Tuntum Clearing; it was a work night for her. They anchored the boat, went ashore on a dinghy, and took the Tuntum trail, as if they had set an appointment with Patrício Macário, coming from the opposite direction.

Patrício Macário left the stump where he was sitting and decided to go nearer the group around the crossing. He wanted to see better what was going on and to listen to what they were saying. There was obviously a kind of chief priestess who was in command of the proceedings and demonstrated a very curious behavior, alternating calm periods near her candles and fetishes with moments in which she danced, ran, jumped, moved about, and made speeches in a slurred patter that sounded like a kind of badly spoken Galician. From where he was, he could not make any sense of what she was saying. Was she giving out prescriptions, predicting the future, casting curses?

Careful not to make any noise, he started to go around the edge of the clearing, keeping behind the bushes. As he approached the crossing, a new group appeared, coming from the other side, four or five people, including one who seemed to be a very tall, hooded woman. He thought it was better not to go on; he could see things very well from where he was now. Unable to find another stump to sit on, he leaned against a tree. And what if that witch could really work magic? He had always heard stories, he knew people who swore by the truthfulness of many things brought about by the power of spells and sortileges. No, that was silly, it was all fabrication, distorted versions of normal events. Nevertheless, it was cold near the group, a strange cold, and the woods did not appear tranquil as they had around the villa. He shivered, pulled up the collar of his coat, glanced around to make sure he was really alone, and turned his attention back to the ceremony. Who was that broad-shouldered, frizzy-haired newcomer? It was someone he knew. But of course, it was his former soldier Corporal José Hipólito, Zé Popó! Patrício

Macário almost left his hiding place to talk to him, but thought better of it. Now people other than the priestess seemed possessed by something, acting as if they were out of control. A handsome girl in a wide, colorful skirt, with whom Zé Popó was starting to speak, pulled away from him and, spinning like a top, dashed into the woods. A little unsteady, the priestess took her cigar out of her mouth and made a few circles in the air in the girl's direction.

"Leave 'r alone! Leave 'r! Leave 'r!" she shouted at those who tried to follow the girl. "Let 'er go!"

Suddenly a complete silence established itself in the group, crickets and toads started being heard again, the wind rustled the leaves of the trees, and he shivered again. It was really a weird place, where everything seemed to be alive and the air kept something permanently cocked. No, it was not pleasant there, and he began to consider going back. And what the devil was that noise now, as if someone was threshing the bushes? Some animal, maybe? But what animal could it be, to make a noise of this type? He pulled away from the tree, turned in the direction of the noise, and had such a shock he went speechless. In front of him, with a terrifying expression on her face, her eyes shining, her hair mussed up, her teeth showing in a disagreeably cocky grin, her arms open as if to hug him, the girl in the colorful skirt had halted, and she raised her chin toward him two or three times.

"Comenzeheeah! Comenzeheeah!" she almost snarled, in a voice that did not seem to be hers. "Fu! Ach-goot-goot-goot! Fu! Comenzeheeah noo, ahn? Fu! Noor eest goot-goot-goot, yah, leebeshen Fu? Comenzeheeah!"

Though still harsh, her voice sweetened a bit, her expression became tender, she bent her neck with a friendly smile. Patrício Macário hesitated, not knowing how to react.

"What do you want?" he said, trying to sound firm but not hostile.

"Fu! Fu!"

Moving swiftly, she hugged him, pressed her face against his, and started to stroke his back, but he was startled and pushed her away with an involuntary cry. At once the group of the crossing, as though it had been there ever since her arrival, surrounded them both, the woman with the cigar in the lead.

"Hoom!" she said very loud, coming close to Patrício Macário and inspecting him from head to toe. "Hoom!"

The others, as if they trusted the woman to protect them in case that white man wanted to do something against them for catching them at forbidden practices, did not move, their eyes fixed on her. Patrício Macário pulled out of the girl's embrace and was going to address the woman with the cigar, when he noticed Zé Popó.

"Is that you, sir, here?"

"I'm glad to see you, Corporal, because this situation is very odd. I came here by chance and was just watching what was going on, when this girl

367

attacked me. Actually I'm not sure she really attacked me, but at least she grabbed me. I haven't got anything against your practices, I have no intention of interfering in them, but I think this is going too far."

Zé Popó smiled. He thought it was natural that the major, being unfamiliar with all that, had not understood what had happened, in fact something quite harmless. They were receiving entities, *cabocos,* spirits, souls of ancestors, relatives, and friends, and most likely the entity now incorporated by his sister Rita knew the major; it could even be one of his subordinates killed in the war. Patrício Macário stared at the girl, now standing quietly next to the woman with the cigar but still aiming at him her disquieting gaze. He barely listened when Zé Popó explained that those people neither wanted nor were going to do anything wrong; they were just engaging in a practice that had started many years ago, passing on from generation to generation. He was asking the major to forgive them, not to take offense; many of them were poor slaves who had no joy in life, except those short, secret moments.

"Huh?" Patrício Macário said when Zé Popó asked him a question.

"I asked if you are going to take any measures against them, sir."

"Measures? Why? What you mean, measures? No, of course not, I'm not a policeman, and I could never think of taking such measures. On the contrary, I'm extremely curious. You said this girl is . . ."

"Is incorporating an entity."

"Yes, incorporating . . . incorporating an entity. You said this girl is incorporating an entity that knows me? How can that be? What do you mean when you say it knows me?"

"Well, that might be difficult to find out, Major. I myself don't know too much about those subjects. I'm here because my mother . . . my mother is this lady here."

Patrício Macário recovered quickly from his surprise and set out to greet Rufina, but she, her eyes upturned and her right hand resting nonchalantly on her hip, ignored him, and Zé Popó went on talking.

"My mother," Zé Popó said, "is the heir to a great tradition. Everything she knows she learned with the late Mother Inácia, whom you probably never heard about, but she belonged to a kind of lineage, a lineage which has a certain nobility, which comes from Mother Dadinha, Mother Inácia, and others, all very unique and cherished by all the people. But those are things of the people, things you're probably not too interested in; they're really things of the people."

"No, I'm interested, I really am. You mean your mother . . . Very interesting, very curious. I could never imagine . . . What a coincidence, to meet you here on a night like this."

"Yes, Major, quite a coincidence; I come here very seldom; I don't live here."

"Yes; neither do I, of course. But getting back to your sister—she is your sister?"

"My sister Rita."

"Well, then, getting back to your sister, how can I hear about this entity that knows me? If it knows me, it must know something about me. That would be an interesting confirmation of phenomena in which I've never believed. Is it possible for me to talk to her, with her in this condition?"

Zé Popó was going to say something, but Rufina anticipated him, letting out a new, very loud "Hoom."

"Hoom! I don't think so," she slurred. "It's Seeneeky there. I'll see if he'll go away for a moment, and then I'll explain what's happening. It's not going to be easy, because he's pretty obsessed."

"It's who? I'm sorry. I didn't understand it."

"Seeneeky is a *caboco*," Zé Popó explained. "I've heard a lot about this Seeneeky; he's a strong *caboco*, a Dutchman, it seems, a very foul-mouthed *caboco* who likes to tear down fences."

Rita Popó jerked herself loose from her mother, who was holding her by her arm and putting her hand alternately on her daughter's forehead and the nape of her neck.

"Nine, nine, nine!" she shouted in the same gruff voice as before. "Ish nisht go, Ish nisht go, Ish nisht go! Ish shtay! Ish nisht go!"

"He's really obsessed," Rufina said. "I'll see if I can take him over there to talk, see if I can make him take it easy."

"He?" Patrício Macário asked Zé Popó, while Rufina walked away toward the crossing in Rita's company. "I know that she, as you say, has incorporated an entity, but in that case she stops being herself at all?"

"Yes; that's just her body there. Here people say she's this *caboco*'s horse."

"And why would this *caboco* have any interest in me? I thought you said it was someone who knew me, but if it's this *caboco*, how could he possibly know me? By the way, there's another curious thing: didn't you say a Dutch *caboco*?"

"Yes; that's what I've been taught. It's a complicated story, maybe a little crazy. They say he was a Dutchman who was left behind when they fled after the invasion, and then he became part of *caboco* Capiroba's livestock. Capiroba is another famous *caboco*, but he hasn't appeared anywhere for a long time now, not even in Amoreiras, where they say all spirits gather together—they all show up, even if they are not summoned."

"Part of *caboco* Capiroba's livestock? Did you say 'livestock'?"

"That's right, more or less. The story goes that this *caboco* Capiroba, before turning into a spirit who protects Indians, blacks, and the common people, used to live in the marshes and raise Dutchmen for beef. He used to fatten the Dutchmen in a kind of coop, and when the right time came he'd slaughter one to eat, together with his women and daughters. They say he had many women and only daughters, never sons."

"You're right, it's a completely crazy story. But you believe in it, don't you?"

"I neither believe nor disbelieve in it. But the truth is, I have seen many things."

"Sure, with your mother exercising this activity. Does she have any official designation—a position, so to speak?"

"No, no; they don't see things that way; for them things are not organized that way. They call her Mother Rufina, mother, great mother, witch—everyone calls her what they think she is; it varies from person to person, or from group to group, maybe."

"Very interesting, very, very curious. She commands a great deal of respect, doesn't she? She has a look of strong authority, in spite of her speech being so hard to understand."

"That also varies. I mean, not what you call authority, because that's something she'll always have; after all, her powers and her science really exist for all these people, and very few can match her in that respect. But the speech varies. When she's incorporating—"

"Oh, does she incorporate too? Sure; what a question; of course she must incorporate—after all, she's a kind of high priestess."

"Yes, she does incorporate, and then she speaks *caboco* talk, and this language itself varies from *caboco* to *caboco,* according to his origin, the time he lived, even his whims. It's complicated."

"I see, obviously, sure. So that's the reason for your sister's voice and that strange jabber."

"Yes; it was Seeneeky talking."

"And was Dona Rufina incorporating? I thought her speech was strange too, although hardly as much as the Dutchman's."

"No; it's just that she's drunk nearly a whole jug of rum, to judge from what she left at the crossing."

"She drank rum? Is this part of the ritual—is it indispensable, so to speak, for the conjuring of the spirits?"

"I'm not sure. She has always drunk rum, and Mother Inácia used to drink too. They say Mother Dadinha, the most famous and reputed of them all, did not use to drink. But my mother does, she drinks every time she has to work here at the crossing, though normally she doesn't touch alcoholic beverages."

"Fascinating! But then the *cabocos* also fall under the influence of the rum. Sure, because if they are in the body of someone who got drunk . . ."

"No, that doesn't happen. If you stay here, you'll see."

"Of course I'm going to stay! Nothing would get me out of here. I've always been very curious about these things, especially now that I discovered this *caboco*'s mysterious interest in me. Unless, of course, my presence becomes inconvenient for some reason."

"Now, Major, how could your presence be inconvenient? They're grateful to you for having shown so much understanding. Someone else might rebuke them and probably try to denounce them. As a matter of fact, I'm grateful too."

"Nonsense, Corporal; one of my brothers is a priest, and I believe in his Latin prattle even less than I believe in these things, meaning no offense to anyone, of course. In matters of religion, I might say I'm an agnostic, although I practice Catholic acts on occasions I cannot avoid. And in matters of customs I think I might be considered a liberal; I couldn't care less if the blacks go on with their fetishist practices, as long as they do it without offending anyone or letting it interfere with their work."

"Yes, but not everyone thinks that way. As a matter of fact, very few people think that way."

"I've always had a reputation for being hotheaded, and I really am. I'm hotheaded because I can't stand seeing rights I consider sacred being violated. So I have sympathy for those who try to exercise rights that to me would be sacred."

"Remember this involves the freeing of the blacks, Major. . . ."

"I'll tell you the truth: I'm for it. I've always been, and even more now, after having fought alongside so many Negroes during the campaign. But let's not talk politics now; I've just escaped a political meeting, which was infinitely less interesting than this. Is Dona Rufina going to take long? It's not that I'm in a hurry—I'm on vacation—but I'm very curious."

At a relatively short distance they could see Rufina and Rita squatting at the crossing. Sometimes standing up excitedly and gesturing wildly, Rita seemed to be telling Rufina a very long story, interrupted by exclamations and almost tearful appeals. Rufina limited herself to holding down her daughter's agitated movements and to listening to the story with slow, judicious nods. But when she spoke, her daughter paid no attention, even tugging at her hair in exasperation and trying to run off to the woods.

"I think that's going to take some time," Zé Popó said. "Wouldn't you like to drink something, sir? Eat something?"

"Eat, drink? Don't tell me they have a commissary here! Corporal, I'm more and more astounded at how many things happen around us, right under our noses, and we are not aware of them! Is there food and drink here?"

"Not of the type you're used to, sir. The food, for example, is good, but I don't think you've ever seen it, maybe only at an open-air market or a popular feast. Most of it is made with palm oil."

"I've seen it, I've tasted it, I like it! It's a little strong, but I like it."

"It's poor people's food, made from beans, pluck, and leaves found in the woods—real poor people's food, but it's good."

"Go on, Corporal; this adventure is much better than anything I might have expected. And drinks, did you say?"

"Yes, poor people's drinks too. Pineapple *alooah*—"

"Pineapple juice?"

"No, it's a drink made by steeping pineapple rind in water; it's very tasty."

"But isn't there anything stronger? I mean, this whatsit doesn't have any alcohol, does it?"

"No, it doesn't. But they have other drinks that do. This time of the year they make a lot of flavored liquor, with genipaps, granadillas, pitangas, aromatic leaves, milk . . ."

"You don't say, Corporal! If you were still in the army, I'd have you promoted to sergeant tomorrow."

They went around the crossing without getting too close to it, and arrived at a spot where the grass was short and food was displayed on pieces of cloth and wood slabs. On the right side, arranged like a row of toy soldiers, were the jugs with the liquor. Patrício Macário uncorked and sniffed them one by one, and helped himself to a generous shot of a genipap drink.

"Aren't you going to help yourself too, Corporal? You don't like them?"

"I'll join you, sir. Just a short one, because I still have to travel before daybreak."

"To our health, Corporal! And in a way, I owe you my health, hah-hah!"

"That's very kind of you, Major. Here's to us!"

"It's a pity I left my cigars back in the villa. I could use a good cigar now. Do you happen to have one?"

"No, sir; I don't smoke."

"Surely someone around here has one. Look, those men are smoking cigarillos."

"But that's not tobacco, Major, it's something else; it's Angolan *lyamba*."

"Really? Never heard of it. May I try it?"

"Well, they smoke it in order to feel things."

"Feel things? What do you mean—that they smoke and actually feel things? Do you believe that? Do you think it's possible for a man to smoke a cigarillo and feel things?"

"I'm not sure. Anyway, it's very different from regular tobacco."

"Get me one, Corporal; I want to try it."

"Glad to, Major."

Patrício Macário inhaled the smoke from the straw-wrapped cigarillo Zé Popó brought him, and did not like its taste at first, but after a sip of his drink he thought the combination was good. He sat down on a stool, invited Zé Popó to take another one, and leaned against a tree. He stretched out his legs, inhaled once again, had another sip, and felt infinitely well, very light, almost weightless, the whole scene acquiring a new charm.

"Corporal José Hipólito, I must thank you. I was having an exceptionally boresome evening, and now you afford me an extraordinary well-being. Wonderful drink, wonderful smoke."

Enraptured by everything around him, he ended up forgetting about the cigarillo, which went out and dropped from his relaxed fingers. And he was not sure it was not a dream when, taken by his arm to the crossing by Zé Popó, he was left alone with Rufina and heard a story he understood and at the same time did not understand, but was fascinated by just the same, so much so that at times he seemed to be living the episodes, in a world of diffuse light and imprecise contours. Rufina told him he had the same soul as Vu, Capiroba's daughter, and therefore in a certain way he was Vu. Vu had been *caboco* Seeneeky's woman, and for that reason Seeneeky, now that Vu's soul had incarnated in a man, had come down as a woman so she could kiss him. She said furthermore that maybe he wouldn't be able to understand those things, but Seeneeky had told her that he, Patrício Macário, would soon meet a woman who used to be *caboco* Capiroba, and that woman and he would love each other. She then showed him, narrating everything in detail, how this woman, whose identity she knew but could not reveal, was also a natural descendant of *caboco* Capiroba, Vu's father, Dadinha's great-grandfather, Turíbio Cafubá's great-great-grandfather, Venância's, also called Vevé, great-great-great-grandfather, and this woman's grandfather in the fifth degree. The woman was therefore her own ancestor—and this had to mean something, though Rufina didn't know what. He should also know that this woman and he, because he had Vu's soul, were in a way related souls, Vu having been the daughter who took after Capiroba the most—and this surely meant something, which the major would discover in due time. Something was positive, absolutely positive: All that had been set up, it was intentional, it had been orchestrated, let him make no mistake about that and try to learn. He might not believe it, but he was part of that people, maybe not in his flesh but in something much deeper, his soul—and he was there for some reason, it wasn't for nothing.

With her hand on his shoulder, she looked at him and smiled.

"You're being enchanted," she said. "Aren't you?"

Almost in a trance, he did not answer, but thought, with the most complete serenity he had ever felt in his life, that indeed he was being enchanted, he was entering a new world, he was opening a previously unsuspected door, but strangely enough he didn't feel insecure, he had the sensation that the unknown was somehow not unknown but familiar. And he was not even surprised when he raised his face and found himself looking at the tall figure of Maria da Fé, standing in front of him, as lovely as before, her green eyes reflecting the light of the bonfires, her head framed by the hood she had pulled back. So that was it, yes, that was it, it was all very clear, nothing called for explanations, all was dazzlingly clear, and he held out his hand to her, and she helped him get up. Yes, he had been touched by that hand before, he had come very close to that face of indescribable beauty before. They spoke nothing at first, standing hand in hand near the crossing, while *cabocos* and souls, jumping back and forth and entering every available head, staged their colloquy of jumbled speech and memories, a festive, happy celebration. With Patrício Macário going deeper and deeper into his enchantment, friends and relatives dropped by, including Leléu, who blessed his granddaughter, Turíbio Cafubá, who also blessed his granddaughter, Dadinha, who blessed them both, Ackee-mun, all curved and saluting both of them in a mixture of Dutch and Castilian, Seeneeky, who pinched Patrício Macário and showed his tongue to Maria da Fé, even the black Esmeralda, all smiles, and dancing with her skirt tucked up. The moon finished her trip over the treetops above the crossing, the night became darker, Patrício Macário found himself completely enchanted.

16

Would Tico know the language of flowers? Henriqueta felt a prickly warmth climbing up her neck to her ears, while she arranged a big bunch of small jasmines in the Macao vase that stood on the chest of drawers in her brother-in-law's bedroom. She plucked out a few leaves to enhance the flowers, stepped back a bit to see the result, and decided everything was perfect. She picked up near the vase a pink-bound copy of *The Calepin of Lovers,* opened it in the chapter entitled "Flowers Speak," and checked: small jasmines signified passion. She blushed again, asking herself if she had chosen the right message. Maybe it was a bit strong, a bit too forward, but the heck with it, she had always had that kind of temperament anyway, and she no longer had any patience for anything, leading this suffocating life. The problem was whether he was going to understand the message, because in spite of being very popular with women, Tico was not the romantic type. But it would be perfect madness, complete folly, to leave the *Calepin* lying around so he could consult it. Too obvious, too audacious. Besides, if the book wasn't around, she would be able to deny she knew the meaning of those flowers, she would keep things within the ambiguity suitable for situations of this type. Yes, she might have read the book in a moment of frivolity, but of course she couldn't recall the meaning of flowers, that romantic nonsense didn't occupy her mind. She imagined herself saying this to her brother-in-law, with an expression entirely opposite to the meaning of her words, leaving him in the most delicious doubt. These maneuvers had a great deal of charm and required a delicate sense of subtlety, but what impatience she felt! She opened the perfumed envelope in which she had slipped the note she was going to leave by the vase. What nervousness, having to choose words, to act with kid gloves, to avoid a single misstep! All right, but the little note was well written, the perfect balance between the simple, affectionate courtesy of a sister-in-law and provocation. "Welcome home," it said. "I have brought you these flowers that I myself chose with particular care, to enliven your room and help fill your mind with pleasant thoughts. Think about them, it will do you good. Affectionately, H." Well, maybe she should address him more informally; after all, he wasn't that much older than she and was her brother-in-law. And the expression "with particular care" wasn't precisely what she had in mind to indicate it was a message through flowers. She'd wanted to say something more incisive, though not too transparent. And "it will do you good": was it really necessary? Why not simply "think about them"? How unnerving to need to pinch little words, if what she really wanted was to write him a letter overflowing with passion and ardor, to do the same things as wily Charlotte, the main character in the libertine novel she had secretly borrowed from Titiza, who wouldn't shy away from anything when she decided to receive a man in her bedchamber. Oh, what a frisson! She slipped the note back in the envelope and balanced it near the vase, thinking at the last moment she had been too restrained. She remembered Madame d'Arconville's thought that she had underlined with her fingernail in the book: *"Les hommes admirent la vertu, mais c'est la coquetterie qui les subjugue.* But *coquetterie* and elegance in Bahia? Banana trees would grow in London parks first. Oh London, oh Paris, oh civilization! She made a weary gesture, wiped off a droplet of water that had fallen from the vase onto the chest's top, arranged the curtains, and left, closing the door. It was almost time for Titiza to arrive to help with the furnishing of the music room, where they would put all the novelties she had brought from Europe. And to have tea and eat biscuits, and talk, talk, talk!

If it weren't for Titiza, my God in heaven, she would be crazy by now, *absolument détraquée.* Titiza was her companion of suffering in this monotonous, little-minded town, full of stupid, unrefined people, in which there was nothing to do, nothing times nothing times nothing times nothing! She had said to Bonifácio Odulfo on several occasions: After being in Europe it was impossible to live in this veritable farm, where there wasn't one decent theater, an opera was staged every two years, social life was boorish, and one could not even have the pleasure of putting on a pretty dress because there was no place to go in it. What for? To suffer while the schoolmistress Maria do Carmo Machado massacred *L'Elisir d'Amore,* accompanied by Bachelor Armindo Barros's no less vile pianoforte? To want to die, truly want to die at the terrifying hour when old Commander Laudelino Proença munched up his endless wedding poems, incomprehensible both for their turgid construction and for the blows of his loose denture he inflicted on the syllables. No, no, no, a thousand times no! They must move to Rio de Janeiro before she had to enter a clinic for nervous diseases—and never come out if it was to go on living in Bahia. She was still a girl when the tragedy had happened, so they hadn't told her anything, but now that she knew the truth about her sister-in-law Carlota Borroméia's death, she would bet anything in the world and swear by every saint that Carlota had become desperate on account of the life imposed on her, especially her being married to that hippopotamus Vasco Miguel. Titiza could corroborate that, and she actually did so in the many confidences they exchanged. Of course Titiza had married Vasco Miguel for money. She wouldn't admit it openly even to Henriqueta, but it was plain to see. What other reason would a pretty, intelligent girl, much younger than he, have had to accept living beside a mumbling, snail-like pachyderm with eyes like a dead chicken's? Her father, a semi-ruined farmer with a lot of land but sinking in debts, must have arranged the whole thing, and Vasco Miguel found himself in possession of the girl and the land. But of course he got the better part of the deal, for if materially speaking everything was provided, spiritually they lived in a desert even worse than hers with Bonifácio Odulfo, who at least still had a little vivacity, though tiresome with his bathos and subservience in private. No, no, no, Titiza and she would win the campaign to move to Rio! Hadn't Bonifácio Odulfo been having conversations about a need for the bank and several of his firms to establish branches or even transfer their main offices to Rio de Janeiro, the court, where everything happened and they wouldn't be limited by the impoverished, narrow horizons of the province? So that was it: a little more persistence, and they would make their husbands take the big step, moving them and their precious bank to Rio de Janeiro.

Come to think of it, there was this joy delineating itself in the future, their change of residence was a sure thing, it would happen sooner or later. Not bad, considering the somber perspectives that haunted her like horrendous incubi on the trip back from Europe. Life went on as cheerlessly as before, but now she knew they were going to live in the court, and her so beautiful and masculine brother-in-law had reappeared after a mysterious vacation he had spent no one knew where. He hadn't told anybody where he had been, but it didn't matter, he had always been a bit eccentric, and this only increased his charm and appeal—a real man, in the full meaning of the word! Maybe a little rough, a bit too blunt, but he had good manners, though distant most of the time, and knew how to conduct himself in society. What a difference from Bonifácio Odulfo's pedantic chatter, what a difference to be in his muscular arms and not entwined in her husband's hairy tentacles, with him practically asking her to whip him. No, not practically; he did ask her once, and only when she was scandalized did he pretend it had all been a joke. If it had all been a joke, why that little whip in their bedroom, with which he had given himself a couple of light lashes before suggesting she use it on him? That had been no joke, the same way it had been no joke when the key to one of the study's bookcases remained in its lock, as if it had been forgotten. How could it have been forgotten, if it was always fastened to the key holder he took with him everywhere? Of course it hadn't been forgotten; it had been left there so she could see what was inside, as for instance the books in the central shelf, which were very different from the ones that circulated habitually around the house; they were brochures printed in unusual colors and odd formats. Right in front, a collection of little tomes with faded red covers: *Collection "Le Fouet."* Didn't *fouet* mean "whip"? Of course it did, and this was confirmed by the engravings. What engravings! That one showing a room filled with leather armchairs, in which a man in tailcoat, with sideburns à la Empire, a bristling mustache, and an obscene smirk, brandished a kind of quince tree branch with which he flogged a *gamine*'s plump behind, under the stern supervision of a gimlet-eyed older woman! She had shown that and other engravings to Titiza, a real scandal! It had been the first time they ever used the word "ass" between themselves—how they had bare asses in those books! Men's asses too, the same debaucher with the little mustache in his shirt, boots, and nothing else, whipping a girl dressed only in a corset. And what events were described in the stories! As far as they could make them out—for the text was in low French, which was not spoken in salons, let alone taught to girls—there was always a man who punished a woman, to later comfort her and take her to bed for the most depraved acts imaginable. But also among those books there was one, only one, in which beautiful young women whipped men of several types and ages, including a gentleman with a bushy mustache who reminded them a little of Bonifácio Odulfo when he had been over-weight. They had laughed their hearts out, locked in the study to look at those big, hairy asses being strapped by women in black lace underwear with their breasts showing. Henriqueta had confidentially told Titiza the strange story of Bonifácio Odulfo's whip, and Titiza was greatly excited and said that in Henriqueta's place she would use it. No such hope with Vasco Miguel, because—believe me, my dear!—he was the one who wanted to do the whipping; he had even started it once, slapping her face a couple of times. If she hadn't been affirmative and threatened to tell her father, he would have gone ahead, but he still made insinuations now and then, which of course she pretended she didn't understand.

One of these days, Henriqueta thought, I just might follow Titiza's advice and give Bonifácio Odulfo a good thrashing. He was the one who asked for it after all, and maybe she'd derive some satisfaction from it, who knew? At least the satisfaction of making up for all her resentment toward the hum-drum life he compelled her to lead, in a town too small for her. Who could understand here the great ideals of the eternal feminine, the longing for subtlety and romanticism, the whims characteristic of a woman of high class, the exquisite sensitivity of a lady like her? "Have you seen my key?" he had asked, and without altering her serious face she answered, looking him in the eye, yes, she had seen it, she had closed the bookcase and kept the key, did he need it now? She didn't say anything about the books, though she did consider it but decided he could go on burning for it until she changed her mind, if ever. *La femme est pour son mari ce que son mari l'a faite*; therefore he was even responsible for her wanting to become Patrício Macário's mistress—and the word "mistress," even if not uttered, left her in an almost uncontrollable excitement.

A coach had stopped outside; it must be Titiza arriving. A black girl came upstairs to announce that *Senhora* Dona Beatriz had just been ushered in, and Henriqueta rushed to meet her. How nice to see her, she was late already, how pretty she was, where had she bought such a delicate camlet, it had to be imported, it suited that style so well, and how lovely the tulle of her mantilla, wasn't it imported too? They kissed profusely and went up to the music room. They had so much to talk about! The most important news had to be given right away, and Titiza couldn't control herself, whispering as they walked upstairs. It was practically certain that they would move to Rio! Very confidentially, because Bonifácio Odulfo wanted to surprise Henriqueta, Vasco Miguel had assured her it was now a matter of months; weeks, even! What news, oh what news! Was Titiza sure, was she sure, Titizinha? Of course she was, or she wouldn't have said anything, because she knew it was what they wanted most in the world. And the whole family would go, only the monsignor would stay, for he would never leave his boys and his charities. What? The whole family, even Tic—even Patrício Macário? Absolutely; that had also been told to her by Vasco Miguel, who heard about it from Patrício Macário himself, when the latter had dropped by the bank to settle a few matters. He also said Patrício Macário didn't want to go, because everything seemed to indicate he was going to be appointed to some bureaucratic job in the ministry, something he abominated. But it would be great if Patrício Macário went too, wouldn't it? And they could go on living in the same house, an authentic close family!

Henriqueta thought she had noticed something suspicious in her friend's eyes when she mentioned Tico. And a certain hesitation in her voice, something suggesting dissimulation. So Titiza had an eye on Tico too? Better forget it! Now she really wouldn't tell Titiza about her plans; she was no fool. Maybe the best tactic would be to encourage her friend to make a clean breast of it, because that way she would have all the information she needed to guarantee her victory. Well, she'd find out about everything in due time; rushing things might interfere with her plans. They went into the music room. Henriqueta put her hands to her head: had anyone ever seen such a mess? Everything still partially in boxes, everything in disorder, everything to be done. But would it be worth it to do anything, now that their moving was certain? Oh, in Rio she was going to take the opportunity to get rid of that awful Virginian furniture, those charmless things, so lacking in imagination. She would even get rid of those chandeliers with branches as lugubrious as moth wings, no matter how Bonifácio Odulfo cherished them for having belonged to the baron of Pirapuama's house. No, no, darling, damask, lots of damask, and objects in the style of the Second Empire—not this one, of course, but the French one. And to change the subject, did Titiza know there was nobody, absolutely nobody, of any distinction in Rio de Janeiro who didn't have her hair done by a French *coiffeuse*? What did Titiza think: would she look well with a *coiffure en papillote*? This season . . .

No time seemed to have passed when Titiza said goodbye. It was getting late, the blacks had by now heated the water for her bath, and Henriqueta ordered them to fill the bathtub. She went into the bathroom, which had been renovated after considerable resistance by Bonifácio Odulfo, who ever since his days as a poet had never quite understood the insistence of certain people on taking frequent, prolonged baths. Now the bathroom was even attractive, with a large Regency-style mirror, spacious closets, a Wedgwood washbasin with two handles so the water could be poured out, a big marble bathtub alongside the wall. Henriqueta sighed contentedly. She loved to immerse herself in the warm water and daydream. Taking off her clothes, she looked at herself in the mirror. She thought of Tico once more. In a short while he would be home. How good it would be if she could show herself to him like this, without any obstacles! She closed her eyes, stroked her hips, pressed the palm of her right hand on her pubis. For a long time she pressed her thighs together, feeling so much pleasure she had to hold on to a towel rack not to drop down. She stepped into the tub; the water was very warm, the way she liked it. Opening her legs, she noticed that mixing with the water, her own juice was trickling out, slow, almost oily, making her so soft between her thighs that there could be nothing more delicious to touch and fondle. There was, yes, there was, yes, but it wasn't there. She reached out behind her, picked up a brush with a smooth, round-tipped wood handle, closed her eyes again, clasped the handle firmly, stroked with the back of her other hand the rather rough bristles of the brush, and taking care not to hurt herself, slipped the handle into herself with a purring moan. Almost at the same instant, while her heart pounded and her breathing became fast, she whispered Tico's name and came for so long she thought she was going to die.

Our Lady Point, June 30, 1871

Rising from his rush mat, Patrício Macário peered out the open window and saw it was a beautiful, sunny day. Once more when he set foot out of the house, to stretch a bit and walk to the bluff's edge to watch the sea, he would meet Agostinho, who would comment on how it was a beautiful day and how it's usually very cold and rainy this time of the year. Then he would report if the tide was coming in or going out and would say he hadn't seen a whale in so many days—to think how it used to be, this time of year! Patrício

Macário smiled, looked at Maria da Fé, who was still asleep, wrapped in a bedsheet, and his heart warmed, as always happened when he gazed at her silently. How proud he felt to be there with her, to share her mat, to be loved by her! Proud because there had never been such a beautiful woman anywhere in the world, and he couldn't describe this pride, which would come to him when he noticed her eyes fixed on him with admiration or desire, when she touched him, when she embraced him, when she let herself be seen stunningly naked, his, his, entirely his because she loved him, he knew. And also proud that he knew she could only love a man who was either identical or similar to her, and this meant he had at least some of her spontaneous and quick intelligence, her clear laughter that brightened everything, her determination and courage, her nobility and dignity, and the certainty she infused in everyone that she would never be disrespected or humiliated. And it was this high-spirited, beautiful woman, indomitable by words or by force, who was there by his side, who loved him, who lay down under him and pulled him to her as if she wanted to merge with him.

He felt an emotion so strong that his eyes became watery. Because he loved her too, with so much intensity that it scared him sometimes, sometimes he thought he had really been enchanted, as Rufina had told him. But Rufina had asked for his confirmation, so that might mean that the enchantment depended in part on the enchanted one. Yes, of course he was enchanted, of course the world had a new brightness and he would never, could never, be the same. He didn't know whether to believe Rufina's complicated story or not, he even avoided confronting that doubt. But the truth was, he didn't see things the same way as before. Neither people, white or black, nor things, nor events. He had learned at first, very vividly, that contrary to what he had thought, everything can be seen in different ways, very different from that which people think is the only one, the correct one. And besides, story or no story, he had started feeling a great affinity to these people. Not an affinity meaning the assumption of a life identical to theirs, but one that made all his former existence absurd, spent as if those people had no significance, as if they were not part of him, as if the whole nation were restricted to those in his sphere, actually a minority that thought it was composed of transplanted Europeans and knew nothing of what was going on. How could a country be built like that? So powerless and depersonalized, how could it stop being, one way or another, a colony?

He could not think very clearly about those things, because he was absorbed by a tumult of new sensations and intuitions, which he was unable to unravel with precision, a source of some anxiety. Some of those things were just glimpsed and others only suspected, which increased his frustration as he anticipated never being able to explain to others a patent truth, for he would have no way to transmit it. Besides, in his long conversations with Maria da Fé after they had departed from Tuntum Clearing before daybreak and had been left practically alone in Our Lady Point, what she told him seemed to him to be fragmentary and disconnected, so that he was never able to put all the pieces together right. But when he spoke to her about his perplexity, she had answered that she, too, did not know how to put together the pieces, her life was more like a search than anything else. She felt as if there was a kind of trunk, a chest, where through the work of people like her, of whom there were more than it was thought, answers would accumulate until somebody could weave them into a whole. The only thing she knew was the power of the people, a power of which it must have consciousness, a power not only of numbers but of what it produced with its hands, heads, and voices, because the people was the real owner of the country, not those who subjugated it for the satisfaction of their own interests. She was sure this was going to be recognized someday, that there would be freedom and justice. Now, how this day was supposed to come about she didn't know, but that couldn't be used as an excuse for her to keep her arms crossed, because there were certain things that could be done. At least the minds, at least the minds! she had said with an impassioned voice. At least the minds should be opened, should be liberated so they could see their truth, not the truth of those who dominated them. She was sure there was a fraternity, a kind of brotherhood whose concrete bases she couldn't specify but to which she belonged, and this brotherhood, no matter how heavy the oppression and no matter how they killed the voices of the people, would always persist, and there would always be one of those brothers, wherever you went. She called this brotherhood the Brotherhood of the Brazilian People, and insisted it wasn't a poetic invention but a reality, though a reality concealed by others, to which people are accustomed. How could one who belonged to this brotherhood be recognized? Those who belong to the Brotherhood, she answered, recognize one another: by their acts, their words, the way they walk, their gestures, their voices, their demeanor, and many other things that those who belong to the Brotherhood know. You are the first to know when you belong to the Brotherhood, she added, although she didn't know how this happened. She imagined that those of the Brotherhood found each other because they dedicated themselves, for whoever dedicated himself would find it, it was something that came from inside and outside at the same time.

Did he believe in God? She did, maybe in a special way, but she did. And for that reason she also believed in the great responsibility of free will. If there was no free will, man would be nothing, could not aspire to dignity, as he would not have any responsibility. But since free will exists, our great responsibility if we want the world to improve is to do something for it to improve, since the world belongs to us, it was given to man. One cannot want God to solve man's problems, because if God did it, He would take away from man his responsibility and consequently his free will. What was

382

clear to her, then, was that every dedicated work aimed at its own excellence, but subordinating this excellence to God contributed to improve the world; yet things were not so simple, and oppression and injustice did not make them any simpler. In her case, the work was to fight oppression and injustice, to try to understand them and to know what were the remedies against them and how to administer them. In her case, moreover, her sense of responsibility led her to put in this fight not her life but her soul. She did not know how this happened, either, but she knew, and this was her commitment.

She mentioned her commitment again in midmorning, when they were getting back from the crab fishing they had done with Agostinho's hand nets. The reason she did so was that after they had had a great deal of fun chasing the crabs that had escaped from the basket he was carrying, he hugged her and said they would never part.

"But of course we will," she said. "Your vacation is nearly over. And I suppose you could say mine too."

"I thought we had settled all this," he said with some impatience. "Just yesterday you said we'd never part."

"You know very well what I meant to say. What I meant to say was that my love for you will never die and will follow you forever. And your love will always follow me, I know."

"To me this is insane, it's stupid. If I love you and you love me, if never has such a passion happened to us, such an identification, such a fervor, such an ecstasy, why, in the name of what, are we going to part?"

"We've talked so much about that . . ."

"We have, we have, but I still don't accept it."

"It's not a matter of accepting it; it's just how it has to be. It's not something I want but something that has to be."

"Maybe it has to be, in the light of those crazy things we know or think we know. But as far as daily, practical, tangible life is concerned, it's not something that has to be; it's a choice."

"A choice is often something that has to be. And besides, do you really think those crazy things are that crazy? I can't be your wife. Even if my being a black or a mulatto or whatever those who worry about those words might say was not a problem, I couldn't be your wife. I couldn't serve you, I couldn't accompany you, I couldn't give you children—in short, I couldn't be your wife, and I would only be your wife if I could be your wife."

"But I can be your husband. And I can stay by your side."

Maria da Fé's eyes filled with tears, one of which ran down to her lips. Without wiping it, she dropped the nets and hugged him for a long time, putting her hand on his lips when he tried to speak.

"You know," she said very softly and looking the other way, "I myself sometimes think I don't exist; I think I'm a legend, as they say I am. And in the future you yourself may come to think I'm a legend too. I don't know if that would be bad for you, because I love you and don't want you to suffer anything ever, ever, ever, and maybe after you convince yourself I'm a legend you won't suffer so much."

"This makes no sense, it's completely absurd; of course you're not a legend: You're my woman, you're my life, you're—"

"I'm not your life; I'm your love. Remember that if we wanted to live together one of us would have to stop being what we each are. And it's not right for me to stop being what I am and doing what I do, nor is it right for you to stop being what you are and doing what you do."

"But I don't do anything. And besides, one can always change."

"Of course you do something and will go on doing something. As for changing, it's impossible."

"What do you mean, impossible? I still say it makes no sense."

"Because I love you the way you are, not the man you'd turn into. And you love me the way I am, not the woman I'd turn into. And of course everything makes sense, everything always makes sense; you say it doesn't because we usually find sense where it interests us to find it. Have you looked for any sense, any reason for what's happened to us? Why have we fallen into each other's arms without saying a word, why do we feel we know each other more than anybody knows anything? Why has it all happened this way? Do you think it just happened, it didn't have to be?"

"No, no, of course it had to be."

"You see? So there are things that have to be, you said so yourself."

There wasn't a living soul, there wasn't anything, not even a little bird, when they lay down on the soft grass under an ancient mango tree and did everything all passionate lovers have ever done, and time ceased to exist. It only began to exist again when Patrício Macário, having unknowingly drunk an infusion of the same herb she had given him the first time, woke up alone in a little house in Good Dispatch where there wasn't a living soul, either, nor did its scant neighbors know to whom it belonged. He woke up impregnated with her smell and with a letter in his hand he never showed anybody.

Settlement of Saint Ignatius, backlands of Bahia, February 29, 1896

Night came down all of a sudden, and a dry chill covered the area around Gentio do Ouro and Xique-Xique, a good many leagues from the gullies of Saint Francis River, where the settlement hides among mountains. It hides because it is an outlaw settlement, a lair of bandits, runaway gunmen, and marauders, where no one sleeps naked or unarmed, and entrance is only by permission. Now that the wilds have blanketed their ferocious plants under a mantle of coldness, and even the dust in the streets has settled down, nothing can be seen but the yellowish glare of a few lamps passing through the squares formed by the walls of clay huts. Up Middle Street, a bonfire is burning in the porch of a large house in ruins, though its stonework walls and tiled roof are still serviceable, which is called by everyone Andrade's Ruin, no one knows why. The history of the Settlement of Saint Ignatius is unknown, as is most of the history of these whereabouts and the people who live in them.

Filomeno Cabrito adjusted his two poniards so their handles would be slanted forward as he liked them, and looked around the hovel, where he had been eating ground dry beef and manioc flour, to see if everything was in order. He picked up his muzzleloader and his leather bag and started out on his way to the Ruin. He did not want to miss the visit of the blindman Faustino, who had arrived from Vila Nova da Rainha preceded by great fame as a storyteller. He was in a hurry because maybe he was late, for the blindman had announced that the true story he was going to tell was long and therefore had to start by nightfall; he would not start it in daytime only because he did not want to grow a tail. And in fact when Filomeno Cabrito went up the corroded steps of the big house, the old man, warming his hands over a little bonfire and wrapped in a black blanket, was already talking to a group of more than twenty men, some of them hatless, almost as contrite as if they were in a church. Filomeno Cabrito excused himself, took off his hat too, and hunkered down next to a half-toppled pillar.

The blindman Faustino's story was indeed long, because it started when the world was made, before Brazil was discovered. He told them there was already a world before Brazil existed, there were Portuguese, Frenchmen, Galicians, Germans, and many others. He explained how the world was made by God, and how, much later, very upset with man's sinfulness, which had engendered even Sodom and Gomorrah, He sent down the Universal Deluge, which drowned all creatures, except Saint Noah, his family, and a couple of each animal, at a time when animals spoke. And then the world went on with all its great history, the kings of Spain, General Napoleon of France, the princes and princesses of Brazil, the emperors, Princess Isabel, and the men who sent the emperor away to bring in the Law of the Devil.

But, the blindman explained, history is not just the one that's written in the books, if for no other reason than that many of those who write books lie much more than those who tell fairy tales. In the time of ancient Egypt, in King Solomon's land, near the Queen of Sheba's land, above the Jewish Kingdom, there was a great library, which contained all knowledge, called Alczander. So very well, so one day this great library catches fire and all that knowledge goes up in smoke, with even the names of those who had more of that knowledge and had written the books kept there. Since that day it's known that all history is false or half false, and each generation that arrives decides about what happened before it, and so book history is as invented as newspaper history, where you read so many lies your hair stands on end. There are very few books that can be trusted, just as there are few people who can be trusted; it's the same thing.

Besides, the blindman went on, history told in paper leaves aside everything that wasn't put on paper, and you only put on paper what interests you. Who can believe that someone with the knowledge of the writing art will take pen and paper to write what doesn't interest him? Does anyone who stole write that he stole, does he who killed write that he killed, does he who gave false testimony confess he lied? He doesn't. Does anyone write well of his enemy? No, he doesn't. Then all paper history is in somebody's interest.

And there's more, the blindman said: What is pitch black for one man may be lily white for another. What for one may be food or valuable metal, for another is poison or tin. What for one is a great event, for another is a shame to be denied. What for one is important, for another doesn't exist. Therefore most of history is hidden in the conscience of men, and that's why no one will ever know most of it, not to mention things like Alczander, which kill memory.

But the story I'm going to tell, the blindman said, is true, as true as God in heaven. And then he told them that once upon a time there was a baron of the Empire who lived in Bahia, where he was the lord of all the fish they fished there, not one fish being fished without his permission. This baron had great wealth and many vast dominions, a large number of slaves, and everything he wanted from life. This happened on account of many facts, among them that the baron had been a hero in the War of Independence, which was why he was appointed a baron, for after the war all the heroes were greatly rewarded, receiving land and gifts from the king Emperor Dom Pedro.

But this baron was very cruel. His heroism in the war was that he secretly killed a slave by the name of Inocêncio and he smeared himself with the blood of this slave and bandaged himself to make believe he had been wounded in combat. Imagine what a heinous thing, but that was precisely what he did. Very well, he smeared himself with this slave's blood, presented himself as a casualty, hid away for some time, and then reappeared and became known as a great war hero and received even more money than he had before and was appointed baron. However, there was a detail: when the slave Inocêncio was bled to death, another slave, by the name of Feliciano, was present and saw everything. He saw all that, but being a wicked master's poor slave, there was nothing he could do and kept silent about it. But then the baron sent for this slave, and when he came he ordered them to cut off his tongue, so he would never tell anyone about what had happened. They chopped it off near its root, and he was never again in his right mind, not really.

So the baron keeps on getting richer all the time, owning all the sugarcane in Bahia and all the fish and God knows how many other things, but his great badness doesn't cease. So it happens that one night, Saint Anthony's Day eve, he sends for a slave girl who was an African princess of great beauty and deflowers this slave girl after beating her up harder than anyone had ever been beaten up in his great slave quarters. But he was never informed that this slave girl, who was called Daê, became pregnant with his child that same night. He never knew because he sent for a freed Negro he trusted, and ordered this Negro to take the slave girl with him to keep or to kill in some faraway place, very distant from him.

The baron's wickedness was punished. Right after this episode in which he abused the slave girl, there appeared a great Brotherhood in the flour house of his own farm, led by a black wizard called Dandão and by an eight-foot-tall black called Budião. These two blacks of the powerful Brotherhood of the Flour House had a chest in which they kept many secrets about the fate of the people, many defenses and many prescriptions, incantations, and spells. And by means of those incantations and spells, as well as the help of others like them, they managed to give the baron a certain drink, and he got more and more bloated little by little, until he died one of the worst deaths ever seen in Bahia, including the plagues.

While this was happening, the slave girl became a great fisherwoman, with the protection of the freed black who had received her from the baron. This black, by means of many, many tricks, fooling whites and making the best of it here and there, saved money and became more or less well-off, had his house, had his pair of shoes, had his Sunday suit, had food on his table, he was a well-to-do Negro. Then the daughter of the fisherwoman Daê, who was also the daughter of the bad baron, was born and the old Negro took a liking to her, raised her as his granddaughter, sent her to a boarding school, and gave her everything he could. His granddaughter became a beautiful girl, a very tall, green-eyed mulatto, and they say prettier than a flower garden and more intelligent than bees. But it happened that one day, as she was coming back from a fishing trip, eight whites attacked her and her mother to abuse them. Her mother defended herself with a fisherman's club she had inherited from Africa, the name of which was *oriçanga,* so the whites stabbed her to death and fled. The girl was never the same again, always thinking of that crime, a crime that wasn't a crime because the law did not punish a Negro's death, always revolted with lack of justice and freedom. Even after the Brotherhood saw to it that the whites were swallowed by a huge sea wave and not a sign of them was seen ever since, even after this revenge, she wouldn't resign herself.

It's not known how she found out about the Brotherhood, nor about the chest, nor about Dandão and Budião, but the fact is that she found out, and when she did she joined them. The old Negro was greatly upset—my baby, why are you going to do a terrible thing like that, to abandon your old grandfather, to leave a comfortable life to involve yourself in this sedition—but she wouldn't listen—I'm going, no one can make me change my mind, I have to follow my destiny—until the old man decided to back her up, and even gave her the money he had hoarded all those years.

What happened to the girl? She disappeared in the world, fighting injustice in the company of a militia called the People's Militia. She freed the black Budião, who had been arrested in a great fortress defended by more than one thousand soldiers with shooting irons, bayonets, and cannons. With him as her partner in command, she confronted army troops in many battles, the first of which was on an island called Itaparica, not this Itaparica we have nearby but another, a very distant one, a great island surrounded by salt water, and in this battle she defeated the military, and afterwards had the two commanding officers dance naked among the people of the island. Where she is and what she's going to do is never known, but it's known she's been around all these parts and made many revolutions no one talks about. More than a few landowner barons had the same fate given the first, and more than a few slaves were freed. There were many, many of them, all around these parts.

But she soon noticed that the fight was much too uneven and would go on like that if she couldn't show everyone, all the people who suffer the tyranny of the powerful, that it's necessary for everyone to fight, each one in his own way, to bring about freedom and justice. And so, besides fighting, she took up teaching and made many schools for the people in the middle of the wilds of several places, where she put her teachers and now and then showed up herself to give lessons, always starting each of them with the following sentence: "Now I am going to teach you how to have pride." To the blacks she taught how to be proud of being black and of everything related to blackness, from their hair to their speech. To the Indians she taught the same thing. To the people, the same thing, as well as that the people is the owner of Brazil.

This made her more and more hated, and every time they discovered one of her schools they'd hang the teachers, put the students in stocks, curse the place, and do all they could to destroy what she had built. She kept hiding from the army, which is the worst and most powerful police of all. But the people liked her, and wherever she went she'd have a place to hide, and no one would inform strangers about where she was hiding, and many thought she was a saint in all her pure beauty.

About her being a saint there's no certainty, but it's certain she had a great love, which was for a high-ranking army officer who never wanted to fight against the people, and when they met he felt their souls were twins and their hearts were in harmony, so he proposed she become his lawfully wedded wife. She, who had fallen much in love with him, cried rivers and rivers of sorrowful tears. It wasn't because she had black blood, it wasn't anything like that that made her refuse; it was her elevated mission. She said to the officer:

"I am not going with you. My heart is broken in a thousand little bits, a thorn is stabbing my bosom with a most immense torment, the hoof of a horse is trampling on my head, there are tears in each of my eyes enough to fill a pail. I'm not going, but I'm going to weep forever for having given my soul to the people and not being able to give it to my man."

They say that from that day on her laughter, which was known for its gaiety, was very seldom heard. But that didn't make her forsake her ideals, though some people even thought she had gone mad. The emancipation of the slaves came, and she preached that that did not free any slaves and that the people couldn't expect anything to be given from above, and if they gave this freedom it was because it interested them, and a good thing for the people it was sure not to be. The Republic came, and she preached that nothing at all had changed, because neither kings nor presidents were thinking about the people, and they could even expect life to become worse. And in fact it was just what happened later, the droughts getting worse, the land being taken from the poor, slavery even worse than before, country political bosses with more power than the emperor of Rome, the people with their heads low, the dispossessed becoming more and more so and likewise the possessors, which is why it's said the Republic brought the Law of the Devil.

So Maria da Fé, which is the name of this great warrior, came to the backlands with her militiamen because she had heard that many people in the backlands were discontented and willing to take arms against tyranny. And here in the backlands people know she has shown up here and there, sometimes making war to make justice if she could, sometimes spreading the Brotherhood of the Flour House and pride. Many times she tried to unite the discontented of the wilds so they could fight together, but this became more and more difficult, with her being persecuted by police, by political bosses, by farmers, and by everyone else who felt threatened by her work. But she didn't give up fighting, and right here in this place where they were, which used to belong to Crescêncio Andrade, a bushwhacker, chief of hired guns, and farmer, the pockmarks made by her bullets are still on the wall, when she joined a revolt of sharecroppers and won, though after she left, a great force came and killed all the sharecroppers, making them dig their own graves and chopping off the heads of the bravest ones to show to the people. That's why this here is called Andrade's Ruin, and no one ever again planted or raised anything here, and it turned into this haunted place, where the souls of the good keep on struggling against the souls of the bad, day and night.

No one knows where Maria da Fé is now, nor what she's doing. But everyone knows that, as the word "faith" that's in her name indicates, she still believes that someday she'll triumph, even if not personally but through someone who inherits her ideas and courage, and she thinks there are many of those. Since she was born around Independence time, she must be old now but alive, because no one ever managed to chop off her head. And maybe she isn't even old, because people know her birthdays are only every four years, as she was born on February 29.

"She may even be around here somewhere," the old man said, pouting and turning his head slowly, as if he was trying to see with his clouded eyes. "Because today's the twenty-ninth of February, and that's why I chose this story to tell you."

Filomeno Cabrito shuddered, and he saw that the other men were feeling more or less like him, starting to move about and talk, as if to air the heavy atmosphere a little. Some said they hadn't enjoyed the story more than they had because it had no end, but the blindman retorted that no story has an end, they were mistaken if they thought that stories had ends. Others asked if he belonged to the great Brotherhood, and he said no but also said that if he did he wouldn't tell them, so the question was useless. Filomeno became interested in the questions and answers, and in the discussion that followed, and imagined that if he stayed there he would learn many, many more things, including things about Maria da Fé, of whom he had heard only very vaguely before. But he got up, went over to the blindman, put a coin in his hand, picked up his bag, put his hat back on, said good night to the others, and set out for his hovel without looking sideways, because he did not want to see ghosts, he did not even want to see Maria da Fé materialize suddenly in the wilds, he only wanted to have a dreamless sleep. He could not stay, it was very late, he had to rise early, he still had a very long way to go and he was not very familiar with the area, having traveled from Piauí by entangled trails until he got there. But he hoped that by persevering and walking briskly, with faith in Christ and the Most Holy Virgin, in a few more days he would be arriving in the place where he was going in pilgrimage or perhaps to live, the renowned Settlement of Canudos, governed by a man known as the Counselor.

Rio de Janeiro, December 16, 1871

"Never! Never! Never!" Henriqueta stomped her feet in front of her bedroom mirror and began a crying fit. "Dadeca, I'm going to use the *décolleté*, nothing will force me to be portrayed in this awful old lady's *jabot*, oh no, oh no, oh no!"

"Madame, *madamezinha*, don't cry, *madamezinha*, you're going to wet your face powder, it's taken so much trouble to get it right," the black woman Dadeca said. "No, it's not bad, it's pretty, you're just like a great lady!"

"Like a great lady? Like an old hag would be better put; I even seem to have a double chin with this thing on! And how many times will I have to tell you not to call me *madamezinha*? "Madame" is a French word, *madamezinha* is a barbarism, something only blacks say; won't you ever learn anything? Oh my God, why did I have to ask my husband's opinion, for him to insist on this museum piece? How can I ever show the portrait to my friends, to anybody? No, I'm not going to feel ridiculous; no one can make me, ever! Come on, Dadeca, move, go to my wardrobe—the one on the right-hand side, the one on the right-hand side!—and bring me my *décolleté* dress, the *moiré* one, that one, help me take off these horrifying rags!"

What a life, what heat, never a moment of peace and quiet! They said it was hot up north, but hot weather like in Rio de Janeiro, my God in heaven! When they first arrived, she was thrilled by the mansion Bonifácio Odulfo bought in Caminho Novo de Botafogo, inside a very large park, with stables, a garden, and a lake with little boats and statues of Nereids and Tritons. But now she no longer thought it so magnificent, she was even a bit envious of Titiza's house in Cosme Velho, which seemed to her to have a more aristocratic touch. She became even angrier at the heat, at everything in the world, and at Dadeca, who just now was taking too long to unfasten the hooks of her corset.

"Does everything have to be extraordinarily difficult for you? And there are those who say the Negro race has intelligence! If apes have intelligence, then Negroes have intelligence too, the intelligence of apes!"

What suffering, my God in heaven! Imagine if a Negress like that had the responsibilities of a lady. That's why Negro tribes have never been anything but bands of cannibals and are despised all over the world. Of course she didn't want to be a Negress, she couldn't even think about it, but sometimes she envied the life of simple people. Everyone thinks that people who have money have no problems, but what a mistake, what a terrible mistake! Simple people are the ones who don't have problems, who don't know anything, don't need anything, have no spiritual yearnings and no responsibility, steal from their bosses, work as little as they can, and lead easy lives, in a bed of roses, as they say. Oh, if they knew about the life of a great lady! But it was no use thinking they might understand it; they wouldn't understand anything; they would just keep on being envious. What paltry people, this Brazilian people! How much exertion, how much suffering, how much anguish she had had to go through just to get Jean-Louis Gaillard to paint her portrait. First she had to concoct a plan to persuade Bonifácio Odulfo, who found the Frenchman's price outrageous—what a mentality, my God in heaven, as if art had a price, as if Jean-Louis Gaillard was not a universal name, one of those portraitists who are born only once each century! What a tribute she had paid, my God in heaven! She had paid it and had gone on paying it, because when she suggested exchanging whipping him for his approval of the portrait, she couldn't have imagined she would be a slave of that practice apparently for the rest of her life. If in the beginning he was ashamed of asking for more, now he did it with the greatest cynicism; it was hell, a veritable hell, that kind of thing is tiresome! How hot it is! And then came the doubt about whether the painter would agree to do her portrait. Yes, on top of it all she had had to deal with that! Every woman wanted to have a portrait painted by him, absolutely every one of them, my God in heaven! What an effort, what tolerance toward the countess of Penha's flabby mouth just because she was a friend of Jean-Louis Gaillard's and he was her houseguest. But Teresa Henriqueta wasn't a woman who gave up easily, and the painter had finally set the time for the first session, for which she was so laboriously preparing herself, assisted by the ineptness of an obtuse Negress. How everything in this country is difficult, my God in heaven! It's so hot! It's so hot!

With the new dress on, she looked at herself in the mirror, found herself pretty, and felt a little better. Maybe her shoulders were a bit shiny, maybe her bust too; wouldn't a touch of powder solve that problem? It was the accursed heat, which left people glistening as if they had been waxed. She smiled provocatively at the mirror, inclined her body in several positions, looked at herself sideways, once again found herself pretty, very pretty really, beautiful, why not say it? She liked that dress, it gave her such . . . such a jaunty, perky, merry look! And at the same time it enhanced a woman, not a girl, a real woman, whose charm and depth could not be denied. She thrust out her bust a little. How about a beauty spot right here, a tiny beauty spot for just a subtle touch of naughtiness?

"What you think of a beauty spot right here?" she asked Dadeca, her little finger pointing to her left breast.

Dadeca was gaping, her eyes fixed on Henriqueta's neckline, and did not hear the question.

"What are you doing, standing there like a dummy? Didn't you hear what I asked you? Don't you think a little spot here . . ."

She noticed Dadeca was shocked by her dress, and raised her hands. What a mentality, my God in heaven! Would she always be condemned to live among so much backwardness, an exile in the very country where she had had the misfortune to be born? What was wrong with that dress, my God in heaven, what was wrong with it? It was modest in comparison to what she had seen in Europe and what she kept seeing in reviews and catalogues—what was wrong with it?

"A little spot, madame?"

Henriqueta laughed. Poor stupid creature, how could the poor devil understand the mind of a superior person? She had to be patient with her, she wasn't so bad, at least she was a Negress that could be trusted. She clasped her hands together on her lap, looked at her with her head inclined, and laughed for a long time. Dadeca ended up laughing too.

"My goodness, madame, this dress . . ."

"What's wrong with this dress, Dadeca?"

"The decotelay, isn't the decotelay too low? Master Bonifácio Odulfo, won't he . . ."

"What? The decotelay? Oh, Dadeca, if you hadn't been born they'd have to invent you! So my decotelay is too low? Not at all. Maybe it's too low for this place, for a backward city and a backward society."

"But madame lives here."

"I have to agree with you on that, Dadeca; now and then, God knows how, you have an intelligent thought. But living here doesn't make a woman like me—"

"A woman! Holy Virgin, madame! A woman?"

"A woman, a woman, yes, what's wrong with that word? A woman, a woman, *une femme, a woman,* a woman! Women will someday free themselves from this fate that makes it embarrassing for them to mention their own condition. A man can say he's a man, but a woman cannot say she's a woman? No, no, the feminine spirit will show its worth someday, I'm sure of that. Yes. I'm a woman, Dadeca, and as I was telling you, living here—*là-bas,* as they say—won't make a woman like me, with no exaggeration, of course, but with the daring a woman knows how to use in a precise measure, give up fighting against these ridiculous, old-fashioned restrictions. A modern woman is not like you think at all, she's not a shrinking violet. A modern woman does her own thinking, and if it depends on me, she'll make her own decisions about the size of her *décolletage* and will assume her natural *coquetterie.* A woman is a being of innuendos, a being of indirect approaches, a being who doesn't submit herself to the dry dictates of reason."

She sighed. What was she doing, having an erudite, intellectual conversation with Dadeca? She felt a little sorry for herself. For centuries now, women like her had been shining in the courts and salons of Europe, and here she was, my God in heaven, wasting her *bons mots* and her culture on an illiterate piece of coal. It's so hot!

"But you're right, Dadeca, I'll sacrifice the spot this time. And if my neckline seems too bold to you, I'll make another concession to the rustics of this hamlet, I'll put on the boa, the white one, what do you say? Oh, I'm feeling Parisian! You think the pink one is better? No, no, too showy; I'll wear the white one. Oh, I don't know. Do you have an idea, Dadeca?"

"It's very pretty, madame, it's really very pretty."

"Why do I ask you about anything? All you know how to do is to say it's pretty or goggle at me like a scared monkey because of my neckline."

"Yes, madame."

"I'll tell you what I'm going to do, Dadeca. I'm going to wear the blue *pèlerine,* the light-colored one. It's obvious—why didn't I think of that before? The *pèlerine* is perfect, it hides but doesn't hide, you just leave it unbuttoned here this way. . . . No, these two buttons. Huh? There! Perfect, perfect! Dadeca, I look gorgeous! Don't I?"

"Very gorgeous, madame, very, very gorgeous, very gorgeous!"

"Thank you, Dadeca, it's true. Now I just have to change these combs; they're horrible; they look like the teeth of some fierce animal trying to swallow my head. They're too big; bring me the small ones, the Spanish ones. They're not as good as they look, they slip a little, but they are a good match for this dress, maybe because of the little gems it's studded with. Hurry up! Am I late? What time is it?"

"It just struck two."

"Two. Are you sure? Go check it."

"But, madame, there's still time. Didn't the painter say he was only coming at three, didn't he say three o'clock? Didn't madame ask me to remind her it was today at three?"

"Dadeca, what an unnerving habit you have of trying to discuss my orders to you! Didn't I tell you to go see what time it is? So go see what time it is; don't argue with me! And hand over those *mitaines* before you leave. Yes, those gloves; don't you ever learn? My God in heaven!"

The painter had indeed set the first session for three o'clock. But Dadeca didn't know, and couldn't know, that the day promised more excitement than a mere posing session, no matter who the artist was. It was the day, it was finally the day she'd fall into Tico's arms, the day—and she felt a tickle below her navel—he would—yes, that was the word, the divine word—possess her! It's so hot!

If it was two o'clock, he'd be arriving by now. What an indescribable sensation! After a campaign during which she had often despaired of making him understand her passion, and had used every ruse and bait that had crossed her mind, even a couple of things she now admitted had been foolhardy, it had finally happened! And in such an unexpected, poetic, beautiful way, so fitting for an affair that had started with a message through flowers! Well, actually for him it had not started then, but at least for her it had. He either ignored or didn't understand the message of the jasmines, just as he didn't dozens of insinuations, made even during the trip to Rio. He had just pretended he wasn't understanding, could that be it? Well, it didn't make any difference now, because it had finally happened, it had happened, it had happened!

It had happened in the hothouse, among orchids, ferns, and exotic flowers, such a damp environment that the glass walls and roof were always fogged. Well, it had almost happened. How did Ovid put it, in that little French edition of *L'Art d'Aimer*? How did he put it? He said more or less that a lover who wins a kiss and nothing else didn't deserve that first kiss. What difference is there between a kiss, an eager kiss on someone's lips, which makes one's whole body tremble and melt, and the most intimate acts of love? None. Therefore it had happened: only an avid, hurried kiss inside the hothouse, such a fervid kiss that when they pulled apart because they heard the footsteps of a gardener among the shrubs, his lip took a little long to part from her mouth, coming loose after a positively inebriating sound, something inexpressible she had never experienced before. And his thigh touching hers during that instant of complete ecstasy, her breast pressed hard by her against his arm—had he noticed it? Of course he had; of all the silly doubts.

Why had he said at lunchtime, as if he wanted to make sure she would listen, that today he was going to come back from the ministry earlier? Exactly because of that, because he wanted her to know about it and create an opportunity for their being together, finally together, finally the great moment for her sensitive and ardently feminine soul. And she knew what she was going to do: she was going to do the same thing as Charlotte, the astute Charlotte of the novel. Isn't it amazing how things coincide in life; doesn't everything seem to have been plotted? First, the coincidence of the flowers. Second, the coincidence of the scene with Charlotte and M. Dubois in the library. Bent on seducing M. Dubois, but hindered by his inexperience, Charlotte didn't think twice. Through astounding machinations with the help of the mulatto girl Kiki, her very clever Antillean chambermaid, she managed to lock herself in her husband's library in the company of a shy, stuttering Dubois, and when she saw he would never take the initiative, she swooned in his arms in such a position that she fell down on the *sommier,* with him on top of her. *"Ah, chéri, tu es si fort, je suis vaincue,"* Charlotte said then, pulling the young man's head toward her panting bosom and slipping her enthusiastic hand under his shirt.

Oh, she wouldn't have to faint. Tico might be clumsy but was no nincompoop like Dubois. And anyway, there was a *sommier* in the library, and the library was just the place where Tico would go when he returned home early. Maybe the coincidences would not follow, but if Destiny commanded it, she would faint.

"Tico, Tico," she murmured almost inaudibly. "I'm overwhelmed, I'm yours!"

"Is madame praying?" asked Dadeca, who had stood behind her ever since she had returned from looking at the clock. "Are you feeling something, madame?"

Henriqueta came to her senses. She had almost betrayed herself, my God in heaven. But she did not disclaim her embarrassment, and simply asked why the black had not told her yet what time it was and had stayed there like a ghost to startle her.

"But I told you, madame. I told you twice, and then I thought madame didn't want to know anymore, madame is so nervous today. . . ."

"What is this? What kind of familiarity is that? Is it true, do I seem nervous to you? Do I really? Why do you say that?"

"Oh, I don't know; madame can't stand still, seems annoyed and at the same time happy . . ."

"It must be the heat. But it's nothing to be discussed with you—stay in your place! What time is it, after all?"

"A quarter past two."

"Very well, I'm ready. I'll put on the *pèlerine* when Monsieur Jean-Louis Gaillard arrives; the rest is all right, everything's ready, you may go. What are you waiting for? You may go!"

She closed the door behind Dadeca, ran to the balcony, leaned over, and saw Patrício Macário's unhitched cabriolet near the first shed of the stables. He had arrived; there was no time to lose. Soon the painter would show up, and such a perfect opportunity might never repeat itself. She primped once more in front of the mirror, dabbed two droplets of a French perfume behind each of her ears and between her breasts, and left the room quietly to go downstairs. On her way down, she thought she was being too precipitate, too anxious. She was nervous, yes, but that shouldn't happen. She stopped, breathed deeply, and gazed at her face in the large jacaranda-framed mirror. Easy, easy. She rehearsed a smile, wiped off a nonexistent little spot on the corner of her mouth, and was going to proceed, when she saw a crystal bottle among the goblets on the small sideboard, almost crimson because of the port filling it. Nothing better for nervousness than a small goblet of port, everyone said that; she herself had drunk some once when she had a palpitation, and had enjoyed it very much. Not a goblet, just a tiny serving; a whole goblet might be too strong. On the other hand, why not a whole goblet? The worst that could happen was for her eyes to become a little moist, but that wasn't entirely bad, it gave them a special glow. She drank a full goblet, and immediately her head felt light and a serene confidence came over her; she was sure everything would turn out well. She entered the corridor leading to the library, looked at herself in the hatstand mirror, pressed down both combs in her hair, and, ready to affect a look of surprise, opened the door and went in.

Patrício Macário, his back to the door, was picking books out of a bookcase to stack on the bureau, but hearing the noise she made, he turned around.

"You here?" Henriqueta said, opening her eyes very wide. "I didn't see you arriving."

"Are you going to a party?" he asked, looking at her from head to toe.

"A party? What do you . . . oh, is it because of my dress? No, it's not a party; it's just that today the portraitist Jean-Louis Gaillard is coming for our first sitting. You don't want me to be seen by posterity in stay-at-home clothes, do you? Do you like it? I'm not sure it's a good choice. What do you say?"

"It's beautiful, really very beautiful. And anyway, any dress becomes beautiful on you."

She felt she had blushed, was a little disconcerted, and picked up one of the books he had laid down on the bureau. Would she now say what had instantly come to her mind? Would she? Would she have the courage? Charlotte would say it!

"If you hadn't liked it, I'd change it right away," she said, blushing again, while pretending to be paying attention to some detail of the book's cover.

She raised her eyes firmly and stared at him unsmilingly. She was near the *sommier,* she had bolted the door on her way in, the moment was now. She walked over to him, her heart pounding, her mouth dry, her hands shaking a little, but with a determination that surprised even herself.

"You drive me crazy, you know?" she said, very close to him. "After that kiss, I haven't had any rest. Why did you do that, why did you take my peace away? I know it's madness, but when you said at the table today that you'd be home early, I fought with all my strength to resist coming here and couldn't do it, I couldn't! Oh, why did you do that? You drive me crazy!"

She looked down, expecting him to take hold of her chin as he had done the first time. But instead of that he went around the *sommier* and strode over to the other side of the room.

"Henriqueta," he began, looking a little embarrassed. "There's something I've been wanting to tell you. That kiss . . . that kiss . . ."

"You don't have to say anything; I know what you're going to say. That kiss was folly—divine folly, but folly. And still more folly because I can't get it out of my mind, and honestly, if you kissed me again I don't know if I would be able to resist. I know I shouldn't talk like that, that I may seem too rash and immodest, but it's the truth. After that kiss, how can I hide the truth of my passion?"

"Henriqueta . . ."

"You're beautiful, so strong, so fragile. . . . My God in heaven, what am I saying, I'm beside myself, why have you seduced me? Tico—"

"Wait just a moment, Henriqueta, just one moment. What I wanted to tell you . . . what I wanted to tell you is very difficult. I don't want you to think I was frivolous when I kissed you. That is, I was, yes, I was, because after all you're my brother's wife and I had no right to act the way I did. But I want you to know it wasn't something I would do with just any woman, it's not something you have to be ashamed of, because I had for you, and still have, the greatest affection and respect."

"I—"

"Wait just a moment. This is difficult in itself; don't make it still more difficult. I'm not made of stone, and a woman like you, with your charm and beauty, is not easy to find."

"I—"

"Please, just a few more minutes, please. What I mean is . . . Do you see these books? They're mine, the few I have, things of my youth which I left with my brother. I'm taking the books out of the bookcase because I'm taking them with me. I'm moving out."

"You're moving out? But how come? Moving out? Another transfer? But now that . . . I don't understand!"

"No, I haven't been transferred; I'm staying in Rio. But not here; I don't think I should stay in this house."

"But why—what's the reason for that? Now that we have discovered each other, now that fate—"

"That's precisely the reason. We can't live under the same roof."

"We can't live under the same roof? Where is it written that lovers cannot live under the same roof?"

"Don't talk like that, Henriqueta; you're too wrought up. Don't talk like that. We're not lovers. That kiss was something fortuitous, a serious mistake, and if we can't undo it, we can at least try not to repeat it."

"Yes, I understand. You've made a fool of me."

"I didn't make a fool of you, I yielded to an impulse. And you must admit you provoked me, you've always provoked me. Then there's always a moment of weakness, and—"

"Not a moment, a life of weakness! I did provoke you, yes, I did, and why not? Because I'm a woman? And because I'm a woman I'm forced to accept passively everything men impose on me, and not fight to conquer what I want? My shame comes not from what I did but from whom I did it for, namely you, who conforms so well to your family's tradition of hypocritical softies. Can you by any chance erase the kiss you gave me? What difference is there between what happened and what could have happened? Could it be the petty, fatuous masculine pleasure of conquering only to reject afterwards?"

"But I'm not rejecting you, try to understand that."

"I won't try to understand anything! And you're right, you're not rejecting me; I am the one who's doing the rejecting, because if before I thought you had the greatness of soul and elevation to realize that love is not dependent upon conventions, now I know you're nothing but a pampered little soldier, maybe even as spineless as your eldest brother and as flaccid as the other."

"That's no way to talk, Henriqueta, you're upset, there's no reason—"

"Of course there's no reason. But remember this: If today the shame is mine for believing in the existence of better people than run-of-the-mill hypocrites like the one you have shown yourself to be, tomorrow the shame will be upon those who behave like you, savage, dubious, immoral moralists, for women are the force of progress, and not men, not those who brandish swords but are afraid of shadows!"

She had intended to say more, but she felt she was going to cry, and did not want him to notice it. She turned her back on him almost with a military about-face, slammed the door, and ran upstairs, feeling like shouting. In her room, she threw herself upon the bed, pommeling bedspreads and pillows.

"I'll never forgive him, never, never, never! Never!"

She got up with her dress crumpled and her hair loose on one side, looked in the full-length mirror, and felt immensely sorry for herself, felt such self-pity that it brought an oppressive pain to her chest and made her want to disappear, and she cried standing up. But some time later, wearing another dress, with a slightly lower neckline than the first, she pulled the bell cord to call Dadeca.

"Help me here, Dadeca, I have to get ready. I suddenly decided I couldn't stand that other dress. I don't ever want to set eyes on it again."

"Yes, madame. It's almost three, madame; the painter must be arriving."

"He can wait. A gentleman always waits for a lady. And besides, he's being very well paid. Loosen my hair; I don't want it combed down."

"Loosen your hair, madame? Stay with your hair loose? Sit for the portrait with your hair loose?"

"Did you hear what I said? My God in heaven, give me patience with imbecility and narrow-mindedness! I spoke clearly, Dadeca: loosen my hair!"

"Yes, madame."

She couldn't have been prettier, in vaporous sky blue, enveloped by a delicate cloud of perfume, her hair arranged in gracious curls, her smile bright, unreticent, when she entered the drawing room to speak to the painter, who was waiting for her near a window, contemplating the garden.

"M'sieu Jean-Louis Gaillard?" she said, speaking exactly like the actresses she had seen in Paris theaters.

The Frenchman stood up, and after looking at her like someone who is seeing a mirage, bowed down to kiss her hand.

"Je suis ravi, madame."

His kiss on her hand was really a kiss, not one of those grotesque clicks in the air Brazilian men did. While commenting absentmindedly on female impunctuality, she appraised M. Gaillard with interest. Much younger than she had thought, and good-looking too, in spite of his paleness and his excessively bulging forehead. Beautiful lips, very fleshy for a European, sensitive brown eyes, strong hands, and his arms and legs ought to be thick too.

"Est-ce qu'on pourra commencer aujourd'hui?" she asked, biting her lower lip and looking straight into his eyes.

17

Rio de Janeiro, November 14, 1889

"I am alarmed," Monsignor Clemente André said in his letter, read by a frowning Bonifácio Odulfo. "Would 'alarmed' be the right term? No, my affectionate, dear brother, I am, you might say, in a panic. I know, very well, that age is weighing me down, and makes me skeptical of man, so many have been the iniquities I have witnessed, in my life as a priest. On the other hand, I am not unaware of the fact that, consumed by the ailments of life's winter (I was almost led to the grave, by erysipelas, and today I no longer enjoy, at all, even one day, one hour, of complete well-being), I may be seeing the world with a certain bitterness. But nobody, in good conscience, can disavow the pessimism, which dominates men of goodwill, before the desolating—pardon the gallicism, which I used, here, because it is expressive, for the case in question—picture which we are facing.

"How do you see the situation there, at the court? Give me some relief, send me a tranquilizing word. In Bahia, news are late, or they do not arrive at all, in Bahia, we hear terrifying rumors each moment, unrest surrounds, like an infernal ghost, every heart. All people talk about is the Republic, as if the toppling of a legitimate sovereign could constitute a foundation, upon which to build a Nation. In truth, with the exception of an occasional, misled, decent man, it is nothing but a mob of remiss, troublemaking students, second-rate pamphleteers, and orators, causing all this anarchic, slanderous, destructive hubbub. But (alas, we, who bear on our backs an ignorant, backward people, have only hopelessness, as a companion), we live in a country where small groups of rabble-rousers have always been able, by taking advantage of the people's pacific disposition (some will say: ovine; with which I am inclined to agree), to do with the Nation whatever comes to their minds. Fortunately, I am positive that the Empire is solid, and that His Majesty is attentive to what is going on. May God illuminate him, and strengthen his hand, because, at a time like this, one cannot, absolutely, act with little rigor.

"But I tremble, my most esteemed brother, because the symptoms, which strike the eye, are, indeed, disturbing. One can no longer go out in the street in peace, especially at night. One can no longer frequent any public place, given the presence, more and more oppressive, of a throng of jobless, panhandling Negroes and Browns, a riffraff of the worst kind, whose language and whose appearance make us, always, seem to be traversing the *Cour des Miracles.* Emancipation, as I had feared, turned out to be a great evil. The Negroes were not, and are not yet, prepared for freedom. Obtuse, oxlike, illiterate, unclean, given to unacceptable practices, they now exercise, freely, their deleterious, corrupting influence, over customs and race. There is no foundation to the allegation that they are bums and tramps because there is no work. There is work, there has always been, for those who seek it, and for those who do not seek it, out of indolence and weakness of character, there never is. But no one takes, incredible as it may seem, measures to contain, efficaciously, this slothfulness. When they wake up, the rulers, it will be too late to overcome such a social and moral ulcer, which threatens to destroy everything the construction of which, laboriously, has been attempted along centuries of dedication and suffering.

"We are living in a crisis of authority, a crisis of command, a crisis of values, a deadly crisis of the deepest gravity, and we do not take notice of it, we do not do anything to quell it. Religious sentiment keeps crumbling down, the barbarian practice of fetishism resists the feeble, inept opposition offered by police organs and by the army, on which, undoubtedly, the solemn responsibility would be incumbnt, of defending the spiritual integrity of the population. Honesty is a most rare exception; felony is the rule. Disrespect is becoming a norm in social intercourse, the greed of merchants is raising the cost of living to unbearable heights, letters and culture are decaying appallingly, and disorder looms, in the horizon.

"All this cannot but cause, in me, a great despondence. And it is the main reason why I am writing you this letter. I know you shall be enormously surprised, but the fact is, I intend to forsake my activities. Disillusion, the burden of my fifty-nine years of toil and vain fatigue, compel me to withdraw from the arena. I intend to finish my days in Rome, in spiritual seclusion and devotion, for which I am, thank God, truly vocationed.

"The necessary steps, all of them, have been taken. I remain as Honorary President of the Charitable Works; I am not severing entirely the ties that bind me to the Orphanage and the Educational Institution, and indeed doing that would be, for me, unthinkable, as they are the fruit of my modest labors. I have encountered support, on the part of the Most Reverend Archbishop, who was very considerate, as usual. I shall sail out on the twenty-second, on the *Prince William,* bound to Rio de Janeiro, where I shall sojourn, for a while, to ascertain a few details with you. I shall proceed to Europe on the *Maria Eugênia,* on the eighth of December. I am taking along, exclusively, my personal belongings, a few books, and as company, solely, my faithful secretary, the young seminarist Luciano do Couto Salles Menezes, whose studies I intend to sponsor, in Rome, in exchange for the dedicated services I am provided by him, a young man from an excellent family, with an impeccable upbringing, and no less culture. We will not disturb you; you may rest assured.

"Recommend me to Dona Henriqueta, your saintly wife, and to my dear niece and nephew, whom I anticipate, joyfully, seeing again. I hope, also, to have the opportunity, so I can bid farewell to him, to be with our youngest brother, Colonel Patrício Macário, although I know that you and he have been very distant lately, something which I, sincerely, regret, although I know reason lies with you, for our Tico was never among the most sensible members of our family, nor has the military career, which, at first, seemed to be so favorable to him, seemed to have given him a satisfactory shelter, since I know, from reliable sources, that in the army it is considered— pardon the vulgarity—an easy bet that he will not ascend to the generalcy. I hope I will be able to address to him a few words, which might work for him as an incentive and a spiritual support, because I am sure that his principal problem is the absence of religious feeling, a condition which, thanks to Divine Providence, does not afflict you, which is confirmed by the blessings poured by the Creator, over your head."

The letter went on, because as usual the monsignor dealt with his intricate financial problems only at the end. Bonifácio Odulfo, however, interrupted his reading, not so much because he feared new expenses but because an unexpected sentiment overcame him. He folded the letter over his stomach, stretched his legs beneath the table, and remembered his family. It was true, the monsignor had been born in 1830, so he really was fifty-nine. Almost a sexagenarian—how time passes! Just the other day in Salvador, he was only a playful seminarist, and now the person writing to him was an old man, a sixty-year-old man, with that heavy, stodgy punctuation he insisted was the correct one, for he considered himself a master of prose, in which he wasn't entirely wrong. A dense, ponderous style, but elegant and classic. Solid ideas too, though maybe a little bit too rigid. If he hadn't dedicated his life to the education and reclamation of wayward boys, his future in the Church would have been brilliant, but this future was suddenly the past now.

Bonifácio Odulfo was no adolescent, either, with fifty-five years on his back. Fifty-five years! It didn't matter if he was in good shape, fifty-five years were fifty-five years, over half a century. Yes, sir, over half a century. With the exception of a dry cough that had started to beset him persistently, his health was excellent, he felt fine, his energy was unimpaired, his appearance unaltered but for a few white hairs on his sideburns and chest. But it was undeniable that he had gone through much more than half of his existence, no doubt about it. One fine day his hour would come—and the idea of death made him rise to pace around the room. Death, something that only happens to others, suddenly appears to be over there somewhere, in some unsuspected corner, waiting for the appointment from which no one escapes. How would his death be? He cracked his fingers nervously and decided to think about something else. Why the hell was he thinking about dying?

The family, the family. After a certain age, a man sees things in a very different way, sometimes diametrically opposed to the way he saw things in his youth. He imagined amusedly that if he met now a young man similar to the one he was until about thirty, he wouldn't bear the presence of such a pedantic, presumptuous whippersnapper, always declaiming inanities *ore rotundo* as if he were the voice of Nature. He was another person, they were all other persons now. The family, the family, the family, too, is something you see differently in maturity. That which oppresses in spring protects in winter. He decided to write down this thought for a vague book he was scribbling intermittently in English, called only for himself "Thoughts on Thoughts," which consisted of observations about maxims, aphorisms, proverbs, sayings, and *mots d'esprit*. But he stopped on the way to his desk: He would never finish the book, and if he did he wouldn't publish it. For a long time now he had decided it was useless to try to communicate his extremely rich and variegated experience, which he considered a march in the direction of wisdom, a wisdom he increasingly perceived as being an inseparable part of his personality. It was impossible to share such a journey with anybody, to reconstitute every step, all the more so because he viewed himself as a leader, a man capable of influencing the destiny of the nation. How often, in solitary, pensive moments, he had understood reality with such clearness that it dazzled him, how often he had the experience of seeing truth in all its luminous transparence! But how could he communicate that, how could he make somebody else see something that depended so much on sensitive, intelligent observation, in the course of an undeniably stimulating life? How could he speak of civilization to people who had never been to Europe and thought they knew something through the pale images offered by books? Impossible; it even caused him some despair. After all, it was more or less like being a foreigner in his own country. And he wasn't a European, either; in a way, he didn't have a nationality in the spiritual sense. Would that be the fate of men of the elite? What loneliness is brought by genius, by knowledge, by sensitivity; it's even melancholic.

And now Clemente André's letter reminded him of so many things. . . . Yes, why this estrangement within the family, this distance, if they were so few and getting old, and should be much closer? He had never gone back to Bahia except on two occasions, which he hadn't been able to avoid. As a matter of fact, like Henriqueta he had begun to abhor Bahia, a backward place, with small-minded, limited people; a filthy, uncomfortable town, its conversations destitute of interest; the general mongrelization there couldn't but shock a man of good upbringing. Dr. Noêmio took very good care of his businesses there, and Vasco Miguel's eldest son—how amazing, who would think six years had already passed since his brother-in-law had died, as apathetically as he had lived, six years!—was demonstrating he had not taken after his father and proving to be a talented business administrator, unlike his stolidly placid, however dear to him, late brother-in-law. And now? Vasco Miguel was dead, his nephews were in Bahia, the monsignor was leaving for Rome, and that breakup with Patrício Macário, a breakup lasting how long now? More than fifteen years for sure, almost twenty. Almost twenty years in which they practically saw each other only at Vasco Miguel's funeral, and even there without speaking.

Of course he was right: what Patrício Macário had done could be neither forgiven nor justified. He still remembered vividly the day Henriqueta, very nervous, distraught and unable to hold back her tears, had told him Tico was importuning her. His own brother, in his own home! He had almost lost his head, but Henriqueta, always an extraordinary woman, had made him see things dispassionately. No radical action was necessary, no scandal had to be caused, for after all nothing concrete had happened. Patrício Macário had fully assimilated her repulse, and at least had had the dignity to take the initiative of leaving their house. The thing to do now was to forget about him, let him live his life, explain to whoever asked about him that his military duties compelled him to live away from his family. After a sleepless night in which only Henriqueta's fortitude had kept him from having a nervous collapse, maybe even a stroke, Bonifácio Odulfo had accepted the facts calmly. But of course when his brother tried to see him the next day to say goodbye, he refused to receive him and instead sent Octaviano to deliver a simple, dignified note, through which relations between them were broken in a gentlemanly way. As Henriqueta—what an extraordinary woman!—had emphasized, it was a gesture of superiority, which perhaps would strike Patrício Macário's conscience someday.

But after so many years, his resentment had diluted itself, it was just a yellowish shadow, a stain whose importance had been deleted by time. Poor Tico, always a bit empty-headed, a primitive, impulsive person, a head-strong rebel who, as the monsignor had remarked in his letter, had not had too much luck in military life, where initially it had seemed he would get along fine. After a participation in the Paraguay campaign reputed as brilliant and a subsequent almost dizzying succession of promotions, his career had stagnated, he moved from bureaucratic post to bureaucratic post and was really an obscure officer. Poor fellow, he lacked learning, he lacked skills, he lacked so many qualities Nature had lavished on his brothers and withheld from him. Bonifácio Odulfo looked again at the monsignor's letter, his eyes filled with tears. What sense did it make now to prolong Patrício Macário's ostracism? Hadn't life itself punished him enough? People said he had become taciturn and self-absorbed, living like a hermit in a little house in the neighborhood of Matacavalos, almost friendless, though involved with republicans.

Yes, that on top of everything. Involved with republicans, who considered themselves a kind of intellectual vanguard, a pretension visible to the reader of the pamphlets and cheap sheets that infested Rio de Janeiro, but were nothing but—what was the extremely appropriate word the monsignor had used?—yes, troublemakers. A police case, even, a mere police case, for hadn't the chief of police forbidden any demonstration, even if purely personal, in favor of republican ideas? True, rumors were rifer and rifer, but they were nothing but rumors, and the calm displayed by the viscount of Ouro Preto, minister of the Empire, with whom he had talked not too long ago, made it clear that the situation was stable. It had to be, because what sense did it make to alter the form of government; what was the objective of such a radical step? England, an example of social, administrative, cultural, moral, religious, and economic superiority, was a monarchy. On the other hand, France, with its so-called Third Republic, struggled under one crisis after another. The United States of America were a republic, but why follow the example of a primitive, traditionless country, whose breakup with England had only alienated it from the mainstream of the progress of mankind? It was just this Brazilian fickleness, a childish fascination with fads, a penchant for novelties, which perhaps constitute the most negative character trait of an undefined, futureless people. And there was Patrício Macário, involved in this harebrained adventure, this senseless waste of time, this quixotic caper that would be funny if it were not irritating.

No, no, something had to be done to reunify the family. He might not be the eldest brother, but he was incontestably their father's heir, therefore their patriarch. That entailed higher duties than the dictates of personal convenience and accumulated grudges, no matter how just. The monsignor's letter had come as a kind of alert, a powerful reminder of a neglected duty. Fortunately, everything happens at its appointed time. He was not ready before, and the circumstances were not the most appropriate, either. Now, yes, now was the moment to give a lesson of greatness, discernment, and responsibility.

He took pride in the natural, and for that very reason edifying, way he had arrived at such an obvious, balanced conclusion. Here was the wisdom, the fairness, that distinguished him from other people—this wonderful ability to be always renewing himself, to adapt to unexpected situations, to visualize what was the right thing to do at the right time. There remained Henriqueta's resistance to be faced. She never uttered Tico's name; it was as if he had died. But he knew her heart, generous, incautious, impulsive, and the same way it would run into a fury of short duration, it would forgive in a loving impulse as shorn of covert intentions as the affection of a child. It wasn't a coincidence that in all of Rio de Janeiro's high society no lady was as esteemed as she, whether for her tireless sponsorship of the arts, giving support to a score of young artists, who truly worshiped her, or for the salons she presided over, where the keynotes were good taste, refinement, and aristocratic courtesy. He was sure she would accept the idea that had just taken shape in his mind: a family reunion, a gathering where uncomfortable differences might be passed over, lost goodwill might be reestablished, and loose ties might be renewed. The monsignor's visit was opportune. He would show her how good it would be for Clemente André, who was moving so far away, maybe never to be with them again, at least in Brazil. And how good it would be for their sense of heritage, of dynastic lineage, of family pride, which he made it a point of honor to inculcate in his children, Luiz-Phelippe and Isabel Regina, who hardly knew their relatives. Yes, that was an important point, a most important point. The decision had been made. He would gather the family together festively, would forgive Tico and give his other brother a proper send-off. It was the duty of the head of a family that, if not one of the most important in Brazil, was inevitably bound to be.

With a contented smile, he went back to his seat. He thumbed musingly through his brother's letter for a few moments, recalling colorful images of his childhood: the lunch table presided over by Amleto on sunny Sundays, Teolina happy in spite of her permanently suffering look, Carlota Borroméia, pale and elusive, laughing as she told them about her piano lessons, the garden outside resplendent in every hue, the breeze filling the drapes, friends talking about things that at that time sounded extremely elevated, intelligent, and out of the reach of anybody who did not have a lot of learning and experience, steaming tureens sailing down the corridors like little flying ships in the arms of black women, smells and tastes never to be recovered, enchantments never to be relived. He pursed his lips so hard that his cheeks quivered, and he thought he would not be able to avoid crying. If forced to, he probably wouldn't have talked about those reminiscences, but fortunately he was alone, the master of his dominions, and he could do anything he wanted, anything at all, even decree a holiday for the hundreds of employees working out there, unaware of the sentiments that affected so deeply the soul of that lonely, insulated man, a general surveying the battle from on high with his spirit afire, while the soldiers, mere puppets in history's magnificent panorama, fight on without sharing the deepest suffering—to wit, the suffering of the man who commands and knows the implications of the great episodes by which the fates of peoples are shaped.

For almost a minute, his smile turning little by little into a resolute expression, he remained with his hands gripping the edges of his desk. And as if a sudden force had overtaken him, he moved from contemplation to action. He pulled out the first page of a notepad, dipped his pen in the inkstand, and after crumpling several sheets of paper, wrote a telegram to Clemente André, in language at first excessively gushy and then corrected by vigorous pen strokes, which even punctured the paper, in which he exhorted him to come as soon as he could, to be greeted joyously by a united, loving family. Stretching out his arm to see better what he had written, he found the result to his satisfaction, added two commas so his brother would not reproach him for his carelessness toward independent clauses, and pressed his blotter down on the paper with both hands. It was finished, definitive, unretouchable, as was everything he authored. Stretching out his forefinger to avoid exposing himself to some unpredictable accident, he pressed the button of the electric buzzer he had reluctantly installed, because contrary to Henriqueta, he suspected there was something explosive in things that went off without being wound up by anyone. Since his office was entrenched behind a labyrinthine barrier of doors, nooks, and elephantine furniture, he could not hear the buzzer, which ought to be sounding in the anteroom where Octaviano worked. Modern things, exasperating things, he thought, while as though he had trouble stopping, he pecked at the black, shiny button with his finger.

It occurred to him that Octaviano, too, had aged and was now the very image of no longer incipient decrepitude; almost a gnarled old man, his posture so stooped that he sometimes gave the impression of not being able to look ahead, he presented the worn-out, disillusioned aspect of someone who had not known how to rise in life in spite of the opportunities offered by his job. Octaviano appeared at the door, straightening his coat.

"Yes, sir. Anything serious? The buzzer . . ."

"The buzzer is here to call you, *Senhor* Octaviano; there's nothing unusual in my using it to call you."

"Yes, sir, of course. It was just that the buzzing was so insistent I thought . . ."

"Think less, *Senhor* Octaviano, and do more."

"Yes, sir."

"Here is a telegram I just wrote, and I need to dispatch it at once."

"Yes, sir. Special delivery?"

"Special delivery. Read it to see if you understand everything that's written there."

"By all means, Dr. Bonifácio Odulfo. By all means, it's perfectly clear, by all means."

"Are you sure? It wouldn't be the first time I give you a flawless original, only to be brought an incorrect copy."

"Yes, sir, but everything is perfect, very clear, very clear. Do you want me to read it aloud?"

"Go ahead."

He kept looking at the ceiling, while Octaviano, straightening his glasses with trembling fingers, read the twelve lines of the telegram like a recitation.

"Just a moment. Where it's written 'plenarily,' substitute 'without stint.' "

"Without stint. Yes, sir."

"Read it again. No, no, 'plenarily' is better. The telegraph operator might mistake 'stint' for some other word; one should never underestimate the ignorance of Brazilian functionaries."

"Yes, sir. Plenarily."

"Yes, now read it again."

This time he nodded as he listened. Very well written, really very well written.

"All right, *Senhor* Octaviano. Very well, you may dispatch the telegram. Oh yes, just a minute. Do you have the key to the telephone room with you?"

"Yes, sir. Do you need it?"

"Of course not. What would I do with it? What I want you to do is to arrange for me to make a telephone call. Is the telephone working today?"

"I haven't checked it yet, Dr. Bonifácio Odulfo. Maybe it isn't. Those objects are very delicate, they keep getting out of order, and maybe today's problems are having some influence on them."

"Problems? What problems?"

"It's in the papers, sir. It's the talk of the town."

"You know very well I don't read Brazilian papers, let alone this anarchic-republican trash that seems to be the only thing published in this country. Nor do I have time to pay attention to rumors. But what's new, anyway?"

"The news is that Marshal Deodoro da Fonseca and a few other republican leaders are going to be arrested tomorrow. There is an atmosphere of great agitation; all people talk about is the fall of the government."

"Nonsense. If they are arrested, so much the better for the country. Nothing whatsoever is going to happen; I'm used to this type of rumor-mongering. It has another name. It's called having nothing better to do. Go check if the telephone is working. Then see if it's possible to make a call to the army department where my brother Colonel Patrício Macário works. I don't know which one it is; I never cared to find out. Try to do this as quickly as possible, and report back to me."

"Yes, sir."

Octaviano left, and Bonifácio Odulfo got up to go to the window and look at Glória Square down below. A great idea, to use the telephone. This way he would avoid a letter, which could be compromising, and would speak to his brother viva voce, in the precise condescending tone he was planning to use. What a beautiful invention, the telephone; possessing money and prestige had its advantages. Too bad it took so long, leaving him anxious and unable to pay attention to the papers on his desk. Just the same, he sat down, pulled over the stack of papers, and started to examine them, but after almost half an hour, he realized that if someone were to ask him what he had just read, he would not know how to answer. Dammit, would that ass Octaviano never manage to make that connection? He rang the buzzer again. Octaviano came in a little breathless, his hair out of place, his coat hanging sideways as though he had put it on in a hurry.

"Yes, sir! If it's about the connection, Dr. Bonifácio Odulfo, we're almost getting through!"

"It's been nearly an hour, *Senhor* Octaviano; I don't have all day."

"I know, Dr. Bonifácio Odulfo; it's just that there was a small fire at the telephone company and connections have become a little slow, but the telephonist—"

"The what?"

"The telephonist, the attendant who's in charge of the connection service. The telephonist has guaranteed that within a few minutes we'll complete the connection."

"The telephonist . . . Pretty soon this new barbarism will be recorded in dictionaries. Telephonist, indeed . . . All right, *Senhor* Octaviano, but if your telephonist—what a word, my God!—cannot complete the connection within a quarter of an hour, let me know, because it's an urgent matter, and in that case I'll send a messenger."

"Yes, sir, but that will not be necessary. I'm sure it will be a success, sir. Do I have your permission?"

"Go, go, go, get this over with."

"Yes, sir."

Octaviano left as hurriedly as he had arrived, and had barely closed the door behind him before he rushed back.

"The connection, sir!"

Bonifácio Odulfo got up, stiffened, adjusted his clothes, ran his hand through his hair hastily, cleared his throat, made a stern face, and followed Octaviano to the telephone room, from which other employees, at whom he directed an annoyed look, were emerging as though they had just witnessed a miracle. He went into the little room, cleared his throat again, took from Octaviano's hand the listening piece of his very modern German apparatus, and sat down, bending forward in the chair placed for him in front of the console.

"You may leave," he said. "It's a private conversation."

"Yes, sir."

But the conversation was difficult. Patrício Macário's voice, sounding like the squeaks of a malfunctioning music box, converted every vowel into a

409

closed *e,* and little of what he spoke could be understood, in waves that rose and then seemed to flow away to an unreachable distance. Nevertheless, his brother was able at least to understand, among shouts so loud that they burst out through the interstices of the door, that Patrício Macário was promising to come to see him as soon as he could, right after the resolution of some important events, which would be set into motion at any time. He couldn't speak now, not only because certain things should not be said on the phone but also because time was short. Bonifácio Odulfo wanted to know what all those serious events were.

"Is there any truth to the rumors?"

"What?"

"What people keep saying!"

"What?"

"Do you mean events concerning the government?"

"Yes, yes! Don't ask me anything now; I'll explain it later!"

"Don't you think it's just rumors, just rumors?"

"What?"

"Rumors! Rumors!"

"How's that again?"

"Rumors!"

"I didn't understand! I'll talk to you later, because—"

The telephone went dead, there remaining only an alarming succession of clicks, crackles, and hisses, which could be a sign that the contraption was about to explode or go up in flames. Bonifácio Odulfo opened the door and called Octaviano to tell him to disconnect the apparatus and observe carefully the safety recommendaions, so it would not overheat and set fire to the building, as had happened at the central station. He walked out satisfied with the contact he had made, despite some small difficulties, which are quite natural when one employs unusual instruments, though perfected by modern techniques. Patrício Macário was going to come to him, and everything was going to happen the way he wished. No one could ignore a telephone call.

Cocorobó, backlands of Bahia, March 1, 1897

Like every good pack leader, the mule Parakeet does not stumble, does not toss her head, does not change her pace for just any reason, does not get her hooves tangled up in ground vines, but paces steadily through the wilds, not needing anyone to teach her the way to the places she knows. Then why did she stall when she got to the foot of that little tableland she has known ever since she was born? And after proceeding reluctantly, didn't she almost rear, her nostrils flaring, her head shaking, her front hooves rising as if she were ready to prance?

"Whoa, Parakeet!" Filomeno Cabrito said, rushing to stand next to her head and hold her halter. "Whoa there!"

What the devil had happened to this mule, always so trustworthy, always a serious worker, now acting up all of a sudden, startling the others and slowing their progress? They had gone a good many leagues with that little mule pack, carrying gunpowder, cartridges, and weapons to the Settlement of Canudos, and there was still a long way to go, with detours because of the soldiers who were swarming around; how could she decide to make things more difficult? Without letting go of the halter, he examined the mule and patted her rump. She seemed to be calming down, though she still snorted and shook her head now and then. He looked inside her ears to see if some bug had gone into them, but did not find any. It was past noon; maybe the soldiers were already in the Rosary Settlement, right by Canudos, and ready to attack. Could it be that the mule was scenting them, the government monkeys? He whistled softly to call the boy Caruá, who had stayed in the rear, holding the last two mules still, and took a while to come.

"You think this mule is scenting something?" Filomeno asked. "I never saw her act so strange."

"They're all like that; the other four are like that too. I think they really are scenting something; I'm sure they are. I don't know what it is, but they don't behave this way just like that; it's got to be something. But she's better now; she isn't even snorting anymore."

"Yes, but if it was something she scented, it can't have gone away all of a sudden; only if it can fly."

"Well, we have to march on—isn't that what we're here for?"

"Yes, better get going now. Giddap, mule Parakeet! Muuule!"

Caruá ran to the back of the pack, crossed himself, looking at the wilds around, and thought he, too, had scented something. It might not even be a bad thing, it could be a good thing, a protection sent from on high for that dangerous mission. He who has God and Our Lady on his side fears nothing, he thought, and crossed himself again.

Though he'd decided not to leave Parakeet's side anymore, Filomeno ended up forgetting what had happened, all the more because the mule was now marching placidly, her stoic head going up and down as she opened her way through the wilds as if in a hurry. Good mule, good pace, and Filomeno breathed deeply. After the light rain that had fallen a while before, the earth was smelling good and the backlands were a great live beauty, making him joyful like a young goat let loose, a contentment that made him leap as he trudged on. He was happy, very happy; he had found the life he wanted—not only life but hope. Life was no longer as it had been in the wastelands of Conceição do Canindé, he was no longer leading a life worse than a black slave's, no longer hungry, no longer feeling there was no place in the world for him. Now there was this place he was proudly occupying alongside the mule Parakeet, taking arms for the holy combat in which once again they would show the tyrants—who wanted to subjugate and humiliate them, submit them to ungodly laws brought from no one knew where—that there was no way to overcome faith and love for the land. They would not win, they would never win, they would never take away from him the good fortune of living the way he had always wanted to live, in his homeland, speaking his words, eating his food, knowing his answers, not seeing anyone as a stranger, everything as it should be in the world, everything in the world exactly as it should be. It was not really that way yet, but it would be, and the day this would happen was not far off, but even close, very close.

Filomeno smiled, not noticing that though the mule was not tossing her head, she was disquieted once again. But Caruá dashed over to his side and asked him if he had not perceived anything. No, no, he had neither seen nor heard anything; he had been absorbed in his own thoughts, musing about the beauties of life and God's kindness. But for the Redeemer's sake, Master Filomeno, don't you see these wilds are alive with people? Filomeno halted his mule and scrutinized their surroundings. Yes, what a suspicious silence; it wasn't a good silence. He started examining plants to see if he would find signs of people, but did not have time even to inspect a low cactus that seemed to have been stepped on and had attracted his attention, because he heard a noise and felt a banging lightning in his head. He woke up later with a very strong pain, tied hand and foot on the ground, in front of a uniformed man who was kicking his ribs.

"Hey! Wake up, you bastard! Wake up, you no-good stinker, where's your bandit's bravery? Wake up, you trash!"

Filomeno wanted to turn around to face the man but could not move because they had laid him on his side, his hands and feet tied together at his back.

"You don't have to turn around to speak—stay just the way you are!" the man shouted, kicking him again.

"What happened?"

"You're not supposed to ask any questions, you dog!"

He gave Filomeno another kick, more powerful than the previous ones, and Filomeno had a coughing fit.

"Which one of you is responsible for this smuggling?" asked another man, whom Filomeno could not see.

"It must be this one here," said the one who was doing the kicking. "He's the older one."

"Yes, I'm responsible, I'm the one who's responsible!" Filomeno shouted when he realized they were talking about Caruá. "He doesn't even know what I'm carrying; he's only a boy I hired to take care of the mules."

"Yes, he must be the leader," the second man said. "Then shoot this one here; we need just one for questioning. We're late already."

"You're going to kill the boy? But the boy didn't do anything—I am the one who's responsible!"

"Shut up!" the first man said, with a new kick, this time to Filomeno's stomach, and unable to bend with the pain, Filomeno lost consciousness for a few moments. But he came to in time to hear muted voices talking a short distance from him and shortly afterward three shots, the first one followed by a muffled moan, and the next two by the sounds of birds roused by the noise.

"Are we going to bury him?" a sharp voice asked.

"And leave the buzzards hungry?" answered the man who had given the order for the execution. "When they kill one of us, they don't bury him; with me it's an eye for an eye."

"Yes, sir. May I take his belt? It's a beautiful belt; it would be a shame to leave it here, Lieutenant."

"Take it, take it."

They came close to Filomeno, this time from all sides. There were ten or twelve of them, probably a picket that had lost its way—a sign that the army was closer than expected; could it have attacked Canudos already? He listened to the discussion about his fate. The first man asked the second if they were going to interrogate him right there; it should not be difficult to make him speak with a couple of whacks. But the second man said no, they already knew everything they needed at the moment. Those were weapons for the fanatics, and they had intercepted them to take them to Angico. The rest—how they had been acquired and who had acquired them—would be known later; it did not matter now. Maybe it would be dark before they got to Angico, and tired as they were, it would not be a good idea to march at night in unfamiliar surroundings. He ordered them to untie Filomeno's legs and help him up, but he was not able to stand on his feet and had to be supported by two privates.

"You know the way to Angico?" asked a young infantry officer, whose face, bearded and with a waxed mustache, he could now see clearly, in spite of his dizziness.

"Yes."

"Yes, sir!" the officer corrected him imperiously.

"Do you know it too?"

The officer took a step forward, raised his right arm, and slapped Filomeno's face as hard as he could.

"I won't take any insolence from you!" he yelled. "Scum! Ignorant fanatic! We'll teach you and all your degenerate rabble how to treat an officer of the

Army of the Republic! We'll either teach you or eliminate you—people like you are the shame of the nation!"

He calmed down suddenly, came close to Filomeno, and spoke near his face.

"Listen well. You're going to guide us to the old farm in Angico. We have two soldiers who are mule drivers and who are going to lead the mules according to your indications. Another soldier is going to be glued to your back to bust your brains if you try to deceive us. If we fall in an ambush or are guided to the wrong place, you're going to be the first one to die, that I can assure you. I know we have to go southeast more or less, and I have a device that tells me in what direction we're going. So don't try to fool me, because it won't be possible."

Staggering at first, but soon managing to navigate steadily, Filomeno walked over to the front of the mule line and saw from the corner of his eyes Parakeet trying to shake her halter from the hands of a black soldier, who was whipping her hard without being able to dominate her.

"Whoa," Filomeno said to her, because he did not want her to be beaten, and she stopped.

"Let's get going," said the soldier assigned to accompany him, his pistol in his hand.

"Lieutenant, don't you think we're running a risk, being guided by this man?" someone asked.

"He'd better not try to fool me. Picanço is right behind him with a pistol pointed to his head, and I'm keeping an eye on the compass, I know the direction is southeast, I just don't know the trails. These people don't think, they are instinctive—they are on the borderline between human and animal. Don't worry."

So on to Angico. In that case, Filomeno had to walk ahead of the mule, because she had been heading to the settlement. But would he really take these people to Angico, for them to join their companions and together torture him to death? It was certain death in any case, and he would rather have a decent death which served some purpose than a meaningless death, useful only for the enemy. But how about the lieutenant's device? The hell with it—if the device were any good, they wouldn't need a guide. He glanced at Parakeet, persisting in her steady pace toward the settlement, felt proud of her, and went on pretending he was guiding her. All was in God's hands.

Nevertheless, now that the column had become silent and all they heard was the sound of footsteps and of men and mules brushing against leaves, he was sure the wilds were still alive with people. He was not a tracker, but he could see human signs and register a few strong smells—of a tamped-down fire, of coffee dregs poured on the ground. And they were not strangers, because they had not damaged plants as they passed; they were people who knew how to walk there and were sure about where they were going. His people, the

Counselor's people? At first it was just something he wanted to believe, but he soon decided he was sure of it and became happy without altering his pace or his face; now it was a matter of time. Yes, and also time to die, because soldier Picanço had tied the rope binding Filomeno to his own waist and kept the pistol pointed, only changing hands now and then. Filomeno wondered if he would go to heaven after such a violent death, without confession, communion, and extreme unction. Maybe he wouldn't, but on the other hand maybe he would, because in a case of this type, God will see that it happened against the victim's will. But anyway he started to pray silently, and in the end he commended his soul with simplicity, asking forgiveness for his sins.

Maybe he was still praying, or again lost in thought, when the officer ordered them to halt. He wanted to check the timing of their march, to know how much longer it would take to get to Angico, and whether they would arrive before nightfall. Filomeno answered that night usually fell suddenly thereabouts, especially if it rained, as seemed likely, so the best guess was it would be dark before they got there; they would have to march at night. The officer did not like the information and threatened to have him whipped or executed right then and there. He picked up his device, raised a kind of lid, and, taking several positions in the wooded area where they were, made a series of readings with a very intent expression. He called a private and asked him for a map, which he folded so as to study it more easily. He took a few notes, made computations and called his next in command to show him what he was doing. After a long talk, he nodded vigorously at something the other spoke, and made a sign for the march to proceed. Filomeno found all that ritual funny, but no change was noticeable in his face when he clicked his tongue at Parakeet to resume their trip.

Yes, night falls suddenly in those wilds, so suddenly that sometimes it seems the passerby just blinks, and when his eyes open he sees night has taken the place of day. And this happened to all in that troop except Filomeno, who knew every sign of night, and knew it was coming at the usual pace, neither hurriedly nor unhurriedly. The commanding officer had two lanterns lit, one at the front and one at the rear, the column took Old Man Trail, and suddenly a succession of closely spaced detonations burst from the woods, the lights went out, and after two jerks, Picanço collapsed on the ground, among people shouting and running about and mules prancing. Unable to see anything but the flashes that preceded the bangs, Filomeno lying on the ground next to the soldier, saw at once that he was dead and tried in vain to get rid of the rope that tied them together. The shooting ceased as unexpectedly as it had started, and all that remained was the sound of voices—a few shouts, some incomprehensible orders, words that sounded like name-calling. Who could they be? Soon that stopped too, though one could see a lot of people moving about. And lights too—not the lanterns, which had probably been destroyed by shots from the ambushers, but tin lamps. Who could they be? A squad of Chico Ema's raiders, irrupting through the wilds to search and kill the monkeys? Maybe something led by the old devil Macambira, who knew how to stalk soldiers better than a hunting dog knew how to stalk cavies? Whoever they were, they were friends.

"Here!" Filomeno shouted in the direction of one of the lamps. "Here!"

Two men he had never seen before came near him. The older one, a man perhaps fifty years of age, crouched down with a knife in his hand and asked the other to bring over the lamp so he could see Filomeno's face. His hat, similar to the ones worn by backlands bandits, was hanging from his neck by its chin strap, showing a white, curly-haired head.

"You hurt?" he asked, and only then did Filomeno notice soldier Picanço's blood splattered on his face and leather jacket.

"No; it's his blood. I'm tied to him."

"Oh. Give me a hand here, Lourenço."

Lourenço took the knife from the older one, cut the rope, and helped Filomeno up.

"The mules!" Filomeno said as soon as he stood up, remembering his cargo. "Did the mules stampede?"

"Take it easy. Only one of them scampered away, but they found her right there by the bumelia tree. You were taking those supplies with this little pack, and then they—"

"Yes, yes, but—please excuse me, I'm very thankful for this rescue, please forgive my ignorance—you're not Good Jesus the Counselor's people, are you?"

"No. Just in a certain way. We are not his people, but we're on his side."

"Against the Republic?"

"No, against tyranny and injustice in the first place."

Filomeno found this answer very odd; he had never heard anything like it. Were they bandits? More or less, the man said, more or less. Filomeno wanted to ask another question, but the man waved at him, as if trying to excuse himself, and walked off toward the others. Now Filomeno could see that not all the soldiers had died at the ambush. Most of them, yes, but about three were left, besides the two higher-ranking men, now surrounded by the strange combatants who had come out of nowhere. His head felt hot, and he ran over there and almost bumped into the woolly-haired man, who was supervising the tethering of the two officers.

"You're going to hang them?" he asked when he saw the ropes.

"No," the man answered. "At least not now."

"You're going to bleed them?"

"No, no; we're going to leave them just as they are. We'll make a decision later."

"This one ordered Caruá shot, a boy who was coming with me, a boy who couldn't be over fourteen. I don't even know if he didn't do it himself, because I was tied up with my back to them. Bastard! Creature of the Devil!"

"Take it easy. We've got him, he's not going to kill any other boy, he's not going to kill anyone else—take it easy."

"I was just going to slap him good, because he slapped me while the others held me when I was caught. And he kicked me a lot too. I don't even know if it was this one or the other."

"Oh, you want to let him have it a little?"

"Sure do. Just one or two, not really a big thing, just to get even, really, something not too heavy."

"Lourenço!"

"What is it?"

"This comrade here has a justified reason to give the two starred monkeys here a couple of wallops. Prepare the two monkeys to get thrashed. Are your hands all you're going to use, friend?"

"This is no way to treat a prisoner of war!" the commanding officer shouted.

"It's a war now that you're all roped up right here. When one of us is roped up, it's not a war, it's a punitive expedition. Shut up, monkey, before I have you hanged by your big toe and spanked with a flowering cactus. Just the hands, friend?"

"Yes, sir, that's right. Can I do it now?"

"Just a moment, please," the curly-haired one answered, turning to the officer. "You, Lieutenant, are going to get a couple of swats in the name of the people you came to kill. All right, friend, enjoy settling your account."

"Could you please raise the lamp this high, so I can hit him in the same place where he hit me?"

"Raise the lamp, Lourenço."

"Much obliged."

"Don't mention it."

The light was reflected on the sweaty face of the lieutenant, who, trying to flaunt an air of courage and contempt, could not manage to make his lips stop quivering. Filomeno raised his hand, but before that he felt like insulting him, like telling him something that would offend him, to get even with that too. He could not find what to say; he thought their languages were different, and although he understood the officer's insults, the officer would not understand his. He raised his arm even higher and hit with the palm of his hand, putting his whole weight in the blow. The officer groaned, raised his head—which had been thrown off balance by the slap—with an expression he intended to be defiant, but did not manage to control his muscles, and his head hung low again. Filomeno got ready to slap him once again, but ended up turning his back on him and walking away. On his way back, he faced the other officer, thought of hitting him too, but decided just to spit.

"You through?" the curly-haired man asked.

"Yes, yes."

"That was quick."

"Yes, I got sick of it the first time. I don't like to beat a man who's tied up; it's no fun."

"I know how you feel; it's the same with me."

"But aren't you really going to bleed them? Is it true? What is that trash good for?"

"We still don't know. We have a custom here. Before we do anything, we first think about it."

"What do you mean, think? What is there to think about?"

The man smiled at him and asked him to take it easy, soon he would have answers for all his questions. He put his hand on Filomeno's shoulder and pointed to a trail ahead. He said he knew Filomeno was taking weapons to the settlement, but he should not worry, he could complete his mission early tomorrow; the army troops were still grouping in Angico; they were not going to attack the settlement before the third or fourth. For the time being, they could rest at a camp they had nearby. Filomeno had taken a rough beating, hadn't he? He needed a rest, he needed to eat something, and besides, didn't he want the answers to all those questions? Filomeno thought of refusing, of making more questions, of demanding that they tell him who they were, but after all, they really had saved him, together with his cargo, and he really was aching, tired, and hungry.

"Yes, yes," he said. "You're right."

"Can you walk?"

"Sure, don't worry."

But they did not have to walk too far, because in a short while they were in a kind of grotto, which Filomeno did not know, though he had passed nearby many times. Beside two huge rocks leaning against each other and forming a triangular arch, they had set up three spacious tents of a type Filomeno had never seen. At the center, a small bonfire, with a kettle hanging from a wood tripod over it. In two or three spots, field lanterns shining, similar to the ones the soldiers had. Many men circulating, a few women, a peaceful atmosphere, like a hunting camp after work. From the side of one of the tents, a smell of something frying came to Filomeno's nose, and he looked interrogatively at the others. The white-haired man smiled, pointing his chin toward the food, and they went over there together, to find a stone range where a fat black was handling a few pans.

"We got salted meat, we got beans, we got land tortoise, we got manioc flour, we even got a little leftover armadillo stew," the black said with such joy that it seemed out of place. "We got sweet banana paste!"

Filomeno squatted down to eat with the others, and felt a little dizzy when the first warm morsels got to his stomach. On the other side he could see the soldiers being tied to a scraggly hog plum tree in the company of their chiefs.

Four or five armed men bearing carbines and machetes positioned themselves nearby, mounting guard, and except for that the place was now a farmyard, a placid, quiet yard where, had small livestock only been grubbing in the dirt, Filomeno would have felt he had been taken to a place very distant from those backlands. Almost no noise, only the tin plates, the chewing of squatting men, crickets chirping, a piece of firewood popping in the bonfire now and then. Filomeno thought again about talking and making questions, but decided to wait; something was bound to happen.

Much later, sucking on a piece of brown sugar taffy, he was invited to go with the others inside the opening between the rocks, which seen from inside was much bigger than it seemed at first sight. It formed a kind of very high-ceilinged salon, illuminated by lamps fixed to its stone walls. On the ground, which had been swept to the point of appearing to be made of cement, two large benches, each one a long board on four low trestles, a few stools with seats of raw leather, two or three straw mats, and a chest in a corner, covered by a crazy-quilt cloth. The flames of the lamps, whose smoke went up and disappeared as if there was a chimney farther than the eye could see among the crannies of the roof, illuminated everything very clearly, with the exception of the corner farthest from the entrance, which was so dark it seemed to be protected by some barrier of a solid, opaque blackness. Filomeno stared at that corner, intrigued because light seemed to stop before getting to it, but he did not have much time to think about it, for it was obvious that something quite solemn was about to take place, maybe a decision about the fate of the prisoners. Especially because the six soldiers, two officers and four privates, tied together like a string of fishes, were sitting on one of the benches, the officers' knees shaking incessantly, though their ankles were trussed up.

After all the newcomers had made themselves comfortable, some on the other bench, facing the prisoners, some on the stools, and some on the ground, Filomeno's friend got up and spoke to the prisoners almost without altering his tone, as if he were just making a casual comment.

"You have been imprisoned as members of a hostile expedition against the people of this land, come here to destroy and kill. The right thing to do would be to kill you at once, because that's the logic of those things. However, to kill just for killing, even when the motive is revenge, isn't part of our practice. You," he said, pointing at the commanding officer, "are already responsible for the murder of a child, and as such are guilty—the same way, incidentally, as all your accomplices."

"I protest!" the officer said, trying futilely to stand up. "This is an act of banditry against the institutions of the Republic, the integrity of the nation, the established powers! Just to make things clear, and not because I attach any importance to the judgment of fanatic, ignorant, illiterate peasants, I have to identify myself. I am Lieutenant—"

"Shut up! Here we don't care about what you think, because everything you think, or think you think, is what they put in your mouth and in your head, and that we already know. Nor are we interested in your identity, for your identity signifies only for you; for us you have no identity, you have the same identity as the others who came in your company—just as for you we don't have identities, either, we don't have faces, we have only one face. Nor do we care about what you say or might say about the judgment we make of your actions, because the only judgment that interests you is the one made according to your standards. Your established power to me is shit, your institutions for me are dung. You call money an allocation or assets, you call stealing expropriation, appointments are elections, murders are executions, you wear fancy costumes and use words you think are nice-sounding, thus concluding that your acts are legitimate. They may be legitimate to you, but not to us, who have never been listened to and have to accept whatever you decide for us and even what you think for us. So because he who condemns a man to starvation and dire poverty has a piece of paper in his hand, is it less immoral, is it right in some way? You come to tell us truths. What truths are those, which humiliate us, diminish us, transform us into nothing—how can that be the truth to us? To me, you are the incarnation of falsehood and death. But even so, it's our practice to let people speak in their defense. However, speak in your defense and not to attack us, because I'll make you shut up once again. Here we have no need for the clownings of your justice, which sets up great pantomimes to mask what we know beforehand it will do: punish the poor man and reward the rich man. Therefore the reason for letting you speak, if you care to, is not that we believe that by speaking you'll stop being the scoundrelly traitors of the people you are. But you may say something that interests us. Speak, any of you, if you like."

The officer tried again to stand, and again the ropes stopped him.

"Aren't you going to allow me to stand up to speak?"

"No; you can speak just the way you are."

"Well, I know it's useless to speak, and if it were not for my subordinates here, for whom I'm responsible, I would not say anything. With your exception, though I don't know who you are, I don't believe any of you can understand my words. We are here on an official mission, with the objective of suppressing a rebellion against the integrity of the Republic. The Republic is a dominion of the Brazilian people, and it cannot allow a challenge against it to go unpunished. You do not owe allegiance to the Crown of Bragança, as you disobediently and seditiously profess, breaking the law and affronting authority. You—"

". . . do not owe anything to anybody; everybody owes us!" a woman's voice said from the dark corner of the salon.

Filomeno was startled. He straightened up on his stool to look at the spot where the words had come from, and did not see anything but the same thick blackness as before. But as the woman went on speaking, her clear voice filled the salon, his face lit up in bedazzled surprise, because as though a white light were sprouting from the ground and the walls, the figure of a very tall woman started to take shape on that spot that was so tenebrous before, her hair loose over her shoulders, a wood staff in her right hand, and very big eyes, initially enveloped by the same haze as her face, but now shining with an intense green, deflecting the light. Her face, sculptured in firm lines, seemed to be ageless. She was not young, she was not old; one could only see she had lived a lot. Filomeno thought he was watching a miracle, the vision of a saint, and wanted to fall on his knees, but the man at his side held him by his shoulder.

"It's all right," he said. "It's Dona Maria da Fé."

"It's who? Dona Maria da Fé? Herself?"

"Yes. She's been there all the time."

"Jesus on the Cross!" Filomeno exclaimed, goggling his eyes, while the woman leaned against a high stool, with a foot on the ground and the other foot on one of the stool's transverse supports.

"The Brazilian people does not owe anything to anybody, Lieutenant," she said. "They owe the Brazilian people, they have always owed, they want to go on owing forever. You parrot the lies you hear because to know the truth does not interest the powerful, but only what suits them. You say we are monarchists, loyal to the Crown of Bragança. And I tell you it is up to the Crown to be loyal to the subjects and not the subjects to the Crown, just as it is up to the Republic to be loyal to the citizens and not to itself. How can you expect a people kept in the deepest ignorance to believe that the Republic is not responsible for all their misfortunes? If everything is getting worse, if poverty increases, if oppression becomes more unbearable every day, if to be hungry and landless is everyone's fate while you save the nation in the capital, writing laws to privilege those who have always been privileged? If the people owes nothing to the Monarchy, it owes still less to the Republic. What does the Republic give us? It gives us more poverty. What does the Republic send us? It sends its army to kill us. If we had not rebelled, what would it send us? It would send hunger and exploitation to kill us. Today there is more hatred against us than there ever was against any foreign enemy. And are you the people, the owners of the country? No. We are the people. However, it is against us that the power of the country is turned, it is against us that its hatred is turned, as it was against the slaves that the hatred and the power of the country used to turn."

"The government cannot give explanations to any rabble that decides to violate the principle of authority!"

"Authority? Who gave you authority? Where does your authority come from? What changed after the Republic, what progress came, what horizon opened itself for the people? What do you know besides killing, trampling, humiliating, and denying freedom and justice? Who ever asked us anything?

Who ever asked what we suffered, what we dreamed, what we wanted from the world, what we could and wished to give? No one asked us anything, and even the gift of language you want to take away from us, through ignorance and through the tyranny of the speech you use, which is the only one you consider correct, although it is good only to hide lies under the guise of truth and eclipse our spirit."

"If you admit the ignorance of your people, then you admit that those who are not ignorant have the duty to lead the rest."

"And you don't find yourselves ignorant? Do you know how to weave the cloth that's covering you? Do you know how to tan, treat, and sew the leather you have on your feet? Do you know how to raise, slaughter, and cook the steer that feeds you? Do you know how to forge the iron of which your gun is made? Your ignorance is greater than ours. You don't know what is good for us, you don't even know what is good for you. You don't even know about us. Perhaps there'll come a day when one of us will seem more foreign to you than any of the foreigners of whom you are vassals. The Brazilian people are we, it's we who are you, you are nothing without us. You cannot teach us anything because you don't want to teach, for every teaching requires the teacher to learn too, and you don't want to learn: you want to impose, you want to mold, you want to dominate."

"This makes no sense, it's a collection of absurdities, it's—"

"This is the only thing that makes sense: it's to see ourselves the way we ought to, not the way you want us to. Your history has always been one of war against the people of your own nation, and even here you're under the command of an officer who won his renown for having Brazilians shot and for being a murderer. And you speak to us of your Republic? Why don't you speak to us about food, land, and freedom? Why, as you hypocritically free the blacks because you no longer need them, do you create new slaves, helping to keep your country the land of a humiliated, voiceless people? Your Republic is a new imposture among the many you have perpetrated and will go on perpetrating, for I have no illusions about who's going to win this Canudos civil war."

"Civil war? What civil war?"

"A civil war! But this civil war will not end here, with our defeat in this battle; this civil war will go on for all time to come, it will assume many faces and will never stop haunting you, until we no longer live in a country that instead of rulers has owners, has slaves instead of a people, shame instead of pride. The power of the people exists, it will persist. The people has its heroes too, heroes you don't know, the real heroes because they are heroes of life, while yours are heroes of death. Here in these backlands, many of those heroes will die, but the people won't die, because it's impossible for the people to die, and it's impossible for the people to be forever stifled. You are traitors of your people, and so you ought to die. And you will die, because this expedition

422

won't be the one that will crush the people of Canudos. The hatred you have for the people will have to manifest itself in all its cruelty, and believe me, the martyrdom of this people may come to be forgotten, may not be understood, may come to be buried under the lies you make up for your own benefit, but one day this martyrdom will prove not to have been in vain. You will have to kill one by one, to destroy house after house, to leave not one stone unturned. And even so, you won't win the war. Only the Brazilian people will win the war. Long live the Brazilian people! Long live we!"

She raised her staff high, the men got up, and without thinking about it, Filomeno found himself repeating with them the salute she had made. And he did not understand the strange pride he felt when he heard her words, as if they had been inside him all his life and only now had taken shape. He looked at the soldiers and thought they were different, very different from the moment when he had faced them for the first time. But instead of keeping his eyes on them, he chose to gaze at Maria da Fé, now so close he could touch her, while she talked to her men and, not giving orders but speaking like someone who was expressing an opinion, said they should free the soldiers without their arms, so they would go back to their camp. Better than simply to kill them was to send them back to their soon to be defeated expedition, after having seen and heard what they had seen and heard.

"If we kill them," she said with a smile, "they will know we exist, but this knowledge won't go beyond them. If we don't kill them, at least they'll be sure I exist, because they are always trying to think I don't exist."

Filomeno did not understand what she said, but laughed with the others; there must be something funny about all that.

"Isn't that right, friend?" she said affectionately, patting his shoulder. "Let's get a rest now. Before midnight we turn these men loose in the wilds, and tomorrow you take your mules to the settlement. Good night, friend."

Before falling asleep, Filomeno Cabrito imagined he was dreaming, and pinched himself; he stayed awake for a long time. And he went on thinking he was dreaming when he woke up the next day in the company of his mules and in an absolutely deserted camp, as if no one had ever been here. But there had been people there, he remembered, scratching his head while going down the trail that led to Canudos alongside the mule Parakeet. At least he would not forget the vision of Maria da Fé and the friendly look of the white-haired man, who before retiring gave him a farewell pat in the back and told him his name was Zé Popó.

18

In spite of the stern look with which he returned the compliments of neighbors who passed by his gate coming back from Mass, General Patrício Macário was not having serious thoughts. He was once again considering an impulse that had followed him all his life, but never as frequently as in the past few years, to suddenly do something crazy in public—for example, to tousle his hair, and when one of those ladies in Sunday clothes said good morning to him, to stretch out his tongue as much as he could, roll his eyes, and wave his hands with his thumbs in his ears. He found the idea extremely funny, almost irresistible. Would he someday yield to an impulse of this kind; was he really going crazy and not just thinking of an eventual innocent prank? There were dreams too, in a way related to those moments of silliness, in which he appeared completely naked on solemn occasions or while commanding troops. Each dream began pleasantly, then turned into a nightmare, from which he woke up relieved. Yes, maybe he was going crazy; so what?

He pulled up the loose pants he wore to putter around the garden and the backyard, turned his back to the gate, and decided he would take care of the front-yard plants later, after that coming and going outside his gate had stopped and he did not have to greet strange people and find himself closer to the brink of madness than usual. As a matter of fact, he was just being stubborn, because he knew what would happen, yet insisted on not changing his routine: wake up at five, wash, get dressed, go to the backyard to see the chickens and spend an hour with them, inspect the other animals, go into the house through the side door, have his breakfast while reading the paper, light a pipe, smoke and read for a half hour, and then start his gardening at the front yard. That was the problem. On Sundays he could not start there;

he had to finish there. He grumbled about how outrageous it is for a man to change solid, rational habits because of other people.

Besides, at that time Adalícia would be in the backyard and try to carry on a conversation, even if he did not reply or shouted at her to shut up. Funny that people had wanted him to get married; Adalícia, with the exception of his bed, performed every function of a wife, from running the house abominably to saturating his patience with chatter that was impossible to contain, which persecuted him until he holed up in his study, because when she had no one to talk to she would talk to everything around, even pans and animals. Which was precisely what she was doing in the backyard. She was chitchatting animatedly with the mulberry trees, while hanging newly washed linen on a clothesline. Oh no, he couldn't stand that, so he turned around to go into the house, stepping lightly to keep her from noticing his passage.

He had got up feeling well, even very well, a rather unexpected condition for someone who had gone to bed depressed and irritated, as incidentally he had been all week. Or come to think of it, as he spent most of his time now. Just an old man's crankiness, that was probably the general view. It could be, and it could also be that craziness. But nothing prevented him from understanding the deepest roots of his despondency. Of course his disillusionment with his career, aggravated by his disillusionment with his profession, probably influenced his state of mind. To see people like Vieira ascend to the highest ranks and be honored in every way, to witness cowardice, duplicity, corruption, and venality go unpunished or even rewarded, to watch the difficulties of the good and the victories of the bad, all of that left him sad, angry, powerless, rancorous. And maybe it was still too soon, as some of the very few friends he had kept used to say, to evaluate what good the Republic had done the country. Yes, maybe it was too soon, but for him things had more and more the shape visualized and demonstrated by Maria da Fé. True, just as when he was in her company so many years ago, he still could not put together all the pieces of a picture whose existence was nevertheless unquestionable. How could he have faith in progress and science, have faith in the technicians and specialists who theoretically were supposed to run the country, if criteria and objectives were always set by the interests of a few? How much longer would this go on? Until they lost power—and would they ever? How could this be possible? But it was possible. He knew about the existence of the people, about the toiling and suffering of the majority, and also knew how everything was decided from above, without taking that majority into account. The army, that repressive instrument, under the excuse of maintaining national unity, was in fact being used to guarantee the power of political factions that were nothing but different appearances of the same thing, in their games of confrontation and balance.

And now, after an unprecedented hysteria against the so-called monarchist fanatics of the backlands, the Canudos campaign had ended, with the settlement destroyed like Carthage by the Romans, house by house, stone by stone, life by life. Why, why did it have to happen this way—what a useless, stupid thing! Monarchists! Yes, maybe out of ignorance they might call themselves monarchists. But actually they were poverty-stricken Brazilians, kept in penury and servility, Brazilians turned into foreigners by those in the cities, who clamored for their extermination, and hated and feared them as one hates and fears the Devil. Now death and more death would come, he was sure, because the established power would continue to crush people, and crushed people inevitably revolt. He shuddered. Those had been her words, once in Our Lady Point. Where would she be now? Would she be alive? She herself had said that one day he, too, would doubt her existence. But he did not doubt it; he was sure of it, he felt her presence often, sometimes even angrily, because while he loved her, he also resented her for having condemned him to solitude, a solitude that only recently he had got completely used to, though people thought the contrary. How could he face the ridicule of explaining he did not want a lasting relationship with any woman because after he had known her, no woman had any appeal to him, and he considered himself married to her? Stories about her still circulated, and now and then one of them would reach him, and he listened to them, affecting an amused interest and the same skepticism as others. They were legends, after all, stories told by people who can do nothing and keep fantasizing.

He did not know why, but he thought she had been in Canudos. Maybe because people said she had gone to the backlands, maybe because something told him so, something odd in the anxiety with which he read and heard news of the campaign, an anxiety that could not be only because of the tragedy that was happening. Nonsense, an old man's notions as he neared his sixtieth year. She was dead, yes, she was probably dead. Only in one sense she was not. In one sense she was truly immortal, as she herself had said to him, she with her beautiful loose hair and her silvery voice. She would not die, she would never die, because the spirit of her struggle would remain with the people despite all difficulties, she was sure of that, as sure as she was of their love for each other.

And there was the Brotherhood too. Was there really a Brotherhood? She herself had been a little vague when she mentioned the Brotherhood; it was like something that existed and did not exist. Would everything in life be like that, existing and not existing? The one who belongs to the Brotherhood is the first to know, she had also said. And he had often thought he knew, but also thought it was part of that craziness, which he could not afford to cultivate. How could he be sure? He missed her, that was the only truth; he missed her as if everything had happened yesterday. Dammit, would the old melancholy come back? This blessed Brotherhood really ought to exist, so he would not feel so alone, with so many things in his mind. That was the worst thing of all, to feel alone, with so many things in his head, things he needed to say, to show, to prove, but he did not know how, he could not see how. Damned useless life, absurd life. What could he do—conspire, make speeches, write? He had done all that, and nothing had changed anything; rather he had been discouraged even more. Even the most idealistic, pure-minded people, very, very rare people, did not see beyond a certain point, did not go beyond narrow limits of which they were not conscious. Everything useless, everything a perpetual frustration, everything an impregnable loneliness.

Nonetheless, he kept on writing. No one knew, but he was writing. The sadness that had returned after the brief interval at the garden did not go away, but now it was mixed with a comforting joy—like that of someone who encounters an old toy with renewed interest—when he pulled out of a drawer in his study two thick stacks of ruled paper that contained over half of his memoirs. He had started to write so long ago that the first sheets were brownish and frayed, the faded ink barely visible under the light that came through the smaller study window. He walked over to the other side, opened the big window, and hefted the first volume as if amazed at having written all that. But he had, and was not going to give it up, although he was not sure he would publish it in his lifetime. Anyway, if he did, he was positive people would try to kill, arrest, or interdict him, or perhaps all three. Because through an initially difficult effort, but later more and more easily, he had purified his style and language to such an extent that he was proud he had not used a single euphemism in his story. A thief was called a thief, an idiot was called an idiot, a coward was called a coward. The part concerning the Paraguay campaign, so different from the official pack of lies and from the reports by the panegyrical historians who were the majority, was certain to be contested word for word. And worse, it would be he who would be called a liar.

But that did not take away his contentment in writing and his vague anticipation of seeing it all published. He feared only that even if he paid for publication out of his own pocket, its circulation would be forbidden. The idea of turning everything into a novel under a pen name had not entirely left his mind, although the two or three attempts he had made convinced him he would not be able to do it. Besides, he did not want anything he was telling to be taken for a mere invention, the product of an unknown, unimportant writer's imagination. Well, it was no use going on thinking about such things; what was important was to write. Preparing himself to forget about everything, even the garden, he picked up the bottom sheets and with an immense pleasure began to revise them, a pencil in his hand, reading a sentence aloud now and then.

He did not hear the gate bell ring repeatedly, or the sound of women's and

427

children's voices take over the garden. He noticed someone had arrived only when General and Marshal, his two little dogs, started to bark and yelp with excitement, while in a shrill speech Adalícia threatened to lock them up. Not just someone, but a lot of people; who the devil could it be? He thought he might lock his door and pretend he was asleep until they gave up, but had hardly collected the papers on his desk and started to open a drawer in which to slip them, when the door burst open and a young matron with a vivacious smile, wearing a flowery hat, a colorful dress, and a lace umbrella, threw herself at him with outstretched arms.

"Uncle! I miss you! Oh, I really do miss you! Let me see you! You look like a boy; you're getting younger all the time! And what do you do? You stay here locked like a monk in his cell; who ever heard of a thing like that? Isn't it enough for you to spend the whole week holed up in this lair of yours—do you have to hide on Sundays too, when everyone is having fun? No, sir, let's get up from that chair, let's talk; how long has it been since we've talked? Are those new glasses? Hmmm . . . They go very well with you; they're in fashion now! So? What's new? What have you got to tell me?"

"How can I say anything," Patrício Macário said, feigning indignation, "if you speak more than your mother and Adalícia put together?"

"It's just to compensate: you never speak!"

"That way I don't make a fool of myself. Where did you get this hat? It looks like a botanical garden."

"You don't like it? I think it's so pretty; it fits me so well, don't you think? José Eulálio likes it."

"José Eulálio is from São Paulo; his taste has to be strange."

"Oh, don't say that, Uncle—he married me!"

"Didn't I say his taste was strange?"

He looked affectionately at his niece. She spoke too much, yes, and she had no business interrupting him at such an inconvenient moment, but she was absolutely the best person in the family. At least from his viewpoint, because since the day Bonifácio Odulfo for no apparent reason had contacted him for a reconciliation, Isabel Regina had taken a liking to him and had never stopped being his friend, in that light-headed way which sometimes bothered him but never irritated him. No, not just that, it even pleased him, though he did not know why. He looked at her curly hair coming out under the brim of her hat and noticed once again that her nose was just a little bit flat, and though her skin was so pinkish white that anything special made two ruddy circles appear on her cheeks, she looked like him. He took her hands between his and smiled.

"And how about you, dear, how are you? Is everything all right? How do you like living in São Paulo?"

"Oh, I'm fine! And I know hardly anything about São Paulo. Not even

José Eulálio likes to stay there; he only goes there because of his farms. He himself says that São Paulo is, and always will be, a kind of suburb. But I like to visit the farms, I go every chance I get. I haven't been able to do it lately only because of the children. Oh, I've brought my boys to see you! They love coming here!"

"Are they here? Tell the older one . . . what is the older one's name?"

"Bonifácio Odulfo, Uncle! What a terrible thing, it's such an easy name to remember—it's Dad's name!"

"The poor child; how could you give him a name like that? That must be the reason I keep forgetting it."

"To tell the truth, I did want to give him another name, Grandpa's name."

"Amleto Henrique? You must be crazy—that's even worse! And the boy would run the risk of taking after the old man."

"No, no, it wouldn't be Amleto, it would be just Henrique, because that would be in Mother's honor too."

"That would be still more serious: the boy could take after them both."

"My, aren't we crabby today!"

"Tell little Bonifácio Odulfo to keep away from my chicken coop. The last time he went in there he caused a devastation my chickens haven't recovered from to this day. I think he has the impression chickens are horses, and wants to ride them."

"That's not too bad; maybe he'll ride one really well, and we'll have chicken stew for lunch."

"Never in your life. My chickens are not to be eaten!"

"Who ever heard of that? Every chicken is to eat!"

"Not mine. Lots of people raise animals that are not supposed to be eaten. So I raise chickens that are not supposed to be eaten, pet chickens."

"That's really something, Uncle Tico. You mean—"

"Don't get overfamiliar with me, calling me Uncle Tico; have some respect for me. I'm General Patrício Macário. I became a general only upon retirement, but I'm a general anyway, and if they put my medals on a scale, with you on the other side, the dish with the medals will be the one that will go down. Don't get fresh, young woman!"

"Yes, sir, Uncle General Tico, tico-tico-tico-tico!"

"Stop that, you're tickling me! Can't you hold still for a second? What an incredible commotion!"

"Oh, Uncle, it makes me sad to see you here in the company of only Adalícia and the chickens . . ."

"And of Marshal and General, don't forget. And of the other animals, the birds, the plants . . . As for Adalícia, you're right, she's a kind of pre-Purgatory, maybe to keep me from going straight to hell. But as for the chickens, no, the chickens are excellent company, better than many fraternities and academies. You don't know anything about chickens; there's nothing you can say on the subject."

"But you don't talk to the chickens."

"Of course I do!"

"But it's not conversation such as you'd have with a feminine companion, a wife. . . ."

"No, no, it's much better. Chickens have a much larger vocabulary than those ladies who frequent Dona Henriqueta's salons. And more moderate habits too. You know, once after I started going to your house again and your mother decided I had to acquire not only musical culture but also a wife among her friends, there was a soirée in which the baron of Whatsit's daughter, a horrendous-looking widow, with teeth more gaping than a corral fence—"

"Don't change the subject, Uncle; you always change the subject when I mention that."

"But of course I change the subject. It's about time you gave up this featherbrained idea to get me married. Married at this age—whatever for? To lose my peace and bring to my house someone to establish rules on how I should wear my slippers, how and when I have to eat and how I should speak, to take me to the theater and entertain her friends at home? Never! Forget it, change the subject, I'd rather listen to you speak about feminine fashions; I consider that a more interesting subject. At the place where you bought this hat do they sell watering cans too?"

"Aunt Titiza is no horrendous-looking widow. And she likes you; Mother told me so many times. Aunt Titiza is still very handsome; you can't say she's not pretty."

"Pretty? A gabby old hag over fifty years old?"

"She's not over fifty; I think she's not forty-six yet."

"The same way your mother isn't thirty-five yet. Is she thirty yet, by the way?"

"You're changing the subject again."

"I'm not changing anything; I'm even going to be very direct. I will not submit to this conspiracy you and your mother and Aunt Titiza and God knows who else have been setting up for me to get married. I absolutely refuse to get married, particularly to any Titiza, Totoza, or Tutuza."

"You're mistaken, there's no conspiracy at all. It's my idea, I'm the one who thinks about it. If not Aunt Titiza, why not—"

"Enough of that! Under no circumstances! Enough!"

"But that's absurd, a man like you, still so spry, hiding here. . . . Is this what you're doing? Are you writing a book, Uncle? Memoirs?"

"Leave that alone, don't pry! Yes, that's what I've been doing, and that's what you want me to give up in exchange for an old nag in the house."

"It doesn't have to be an old nag."

"Every woman is a nag!"

"May I read it?"

"Huh? No, give me that! Come on, hand it over—it's dangerous reading."

"But isn't it going to be published?"

"I don't know yet. Come on, give it to me."

"Please, Uncle, just a short moment; it looks so interesting. . . ."

"Much more interesting than you think. So interesting I'm not sure I want anyone to read it."

"Come on, Uncle; if you really didn't want anyone to read it, you wouldn't be writing it."

"Stop being intelligent; women are not supposed to be intelligent—they become too dangerous."

" '. . . the notion of a military aristocracy, a concept dangerous in itself, acquires more ominous aspects if viewed in the light of our intended institutional stability. The reasons for that are countless, and one of them stands out: The distance between an aristocracy and a privileged caste is very short, much shorter than some well-intentioned minds think. The notion of aristocracy involves necessarily the notion of the existence of "better people," and also necessarily defines that which is "better," so anything that does not fit those criteria is not "better." And will not those criteria be just those which embody the interests and values of the members of the aristocracy?' Uncle, you're a good writer! I'm going to have to read it again to understand it well, but you're a good writer!"

"Nonsense. As you were reading this aloud I realized how badly written it is."

"It's not badly written at all! It's very, very, very well written, that's what it is! What comes next?"

"Yes, it's badly written. I write with great difficulty—just look at the number of corrections."

"I don't agree; there are almost no corrections. Now tell me, what comes next?"

"What do you mean, what comes next?"

"What comes next, what comes next! You say that the military . . ."

"My dear child, I don't know what comes next, and it wouldn't make a difference if I did. Those things can't interest you; they are arid things, an old man's crotchets."

"I don't think so, I think it must be interesting. You're making an analysis of the role of the military in government, aren't you?"

"That's right, yes, it's more or less that. You're really intelligent; you sure didn't take after me."

"So what comes next?"

"Do you really want to know?"

"If I didn't, I wouldn't have asked."

"It's because . . . All right, what I think, what I fear, is something I once believed in but can't believe in anymore. It's government by technicians, specialists, wise men, the 'better people' I mentioned. As I said, there was a time when I believed that this would be the best government, such as Plato had imagined in his *Republic,* for after all, those he called philosophers were nothing but what we call scientists today, since the classification of sciences would only come much later."

"You talk so beautifully! And you're going to write all that?"

"Yes, yes. I mean, I don't have enough culture for certain things, there are aspects I want to touch and don't feel secure about, I feel I should be better informed, have a better basis. But thank you anyway."

"For what?"

"For having so graciously pretended so many pleasant things for your old uncle. The truth is, you're the first person to set eyes on these papers, and I don't regret it, I'm happy about it. Perhaps you'll also be the last person to see them, and that makes me equally happy."

"Why, I never heard so much nonsense! I didn't pretend anything. You're writing an interesting book; it has to be interesting, considering your experience and ability. You ought to show it to your friends. Why don't you show it to Dad?"

"God forbid! Your father would be outraged. No, sir. You have to promise me something. Do you promise?"

"What?"

"Promise?"

"I promise."

"You're not going to speak to anyone, absolutely anyone, about this book—it's a big favor you're doing your uncle. Do you promise?"

"But why? I don't see any reason for that."

"Promise me; you'll be doing me a favor. Come on, promise."

"I solemnly promise . . . Just a moment! Only if you promise me something too."

"Nothing of that sort, that's got nothing to do with it, you can't do a thing like that. Especially if it's something having to do with your ideas about a marriage for me. I mean it!"

"No, it's not that at all; it's very simple. You promise?"

"All right. But I reserve the right—"

"A promise is a promise. You promise?"

"All right, I promise."

"All right, then I'll promise first. I solemnly promise not to tell anyone, not even in dreams, that my dearest Uncle Tico is writing a book, either of memoirs or of anything else."

"Perfect, perfect; thank you very much."

"As long . . . as long as Uncle Tico comes to lunch with us at Dad's!"

"Oh no! Anything but that! No, never! I don't intend to go out for anything today. Ask anything else but not that."

"You promised!"

"I said I'd reserve the right to refuse certain promises."

"You said nothing of the kind!"

"That was because you didn't let me, but I was going to say it. No, ask for anything else, anything."

"Dad's health hasn't been too good lately; it would do him so much good to see you. . . ."

"Don't be a liar. He's a new edition of old Amleto, who always got worse, however he was feeling, when I showed up."

"That's not true; you're not being fair to him. Dad likes you so much; he keeps complaining about not seeing you more often."

"He's a liar, then. He's always found me the family's scapegrace. In which he may be right, but . . ."

"Do you have to be so grouchy? That's terrible! I don't know why it's such a great sacrifice for General Patrício Macário to have lunch at his brother's, to see his relatives and remember he has a family, and to cool his head, now so busy with this work."

"Do you think remembering our family cools my head? Let alone seeing it!"

"Uncle Clemente André wrote from Rome; he's very ill."

"Is that true? The monsignor is sick? What's wrong with him?"

"I don't really know, but I know it's serious."

"What a pity; the monsignor . . ."

"Come on, Uncle, everyone's going to be there. José Eulálio is going to be there, absolutely everyone is going to be there: how often can a family get together like that?"

"You should have been born a man—you'd be an extraordinary lawyer."

"I'm glad I wasn't, because then I wouldn't be able to kiss you whenever I wanted, like that, like that, like that! All settled, then. Let's change those clothes—what kind of clothes are those for a general, my God in heaven! Go on, go change your clothes; it must be almost nine or more, and I promised the children we'd go for a boat ride in the pond. Do you have a fishing rod? José Eulálio had them put fish in the lake, and now he guarantees we can fish—isn't that going to be fun? Oh, Uncle, if you had acted this way in your battles, we'd have lost the Paraguay war. Why are you standing there—go change!"

"Do you by any chance want me to go in my dress uniform?"

"Can you? Is it pressed? What a beautiful idea, your dress uniform with those golden things all over it, all the medals, a plumed hat, sashes, swords, stars, everything! Are you really going to wear it?"

"Of course not; I'm not as addlepated as you."

"Oh, that's a shame! The boys would be so proud; they keep saying their great-uncle is one of the greatest heroes of Brazil."

"I wish they were right."

"Of course they are! And since you're not going in your dashing dress uniform, at least make yourself as elegant as possible. Today's a day for new clothes. Go change, Uncle; it's getting late!"

"You forget I'm from Bahia too," Bonifácio Odulfo pontificated, halting for a moment while pacing back and forth in his library, and raising his forefinger. "Yes, you forget I'm from Bahia too! And being from Bahia, I know it as well as you do, perhaps better! Perhaps better!"

Patrício Macário sank down in his armchair. No, no, he wasn't going to argue anymore, he wasn't going to discuss anything, he was going to let him say whatever he pleased, he'd occupy his mind with something else. That was normally easy, but Bonifácio Odulfo had the habit of staring motionlessly at his interlocutor after an utterance he considered striking, and not saying anything else until he noticed some reaction. If it weren't for this unnerving habit, he could be totally ignored, as he started, not as worked up as before, a lecture about Brazil for his brother, his son-in-law, and his son. A few minutes before, Patrício Macário, thinking he would encounter some sympathy, had mentioned Canudos, and his brother had stood up in a rage. Was it possible that a military man whose comrades had been decimated in such large numbers by those illiterate fanatics, veritable primitive animals and enemies of the Republic, was it possible for a military man, a general, to regret the slaughtering of backlands bandits? And how about the slaughtering of soldiers?

"I regret it too, of course," Patrício Macário had answered. "I regret it especially because the army was once more used against Brazilians. We're getting into the habit of dealing with any dissension this way."

"Not any dissension! There are constitutional guarantees, everyone knows that."

"What constitutional guarantees? What constitutional guarantees has a poor backlands yokel, reduced to the most complete ignorance and penury, with no access to justice, no access to anything?"

"Don't be melodramatic, my dear brother, don't picture things as worse than they are. We're in a country of abundance, and precisely because of that, people cultivate lazy habits, have no initiative, live from what they pick in the woods and in other people's farms; that's the problem. Ask José Eulálio here about the difference between our farmworkers and immigrant settlers. It's a matter of upbringing, of national temperament; it cannot be the object of bleeding-heart reforms. And besides, you speak as if they weren't enemies of the regime."

"Don't give me this talk about enemies of the regime. Does this regime have enemies?"

"Does it not? Are you going to say that the regime has no enemies? That is the most unbelievable statement I've heard in years!"

"The enemies of the regime are those who despite being economically privileged feel occasionally penalized and cause this self-interested, ridiculous bickering which doesn't really interest the people, the nation. What benefits did the Republic bring the people?"

"In that case, what benefits did the Monarchy bring?"

"None. It's not a question of monarchy or republic; it's a question of acknowledging that we won't be able to eternally muzzle through military actions the voice of the dispossessed, the oppressed, and the wronged, who are the great majority. It's a question of establishing a regime that instead of trying to solidify the privileges of its beneficiaries tries to understand that the country will only be great as long as it doesn't keep its people impoverished, enslaved, ignorant, and hungry. This seems elementary to me. Do you know the despair, the misery, the hopelessness of the people of the backlands? So? So what the Republic does is to send them soldiers to kill them, to sweep them off the face of the earth. Is that how things should be dealt with?"

"In this particular case, yes! That's how you strengthen the regime!"

"That's how you weaken the regime!"

"That's how you strengthen the regime! That's the way to do it! Are we going to allow degenerate, unintelligent mongrels with no firmness of character and no positive qualities but their instinctive love for life to interfere in the affairs of the Republic? How far would that take us?"

"At least as far as their lives are concerned, they should have the right to interfere."

"And from where does that right emanate? What understanding do they have of that right? What good fortune would come to them from the understanding of that right, which incidentally is very arguable?"

"You speak as if those people were foreign to you, as if they didn't belong to the same species as we."

"And do you think those people and you are the same thing?"

"They're human beings like us, and Brazilian."

"There are those who would question calling them human, but let's consider that my handicap in the discussion, as they say. Do you contend that those people are really our people, that they are representative of our people as a whole? Imagine a bumpkin as a deputy, a rustic as an ambassador, a lout as a senator. What a fine show we'd put on, what a fine show! Things must be seen clearly! In this world, some were made to lead and the majority to obey; that's the reality!"

"But to lead may mean to govern honestly, not to oppress."

"What do you call oppression? What else can we do for those people? Give them bathrooms? They'll go on relieving themselves in the bushes! Give them money? They'll spend everything on liquor and sprees. You've got to see reality; we must contain the action of delirious progressives such as you, so the country won't fall into anarchy and chaos. The few conquests we have obtained will not be taken from us! You will take nothing from us! You will not turn this country into—"

A coughing fit interrupted his shouting, and the two younger men rose to help him. He refused a glass of water, leaned against a column, breathed deeply, and wiped his eyes, which had become filled with tears from his intense coughing. Impressed with his vehemence, Patrício Macário decided they were speaking in different orbits; it was no use arguing. He even thought of going out for a stroll in the gardens before lunch, and was about to rise from his armchair, when his brother, with a nervous grin, made a sign for him to wait, as if he was promising tacitly he was going to calm down. He apologized, saying this subject always aroused him, and not without reason, because he had studied it deeply and sometimes did not realize that other people had of course not reached his level of understanding.

"You forget I'm from Bahia too," he said then, at first just in a professorial tone, but soon becoming inflamed once again, though not as before. "Yes, you forget I'm from Bahia too. And being from Bahia, I know it as well as you do, perhaps better. Perhaps better!"

From the bottom of the armchair, Patrício Macário tried to avoid the intense stare his brother was directing at him as he waited for a comment about what he had said, but evasive maneuvers were of no use, because he stood in front of the armchair with his arms crossed.

"Perhaps better!" he repeated.

"All right," Patrício Macário said wearily. "Certainly better."

"You say that ironically, but it's true. I have farms, I know the backlands, I deal with agriculture and cattle raising. Therefore I know what I'm talking about."

"Right, right."

"You amaze me. Such an ardent republican—a republican, if I'm not mistaken, from the first hour, who was even punished more than once for his activities, made enemies because of them, and didn't have the career he might have had because of them—a republican like you now repudiating his ideas."

"I'm not repudiating my ideas; I'm just disillusioned with the Republic, that's all. I haven't seen any change for the better. The old functionaries of the Monarchy still occupy their positions and have the same influence and prestige as before. Our elections are rigged, public administration is motivated by self-interest, people steal here more than anywhere in the world, the people become poorer every day . . ."

436

"My dear brother, you're a utopian, that's what you are. Did you want the Republic to change the natural order? The men who are exercising influence are doing so because they are qualified for that. What did you want, did you want the rabble to take command of the Republic? What do you want, do you want the elections not to reflect the social and political forces that are truly significant for the country and for each region? They are rigged because the voters don't have enough discernment to perceive often subtle social needs, and therefore it's necessary for the ruling elite to take upon itself the organization of power. You don't know any strong nation without a strong government, a strong nation in which the common people, the unqualified, have an active voice."

"What the hell is the people you refer to? For you, everyone is the common people, with the exception of the four or five characters you think are comparable to you. What common people? Everyone? Because you refer to everyone, every Brazilian, with that same contempt. I don't advocate the taking away of your blessed privileges, you can keep them, but see that in order for that to be so, it's not necessary to enslave the people, to keep it in poverty, ignorance, and disease. Don't you see there can't be a decent country, a strong country, as you say, whose people is composed of diseased, hungry slaves and paupers?"

"Poverty exists everywhere!"

"To begin with, that's not a justification. Second, it's not true, at least not as much as here. We were one of the last countries in the world to abolish slavery, and we abolished it only on paper, as you know better than I do. You can't go on thinking this country is the property of people like you! And even if you can't stop thinking like that privately, why do you treat it in a way no farmer treats his farm? Why don't you give it anything? All you want is to receive. Why do you hate it this way—ashamed of it and of everything related to it, thinking of yourselves as exiled Europeans, and hating even the language you speak? Plunderers, pirates, pillagers, you view this country as something that has nothing to do with you; you don't want to give, you only want to take!"

"That's not true!"

"Yes, it's true! There's nothing foreign about the peasants of Canudos, as you think. It's people like you who are the foreigners, people who have never accepted being born and living here, your kind of people! You people can pervert anything! The Republic, an ideal of progress, prosperity, and justice, immediately became the vehicle for you people to make more money, to gain more power, to profit in every possible imaginable way, robbers of your own country, traitors of your own people, scound—"

"My God in heaven, how those men shout! Gentlemen, gentlemen, has a war broken out?"

Carrying a fruit basket and pouting in a way she considered youthful,

Henriqueta appeared at the library door and halted in exaggerated horror as she surprised Patrício Macário, very pale and wild-eyed, marching to his brother with his fist extended.

"It's not pugilism, is it?" she asked, smiling nervously. "It's not fair, Tico; you're in much better physical condition than he, and spent all your life using your muscles while your brother was using his mind. Bonifácio Odulfo, have you been coughing again? Are you all right? Do you want me to order something for you, a cordial?"

"No, no, thank you. I had forgotten my brother's temperament. I think we both got unduly worked up. It's silly to get worked up like that over nothing."

"You insist on provoking me!"

"You're right, but it's not for provocation's sake; it's just that I think a dialogue with a man of your profession is interesting."

"But it's not a dialogue, it's preaching. And one of the most . . . All right, let's not be rude. I'm sorry, Henriqueta."

"Now really, don't mention it, I'm used to the family. But may I ask what's the reason for so much ado, so much indignation?"

"Nothing, really. The general and I were discussing the people, and we had a few divergences, but all is forgotten, isn't it, Tico?"

"Discussing what?"

"The people, the Brazilian people."

"My God in heaven, and because of that you almost got into a scrap? The people? They say women are enigmatic, but on my part I assure you I shall never understand men. But what people—the common people, employees, housemaids, store clerks, laborers, farmworkers? Isn't it enough having to put up with them—do we have to fight over them?"

"All right, Henriqueta, let's change the subject."

"Yes, let's! Let's change the subject at once! The subject and the ambience, because I've got a surprise. Guess who's coming to lunch too!"

"I have no idea."

"Well, it really was supposed to be a surprise. Madame Renard! My dear friend Madame Renard! Isn't it wonderful?"

"Wonderful? Yes, it's wonderful. Where is she now?"

"In the music room, with Titiza and Isabel Regina."

"And she's going to play? Now?"

"My God in heaven, isn't it fantastic? Yes, she is! And guess what!"

"I don't know; something modern?"

"Very, very modern. Chopin! Chopin! One of my greatest embarrassments was to know the great Alexander Chopin only by references and from having read about him, without having ever listened to his music, which everyone considers divine."

"Isn't that Frédéric Chopin? I thought . . ."

"Frédéric, yes; I always get Alexander mixed up with Frédéric."

"Alexander the Great, Frédéric the Great . . ."

"How clever! But of course! We're going to listen to a polonaise, that was what she told me, one of the famous polonaises everyone talks about but no one plays! Shall we go, then?"

"Yes, yes. Isn't that chic, listening to music before lunch? And Chopin!"

"And Madame Renard! Come on, let's go; it's something for kings! As soon as she laid eyes on our piano—didn't I tell you a German piano was worth its weight in gold?—she felt her fingers itch; she told me that herself. Shall we go, shall we go? It's almost ten o'clock; pretty soon we're going to have lunch, and those pieces aren't short. Shall we go, my dear general and brother-in-law?"

"Yes, though honesty commands me to confess I've never heard of Chopin. Is he French?"

"Of course he is; everything that's worthwhile is French. Shall we?"

She did not wait for an answer but took her husband's arm and headed for the stairway that led to the music room. Patrício Macário sighed. And anyway, it was better than to go on listening to his brother's foaming diatribes. He knew the music room, he knew there was a corner near the small balcony that offered a view of the garden and the pond, and at least no one would speak while the music was playing. There was a time when he would not have forgotten the incident so easily, but now he was realizing, not without a certain wistfulness, that what his brother thought was indifferent to him, profoundly indifferent. He annoyed him when he spoke aggressively or authoritatively, but the annoyance lasted only while it was being directly provoked.

Maybe it was better that way, he thought wearily, going slowly up the stairs. He had a vague idea about who this Madame Renard was. She was a French concert pianist who had come to Rio for one season and decided to stay on, most likely because no one gave her any notice in France, and here she was treated as she had never been treated in her life. But he did not dislike her when Henriqueta introduced them. Although Henriqueta spoke in French, Madame Renard answered in Portuguese, shaking his hand warmly. She was glad to hear he was a general, and a war hero besides, because she was going to play a piece alluding to the heroism of the Polish people. Right at its beginning, he would be able to notice almost a description of a troop movement. Therefore her performance would be dedicated to him, it would be in his honor. She liked Brazilians so much; such a simple, good people . . .

Patrício Macário thanked her, and if at first he worried about the dedication, because it meant he would have to pay attention to the music, he soon decided it did not matter. He would stay at the same balcony where he had planned to stay, he would affect an extraordinary interest, and in the end he would make some complimentary remark. He was about to sit down, when he saw Isabel Regina, who ran over to him.

"Uncle, we caught two fish! You said you were going to fish with us but never showed up!"

"I wish I had a rod now—a birch rod, to show you what you deserve for getting me into this."

"Now really, Uncle, it's been all a lot of fun today. And Madame Renard is a great pianist; it's going to be wonderful."

"Yes, wonderful. That's what I've been told. But the least you could do to redeem yourself is to accomplish a most important mission for your uncle here."

"Yes, sir, General, sir, at your service!"

"Then step to it. Go inside and with all discretion get me a carafe of sugarcane rum and a little glass, bring them without letting anyone see it, and leave them here with me."

"Sugarcane rum?"

"You can stop looking like that; I know there's rum in the kitchen. Hop to it before the music starts—go on!"

She did not play badly, Madame Renard. In fact she played very well, and Patrício Macário, while noticing it was one of those days when alcohol went straight to his head, took his eyes away from the scenery to follow the pianist's energetic movements. Very beautiful, really. The rum was not the only thing inebriating him; it was also the clean, fresh air coming from the balcony, and it was especially the music, which brought him a feeling of plenitude and freedom, a kind of quiet elation, of confidence in something he did not know. Yes, freedom, of course, a freedom that was at hand, and out of blindness or even morbid self-indulgence he failed to embrace it. Yes, what was he doing in Rio, uneasy, embittered, surly, rootless? He was in Rio because he had got used to it, but he was doing nothing that depended on it, nothing actually bound him to it except habit, the routine now ingrained in him. He remembered All Saints Bay, he seemed to be floating above it, riding the music, and hovered over the rounded contours of the island of Itaparica, while Madame Renard made the piano peal like a carillon. He made up his mind: He would go to Itaparica at once. Everything was there, everything important had happened there, knowledge was hidden there—it was the only place where he could be free. Or at least know if he could ever be free, full-sailed and free as he was now, flying over the vast green-blue gulf, in the company of winged fishes and of the most secret memories a heart can have.

440

Folks, what a beautiful puffer fish stew is a-bubbling in the big clay pan! Steaming fillets white as angelicas, almost reaching the perfect point, smelling beautiful and surrounded by broken-tipped okras chosen scrupulously, over a hand span long, properly gooey and dominating the dish. A lot of gherkin, a little bitter eggplant, a few plantains, two or three big sweet potatoes, several slices of squash, tomatoes in various states of ripeness, white potatoes, a sweet cassava, a big slice of yam, cabbage, kale, and breadfruit. Everything first class, the best ingredients of a great fish stew, seasoned with lemon juice, hot red pepper, a little garlic clove, a little salt, purple onions, and coriander as if it were grass, all pounded together in a small mortar.

It is thus understandable why Florisvaldo Balão, the witch Rita Popó's man, who is just coming for lunch, stops in front of the beautiful big pan gurgling over live coals and snuffs in voluptuously the salt-and-peppered air dampened by the steam of the puffer fish, renowned as the best fish of the sea, a delicacy for homages and fraternizations, whose taste and tenderness are reputed as without equal. Appraising the gravy, in which a few okras are already starting to come apart, he anticipates the mush of fine manioc flour, expertly scalded and mixed, and closes his eyes delightedly. So maybe it is not as easy to understand the reason why, after so much enchantment, Florisvaldo changes his expression and, glancing suspiciously at the pan, crosses himself and murmurs a strong prayer. That is because in addition to being the best fish of the sea, the puffer fish is also poisonous, routinely killing very fast those who eat it without knowing how to prepare it. Fortunately, there are those who know how to prepare it with competence. It is enough, for example, to remove its skin. No, no, removing the skin is not enough, the skin has got no poison, there are even people who eat the skin. The problem is in its belly button. The puffer fish has that lumpy little belly button, and that is where the poison is, it being therefore sufficient in order to avoid danger to make a kind of wedge in the fish's pulpy flesh, right on the belly button's spot. Of course it is very true that the seat of the venom may be its head, so perhaps the safest thing to do is to throw away the head. But surely it is quite possible that reason may lie with those who affirm that the poison is in the whole fish, but if it is cooked for a long time in an uncovered pan, the poison will turn into smoke and go away. No, no, the problem is entirely different, for it is nothing but complete folly to eat puffer fish if the moon is full, or maybe waning, or, who knows, crescent, perhaps new. No, forget about the moon; the secret is the month in which you eat the puffer fish, because you are not supposed to eat it in months that do not have the letter *r* in their names, or in the ones that do, or during Holy Week or all of Lent, or fifteen days before and fifteen days after Christmas Eve.

To eat a puffer fish stew is consequently an important experience, and there are people who eat it regularly even for years and years with just one or two deaths in the family, and the case is not known of anyone having died from eating puffer fish without being used to eating puffer fish, because those who are used to it are the only ones who eat it, since those who are not used to it may die if they eat it. Florisvaldo Balão and Rita Popó are used to eating puffer fish, everyone who is going to share the lunch is used to eating puffer fish, and that was why he crossed himself and made his prayer not to die this time yet. Then he stepped over to the dining room, where he was being awaited by some of the ten or twelve guests who were going to join him and Rita, as happened every Sunday. And he walked in smiling, because he knew what the subject of the conversation was, for it was always the same when they served puffer fish, that is to say, stories of people who had died from eating puffer fish. Like the one Edésia Odd Speech was finishing, about her five friends who ate fuffer-fish, went to bved, and neper woke up exceft one, bvut he got crazy in the bvrain.

"Were those the people who died in Rail Point?"

"No, those Rail Point people were another case," explained Ramiro Grande, who became famous for having once quit eating puffer fish and having gone back to it when he seemed to have got rid of the temptation. "In the Rail Point case, the oldest girl in the house would not eat puffer fish, but she ate the chicken that ate the puffer fish's insides, and then the people who had eaten the fish died, and so did those who had eaten the chicken, and even those who ate a soup made of said chicken, and the dogs who ate the leftovers."

"Who prepared the puffer fish today?"

"Désia."

"Not me; I ony did three of them; *Sa* Rita did the rest."

"Puffer fish by four hands?"

"What's wrong with it? Same system."

"A four-hand puffer fish, huh? I've always heard a four-hand puffer fish is not a good thing."

And they were still discussing the puffer fish when Rita Popó, so fat she found it more comfortable to go through the door sideways in spite of her huge bosom, came back from a room outside the house she called the little chamber, stopped at the kitchen, tried the texture of the fish with the tip of a wooden spoon, poured a little more water in the pan, fanned the fire, and came into the room. She addressed them a not very affable grin, accepted with a certain weariness their respectful salutes, and said she was tired, she had done a heck of a lot of work. Florisvaldo called her aside for a private talk.

"The general, is the general still in the little chamber?"

"Yes, yes."

"Don't you think it's about time he left? How long's he been there? It must be almost fifteen days now, isn't it?"

"It's going to be. It must be ten or twelve."

"You're telling me you don't know how many days he's got to stay there? Aren't you counting the days? What kind of a funny ritual is that?"

"Don't talk about things you don't understand. This isn't really a ritual, it's another type of thing."

"But is he never coming out? This scares me: he's a general, he's important, one of these days they'll decide to look for him, and we'll be the ones who will carry the can."

"The door isn't locked, nobody's forcing him to stay there, he can leave anytime he wants. He's staying because he wants to; he thinks it's important for him to stay there as long as necessary."

"Necessary for what?"

"For him to discover something."

"What something?"

"If he hasn't discovered it yet, how am I supposed to know?"

"But you were the one who made him do all this, you gave him advice."

"I talked to him, that was all I did. He came to see me on his own, you know that, no one called him. He used to know me, and then he came to see me."

"He used to know you from where?"

"He's known me for a long time, from the time of my late mother Rufina, from the time Zé Popó still lived around here. He talked to my mother once, it was something very important for him, so he came back, thinking she might still be alive. He went to Tuntum, to Little Swamp, and to Holy Port, he searched everywhere until he found me. I didn't hear the talk my mother had with him because I was possessed at the time—and by Seeneeky at that, who leaves me all bruised when he goes out to tear down fences, railings, and chicken coops—but he told me everything."

"Everything what—what was the story he told you?"

"Now, that I can't tell you. It's his story, not mine; he's the only one who can tell it; my duty is to stay silent."

"Don't you think this is all very strange? This man there, an important white, a general, locked up like a madman in the little chamber . . ."

"He's not like a madman; he's thinking and learning in the little chamber all by himself. And besides, you've got nothing to do with that, leave this matter to me, don't get involved with it, it may not be good for you."

"All right, all right, it's just that I worry; you forget the little people are always the ones who get the blame. But all right, you know what you're doing. Isn't the stew ready yet?"

"It should be. Edésia, dear, help me here with the mush; that's a heavy pan."

Soon they were sitting down to eat, joyful with their reunion and with vainglory, which is the real reason one eats puffer fish, for a person who eats puffer fish is not like others. And also what a lovely day it was, the January midday sun rebounding on the bluest possible sea under a sky like no other, a northeasterly cooling the water jugs on the windows, the shadows of the trees coming and going with the wind and drawing mosaics on the ground, flycatchers singing as if to show they were having a party, no ampler comfort being possible for any creature in this world. Florisvaldo remarked what a beautiful day it was, filled his wood bowl, crossed himself, said a prayer, kissed the medal and the beads hanging from his chest, and started his lunch, praising its taste very highly. Ramiro asked them if anything happened to him to send a message for his wife to come and make arrangements for his funeral, because she was in Incarnation Village, spending some time with her mother, who had become ill after eating puffer fish in palm oil. Someone asked if Edésia, who was the earliest puffer fish eater among them, had ever felt anything, and she said, only once. Her lifs itched, her pingertifs itched, her legs pelt prickly. Then she bvecame dizzy, bvut with a good dizziness, bvetter than wine dizziness. And then she felt a little numb for over a fortnight, but that was all that happened, if she said otherwise she'd be a liar. Rita Popó smiled and got up to take a full plate for the general, full not with puffer fish, which you only give to those who ask for it, but with two mojarras she had cooked separately, with rice, kidney beans, and a few vegetables.

Inside the little chamber, right after Rita Popó left to go fetch his lunch, Patrício Macário asked himself how many days he had been there, and realized he would find out only if he asked, because he had lost the notion of time, and if it were not for the brightness that, though scantily, entered the room, he would not even know whether it was day or night. What a curious experience! And after all, how time mattered so little, how in a certain way it did not exist outside people, only inside them. He knew and imagined everyone knew that time shifts back and forth in its several durations, and one hour can be extremely long or instantaneous, but now he also knew something deeper, which perhaps he would be unable to explain to anyone who had not gone through a similar experience. He had gained a new intimacy with time, locked there with no watch, no calendar, no worries, and no conversation, except for Rita Popó's visits. Maybe not intimacy but independence, maybe indifference, maybe even the contempt in which one starts holding something whose heretofore feared power is suddenly exposed as a sham. In short, as that very strange woman had said, those are things that cannot be learned by means of words and consequently cannot be taught by means of words.

Yes, a most strange woman, coarse and illiterate and at the same time wise, in relation not only to her occupation as a witch but also to other things, which one would not expect from people like her. Although of course her links to Maria da Fé led him to believe there was something special about her, there probably was, sure there was. He had first looked for her mother but then found out she had both inherited her mother's position and acquired a still greater fame. She had grown prodigiously fat since the day he had seen her first, to the point where he did not recognize her when he met her this time. Now she was an imposing, monumental figure, whose appearance would elicit respect even in places where she did not have the same high status as she had among her people.

Patrício Macário, riding slowly up to the yard, noticed that people were moving away as he got closer, so he dismounted, thinking maybe this way he would not intimidate them. But their behavior did not change, and he decided to walk toward the largest house, where many of them were rushing as if there was someone there they should alert about his arrival. Speckled with bits of hardened mud, even on his beard, he was probably very disquieting for people who were used to having their religious places and objects depredated by whites. He wondered if he should smile, and was still thinking about how he would act at the doorstep, when she came to the porch as though his presence there were an everyday occurrence, greeted him with a gesture, and said:

"Welcome, General Patrício Macário. You took a long time to come, but you're finally here, welcome. You can hand your horse over to this boy at your side and come in, please. We're very glad to see you in our house."

"Thank you very much," was all he managed to say, surprised, handing the reins to the boy and hammering his feet down on the ground to shake the mud from his boots before going in.

He apologized for his appearance, explaining that he had come from the city of Itaparica, normally a short trip to Amoreiras, but made difficult today by the mud. And he was about to start a little anxiously to tell her why he had been looking for Sa Rufina and now for her, but she interrupted him, saying there was no hurry, he shouldn't rush things, he ought to finish arriving, take a bath, change clothes, there was no need to worry, later on they would have all the time in the world to talk, she already had an idea of what he was after.

Because she said that, he could hardly restrain his impatience as he took a bath, put on the clothes he had brought in a little valise behind his saddle and the boots they had cleaned for him, drank two glasses of water, and waited, walking back and forth, for her to come. At first he was disappointed, because when he asked her about Maria da Fé, the Brotherhood, even Zé Popó, she gave him vague and evasive-sounding answers, which even irritated him a little. But she noticed that, and explained to him in a patient, monotonous voice that contrary to what people think, magic is made not from outside but from inside. That was why people mentioned so much the need to have faith for things to happen, for after all, faith is nothing but a way to see the world that makes it possible for the things you wish to happen. Faith, therefore, is a knowledge, a knowledge he didn't have and no one could give him, only he himself could do it, though he could be helped. She was willing to help him if he wanted, and as long as he understood that the world can be seen in many ways. He certainly knew that people who are excessively sure that there's only one way and one truth, a truth entirely known to them, are dangerous and prone to all types of crime. To know the truth and try to impose it on others, in a world where everything changes and is cloaked under all kinds of appearances, is a serious madness. That is the reason why mad people like them do not understand the Gospel of the priests. It says you should turn your other cheek if you are slapped, but it also shows you should whip the asses of the moneychangers of the temple. Which way is right? A backward mind, a hardened mind, a mind that hasn't ventured through paths that would have opened other entrances to it, will choose one of the two ways and will start condemning the other way, making up the most stupid reasons for the other way to be despised. This is because they don't understand that you must both turn the other cheek and get into a good brawl, because life is like this, it says one thing here and a different thing there, life isn't written on little slates, nor is its functioning ordered like those madmen want, the only fully ordered things are lies, which are always perfect explanations. She could see disappointment in his face for not having received direct answers, but he should please try to realize she couldn't give that type of answer; there were things that depended on his head.

He went on listening to her, almost dizzy, at times impatient and at times fascinated, not knowing what to think about that speech, which sounded simultaneously brilliant and delirious, sensible and ranting. He even interrupted her in a moment of exasperation to ask if the way she greeted him, saying he had taken long to come, had not been an imposture to impress him, making him think she knew beforehand about his coming. How did she know? She sighed and said that to do that she didn't have to be a diviner, because it was obvious from the part of his history known to her that he had an obsession with his past, and therefore sooner or later he would come to try to dissolve that obsession.

Oh my God, she said, what a complication, having to explain that the way you ask a question chooses its answer. She apologized for her frankness and told him he didn't know how to ask, he only asked in a certain way, and for that certain way he already knew the answers he would get, for they were always the same. But there were things that couldn't be explained with words, all the more so because words are tyrants and always cling to each person's experience, thus enslaving people's minds. She would help him if he wanted, she said again. There was no prearranged route, it wasn't like in a school, where you learn lessons; it was something that depended a great deal on him—how difficult it was to explain that, my God! It was as though he could learn only if he knew and know only if he learned. It was like slacking off, he should get into a kind of slackness, of forgetfulness, did he understand that?

No, he didn't. Yes, she knew it was difficult, it wasn't something that could be taught with goddamned, accursed words, so the only help she could offer was to let him try to learn there, and she knew the best method, which she would teach him if he wanted. He did. Did he really? Yes, yes, he did, why not, at least it would be something new in his life, a different experience.

"A different experience, yes," she said, "but not a new thing. It's an old thing."

The first instruction was that he didn't have to agree with anything, he just had to follow on. What did she mean by that? Follow on. Yes, but how? Just follow on. You know what "follow" is? So follow on. The second instruction was for him to feel free, nothing would be forced on him. If he didn't want his door to be shut, he could open it; if he didn't want to stay alone, he could go out to talk; if he didn't want to sit still, he could move about as he pleased. But he should want something. For example? For example, what kind of thing could he want? Oh, how could she know? Anything! Just go on wanting something. He wasn't being forced to want something, he wasn't being forced to do anything, but if he didn't want something he wouldn't be there, right? But what? How should I know? she said.

Very well, third, fourth, fifth, and sixth instructions, all quite simple, and there he was, cloistered. In the first two days, he doubted he was going to stay there, he believed his sense of the ridiculous would disallow him to spend too much time in this experience. But in the third day, when he got up to open the door, which he knew was not locked, he stopped before holding out his arm and did not step out, returning to where he had been sitting. When Rita Popó showed up for the first time that day, he made a point of being ironical about his situation, but she seemed not to understand what he meant. After that he asked her for a book, a publication, something to read. She appeared very surprised, almost as if she did not know what those words meant. Books, what did he mean by books, if no one there knew how to read? And why did he want to read, why didn't he try to learn by other means? But he insisted, and she ended up remembering she had seen a book at the home of a relative of Florisvaldo Balão's who lived nearby, and she was going to have someone pick it up, since it was so important to him. A little later she returned with the book, a yellowish, coverless paperback, with a few loose pages and others missing. Under her curious gaze, Patrício Macário thumbed through the book, and some passing titles led him to the conclusion that it was a collection of narratives of travels, adventures, and explorations. Better than nothing; he was going to read that; now he just wanted another little favor. He was feeling like having a drink; wouldn't she please get him some firewater?

He drank much more than he had planned, and shortly before noon he found himself rolling on the ground with laughter, in the middle of a story fraught with perils, deaths, and heroic deeds, in which Spanish navigators battled Moorish pirates on the African coast, had a shipwreck, and were forced to confront the Pygmy People, a most ferocious lot, with razorlike teeth and poison-darted blowguns, in spite of an average height of just two feet.

"I'm learning, I'm learning!" he said, laughing, to Rita Popó when she brought him his dinner.

"With the book? Is it a good book?"

"It's wonderful! I was reading a story about the Pygmies, a people with an average height of two . . . two . . . two feet!"

He tried to go on telling the story, but his laughter stopped him and caught her too, who laughed and picked up a little cup to help herself to a shot of firewater. Patrício Macário applauded her and tried to make a toast, but he burst out in a new fit of laughter, pressing his arms on his stomach. She had another cup of firewater and complained she didn't like it without mixing it with something—wouldn't he like to taste an infusion she had in her place? But of course he did; nothing like a few little libations before lunch!

Later on, not knowing how much time had passed and not even whether he had had lunch or whether it was day or night, he thought of getting up to open the wicket and check whether there was light outside, but then he decided it was just a stupid, senseless habit to keep finding out what time it was. What difference did it make, why should he get up to submit to a senseless thing? He felt very happy with his decision not to get up. As a matter of fact, he felt extraordinarily well, contrary to what someone who had drunk so much liquor might expect. It must have been that infusion, one of the miraculous herbs these people know and keep secret. But he was going to get up anyway; he wanted the book, which was a few steps from him. However, when he tried to move, he couldn't do it. What was that, was he paralyzed? But he only had one moment of panic, because he realized right away with great calm that he was not paralyzed, it was as if one side of his will wanted to experience being unable to move. He could move, he wanted to move, but also he neither could nor wanted to move. Was it possible to understand that? But it was happening, and then he remained absolutely motionless, sitting on his cot near its head, with his back against the wall. Maybe it would be better if he made himself more comfortable, perhaps stretching his leg so it would be completely relaxed, but he soon understood he did not need that, because his body seemed more and more to be abstracting itself from his mind, or vice versa, so his position was increasingly losing its importance. Had he read the book in this mysterious time that had passed? Probably yes, because although he did not remember anything about it except the story of the Pygmies, he could now look at it and read it without touching or opening it, as if it unfolded in front of him by itself—not in letters, not in images, not in anything defined, but very clear. All he had to do was lay his eyes on it, and it became alive and transparent. As he realized something extraordinary was happening, Patrício Macário also realized suddenly what Rita Popó had meant when she advised him just to follow on. He just followed on, letting his attention stray from the book and starting to observe how the walls took on the colors and textures he wanted, how everything was funny or sad according to his wishes, how the roof would open up or rise if he wished. And why didn't he wish it, just to prove it? Because suddenly it did not interest him to see a roof rise through the strength of a wish; all that interested him was that it would move if he wished, just as his motionless muscles would move if he wished. How could he describe to anyone the feeling he was experiencing? Would he say it was joy, euphoria? Yes, but a little more and a little less than that. Triumph, power? No, something like that, but with a difference that made it impossible to use those two words. Neither asleep nor awake, his eyes neither closed nor open, he surrendered to a sea of waves and forms that engulfed him, without his worrying about where he was going, how he was going, what he was going to find, if anything; he was just going.

And now, just a while before Rita Popó was to bring the two mojarras, he was finishing solidifying the serenity that for at least two days now he felt coming over him, stronger and stronger, a kind of calm assuredness, silent joy and strength. He did not bother to try to find out if it was all just an illusion the same way he had given up trying to find out if everything that had happened to him had really happened or been imagined. Nor was he disturbed as he would have been before by the circumstance that he would never be able to systematize or organize in a logical way this unbelievable sojourn in the little chamber. He remembered having talked to many people, having heard and told stories, having had mental adventures he would never forget. He also remembered the time he was laughing his head off in Rita Popó's company and had asked her if by any chance he was going crazy. She said no, he might have been crazy before, and if things now looked extraordinarily funny, it was because he was seeing them with the new eyes he was acquiring and learning how to use. He agreed, but insisted that anyway he was no longer the same. Of course not, she answered, because your head has changed.

They had become good friends, they had even developed a comfortable closeness, and sometimes they did not really have to speak in order to converse, nor did they need to comment on his experience, because she was right, it was not like school learning. As a matter of fact, maybe the learning would actually start now, when he got back to the world outside to see everything he already knew as though it were the first time. He knew he was finally going to leave, he was going to open the door and leave, he was ready to leave. He just wanted to wait for her, to have one final talk and at last say goodbye. He had discovered nothing about Maria da Fé, except a few vague stories. Little was known about Zé Popó, either, and as for the Brotherhood, Rita Popó would simply change the subject. Well, it had been worth it anyway, as he intended to tell her. He thought it was amusing that if somebody, even one of his friends, asked him what he had been doing all this time, he would not know how to answer even if he wanted to, and this was surely the reason why all those things were secret, because they were incommunicable except through experience. He heard her footsteps outside and rose to wait by the door.

"But, creature of god, have you lost your mind?" Florisvaldo said to Rita Popó. "Take back the man's mojarra; tell him to forget about this puffer fish thing!"

"You want the puffer fish all for yourself?" she answered, without interrupting what she was doing in the kitchen. "There's plenty, don't worry."

"It's not that I want the fish for myself; it's just that I'm thinking if this man dies here they'll say we poisoned him."

"If he dies, we die too; it's the same stew."

"Not at all. It may happen that one dies and the other doesn't, everyone knows that."

"It's no use, Florisvaldo. I'm going to take puffer fish for him."

"But what kind of a half-witted idea is that, why did you have to tell him we were having puffer fish here?"

"I don't know. I don't know, but I did tell him, and when I did, he said he didn't want the mojarra anymore, he wanted some of the puffer fish stew too."

"But didn't you tell him it could kill him, didn't you explain to him what a puffer fish was?"

"I did, I did. But he didn't change his mind, and he didn't come to have lunch here only because it's his last day in the little chamber and he wants to have lunch there. And I'm going to join him."

"Why? Are you supposed to?"

"More or less. Now excuse me, I'm going to take the food, excuse me."

"I still say I'm against it. If this general dies, there'll be no shortage of hanging rope for any of us."

"That's all hogwash; you've had some of the puffer fish already and nothing happened to you."

"But I haven't finished, and the effect comes only after you have finished."

"And you'll never finish if you keep on talking like that. Excuse me, excuse me. I'll be back soon."

She covered with a piece of cloth the bowl filled with stew she was going to take, put an overturned plate over the dish of mush, put everything on a wood tray, and left with it on her head, just one of her hands touching it lightly at the edge to balance it. When she got to the little chamber, the general looked much tidier than before, and he beamed as he opened the door.

"Excellent! And what a beautiful idea, bringing this wood tray! It'll serve as a table; we can arrange it here on top of those two stools. Splendid! It smells fine! It's the first time I feel hungry here, the first time I'm really hungry in years!"

"The others didn't believe me when I told them you were going to eat puffer fish."

"They don't know me. But let me see, may I lift that cloth? It's this here, isn't it? Splendid! Really splendid; are they always white like that, or is it the preparation?"

"No, its flesh is naturally white like that; it's the best fish of the sea."

"I can tell by the smell; it's enough to give you the idea."

They sat down on two other stools, and brandishing a wooden spoon, he asked if he could serve her. No, no, she would serve him, he was the visitor, he had a right to the best pieces, though everything there was of the very best quality. She served a brimming plate for him, dug a depression in the middle of the mush with the back of the spoon, and poured gravy over it. My, that smells good! Could they really be true, those stories of deaths provoked by such a delicious-looking fish? Yes, they were, because the puffer fish is a fish for princes and noblemen of the highest lineages, it's the fish of the king of Japan, where it's called foo-goo fish and can only be eaten by permission of the king, out of consideration or esteem; it's a mysterious fish. So, my dear Sa Rita, we're having a banquet for kings, and they wanted to deny me this privilege on the insignificant possibility that I might die after lunch? What happens to the dignity of someone who sees others taste a delicacy and doesn't do it too, out of cowardice? And what happens to real indifference to death? It's easy when it's out of duty; the real proof is when it's out of pleasure. You're right, Sa Rita. To eat of this fish is such a rich experience that books could be written about it.

He thrust his big three-pronged fork into the stew and started to eat. How tasty it was; he could understand the king of Japan's zeal! And wasn't *Sa* Rita going to eat? Oh, this is a beautiful conclusion for this phenomenal stay!

"I have to admit," he said, after remarking that the fish had no bones and was incomparably delicate, "I'm going away without having resolved my obsession. Remember you said I had come here to resolve an obsession? It's true, I still want to resolve this obsession, but I don't seem to be able to do it, it's still very solid. That of course doesn't mean I regret all this; much to the contrary, I . . . What an excellent fish? Splendid, really, splendid!"

"It's still too soon for you to know if you have resolved your obsession."

"Maybe, but as I told you, I'm leaving today. And of course I don't want to go away without thanking you for everything, really thanking you from the bottom of my heart."

"You have nothing to thank me for, General."

"Yes, I do; I have a lot to thank you for; yes, I do. But naturally that doesn't stop us from enjoying this extraordinary fish. Splendid!"

After helping himself three times, he commented that he had never eaten so well in his life, pulled the stool near the wall, which he leaned on, his legs outstretched. He asked Rita Popó in how much time a poisonous puffer fish would take effect, and she said she didn't know; it depended on a lot of things. Anyway, it would be a fine death, he observed; I've never felt so well. Was she also seeing the king of Japan right in front of them, his fists closed on his waist, extremely angry because they ate the royal puffer fish? Was she? Very well, *Sa* Rita, we'll ignore the king of Japan—that is to say, if he shuts his mouth, even though I don't understand a word of Japanese. And I shall take the liberty to make a small change in my plans. After a meal like this, I cannot dispense with a little rest, counting once more upon your hospitality. I'm going to sleep a little here and then leave. The weather is dry now, isn't it? So, so it's going to be a very brief trip back, and honestly I don't know how many days I have spent here. I feel a kind of tickling in my lips—does hot pepper do that? Not only am I feeling my lips tingling but also I feel a sort of torpor, and my legs are going numb. But it's not an unpleasant sensation; much to the contrary. Do you feel the same thing too, *Sa* Rita? Do you believe the puffer fish was poisonous, then? So could we possibly be dying? Is that correct? Are we dying?

"Are we dying?" he asked, after raising his torso in a world turned absolutely silent, where his voice was the only sound in the air.

Rita Popó turned around, and he noticed she did not know if she was dying, either.

"I don't know," she said. "Maybe a little, maybe much."

"Are we lying down or sitting?"

"I don't know. I feel I'm kind of floating."

"You're right. Now that you tell me, I can see I'm floating, we're both floating. Floating, yes! It doesn't make too much sense to want to know if we're standing or lying down; we're in every position, of course."

"Yes, in every position, that's true."

"You think the others are like this too? Is it also possible that we may be dreaming together? Are we dreaming together?"

"We may be dreaming together."

"Shouldn't we go looking for the others? After all . . ."

"Well, in that case, I'm going; you can stay here."

"Don't you want me to go with you? Granted that I'm still not sure I'm going to be able to move."

"No, go on resting; I'll take care of that."

He saw her stand up, not like someone who's rising but as if she was unfolding abnormal articulations, sliding toward the door and leaving before he found out whether she had really opened it or had disappeared through the wood. He thought of doing the same thing and felt he was twirling in the air like a windblown leaf and saw himself articulated in the same odd way, but he realized he could go to the door if he wanted. However, he never found out if he would be able to go through it, because it opened slowly and Rita Popó came in, followed by a tall, dark man, whose features made him tremble.

"This last day," Rita Popó said, her voice like the reverberation inside an empty pot, "you are having a visitor. Here is Lourenço, your son, Maria da Fé's only son."

Patrício Macário heard his chest pound as if it had climbed up to his head, and he raised his hands.

"My son?" he asked, though he had known it was true as soon as he saw him. "My son?"

But Rita Popó had disappeared unnoticed. The man walked to him and held out his arms.

"My son? Lourenço? I never . . . I . . ."

He embraced his son, and they remained embraced while he cried silently, without feeling like asking about anything, even knowing beforehand the answers to much of what he could ask.

"My son . . . Lourenço . . . Your mother . . . Oh my God, my son! How old are you? No, that doesn't matter, to me you were born now, my son, my son! My son! My son! My son! My son!"

They sat down hand in hand to talk. How Lourenço looked like his mother! Did he know he had the most beautiful mother there ever was, so beautiful and perfect that she herself had said that even Patrício Macário would someday think she was nothing but a legend? Yes, a son, she had become pregnant by him, he could never have expected such a supreme gift! Did Lourenço know what happiness was? Maybe he did, although he was still too young to really know, but he should know: Happiness was what he was feeling in front of his son with Maria da Fé, in front of the deepest proof that she had loved him, in front of the infinite and the wonder of life. No, happiness wasn't an abstract concept, happiness was something concrete and corporealized, happiness was he! My son!

He also knew the answer for what he was going to ask next, but he had to hear it loud and clear to get rid of that persistent ghost in his mind. What had happened to Maria da Fé, hadn't she, for example, been in Canudos? Lourenço said yes, she had been in Canudos, she had kept on fighting for the rest of her life, for she was dead, yes, she was dead, though no one knew how, because already old but still strong, she had disappeared one day, after having sailed out alone on a little boat off the cliffs around Our Lady Point. Our Lady Point? Yes, Our Lady Point, in whose surroundings or anywhere else no trace of her or her boat was ever found, not one vestige. The only things that belonged to her they had found were those he was now handing over to his father. They were three mementos: The weapon called *araçanga,* which had belonged to her grandfather and to her mother the fisherwoman Daê, which was the symbol of proud work, either for attack or for defense; a stingray spine sheathed in a cloth tube, which had belonged to her famous grandfather, Black Leléu, and which was the symbol that showed the people has more hidden weapons than is thought or imagined; and a little blue glass bottle with a sealed lid, in which she had kept the tears she shed right after their separation. Let him keep that bottle to pour on the sea whence everything came, the day there was the freedom that there was not for their love, a freedom that someday would be lived by either their children, their grandchildren, their great-grandchildren, or even descendants so remote they might never have heard of them but just bore their heritage, which should be proud and happy. Those three things were found on the fork of a tree by the edge of Our Lady Point's great cliff, a place she would always go back to when she revisited the bay lands. They had been bundled together in a handkerchief with the monogram *PM,* a handkerchief she had taken secretly from him to keep in her cleavage for the rest of her life, and which she was now returning because their smells were mixed in it, as their beings were mixed in their son Lourenço.

"I can die now, can't I, son?" Patrício Macário said. "Can't I? Not because I want to die, but because I'm finally so happy that I ask nothing else from life, nothing else."

Lourenço answered no, of course not, he should think about living, never about dying, all the more so because those who really live never really die, nothing alive really dies. Death is the kingdom of those who serve no one but themselves, of those who have the shadow of the Curukere moth hovering over their heads, bad priests, bad leaders, bad brothers, bad neighbors, robbers of the spirit of the belief in God, life, and hope.

"What do you do, my son?" Patrício Macário asked, enthralled by seeing in the young man his demeanor and his features when he was younger, distilled by the light and fervor of his mother, which sparkled in each of his gestures.

"I'm a revolution maker, my father," Lourenço answered. "Ever since my mother's time, even before that, we've been looking for a conscience of what we are. And before that we didn't even know we were looking for something, we just rebelled. But as time passed we accumulated wisdom through practice and thought, and today we know we are searching for this conscience and are finding this conscience. We don't have enough weapons to overcome oppression and never will, although it's our duty to fight whenever our survival and our honor have to be defended. But our weapon must be the mind, each and every one's mind, which must not be dominated and have to assert itself. Our objective is not really equality, rather it's justice, freedom, pride, dignity, good coexistence. This is a fight that will go across centuries, because our enemies are very strong. The bullwhip still prevails, poverty increases, nothing has changed. Emancipation didn't abolish slavery, it created new slaves. The Republic didn't abolish oppression, it created new oppressors. The people doesn't know about itself, has no conscience, nothing it does is seen, and all it is taught is contempt for itself, for its speech, for its appearance, for its food, for its clothing, for what it is. But we are making this revolution of small and great battles, some bloody, some muffled, some secret, and this is what I do, my father."

His father also asked him about the Brotherhood. Lourenço answered that there was a Brotherhood of the Brazilian People and a Brotherhood of Man, no question about that. Haven't wondrous things happened and aren't they still happening, not only to themselves but to others, even the most destitute? If you think well, you'll see that nothing is by chance, but common sense, which is a way to bind conscience and shackle freedom, denies that and prefers to go on believing in old, worn-out truths. Isn't there hope? Yes, there is hope, there has always been hope, there is hope. His mother always used to explain that you knew when you belonged to the Brotherhood. And it was true! How could his father ignore that he belonged to it, and it had always been so, now more than ever? All he had to do was to see with his new eyes, to think with his new head, and mainly to remember there is a Spirit of Man, and this Spirit of Man has as its noblest and strongest impulse not only to survive but to prevail, because the failure of the world it inherited will not be God's failure but the failure of the Spirit of Man, and this failure is the only way for a spirit to degrade itself, the only form of death. This Spirit is contradictory to Death, and therefore the Brotherhood exists, because this Spirit needs Good as fish need water. And there are sacrifices for this Brotherhood each minute, there are thousands and thousands of unknown struggles and heroism about which only the Brotherhood knows and

455

of which they have preserved mementos since the time of the flour house conspirators, since before the conspirators, through many, many years. And he also spoke about Júlio Dandão's chest, and said Patrício Macário would be its guardian and should not worry about what to do, because that would also come to him naturally, he wouldn't have to be taught anything.

Maybe because his son said that the Spirit needs Good as fish need water, Patrício Macário, feeling such a strong love that he could sense no more than light and warmth, noticed he was inside a translucent liquid with his son, and so patently it would exasperate him to have to explain it to someone else, they were different and were the same man. He looked at his son, saw him as a little boy learning to walk, followed with tears in his eyes all his childhood, put him in his lap, sat down on a porch thinking about the miracle of his little boy for the first time using words, for the first time having an opinion, for the first time doing something for no reason, as is proper of man, for the first time understanding he had a father, for the first time wetting his hands in rainwater, for the first time dealing with animals, for the first time smelling a fruit, for the first time discovering he couldn't look at the sun, for the first time seeing a fish, for the first time looking for a reason, for the first time running over the sand on a beach, for the first time tasting salt, for the first time shaking his body when hearing music, for the first time staying by himself in a corner with dreams and thoughts all his own, for the first time trusting a friend, for the first time gazing in wonderment at his hands. How can one who feels avoid turning into a spiral of fire, just from witnessing life?

He soared up in the air toward the Infinite, where he found himself in a dark place in which everything had colors and was neither hot nor cold, and all distances could be covered by thought. And thought shaped everything, though not as it wanted but as it must, though what it must was what it wanted, though as it went where it wanted it went where it must go. Oh, boys and girls, how many lovely things are showing here, why are those things not seen? They gave me the eyes of a child, and so I can be a wise man. They gave me wings, and so I can navigate among the stars and foreglimpse the Absolute and have Faith, as a gift as well as a conquest. Souls, souls, souls! Souls! I! We! All! I! Souls! We and I! Souls! The soul!

Almost at midnight, in the very dark little chamber, Patrício Macário got up, and the first thing he did was to inhale so deeply he thought he would never stop. What had happened, what was happening? Had he died a little, as Rita Popó had said? Had he died and then returned? Was he dead? He felt himself, shook his head, rubbed his eyes, and heard someone move by his side.

Sa Rita?

He struck a match on the sole of his boot, found a lamp, lit it, raised it

456

toward the place from where the sound had come, and illuminated Rita Popó's face as she smiled softly.

"We . . ." he began, but she made a gesture as if saying they should not speak. "The others . . ."

A new gesture, and he shut up. There was no longer that stony silence outside, the night now pierced by the songs of crickets and toads and by the hooting of owls. He went to the door, opened it, looked at Rita Popó's house, and saw that they were lighting lamps too. So they also . . . He stepped outside and stopped while the door of the house opened and two people, a man and a woman, also stepped outside and halted at a short distance from the house. They looked at him, and he realized they would not speak about what had happened, either, it was not something one could talk about, it was not, come to think of it, something he himself wanted to talk about. He got back to the little chamber, looked for signs of his son's visit, and found none. And the objects he had given him, where were they? They had disappeared too. He smiled. He was happy anyway, and was now suspicious of the habit he was already losing of trying to make excessively clear distinctions between illusion and reality; it seemed to him now a simpleminded attitude.

He was leaving right now. The night was clear, and the low tide would let him ride down the beach, which could be seen from afar, reflecting the moon. He felt in excellent condition; it would be a very pleasant trip, he was sure. He embraced Rita Popó for a long time and told her he would be back, and she said yes, he should return as often as he liked, he would be most welcome every time. He looked around, picked up a few objects and his coat from the cot, and only then saw, folded in the coat's front pocket, a rumpled handkerchief with the initials PM. He pulled out the handkerchief, took it to his nose, smelled it with his eyes closed, pressed it against his heart, and slipped it under his shirt, next to his skin. Rita Popó, by his side, did not seem to have seen anything, nor did he make any comment about what he had done. He embraced her again, left the little chamber, went to the small donkey stable where his horse was, harnessed it, mounted, and rode out to the beach, tying his hat to his saddle pommel so he could feel the wind on his head.

On the beach, he set out to Itaparica at a marching pace but soon loosened his reins, and his horse started galloping happily over the sloshing sand of the sandbanks. There really could be no place as beautiful as this, an opalescent infinitude embedded in the night, the wind casting into space water droplets that seemed to mix with the stars, scintillating just like them, and coloring everything in sight. He pressed the handkerchief against his chest once again—could there be a fuller happiness than his? Of course he did not know that when he got home, a few minutes later, the noise would wake Adalícia, and after nervously blessing his return she would show him

457

a chest, an odd-looking trunk, which someone had left there in his absence, she did not know how, and which she had not known how to open. On top of that chest he would also see a cloth-wrapped package she had no memory of, and as he opened the package he would find a very dented hardwood club, a sheath of cloth with a stingray spine inside, and a little blue bottle filled with tears.

19

Resort Town of Itaparica, January 7, 1977

Will Stalin José make his speech? Will he do as he promised—climb up to the official platform, tear open his shirt over his chest, and make an ad-libbed speech denouncing the corruption of the ruling classes, the vampirism of multinational companies, North American imperialism, and the violence of the dictatorship that's crushing the Brazilian people? Will he once more accuse the authorities, those present and those represented, and again be hauled into jail under the National Security Law, to take a couple of whacks, electric shocks in his nuts, ferule strokes on the soles of his feet, and "telephone calls" with blows by cupped hands on his ears as he hangs upside down from a rack? Isn't it enough that he's already lame and a little deaf on account of those sports, besides, as it's bruited privately, having to use rubber panties because after the shocks he can't hold his urine anymore? Isn't it enough that in '38, or maybe '39, Getúlio Vargas ordered his father, the oldtime Communist Teodomiro Longshoreman, strangled by a secret agent named Luiz Sledgehammer, who used to brag about having strangled over ten Communists, using only his hands? And his niece, his sister's daughter, who was arrested because she was necking in a station wagon with a subversive, was raped by six men and then dumped dead on a beach, the coroner's report indicating drowning as the cause of death? It was a crazy family because of the old man's influence, and he was crazier than the old man. What business does he have, at times like these, to keep making provocations? What good does it do? The system is very solid, the armed forces are united and cohesive, the nation is warned against incendiary extremism and the small groups bent on establishing the chaos propitious to the implantation of alien ideologies so discordant with the Brazilian people's orderly, peaceful traditions—there is full democracy, so who needs change?

But Stalin José is really a bit round the bend and guarantees he's going to speak, he says they may kill him, but he won't shut up. Will he really make the speech?

These and other questions are repeated all over the city, in the domino-playing circles of Greengrocer Square, in the fish stalls of the market, in the humblest and the most prosperous homes, such as Ioiô Lavínio's, where the only drink offered is Scotch, among other reasons because his oldest son, Lavinoel, works for the federal police and has access to smuggled bottles. And they are drinking a lot of White Horse with coconut-water ice and guarana soda pop, and having as hors d'oeuvres clams and white cheese sprinkled with Worcestershire sauce, while they wait, around nine o'clock, for the preparation of the big jewfish-head stew with which Ioiô Lavínio keeps up the tradition of not letting the Seventh of January pass by without some kind of celebration. It's a family thing, because Ioiô descends from the legendary patriarch João Popó through Labatut Popó—that is to say, the legitimate branch of the family. Nowadays there are no more men like João Popó, men with a capital *M*, and today's conditions do not permit celebrations like the ones he had. Old people used to say that during the whole Seventh of January week he paid out of his own pocket for the meals of the town's poor, besides having several steers slaughtered to distribute meat among the people. He was a stern man of austere habits, who allowed no familiarities, a brand of man that indeed doesn't exist anymore.

That doesn't mean Ioiô Lavínio is not also a patriot of deeply rooted convictions and civic courage recognized by all. A revolutionary from the word go in 1964, he personally conducted the arrest of the aldermen Lóydson Barreto, Juracy Bonfim, Radclife Luz, and Ruy Castro Alves da Conceição, not because they were his personal enemies and had forced that rascal Mayor Oldismair das Neves, a clown with neither moral authority nor qualifications to be the mayor of a town like Itaparica, to charge him an extortionate tax for the Municipal Market concession, but because they were Communists, or fellow travelers, which comes down to the same thing. Arrant Communists, all four of them, shameless crooks; where in Russia would a pretentious mulatto like Ruy Castro Alves have the freedom he has here? The truth is that every Communist is a frustrated individual, moved by spite, by envy, and by a feeling of inferiority, for which he has to compensate at any cost, even if it means the ruination of decent men and of the prevailing morality. So he arrested the four of them and wired his son at the federal police to suggest that they at least be put in solitary confinement, and when the proper police and military inquiry was started against them they should be treated rigorously, even using the American apparatuses to do the job because the American machines are superior to any of the ones used here and hardly ever kill or cripple. Ioiô Lavínio had right on his side, but he didn't want those wretches to die; it wasn't compatible with his Christian spirit.

When the glorious revolution of '64 broke out, he led the Gold for Brazil campaign on the island and personally donated his accountant's graduation ring, their wedding bands, a tie clip, a necklace, and a watchband. He pressured the police commissioner to forbid everyone, whether permanent or summer resident, to circulate in swimming attire that was offensive to public decorum. He suggested searching the baggage of apparent hippies who landed on the island, to prevent an influx of drugs and pornographic material. He obtained the banning of the play *Lieutenant Botas—Hero or Mercenary?*, which the Maria Felipa Theater Ensemble was going to stage, by demonstrating that it maligned patriotic ideals and denigrated an illustrious figure of our history, from what was obviously a Bolshevik standpoint. He founded the March 31 Youth Club with the collaboration of an army officer who was a friend of his, Major Eduardo da Vinci Mota, its aim being to stimulate among young people a love for Brazil and the basic values of our Christian, peace-loving, harmonious society, besides offering wholesome sports in the complex they were going to build, which circumstances prevented their finishing or in fact even starting, though the sale of its shares was a complete success, particularly because of the major's talents as a salesman who was very well received by all the town's small merchants he visited, who often even bought more than a share.

Consistent with his past, he remained against Getúlio even after the 1937 coup, although he admitted it was a necessary step to impose order upon a country on the brink of an abyss. The promulgation of labor laws had left him so upset that he considered emigrating, and didn't do it only because his family managed to dissuade him. And though not fascist inclined, like many of his friends, he was outraged by the treason committed against the nationalist group Integralist Action, which they had tried to crush by reducing it to the condition of a social club. Appointed a state tax inspector because of his unbending loyalty to the province's provisional administrator, Juracy Magalhães, and later to the National Democratic Union, he ascended rapidly in his public career, in which he excelled through his diligence and his courteous manner, acknowledged by the very people he investigated, who always lavished on him very generous gifts, such as the house given to him by the late Commander Inácio Pantaleão Pimenta, owner of a chain of textile and grocery stores, and others, many others, so that without his needing to renounce his unyielding principles, he had been enabled to lead a comfortable, worriless life. All the more so because he retired quite young, taking advantage of a law that besides retiring him three levels above his own career rank, allowed him to double two thirds of his years of service, for having carried out several selfless missions on committees and specially paid assignments. He'd still had two years to go, but this was taken care of by an affidavit attesting his ill health, obtained from a very influential doctor friend of his, whose word no one would dare to doubt.

Back on the island, he dedicated himself to politics for some time, but soon gave up direct involvement. In the first place, his frank, no-nonsense nature, which made him incapable of lying and beating around the bush, of treachery and dirty blows, abhorred the sordidness of politics, shady deals, collusion, treason, the misuse of public money. He was so strict about those things that when one of his sons, then eight years old, found a two-milreis bill lying on the ground, he made him look for its owner all over town until he finally returned it. In the second place, there was the painful rupture of his old friendship with Dr. Gilson Duarte, who had not complied with his written request to give some help to Lavinoel, who was going to take the law school entrance examination but was a little unprepared in Latin, sociology, and Portuguese, though he knew some French and had memorized the first ten lines of each of the texts that might be assigned for translation in the exam. Lavinoel's subsequent flunking and Dr. Gilson's attempt to explain it constituted a rude blow to a long-standing friendship, because the professor, who was also a brilliant orator at the State Assembly, had always counted on the votes controlled by Ioiô Lavínio, which were not few, considering how many people depended on him. Dr. Gilson should not have denied him that banal favor, since his own son, regarded as a brilliant student in the same school, was obviously the beneficiary of his father's position and influence. The consequence was that Lavinoel had to take a new entrance examination, this time in a diploma mill in Niterói, involving expenses and worries because of so trifling a matter. But he who laughs last laughs best, and Lavinoel is now very well placed at the federal police. An enterprising man, he is respected and well-to-do, with a nice house in the Pituba neighborhood, a late-model twenty-five-foot motorboat, a late-model car, and three wonderful children, Marcus Vinicius, Vanessa, and Priscilla Alessandra.

Incidentally, Ioiô Lavínio managed to get a college education and good jobs for all his four children. Lavínia Graça, the eldest after Lavinoel, didn't have a very good academic mind but managed to graduate from the Fine Arts School, not long before causing her parents so great a mortification as almost to have killed them. She lost her virginity to Ronaldo Jataí, one of the island's many loafers, who belongs to a family that had some means in the past but who now lives off the rent of his grandfather's old mansion, turned into a rooming house and lodging at least thirty families. And worse, she became pregnant. If it weren't for the beneficence of Dr. Plínio Lobo, a longtime friend of the family, the situation might have become untenable. Fortunately, Dr. Plínio was the owner of a clinic that had a contract with a federal medical insurance agency, and he performed her abortion there, moving heaven and earth to spare expenses with the hospitalization and the procedure, since Lavínia Graça was not insured by that agency. But the good Lord, who sees everything, provided her with a back-dated card and forged documents, a task made difficult because the man who took care of those

462

things for Dr. Plínio was ill, and they had trouble finding another one with enough experience. But finally everything was settled, and Ioiô Lavínio was almost speechless with gratitude as he signed his daughter's release papers, on which, though she had spent only a day and a half in the hospital, major surgery and a forty-day hospitalization were reported, besides some medicines and expenses. A real fortune for the agency to pay, but in such matters money has to be no object, and it was only fair for Dr. Plínio to be rewarded for the risks he took and the charitable deed he performed. Not to mention that he also referred a colleague of his in Rio de Janeiro to restore her hymen, something that was taken care of that same year, with the excellent results that Lavínia Graça recovered very quickly from her trauma and married Dr. Domingos Mendonça, graduate of the School of Electromechanics now working as a real estate agent, having made a fortune during the boom of government-financed housing mainly by selling housing projects for low-income groups, earning in commissions a sum that, as his father-in-law says, would be enough to build about twenty more of such projects. Lavínia Graça now turns up once in a while in the social pages of the papers and, with the collaboration and incentive of the Lions Club, has held an exhibit of her collages, entitled "Repaintescence," which was even praised in the press. Dr. Domingos, whose two daughters, Monika and Erika, he intends to have educated in Switzerland, is an excellent son-in-law, although Lavínia Graça, on account of that artistic temperament of hers, has talked of separation a couple of times. Psychoanalysis, however, has been helping them both, and they now go on conjugal vacations every year, and apparently live more happily than ever before.

Lavindonor, the son that came after Lavínia Graça, had given them even more trouble, because he had his way with two girls of the people, people of low extraction really, and one of those times it seems he forced himself on one of the girls in the company of two friends. Of course that's what the Negress says, because you can't accept the word of those sluts who walk around bare-assed and practice the filthiest acts imaginable, baiting boys and looking for trouble. Anyway, if Lavinoel hadn't been very influential with the Secretary of Public Security, they'd have had quite a problem; even in spite of his influence Lavinoel was force to allege that Lavindonor's arrest was not in the interest of federal security agencies, for reasons he could not reveal. They dropped the charges, but the boy continued to strike an occasional bad patch. He ran over a six-year-old child as he was driving a little juiced up, but fortunately the boy didn't die, just got one of his legs crippled and lost an eye, which was compensated by a job Ioiô got for his father as night watchman at a supermarket, in exchange for his not filing a complaint. Lavindonor involved himself with a group of dope smokers and rowdies, and was once arrested for taking part in a gas station holdup, but fortunately it was later proved that it had all been a joke after a drinking spree. Finally, because of the policemen who became his friends after they arrested him and found out he was Lavinoel's brother, he tried, without a recommendation, to pass a civil service examination to become a police investigator and failed, but even so he took to participating in manhunts, and was even accused of the murder of a rich man's spoiled kid who got involved with drugs and was found hogtied and shot dead in a thicket in the town of Lauro de Freitas, in what was later demonstrated to have been self-defense on Lavindonor's part. Fortunately, God helps those who trust Him, so when Lavindonor seemed to be a lost case, he was saved by the love of a girl from an excellent family from the state of Sergipe, rather homely but very gifted and good homemaker, the only daughter of a big farmer in the region of Itabaiana. This girl has been a real blessing in Lavindonor's life, and he now helps with his father-in-law's business and dedicates himself to his home, in the company of his wife and his sons, Robson, Rickson, Rockson, and Rodney. In his spare time he works with two army colonels, selling retirement plans, pensions, and investment funds for the Great Civil-Military Family of Brazil Savings and Pension Fund, an organization owned by a group of Syrian-Lebanese businessmen from São Paulo but managed by a northeastern general, which has been performing excellently.

Finally, Lavinette, the youngest, married very early and had two daughters, Tatiana and Andréa, but even so managed to get a degree in Social Sciences. Her husband, a bank clerk, was very jealous, a very limited young man who did not view favorably either her work, or her schoolmates, or her attitudes, so their separation became inevitable, and Lavinette these days has an open marriage with a composer called Jorge Mayflower, from Ituberá, who at the moment is in Rio de Janeiro to record his first single, leaving his daughter, Alga Marinha, in the company of her mother and grandparents.

There was nothing like the joy of seeing almost the whole family together, plus their closest friends—a full house—and the prospect of a superb fish stew, after which anyone who wished could go to the civic parade. In spite of his displeasure at the speech to be made by Stalin José, to whom people said he was related through one of his family's illegitimate lines, though he didn't acknowledge it, he would not miss the parade, nor would he be absent from the group that would pull the Indian float, the symbol of Itaparica's fight for Independence. He couldn't miss it, it was a tradition, though he himself would not make any speech, as formerly, on account of his disappointments with politics.

But he had no business thinking about those things, as he drank a Scotch one could see was genuine by the circle of bubbles it formed when you shook the bottle—not with tidbits of this quality, with this life which is here to be lived, for the life you lead is all that matters in life. Inside, in blue bermuda shorts and a commodore's cap, Dr. Domingos was demonstrating his new stereo, brought back from an excursion to Disney World. He had bought two of them, by the way, one for himself and another for Lavinoel, who didn't have any trouble getting them through customs, together with the merchandise for the boutique Lavínia Graça ran at her home, just as a hobby. Ioiô Lavíno decided to go in there, not only to examine the sound system but also to ask them to put something softer on, a classic such as the ones he liked, "Over the Waves," maybe a nocturne by Chopin. He went looking for his records in his ivorywood bookcase with its tapered legs. Dammit, they had rearranged the bookcase again, and when they did that everything disappeared. He looked among the hardcover tomes of the *Home and Office Encyclopaedia*, the *Light and Wisdom* collection, a set of spirit-written works by the most famous mediums, works of Humberto de Campos, Ruy Barbosa's selected speeches, Vargas Villa's much-thumbed books, the Army Library volumes, and the photo albums. He did not find what he wanted, and was going to shout something to the others in exasperation, when he decided to open the little latticework wicket, found the records, and, right behind the LP *Carnival in the Good Old Days*, saw *Classics at the Piano #2*. Oh, "Ritual Fire Dance," that's it! Of course! Delighted, he did not even bother to close the wicket, and hurried to the dining room, where the sound system, sprouting from a tangle of cords and boxes, filled the house with the sound of "Besame Mucho," from a cassette recorded by Ray Conniff and bought in Miami.

"Turn this thing off and put this on," Ioiô said. "This is real music! Do you know 'Ritual Fire Dance'?"

"Come on, Dad, everybody loves this Ray Conniff interpretation, he gives new life to this song. You remember this—I think they played it in your time. '*Besame, besame mucho! Como si fuera esta noche la última vez! Besame . . .*' "

"I'll admit it's nice. But you can't compare that to classical music. Classical music is the true music. Not for every occasion, I agree, but it's the true music."

"All right, Dad, I want to try the record player anyway. This record player is a genuine Garrard, diamond stylus, stroboscopic synchronizer. . . . See, if you look at these little stripes on the turntable you can adjust its speed; it's a wonderful thing, state-of-the-art technology. You see the head of the pickup arm, how it moves in two directions simultaneously to follow the grooves of the records? Wow, this record of yours is filthy! I have an electrostatic spray that will take care of that in no time. A spray and a brush with special bristles. God, it's really filthy!"

He finally placed the record on the turntable, and no sound came out at first. He pressed two buttons frantically, commented he had forgotten to turn on the switch for the record player's input, pressed a third button, and the room was inundated by the Dance's precipitous eighth notes. Ioiô Lavínio was dazzled: What a sound! He ran outside to call more people to listen, came back and sat in front of the loudspeakers, his eyes closed.

"Yes, sir, what a magnificent sound! It's really something, really something! Americans really know how to do a good job."

"Americans and the Japanese. The Japanese beat the Americans in certain areas."

"Yes, but America will always be America. There can't be any comparison between a country like the United States and a country it defeated in the war."

"But they had to use the atomic bomb."

"No, they didn't; victory was already theirs. The atomic bomb was more like a moral effect thing. It had mainly a moral effect. Japan exists today because the Americans led it to recovery through the great General MacArthur, one of the greatest geniuses of mankind in this century."

"I agree, a great general, really a great general. Wasn't it Gregory Peck that played him? Yes, it was Gregory Peck, I'm almost sure."

"The Japanese are indeed an industrious people, with a very different outlook from ours; for them, work is everything. Give a piece of land to a Brazilian, give another one just like it to a Japanese, and you'll see that within a year the Japanese will be rich and the Brazilian will have sold his plot to get drunk and make children; that's the reality. It's a question of character, of mentality. As General de Gaulle said, Brazil is not a serious country. And the blame for our situation cannot be put on the Americans, as the left keeps saying in order to make Soviet propaganda; it's ours, it comes from amorality, lack of seriousness, lack of persistence, lack of public spirit, lack of character, really. The truth is, if it weren't for the Americans, woe to us, woe to the world. There are other great peoples, such as the Japanese themselves, the Germans—"

"Lavinoel here told me once he was an admirer of Hitler!"

"And in many ways I really am! I don't agree with everything he did, but to a large extent I do, he was right in many things."

"The Jews, tell them your theory about the Jews."

"It's not a theory, it's something everyone knows. The Jews . . . Have you ever read *The Protocols of the Learned Elders of Zion?* No? Better read it, then! It's going to be difficult to find it at a bookstore, because whenever someone publishes an edition, the Jews buy all the copies to destroy them. But I have a copy, and you can borrow it to see for yourself. Dad's read a few sections."

"Yes, yes, I have; it's pretty awesome."

" 'Awesome' is a weak word; it's terrifying. You can tell by the Jews we know. They themselves seek isolation, they all hole up in the Nazaré neighborhood. You remember your classmate Jaime? Jaime, a fat little fellow who was very popular—you remember him! He used to go steady with a Christian girl in school, but when he had to get married he picked one of their Sarahs; it's always like that. They have contempt for us. The Jews will destroy mankind, you'll see."

"You mean you're for the extermination of the Jews?"

"My political position is known to everyone: I'm for Swedish socialism, which is the most perfect system on earth. You remember the story they told about Jaime back in school? That he kept two little soap bars, labeled 'Grandpa' and 'Grandma'? Hah-hah-hah! Get it? Grandpa and Grandma, hah-hah!"

"I can't hear the music, with all this laughter!"

"I'll remember to tell you the joke later, Dad, don't worry. That's a good one, Grandpa and Grandma, hah-hah! Did anyone tell that to Jaime?"

"Of course they did, there's always a joker to tell those things. Waldir told him; Waldir has always been the prankster type. You remember Waldir?"

"Will you keep quiet—I want to listen to the music!"

"You were the one who brought up the subject."

"Yes, but it was a serious conversation; I didn't mean to make any jokes."

"You can't hold a conversation in Brazil without jokes, Dad, don't you know how Brazilians are? Brazilians are women, booze, soccer, carnival, and dirty jokes, you know that."

"That's sadly true, yes, it's true. I feel very sad for having to agree with that, but it's true, it's really true. Remember the only places in Brazil where there is some progress are precisely the ones where foreign blood penetrated—Germans, Italians, Japanese. Here in Bahia, what do we have? Negroes and the dregs of Europe, the Portuguese and the Spanish, and things are as they are. The whole Northeast is like that. Can you carry water in a sieve? Truth is tough but has to be told. If we had been colonized by the Dutch—"

"By the British, by the British!"

"Or by the British! We had the misfortune of having been colonized by Portugal, which incidentally sent only its felons here. That's why the Seventh of January is for me the happiest date there is, because that's when we celebrate the kicking out of that scum. It didn't do any good, because all the harm had already been accomplished, but at least we had that pleasure. I can't stand the Portuguese, I don't even like to talk to them; it makes me mad."

"Really, Dad, that's all nonsense; it's the structures that are to blame," said Lavinette, who had come in the room unexpectedly, her eyes a bit bloodshot and heavy-lidded.

"There you go again with this structure talk. I want to know how structure explains illiteracy, indolence, disease . . ."

"You bet it does! It's just that I can't talk to a square; squares just don't dig it, they simply don't dig it."

467

"I'm not a square! I'm not an old mossback. If there's an old man who can't be called a square, I'm that man. I sit in bars in the company of young people all the time and get along fine with them; I'm very well received. The trouble is, you're prejudiced, like many in your generation."

"That's not the point, Daddy, I didn't mean it that way. But wasn't Dutch Guiana colonized by the Dutch? Wasn't India colonized by the British, and Nigeria, and British Guiana?"

"But those are very different cases."

"There's nothing different about them. You have to have a grasp of the structures to be able to understand that. Portugal, you know, had a different structure, and this structure is what caused . . . Don't give me this inferiority talk, that's really the end. You have to get a grasp of the structure."

"You know the story about God creating the world and giving Brazil everything, and then the assistant angel says it's not fair, and then God says, wait till you see the bunch of bast—the bunch of rascals I'm going to give it for a people?" Domingos said, putting his arm on his sister-in-law's shoulder and taking the opportunity to rub his arm on her breast a little, which she pretended not to notice. "I'm friends with a lot of chicks; you don't know me, I know all about the younger set. Don't you have a reefer with you? I'd like to have the experience; everyone says it . . . Is it true that you acquire a new consciousness? I'm not like you think, you know. I read a lot of poetry, I'm a big art fan. I . . ."

Ioiô Lavínio saw them leaving the room and smiled affectionately. A family, what a beautiful thing! The Motherland is an amplified family, he thought, proud he knew by heart countless passages by Ruy Barbosa. His eyes moist with self-satisfaction and gratitude to God for the happiness He had bestowed on his life, he turned to the window that faced the great, waveless tide, heavy and plumbous like an ocean of mercury. With a quick about-face, which made him spill some of the Scotch he was about to sip as he stepped out to the porch with Lavinette, Domingos rushed back to the record player, flipped the "repeat" switch, and the "Fire Dance" burst forth from the speakers like a maelstrom. How could Ioiô Lavínio possibly communicate this emotion, how could he share it? A family reunion, a luminous Seventh of January, this drink, this music, this feeling . . . Instead of hostility, for the first time he felt commiseration for Stalin José. Would he make his speech? Why did he persist in that folly, which led nowhere? Why couldn't he adapt to life as it is, in a country that does have its problems but is so cordial, so peace-loving, so abundant, so rich in opportunities, so generous?

And there's more! A country with a mirthful, merrymaking people dancing through all difficulties with its celebrated talent for always finding a way, a happy country! And more! A people that never endured wars, plagues, volcanoes, earthquakes, or fratricidal struggles. And more! A people that

468

lives in harmony and courtesy, an obliging, kindhearted people, in which every race and color mix freely, since racial prejudice is unknown here, because here prejudice is only of an economic nature. And more! A people of extraordinary musicality, able to use improvised instruments such as matchboxes, glasses, dishes, and old cans to make music and impress any foreigner, like those tourists who stopped at Greengrocer Square to watch a group doing the samba in Naninho's stall.

"Isn't that right?" Stalin José was asked by Aloísio Pontes, a potbellied, straw-hatted, beaming summer resident who was coming back from the market with a bunch of squid for bait and stopped in front of the stall, where an epiphany of love for Brazil had erupted in him. "This really is a catching rhythm, huh?" he added, with a few little hops, twirling the plastic bag with the squid over his head. "*Saravá, heh, vatapá, cangerê, ioiô, esquidô-esquidô!* Atta boy! Isn't that right, *bichinho?*"

Stalin José smiled, not only because he found the other man's excitement amusing but also because of that *saravá* and other words he had used, besides his being another Rio native who thought people in Bahia called each other *bichinho*, and therefore they hear *bichinho* and say *bichinho* all the time, although they are the only ones who say *bichinho*. He remembered the time these things annoyed him to the point of making him want to start a fight, particularly when he drank a little. But nothing of the kind annoyed him any longer; very few things still managed to annoy him. Even those he made a point of being annoyed at needed a certain cultivation, as if annoyance were a plant requiring special attention. Even his frustration for not knowing how to sing, not having ever sung anything in his life, was not as strong now as it had been, though seeing those people making rhymes and frolicking made him kind of miss something he never had before. He felt with his tongue the crudely made bridgework that replaced his front teeth and remembered that because of his inability to sing he had lost three of those teeth, when just after the beginning of the Redeeming Revolution a captain had ordered him to sing the national anthem. He answered he did not know how to sing, and offered to recite the words, but the captain interpreted that as another taunt from a sophisticated subversive and punched him in his mouth, breaking those three teeth. The other teeth, well, each of the others had its story: the Petrobrás one, the parliamentary one, the one at the demonstration in '68 . . . He did not even remember how he had lost some of them; he did not care for his teeth; he did not care about almost anything.

"Don't you sing?" Aloísio Pontes asked. "A certified, card-carrying Bahian like you?"

How had he met this fellow? It must have been in another summer, at the early-morning breakfast at the market or at Honorina's stand, at Aprígio's stand, Walter's store, Wide Pants's joint, someplace like that. He was difficult to forget because of his invariably cheerful look, a rather compulsive, overly permanent happiness, his face always quivering as if preparing another giggle even when what was being said to him was not funny at all.

"How about it, *bichinho?*" Aloísio said. "Hail to Bahia, *iaiá*! Hail to Bahia, *ioiô! Ziriguidum!*"

"I can't sing." Stalin José answered the question Aloísio had already forgotten.

"What a mulatto bombshell, huh? A rump like that . . . What a bombshell! What did you say?"

"Nothing, really; I just said I can't sing."

"Well, I can't, either, but I sing just the same. Singing shoos the doldrums away!"

What a predicament, really, not to be able to intone a single note, not even when his jailmates sang anthems in defiance of their jailers. Whom had he taken after, with this specialized deafness? He wasn't sure, because in all the descendants of João Popó, so numerous they could not be counted and diversified in so many ways, as far as he knew there were many people with musical talent. Well, there was a bit of everything among the Popós, even a fellow like him, who even before his ears started buzzing all the time because of the beatings could not tell one melody from another, to him it was all a jumble of disconnected noises. Interesting, because old Teodomiro, his father, had been a musician. That is, not exactly a musician, because he was never able to be a professional, and his son never saw him playing any instrument; he knew his father was a musician only because he had been told. With the help of his godfather, the late Commander Miranda, although he was the son of an impoverished sharecropper, Teodomiro had managed to go to a conservatory in Salvador and was considered the best student they had ever heard, in spite of being brown. But his father died all swollen up with schistosomiasis, his two brothers had the same disease and were too weak to work, the sisters did all they could, but one was bowlegged because of a bone disease and could barely walk, and the two others fell sick with malaria, and his nephews were stunted and full of worms, so he had to abandon his art to support his family. He improved their house, planted a vegetable patch and an orchard, set up a vegetable store in Duck Street, even managed to own three donkeys and a cow, to start raising chickens and to put his mother in a charity hospital with the help of his godfather to treat her elephantiasis, which did not allow her to stand on her feet anymore. But one fine morning his fate changed, because a stranger arrived with a deed for the plot he lived on and farmed, and told him to leave immediately because he needed the area to raise horses and did not want anyone around. Teodomiro pointed out that his family had always lived there and that the former owner collected only a percentage of what the vegetable patch and the orchard produced, besides receiving three dozen eggs a week of the five he produced—couldn't he at least keep the house and the vegetable patch? No, he could not, and the next day they brought a cart, piled on it everything he owned, tore down the house, destroyed the vegetable beds, and razed the chicken coop. The priest let them sleep for a few days in the yard of Saint Lawrence Church together with the beggars, until he got his two sisters jobs at the house of a summer resident and settled in Areia do Sete in an old shed he renovated little by little with dry coconut leaves. But when he set up his vegetable stall once more, this time to sell other people's produce, the town administration confiscated everything because he was neither registered nor licensed, besides being a minor and thus barred from doing business. The owner of the Areia do Sete plot gave him seven days to get out, or he would call the police to arrest him, and since he no longer had his godfather, who had died, leaving his political adversaries in power, he decided to take all fourteen members of his family to Salvador, where at least there would be a bridge under which they might sleep. However, it took him a long time to sell the two donkeys he still had, because everybody knew he was in a pinch and offered next to nothing for them, which he ended up having to accept. But then the time for him to leave the plot had run out, so the police tore down the shed's straw walls, set fire to his clothes and sleeping mats, and arrested him. At the police station he was paddled on his hands, the soles of his feet, and his behind because he tried to defend himself and insulted the police soldier who took the money he had on him from the sale of the donkeys. Because the Itaparica jail was falling apart, they took him to Salvador and dumped him in a communal cell for dangerous prisoners, where in the first night he was grabbed by five of the others and buggered by all of them in a row, a routine that repeated itself for three successive nights, until a commissary sent for him because he had decided to investigate his participation in a great burglary that had happened on the island a short time before his arrest. They beat him on his face, and he was about to admit guilt though he did not even know exactly what had been stolen, when they arrested the real burglar and let him out in the street wearing only shorts, warning him that if they ran across him again they would arrest him for vagrancy, unless he could prove he had a job. He managed to do an odd job at the port, a fellow odd-jobber gave him a torn shirt, and he started sleeping under a marquee in the Priests' Crane neighborhood. Finally he became a longshoreman, and began working mornings, afternoons, nights, Sundays, and holidays without complaining, until the day a foreman tried to horsewhip a black porter who did not want to carry a muriatic acid crate on his head because one of the bottles was broken and leaking, and when Teodomiro protested he was threatened with the whip too. He did not accept the punishment, thrashed the foreman, was later protected by some of his closer companions, and ended up becoming friends with a very silent, wild-eyed fellow longshoreman, who showed him old copies of a newspaper called *Free Land*, issued in São Paulo. This man told him about many things he had never heard of, and said it was possible to resist not only what the foreman had tried but many other things. Contrary to what Teodomiro thought, the world wasn't all like that, it was like that only where the oppressed had not resisted. There were places in the world where people like them were respected, made decent money, and had enforceable rights, believe it or not. But Teodomiro doubted he was telling the truth, because he could not imagine a world where things were different; were there several worlds, then? But little by little, laboriously reading the papers his friend showed him, he started believing that all that had happened to him, and was still happening, was actually not as natural as he had thought. He listened with great wonderment about comrades of his from distant places who were already engaged in those struggles. He felt proud to have those comrades and to also be someone's comrade, and became interested in hearing about that they did. While they gathered around a fire in the hovel where they lived, covered by tin plates and perched on the Big Nail scarps, he heard that the streetcar coachmen of Rio de Janeiro once stopped the streetcars and faced up to the guns of the police so as not to be humiliated. He heard the stories of the Sorocabana railroad workers, of the strike by Rio factory workers, of the Great Western strike in Recife, of the unloading of coal blocked by the longshoremen of Recife until they got a pay raise, of the gas strike in Rio, the railroad workers' strikes in Alagoas, Paraíba, and Pernambuco, the strikes in Rio Grande do Sul, strikes everywhere, struggles, combats, martyrizations, lies, humiliations, tortures, cruelties. He learned about the Campinas Workers League and the Brazilian Workers Confederation, he learned about Italians, Germans, Spanish, Portuguese, Syrians, all of them struggling, about trampled Brazilian workers, he learned about socialists, anarchists, maximalists, and revolutionists. With tears in his eyes, he listened to the whole story of the Whip Revolt, involving a flog like the one he had almost thought it natural for the foreman to use against a lowly longshoreman. During the telling of the story of the Whip Revolt, so secret it will never be told outside the tin-roofed hovels on the steep scarps around the old Big Nail slave quarters, he asked for repetitions and explanations like a child, and had a fever and trouble closing his eyes when he tried to sleep after listening to them. Tied up on the great warship *Minas Gerais* in front of all his companions, the sailor Marcelino Menezes was given twenty-five lashes, while they played bass drums and snare drums. Why? Because he wanted to complain, he wanted to tell people that the glory of battles sailed on hunger, on people sleeping on coal piles, on people dying of suffocation inside the hollows of the ships, on people getting beaten, on downtrodden, muzzled people, people no one wanted to know about and nobody knew about. And then the great fleet of the seaman João Cândido making maneuvers in the sea in a way said not to be possible for someone who was not white and star-studded, battleships resolved to bite in the name of the whipped ones, aiming the dark mouths of their cannons at the great city of Rio de Janeiro, the capital of the Republic, which thus heard for the first time, and heard in fear, that in the bellies of those bedecked, shiny ships there were men like worms in reverse, men who gave life and had no life. He shuddered when he was told that they had promised to pardon João Cândido, but arrested and mistreated him, and sent him to a madhouse and later to prison; that they had sent many others to die of malaria in rubber forests up North; and that still many others had been locked in a basement on Snake Island, where quicklime and water was poured to asphyxiate them. That was how he first turned anarchist and later Communist, named the two boys he had Lenine Antônio, deceased, and Stalin José, worked hard at organizing longshoremen, and was arrested several times, to be finally strangled by Luiz Sledgehammer, who afterward commented with admiration how his neck was tough, because he had not managed to choke him with his bare hands and had been forced to use a steel wire fastened to two wood handles, which he fortunately always had around for any such eventuality.

"Every Brazilian is a musician!" Aloísio shouted, while the samba players danced off to Fort Park.

"I know," Stalin José said, rising to get a shot glass of sugarcane liquor in the bar. "My father was a musician."

He wasn't going to stay in the bar, sitting with his third glass of firewater, waiting for the school parade. The procession of cretins, pharisees, bootlickers, demagogues, and secret criminals behind the Indian float was one thing; the school parade was another. Especially now that he had had a couple of drinks, he was sure he would feel like crying. Not that it bothered him; it actually gave him an odd, rather incongruous contentment. But he would have no one to talk to, and even the few friends who still spoke to him on the island, mostly childhood friends, the simplest ones, would not understand whatever explanation he tried to give about his uncontrollable urge to cry when he saw the children of Itaparica marching in civic parades. He was no longer close to anyone; he had grown so accustomed to it he did not even notice it. He bent over with a sharp pain above his navel and remembered what the doctor had told him about drinking alcohol: certain death sooner or later, all of a sudden, wherever he might be. And it wasn't just ulcers on his stomach wall; it was the whole wreckage in which he had been dragging himself along, nothing functioning properly in a body that every now and then started to sputter like an old jalopy on the verge of disintegrating. Oh, fuck it, he had nothing to explain to anyone, there was no one to be affected by anything that happened to him, and the only reason he was not going to stay for the school parade was that the last person in front of whom he had permitted himself to cry had been Jandira, and he had no idea where she was, and it would be of no use if he had.

He picked up the book he had brought along thinking he would manage to read in the square while basking in the sun a little, and sharpened his eyes to read the words stamped in a circle over the logotype of the publishing house Editorial Vitória. It was an old paperback, which had escaped confiscation and burning the day they came to their house at night, hooded him, and took him to a place whose location he never found out to threaten him and beat him up; it had not been among the books he kept at home, it had been forgotten in Itaparica. But of course he did not have to try hard to decipher the fading letters; it was the seal of old Acúrcio Bastos's bookstore. He suddenly felt an immense nostalgia for Acúrcio Bastos and his little bookstore, shut down so often, plundered, and even burned. But he, a lean mulatto with thinning gray hair, who never smiled although he was always in a pleasant mood, would find a way of reappearing like a sauba ant hill sprouting back up after having been buried. And then he would return to his place behind the counter, his glasses on the tip of his nose, his shirts frayed at the cuffs and collars but scrupulously starched, smoking his cigar after lunch, his only one, not out of preference but because he did not have the money for more than one, while he pretended he was not being benevolent as he went on giving credit to those who never paid him, making meticulous notes on their files, as if he actually expected to receive the money.

He stroked the book and almost smiled. He remembered it, he remembered it, it was in his hands the day they were alone at the bookstore after 6 P.M., talking about literature, and by such a quick impulse that when he noticed it he had already obeyed it, he decided to open his heart to the old man. Had that been why he had forgotten the book in Itaparica, leaving it behind as if on purpose?

"I know how Dom Casmurro felt," he had said abruptly, and the old man seemed not to have understood. "No, this scene, this scene we were commenting on, this scene with Escobar dead and Capitu gazing at him. I know how that look is, I've felt that. I saw my wife looking at another man like that; there's nothing more terrible than that, there's nothing worse than this look the woman you love throws at another man, because it's the truest, the most involuntary, the most undeniable, the most indisputable, and nevertheless the most intangible look there is. Because it's only for an instant, sometimes a fraction of a second, nothing can be proved, nothing can be discussed, and that which existed so visibly and powerfully flashes like lightning in the middle of a conversation and is subject to every doubt, except the doubt of the author of the look and that of the one it hurt."

He spoke with such intensity that the old man took his hands from the counter where they had been resting all this time, made himself comfortable behind his little desk, pushed his glasses up to his forehead, and looked at him with the expression of someone who is going to listen to something deep. And he did, because Stalin José told him how Jandira and he had been

474

in love, how she had believed he would have a glorious destiny, how they had faced one difficulty after another with bravery and dedication. Then there was the first look, after his seventeen-month stay in jail, during which his lower jaw was cracked, and he came back home broken down, his jawbone tied up by wires, a frozen trismus that allowed him to feed himself only through a straw and even so with difficulty, and did not let him grunt more than one or two unintelligibly consonanted words at a time. She hugged him, held him while he sat down in the only armchair they had, and then addressed that look at him, a long look underlined by the pale smile of one who is showing commiseration but not love.

There were other looks, many looks, but only at him, never at anyone else, so he could still nurse the hope that all would be back to normal as soon as things changed. But things did not change, clandestinity made him stay away from home for months, even years on end, her relatives had to support her, and he could not help feeling ashamed, no matter how he exhorted himself otherwise, for not having anything, not giving anything, not offering anything, not being a man like the others, who did things, decided things, knew about business, made money, and had fun. Why did he have to be like that, why had he got to be like that? Had he embraced a religion, a crazy priesthood, after all? At any event, it was no use speculating, because he started to discover gradually that they no longer knew each other, and she used ready-made sentences pronounced monotonically for the performance of the petrified rites of their marriage, from what she spoke to him in bed to her answers when he asked for a comment on something he had done.

It was then that the same look that pierced Dom Casmurro's chest came about, as they were sitting at a table having a beer and she laughed at something their friend Rogério Lopes had said, and as if her eyes had tripped on something as they followed her head moving with laughter, the look at the other happened, a short but infinitely lasting look, a look he did not remember having ever received from her, not a look by someone who is flirting but one that instantly showed her to be vulnerable to the other. He remembered how he suffered, his stomach shrinking and a pain in his chest that seemed determined to kill him, because another thing identified him with Dom Casmurro, something that had never crossed his mind but now was as clear as water: his son Camilo Ernesto's features were very much like Rogério Lopes's, and they even walked in a similar way. And then, after spending a few days suffocated by this pain, he packed his valise in secret, wrote a note saying he would be back to pick up his books and a few odds and ends, and left the house by daybreak.

He finished telling old Acúrcio everything, and realized he was flustered, had sweat on his brow, and was panting instead of breathing. Staring at the floor, he thanked the old man for listening to him with so much patience and apologized for having told him such a banal story, which could not be important to someone who was dedicated to a superior cause like himself; he should even have expected it to happen, for militancy involves many sacrifices, and that one could not even be considered one of the greatest if compared to the suffering of many of their comrades. He raised his face, hoping to hear something back, and saw that the old man had been gazing at him with a tenderness he had never seen in his face before, and a tear was slowly trickling down his cheek. Stalin José embraced him, kissed his face, and left without looking back, and it was the last time he saw Acúrcio, his good friend he had never met outside the bookstore, whose memory now arose so vividly, in front of an old book that an old Communist was holding in his lap in Greengrocer Square.

A skyrocket hissed, bolted up, and exploded in three little smoke balls over the tower of the Mother Church. Holding his fourth shot glass of sugarcane rum, Stalin José walked to the corner of Straight Street and saw from afar the school parade coming, a majorette about twelve years old ahead of the drums in a white leotard, a short skirt, and a little green and yellow hat. It was too late to leave; now he had to stay and see it. And why did he have to stay, for what reason? He no longer saw a reason for anything; he felt his mind was indifferent and shapeless like beaten egg whites, nothing of what he had done made sense anymore, so many things, so many visions, so many words and phrases: provocation, agitprop, comrade, basic organization, terrorism, Trotskyism, revisionism, Albanian line, personality cult, armed struggle, national bourgeoisie, *campesinos*, *lumpenproletariat*, feudalism, capitalism, self-criticism, reeducation, Maoism, urban guerrilla, purges, socialist paradise, missions, communications to the plenum, petit bourgeoisie, life is the natural state of existence of albuminoids, ¡*no pasarán!*, the history of all heretofore existing society is the history of class struggles, plebeians against patricians, slaves against masters, proletarians against . . . Stalin José, not knowing if he was dizzy because of a weakness in his head, because of the madness that was splattering his fluffy brain, or because an impulse to fly was dominating his arms, found himself with his chin quivering, his lips out of control, and his eyes becoming misty, at the same moment that the little majorette, her leotard crudely darned at two small spots near her waist, marched by in front of him, her face raised toward the sun and with pride in her demeanor, lifting her skinny legs and twirling in the air a baton ornamented with the colors of the Republic. Was he going to cry, was he going to have to run to a corner like a bat hiding from light, was he once more going to wonder why he was crying without ever, ever stopping? Behind the majorette were two signs, one carried by two black girls who would never know how beautiful they were and would not believe it if they were told so—THE INTREPID VILLAGE OF ITAPARICA IS PROUD OF THE HEROES IT GAVE BRAZIL—and the other carried by two boys, the first flashing his teeth and the second staring unsmiling at the sky, both stomping their right feet on the ground at each beat of the bass drum—PEOPLE OF ITAPARICA, BE PROUD OF YOUR BROTHERS NORTH AND SOUTH. Would he have to cry, would he have to cry? How could they, so ignored and despised, raise their heads in such a way not because they had rehearsed it but as if they knew something no one else knew, except an old, drunken, repentant, nonrepentant Communist, except that staggering man from whom a lady stood back when he came near her to lean against a pottery tree, except that prematurely old person, nothing, nothing, nothing, Stalin José! Crying without worrying about covering his face or hiding, as he used to do, he looked at the little heads crowned by green and yellow cardboard, put his hands on his ears not to hear the drums that set the rhythm for the short little steps of the children from the nuns' orphanage, guessed he had a dynamite stick hissing in his stomach, felt sure he was going to die, and imagined that he, too, had one of those hats on his head and that he could hug those little countrymen of his and kiss them and tell them he loved them, he loved them, he loved them so deeply that as he saw them he could even come to believe in God, for He was giving him the best death he could aspire to.

He died by the pottery tree, which still had the little iron fence from the time Coffeepot Snout was the mayor, vomiting so much blood that the ground around the tree remained dark for several days. They took him to the medical station to see if the assistant nurse could do anything, but he was dead on arrival. If it were not for the fellow feeling, the innate kindness, and the sentiment of solidarity of the Brazilian people, a people capable of forgiving anything, maybe he would not even have been given a coffin and would have been buried wrapped in a bedsheet, because nothing of value was found in the boardinghouse room where he lived, just a few grimy books, a few pieces of clothing, a few faded photographs, some illegible notes, a sewing kit, a box full of medicines, and an old letter signed by a certain Camilo Ernesto, which ended with the words "I never had a father." They took the books to the library, which refused them because they were sure to be subversive material, they gave the clothes to the nuns and discarded the other things, with the exception of two empty boxes, which Leovigildo, the boardinghouse owner, filled with wood shavings and used as nests for two broody hens he had in his backyard. But everyone took pity on him, because after all the poor devil had never harmed anyone, and even Ioiô Lavínio, who complained that the death had spoiled the holiday, insisted on donating a certain amount for the funeral expenses and on attending the burial. On the way up to the cemetery, he was complimented for his generosity toward someone who had done nothing to deserve it, but asked people not to mention it because he had acted out of a Christian impulse, for in spite of having been a bad Brazilian and the son of another bad Brazilian, deep down the deceased had been nothing but a disoriented idealist who after all was his distant relative, as was everyone else on the island, come to think of it.

20

"Entre abogados te veas" is really the definitive curse, a masterpiece of concision and malice, to which only a fool would rather expose himself than to apparently worse but infinitely milder ones, such as "Go to hell" or "May you spend the rest of your life eating Bahian food." He had learned it from a Mexican he had met in New York and who had become his friend for a while, before losing more than eighty thousand dollars in a poker game he had set up himself. He had not felt sorry for the Mexican, for after all, that's what gambling is all about, and besides, the worst that could happen to him would be to spend two days without snorting coke while his father smuggled out more money for him. But he had disappeared after the game, and now the winner, Dr. Eulálio Henrique Martins Braga Ferraz, a descendant of the legendary banker Bonifácio Odulfo Nobre dos Reis Ferreira-Dutton by way of his daughter Isabel Regina's marriage to José Eulálio Venceslau de Almeida Braga Ferraz, the scion of a powerful São Paulo family, leaned back in a Swedish armchair in his vast office and sighed with the conviction that the Mexican had not limited himself to teaching the curse; he had also called it down upon him. Would he never do anything in his life other than deal with lawyers, every one of them as sinister as they come, writing in a language full of tortuous constructions and drawing up somber scenarios if this or that was not done? Lawyers from the commercial bank, lawyers from the investment bank, lawyers from the savings and loan company, lawyers from the farming and cattle-raising holding, lawyers from the insurance company, family lawyers, lawyers, lawyers, lawyers, a sea of lawyers, ipso factos, in limines, and sub judices capable of wrecking anyone's mental balance. Yes, the Mexican really had called the curse on him after losing those eighty thousand dollars and, ashen, leaving the New York Hilton suite where the game had taken place. It had been a neat bluff, he had won the game with chip power,

he had made the little brown brother from the north run. In exchange for that, *los abogados*.

He glanced at his watch and sighed again, regretting having summoned that lawyer Chagas Borges to clarify the legal complications that would be caused by the marriage of his cousin Luiz-Phelippe Ferreira-Dutton Filho, the youngest son of his grandmother Isabel Regina's brother. He had never managed to have a perfect understanding of kinship lines beyond cousins and brothers-in-law, and his confusion became much worse with Chagas Borges's interminable explanation, over one hour of talk about agnates, cognates, putatives, germanes, and other monstrosities, to wrap it all up by declaring he would have to study the matter in more detail in order to form an opinion, since there was no more complex branch of civil law than family and inheritance law. And all that just to answer what should be a relatively simple question: What would be the consequences of the harebrained marriage planned by Uncle Luiz-Phelippe, by now about sixty-five years old, for the patrimonial security of his family? That was all, period. Luiz-Phelippe's kids, Luiz-Phelippe Neto, Sílvia, and Henriqueta—on second thought, not exactly kids anymore, since Henriqueta, the youngest, should be pushing thirty—were worried, really terribly worried, and had asked him to interfere, for the love of God. The old man ought to be used to living alone after twelve years as a widower; what the hell did he want to get married for? Didn't he have everything he wanted, didn't he do everything he wanted, not having to work for a living and leading a life anyone would pray for? Why marry, then? And whom! A Bahian widow who fancied herself an aristocrat but was actually a mulattoish, penniless farm owner of dubious origin, who had now found a haven and made the old boy completely blind, completely mindless. Eulálio had to interfere, he had to talk to Luiz-Phelippe, who greatly respected his opinion. All three of them had been waging fierce opposition, but it was getting nowhere, and maybe only Eulálio, the most influential, powerful member of the family, could bring the old boy back to normality.

And to top it all, Uncle Luiz-Phelippe had phoned him too, to tell him he was coming to São Paulo to ask for his help in settling a delicate matter. Of course it was the same problem, and now he was involved with the two poles of this family squabble he had nothing with. For a long time now the Rio members of the family had been dissociating themselves from their businesses, with the exception of cousin Aloísio Henrique, son of Amleto Henrique, Uncle Luiz-Phelippe's older brother. When Aloísio wasn't at the Jockey Club, he ran the brokerage house in Rio. The others lived on a still considerable unearned income or were involved with other things. He couldn't even remember too well his twice-removed—or would that be thrice-removed—cousins' names. One of them was an architect. Luiz Eugênio, Uncle Bonifácio Vicente's son, was a fruit and lived in Paris, Henriqueta kept on marrying and unmarrying, Sílva had got married to an American and had been living in Detroit until she got a divorce, and was now involved with theater work in Rio, and so forth. Therefore, therefore they had no business dragging him into this. The old boy could throw away everything he had, including his participation in the trust, and it wouldn't make any difference, it was just a drop in the ocean, which held no interest even as a topic for discussion.

Yes, but on the other hand there are emotional obligations, family obligations, really. It's necessary to maintain a family sense, a sense of lineage. He picked up once again the monograph on the Ferreira-Duttons made by the British-American Institute for Genealogical Research, which he had been showing to Chagas Borges in the vain hope he would shut his mouth. The gringos know how to do those things; something like that, with so much class, would never be done in Brazil. It was only part of the study commissioned by his uncle Bonifácio Vicente, who had let him borrow one of the two copies he had received. The rest was still being completed, but Uncle Bonifácio's well-known impatience made him ask them to organize in an album the material available, and there was the result. A little history of the family, written in very elegant English, portraits of ancestors and people connected to their house, diagrams showing kinship lines.

He opened the page where they had printed the portrait of the first Ferreira-Dutton, Amleto Henrique Nobre Ferreira-Dutton. An extensive biography. The name Dutton must in actuality have originated from Hutton, the discrepancy being attributable to the confusing way capital letters were written at the time and the bad condition of the documents researched. Admitting this as the most likely hypothesis, the lineage can be traced back to George Hutton—from a family related to the house of Windsor by way of the duchess of Kent—who came to Brazil because he wanted to run a farm in the tropics for adventure's sake. Here he met a girl, possibly Ana Teresa Rawlings Ferreira, the daughter of an English Catholic mother, who descended from landed gentry, and a Brazilian father, the eldest heir of the viscount of Casa Alta. This part of the story was the hardest to check, given the circumstances, for the truth is that Ana Teresa became pregnant by George Hutton out of wedlock, which in view of the prejudices of the time was tantamount to a calamity, muffled only through her family's great influence. A letter found by the researchers, very hard to read because the writing is faded in several places, gives them reason to believe that not long before Ana Teresa gave birth, George Hutton, who had not known about her pregnancy because he was away on a trip to Grão-Pará, married her, but she died after giving birth to the boy Amleto, who was lovingly raised by his grandparents after his father was summoned to His Majesty's service back in England. Then the association with the baron of Pirapuama, the talent that saved the baron's half-ruined businesses, the banking house, blah-blah-blah, blah-blah-blah, the rest is known history.

He looked at his great-great-grandfather's portrait—his stern face, high collar, stiffened neck, knitted eyebrows. So white that his skin seemed milky, his thinning, very smooth hair running down the sides of his head, he might very well be an Englishman, as indeed he would have been if only he had been born in England. Visibly Nordic features. What would he be like in daily life, what kind of voice would he have? It was obvious he was one of those old fogies, a reservoir of honesty and austerity, which had its positive aspects but was sure to have caused him problems with his businesses, because people like him, excessively attached to principles and scruples, tend to follow a very rigid line of conduct, rather losing money than violating their ethical standards. Yes, he must have been a terrible old curmudgeon but an interesting figure, a man one could not help being fascinated by.

Bonifácio Odulfo, his great-grandfather . . . Henriqueta, his great-grandmother . . . He looked like his father, the same air of severity, even surliness. And she was the embodiment of sweetness; he could see she had been a sensitive person, certainly stifled by the cloistered life imposed upon women at that time. He smiled at his great-grandmother and felt a kind of nostalgia for the time of young black house girls and large country mansions, a simple, wholesome time, without today's violence, without the pressures that keep contemporary men in permanent tension. What would Great-grandma say if she could watch the behavior of her female descendants, of today's women in general? He laughed again. Poor Grandma, she would think she was in Sodom and Gomorrah; she would ask to go back to her tomb. And what about the general here? An attractive man, with a strangely placid face for someone who had raised hell in the Paraguayan war and was known as hot-tempered. Whom did he look like? He must have taken after his mother's relatives, some Arab hidden among old Teolina's ancestors, from the time the Moors occupied the Iberian Peninsula. That's the reason for that dark skin, those good-looking but hard features, different from the delicate cast of the others'. In spite of that, he did look a bit like the monsignor. The monsignor . . .

"Dr. Eulálio, excuse me," a woman's voice said over the intercom.

He had been daydreaming so much that it took him some time to realize who was calling. He left the album open on the table and bent over toward the intercom, a little annoyed.

"What is it, Dona Shirley?"

"Dr. Luiz-Phelippe is here."

"Oh, send him in."

Dammit, he hadn't even prepared a strategy for their meeting. But then he hadn't decided what side to take, he didn't know his uncle's fiancée, he didn't know anything. But he sympathized with his uncle's children's concern; after all, they didn't know how to do anything and were used to living well—it was natural for them to get nervous at the prospect of that marriage. Well, he'd dance to whatever tune was played, he'd improvise, he would see what he could do for the kids without compromising himself too much.

"Dr. Luiz-Phelippe, I'm happy to see you! How are you? You're looking younger than ever!"

"You think so?" Luiz-Phelippe asked, his pudgy little face beaming. "You know, I think so too. And how about you, how are you?"

They embraced; Luiz-Phelippe complained about having to use an identification tag to get into the building—and by the way, what a building! Yes, it had become impossible for them to stay at the old headquarters; they had had to build this new one on Paulista Avenue. And as for the tag, Uncle knew very well about security problems. Even with their rigorous controls, hadn't a bomb been planted in their Osasco factory? Yes, it had, it had, it was a horrible thing, no one can be trusted anymore. He hadn't been in São Paulo for a long time now. And Guida, how is she?

"Were you taking a look at the family portraits?" he asked when he saw the album on the table.

"Yes, yes. Have you seen it? It's interesting."

"I've seen it; Boni showed it to me. What a face the monsignor had, huh? Don't you think he looked a little rakish?"

"Yes, a bit rakish, a bit naughty, it's true."

"And that's how he was! Haven't you ever heard the stories about him? He used to screw all those devout women who hung around him! They say he had an apartment behind the sacristy of a church back in Bahia, where he used to give spiritual counsel to them. Now dig the furniture of the apartment: a chair, a little closet, and a bed! Hah-hah! Look at his face! I'm sure we have a whole lot of, so to speak, ecclesiastical cousins in Bahia."

"You bet, and all of them darkies."

"Mulattoish."

"Darkies. Every Bahian is a darky. Bahians are responsible for this irritating practice of saying all over the world that every Brazilian has Negro blood. I've even had an argument with one of those bastards in Canada. I told him that might be true about Bahians such as he, who eat those gooey, yellowish foods and have rotten teeth and Negroid faces, but not me! I had been drinking a little—you know the Toronto Hilton bar, the one in the lobby near the swimming pool? I remember I had knocked off a whole bottle of Queen Anne all by myself—and then it really pissed me off when that bastard started that crap."

"You're right; it's the same kind of thing they used to say some time ago: Every Brazilian has syphilis."

"I remember that, I remember! I couldn't screw this American girl when I was working for my master's degree at UCLA because another bastard like that Bahian bastard in Canada told her that, looking as if he was making a great revelation. I didn't bash his face in right then and there because I was in Los Angeles, and Americans lock up anyone who punches anyone else's nose, but if it was here, that Bahian would be in bad shape."

"Were they both Bahians, really? Bahians . . ."

"Who gives a shit? From Bahia, from Ceará, from Pernambuco, they're all the same to me, I don't even like to see them. When one of them shows up on television I turn the sound down—I can't stand that lah-lah-lah, lah-lah-lah speech, as if an animal was trying to come out of their mouths. I'm fed up with this talk that's now fashionable in the press—I'm glad I almost don't read Brazilian papers anymore—and everywhere, that Northeasterners built São Paulo, that they built this and that. The fuck they did; we were the ones who built São Paulo, it was people like our family, it was our family that carried this shit on their backs, founded Higienópolis, didn't leave a fucking stone unturned. I'd like to turn loose a bunch of those yokels here when this here was a mule drivers' overnight stop, to see what they would build. They would build those rat holes they live in, two hundred churches, and acres of those stalls to sell that yellowy, noisome food they eat there —that's what they would build. In that case, why didn't they build anything back there? If you say the wops helped, I'll grant you that. I'll grant you the Japanese. I'll grant you even the Arabs, though most of them are thieves, just like the Jews, who do nothing productive and are always involved in some clandestine-looking trade. But this talk about Northeasterners having done any building I can't accept. They laid bricks, but that's not building, that's the least important part, anyone can do it, and that's why they do it. The truth is, we're giving them jobs, in exchange for their changing São Paulo into a kind of Bahian outdoor market, crawling with blacks and drowned by that insufferable music even on stations that formerly only played decent music."

"You get all worked up when you talk about that, don't you?"

"Yes, I do, I really do! Overvaluing people without the slightest qualification, overemphasizing the role of hard-hats in development and production, all that is going too far, and the consequences are right in front of us, everywhere. Ask anyone who deals with metalworkers, ask Nino, ask Alfredo, ask Cazzarelli, who's now yanking out what little hair he still has: You should see the arrogance of those characters; you'd think they owned the factories. What else do they want? They already have the most incredible labor laws in the world, something that can only happen in Brazil! Kick one of those sons of bitches out, and he'll go to a labor court and rip his boss off, not to mention social security costs, which everyone thinks are borne by them and are actually on our backs, as any businessman can show you in hard figures. If you knew about the tax, social security, and labor load companies have to bear, your jaw would drop; it's absolutely unbelievable. And how about bureaucracy? Every day they think up something new, every day you have to hire a new lawyer to get through the bureaucratic mess they create. Why don't they decide once and for all if we have free enterprise or socialism in this shit? It just can't go on as it is! If it's socialism, all right, I'll get the hell out of here, depending on how it looks. But we just can't go on this way."

"But things seem to be pretty much under control at the moment. The government—"

"Nothing is under control! Press censorship itself is full of holes, they publish anything they want, if you can read between the lines. A decree is issued, with congressional approval and everything—that is to say, everything by the book, everything legal, mandating prepublication censorship for books, which is a logical consequence of press censorship. If you're going to have censorship, you've got to censor everything; you can't leave any loopholes or it will all turn into a comedy. Very well, the law is passed, just because Jorge Amado, who, mind you, never quit being a Communist but is free to go around and is received by everyone, and Érico Veríssimo, who's probably gaga now and ought to be arrested, too, for defying the law and affronting authority—those two dingbats, who never did anything in their lives but write novels, something that doesn't contribute anything, doesn't teach anything, and only people with time to waste read, those two clowns come out and bumptiously announce they won't submit their books to censorship, and nothing happens and no one does anything about it and the law becomes a dead letter. Everything here is like that, it's all a big joke, those two should have been thrown in jail, and it's because of these contradictions that I don't believe in the regime. Didn't they institute the death penalty? Did they condemn a guy the other day? Very well, how much do you want to bet that at the last minute they'll decide not to execute him, and I wouldn't be surprised if in years to come he ended up being decorated. I'll bet a case of Chivas against a bottle they won't knock him off. You game?"

"You say he won't be executed."

"Right. I say he won't be executed, and you say he will."

"All right, I say he will. I think this case of Scotch is in the bag; the military will fix this guy if it's the last thing they do."

"We'll see."

"Well, if he's executed, we'll get drunk on a case; if he's not, we'll get drunk on a bottle. It doesn't matter."

Now calmer, Dr. Eulálio noticed his uncle was looking for an opportunity to mention the subject that had brought him to Sáo Paulo, because he acted as if he was talking about other things only not to be rude. So he asked him to sit down in one of the two leather-bound armchairs near the picture

484

window and asked him if he wouldn't like a drink; after all, it was almost lunchtime—they were having lunch together, weren't they? So how about the drink? He went over to the bar, took some ice from a thermos bucket, asked if his uncle also liked his Scotch in a short glass, and commented that in a colored or a thick glass the taste of Scotch changes. After he had served them both, he finally sat down to listen to Luiz-Phelippe's story, which began the day his uncle had lost his unforgettable Cizinha, twelve years before. He discoursed about lonely nights, his children's indifference, his friends' inconstancy, and the futility of social life, which he still hadn't given up though it almost made him nauseous because of all those hypocritical, vacuous people. Then he had met Maria Dulce, an extraordinary woman whose depth and culture he had never encountered in another woman, and all this combined with a ripened, sensual beauty, with an extraordinarily firm character—she wouldn't even let him give her expensive presents!—and a sweetness confirmed by her name: a perfect woman. And he wouldn't say this if he weren't speaking to Eulálio, a relative and such a close, trusted friend, but how well they got along in bed! Modesty aside, he had no need to brag, and he wouldn't say this, his really wouldn't, if it weren't the gospel truth, but he had always been very vigorous sexually, and the truth was, he had never failed to get an erection, not once, ever, not even one single time, even with the trashiest women, an old bag with so many skin folds that you couldn't see her twat, a very, very black woman, a Lapa neighborhood whore, it could be anything, nothing of that sort was a problem to him, it was just a special sensitivity to sex that he had, and thank God, an iron constitution despite his excesses. But even taking those facts into account, the rapport between Maria Dulce and him was something he had never experienced before. Hadn't Eulálio himself said he looked younger? Well, he really was, and besides, age, let no one be mistaken about that, is a state of mind, a psychological condition above all!

All right, now that he wanted to get married, his children, whom Maria Dulce had done everything to please, to no avail, were setting up such a terrible opposition Eulálio had to see it to believe it. What was the reason for that? Maria Dulce was a woman of means, she had a lot of land in Bahia and insisted on keeping their estates legally separate, even though the law made that mandatory anyway, due to his age. Her children were practically independent, and they were her children, not his, so they wouldn't inherit anything from him. His children's situation would be kept exactly as it was; he had no intention of altering their financial condition in the least. So what was the problem, except their prejudice? And after all, he was still alive; it was his money, not theirs, wasn't it?

"No," Dr. Eulálio said. "When you have as much money as you do, it's never your money. It may not be right, but it's so. I can understand why your kids are worrying. According to Sílvia, you're even thinking of investing in the modernization of her farms. You don't know the first thing about farming, you're going to spend a hell of a lot of money, and you might take a beating. And if that happens, what will happen to the kids?"

"But why can't I invest my money the way I want? And what if I wanted to invest anyway, without marrying her?"

"No, you can't do that; you've got responsibilities. Why don't you just live with her, instead of marrying her? It comes down to the same thing and will avoid a lot of problems. You draw up an agreement with her, offer her a few guarantees, make a kind of contract. I'll help you if you want; I have good lawyers."

"I've thought about that, but she won't hear of it. I mentioned it once, and she almost broke up with me; she was terribly insulted by it."

"Uncle, do you want me to be honest with you? May I be honest with you?"

"I know what you're going to say, you're going to say she's interested in my money. I expected a different attitude from you; you're an experienced, modern man, you should have gotten rid of those prejudices."

"It's precisely because I'm experienced and modern that I think she's interested in your money. In your money, your name, your position . . . But on the other hand, even when in love, every woman deep down is always interested in those things, one way or another. I'm not blaming her; I'm a realistic man. And because I'm realistic I can't ignore that motivation in her; the truth's got to be looked at without fear. What you have to do is to balance the interests of your children with the facts of this situation."

"But how? I'll tell you one thing: No matter what, even against your opinion, I'm going to marry Maria Dulce."

"Of course you're going to marry Maria Dulce. But you're not going to invest anything in her farms."

"But I promised; I can't pull back now."

"You promised already? She's fast, isn't she?"

"You shouldn't talk like that!"

"All right, Uncle. You promised, but that doesn't mean you have to keep the promise with your money. I'll work things out for you."

"You'll work things out? What do you mean?"

"There's something I can do; I'll tell you in a minute. But first you have to accept one condition, which is to let a lawyer I have complete trust in—Dr. Chagas Borges, the greatest old fox in the courts of São Paulo and a University of São Paulo professor, really top of the line, you must have heard of him—draw up the conditions for your marriage. I mean, let him draw up a plan that will guarantee the kids' rights and avoid future problems, and this involves arrangements preceding the wedding. There are all kinds of legal means; don't worry."

"But to guarantee the interests of the kids, I'm going to have to forget about associating myself with her in her farming."

"You're not going to have to forget about anything. I've got a first-rate projects department, I've got people at the Northeastern Development Agency who will rush through anything I want; everything is in my hands. So what we're going to do is to arrange a financial package for Aunt Maria Dulce, taking money from one of those funds—there're so many I forget their acronyms, but I pay a lot of people not to forget them. What type of farmland does Aunt Maria Dulce have?"

"Sisal. Her lands are in sisal country."

"That's shit. But it doesn't matter, because we can settle this; we can set up market research on something, we'll annex heavy stuff to the project, and even if it has nothing to do with sisal, even if it's castor beans, wrapping paper, fountain pens, we'll find something, that's no problem, no problem, don't think about it, I'll take care of everything. It may be a relatively complex package; we might issue bonds, manage the financing. . . . I'll take care of everything. Do you trust me?"

"I do, I do! But I still don't know what you're getting at."

"My dear Uncle Phelippe, the money exists; it doesn't have to be your money. The money exists, all you need is to know how to lay your hands on it, and this is what this organization whose building you admired so much is all about. She has the land, and she must have done something on it, and we can configure it in a way that will suit our interests; that's a simple thing. This isn't going to cost either of us one centavo; on the contrary, we'll even make money with it, because the financial processing is not done gratuitously and we ourselves are going to take care of it, here at the bank and through other companies. There are special maturity periods, special interest rates, there are all kinds of things. The bonds may be marketed at normal interest rates applicable to any commercial transaction but financing a project with much lower financial costs."

"I get it, I get it—you're really a genius."

"No, I'm not, this is routine, everyone knows about what I just told you, I wish everything were so simple. Now to get back to the matter at hand: You have to trust me. I'll set up this operation where everyone's going to come out a winner, you'll marry your Maria Dulce, the kids won't get jumpy, everything's going to be just fine."

"But this scares me a little. You yourself said sisal is shit and I can take a beating."

"I also said you'll have to trust me, didn't I?"

"Yes, yes."

"So? In the first place, I've got people who can aid this project, during its implementation, I mean. All of that can be entirely paid by the operational budget—that is, it won't cost anything, nothing will cost anything; the money exists, Uncle! The only way not to take a beating is not to put your money into this thing; there's money to be put into it that doesn't belong to you, with no risk involved, no threat to your estate nor to the kids'. These days, to put your own money on a project is crazy, is irrational, it's simply not done. The money is there, it was appropriated for that purpose, and it's actually sinful to ignore opportunities like that."

"Oh, you mean you find all this an excellent opportunity?"

"Yes, I do. As I said, leave it to me. When I have finished setting up this economic-matrimonial package, I'll call you or I'll go to Rio to see you—it's been a long time since I've been there; there are even people there I want to see, if you know what I mean, hah-hah. Leave it to me. I just need all the elements. As soon as you get back, send me everything concerning her properties—locations, areas, deeds, balance sheets, everything. I'm going to assign Menezes, a guy I have here who's a whiz at this type of thing, to oversee this deal. He's away on a trip to Maranhão now, supervising a babassu project—it's big thing there now. But he'll be back in a couple of days, and I'm going to turn everything over to him. It's all too complicated to explain in detail now, but don't worry, it's all clear in my head. The government gives out money for this type of thing, don't worry. There's no chance of your taking a beating; to take a beating would be if you put your hard-earned money in an adventure like that, which will never work except for a monumental fluke."

"Well, I still don't understand it too well, but I trust you, you're really taking a weight off my back. You don't know how grateful I am!"

"Come on, that's what relatives are for. And as you said yourself, we've always been friends. It's no trouble at all; on the contrary, it will be a great pleasure to help you be happy with your Maria Dulce—it's my wedding present."

"Will you speak to the kids?"

"Yes, yes, I'll call Sílvia or Henriqueta later today; don't worry. I'm just going to call Dona Shirley to take a few notes, and then we'll go out to lunch, all right?"

But his uncle, now very excited at the unexpected solution to his problem, said he couldn't go because Maria Dulce had taken the opportunity to come to São Paulo with him to do some shopping and go to a few restaurants—she loved Arab food, she loved Italian food, she loved to eat in São Paulo, for São Paulo, you can't deny it, is where you eat best in Brazil—and do some sightseeing. She should be waiting for him at the hotel, and he was going to give her the great news, and celebrate, celebrate! Dr. Eulálio understood. The old man wanted to ball his lady a little in São Paulo; these changes of atmosphere are always stimulating. He embraced him affectionately, took him to the door with a hand on his shoulder, said goodbye with another embrace, and followed him with his eyes while he crossed the waiting room, a rather anserine grin on his chubby little face.

He closed the door and returned slowly to his desk with the warm feeling one gets from doing a good deed. And from having worked out an excellent deal for the bank. He wrote down a reminder on a memo pad to tell Dona Shirley to make up a list of all official funds and programs whose resources the bank might pass on to agricultural and industrial initiatives in the Northeast. And to tell Menezes to come see him as soon as he got back from Maranhão.

He pulled the album closer to him and gazed for a long time at his great-great-grandfather's portrait. Indeed, a lineage is a lineage, good blood is good blood, his family had a destiny, a destiny for greatness, for belonging to the elite. Had he inherited the patriarch's talent after so many generations? Of course he had, especially because that talent had been augmented by his great-grandfather Bonifácio Odulfo, an extraordinary man, an entrepreneur much ahead of his time, with a multifaceted intelligence, which afforded him even a high-quality literary avocation, practiced secretly in his scant spare time. Curiously enough, he had died of a lung disease, as if the disease of the poets of his time had caught up with him in his ripe years. Eulálio Henrique started to daydream again, and only much later did he order a lunch to be eaten right there in the office, because with all that conversation and the memories of his family—his grandmother Isabel Regina, the only time he had seen his great-uncle Patrício Macário, at his hundredth birthday, and so many other things—he had forgotten he was supposed to make an important speech at the Federation of Industrial Companies. Even though his staff had already written practically everything, he made a point of giving a personal touch to his pronouncements, incorporating a few subtle messages, making some veiled personal allusions. He couldn't fail; the ceremony would get nationwide coverage. His lunch, broiled fish with lemon sauce, a salad, a glass of German white wine, whole-rye bread, and half a small papaya, did not take long to arrive and found him poring over a notepad covered with scrawls and brusquely corrected sentences. He did not raise his eyes to the uniformed waiter who had brought his lunch, and waved his hand for him to set everything down on the round table near the leather armchairs. He had had another double shot of Scotch, and maybe that was the reason why he was inflamed and vehement, even transported, when two minutes later he got up to go to his lunch table, reciting between his teeth what he had written. The corporate leaders of Brazil are conscious of their grave responsibilities toward the nation and the Brazilian people! In Brazil today there is a new brand of businessman, a new mentality, a new consciousness of the social role to be played by business, which has become crucially important in today's Brazil! No, no, two "today"'s and two "Brazil"'s, better change that, change that. But essentially it was good, it was just fine, and should go over big with the audience, particularly because they were sincere statements, as everyone knew who knew him.

Resort Town of Itaparica, March 10, 1939

The steamboat chartered by Dona Isabel Regina left Salvador at 7 A.M. and should have got to Itaparica around nine, but a strong ebb current and a relentless northeasterly wind were holding back the *10th of November*, which was rising and falling in the waves like a merry-go-round horse. She was impatient with the delay and regretted not sailing out with the official visitors' boat, which had left half an hour before and ought to be docking on the island by now. But Eulálio Henrique and Bonifácio Odulfo III, her two grandchildren, who were traveling with her, did not want the trip to finish, because they kept discovering in the sea things they had never seen before—dolphin schools chasing mullet, fish flying alongside the ship, large, grayish birds diving down to fish.

"Boys," she said, glancing at her watch, "don't stay that close to the rail. Why don't you look at the sea from this little window?"

"Aw, Grandma, it's no fun that way. We're not hanging out, we're just near the rail."

The boy was right; there was no reason to keep them from having fun. They lived on the Itu farm and in a boarding school in São Paulo; it was a rare occasion for them, and besides, they really weren't running any risk near the rail. She shouldn't vent her nervousness on the children. She joined them by the rail and showed them the part of the coast where the famous baron of Pirapuama's whale fishery used to be. The baron was their relative in a certain way, because one of his children, the great banker Dr. Vasco Miguel, had married Carlota Borroméia, Big Grandpa Amleto Henrique's only daughter, Little Grandpa Bonifácio Odulfo's and Uncle Grandpa the General's sister, who had died of a heart attack still very young—who knows, if it had happened today maybe she would have been saved, huh? The boys aimed their binoculars at the distant beach and were not too impressed by what they saw: a few grimy ruins, a heeled-over lighter, two or three little canoes, a partially destroyed whalebone fence winding away to disappear in the woods.

"There's nothing there," Eulálio Henrique said. "Nothing."

Grandma Isabel Regina, remembering something she had read in a chrestomathy she had found very instructive for young people, about how apparently lifeless ruins and landscapes are in reality silent witnesses of history, loaded with the weight of time and inhabited by everything that ever happened among them, turned to her grandson, raising her forefinger in the posture of someone who's going to give a short lecture. But she didn't even begin to speak, because when she opened her eyes, which she had closed for a moment to organize what she was going to say, she let out a horrified cry. Over Eulálio Henrique's head, fluttering limply as if it were made of gelatin, a black creature, maybe a bat, maybe a huge moth, seemed to be going to alight. Scared by his grandmother's cry, the boy stroked the back of his head, and the creature set down on his hands and would not fly away no matter how desperately he shook them, unable to cry, so intense was his panic. Isabel Regina hesitated, raised her handbag to strike at the creature, but took a little long because she was afraid, giving time for a broad-shouldered black sailor to come across the deck and with a kind of staff touch the creature, which immediately took wing, hovered awhile in front of the group, and, opening its wings very wide, glided in the wind toward the beach.

"My God, what a horrible animal! Are you all right, son? It was nothing, it was nothing, it was just a scare. Did it bite you? Let me see your hand. No, it didn't bite, everything's all right. My God, what a horrible animal; I have never seen a creature like that!"

"It's the Curukere," the black sailor said, with an expression Isabel Regina found disagreeable, almost scary.

"What are you doing standing there?" she said forcefully. "Get a glass of water for the child, water with sugar, go on!"

She hugged her grandson, went on calming him down, and promised him a present, many presents, now he could stop crying, it was all over now. And while she held his head against her bosom, she raised her eyes, looked at the now surprisingly near beach, and shuddered, because she felt coming from it a kind of muffled malevolence, a deceptive peace, pregnant with invisible threats. She shuddered again and thought she was becoming too impressionable, she was acting like a naive child. The sugar water arrived, brought not by the strange-looking black but by a young man who was probably a kind of officer, and very courteous. He talked to the boy, asked if there was anything else he could do, and offered to take the two brothers for a tour of the ship. Isabel Regina refused; the trip was almost over now, and she'd rather stay in their company. And as long as he was there, could he tell her what kind of animal that was, that had scared the boy so much? The sailor had said it was a Curukere, or something like that. But the young officer said he had never heard of such an animal; it must be a black word. Isabel Regina gestured what seemed to be agreement and decided to forget about everything and get ready to land. She could already see the church towers, the boulevard houses, the Getúlio Vargas Square trees—yes, they were arriving at last; it was about time.

Mass would be at ten, and it was just nine-thirty, but she wanted to go ashore as quickly as possible, she wanted to see a lot of people, to supervise personally the last details for the party, and especially to have time to be with her dear Uncle Tico, so old, the poor dear, though very sharp and rather spry for his age. One hundred years, that was beautiful! A man who had lived through such important moments of Brazilian history, had known the time when there was slavery, had fought in Paraguay—truly a living monument. One hundred years of life, there in the placidness of Feira de Santana, secluded among his studies, his plants, his animals, his eccentricities, his friends of inferior social condition, who esteemed him so, and his memories, which were sure to be extraordinarily rich. Of course she had been right in moving heaven and earth for her uncle to have a hundredth birthday party worthy of his importance and their family's importance. True, most of their relatives, who lived in Rio and São Paulo, were not going to participate in the celebrations—the Mass, the small reception, and the intimate luncheon, besides the game and food stalls she had ordered set up for the townspeople, the military police band she had asked for, and a few other things she had found appropriate for the celebrations. But the ship that had preceded the *10th of November* had brought officials, journalists, and very important people from Bahia to the party; it would be a complete success even without the relatives.

The most complicated task upon her arrival was the unloading of the automobile she had insisted on bringing over to transport the general from his house on Channel Street to the little Church of Saint Lawrence. The distance was small, but he would probably have trouble walking, and a dignified means of transportation was necessary, in a town where there were only a pair of jalopies and a multitude of donkeys and carts. A little annoyed, she remembered the general had not agreed to have the Mass said in the Mother Church of the Consecrated Host, a church whose size and importance matched the event; he had written her a letter, which stated in a firm handwriting that he would leave his house only if the Mass was said in the Church of Saint Lawrence, almost a chapel, a poor, desolate building which the Jesuits built for the Indians. Yes, she had to respect the old man's whims, and after all, the church had some historical value, despite its bareness.

She did not wait for them to finish unloading the car, exhorted them to hurry up, and ran down the pier like a young girl, hand in hand with her grandsons, but soon she got hold of herself, adjusted her hat, and walked briskly the rest of the way, looking straight ahead so as not to have to talk to anyone and be even later than she was. She found the old man sitting smiling, in a wicker armchair, surrounded by a numerous group listening to something he was saying. She rushed over to him, hugged and kissed him, and showed him his two great-grandnephews, little Bonifácio Odulfo and Eulálio Henrique. The old man laughed: pity this family's children, who keep inheriting those horrible names. His voice failed now and then, and they often had to bring their ears close to his mouth to hear him, but otherwise he looked very fit, really very fit. It's been such a long time, dearest Uncle Tico! It seemed to have been yesterday that he lived in Rio de Janeiro and she used to go visit him, not with her grandchildren, but with her children. How time passed! And how beautiful to live to be a hundred with such lucidity, such joy, such vivacity! So many things seen and felt, so many stories to tell! And by the way, how about those memoirs he was writing: they had been finished for a long time now, hadn't they?

"Oh, that," the general answered with an almost impish smile. "I locked everything in a chest."

"A chest? Did you say a chest? A trunk?"

"Yes, yes, a chest, a trunk, a chest—I don't speak Greek. I put everything in a chest."

"What chest?"

"What do you want to know that for? It's locked; it's not supposed to be opened before my death."

"Gee, don't talk like that, Uncle, what a horrible thought."

"But it's true. What do you want? I'm not immortal and I'm already indecently old; to live so long is an exaggeration, it's in bad taste."

"I don't think so. I'd like to live as long as you myself."

"Don't be silly. After a certain age, life seems . . ."

But she never learned how life seemed after a certain age, because the celebration was breaking out inside and outside the house, with skyrockets, marches played by the band, people coming in and out, hugs, compliments, *vivas*. Rising to go to the Mass, the general insisted on walking for a while, but finally acknowledged it would be too tiring and slow, and agreed to go in the car, which he boarded under applause and a rain of flower petals. With the band, now in formation by the little church's door, breaking into drum rolls and fanfares at his arrival, the general stepped out, smiling, made a military salute to the musicians, and waved at the crowd extending from Mother Church Square to Greengrocer Square. A string quintet from Rio de Janeiro was in charge of the music accompanying a soprano and a baritone, and the Mass was celebrated by the assistant bishop, who delivered a long, erudite sermon that was greeted as a veritable lesson in history, then declaimed the sacred oratory in glorious tones, while the general, sitting in the front pew, snored lightly, a smile seeming to take shape on his face.

Back at the house, both Dona Dalva, his nurse and housekeeper, and Isabel Regina wanted him to rest, to have a light meal and sleep until midafternoon, when he would reappear to say goodbye to their guests and talk a little more. But he answered that he had no intention of complying, and besides, he had slept magnificently not too long before, during the opportunity provided by Dom Ludovico's outstanding sermon. He sat down in the same wicker chair as before, argued with the women of the house because they would not bring him a slug of sugarcane liquor, and reluctantly consented to a little glass of claret, which he drank in little sips, pronouncing it a sour syrup. He asked what they were going to have for lunch, and when they told him about all the food they had prepared for the guests, he complained that not even on his birthday would they give him a chance not to eat that abominable pap they forced down his throat. He started to give a funny lecture, with people sitting on the floor to listen, about a curve he had traced for human life, and how curious it was that everything was indeed circular, and when a man became too old he returned to childhood, both in wisdom and in the restrictions this wisdom elicited in adults, who monopolize wisdom, but since they know it's just as false as any other, they are afraid of the disengagement proper to extreme youth or extreme old age, and then forbid children and old people to do or even say anything that will challenge their convictions.

"What a thought!" someone in his audience exclaimed, among solemn nods by others, but the general clicked his tongue disparagingly and said it was nothing of the sort, it was something that had been known and said since Creation, and it carried some weight only because a hundred-year-old person was saying it. He went silent for some time, smiled, became serious again, and crossed his arms.

"I thought I'd tell you people a couple of stories," he said, his voice weaker than before.

A boy who was staring intensely at him, seeming at the same time to be about to cry, ran inside to call more people to listen to the general's stories, the general was going to tell stories, what stories he had to tell! But the general, lowering his head as if he was looking at something inside himself, said no, he had only thought about telling stories, because he had always known he would not tell them, he would never tell stories, others would do it, there would always be someone to tell stories. He wanted, he went on, his voice more and more tenuous, to say something about the Brazilian people, because he had learned a great deal from the Brazilian people, he knew about the Brazilian people. But that was a life, and you can't tell a life, you just live it. He would also like to share a few secrets; he also knew many secrets. But he could not tell any of those secrets, because their secret condition did not depend on their being kept secret at the cost of sanctions. Not at all; in a certain way they were secrets in their own essence, to be secret was part of their nature, their being secret did not depend on them, it depended on those who discovered them. Therefore it was no use revealing them, because even if they were revealed they would not stop being secrets, for no one there would know the right way to believe them.

He would also like to say he was happy, but he wasn't, not for himself but for them. For himself alone he would be happy, but this of course is not possible. He wasn't happy because he was now one hundred years old and the Brazilian people still didn't know about itself, didn't know anything about itself! Did they realize what that meant, not to know about oneself? No, they thought they realized it, but they didn't, and would still suffer much before they did know, and that was why he wasn't happy. He wasn't happy even with the profession that had been chosen for him but later turned into a part of him, because he had never managed to be a Brazilian soldier—and he almost shouted, his faint voice quavering with emotion—a true Brazilian soldier, a soldier of the people, a soldier with the people, a soldier who doesn't give orders to the people but is part of the people, a soldier who doesn't kill the people but dies for the people, a soldier who deserves the statue, the tears, the memories, the hearts, a soldier who doesn't hate but loves, a soldier who doesn't want to teach but wants to learn, a soldier who feels shame at hunger and oppression, a soldier who's ashamed to be a policeman for the government against the people, a soldier who doesn't squander his bravery uselessly, fighting in vain, dying in vain, and, what's worse, killing in vain, battling against himself, giving his life so his people will go on losing theirs. But he had not managed to become that soldier, in spite of himself, like many others before him or after him, who had only suffered intensely, usually under a silence more painful than war wounds. Would the day come when soldiers would be so distant from the people that they would have to deny that distance all the time, without convincing anyone? The day they would be afraid to go out in the street in uniform, except when on duty? No, not afraid, for they have power, much more power than they should have; they wouldn't have any fear. Shame? Yes, shame, not really of the uniform, because there have always been those who honored it. But a subtle shame, a sneaking, treacherous shame, shame for not being fellowmen, shame because the others do not dare to treat them as equals. Because when they put on their uniforms, they know they intimidate; when they put on their uniforms, they know they are not told the whole truth; when they put on their uniforms, there are people who avoid them; when they put on their uniforms, they never know if they are being treated well because they are liked or because people are afraid of them and think they must please them. And they know they cause fear because their uniform has been excessively misused, maybe by themselves. It's this shame, the shame that comes from being not soldiers but, more and more, tutors or tyrants, a shame that will always increase, because power wants more power, and odious power can be preserved only by increasing this shame. Worst of all, with all this power, the enjoyment of which shall always leave a bitter aftertaste and will produce nothing but a shallow happiness, they will not be the real masters but taskmasters of their own people, seduced by false honors and by the crumbs from the rich and the aristocrats, whose life they will never be allowed to know. Servants, high-ranking servants, but servants. They would not be servants only if their service was to the only sovereign entity, the people of which they don't want to be part, though they lie about it.

He let a tear run down freely from each of his eyes, pushed away a handkerchief a solicitous hand proffered near his face, and said, his voice so tiny that almost no one heard him, that he didn't mean anything to happen because of what he had spoken or might speak. He didn't mean anything to happen, he wasn't predicting anything, he was just giving a testimony, a testimony they might or might not put faith in, but it was a testimony. He could not die without telling them he knew one thing for sure, which in its turn made him sure of another thing—that the people thinks, that the people pulsates, that the people has a mind which transcends the minds of individuals, that it will not be exterminated, even if everything is done to effect that, as it's being done and it will continue to be done. And the first thing he was sure about was the Spirit of Man.

"I cannot die before I assure you," he said, raising his head without looking anywhere, "that the Brazilian people is not alone. Not because it has allies, for only rulers have allies, but because there is a cause common to all men, even if it doesn't look that way, since Evil exists. But the Spirit of Man also exists, not as a chimera, not as something invented out of need. Everything else was invented out of need, and the only thing that wasn't, though it's the only one that exists by necessity, is the Spirit of Man. The Spirit of Man is universal, aspires to plenitude and grace, and has as a common cause for all its consciences this aspiration, which translates itself into the final peace of existing without perceiving existence, existing as an essence, just existing, because the Spirit of Man yearns for perfection, that is to say, Good."

He tilted his head sideways, and went on talking as though he were just sighing and only the soundless air was modulating his thought. No one was able any longer to hear what he was saying, and many even thought he was sleeping and just moving his lips, but he still spoke a little, saying the Spirit of Man would triumph, and therefore the people would triumph. He breathed deeply, looked amused, waved his forefinger at the young boy who had been staring into his eyes ever since he had started talking, and asked him to come as close as possible.

"What I'm going to tell you is useless for the time being," he whispered. "Perhaps forever, because I may be just a doting old man without knowing it. Pssst! You'll only be able to be anything after you are you! Pssst! Understand? Sounds silly, but it isn't! We may be everything, but before that we have to be ourselves, understand? What's your name? Everything, everything, everything! Pssst! Long live the Brazilian people, long live we!"

He straightened his neck, crossed his arms, breathed even more deeply than before, kept his lungs filled for a few seconds and suddenly blew out air like someone who's puffing out cigarette smoke, and no longer moved.

"Is he asleep?" Isabel Regina asked, returning from a short trip to the kitchen, to see how things were coming along.

496

"I don't know." the boy said. "I thought he was sleeping before, but then he called me to tell me something."

"What did he tell you?"

"I didn't understand it too well; he spoke very softly and said it might be just something a doting old man would say. And he ended by saying long live the Brazilian people."

"Yes, he never loses his old ways, I know how he is," Isabel Regina said, looking tenderly at the old man, but when she hugged him his head slumped down, and he fell on her lap. "Uncle! Uncle Tico! Help here, for heaven's sake! Uncle Tico, oh, dear Uncle Tico!"

But neither the state secretary of health, a famous doctor, nor the other doctors present and those who were spending the summer on the island and were called in a hurry, managed to revive the old general, in spite of chest massages and the injection of a heart stimulant. His heart had stopped for good, the party was over, now all that was left was to have his wake and bury him. Pale, but resolute and calm, Isabel Regina took all the necessary measures. The wake would not be at the Mother Church; it would be at the old little Church of Saint Lawrence, so dear to the general. The assistant bishop would celebrate the funeral Mass; he could not refuse to stay overnight in Itaparica to comply with this request of hers. The 10th of November sailed out, taking a friend of the family to buy a coffin, the representative of the Sixth Military District's commander to communicate the general's decease to his superiors and request the appropriate military honors, a messenger to send cables to members of the family, and a few journalists to publish the story in the next day's editions. The mayor decreed a seven-day mourning period and refused the customary payment to keep the generator working all night, instead of turning it off at ten as usual. All the people of the little town, talking in whispers as though they were in a church, came to the door of the general's house to make sure he had really died and to see him for the last time.

At 7 P.M., submerged in angelicas, gladioli, chrysanthemums, carnations, dahlias, and daisies, Patrício Macário's body lay in state in the little church's nave, where it had been carried by so many hands that many of them did not even touch the coffin, as the band, erect, played Beethoven's Funeral March, the sergeant, very black, in his white, gold-frogged uniform, crying, with one of his hands brandishing his baton and the other exhorting his musicians' sorrowful attacks, the tuba playing off key and making the piece's solemn C's sound like desperate A minors.

Very tired, Isabel Regina was persuaded to go back to the house around ten o'clock, to take a bath and rest a little. But she could not fall asleep in spite of a warm bath, and stayed up talking to Dalva in the dining room. She asked her to go on living in that house until they decided what to do with it. Couldn't Dona Dalva, with proper compensation, of course, remain in the

497

house for good, keeping it as a kind of memorial for the general? Better yet, why didn't they make a museum out of the house, the Patrício Macário Museum, keeping everything that belonged to him and a few other objects related to Itaparica's role in the war? Wasn't it a good idea? The general had had a very rich life, he had gathered many things over a great many years, he had even written his memoirs. The memoirs! Yes, what a fortunate coincidence: he happened to have told her he had kept his memoirs in a chest that could only be opened after his death. Did Dona Dalva know what chest that was? Yes, she did; it had to be an odd-looking one he kept in the study, always covered by a cloth. She rarely saw it, because the general used to keep his study locked and would allow it to be tidied up only in his presence.

"Where's the key to the study?" Isabel Regina asked, rising so abruptly that she knocked down her chair.

"It should be on his key ring, in his night table drawer."

They picked up the bunch of keys, rushed to the study, opened the door, and to Dona Dalva's surprise, found the big window fully open and the drapes fluttering. And in the place where the chest ought to have been they found nothing; it had disappeared.

Not content with the thorough cleanup they did from Fair Park to Glory Square, taking advantage of the fact that many people had left their houses because of the general's party, the thieves Leucino Potato, Nonô from Candeal, and Virgílio Mackerel also spirited away the three donkeys of Astério from the Fountain, with their packsaddles, panniers, and all the rest of their trappings, to carry off quickly what they had stolen, before someone noticed something. They had electric radios, silver trays, pearl necklaces, gold chains, luxury clothing, everything, enough to fill the six panniers, with a few things left over for them to carry on their backs. They were also taking the little trunk Nonô had picked up at the general's house, which worried Mackerel, who voted against stealing from the general. But Nonô was a natural-born sneak thief, and it made him almost ill if he saw something lying around unwatched and did not take it. He said it also broke his heart to steal from the great general, whom everybody was so fond of, but they shouldn't have left that window so invitingly open; people just shouldn't do that kind of thing. And besides, there probably wasn't anything in the trunk; it was more like a souvenir for him. He had even tried to open it to prove that all it had inside was nothing but old papers and stuff like that, but he had not succeeded, and moreover they had no time to lose, they had to pack everything up and take a powder. When they got to a safe place later he would open it; it shouldn't be too difficult.

Where the hell had Potato taken it into his head to go? In a night this dark it was scary to run around the woods unarmed, what with all the animals, ghosts, and all sorts of dangers, even pointed tree branches, cockleburs, thorny underbrush, and scratch bushes with leaves so awesomely large they seem to be prickly elephant's ears. But Potato was a stubborn fellow, and they had decided they would split their take only when they got to a safe hiding place. But did he know any hiding place around? No, it wasn't that he knew a place, it was just that there were many abandoned buildings scattered around, many thicket-surrounded ruins, and pretty soon they'd stumble upon one of them.

"I only know the beach trail," Mackerel grumbled. "This is more or less Amoreiras or Little Swamp, isn't it?"

"More or less. Take it easy; pretty soon we'll come across a place where we can stay; they used to do a lot of building around here."

"I hope so, I hope so, because I'm getting nervous with all this, especially because of the trunk Nonô took from the late general. The man died today, his body is still fresh, and his soul might get angry with the stealing of his trunk and come over looking for revenge. I don't like this."

"That's all a lot of crap, man. I've never seen a ghost, and I wish I did, so I could believe in them."

"Don't say that, for your mother's blessing's sake; you may be punished for saying that."

"I want to see one, I want to!"

"Stop that, for Our Lady's sake!"

"You mentioned Our Lady, and she's helping us! You see there, by the creek, near that wild banana clump? You see that white shape—that's a wall. I've been here once; that used to be a flour house, from the time of sugar mills and whales; it still has even a piece of roof. All right, we're here! Come on, you stupid donkey!"

"You sure that place isn't haunted?"

"What do you mean, haunted? Mackerel, don't be such a yellowbelly!"

"I'm not afraid of flesh-and-bone creatures, not any of them, but ghosts are another thing. You should hear the stories I know. Did you use to know the late Cavalla, who used to live in Mercy Village, the father of that boy what's-his-name, the red-haired one? Well, this kid—"

"Save your stories, Mackerel. Better light up the two tin lamps."

"Didn't you get that great big lantern from that house on Duck Street?"

"That's right. Pick it up—you know how to light it?"

"Nothing to it."

Raising the lantern to light their way, Potato went in, followed by the two others and the donkeys. For a ruin abandoned so long, it could be said the flour house was in good condition, with most of its walls standing, a roof section covering the area where the ovens had been, the ground free of weeds and grass, as though the place was still being used. The three of them occupied it, hung their lantern from a lath, and lit up the tin lamps.

"People come here now and then," Potato said, stroking the ground with his foot. "A ghost's foot doesn't trample grass or wear down the ground like this."

"Well, let's get down to business," Mackerel said. "We'll unload these panniers and see who gets what. A donkey and two panniers for each of us, and the rest we figure by value and not item by item, all right?"

They took a long time arguing and getting angry at each other about their allotments, and they were about to get into a fight when Nonô, who had taken the chest to a corner and hadn't managed to open it yet, settled the dispute by relinquishing to the others a few things he was entitled to, in exchange for their letting him keep the trunk. The others were suspicious at first and examined the trunk, shaking it to try to guess it contents, but they knew Nonô was a bit touched in the head and probably wanted the trunk just out of a whim and not because he knew what was inside it, so they finally agreed.

"Why don't you throw the damn thing against the wall to bust it open once and for all, so we can see what's inside?" Mackerel asked.

"No, no, no breaking; this trunk is valuable."

"What value can an old chest like that have, so impossibly heavy, so strange-looking? Who would want a thing like that, especially knowing no one can open it? Where's the lock?"

"It doesn't have a lock; I've checked all over it. It only has three little slits here, and these rings. There must be a secret, a secret you use to open it; if you take your time you'll find it out. It just takes time."

"Well, go ahead and take your time. As for me, I'm going to eat the broiled chicken we got at that white woman's house."

"Go, go, just leave a little piece for me, I won't be long; I'll be through with this in a minute."

But they had finished eating, Potato starting to fall asleep and Mackerel puffing on a stolen cigar, when Nonô cried out from his corner, where he was lying belly down in front of the chest and seemed to have his head glued to it.

"Come over here, come over here! Come over here quick!"

"Why are you talking like that?"

"I'm holding a little latch with my tooth, and if I let it go I don't think I'll be able to open it again! It's strong as hell, and seems to have a spring! Good heavens! Good heavens! Good heavens!"

"Good heavens what, you idiot, what the hell are you seeing there? Are you seeing something there? Is there a hole in it?"

"Yes, where my right eye is, right here, there's something blinking inside! Good heavens!"

"Something blinking?"

"Yes. No! It stopped blinking! Good heavens! Most Holy Virgin! Our Lady of Perpetual Help! Everything's bright! Good heavens!"

500

"Don't be such a big liar, Nonô—you're not seeing anything there, anything, you hear? Move over so I can take a look too."

"No, no, if I move over, this thing will snap shut, and not even a saint will be able to open it again; it was a fluke. Good heavens! I can't believe that—ouch, my eye! Holy Mother of God!"

"Don't be a liar; you're not seeing anything there."

"By the light from above, by everything that's sacred, I swear to you! You want me to tell you what I'm seeing?"

"Tell me, tell me."

"I'm seeing the future!"

"Seeing the future? What you mean, the future?"

"I don't know, I only know it's the future, there's something here that shows it's the future."

"What is it?"

"I don't know how to say it—it's something."

"Come on, stop trying to make fools of us—you're not seeing any future, you're not seeing anything."

"I am, I am, I am!"

"Then tell me what numbers will be the winners in tomorrow's numbers game."

"I'm not seeing that type of future. It's as if there was a voice here whispering in my ear to explain what's inside, though there is no voice, but there is. Good heavens!"

"What are you seeing now?"

"Thieves like ants! It's crawling with thieves—liars and thieves in every nook and cranny!"

"A real lot of thieves?"

"Wow! Whew! You wouldn't believe it! And all of them very well dressed, very classy!"

"How are they dressed—in three-piece suits, two-piece suits, vest and tie?"

"In white linen two-piece suits, gabardine three-piece suits, silk ties, diamond studs, pearl cuff links, crocodile-leather shoes, nice-smelling water under their armpits at twenty thousand a drop! I'm talking about civilians."

"Are there thieves in uniform?"

"You wouldn't believe it! Jesus Christ, see how many there are! Good heavens!"

"All of them breaking into homes and taking other people's things?"

"Not on your life! They don't even touch the money. All of them have these little cards. Money is not called money."

"What is it called?"

"All kinds of names: appropriation, allotment, a certain amount, surcharge, discount, medium of exchange, fees, remuneration, allocation of resources, earmarking of resources, commission, honorarium, compensation, disbursement, credit, transfer, investment—so many names that if I named them all I wouldn't finish today, and there are more things to see. No one mentions money, everyone is ashamed to say money."

"Is there a lot of shame because of money there?"

"A hell of a lot! Everyone sends their money out, and they're so ashamed that when somebody says they sent their money out, it's embarrassing for them, so they have the one who said it arrested, and if this somebody goes on talking about the money they stashed away, they have this somebody killed!"

"A lot of dead people there?"

"Wheee! There's a bomb that doesn't spare even a man's soul, it burns it away together with his body. It's written here: Nothing can survive a thermonucleous explusion, not even little souls, not even little souls!"

"Did they throw the bomb there?"

"Not yet, but they want to throw it to guarantee peace. If people don't behave, everyone dies, even souls in the thermonucleous!"

"But then no one's died so far—they may die, but they haven't."

"Yes, they have! They're dying! There's an eight-year-old boy here who's carrying his two-year-old sister, who was shot by an American by accident after other Americans had dropped a bomb on his father's house by accident when the Americans were invading his land to save him, only no one was left, but everyone was saved. There are also people dying in every way, a lot of them out of hunger, boys skinnier than a bamboo, and buzzards coming to eat them. A lot of fat buzzards!"

"Don't they have any food there?"'

"No, there's even too much food. There are these blond folks putting powder milk in the mixture they use to pave their avenues, so they become smoother. There are plenty of people setting fire to chicks and drowning chicks, there are people killing geese just for their livers, there are people paying other people not to plant anything so there won't be too much food and the price won't go down, there are people trying to castrate other people so they won't have children who may eat the food they throw away—there are things here even God would doubt! There's onion and garlic being dumped in the river, imagine, onion and garlic! And after they dump them in the river, they buy more, only this time from foreigners, so foreigners will respect them."

"A lot of foreigners there?"

"Not many, but all of them calling the shots; it's really something. A man likes something, the foreigner comes and says that's not true, the man likes something else, but he does it artfully. Foreigners command, but it's not really foreigners, it's money. Money is the boss."

"A lot of money there?"

"Wheee! But all of it in their hands!"

"And what's all this money for?"

"For everything! You don't know what they do!"

"What is it that they do?"

"Oh, they kill, they steal, they rob, they lie, they propose and they dispose, they raise all kinds of hell, and nothing happens to them. Think about something, and I'll tell you if I can see it here. Think up something very bad."

"Are they killing heads of families?"

"You can't imagine! Ow! Hail Mary! Ow! You think anyone can go out in the street anymore? If they go, they're shot dead!"

"How about children—are they killing children?"

"They're being liquidated, my friend! They look like flies in vinegar! God, what a terrible thing, what a terrible—ouch, my eyes!"

"What happened there, Nonô?"

"Oh my eyes. I can't believe it, oh my eyes, Our Lady of mine, Most Holy Virgin of mine, forgive my sins, my God in heaven, oh my eyes, oh my dear little eyes, oh what terrible things!"

"Nothing can be done, right?"

"Oh my eyes, I don't want to see it anymore, oh my dear little eyes! There comes more bashing, I don't want to see it anymore, there comes more bashing!"

"Don't let go, see some more!"

"It takes courage, it takes courage!"

"So have courage, man, see some more! Tell us more—what else are you seeing?"

But Nonô could not go on peeping into the chest, because a muffled roar—as though a colossal animal were buried there and wanted to raise the ground to escape—started to agitate everything around: an elephant's roar, a whale's, a jaguar's, a laborious panting that suddenly overtook the world; it was no longer a creature under the ground, it was the ground itself as though it was in labor pains, as if it was going to bite, as if it was going to turn over itself.

"Everything's alive, Our Lady of mine, my Jesus Christ, everything's alive!" Mackerel shouted. "Oh mother of mine!"

The others would not have been able to answer even if they wanted to, because with a cry he had never thought he was able to let out, Potato drew his hand away from the wall on which it had been leaning as he felt trickling over it a thick, warm juice, a red, burning juice, a juice similar to blood, blood oozing out slowly from the walls of the flour house ruins, pouring in slow spurts over the mortar blocks, coming out of every point on the wall, a viscous, silent cascade, blood flowing out of every crack, every dark spot of ancient cement, every hiding place for spiders and scorpions, every grain of sand gathered there, every little pebble. The flour house started to move in the same tempo as the ground underneath it, the blood began to sputter as if pumped up by those great sighs, the donkeys tossed their heads and broke their halters to flee, and the three thieves, without saying anything, stampeded through the wilds, looking for the sea by its smell. In the sky of Amoreiras, nothing could be seen except the January constellations in their inexorable ride. High above the Amoreiras sky, where everything exists and nothing is unbelievable, the Souls' Perch, vibrating with so many restless wings and so many dreams brandished in the indifferent wind of the universe, almost tumbled down with the agitation that came over it, while the earth throbbed down below, and the little souls strove to go down, go down, go down, go down, go down, go down, because they wanted to fight. Why did they want to fight? This is not known, nothing is known, all is chosen. All is chosen, as know the little souls now shivering in the infinite cosmic cold, which makes them sway like the kites flown by the children they miss. Little Brazilian souls, so tiny and guileless they caused pity, but resolved to go back to fight. Little souls, which had learned so little and wanted to learn more, as is the nature of souls, and trembled again when down below three thieves ran away from the old chest, which was covered by blood, by blood, by blood, by mortar which is the same thing, by sweat which is the same thing, by tears which are the same thing, by breast milk which is the same thing. This happened above, God smiling or not, because down below, way down below under the air of Amoreiras, everything was happening or might always be about to happen. The southeasterly wind blew, gathering the clouds, it started to rain in thick, rhythmical drops, all those who were still awake got up to shut their windows and collect the water that would come from the gutters. No one looked up, and so no one saw in the middle of the storm the Spirit of Man, errant but full of hope, hovering over the lightless waters of the great bay.